RAISING CAINE

RAISING CAINE

VOLUME THREE OF
THE TALES OF THE
TERRAN REPUBLIC

CHARLES E. GANNON

Raising Caine: Volume Three of the Tales of the Terran Republic

This is a work of fiction. All the characters and events portrayed in this book are fictional, and any resemblance to real people or incidents is purely coincidental.

A Baen Books Original

Baen Publishing Enterprises
P.O. Box 1403
Riverdale, NY 10471
www.baen.com

ISBN: 978-1-4767-8093-1

Cover art by Bob Eggleton

First Baen printing, October 2015

Distributed by Simon & Schuster
1230 Avenue of the Americas
New York, NY 10020

Library of Congress Cataloging-in-Publication Data

Gannon, Charles E.
    Raising Caine / Charles E. Gannon.
        pages ; cm. — (Tales of the Terran Republic ; Volume 3)
    ISBN 978-1-4767-8093-1 (trade pb)
    I. Title.
    PS3607.A556R35 2015
    813'.6—dc23

                                                    2015025752

10 9 8 7 6 5 4 3 2 1

Pages by Joy Freeman (www.pagesbyjoy.com)
Printed in the United States of America

With Thanks to:

Bob Eggleton, artist extraordinaire, creature designer/
consultant on the water-strider, and all-around great
guy and friend;

Gerald Nordley and **Stephanie Osborne**, for their
generous and expert input on both the planetological
and biological forces that would bear upon the possibility
of life on tidally locked worlds.

And Dedicated to:

My late father, **John Patrick Gannon**, whose love of
intelligent, exacting science fiction was a powerful legacy
to me. Although his interest in alterity was not very
broad, it was very, very deep, and put down enduring
roots in my soul as a child and in my life as an adult.

CONTENTS

Interstellar shift links
(max human range: 8.35 ly)

(Biogenic worlds are labeled in **BOLD FACE**)

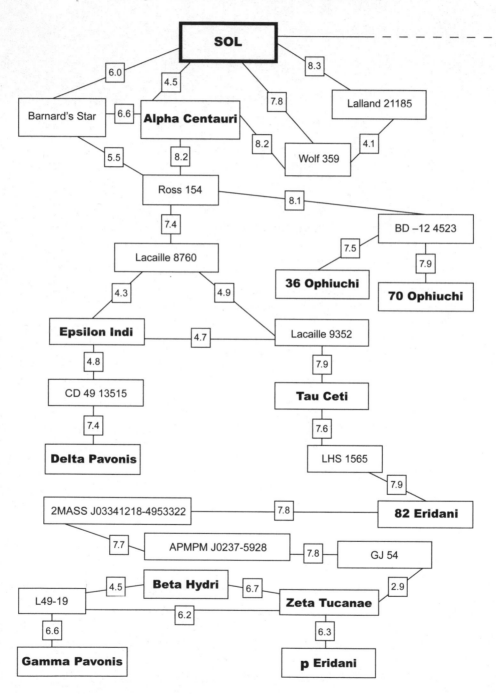

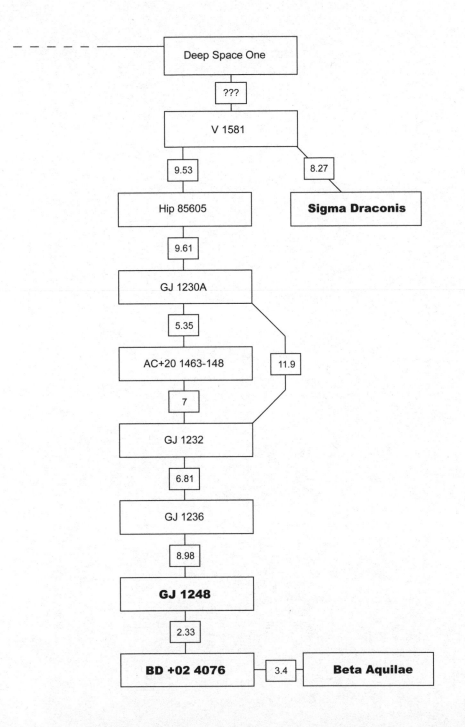

RAISING CAINE

PART ONE

June 2120

Chapter One

Weightless, Caine Riordan escorted the Slaasriithi ambassador to the exit of the free-floating habitation module in which they had met. Nearing the docking hatch, the slender exosapient raised one gibbonlike arm to steady its zero-gee drift and raised the other to lift a tendril-fingered hand in farewell.

Caine returned the wave as the ambassador disappeared into its diplomatic shuttle and wondered, *Will I ever get used to being the point man during first contacts?* It didn't seem likely, not when every new species presented him, and humanity, with yet another disorienting surprise. In the case of the Slaasriithi, the surprise had been in their appearance. Not because they were ghastly—they weren't—but rather, because they were unnervingly familiar. Tightly furred, wasp-waisted, and with a roughly tetrahedral head perched atop an abbreviated ostrich neck, the Slaasriithi were identical to the primitive beings Caine had met on Delta Pavonis Three two years ago. But Ambassador Yiithrii'ah'aash had denied kinship between his race and that one—sort of. Leading Riordan to conclude that there was only one constant when conducting a first contact: each day ended with more questions and mysteries than it had begun.

As the hatch whispered closed, a muffled thump drew Caine's attention to the opposite end of the module: his own retrieval shuttle had completed its hard dock. A voice emerged from the speaker: "Sorry about the bump, Commander Riordan." The voice

3

was mature, matter-of-fact—not one of the young, nervous pilots that predominated here in the recently pacified Sigma Draconis system. The Arat Kur locals, driven all the way back from their invasion of Earth, had put up a stiff fight before conceding. In consequence, there were now slightly fewer young pilots in the fleet, and those who remained were no longer quite so brash as they had been when they arrived. In short, they had grown up.

But this shuttle-jockey sounded as if he had grown up quite some time ago. He expanded upon his brief apology: "Guess I'm getting a bit rusty."

"Hardly felt the bump," Caine lied politely. "Can I get out of this tin can, now?"

"No, sorry, sir. Another half hour and the xenomicrobiologists will be done with the quarantine protocol."

"I'm not 'sir.' Just 'Caine.'"

"Uh . . . not to seem contentious, sir, but it says right here on my orders that you are a full commander, USSF."

"Really? I wasn't when I left the shift-carrier this morning." *Although, for all I know, Downing has put me back on the active duty roster. Again.*

"Well, sir, I wouldn't know anything about that. All I know is what I read in my orders."

"Fair enough. They keep changing my status back and forth so fast, I'm not sure of my title from day to day." *Or whether I'm a soldier, an intelligence operative, an envoy to exosapients, or just a civilian again.* "What about you? Navy?" Caine was slowly drifting back down toward the deck: the pilot of the retrieval craft had imparted a slow rotation to the module. As Caine's toes made contact, the whole world seemed to be sliding subtly, but perpetually, sideways: the Coriolis effect from the spin.

The shuttle-jockey corrected him. "No, sir. I'm not Navy. Commonwealth Survey and Settlement Office."

"You have a name?"

"Karam Tsaami."

Caine, in the course of his travels, met a lot of people whose names were unusual cultural mash-ups, even for this day and age. Still, this was one of the more peculiar combinations. "So you're, uh, Finno-Turkish?"

"By way of Toronto, yes." Tsaami's tone was distinctly wry. "And unless I'm mistaken, sir, you're the guy who reported first contact with the natives on Delta Pavonis Three at the Parthenon Dialogs two years ago."

Yes, the same natives who paradoxically, even impossibly, are dead-ringers for the Slaasriithi I just met with. "That was supposed to remain a closed-room debrief."

"Yeah, well, the story even reached me out where I was ferrying, er, special payloads. In the Delta Pavonis system."

"Special payloads?" Although officially civilians, a lot of SSO jockeys ferried covert operators around the colonies beyond Alpha Centauri. "Spend a lot of time at Delta Pavonis?"

"It's been my home, on and off, for the past three years."

Three years? The pilot's voice suddenly seemed familiar. "Hey, aren't you the guy who flew me out to the illegal CoDevCo facility on DeePeeThree?"

Karam Tsaami sounded pleased. "Yep. That was me. Been a long road since— Hold up. I've got incoming commo, highest priority." The ten-second pause felt like ten minutes. "Commander, we're going dark. Admiral Lord Halifax has called the fleet to battle stations. An Arat-Kur shift cruiser just popped in-system. ETA fifty-five minutes."

"And we're going to hide?"

"Commander, given our size, our best chance in a shooting war would be to become invisible. But since we can't do that, we're going to remain a motionless and inconsequential speck while enemy scanners are filling up with weapons-hot bogeys. So yes, we're going dark. Right now."

The speaker's glowing green indicator winked off. Then the module's lights did the same, leaving Riordan alone in the gently rolling darkness.

Except that, squinting, Caine now noticed a small red light, blinking alongside the hatch through which the Slaasriithi ambassador had exited. Riordan pushed off the floor, drifted to the hatchway: nothing but the aft airlock beyond it. So did the light indicate a pressure leak? A compromised seal?

No, he realized, leaning closer, *that's the activation light for an external commo jack.* So was someone actually outside the module, trying to reach him? Caine punched the manual activation stud. "Hello?"

"Commander Riordan, is that you?"

"Yes. Who's this?"

"Bannor Rulaine, sir."

It made no sense that Bannor, a friend from the war, was floating just outside the airlock. To the best of Caine's knowledge, the ex-Green Beret should still have been babysitting an enemy agent back on the flagship, a liquimix battle rifle aimed at the Ktor bastard's midriff. "Bannor, what the hell are you doing out there?"

"Well, sir, I'm doing what our boss Mr. Downing told me to do: watch over you. I'm not alone. Miles O'Garran is here, too."

"Little Guy" O'Garran, as well? Well, Downing certainly pulled the A-team off the benches for this *overwatch mission.* "So why the heck are you on the *outside* of the module?"

"We're here to make sure you had some unseen backup. Just in case something went sideways."

"Which, thanks to the Arat Kur, has now occurred. You got the alert?"

"Loud and clear. And unexpected. I thought we'd accounted for all the Roaches' ships."

Caine suppressed a sigh. *That's because you're a few steps further down the clearance food chain. Just because we secured the Arat Kurs' home system doesn't mean we're out of the woods.* "Well, your overwatch job ended when the Slaasriithi left, so get in out of the cosmic rays."

"Thanks, sir, but even cracking the outer hatch is contrary to the current blackout protocols. Opening the airlock to free space would produce a thermal differential that could show up on enemy sensors. Besides, our mission isn't over until Mr. Downing says it is. Oh, and Chief O'Garran just reminded me that this is a rare opportunity for us to work on our tans."

Yeah, tans which can be measured in double-digit REM per hour—the kind of tan which causes you to lose hair, and maybe a few years, if it goes on too long.

The green light flashed on the comm panel behind Riordan. "Hold on, Bannor: message coming in."

Karam Tsaami's voice was tense. "Commander, some big shot named Richard Downing wants to put you in the loop. The big loop. As in, patched through directly to Admiral Silverstein's combat information center."

"And when does this happen?"

"Dunno, sir. I'm just standing by like you are."

Riordan heard the weary tone of a long-term professional—a

long-term *government* professional. Who had been his aerial chauffeur on Delta Pavonis Three two years ago. An extraordinary coincidence. *Or probably not,* Caine realized with a smile. "So, Karam, nice to have you ferrying me around during yet another first contact. Pretty small universe, wouldn't you say?"

"What? You don't like me?"

"Oh, I like you just fine, Karam. It's implausible coincidences that I'm not so fond of."

"Yeah, okay. I was your taxi driver to the CoDevCo compound on DeePeeThree because I had the right clearances. But now—well, things are different. When it comes to you, that is."

Huh? "Different how?"

"Caine, er, Commander, it's like I was implying earlier: you don't seem to realize how many people know your name, now. More to the point, you have no idea how many people are probably following your movements. Of course, being at the center of events during the invasion of Earth didn't help matters, if you were trying to stay off the radar."

"Not like I wanted that attention."

"Didn't say you did. You don't seem the type. But even before the fires had burnt out in Jakarta, a bunch of intel types were inviting lots of your prior official contacts to come have a nice quiet chat in a nice secluded place for a nice long time."

"Did they suspect some of you as moles?"

"Maybe, but mostly they were looking for folks with clearance who'd already had direct contact with you. They picked me to be one of the ship jockeys who could also watch your back. But you pretty much fell off the grid after Jakarta."

Did I ever. "That's because I didn't walk away at the end of the Battle of Jakarta. I rode out here to Sigma Draconis in an intensive-care cold cell."

"Ah. Sorry. I didn't know that you— Wait: message coming through."

Tsaami was back on within the minute. "Okay, I'm jumping off the line. Mr. Downing is going to come on in a few moments with brief instructions. He's bouncing this one commo through my lascom and then cutting me out of the loop."

"Good talking to you, Karam."

"Yeah, likewise. We'll have to get a beer someday when you aren't on everyone's watch list."

The circuit switched channels with a pop. Downing's voice—crisp, urgent, and decidedly Oxbridge—crackled out of the speaker: "Caine, if you are reading this, you are to reply with a zero point two second coded lascom pulse with wavelength variation protocol Hotel X-Ray Seven."

Riordan did so, and then, after his pulse's variation fingerprint had cleared the security firewall, asked, "Richard, what the hell is going on? Why would only one Arat Kur ship shift into—?"

"No time now, Caine. You'll be receiving live-feed from my pickup here in the intel situation room. Once you are in that loop, just listen. Do not send. It is unlikely that tight-beam emissions would register on enemy sensors, but we don't want to take a chance. In the meantime, stand by for emergency extraction by us, by the Slaasriithi, or to hear that we are relinquishing command authority over your team—Tsaami, Rulaine, O'Garran—directly to you."

Riordan increased the volume for Bannor's benefit. "So I'm waiting to learn if the shit that's hitting the fan will bury half the fleet. Or more."

Downing only replied, "Stay alert."

The circuit closed and then reopened on a different frequency, this one a loud babble of orders, reports, and counterorders: the sounds of Admiral Ira Silverstein's CIC at red alert and weapons free.

Bannor commented through the external comm circuit: "They sound pretty panicked."

Riordan listened more carefully. "They're scrambling every drone and Hunter-class control sloop they've got on ready status. Problem is, this Arat Kur ship shifted in so close that they don't have the time to push out a full protective hemisphere around our shift-carriers. Whatever happens is going to be close, dirty, and very destructive."

"Makes me glad the Arat Kur only brought one ship."

Caine grunted agreement and listened to the staccato sitreps and flight ops chatter crackling out of the speaker behind him. He recognized Admiral Silverstein's voice laying down a barrage of orders: "I want those Boulton-class cruisers out in front and on our flanks. And Commo, you tell the shift-carrier captains that if I *don't* see them redline their thrusters and un-ass this area of operations, I will personally come to each of their bridges when this is over and bust them down to ensigns. Nothing is more important than our shift hulls. *Nothing.* Signal Halifax on *Trafalgar* that we are now at eighty percent of maximum power output and stand ready to discharge spinal weapons and point defense fire lasers simultaneously."

"Sir," cried another familiar voice—communications officer Lieutenant Brill, if Caine remembered correctly—"I've got incoming signals from the enemy ship. Well, maybe it's *not* an enemy ship."

"Brill, give me clear data or I'll find someone who can."

"Sir, I think— Listen."

Yet another voice, this one unfamiliar, became prominent. "—your fire. I say again: hold your fire. This is prize-ship *Doppelganger*, transmitting on all frequencies, all codes: please respond. Repeat, hold your—"

"Damn it!" Silverstein shouted. "Captain Kagawa, you nearly had us soiling our duty suits over here. We were seconds away from frying that Arat Kur hull you've commandeered. Why the hell didn't you follow protocol and communicate immediately?"

Kagawa sounded harried. "Two problems, Admiral. The first was that the Arat Kur left us some viral surprises in the communications software."

"Damn it, I thought we'd purged all that crap."

"From the coding and management systems, yes, sir. But not from the physical interfaces. The Roaches must have rigged this sleeper virus to activate when the shift drive was engaged without a passkey code. From the moment we came out of shift, we couldn't get the radios or lascoms to realign or transmit."

"Then why the hell didn't you stand off and pulse your power plants to send a Morse code mayday in the clear?"

"Well, sir, that's the second problem."

"More software issues?"

"No, sir. A diplomatic issue."

"A diplomatic issue?" Silverstein repeated.

"Yes, sir. Our ranking passenger—and he officially ranks me, once we entered this system—ordered that we maintain our approach even as we tried to regain control of our communications."

"What? Why? Damn it, who is this ass, anyway?"

"It is I," said another familiar voice, "Ambassador Etienne Gaspard, charged to lead the negotiations with the Arat Kur Wholenest. And now, apparently, I have been promoted to 'ass.'

I am unfamiliar with the duties and prerogatives of that new rank, Admiral, but it shall figure prominently in my report of this event. Of that I assure you."

"What the hell is going on?" Bannor asked, evidently having heard the furor but not the specific words. "Are we being hit by the Arat Kur?"

"No," Riordan answered, "worse."

"Worse? What could be worse?"

"We're being hit by diplomats. Stand by to come in out of the sun, guys."

Chapter Two

As Riordan exited the meeting module into the quarantine section of Ira Silverstein's flagship *Lincoln*, klaxons began yowling and the alert-condition lights began pulsing red.

Richard Downing waved for Riordan to remain on the other side of the clear plastic barrier as the ship lurched into sudden acceleration and the compartment's intercom announced, "Mr. Downing, you're wanted back in the CIC's intel annex."

"Acknowledged. But what in bloody hell is happening *now*?"

"Sorry, sir. Unidentified ship just shifted in."

"*Another* one?"

"Yes sir, and only twenty-five light-seconds beyond geosynchronous orbit. They are not responding to hails, but— Wait a moment, sir. I have more data coming in."

Caine put his hands up against the wall of the plastic box in which he was being held. "Richard, get me out of here."

The commo officer's report resumed before Downing could respond. "Classified update for you, Mr. Downing. The ship identifies itself as a Ktoran vessel operating under 'Autarchy aegis'—whatever that means—and is demanding the immediate repatriation of their ambassador, Tlerek Sirn Shethkador. They are still not acknowledging our hails or altering their trajectory. They're coming straight at us, sir. We're deploying to engage."

"Very well, keep me informed. Downing out."

"Richard, get me the hell out of this box *now*."

"Caine, I—" The quarantine section's commo panel buzzed; Downing rolled his eyes. "Bollocks—now what?" He tapped open the circuit. "Yes?"

"Richard, Ben Hwang here. I just got the lab results: you can release Caine from quarantine."

"Many thanks, Ben. You've heard the situation?"

"I have. And I figured you'd want Caine to be on hand for whatever comes next. He saw through the Ktoran bullshit the first time. He might again."

"Indeed he might."

"One bit of bad news: there's no usable genetic material from the dead skin and hair we harvested from the Ktoran ambassador's first holding cell. He must have been misted by a gene-specific toxin when he emerged from his bogus environment tank. So we're going to need to take a cell sample against his will."

"Not with a Ktoran ship in-system, you're not. He threatened war the first time we tried that. Now he just might be able to carry out that threat. Besides, overriding his diplomatic privilege is a political decision, not military."

"Well, we do have two Republic consuls in the Fleet."

"Yes, but not a lot of time, so start the process, Ben. If you need me, I'll be in the auxiliary bridge's intel annex." Downing closed the channel, instructed the waiting orderly: "Mr. Riordan is to be released immediately. You will forego taking his exit vitals."

Caine refrained from drumming his fingers as the orderly started undoing the box's seals. "What's our job?"

"Since the Ktorans have come looking for Ambassador Shethkador, we have to run real-time technical and diplomatic intelligence."

Caine shrugged. "Well, if our objective is to maximize our safety, the course of action regarding Shethkador is clear."

"Oh?" Downing asked as Caine emerged from the quarantine chamber. "And what course of action is that?"

"You kill him. Immediately."

Downing blinked. He had probably presumed that such ruthless thoughts never entered the former defense analyst's mind. "Caine, I agree that Shethkador is a right bastard, but—he's an ambassador."

"Yes, he's an ambassador who back-shot me in Jakarta while masquerading as a genuine exosapient. In other words, he's also a lying assassin."

Downing shook his head. "I know he deserves to be shown out the nearest airlock, but killing him could start a war."

Riordan shrugged. "I know we can't kill him, even though that *would* be the safest course of action for fleet security. But that's the risk we take for the good of Mother Earth."

"I don't remember you being quite so sarcastic, Caine."

"I don't remember having to be courteous to monsters who've tried to kill me. Multiple times."

Downing seemed to be casting about for an appropriate riposte but didn't find one. He opened the hatch. "We have a job to do."

"Yeah, don't we always?" Caine led the way out.

Standing at the edge of the intel annex's small holotank, Caine watched as the Ktoran ship—signified by a red mote—effortlessly slashed through the screen of defensive drones that had been deployed by European Union, Russlavic Federation, and United Commonwealth warships. The Hunter-class drone control sloops—small blue specks—gave ground before the much larger vessel, which to Caine looked like an ominously effulgent drop of blood.

"They didn't even bother to use any drones of their own," muttered Gray Rinehart, Downing's assistant and adjutant-director of IRIS. "They just took out ours with onboard lasers. Didn't even use their main, spinal mount: just their secondary UV batteries." He shook his head. "Damn, but they're swinging a big brassy set."

"And making a point while they're at it," Caine murmured.

Vassily Sukhinin, senior consul for the Russlavic Federation and a confidante, stared at the plot, frowning. "If you mean that they are trying to show themselves to be unconcerned with our weapons, I wonder if they will be so dismissive when they come within range of our nuke-pumped X-ray laser drones."

Caine shook his head. "I'm not saying that they're invulnerable, just that they have a lot of abilities that we don't."

Sukhinin scanned the flatscreens ringing the space above the holotank like a halo of black rectangles. "Where are the visuals? We littered nearby space with no- and low-metal microsensors. The Ktor must have entered their range by now."

Downing, cupping his hand over his earbud, explained the lack of images. "The Ktor have been eliminating the microsensors as they approach."

Caine nodded. "Which means that they're doing it from ranges greater than fifty thousand kilometers, since we're not getting any visuals first."

Downing glanced up. "According to the comchatter, the Ktor are eliminating the sensors from ranges substantially greater than fifty kiloklicks."

Sukhinin's expression went from surprise to narrow-eyed wariness. "How *much* greater, Richard?"

"One intercept took place at one hundred and fifty kiloklicks."

Sukhinin nodded at Caine. "You have the right of it, then. These *svolochi* are showing off both their muscles and their keen eyes. To be able to intercept a sensor with less than one hundred grams of metal in it, and no larger than a wine bottle, at half a light-second?" He snorted. "That is not good tactics; that is a dominance display. Particularly since their spies within our megacorporations surely informed them that our microsensors have almost no detection abilities beyond one hundred kiloklicks."

Caine nodded, watched the death dance progress in the holotank. *Lincoln* and the two closest shift-carriers were a triad of blue spindles, all making best speed away from the oncoming bogey. Fanning out in their wake were two disk-shaped screens of azure motes: smaller warcraft that had already been deployed when the Ktor arrived or that were now detaching from the cradles of the fleeing carriers. The first screen, mostly comprised of lighter patrol craft—drone-controlling sloops, corvettes, and a few frigates—had formed up around a small hub of destroyers and cruisers that had been scrambled to respond to the false alarm caused by the arrival of the *Doppelganger.*

The second, larger disk was predominantly comprised of capital ships, mostly cruisers of various marks, with destroyers roving ahead and at the periphery. A steady stream of aquamarine mayflies—drones—were emerging from its outer surface, with slightly larger gnats—X-ray missiles or similar decoys—hanging back behind the bow wave of the formation.

Downing touched his earbud again, confirmed what the holotank was showing them. "We are at eighty-five percent deployment, shift-carriers now at one point five gees constant, heading directly away from the intruder."

Caine glanced at the single blood-speck that was chasing half a fleet and closing the distance rapidly. "Ktoran acceleration?"

Downing's reply was muted. "Two point one gees. They will reach our long-range engagement envelope in twenty minutes."

"Which means we shall be within their demonstrated range in ten," Sukhinin grumbled.

Gray Rinehart raised a single, silvery eyebrow. "I thought they were here to pick up their 'ambassador,' not start a war."

Caine shrugged. "They might be multitasking today." Even Sukhinin had a hard time smiling at that gallows humor. "But if they really do mean to fight, they must have more ships around here somewhere."

Downing nodded tightly. "Agreed. Their abilities are far beyond ours, but they are not gods. Our numbers are too great for them to be able to—"

The door toned twice: coded entry had been requested and automatically approved.

The bulkhead-rated portal moaned aside, revealing a Naval Intelligence liaison. Just behind him were several heavily armed guards, clustered around a tall human male in a day-glo orange jumper. "Mr. Downing, I've brought the prisoner as per—"

If Downing's abruptly outthrust and quivering finger had been a discharged pistol, the liaison would have been dead where he stood. "What the bloody hell are you doing? Why the hell is *he* here?"

The human in the day-glo orange jumper smiled faintly.

The liaison blinked and swallowed. "Sir, Mr. Downing, I thought—that is, when the XO ordered that I bring all relevant security assets to your situation room, I—"

"Lieutenant, you will listen to every word I am about to utter very carefully, or you will be swapping that nice blue uniform for a duplicate of the orange jumper being worn by our 'diplomatic guest.' The detainee you are escorting—Tlerek Srin Shethkador—is *not* coded as a routine intelligence asset. He is coded as a level 1-A security risk. He is a known assassin and saboteur, and will readily violate his diplomatic privilege to carry out such acts. The special protocols for handling this individual indicate that he is to be kept in restraints and under guard at all times, and is not to be allowed within two hundred meters of any class-one or -two communication, computation, guidance, or weaponry systems. He is presently within one hundred meters of multiple systems of each type I just enumerated."

Over the course of this clipped-syllable summary, the liaison had flushed, then gone white, and now looked as though he might vomit.

Conversely, his prisoner's smile had widened slowly but steadily. From over the pasty-faced liaison's shoulder, the Ktoran said mildly, "It is always nice to be appreciated."

Downing didn't take his eyes off the ambassador who had very nearly misled the human command staff into believing that the only possible resolution to the war with the Arat Kur was extermination, rather than negotiation. "Mr. Rinehart."

"Sir!"

"You will please take charge of this detachment. You will convey the prisoner back to the secure containment facility in cargo module seventeen-D. He is to be returned to his hermetically sealed quarters therein. You will retask Mr. Wu to resume direct monitoring of this individual. Once Mr. Wu is in place, you shall evacuate the air from the cargo bay and leave a full platoon of Marines on level-two alert in the designated overwatch positions surrounding, and leading to, module seventeen-D. I regret to order that you rouse Major Rulaine to command the entire detachment, but he is the best person for this job. Return here once you have ascertained who gave orders for our 'guest' to be removed from the secure containment facility. That person either ignored, or somehow missed, the authorization level required to do so."

As the Naval Intelligence liaison stepped aside, Gray Rinehart stepped forward, drawing his side-arm: a liquimix NeoCoBro machine-pistol. He leveled it at the Ktoran ambassador. "Mr. Shethkador, I trust you are going to be fully cooperative."

"I have been thus far. This young officer asked that I accompany him to this place. I did so without hesitation or question. I trust that was sufficiently cooperative."

Rinehart made no direct response. "After you, Mr. Shethkador. Lieutenant, you lead the way back. Detachment: weapons off safety. And leave me a clear field of fire."

Murmurs of assent accompanied the group back out the door, which sealed slowly behind them.

"That was strange," Caine said.

"More than strange," Downing amended, still staring at the door. "That should never have happened. When Major Rulaine was taken off the detail to provide overwatch for your meeting with the Slaasriithi ambassador earlier today, I personally replaced him with a new IRIS striker: Peter Wu, one of the tunnel rats who breached the Arat Kur compound in Jakarta."

Sukhinin's frown deepened. "So, this could not simply be a clerical error, a 'glitch' as you say."

"No, it can't. There's a reason I assigned Wu to report directly to me as the watchdog over our Ktoran guest. If anyone tried to countermand our security precautions, he was present to inform them that they may not do so unless they have a bloody executive order. Or one from the Joint Chiefs."

Caine looked up from the holoplot. "So why didn't Wu call in?" *And why is it that, every time the Ktor are involved, there's always something that goes inexplicably awry? Power plants short out, pacemakers stop working, airlocks burst open, computers malfunction, monorails crash…*

Downing shrugged. "Wu's silence is actually not so much suspicious as it is a matter of bad protocol management. All matters pertaining to the disposition and whereabouts of the Ktoran ambassador must remain on a secure channel, so Wu could not use the intercom. But the call to general-quarters shut down his collarcom. Only command-grade intra-hull wireless is permitted during battle stations. Otherwise, there's too much EM emission and too much unnecessary comchatter."

Sukhinin folded his hands. His tone was low and respectful: a sure sign that a circumspect criticism was forthcoming. "So Mr. Wu's inability to report this matter promptly is an operational—er, slip—that shall want redressing, yes?"

Downing's smile was pinched. "Yes, Vassily. I'll get fleet security to change the protocols."

Caine pointed into the holotank. "You're not the only one making changes. Look."

The red mote denoting the Ktoran intruder had now begun to spawn a small swarm of ruby pinpricks.

"Drones." Sukhinin drew in a long breath, then: "Perhaps they have come to fight, after all."

"I don't know," murmured Downing as he rubbed a finger meditatively across his lower lip. "I still think the odds are so heavily stacked against them that—"

The alert-status lights flashed anew and the klaxons emitted a rapid, three-pulse warning.

Sukhinin, who was not intimately familiar with Commonwealth shipboard procedures during general quarters, started. "*Shto*? What is this? We are not already at battle-stations?"

Downing frowned. "We are. This is a special alert, reserved to call attention to an additional, unexpected development or threat."

Caine saw two of the flatscreens over the holotank brighten. He stared, then pointed. "You mean something like that?" The two older men glanced up.

A dim, fragmentary shape—part flattened ellipse, part droop-winged delta—stood out, ghostlike, against the darkened half of the larger of Sigma Draconis' two moons.

"Yes," Downing said quietly, "I mean something like that."

A fleetwide sitrep erupted from the room's speakers: "Unidentified bogey at one-hundred-twelve kiloklicks, bearing 175 by 13, relative ecliptic. Assumed to be hostile. All helms: commence defensive evolution Echo Whiskey Seven Niner in sixty seconds measured from my mark. And...mark. All remote CICs are to activate InPic telepresence systems and prepare for—"

Asked over the torrent of orders, Sukhinin's questions came out as dry-throated croaks: "What ship is that, and where did it come from?"

But as more of the mystery ship came into view, its outline now picked out by a ladar scan, Caine realized that he'd seen that shape before. In fact, it was identical to that of the first exosapient spacecraft that human eyes had ever beheld—

"That's a Dornaani ship, not Ktoran," Caine shouted. "Tell our people to stand down. It's here to aid us, not attack us."

Downing squinted at the image. "Yes, it's rather like the one that carried us to meet our exosapient neighbors at Convocation. But still, it could be a trap. The Ktor are no doubt aware we are familiar with that Dornaani design, might logically use it to fool us, if only briefly, into thinking—"

"Then don't trust your eyes," Caine interrupted. "Get Admiral Silverstein or Admiral Halifax—or whoever you can reach—to run a spectroscopic check on that ship's hull materials. And to analyze the drive emissions, while they're at it. Lemuel Wasserman ran those same scans the first time we saw that ship, said that both yielded distinctive results. So if the comparison produces a match—"

Caine fell silent: Downing, convinced, had turned away, was already busy trying to get in touch with the fleet's commanders.

Sukhinin looked over. He smiled faintly. "You are starting to sound like a genuine naval officer. So perhaps you were *not* sleeping during the classes they rushed you through at Barnard's Star Two-C."

Caine tried to smile, but couldn't. He remembered the classrooms he had occupied for as many as twelve hours a day at the joint Commonwealth and Federation naval base—The Pearl—located beneath the uninhabitable surface of Barney Deucy. "I had great instructors," was all he could say. Because the classrooms and instructors and the Pearl itself were just so much floating detritus now, the residual spoor of the surprise attack with which the Arat Kur had commenced their war upon humanity.

Downing looked up. "Analysis of the new ship's hull is ongoing. There is no thrust signature, so no help there. The vessel is now emitting the transponder code reserved for the Accord's Custodian vessels, although that proves nothing."

"Well," temporized Caine, "it does prove one of three things."

Sukhinin's eyebrows raised. "Oh? And what would those be?"

Caine shrugged. "One, that it's a Custodian ship. Or two, that the Ktor are emulating a Custodial vessel, which is so severe a violation of the Accords that they must be planning to renounce their membership, anyway. Or third, that someone else is trying to run a false-flag operation."

Sukhinin glanced at Downing and added a shrug of his own. "Caine has a point. Well, three of them."

"Probably so," conceded Downing. "But new sensor data is pointing to the first alternative. Hull results match those from the Dornaani ship. Fleet sensor ops are still trying to puzzle out how it was lurking there the whole time and we didn't see it."

Caine remembered some of what Lemuel Wasserman had remarked about the initial readings he got from the Dornaani ship. "Wasserman speculated that their hull was made out of material that had variable physical properties, controllable by the operator. At first, our radar couldn't register it. Attempts to get an active scan outline came back like a froth of random noise. But then all of a sudden, our readings cleared up. As if the Dornaani had hit the 'off' switch on a variable stealth device."

Downing was nodding. "That's what fleet is reporting now: the same 'fade in' effect, only much, much quicker. So, unless the Ktor have the same capabilities and have built a Q-ship that matches the Dornaani design, meter for meter and curve for curve, I rather suspect that our newcomers are—"

The room's speakers reactivated, filled the room with a carrier tone. "Mr. Downing?" The accent could have belonged to a BBC newsreader.

"Yes?"

"This is Commander Mark Lucas, Royal Naval Intelligence aboard HMS *Trafalgar*, contacting you at the instruction of Admiral Lord Halifax, who sends his compliments. We are receiving signals from the Dornaani Custodial ship *Olsloov*. The Dornaani indicate that they are about to initiate a communiqué in which we may not participate, but in which we might have a keen interest."

"Thank you, Commander. If I parse that correctly, our Custodian friends are inviting us to eavesdrop on a conversation they are about to have with the Ktoran intruders."

"That's the gist of it, sir. But I repeat: access is not being offered for our command staff, not even Admiral Lord Halifax. Just *you*. And Commander Riordan."

"And Consul Sukhinin?"

An extended pause. "Yes, sir: the Custodians are pleased to approve Consul Sukhinin, as well."

"Excellent. By the way, did the Custodian communicating with you identify him- or herself?"

"Yes, sir. The Dornaani's name is Alnduul, Senior Mentor of the Custodians' Terran Oversight Group." A pause. "Is that significant, Mr. Downing?"

Chapter Three

Downing turned toward Caine with a broad smile. Riordan reflected that it was probably a match for the one he felt growing on his own face. *So, Alnduul is still in the vicinity. Thank God.*

The British naval intelligence officer cleared his throat. "Mr. Downing? Did you read me? Am I to infer that this 'Alnduul' is a friend?"

"Sorry, Commander. Yes, I did read you. And yes, Alnduul is most assuredly a friend."

About the best damned one we have among the exosapients, Caine added silently. *Maybe the only one we have.*

"Very well, sir. I'm adding you to Alnduul's comm channel." Rather than shutting off, the speakers remained active, a white-noise hum filling the compartment.

Sukhinin was frowning. "These Dornaani: they make me uneasy."

Downing shrugged. "Well, Vassily, they *are* exosapients."

"Bah. I am referring to their actions. Alnduul was with us only a few days ago, yes? He was present when we discovered that the Ktor are not only murderers and liars, but a breed of displaced humans." He literally spat. "So, once all was well, and the Arat Kur had agreed to negotiate with us, Alnduul takes his leave, waving his long fingers like streamers in the wind and wishing us enlightenment. A small ship collects him, swings behind the larger moon and disappears. So we presume that the ship must have contained a miraculously small shift drive and that he is gone.

21

"But today, our Mr. Alnduul shows up in the vicinity of the same moon, commanding a ship that has probably been floating there the whole time. In what should be plain sight. So I must wonder: how many days has it been watching everything we do, eavesdropping on every message we send? No." Sukhinin shook his head. His meaty jowls amplified the motion. "I do not like it."

"Well, he doesn't lie to us," Caine pointed out.

"Perhaps not, *parnishka*, but he doesn't tell us all the truth, either. It would have been nice to know he was perched near the larger moon like a great, invisible vulture, watching us."

"Or watching *over* us, as seems to be the case here."

"Or maybe both." Downing raised his hands to stop the debate. "I think it unwise to either be too wary, or too trusting, of the Dornaani at this point. But Alnduul, at least, has demonstrated his willingness to help us, even at the expense of his reputation among the rest of the Dornaani Collective."

Sukhinin huffed. "So *he* says!"

Richard sighed. "Vassily, while I am quite a fan of Russian caution, not to say cynicism, I must—"

The carrier tone from the speakers acquired a fine thread of static: an open channel. "This is Senior Mentor Alnduul of the Accord Custodians, sending to Ktoran vessel. You are currently in violation of the Thirteenth Accord, which requires that you run a transponder at all times."

"With all due respect," a human voice answered, its tone suggesting that the amount of respect due was very minuscule, "this vessel is running with an active transponder."

"Incorrect. You are running a locator beacon only. The Thirteenth Accord stipulates that your transponder must also relay your ship's polity of origin, its name or code, its master, and any special conditions under which it might be operating."

The human voice was bored and dismissive. "We openly identified our origins and our purpose shortly after shifting into this system."

"You have violated the Accord, even so. All required data must be included in the transponder signal at all times."

"Senior Mentor Alnduul, it would be most agreeable if you do not belabor this matter. It is a quibble."

"It is the law. You will adjust your transponder signal immediately."

Caine wondered if the human voice was going to respond, *Or you'll do what?*

But instead, Downing, who was listening closely to his earbud, pointed to one of the flatscreens. A new wave of transponder data scrolled past, indicating that the vessel was indeed from the Ktoran Sphere, was named *Ferocious Monolith*, listed Olsirkos Shethkador-vah as the acting captain, and had been sent under the auspices of an authority labeled "Autarchal Aegis" to retrieve ambassador Tlerek Srin Shethkador, presumed to be in Arat Kur space.

Alnduul's voice was more crisp than Caine had ever heard it. "Your compliance is appreciated, *Ferocious Monolith*. It is difficult to conceive why the Ktoran Sphere, currently under numerous Custodial sanctions, would fail to instruct its ships to observe the Accords more carefully. Today's violations would be significant at the best of times. Given your polity's suspended membership privileges, it is extremely severe."

"Perhaps we do not attach the same measure of importance to rules-stickling. Our attention is focused upon our mission to retrieve Tlerek Srin Shethkador, a mission which your own superiors approved some weeks ago. Consequently, our arrival here should not cause consternation. Or a violent repulse by the so-called 'Terrans.'"

"I possess a copy of the Custodial travel warrant that confers permission for you to enter this system to retrieve your ambassador. However, that warrant stipulates that you are to arrive no earlier than eight days from now."

"We hope it is understandable that we are eager to reclaim Srin Shethkador. That is the cause of our haste and early arrival."

"Yeah," drawled Caine, "sure it is."

Alnduul wasn't having any of it, either: "Given the Ktoran Sphere's recent violations of various accords and Custodial mandates, these additional infractions do not bode well for reinstatement of your membership."

The reply was unruffled. "I believe the correct terminology is *alleged* violations."

Alnduul's voice was as flat and cold as a skating rink. "Sophistry. Characterizing your violations as 'alleged' is akin to characterizing the laws of gravity as 'tentative.'"

"Yet, until a judgment is made, the term 'alleged' is consonant with the juridical protocols of the Accord and Custodians. Is it not?"

"You are correct." Alnduul sounded as though he would have rather eaten his own leg than agree. "For now, you will immediately cease all offensive operations and terminate your acceleration. Once you have complied, we will communicate the purpose, and legitimacy, of your mission here to the representatives of the Consolidated Terran Republic. We will encourage them to return your ambassador as soon as they may, at which point you are ordered—under Custodial authority—to commence preacceleration and depart the system as quickly as practicable. An approved list of systems whereby you may return to the Ktoran Sphere will be relayed to you at the end of this communiqué. To deviate from that route will lead to swift repercussions."

"We shall be duly attentive to your instructions." The Ktoran carrier wave faded out, followed shortly by an increase in light static: two-way communication was now possible.

Alnduul's voice returned to its customary, milder tone. "Gentlemen, the Ktoran interlopers are no longer on the channel."

Sukhinin didn't waste a second. "Many thanks, *gospodin* Alnduul, for providing us with timely information regarding the Ktor's expected arrival."

Alnduul sounded puzzled. "But . . . I did not."

"Of course not. Nor did you share other relevant information." Sukhinin was flushed now. "You did not let us know you were still in the system, did not let us know that the Ktor were coming, did not immediately intervene when they arrived. Let me see—am I missing anything?"

Sukhinin's sarcasm was no longer lost on Alnduul. "I assure you, it was our intent to apprise you of the Ktor's imminent arrival once the negotiations with the Arat Kur were well under way."

"Why? So that we might enjoy a few more days of blissful ignorance?"

"No. To ensure that the Arat Kur negotiators could not be emboldened by rumors of the pending arrival of their strongest allies. And also to ensure that we remained undetected for as long as possible. That way, the exchanges between yourselves and the Arat Kur could not be accused of taking place under Custodial auspices."

Downing managed to ask a question before Sukhinin could

find another argumentative brickbat to sling at Alnduul. "But wouldn't it be best for the negotiations to have the implicit benefit of Custodial oversight?"

"Although the Arat Kur have violated the most crucial of all the Accord's rules, they are still members, which means that they may still expect equal access to information. On the other hand, humanity is still a protected species, since the Convocation at which you were to have received your membership was derailed by the disputes which led to the late war."

Sukhinin became even more red. "And so you would support these attackers of our homeworld—these *chudovishnie* Roaches—against us in the negotiations, if they asked?"

Alnduul sounded weary. "It is not so simple a matter as that, Consul Sukhinin. No Custodian—indeed, I believe no one in the entirety of the Dornaani Collective—would wish to take the side of the Arat Kur against your interests and claims for reparation. But this scenario is without precedent in the annals of the Accord. Therefore, we felt it best to let the disputatious parties come to their own agreements. Specifically, if you wished to aggressively seek reparations for war damages, we did not wish the Arat Kur to know we were present, and thus, to exercise their right to call upon us for mediation. As they now might, if word reaches them that we are still present in this system."

Downing rubbed his chin. "So perhaps the Ktor's early arrival is not simply a consequence of their excessive enthusiasm for retrieving Tlerek Srin Shethkador."

"I'm sure that the timing of *Ferocious Monolith*'s appearance serves many Ktoran agendas, not the least of which would be to remove the ambassador before his identity as a human was revealed. Of course, they had no way to know that they were already too late to prevent that."

Sukhinin placed a fist on the commo console. "And you still insist that it is wise for us to help these *virodki* hide their true nature?"

Caine leaned toward the Russian. "Vassily, if we *don't*, we lose the only leverage we have over them. I don't know how long the Ktor expect to be able to conceal their speciate identity and their genocidal campaign against the Arat Kur over ten thousand years ago, but evidently they consider it important to suppress that information for now."

Alnduul's eyelids nictated once, quickly. "Caine Riordan is correct. At this moment in time, you are well-advised to protect the secret of the Ktor. Sometimes, a long-term benefit is derived from maintaining a short-term silence. Accordingly, I encourage you to return the Ktoran ambassador to his ship. But I may not *instruct* you to do so, since you are not members of the Accord."

Sukhinin cocked a wicked eyebrow at Downing. "It might be useful, as well as amusing, to keep this *moshennik* Shethkador around for a bit longer, hey? Extract some repayment for what he wanted to extort from humanity? And let his comrades shake their fists."

"Vassily—" Downing began carefully.

"Bah, Richard, you take me too seriously." Sukhinin gestured into the holotank: the red blip and its small cloud of attendant ruby mayflies were still chasing the actinic blue points, albeit lazily. "I know the Ktor have not come just to shake their fists: they will use them, if they become too aggravated. I speak of what I wish to do, not what I recommend we do."

Caine sighed, smiled. "Well, that's a relief."

Sukhinin's eyes moved to meet Caine's, but his wolfish smile did not change. "I'm glad you feel so, *parnishka*."

Caine had learned that when Sukhinin used that familiar appellation, the odds were dead even that he was about to drop a bomb on the person so addressed. "I'm not sure I like the way you said that, Vassily."

Sukhinin had the good grace to look abashed and sounded genuinely apologetic. "Caine, surely you must see what this means."

"What this means—?"

Alnduul's voice intruded. "I believe Consul Sukhinin is suggesting that you escort Ambassador Shethkador back to his ship."

Caine remembered the pasty, nauseous appearance of the hapless security liaison only ten minutes ago and was fairly certain his own face looked like that now. "You're joking."

Downing shook his head. "I'm sorry, but no. Firstly, we can't let any Ktor on our ships. We have seen how much unexplained havoc seems to follow wherever they go. Secondly, whilst Vassily and I are the only ones who *should* go, who have the diplomatic credentials, neither of us are permitted. He is a World Confederation Consul: he shouldn't even be this close to a potential war zone. And in my case, well, there are a few too many of IRIS' secrets up here." Richard tapped the side of his head.

"I'm in IRIS, too," Caine offered lamely.

"Being in IRIS is a great deal different than being in *charge* of IRIS, Caine. Besides, if we do send you over, that might actually help take any enemy spotlight off you."

"Because if you're willing to send me, they'll deduce that I mustn't know anything they're interested in?"

"Exactly."

"And if they decide to dissect me, just to make sure?"

Alnduul broke in hastily. "I would not permit that."

"Alnduul, no disrespect, but you won't be there."

"No, but we may equip you with a biomonitor. If the data stream from it is in any way obstructed, impaired, or altered, my ship will consider it a hostile act against a person who is acting at the behest of the Custodians."

"Does that mean you're . . . uh, deputizing me?"

"Nothing so involved as that. But the twenty-first accord allows me to solicit help from willing parties in accomplishing the mandate of that accord. If you agree to carry out this task, you will have our express protection. Over which I have full and immediate control."

For the first time in many months, Caine felt that he had just become more, rather than less, safe. *But damn it, stepping foot on a Ktoran vessel? Really?* "Look, can't we avoid all this?"

Downing folded his arms. "How?"

"By handling the transfer the same way we handled my meeting with the Slaasriithi ambassador. We rendezvous with the Ktor at a module floating in space. They get Shethkador and go back to their ship. We return and go into quarantine. That way, no one"—*which is to say,* me—"has to journey into the belly of the Ktoran beast." Caine waited for someone to say something, even Alnduul. But no one did. "Well?" he asked.

Downing looked up. "Caine, if we do that, we'll be losing an immense opportunity. By asking for us to return Shethkador, the Ktor are also inviting us to go to their ship. To see it from the inside."

Caine blinked, sputtered. "Well, it's just fine with me if we pass up that 'opportunity.'"

"Caine, our ability to fight the Ktor—which hopefully won't happen for some time, if ever—will be markedly improved by every bit of specific data we can gather about them and their technology."

"Well, then send an engineer, someone who's got that skill set."

"Caine, your powers of observation and deduction are exactly the skill set we need in this circumstance. If we sent an engineer, we might miss important social and cultural details. If we sent a xenologist, we might miss technical components. We need someone who specializes in observation itself, and who has a broad enough knowledge-base to sift out significant factors from background noise. And that specialist is you. That's why you've become the first choice for first contact."

"Richard, you may mean that as flattery, but I hear it as a death sentence."

"I know you do, and it's beastly bad luck that we have to ask you to go back into the bull-ring again, but we've been handed a short-lived opportunity and no time to prepare for it. You have the best skill set, and you also have had the closest prior contact with the Ktor."

"When you say 'close contact,' are you including that arm-spike Shethkador fired into my back in Jakarta? The one that would have done me in if it hadn't been for Dornaani surgeons? Because, I've got to tell you, that kind of 'close contact' is a little *too* close for my tastes. Don't want to repeat it."

"We—and significantly, Alnduul—will not allow that to happen."

Vassily opened his hands in appeal. "Understandable. But if you will not go, you know what will happen, of course."

Caine felt his stomach sink. "You'll send someone else."

Sukhinin shrugged, his expression a hang-dog acceptance that life was inherently unfair. "Of course."

Riordan pushed back from the holotank, disgusted. "I guess I don't have a lot of prep time."

Downing's eyes were sad, apologetic. "No, you don't. Let's get started."

Chapter Four

FAR ORBIT
SIGMA DRACONIS TWO

Strapped into one of the forward acceleration couches in a Commonwealth armored pinnace, Caine glanced back toward the cargo section where Tlerek Srin Shethkador and Miles O'Garran's security detachment were waiting. Downing was alongside Riordan, studying the feed from the forward sensors. "Do we have a visual yet?"

Downing shook his head. "No, but it's still early."

Caine rubbed his hands, felt chilly despite the constant twenty degrees centigrade maintained inside the armored pinnace. "You know, I'm surprised the Ktor agreed to have me come aboard. My prior exchanges with them haven't exactly been pleasant, and I just outed Shethkador—and therefore, all of the Ktor—as humans a couple of days ago. I doubt I'm on their 'favorite Earth-folks' list right now."

Downing's smile was faint. "True, but it's of no consequence. You'll go aboard, present your credentials, participate in whatever ridiculous minuet of courtesies and verbal fencing they elect to impose, and be present long enough to see Shethkador aboard to the satisfaction of this Olsirkos Shethkador-vah."

"Sirs," the copilot called into the passenger compartment, "I have a visual of *Ferocious Monolith*. Feed three, if you want to take a look."

"Very good, Lieutenant," called Downing, who pulled the screen into a position where both he and Caine could study it.

Riordan wasn't convinced he was looking at a shift-carrier at first. It did not have the distinctively freight-train modular appearance of all human and most Arat Kur shift-capable craft. It was shaped rather like a thickened Neolithic arrowhead, a wide, flat delta shape, with a notch separating the warhead from the after part that would be lashed to the shaft. There were no rotating habitats in evidence, and further surface details were hard to discern because, unlike any other spacecraft Riordan had ever seen, its surface was dead black. *Truly dead black*, Caine realized as he looked for reflections and found none. "I think that hull is designed to absorb light," he muttered.

Downing nodded. "The same sort of effect we've noticed with the Dornaani. But this is a damned odd hull design. How do they maintain gravity equivalent in crew quarters? And if that large section aft of the widest part of the delta-shape houses their engineering decks, then how the devil do they shield themselves from the output?"

Answers started presenting themselves. Caine pointed to a pair of transverse seams that had appeared close to the center of the arrowhead. "Something is separating from the hull; a whole band of it is lifting up."

"No," corrected Downing after a moment, "that band of hull is splitting apart along the ship's centerline, dividing into two equal halves that are moving out from its axis."

Caine squinted and then understood what he was looking at. "Those two halves, at the end of those extending pylons: those are the rotational habitats."

Which now underwent a further transformation. The two faces of each segment began to split apart and open like a jackknife. They ultimately unfolded into two hinged, mirror-image halves, the top and bottom faces joined at a one-hundred-twenty-degree angle of incidence. They began to spin around the ship's long axis.

"That's a pretty impressive piece of engineering," Downing murmured.

"I don't think they're done showing off, though," commented Caine, who had noticed movement back along the notch that divided the ship into its forward and aft sections. "Look." From the section behind the notch, fins or sails were extending outward.

Downing frowned. "What the devil—?"

"Sirs!" exclaimed the copilot. "Intruder energy output is spiking, neutrinos increasing sharply. I think their engines are—"

But Caine didn't hear the rest. The fins or sails were becoming a kind of black parasol around the stern of the ship, screening the forward personnel and cargo section from the aft engineering decks.

As the parasol continued to expand outward like a skirt, the copilot reported, "We are no longer in the line of the emissions, sir, but they continue to spike. We can detect the bloom around the edge of that...that stingray's peacock tail."

Downing glanced at Caine. "A peacock-tailed stingray: seems as good a description as any."

Caine shrugged. "Better than anything I'd have come up with."

Downing grinned crookedly. "I thought you were a writer."

Caine tried to return the grin, but couldn't get past the irony of who had whisked him out of that career, thereby destroying it. "Yes, well, two guys from IRIS put an end to that about fifteen years ago, now—*Richard*."

Downing looked like he had swallowed his tongue. Or wanted to. "Caine, I—"

Caine shook his head. "Sorry, Richard. I don't know if I'll ever be able to joke about that. But what's done is done. I'm where I need to be, I guess, and we work well together. Let's leave it at that, yeh?"

Downing nodded, avoided Caine's eyes by focusing intently on the screen. "Look at the thermal image overlay."

Caine did, and frowned. "Damn, with all the energy their power plant is putting out, that flimsy parasol ought to be white-hot by now. The neutrinos alone should be cutting straight through—"

Downing shook his head. "No. It's not just a shield. Look how its rim temperature drops off rapidly, even down where the parasol emerges from the hull. And it's not just a radiator, either."

Caine felt his eyebrows rise slightly. "Advanced thermionic materials?"

Downing shrugged. "What else makes sense? Whatever that parasol is made of, it not only absorbs heat but eliminates it, probably by converting it directly into electricity. And it's doing so at efficiency levels that are at least an order of magnitude greater than anything we have. It's a damper, shield, and power-reclamation system all in one. A pearl of great price."

"Yes, and another bit of purposeful bragging," Caine added. "A ship with a system like that is going to have a much better power-to-mass ratio than ours or the Arat Kurs'."

Downing nodded. "To say nothing of higher operating efficiency and better ready power levels."

Caine sighed, leaned back. "So they've shown us that they can put a tiger worth of hurt in the body of a housecat. But there is one significant drawback to their dominance display."

Downing smiled. "They've shown us how much higher we need to be able to jump if we want to match them. Although I must say that is a high, high bar."

Caine shrugged. "Which means we'd better get hopping." He stood into the zero-gee without remembering to be careful—and discovered that, finally, it was starting to become second nature. "Let's request approach instructions and get this over with."

Shortly after they docked with *Ferocious Monolith*, the Ktoran craft brought its rotating sections to a halt and commenced to spin slowly around its own keel, instead. Caine surmised that was probably because the exchange was likely to take place in the main hull and the Ktor didn't want to go through those formalities in zero-gee. It was pretty hard to look dignified and imposing while floating, unpowered, in midair. Particularly their returning leader, the Srin Tlerek Shethkador.

The *Srin* Shethkador. None of the analysts who had pored over every recorded word of the assassin-ambassador's utterances had been able to determine precisely what a Srin was, nor was Shethkador disposed to clarify the matter for them. It was clearly a title of some importance, but whether it was civil or military, inherited or earned, remained a complete mystery. *And it will probably still be a mystery when this day is over,* Caine reflected as the armored pinnace's docking hatch opened to reveal the Ktoran ship's ingress: a shiny iris valve. After a five-second wait, the plates of the valve dilated with a ringing hiss, revealing four guards in what looked like armored vac suits, unfamiliar weapons at the ready. Faceless behind the black helmet visor that was part of their uniform equipage, one stepped forward and gestured that Caine should approach.

Caine turned and saw that Miles O'Garran was right behind him, the top of his head barely reaching Riordan's shoulder. "Ready, Miles?"

"Whenever you are, sir. But—"

"Yes?"

"Are you *sure* you want me to do this solo, leave my guys back here to keep the ambassador company?"

"I'm sure."

"May I ask why, sir? They're all eager to come along. Real eager."

"That attitude, while laudable, is why I'm leaving them here. For all we know, the Ktor might try to have some fun with us, try to provoke us into making some misstep. I need a seasoned pro who can keep his head clear and his finger away from the trigger if that starts happening. I know you're good for that job. The other guys and gals: they seem a little too heavy on the *oo-rah* and a little light on Zenlike serenity."

O'Garran smiled. "Good working with you again, sir."

"You too, Miles. Let's get this over with."

The corridors to the bridge were masterpieces of defensive architecture: cutbacks, hard-points, doorways, and angles that had been designed to make any hostile boarding attempts a tactical nightmare. *No automated defense blisters or systems of any kind, though,* Caine noted. *Strange.*

Bracketed front and back by their escorts, Caine and O'Garran arrived, without fanfare or much warning, on the bridge of the *Ferocious Monolith.* They passed through a slightly wider auto-mated hatchway and were suddenly in the surprisingly small compartment. Caine peripherally noted various details: that they hadn't come through the largest entry to the bridge; that most of the crew were in plain gray flight suits; that instead of appearing extremely advanced, the bridge was spartan. It even lacked the minimalist elegance Riordan associated with higher technology: it was a triumph of ugly utilitarianism.

But Caine did not focus on any of these, or the hundred other details that vied for his attention. *The best way to look anxious and disoriented is to gawk at my surroundings. And I'm not here to look like a yokel with wide eyes and hat in hand. This is the lair of dominance-obsessed predators; my job is to find the alpha and look him in the eyes and keep looking. And to not blink. Not once.*

Riordan did not have long to wait. A tall, trim Ktoran— much adorned with what were presumably symbols of rank or achievement—turned from a cluster of advisors and faced the human visitors. He stared.

Caine stared back...and did not approach.

The Ktoran frowned. "I am Olsirkos Shethkador-vah, Master of *Ferocious Monolith*. You may approach."

Well, I see we're going to start the wrestling match right away. "I am Commander Caine Riordan, Consolidated Terran Republic Naval Forces. I have *been* approaching since I boarded your ship. I am here to present my credentials and documents concerning the violations, condition, and repatriation of Ambassador Tlerek Srin Shethkador." And he did not move, except to hold up the relevant papers: hard copy only, both to follow diplomatic protocol and because the last thing either human or Ktoran computer experts wanted was to have any contact between their respective systems.

Olsirkos narrowed his eyes. "Evidently you do not understand our customs."

"Probably not. Evidently you do not understand ours, either. I presume you wish to have the Srin returned before I depart?"

"You will not depart without returning the Srin."

"I will if you do not take these documents from me."

"Allow me to rephrase. You shall not be permitted to depart if you do not follow our customs and acknowledge my authority in the appropriate manner before we proceed."

"Allow me to explicate. If I am not allowed to leave when I choose to do so, the Dornaani will see to it that any obstructions are removed. Forcibly. And while you have our cordial respect, your authority is over your own personnel, not us." Caine kept the documents upraised and motionless.

The crewmembers near Olsirkos—mostly officers, from the look of them—glanced at the master of the ship. In contrast, the gray-suited personnel at the duty stations seemed desperate to focus their attention on something else—*anything* else.

Olsirkos' color had begun to change, but then the flush of anger receded—with unnatural speed, it seemed to Caine. As if that involuntary reaction had been explicitly and swiftly countermanded. Instead, the Ktoran smiled. "It would be interesting to see," he commented in an almost diffident tone as he stepped down from the command platform, "how this encounter would have played out in the absence of your Dornaani warders."

"Probably less well for me," Caine admitted, "but no different for you. With or without the support of our Dornaani friends,

Tlerek Srin Shethkador will only be returned when proper protocol is observed."

"And if we had elected to seize your armored pinnace and take
him?" Olsirkos approached slowly.

"You would have discovered that there is a an explosive
decompression setting for the Srin's compartment, rigged to a
deadman switch."

"Which you have just revealed, minimizing its effectiveness."

"True, but you would have less luck neutralizing the bombs
on board the pinnace, since they are activated by both command
detonation controllers and breach-sensitive countdown triggers.
The blast would not only vaporize the Srin, but also severely
damage this ship."

Evidently, Olsirkos Shethkador-vah had not been expecting that
response: he halted at a distance of two meters. He also did not
seem to suspect that the second threat might be a lie; rather, he
seemed to reassess Caine. Who could see, in the Ktor's subtle
shift into a deceptively casual stance, his opponent's decision to
change tactics. "I know you," Olsirkos said.

Caine swatted away a rising edge of anxiety. "Indeed?"

Olsirkos seemed disappointed that the rhetorical shift had not
rattled the human. "Yes, but I thought you were a diplomat, a
delegate to the late, disastrous Convocation where our peoples
first met. Yet here you are, a member of your planet's quaint
military forces."

Ignoring the goad implicit in the adjective "quaint," Caine
shrugged. "Once we discerned that war was imminent, many
people elected to join the fight that led to the defeat of your
allies. I was simply one of them."

Olsirkos fought down his color once again. "You mistake our
role in your late conflict with the Arat Kur and the Hkh'Rkh.
We were not their allies. We merely shared common interests
and provided advisors. Furthermore, the forces you claim to be
invaders were invited planetside by humans—by leaders of some of
your most powerful megacorporations, if the reports are accurate."

"The reports are accurate, but evidently incomplete. The megacorporations have no standing before the Accord, and no power
to speak for the people of Earth or the broader Terran Republic.
And besides, I don't recall anyone inviting the Arat Kur and
Hkh'Rkh to mount their initial sneak attack upon our naval base

at Barnard's Star. As to the matter of whether or not you were their allies, I can only report that they claim you were."

"Yes, the endless war of words." Olsirkos smiled. "We have not declared war upon Earth, and only had advisors present, but you list us along with the actual invaders, who then attempt to embroil us in the hostilities by claiming an alliance that does not exist. Ask them to produce any such official documents or treaties to which we were party with them. You will find none."

And why am I not surprised in the least? "Whatever circumstances are claimed by our respective governments, Tlerek Srin Shethkador committed several crimes while upon Earth—and since, while in our custody."

"Ah, you are referring to his attacks upon yourself and others?"

"Others?" Damn, I wish I had the time to—"Those are among the charges, yes."

"And perhaps they were valid. But they ceased to matter when your World Confederation accepted him as our official representative and ambassador, who then traveled to this system with your fleet. As I understand it, any alleged transgressions he may have committed before that appointment were, of necessity, pardoned. He could hardly be both a felon and an ambassador, after all." Olsirkos' smile was that of a man twisting a knife in an old enemy's heart or, in this case, twisting the robotic arm Shethkador had fired into Caine's back in Jakarta.

"This," Caine commented after a sigh, "has been a diverting conversation, but it grows tiresome. I take it you wish to have the Srin returned promptly?" He waggled the papers in his hand.

Olsirkos' smile faded. "Yes, I do." Without allowing his gaze to drift from Caine's eyes, he snapped an order at a gray-suited crewman to his left. "You, autarchon, fetch the documents."

The gray-suited figure swung around, his eyes avoiding both Caine's and Olsirkos', took the papers gently but firmly from Riordan's hands and transferred them to his superior with a slight bow of his head and bend at his waist.

"Return to your post," Olsirkos muttered as he glanced down at the sheaf of documents and then held it back over his shoulder. "Intendant Hekarem, see that these are in order."

One of the nearby officers fairly leaped forward, took the papers out of Olsirkos Shethkador-vah's hand with an excess of care, and retreated to peruse them.

Caine returned Olsirkos' stare and discovered that he did not have to feign boredom anymore. The dominance duel that had started as riveting had become repetitive, then pointless, and now, childish. *But damn it, I can't look away if he doesn't do so first, so I guess I just have to—*

Olsirkos looked past Caine toward O'Garran. His smile transformed into a smirk. "Pitiful," he said.

Oh, no. Little Guy, don't you dare—

Miles "Little Guy" O'Garran's retaliatory inquiry was quiet, controlled, and full of rage. "Would you care to clarify?"

Damn it, O'Garran, I told you: we're not here to start a war; we're here to end one. Caine cleared his throat for Olsirkos' attention. "It may not be inconsiderate to openly comment upon a stranger in Ktoran culture," Caine observed in a neutral voice. "It is considered offensive in ours."

"Oh, I am familiar enough with your cultures. But you are on our ship, and we will not put our conventions aside for your comfort."

"I was not asking you to." Caine reflected that this first contact—with another branch of humanity—was, in every conceivable way, by far the most unpleasant one he'd ever experienced. "I was simply explaining my companion's reaction."

"Yes. I am aware. Frankly, I was not staring, but examining your servitor. I find it most amusing that you elect to bring the inferiorities of your culture wherever you go. Whether out of blindness or perverse pride, I cannot discern."

"The inferiorities of our culture?"

"But of course." Olsirkos gestured toward O'Garran as if he were a disappointing show dog. "The physical insufficiencies of this servitor alone prove my point. We would never tolerate a genetic deficiency that is so obvious, and so easily corrected. And if we did, we would never make such a specimen a warrior."

O'Garran made no sound, which worried Caine more than if he had. "You know," Riordan said with a mirthless smile, "we have a saying on Earth about combat capability: that it's not the size of the dog in the fight; it's the size of the fight in the dog." And then, over his shoulder: "Sorry, Miles; no offense intended."

Caine could hear the grin in Little Guy's response. "Absolutely none taken, sir. And oo-rah."

Olsirkos matched Caine's stare, smiled when he saw he was not going to win that dominance contest. "Yes, I have heard that inane axiom. All other physical parameters being equal, size is decisive."

"Oh, you must mean as demonstrated by the Hkh'Rkh, who average almost two and a half meters? But I wonder if the example of the Hkh'Rkh adequately supports your implication that Chief O'Garran is an inferior warfighter. Indeed, the accuracy of that claim could have been assessed during the recent fighting in Jakarta." Riordan shrugged. "But it would be difficult to gather the relevant Hkh'Rkhs' opinions on that matter."

"Why so?"

"Because they're all dead. Chief O'Garran was not in a position to take any prisoners that day."

Olsirkos blinked. And Caine responded with a widened smile. *Gotcha, asshole.* "May I presume that our credentials have been verified and that the initial pleasantries are over?"

"They are indeed over." Olsirkos' stare, now openly hostile, reminded Caine of a chained attack dog straining at its collar. "The papers are in order. Return the Srin at once."

Caine folded his hands. "This will go more quickly if you observe proper diplomatic, or even military, etiquette. Such as: since we're not under your command, you will secure our cooperation by making requests, not by giving orders." *And while your enraged eyeballs try to jump right out of your head, I will ignore you and survey my surroundings patiently—and so, observe what I can for the technical intelligence people.*

Affecting disinterested waiting, Riordan could not change the angle of his head too dramatically. He had, at most, one hundred forty degrees of frontal exposure that he could take in, and could not be noticed looking in any one place or at any one object too long.

The most striking item was the crew itself. Its physiognomies and demographics were markedly distinct from any human ship Caine had ever seen or heard about, in any era. The majority of the gray-uniformed drones, one of whom Olsirkos had labeled an "autarchon," were not merely thin, but spindly: probably born, bred, and employed in zero or partial gee. Their tasks—running various ship's systems—were logical extensions of that hypothesis: they were performing duties they'd learned growing up on a space station, a moon, or a ship.

Furthermore, none of the bridge crew appeared to be over thirty-five, forty at the outside, and none of them were women.

Another surprise was the absence of robots. Although consumer and industrial 'bots were rare on Terran ships, most military hulls had a sizeable complement of zero-gee floaters: ROVs that fetched, maintained systems, and carried gear about the ship. No 'bots of any kind, or their ubiquitous charging stations and ready racks, were in evidence on *Ferocious Monolith*.

From what Caine could tell, the Ktoran computers had sophisticated interfaces, but there was a great deal of hard-wire control redundancy. Old-style keyboards, trackballs, and intercom handsets were tucked away in emergency access slots. Clearly, the Ktor preferred hard-wired systems. And come to think of it—

Caine shifted his attention back to the crew, focusing on the officers this time. Sure enough, none of them had collarcoms or their analogs. Instead, they all wore some kind of multipurpose device clipped on their belt, equipped with a spooled cable. But almost no one was using them. In the time he'd been on the bridge, Riordan had seen two autarchons communicating with another part of the ship, and both times, they used one of the numerous—and seemingly anachronistic—hardwired handsets.

While studying the belts of the officers, Riordan also discovered that everyone over the rank of autarchon was armed. All had daggers of some sort, and almost as many had handguns, several of which looked outlandish. But the weapons were not standardized; the greater the apparent importance of any given individual—which Caine inferred to be roughly proportional to their accumulation of medals, insignias, and other official gewgaws—the more profoundly eclectic their gear and attire appeared to be. In fact, the most senior of the bridge crew were all wearing different uniforms. The only common adornment was a small, square, gray shoulder patch.

Peripherally, Caine saw Olsirkos lean in slightly closer. The Ktor muttered, "I request that you return our Srin with all possible speed."

Caine did not hurry to bring his eyes around to meet with the Ktor's. "We are pleased to comply. I will contact the pinnace and have Tlerek Srin Shethkador transferred to your custody."

"Do so."

Riordan tapped a three-tone code into his collarcom. The security detachment would commence unloading the Srin immediately upon receiving it. Making sure that O'Garran was close behind him, he made briskly for the exit.

Chapter Five

Riordan hadn't finished strapping back into his seat aboard the armored pinnace when Downing sealed the hatch to the bridge, snapped off the intercom, activated a white noise generator, and turned toward him urgently. Caine raised his hands: "Richard, calm down. I didn't learn *that* much about the Ktor. I'm sure the debrief—"

"Sod the debrief," Downing said flatly. "It will happen when and if it happens. We've got more pressing matters. We just got a communiqué from the Slaasriithi. They want to go *now*."

"Go where? Home? Well, why's that a problem? They're not needed for the negotiations with the Arat Kur."

"No, Caine. They want to carry human envoys, you and a few others, to their homeworld. And they want to leave in the next twelve hours."

"Richard, that's—that's nuts. They can't just expect us to—"

"They can and they do expect us to accede to their—well, not demand, but very strongly worded exhortation. The arrival of the Ktor seems to worry them. Profoundly. When I pressed them for a slight extension, just a day or two to prepare, they rejected that idea. And how often have you seen the Slaasriithi reject an idea outright?"

"Never."

"Not me, either. Maybe Alnduul will be able to shed a little more light on the matter: I've put in a call to him. But some of

40

the phrasing in the Slaasriithi message—'compromised security' and 'possible infiltration'—leads me to wonder if they already know that the Ktor are actually humans."

Caine saw it. "Damn, of course. If they know that, then they'll realize that the Ktor infiltrated corporations and government agencies on Earth. And each of those infiltrators probably recruited more than a hundred human collaborators. So the longer we stay here, with a Ktor spymaster-assassin now repatriated to one of his own ships, the better the chance they have to activate some sleeper cells that might be in the fleet."

"Exactly. They are probably conjecturing what we already know: that the Ktor can create and control suicidal saboteurs, penetrate many of our data and intelligence networks, and exchange information between their operations cells faster than should be physically possible. Given a few days, they could pull some strings, change some files, and seed any diplomatic team we assemble with one or more of their own operatives. Which, depending upon how and where those operatives struck, could leave the Slaasriithi uncertain of how safe it is to deal with us at all."

The intercom status panel flashed red. Downing jabbed the virtual button. "Yes, Lieutenant?"

"Sorry to interrupt, Mr. Downing, but I have Senior Mentor Alnduul on secure three."

"Thank you, Lieutenant. Patch him through."

The compartment's comm screen brightened, revealing the Dornaani's back-sloping teardrop head and large eyes. Underneath his single nostril, his lamprey mouth was clenched tightly before he began to shape human words. "I have responded as soon as I was able, Richard Downing. I have already been apprised of the situation. The Slaasriithi ambassador, Yiithrii'ah'aash, contacted us as soon as *Ferocious Monolith* revealed its identity. They were unaware that any Ktoran ships were expected in the area, and were alarmed to learn that this one arrived so early. Frankly, I cannot fault the Slaasriithi's reaction. But I also suspect they were more sanguine about inviting a human delegation after meeting with you, Caine Riordan."

"That sounds promising," Downing observed.

"I agree. The Slaasriithi make decisions and act upon them at a much more leisurely pace than the other races of the Accord. For them to tender an invitation regardless of the current pressures says much about the impression Commander Riordan has made upon their leaders. But their acceleration of this diplomatic mission also signifies they fear the Ktor could undermine it. If you refuse to leave promptly, I believe they will withdraw their invitation. They no doubt wish to ensure that envoys from your species would be drawn from a pool of persons unlikely to have been subject to Ktoran influence."

Caine leaned toward the Dornaani's image. "That's an interesting speculation, Alnduul. I don't see how you could arrive at it unless you also presumed that the Slaasriithi have a strong suspicion—or *know*—that the Ktor are another branch of humanity and that therefore they could have infiltrated us earlier."

Alnduul's nictating eyelids cycled even more slowly this time. "I cannot comment on your conjecture, Caine Riordan. But the fundamental logic is inarguable."

Huh. Typical Dornaani. They manage to tell you you're right without coming straight out and telling you that you're right. "Alnduul, am I correct in assuming that you believe it would be in our best interests to comply with the Slaasriithi request?" *Which is to say, go completely unprepared?*

One of Alnduul's hands rose into view: his long fingers trailed like streamers in a sad, slow wind. "As a Custodian, I am unable to share my personal counsel on this matter. However, I have approached the on-site representative of the Dornaani Collective with a request that my ship, the *Olsloov*, be allowed to provide you with transport on your journey." The end of his statement was abrupt, clipped. Among Dornaani, that was the equivalent of a pregnant pause.

Caine managed not to smile. *Okay, so you're willing to piss off your boss to try to get us a high-security ride to the Slaasriithis' party. So, yes; you think it's important that we go.* "Thank you, Alnduul. I am unsure if you're familiar with the human expression, 'a wink is as good as a nod'?"

"I cannot recall hearing that expression," said Alnduul. Who then nictated his left inner eyelid with uncharacteristic speed.

"Did he just wink?" whispered Downing.

"If not, he developed a very timely facial tic," Caine replied.

Alnduul glanced off-screen. "I am summoned to discuss my request to transport you aboard the *Olsloov*."

Downing nodded. "We'll start making our preparations."

Alnduul's fingers made a gesture that somehow used the rotary motion of a pinwheel to impart an impression of a passing ocean swell. "I shall update you with all speed. Enlightenment unto you both." The screen went dark.

Downing leaned back in his acceleration couch. "Well, now we have to find a consul to send along with you as a plenipotentiary ambassador."

"We'll need a world-class technical expert as well. Thank God we've got Lemuel Wasserman traveling with the fleet."

Downing elected—somewhat conspicuously—to begin studying personnel rosters at that very moment. "Doctor Wasserman is no longer with the fleet."

Caine started. "Wait a minute, just two days ago, you said Lemuel had been sent with the fleet to—"

"He'd been sent with the fleet, yes. But he didn't make the shift with us into Sigma Draconis from V 1517. He stayed behind with the two shift-carriers we left there, the *Gyananakashu* and the *Arbitrage.*"

Caine stared at Downing, started breaking down the improbability of Wasserman simply being "left behind." "Lemuel was assigned to assess which Arat Kur technologies we needed to get our hands on. No one else can match his ability to see beyond the current theoretical horizon, even if he *is* a pain in the ass. And he trained for months to do this job. Which now, all of a sudden, he's not doing." Riordan frowned. "So Wasserman saw, or learned, something on the way from Earth to V 1517. Something so important that he's being sent back home."

Downing shrugged. "Assignments change."

Caine sat back slowly. "No, not in the case of someone like Lemuel Wasserman. Assignments like his don't simply 'change.' But they might get preempted if something more urgent comes along." Riordan considered what might warrant that kind of pre-emption and then realized: "Of course—Wasserman has learned how the Dornaani manage to shift to deep space. When the fleet shifted out from Earth with their help, you must have set him up as the technical liaison to the Dornaani when they were temporarily modifying our ships. And, against all odds, Lemuel struck paydirt, learned how they work that magic. And now, he's traveling back with the first of the tankers the Dornaani will help shift back to Earth. Hell, that means he'll also be on hand when they *remove* the modifications: another golden opportunity to gather more data on the underlying physics and the engineering."

Downing put down his slate. "Caine, this is not a need-to-know topic for you."

Riordan shrugged. "Maybe not, but it will influence what our legation to the Slaasriithi should be trying to achieve."

"How so?"

"Come on, Richard. Wasserman may get his hands on the theoretical and technical recipes for how the Dornaani manage to make deep space shifts, but that's only half the objective. To make optimum use of that capability, we need to keep expanding our shift range, and there's no way the Dornaani are going to let our people near their drives. But the Slaasriithi are, by all estimates, more advanced than the Arat Kur, so they are a better place to go seeking that kind of technical assistance."

Downing picked up his slate again. "You posit an interesting theory, Caine, but I can't comment on it. Instead, I've been concentrating on finding technical experts who can replace Wasserman. A number of likely candidates have just arrived on the *Doppelganger,* in fact."

Caine shook his head. "Filling Lemuel's shoes: that's a pretty tall order."

"Yes, it is. Wasserman's broad range of abilities enabled him to coordinate our technical intelligence for a wide array of fields, as well as working as a specialist in high energy and theoretical physics. But fortunately, Earth also sent along naval designer Morgan Lymbery to assess Arat Kur aerospace technology."

"Isn't Lymbery the guy who spearheaded the development programs for the Boulton and Hunter classes?"

"Yes. Bit of a maverick. Eccentric where Wasserman is pugnacious."

"I'd like to meet him."

"I'm sure he'd like to oblige, but he's in cold sleep. Same with most of the other personnel we'll be pulling for your mission: a collection of experts we can thaw out at need."

Caine nodded. "And as you say, we're going to need an ambassador with plenipotentiary powers, too. It's a lucky break that we have three consuls with the fleet."

"Yes, but unfortunately, we have only one choice." Downing ticked off the excluded consuls on his fingers. "Visser can't commit to this mission. She is needed on Earth if she is to prepare for her turn in the proconsular seat. For that reason, Sukhinin has to remain here: he and Visser were the only ones on-site for the breakthrough in communications and negotiations with the Arat Kur. One of those two must continue building upon that personal foundation. Besides, Sukhinin is the only consul whose specialty is in military policy. Rather crucial during the negotiation of a surrender, as well as reparations that involve transfers of strategic technology and skills."

Caine's stomach sunk. "So you mean I've got to travel with Etienne Gaspard?" *The guy who almost got* Doppelganger *destroyed a few hours ago, and tried to rhetorically crucify me at the Parthenon Dialogs last year? Please, no...*

"Yes. Gaspard. And he'll be a right wanker about this, I'll wager." Downing shook his head. "According to the dossier he relayed shortly after arriving on *Doppelganger,* he spent four months preparing to replace Visser on the negotiating team. So he's sure to be hopping mad."

"Great."

"Oh, that's not the half of it, Caine. From what I can tell, the last time he was briefed on the Slaasriithi was when he came to my office in DC last year, just before the invasion. So you'll need to educate him en route."

Caine hadn't intended to recoil, but he did. "I'm supposed to educate Gaspard? On a topic I hardly know any better than he does? C'mon, Richard: how about you send me on a combat mission instead? Direct insertion into a hot LZ? Can't be any worse: probably a damned sight better."

Downing smiled ruefully. "Be careful what you wish for, Caine. You just might get it. Now let's get to work."

Chapter Six

FAR ORBIT
SIGMA DRACONIS TWO

Olsirkos Shethkador-vah was waiting at the embarkation portal when the plates of that outsized iris valve rang open. Tlerek Srin Shethkador stalked over the threshold and dismissively acknowledged the crew's obeisance, offered the moment the *krexyes* horn howled to announce his arrival. Shethkador was gratified to notice that the horn was genuine and not some insulting pseudo-chitin imitation. He nodded irritably at Olsirkos. "'Vah," he muttered, "escort me to the Sensorium at once."

Olsirkos waved four huscarls over. Their composite armor plates thumped dully as they fell in around the Srin and the 'vah. "Srin Shethkador, do you not wish an interval of restoration in your quarters? We have prepared suitable facilities in the rotational habitat, and hope you—"

"I must make contact with the Autarchs immediately. I will take my ease later."

"Fearsome Srin, the orders we carry from the Autarchs do not compel you to—"

"I follow protocols of which you would not be apprised."

Olsirkos averted his eyes deferentially. "Yes, Srin."

"Your diligence in pursuing both your duty and my comfort are noted, Olsirkos."

"The Srin honors me with his regard."

"So I do." *And now that he has been lulled into a false sense of security*—"However, that honor is overshadowed by your handling of my repatriation. You shifted into this system near the main world, knowing that it was surrounded by the Aboriginals? And you entered at combat speed, with the rotational habitats retracted, and without compliance to the Accord transponder requirements? Were you trying to rekindle the recent war, 'vah?"

Olsirkos—who could well expect to lose face, rank, or possibly toes or fingers over such infractions—did not flinch or swallow nervously. "Those orders were not mine, Masterful Srin."

"Ah. At the behest of the Autarchs, then?"

"It is as you say, Srin."

So: more idiocies from dust-covered oligarchs who spend too much time plotting combats rather than engaging in them. "Explain, 'vah."

Olsirkos nodded compliance. "Most of the Autarchs wished to effect your repatriation with a minimum of activity or upset. Several, our own House included, opined that it would be best if we merely sent an away-boat to reclaim you from a neutral facility, such as a free-floating module. But Houses Jerapthere and Falsemmar insisted that this first direct meeting with the Aboriginals should show them how primitive and useless their spacecraft and weapons would be in a confrontation with ours."

"And their rationale for such an idiotic plan?"

"I was not privy to their discussions, Potent Srin. However, the implicit rationale of the orders seems to be this: by striking terror and awe into the Aboriginals, they will be doubly reluctant to engage or confront us, and thereby, be more easily intimidated and manipulated."

"Absurd. The Autarchs have achieved but one thing: they have revealed the standards of innovation and excellence that the Aboriginals must be resolved to meet. And, so, they will become less terrified."

"Fearsome Srin, I do not understand."

Of course you don't. "'Vah, attend and learn. For the Aboriginals, we were *more* terrifying when they lacked any sense of our capabilities. That constant, unbounded fear would have undermined their efforts against us, for they lacked a concrete benchmark which, once achieved, promised greater parity with us.

"Most Aboriginals find such an amorphous competition exhausting: it ultimately erodes their morale and energy. But, thanks to the Autarchs, they now have quantifiable technological intelligence on our midrange space and military capabilities."

"But, seeing how far above them those capabilities are, will that not terrify and cow them?"

No matter how carefully the Breedmothers groom the genelines, the gift for strategic insight remains rare and elusive. "'Vah, you do not understand this phenomenon because you are too accustomed to interacting with helots and huscarls. Like other Wildings, Aboriginals have not been taught to perceive and presume their own innate inferiority. Rather, they will work to catch up to us, if agitated. And this ship's ominous approach has indeed agitated them.

"It is alarming that the Autarchs failed to learn this lesson from the Aboriginal repulse of the recent invasion, since I presume that they all supported this insipid posturing."

"Several objected initially, Srin, but ultimately consented. In return, those reluctant Autarchs received concessions."

"Which were?"

Olsirkos stood taller. "That a member of House Shethkador— namely, myself—should be placed in command of this Aegis hull. As it was, they were unwilling to accord that honor to anyone over the rank of a first-generation Evolved. So I was sent." Olsirkos' voice did not falter, but his gaze did. "I was concerned you might feel insulted that you were retrieved by a mere 'vah, such as myself."

"I am insulted, naturally," Shethkador said with a shrug, "but am neither so stupid nor intemperate as to perceive you as the architect of the insult." *Besides, it's not as though the rival Houses would accept two Awakened Shethkadors as the two senior officers on an Aegis ship. A multi-House command staff is the only means whereby the Autarchs are assured that a hull's actions will not be unduly influenced by factionalism.* "Immediately after I have completed my Reification, I will be consulting the ship's manifest to acquaint myself with our resources. Are there any expended or missing assets of which I should be made aware?"

"Not as such, Srin. But some assets were deployed to observe the Aboriginal activity in the system we passed through immediately prior to this one."

"And that system is?"

"V 1581, Srin. Upon arriving there, we discerned it to be the system where the humans first entered Arat Kur space. They left behind two tankers. One is a megacorporate ship; the other is from the TOCIO bloc. Another craft, the prize hull the humans have renamed *Doppelganger*, was also present, hurrying to make shift here. Since it seemed likely that we would have to reenter V 1581 when we begin our journey back to the Ktoran Sphere, I deployed one of our patrol hunters, *Red Lurker*, with our frontier observation team to gather information on the Aboriginal traffic and activity in the system."

Srin nodded. "Very well. And how long has *Red Lurker* been on station there?"

"Approximately three weeks, but they are furnished for long-duration detached operations. Also, should something untoward befall them, they are quite expendable."

"More so than the rest of *Monolith*'s crew?"

"Yes, Srin. The frontier team assigned by the Aegis overseers were almost all Arrogates, and few have genelines prized by their adoptive Houses. If they are lost, it neither diminishes our ability to project force, nor strikes a hostile spark between any Houses."

Arrogates, who were descended from Extirpated Houses, were noteworthy for their political neutrality, having little reason to prefer one faction above another. But in consequence, they were a polyglot group and, so, often trailed loose ends of mixed loyalties and diverse aspirations.

Tlerek Srin Shethkador did not like loose ends and this situation promised to be rife with them, some of which might be fraying badly at the margins. He would have preferred to immediately peruse the dossiers of the frontier group in detail, but it was urgent that he conclude his contact with the Autarchs swiftly. He restricted himself to one cautionary observation regarding the detached observation team: "It is unwise to leave behind any groups with technology that, if it were to fall into the hands of the Aboriginals, would help them achieve parity with us. Your hands will be forfeit if you have been careless, 'vah."

Olsirkos smiled shrewdly. "In this particular, you need have no misgivings, Fearsome Srin. While the frontier team does have advanced technology with them, it is impossible for the Aboriginals to acquire it."

"That is a most confident, but also a most improbable, assertion. Serendipity favors all combatants equally. How is it, then, that the Aboriginals could not, under some odd inversion of likely outcomes, lay hold to the technology possessed by the frontier team?"

Olsirkos smiled more widely. "Because I put the technology, and the team, someplace that the Aboriginals cannot reach."

Shethkador did not show the extent to which Olsirkos' mysterious comment and confidence intrigued him. He stopped before the entry to the Sensorium. "I require that the honor guard precede me and sweep for any anomalies before I enter." Olsirkos gestured the guards through an iris valve that opened upon a circular, dimly lit chamber. A pong of thick, unctuous musk and decaying incense wafted out.

"I will want a complete operational report when I am done here. Be sure that it is extremely detailed," Shethkador warned Olsirkos. "I may have need of the smallest particulars." His honor guard, finished with their sweep, stood aside at rigid attention as he entered the reeking, domed chamber.

After the antique iris valve rasped closed, Shethkador sealed it with his personal code and crossed to the small, featureless panel where the Catalysites were stored. He passed his hand over the panel, which, sensing the requisite amount of Symbiot in his bloodstream, slid open. He removed one of the tightly sealed opaque vials waiting in a row, tapped for the panel to self-seal, and positioned himself on the cushions he had selected.

Among the Awakened, who were the unofficial meritocrats of the Evolved, some relished the power and reach of a Catalysite-assisted Reification, claiming it to be the ultimate dominative euphoria. Shethkador was not among their number, and secretly contemned such Awakened as weak-minded sybarites. After all, they reveled in the dominion enabled by the Symbiot without bothering to reflect that they were relying upon an external source to attain that acme of power. Well, no matter: that weakness would eventually be their undoing when the genelines of their Houses came to contend with another that was populated by fewer lotos-eaters.

Shethkador elected to forego the meditative preparations; it was superstition rather than effective practice, in his opinion. He popped open the vial and inserted his finger into the complex microecology within until it met the sluglike dermis of the Catalysite.

He contemplated a quadratic equation until the perfusive flood of burning had swept out into his body. It left a singed tingling in its wake and a perception of the universe as a hierarchy of pressure-sensitive control cells, each cluster of which was itself but a small cell in still greater control clusters, and which all expanded upward and outward into a limitless whole that was greater than the sum of its parts, and through which his awareness grew and expanded, rushing toward an infinitely receding periphery that was the demarcation line of—

All things stopped. Were frozen in the impossibly small spatio-temporal lacunae that separated every action from every reaction, even on the level of entangled quanta. Guided by instinct and the Symbiot within him—and he detested being uncertain of where the former ended and the latter began—he found the incomplete cluster he sought: the Autarchs of the Ktor.

Who were slightly more than fifty-five light-years distant.

Chapter Seven

FAR ORBIT
SIGMA DRACONIS TWO

Davros Tval Herelkeom, senior of the five Autarchs who had made themselves available, acknowledged Tlerek's contact: "Your signal is clear, Srin Shethkador. Your House sends its compliments and anticipates a report of success." Which was a strange greeting in that this affirming welcome should have come from Tlerek's great-uncle once removed, the Tval Kromn Shethkador, who was present in the group. *On the other hand, if these walking fossils are currently split among themselves, it might be deemed an unacceptable entreé to House-domination if both Shethkador voices become preeminent in this counsel.*

Tlerek sought a tone of response that was at once direct, assertive, and tinged by the annoyance he felt over the resolution of the war upon Earth. "Regrettably, I must disappoint the anticipations of both my House and the Autarchs. The Aboriginals stayed their vengeance against the Arat Kur homeworld, largely because they discovered my identity as *homo imperiens.*"

A long pause, and then a contentious, angry query from Beren Tval Jerapthere. "You have failed?" Beren's tone bordered on effrontery.

"*I* did not fail, but I report failure. Do you wish my report on the conclusion of the war?"

Beren became peremptory. "Yes, at once."

"I am pleased to comply. The fleets of the so-called Consolidated Terran Republic successfully misled the Arat Kur and Hkh'Rkh into believing that their initial attack upon Barnard's Star was a genuine surprise which decimated their formations. This was a ruse. The human fleets reappeared after the invaders divided their forces and were committed deep within the gravity well of Home, or, as the Aboriginals call it, Earth. Aided by a Dornaani computer virus introduced through a joint Custodian-Aboriginal clandestine operation, the forces of our proxies were neutralized or eliminated, with many of their hulls falling into the hands of the 'Terrans.'"

Davros Tval Herelkeom resumed control, somewhat archly, of the contact. "Current disposition of enemy forces?"

"I am unsure, but the most technologically advanced of the Aboriginal fleets are currently here in far orbit about the Arat Kur Homenest, which has surrendered to them."

"The Arat Kur surrendered?"

"Yes. You may recall my prediction that I would lose the ability to mislead each side into believing that the other was obdurate in their hostility if the Aboriginals discerned my true speciate identity. Which they did."

Ruurun Tval Tharexere, oldest of the Autarchs and of his unity-obsessed House, entered his observations into the contact. "This is most unwelcome news."

"With all respect, Autarch, the course of events followed my misgivings as players follow a script. The Aboriginals detected the forensically inconclusive waste-emissions from the false environmental suit and that, in conjunction with the military and diplomatic peculiarities of the conduct of the conflict, led one of them to hypothesize my true species."

Beren's resentment and rage were palpable through the contact: he had been the architect of many of the stratagems that had gone awry. "You would blame our plans, our technicians, for your own failures? Failures against Aboriginals?"

"Instruct me, Autarch: how were these *my* failures? Did I not point out the risks in the suit's design and the underlying xenobiological conceits? And did I not predict that the Aboriginals had an excellent chance of defeating the Arat Kur?"

"Yes, but their defeat was an acceptable outcome if it created an opportunity to entice the Aboriginals into wholesale genocide. The ostracization they would have faced for that act would surely have pushed them in our direction, and so, under our dominion."

"And I warned, did I not, that the plan's signal weakness was that I had to be physically present in order to obliquely encourage that genocide?"

"Yes, but—"

"By your leave, Autarch, my House will wish to inspect the transcripts of this exchange, and I humbly request that I may finish without interruption."

Beren's almost shuddering response conveyed barely suppressed fury. "You—your request is... granted."

"My thanks, Autarch. I warned, did I not, that being physically present amongst the Aboriginals would give them the time and opportunity to conduct detailed analysis of the suit and its components, even if only by external sensing?"

"I cannot, at this time, find mention of—"

"I asserted this on the third day of tactical planning, Autarch. Please consult the transcripts. It was one of my first objections."

Beren paused. "Ah—yes, now I recall."

"It is happy indeed, Autarch Tval Jerapthere, that your memory now compasses this instance. To conclude, I felt it likely that the Aboriginals would—through inspiration, thoroughness, or serendipity—discover that the environment suit was a deception. They did, and the outcome was as I predicted: they are now aware of our true speciate identity. Furthermore, they have shared it with one Arat Kur of the Ee'ar caste, who will no doubt share it with select members of his own, as well as the Hur, caste. There was also a Custodian present, so the Dornaani discord occasioned by their contending conjectures about our identity are now at an end, and so too is the concomitant drain on the surveillance and intelligence assets they have long dedicated to the matter. Furthermore, the Aboriginals now have full access to Arat Kur technology."

Ulsor Tval Vasarkas' declarative was shaded to suggest that the Autarch would brook no dispute on the matter. "That latter risk was deemed acceptable."

"By the Autarchs, perhaps," Shethkador replied carefully. "However, you may recall that I opined differently. The observable phenomenon of postwar rebuilding on Earth, in the face of the unresolved exosapient threat, was already arising when the Aboriginal fleet departed for its strike against Sigma Draconis. Even now Earth is reverse-engineering key naval technologies: pseudo-singularity capacitors, navigation systems, field-effect generators, spinal-mounted X-ray lasers, high-yield pulse fusion thrusters, antimatter production and retention systems. They will be manufacturing them within two years. In five years' time, these technologies will be commonplace in the Aboriginal formations. In ten years' time, they will be ubiquitous."

Davros' contact was unconcerned. "Let them do so. The economic impact of such rebuilding will cripple them."

"On the contrary, Autarch. It will strengthen the Aboriginals by providing jobs in their market-driven economy and will make them both bolder and more canny opponents."

Beren pushed back to the fore of the contact, and his shading was as reptile-cool as it was hostile. "Are you saying our plans were folly?"

Time to redirect the exchange. "I would not risk my geneline by suggesting that the Autarchs could be so profoundly and singularly mistaken. Let us say that we are all still paying for the error of the rogue elements of House Perekmeres."

Beren's contact was as calm as his animus was clear. "It is always convenient to blame the dead, Srin Shethkador."

"Perhaps, but it is never right—nor wise—to blame the Autarchs, Autarch. And is there any denying that House Perekmeres' unapproved attempt to cripple Earth with an asteroid strike triggered this cascade of disastrous sequelae? Instead of eliminating the Aboriginals as a threat and resetting their cultural paradigms, the so-called Doomsday Rock alerted them to exosapience and interstellar travel and, thereby, accelerated the problem. Were not the lately failed war plans—hasty, forced, inelegant—simply the ineluctable offspring of the Perekmeres's defiance of the Houses and the Autarchs?"

If Ulsor Tval Vasarkas' comment had a subtext, Shethkador could not discern it: "You sound as if you would purge the Perekmeres again, if it were possible."

"I laud the thoroughness of their Extirpation, even down to the fetuses in the EndoWombs. I would have gladly assisted, had I been asked."

This time, Ulsor's contact trod a line between assertion and irony. "Your reputation for dutiful service remains impeccable, Srin Shethkador."

"I would best serve the core values of the Creche worlds if my perspicacity enjoyed equal confidence among the Autarchs."

Ulsor's response was quick and sharp. "Is this insolence, Srin Shethkador?"

"This is simple fact, esteemed Autarch. Did I not fear this outcome? Did I not predict its disastrous progress?"

"You did. So how do we know that you have not had a hand in creating that failure to enhance your reputation for foresight-fulness?"

"Let us assume, as your hypothesis must, that I have lost all loyalty to the Ktoran Sphere. Even so, the scheme you suggest would still be folly for me and my geneline. There is more glory to be had, more fame to be acquired, more improvement of my gene-rating to be enjoyed, in acquiring victory than there is in having been sadly correct in my foresight. Will I be draped in the enemy's skins because I predicted this failure? No. But I might very well have worn that mantle of the flayed remains of our foes had I been able to send word that Earth would soon come under our power. No, esteemed Autarch: though I may be proven right by these events, it is no victory for me."

Tlerek could almost see Ulsor's nod across the dozens of light-years. "Well said. And better still, it is as you say."

Shethkador could feel the strength borrowed from the expended Catalysite's protoplasm beginning to wane rapidly, like a star tuck-ing behind the terminator line of a swiftly rotating world. *And not a moment too soon: these walking corpses would remonstrate and share their dubious wisdom for hours, given the chance...*

Kromn Tval Shethkador's contact reached out across the light-years briefly but sharply. "Your signal fades, Tlerek Srin Sheth-kador. You proceed with our trust in your judgment."

There was a pulse of approval from Ruurun, followed shortly thereafter by Ulsor's clipped, "Your perspicacity does not go unap-preciated, young Shethkador." But the emphasis upon "young," and the absence of praise for other characteristics, was not lost on Tlerek.

He resolved to dominate what was left of the contact with pointless pleasantries, so that none of the Autarchs could utter any last-second directives that might restrict his actions. "I am gratified to represent the Ktoran Sphere in this place, and to attend to the voices of the Autarchs. I shall make further report when I determine whether it is best to reposition *Ferocious Monolith* so that it seems to have commenced its homeward journey as instructed by the Custodians, or to fabricate a pretext to remain and gather further data."

Tlerek Srin Shethkador waited for a response. There was none—and his perception of the universe as a vast membrane comprised of touch-sensitive cells was gone. In its place was the narrow reality contained within the scope of his senses and an annoying feeling of diminishment.

Shethkador was up off the cushions as soon as he became aware of that first tinge of melancholia: down that path lay overuse of, even addiction to, the artificial surges of the Reifying power enabled by the Catalysites. Of course, the Catalysites themselves were not the enemy: they were utterly insensate. The foe was the Symbiot itself, seducing with the temporarily actualized promise of fabulous power—power which came at the cost of one's autonomy. Which was why the Ktoran reflex for dominion was all-important, not merely because it fueled the will to control all other species and planets, but to maintain control over oneself. Resolving not to rub at the painful welt on his index finger, where the caustic fluids of the Catalysite had surged greedily into his bloodstream, Shethkador exited the Sensorium.

Olsirkos was there. Two guards were present also, but hanging well back, out of earshot. "Fearsome Srin," Olsirkos began, "if you should wish to first take some repose in the—"

"I have need of information, not rest. It is also necessary that I make an appearance on the bridge. Attend me." *Because, as the ancient axiom has it, "one cannot assert one's dominion in one's absence."*

Without checking to see if Olsirkos was at his heels—for it was the 'vah's life if he was not—Tlerek Srin Shethkador made swiftly for the bridge.

Chapter Eight

IN THE EXOSPHERE
V 1581 FOUR

Hirkun Morsessar, Tagmator of the Aegis patrol hunter *Red Lurker*, stared at the visual feed from the bow: swirling, dimly lit whorls and clouds. The violent collage was mostly white, but some of the drifts and plumes were bilious. Others were tinged with ochre. Together, they recalled the miasmas that hung about the Creche worlds' shabbiest, unventilated pipehouses, tucked away in grimy urban helot-warrens.

A sharp bump, followed quickly by a sideways shuddering, reminded Hirkun that, despite appearances, they were actually in the upper reaches of the medium-sized gas giant that occupied the fourth orbit around the star the Aboriginals had labeled Cygnus 2, or V 1518. "Attend to your instruments," Morsessar warned the pilot. The Autarch-assigned helmsman—a lictor, equal in status to a huscarl but without affiliation to any House—complied as best he could, but the buffeting downdrafts from the port side were patternless. They defied both his and the flight computer's abilities to predict and stabilize their flight.

"Apologies, Tagmator." The hush in the Houseless pilot's voice sounded more like the product of fear than regret.

This was satisfying and proper. Technically, the maximum disciplinary action available to Hirkun was comparatively limited; lictors were the ward-chattels of the Autarchs themselves, and so could not be harmed too greatly without inviting their masters' censure and consequent reprimands from one's own House and Family. But this lictor was sufficiently fearful of Hirkun's power, even so—one of the few gratifying elements of this accursed observation mission. *A misnomer if there ever was one. Just how much observing can one do from* inside *a gas giant?* "Keep your course, helm; you have strayed twelve degrees from our assigned heading. And make our journey smoother. Exercise greater powers of anticipation."

"Yes, Tagmator."

An impossible feat, of course, but one never maintained dominion by lowering expectations or even making them reasonable. *We exceed our limits only when forced to do so*, as the Progenitors' Axioms had it. And since Hirkun's life and fortunes depended, for now, upon this crew, then it was certainly in his best interests to—

The iris valve to the small bridge scalloped open: a tall, black-haired woman entered and sank, brooding, into the seat that doubled as the XO's position and the backup sensor and comm ops station. She did not make eye contact with Hirkun.

"Problems, Antendant Letlas?"

"No, Tagmator," the willowy Antendant answered curtly.

"Antendant, if you wish a recommendation that will aid your ascent to Intendant-vah, do not trouble your commander with indirect communication. Speak frankly and at once: what troubles you?"

Letlas sat straighter. "Apologies, Tagmator Morsessar. I am annoyed at myself."

That was unexpected. "How so?"

She glanced at the pilot, the only other person on the bridge. "I am uncertain that my concerns are best shared in this place."

Ah. Hirkun turned to the lictor. "Pilot, monitor the Aboriginals' broadcast frequencies through your helmet. Increase the volume to maximum. Be certain you cannot hear me—even my orders."

"Yes, Tagmator," he replied, making haste to comply.

Once the lictor had settled the light duty helmet over his head, with the blasting static still clearly audible, Hirkun nodded. "Proceed, Antendant."

"Tagmator, I am unsure that our chief sensor operator is fully competent."

"You mean Nezdeh, the senior Agra?"

"Yes, she. Tagmator, I shall speak further only at your express encouragement."

That cautious phrasing puzzled Hirkun. "Antendant, that is the formula whereby an Intendant—or an aspirant, such as yourself—warns one of the Evolved that to continue might involve speaking ill of another one of the Evolved."

Letlas avoided Hirkun's eyes. "It is as you say, Tagmator."

Hirkun was too surprised to suppress the frown that he felt bending lines into his face. "Speak clearly, Antendant: do you suspect that Agra Nezdeh is Evolved, but masquerading as non-Evolved?" *Impossible.*

"This is why I was irresolute in expressing myself, Tagmator Morsessar. I know full well how absurd this must sound. But I have watched her manipulate the controls as she tracks the Aboriginal craft that is orbiting just above us, while we remain beneath the storm heads that block their rudimentary sensors."

"Yes, and so far, she has done an adequate job."

"Yes, Tagmator. She does an *adequate* job. But no more. It is not the place of us non-Evolved to merely perform adequately in our specializations. Since we lack the onerous responsibilities of ensuring dominion, we have the luxury of becoming true specialists. Nezdeh has not done so, but rather, shows a great breadth of competencies." Letlas paused. "It is more akin to the skill diversity routinely associated with the Evolved."

"Even among Intendants, to say nothing of huscarls, some non-Evolved have far more promise as generalists than as specialists. It can be frustrating. It can also prove invaluable."

Letlas looked away. "Tagmator, I do not wish to seem obstinate, but—"

"Your insight is sought, Antendant. Speak your mind."

"If Nezdeh were young, I would be less concerned. But by her age, a trend toward generalization at the expense of specialization would have been noticed in one of the non-Evolved. It would have been either corrected or exploited. But for her to come to this ship, at the last moment, touted as a sensor and communications specialist when she is, at best, adequate—this fills me with misgivings."

Hirkun nodded. "It is peculiar." He did not add his own misgivings, which did not concern Nezdeh's skill levels so much as the peculiar manner in which she had been added to *Red Lurker*'s complement. The veteran communications specialist who had been part of the patrol hunter's rota for the last three years—Lokagon Emren Arrepsur-vah—had made his final return to space only four days before *Red Lurker* had been deployed. Wrapped in the winding sheets of a defeated duelist, Emren Arrepsur-vah had been pushed toward the winking red speck that was V 1581, four and a half light-hours away. By the time his remains were embraced and immolated by that red dwarf star, all memory of him, and the House to which he had aspired to add his geneline, would be long gone.

Nezdeh Kresessek-vah had been Arrepsur-vah's logical replacement, recommended by the Aegis database as both capable and seasoned. Her slightly greater age and her status as 'vah—aspirant to having her geneline formally integrated into that of House Kresessek—had led Hirkun to conjecture that she was a promising Intendant, about to come into her own. Now, however, he began to reconsider: it was possible, given her rank, that she was in fact Evolved, a refugee from a House so badly defeated that it had been Extirpated. If so, then that would certainly explain why her skill set was marked more by breadth than depth. He would have to investigate her origins more closely upon the return of *Ferocious Monolith*.

But Hirkun perceived that her current performance might reveal other useful clues as well. "Antendant Letlas, is there any sign that her skills are improving? For instance, was she better than adequate in detecting the departure of *Ferocious Monolith* earlier today?"

Letlas forestalled a shrug. "Tagmator Morsessar, her performance was improved. But I am unsure if it was because her skill with the sensors is improving, or because she had maintained a log of *Monolith*'s telemetry as it preaccelerated to its shift point. She knew exactly where to find the shift-bloom in her sensors. She may have known approximately *when* to look, as well."

Which was not overly peculiar. The customary preacceleration protocols would, if followed, enable a fair estimate of the time at which the ship's velocity—which was to say, its increase above rest-mass—reached the point at which it could engage its shift drive. But typically, sensor operators did not seek the bloom except to confirm that a ship had shifted when and where it said it would. "Are you saying that Nezdeh pinpointed the shift-bloom even before *Ferocious Monolith*'s tight-beam shift notification reached us?"

"Yes, Tagmator."

That was a fairly impressive sensor achievement. But it was also an expenditure of effort without any meaningful gain. "Has Nezdeh put us at risk of discovery by the Aboriginals? Has she been overly bold in shadowing the Aboriginal shift carrier that is refueling above us, the *Arbitrage*?"

"No, Tagmator. If anything, she has been remarkably circum-spect in the performance of that particular task. Indeed, she has shown her greatest skills in trailing the megacorporate craft at considerable distance while remaining beneath various meteorologi-cal disturbances. She was able to track it by the slight ionization path that the craft's passage leaves as it moves through the thin particulate field at the highest level of the gas giant's exosphere." Letlas paused. "Given the ease with which she did it, I suspect she has performed that task many times before."

Hirkun heard the implicit warning in Letlas' observation. "It may be that she is one of the Evolved, and that she has been displaced by the dissolution of her original House. And I intend to inquire into that matter when *Monolith* returns for us. But in the meantime, there is no cause for alarm."

"I hear the dominance and wisdom in your words," recited Letlas carefully. "I was simply perplexed that her dossier con-tained no special mention of her origins, as would be customary if she was Evolved."

Hirkun was resolved not to be schooled by an upstart, a mere aspirant to the ranks of the Intendant class, but he could not bring himself to rebuke her for being both prudent and perceptive. The lack of greater detail surrounding Nezdeh's posting to his command *was* atypical. "Antendant Letlas, your input has been noted. You shall now put this matter from your mind. After all," he waved his hand at the screen's depiction of onrushing vaporous drifts, "we are in the high guard position within a gas giant, unable to exit with-out risking detection by the Aboriginals, and without any means to leave the system until *Monolith* returns to covertly extract us." He leaned back in the wide commander's seat, affecting more ease than he felt. "Even if the irregularities in Nezdeh's posting were, somehow, indicative of a threat, just what could she—what could anyone—hope to achieve in circumstances such as ours?"

The iris valve dilated as if in direct response to Hirkun's rhe-torical question, opening without the prefatory activation tone. *Which is not possible, unless—*

Hirkun was on his feet before his startled blink was completed. He measured—only semi-consciously—the rate of the ship's for-ward momentum, and how that would complicate his rise into a spin-and-draw crouch. Without so much as a wobble, his Evolved senses combined to place him in two-thirds cover behind the command couch's heavy back, his liquid-propellant handgun up, his thumb already adjusting the zero-gee setting to a full-gravity regime. He felt a satisfied smile on his face, exulting in the lethal grace with which he now drew a bead on the iris valve—

And felt two impacts in his chest, very near his heart. They staggered him enough to throw off his aim: three percussive blasts from his pistol drilled expanding rounds into the valve's coaming, less than ten centimeters from where Agra Nezdeh's cheek was resting, her feet braced, her body mostly behind the bulkhead. Two other recent rotations into his crew—the Evolved Antendant cousins Vranut and Ulpreln Balkether—had rolled into the room under the cover of her fire, were already rising with the speed one would expect from their genelines.

Hirkun willed the circulation in the vicinity of his clustered wounds to decrease, boosted both the arterial and venous peristalsis to compensate for the redirection of that blood flow, triggered a full spectrum endorphin and adrenal cascade, and, in the same moment, expanded his peripheral awareness to take stock of Letlas' reaction to the mutiny.

She was sheltering behind her seat, her hand conspicuously far away from her sidearm. *No real surprise: she is no fool.*

Using countervailing hormones to steady the incipient tremor from the adrenal flood, Hirkun tracked over toward Nezdeh. She ducked behind the starboard bulkhead—

—Just as Idrem, the *Red Lurker*'s senior lictor, leaned around the port side rim of the iris valve with a needler. The coil rifle emitted two of its characteristic high-frequency snaps. Hirkun felt two hammers rip through his body, one shattering his left hip, the other blasting through his right lung.

As he fell, struggling against the loss of control, he appreciated the conservative tactics that had been used to kill him. The mutineers had known that they would not have sufficient aiming time to be sure of scoring immediately lethal hits upon him. So they had concentrated on inflicting wounds that cost him initiative and reflexes to counteract. That, in turn, had allowed Nezdeh—the apparent ringleader—to stay exposed just long enough to draw his attention away from where Idrem emerged with the far more lethal, but less handy, needler. The traitor had aimed, wisely, at the center of mass: the shattered hip overcame even an Evolved's ability to stand, and the punctured lung forced Hirkun to choose between conscious control of blood loss, or making a counterattack. In such a rapid exchange as this, there was no time to sequence them: it was one or the other.

Hirkun resolved to shoot as he fell to the deck. He missed, but came close enough to keep the mutineers' heads down.

But only for a moment. As the *Red Lurker*'s master converted his fall into a roll that put him behind his command couch, Vranut Balkether popped around the far edge of Letlas's couch and fired his own liquid propellant handgun into the prostrate, struggling Hirkun. The Tagmator tried to concentrate on how many of that quick flurry of rounds had hit him, where, and how to respond. *I have lost, but as long as I live, I can bargain. And lie. Vengeance can come later.*

But he felt control of his body slipping away along with the fixity of purpose that had allowed him to track and respond to his numerous injuries. He saw Nezdeh's face loom over him and he knew, with dull certainty, that there would be no bargaining.

As her pistol came up level with his forehead, Hirkun reflected that here was the proof of yet another Progenitor Axiom, the one that explained why women should not be sent on field missions:

They are simply too dangerous.

Nezdeh, late of House Perekmeres, stepped over Hirkun Morsessar's corpse, fired two rounds into the cowering pilot, and then leveled the weapon at Letlas. "You. Antendant."

Letlas made the appropriate prostration with reassuring swiftness and enthusiasm. "I hear your words, Agra—no, *Berema* Nezdeh Kresessek-vah."

She laughed. "What an inanity. That you style me a Lady of a House for which I am still ostensibly a 'vah, an Aspirant? Your eagerness to flatter leads you to foolishness."

"I mean to respect, not flatter. But I know not what to call you, Berema."

Nezdeh considered. "There is merit in that point. Scant merit, but merit still. Look up, Antendant, and tell me: do you wish to live?"

Letlas looked up. Before her mouth opened with the answer, her eyes made it clear. "I wish to live, Berema Nezdeh."

As if there had been an iota of doubt. "And will you take service with House Perekmeres, as a probationary Antendant?"

Letlas stammered. "With—with House Perekmeres?"

"Is your hearing impaired?"

"But House Perekmeres was Extirpated, Fearsome Berema."

Ah, she is catching on: she does not know my former rank, but has deduced that I was high enough in the genelines of Perekmeres to warrant the honorific "Fearsome." She thinks quickly. "Extirpation was inflicted upon us," Nezdeh said crisply as more of her mutineers entered the bridge. "That does not mean I accept it, any more than I accepted the vile touch of the Kresessek abomutations who hoped to add my geneline to theirs in the old manner. Now, I shall ask it one more time, since your wits seem addled: will you take service with House Perekmeres?"

"I . . . I will, Fearsome Berema."

"Excellent. Rise. Now, enter the commander's access code for the engineering and helm controls."

"I am but an Antendant, Fearsome Berema."

As Idrem came to stand beside Nezdeh and the deck jounced through another patch of extended turbulence, she brought her pistol to bear on the Antendant once again. "I have observed the bridge routines and who was present, or not, when various systems were accessed or terminated. The XO naturally has a separate but equal set of command codes, but I slew him ten minutes ago in his quarters. There is one crewmember, often of lower rank, who also has access to the commander's codes." She smiled. "I am familiar with these protocols, having captained ships before. You were present at the correct times, and are the correct rank with the correct role. You are the keeper of the codes. I have eliminated all other possibilities. Do not try my patience, Antendant. Enter the overrides."

Letlas averted her eyes, moved to the blood-and-bone-spattered commander's console and entered the codes. She looked up. "How may I serve House Perekmeres now, Fearsome Berema?"

"This way," Nezdeh replied. She raised the pistol and fired two rounds into the Antendant's chest.

Letlas gasped as awkwardly as she fell, blood pumping out of two craters that bracketed her sternum.

Nezdeh stepped closer to watch the light leave the Antendant's eyes. "You hesitated. Had you meant to serve Perekmeres, you would have rejoiced in the opportunity to comply immediately, and thereby prove your loyalty." Letlas was either wheezing for breath or trying to speak, but it did not matter: moments after

Nezdeh had pronounced the epitaph of her insufficiency, the Antendant was dead.

Nezdeh looked about the bridge. *One cannot dominate from behind a wall of silence*, went the axiom of the First Progenitors. She kept faith with their wisdom: "Ulpreln: your hand to the helm. When the bow is steady, don the pilot's helmet so that you may listen in on the briefing." She unreeled and spoke into her beltcom as she waved for two of the mutineers to clear the three bodies. "Brenlor Srin Perekmeres?"

Her earbud crackled with the reply. "Here. Do you have dominion, Nezdeh Srina Perekmeres?"

She smiled. "I do. The rest of the crew?"

"Sworn to service or dead."

"Were any of the uncertain members swayed to our side?"

Brenlor's pause was pregnant. "Not reliably so."

Nezdeh closed her eyes: Brenlor was marginally her superior and had a full measure of what she considered House Perekmeres' most characteristic negative trait: male impulsivity. Which was often expressed through bloodthirsty aggression. "This was necessary, Srin?"

His response had a discernible edge. "It was. Besides, the poison meant to incapacitate the off-duty crew was fatal in three cases."

Nezdeh glanced at Idrem, who shrugged: "As I warned from the outset, dosing and individual susceptibility were variables beyond our control. The outcome was uncertain, at best."

She nodded. "Brenlor, we must hold our briefing promptly. The orbital path of the human shift carrier will soon be optimal."

"Understood. I shall meet you in the ready room."

Nezdeh glanced behind her at the entry to the small compartment which served as commander's office and briefing chamber. "We shall be there." She moved in that direction, turned to the rest of the team that had stormed the bridge. "Follow me."

Nezdeh did not move her eyes to observe the faces of the Evolved and the Intendants wedged in tightly around the briefing table: she merely expanded her peripheral awareness so that the edges of her vision were nearly as acute as the focal core. As Brenlor's assertions of House Perekmeres' imminent resurgence veered increasingly toward stentorian bombast, she surveyed her assets:

Idrem: indispensable and crafty. Unlike Brenlor, who had fled

House Perekmeres' precincts prior to its Extirpation, Idrem had managed to stage his own apparent death, using vat-grown tissue and blood to leave a forensically convincing residue. He had then taken refuge in the one place that subsequent investigation was unlikely to find him: among the ranks of the Autarchs' Aegis forces. He had made his supplication in the guise of a huscarl left masterless by the liquidation of a lesser Family from an entirely different House. By the time the Extirpation occurred, he had been wearing the Aegis gray for nearly a month.

Nezdeh did not like admitting it, but Idrem was probably her intellectual equal, possibly her superior. That thought rankled, but also, oddly, titillated. He was not the most athletic or vigorous of the Evolved, but he was also immune to the unremitting need for making dominance displays. The more impetuous of the Evolved males presumed this indicated passivity, and so were ready to dismiss Idrem. But Nezdeh realized the true source of Idrem's quiet: utter self-assurance in himself and his competence. That made him far more dangerous than most of the boisterous males around him, for he could not be manipulated by his temperament.

Of the other four Evolved, three were young and from Families that were comparatively distant from the progenitorial root of the true House of Perekmeres: first cousins Vranut and Ulpreln Balkether, and an aunt that was their chronological junior, Zurur Deosketer. In a few more generations, their genelines would have become so dilute that their offspring would have had to seek other fortunes. But now, with the blood of the House of Perekmeres wiped from the marble halls of both its greatest and least Hegemons, their fortunes were ascendant: scarcity of a geneline, like any other resource, greatly enhanced its value.

The fourth Evolved, and the third woman on the mission, Tegrese Hreteyarkus, had also been an Arrogate—a war prize—of Perekmeres' Extirpation, and passed to a minor Family of House Vasarkas. Unlike the rape-minded Srinu that Nezdeh had repulsed in House Kresessek, House Vasarkas had allowed Tegrese to exist like a bird in a shabbily gilded cage. Blending her geneline with theirs was left as a matter of her will.

But her will was focused upon escaping her hybrid existence as part-prisoner and part-chattel. She had volunteered for wet-work and received it by convincing her overseers that she meant to learn whether she wished to serve House Vasarkas as a Breedmistress or adventurer. Her actual intent had been to acquire the freedom and mobility to seek out other survivors of House Perekmeres and to plot its restoration.

Two others, Sehtrek and Pehthrum, were former Intendants of the House. Since their genelines had not been Elevated prior to the Extirpation, they had been deemed reliable by the Autarchal Aegis and were Arrogated to it. Their assignment as lictors to *Ferocious Monolith* had been arranged with little effort almost four months ago.

Nezdeh leaned back. Nine persons, and two of them Low Bred, with another six to be added after the first phase of their mission was complete. So, altogether, fifteen renegades of the purged House Perekmeres against the might of the Hegemons of the Great Houses and the juridical authority of the Autarchs, whose ostensible neutrality was a farce. Autarchal decisions almost invariably aligned with the interests of the Hegemons. If Nezdeh's small band could contend with those daunting odds, it would be a story worth telling—if any of them lived to tell it.

When Brenlor finished his oration, Nezdeh stood slowly. "We all know what must be done. We have excellent intelligence on our first target, and it is utterly unsuspecting." She glared around the table. "But do not underestimate the Aboriginals. The Arat Kur and Hkh'Rkh did and they are now paying for it.

"We cannot afford such payments. We have no place to which we may retreat, for there is only one outcome that does not end in our death: absolute victory. So, no bravado. We cannot afford it. No unnecessary destruction. Again, we cannot afford it. No wasted time. Yet again, we cannot afford it. When those who shall carry our restored genelines into the future speak of this battle, they shall recall it not as an arrogant gamble, but as a precise, clinical operation. That shall be our legacy and the source of our glory."

The eyes around the table had kindled to her words, whereas Brenlor's had left them merely smoldering. She was speaking the truth, and they knew it.

Nezdeh pushed back from the conference table. "Report to your stations." She checked her wrist-comp. "We are in position. It is time."

Chapter Nine

IN CLOSE ORBIT and IN THE EXOSPHERE
V 1581 FOUR

Jorge Velho, acting captain of the SS *Arbitrage*, cursed as the navplot stylus slipped out of his hand and—surprisingly, in his experience—fell to the deck. Granted, the speed of its fall was nothing like Earth norm. It was more like a stone sinking to the bottom of a pond, but still, it tricked his space-trained senses. He associated bridge duty with either free-fall or micro-gee, unless the engines were engaged. However, the *Arbitrage*'s proximity to the gas giant that bore the chart label V 1581 Four allowed it to exert almost a quarter gee on them.

Velho's XO, Ayana Tagawa, lifted an eyebrow but said nothing. However, his helmsman, Piet Brackman, emitted a sardonic snort. "Need a lanyard for that, sir?"

Jorge tried to turn a stern gaze on Piet, but couldn't keep a straight face. "Just steer this barge, you *réprobo*. You have little room to talk. You bounced off two walls in the galley before you found your footing, yesterday."

"That is not a fair comparison," Piet complained. "The toruses were still rotating then. I had gee forces in two directions."

"As did the rest of us who were in the toruses. And who did not fall down."

"Eh, go back to Belém. Sir."

"Right after we drop you off in Pretoria. From orbit."

Ayana may have sighed. She often did when the two old friends began chiding each other. Her eyes had not strayed from the navplot: a 2-D representation with a faux-3-D "deep screen." "Sir, we will need to reduce our velocity by four meters per second if we are going to stay within the optimal retrieval envelope for both our tanker-tenders."

Jorge Velho glanced over her almost elfin shoulder. "Is Deal One lagging again?" The pilot of the lead fuel barge was a rather annoying perfectionist, her many minute corrections accumulating into noticeable delays.

"No, Ms. Ho is right on schedule. The difficulty is with Deal Two."

"Piloting errors?"

"No, sir. Mr. Vindar reports that the starboard fuel transfer umbilicus seems loose. He has been taking extra care attaching and detaching from the skimming drogues. He fears that any imprecision during those maneuvers may torque the mating rings and tear the umbilicus free of Deal Two."

Jorge nodded, checked the feed from the long-range camera that was tracking Deal Two. The tanker-tender, shaped like a bus half-transformed into a lifting body, would have to initiate a fuel-costly burn in order to keep its rendezvous with one of the *Arbitrage*'s four smaller, flatter skimmers. The skimmers were remote-operated vehicles designed to move deep into a gas giant's exosphere and lower a drogue into the predominantly hydrogen soup below, drawing it up via pulsed electromagnetic tractoring. Any delay in transferring the harvested hydrogen meant a delay in them returning to their next run, and so on and so forth, causing the logistical dominoes to fall ever further and faster.

"No," Jorge decided. "We're cutting our losses. Bring Deal Two back now. Inform Deal One that she is to finish her current fuel transfer from skimmer three and follow Deal Two back to the barn."

"Sir, that will seriously impact our projected refueling time."

Jorge nodded. "Agreed, but tell me: if we lose one drogue's load, how much will our mission be impacted?"

Ayana returned his nod. "Yes, sir. You are correct: the time it would take to replace the umbilical would be worse."

Piet shook his head. "Much worse. I'm not even sure we have a spare umbilical in stores."

Jorge stared at the deck, was suddenly struck by a mental image of the pale, jaundiced gas giant looming far beneath his feet. "And CoDevCo managed to blank much of that data before *Arbitrage* was impounded for use as a military auxiliary."

Ayana looked at Velho out of the corner of her eye. "Kozakowski might know."

Yes, indeed he might, Jorge allowed, *but I hate having that man within ten meters of me.* Aloud: "Kozakowski might know, but I'm not sure he'd tell the truth."

"So what's new?" Piet asked sourly.

Jorge smiled. "My point exactly. Mr. Kozakowski's loyalty is to the Colonial Development Combine—"

"—which makes him a traitor," Piet supplied.

"—and he has not been forthcoming, despite being granted immunity from prosecution."

Ayana had finished sending the new orders to Deal One and Deal Two. "What exactly did he do, more than any of the other executives, that helped the invaders?"

Jorge shrugged. "I am not sure. Any specific charges were suppressed by the time the Auxiliary Recrewing Command forwarded his dossier to me." *But there was scuttlebutt, as there always is between captains, military and civilian alike. And I would not be at all surprised if the rumors are true: that Kozakowski* had *been a CoDevCo liaison to, and factotum for, the Arat Kur, and maybe even the Ktor.* Although it was hard to see how a human would have come to serve the Ktor, who were reputedly ice-worms that traveled about in environmental tanks that resembled oversized water-heaters on treads.

Kozakowski had been CoDevCo's master aboard (but not captain of) the *Arbitrage* when she was intercepted by a Russlavic Federation cruiser, so it was quite probable that he knew if spare fuel transfer umbilicals were in the ships' stores. But still—

Piet Brackman jutted his prominent chin toward the ventral view monitor: the ever-approaching rim of the gas giant seemed to be fading away, being consumed by the blackness of space itself. "Approaching the terminator, Captain."

"Ten minutes to loss of lascom and line of sight back to the fleet assets near planet two," Tagawa added.

"Very well." Protocol dictated Velho's next orders. "Ms. Tagawa, initiate contact with provisional CINCSYS and advise them we are about to go dark. Attach the estimated time we shall emerge from planet four's comm-shadow. Request immediate confirmation

of receipt of our transmission, and pending day-codes. And—"
Velho paused: Tagawa turned, obviously sensing how his tone
veered toward hesitation rather than finality.

"And yes, Ms. Tagawa, we shall do as you suggest: call Kozakowski to the bridge."

Ulpreln struggled to keep the *Red Lurker*'s bow steady. "Apologies, Srina Perekmeres."

Nezdeh nodded, leaned over so she could read the helm instruments. "I read the wind speed in excess of eight hundred kilometers per hour. Imperfect control is not merely understandable;
it is unavoidable. And as regards the formality of your address:
we shall dispense with that until we once again have our own
compounds and courts. Then, you may style me so nobly."

Ulpreln half turned from his console, a small smile sending
wrinkles into the crescent of his cheek. "As you wish . . . Nezdeh."

The young Evolved's voice was not insolent; it was appreciative.
This was consistent with her greater plan: to bind the group's
loyalty to her. She wished Brenlor no ill, but dominion had to be
split evenly between them, or she would not have enough power
to govern his rash reactions and overly bold plans.

From his post at the sensor station, Sehtrek pointed to one of
the secondary screens. "Our target, Nezdeh."

In the overhead, or spaceside, view, there was a longish spindle
of pristine white, distant through the misty atmosphere.

"Ulpreln, hold relative position. Sehtrek, maximum magnifica-
tion."

"Resolution will be poor, Nezdeh."

"Let it be poor. Show me what is there."

The indistinct spindle was replaced by a long, batonlike ship:
a typical human design. The ship's own fuel, engines, and power
plants—and all their radioactivity—were clustered at the stern,
behind two great disk-shaped shields. The habitation toruses and
command section were located at the bow. In between, large fuel
tanks and a few cargo modules followed the long thin keel, giving
the impression of railway cars on a great length of track. Relatively
close by, a fuel tender was returning to the ship, heading for one
of two large docking cradles just forward of the skimmed fuel
tankage. An identical craft was approaching at a leisurely pace
from the opposite direction.

"Range to objective and predominant wind speed?" Nezdeh demanded.

"Range is just under eight kiloklicks. Wind speed averages three hundred forty kilometers per hour, plus or minus fifty."

Nezdeh nodded and studied the improving image. The human ship's rotational habitats confirmed her cost-cutting, megacorporate origins: the after-torus was a solid design, whereas the forward one was actually a hexagon. Each side was a framework cradling various modules, most of which were hab mods. Most importantly, neither the torus nor the gigantic hexagon were rotating—standard procedure when a ship was under thrust.

"Acceleration of target?"

"None. Its engines are in readiness, but thrust has been discontinued. I believe they are trying to facilitate an earlier retrieval of their tankers and skimmer ROVs."

Could it get any better? "I make our intercept ETA approximately twenty minutes if we sustain three-point-three-gee constant and then counterboost at max."

"Allowing for buffeting, and the gas giant's decreasing gravitational pull, that is a reasonable estimate, Nezdeh."

"Wait for the furthest tanker to be secured in its cradles. Then commence intercept as soon as you have a clear trough between the storm cells and with minimal particulate density. We want as direct and unimpeded a path as possible."

"As you order, Nezdeh."

She toggled the intercom to the EVA ready bay. "Brenlor."

"Here. How long?"

"I would say twenty-five minutes. Are you prepared to strap in? We will be closing at three-point-five-gee sustained."

"We are suited. Strapping in."

She signed off, turned to Idrem at the weapons console. "Readiness?"

"UV laser warm and ready for full charge. All six directional blisters test green. Railgun same." He met her eyes. "I should turn the weapons over to Tegrese."

Tegrese moved toward the weapons station, but kept her eyes on Nezdeh for approval.

Nezdeh frowned. "I mean no slight, Tegrese, but Idrem, you are our best gunner."

He nodded. "Yes. But I am needed more urgently on the EVA team."

Which was, regrettably, true. Not because Idrem had excellent EVA and personal weapon skills—although he did—but because someone with sufficient authority had to be present to ensure that Brenlor's actions in securing the *Arbitrage* did not become too destructive. Nezdeh looked away so that neither Idrem nor Tegrese would see her regret. "Go then, Idrem. Tegrese, stand to the weapons."

"Yes, Nezdeh. Shall I ready missiles, as well?"

Nezdeh shook her head. "No. They are too imprecise." She resumed poring over the intelligence and confidential files they had on the SS *Arbitrage*, courtesy of the many collaborators they had suborned within the ranks of the Colonial Development Combine. *Where greed is great, corruption is simple*, as the Progenitors' axiom had it.

Ulpreln almost sounded excited. "Nezdeh, the second Aboriginal tanker is in contact with the shift-carrier, and I have an acceptable meteorological window."

Without glancing away from the data that had been furnished by traitorous Aboriginals, she reached behind her command chair for the acceleration straps. At the same time, she began consciously adjusting her blood flow to aid her vacuum suit's antipooling systems. "Sehtrek, pass the word: commence acceleration compensation protocols."

She kept reading the human data and the target updates as the announcement went out over the intercom. When it was done, she glanced at Ulpreln. "Activate the navigational holosphere, close tactical scale." He complied: a three-dimensional representation of the surrounding ten kiloklicks blinked into existence at the open center of the bridge. She assessed the conditions and smiled: *perfect. At last, the axe of fate swings for, rather than against, the fortunes of House Perekmeres.*

She elevated her chin slightly. "Commence intercept."

And then, even though she was prepared for it, three point five gees of upward acceleration slammed half the air out of her lungs.

"Captain Velho, please join me at the plot." Ayana Tagawa's voice sounded unusually constricted.

Moving close alongside her, Jorge Velho was briefly afflicted by a familiar melancholy twinge. Proximity to Ayana reminded him of just how profoundly she did not return his romantic interest.

But that sensation did not survive his first glimpse of the new blip in the navplot. "Is that a malfunction?" he asked.

"No, sir. It is not. I have confirmed it with radar, although the return is oddly compromised, in much the same way that stealth coatings dampen and distort detection."

Velho stared at the blip. "But this is not possible. A powered object moving up at us from out of the gas giant?"

Piet had craned his neck to get a look. "Nothing can survive being inside a gas giant. Go too low and you're crushed. But at altitude, the flying conditions are the equivalent of being in a nonstop hurricane." Which Velho knew to be an understatement, whether Piet intended it that way or not. Gas giants the size of V 1581.4 usually had relative wind speeds of up to five hundred kilometers per hour. Especially turbulent ones often exceeded one thousand.

But in the navplot, the impossible contact kept coming up at them. And it was coming fast. "Cross sectional analysis: does the database have a ship-type identification?"

Ayana shook her head sharply. "No recognition from the ship form database, and we have the postwar update running. Also, while the approaching craft's thrust agency is clearly magnetically accelerated plasma, this specific signature is unknown. But the metrics indicate that the energy density of the drive is unprecedented. Nothing in our inventory, or even the Arat Kur's, can put out that kind of power, given the limits of its size."

Damn it, I'm going to sound like a madman reporting this contact, but—"Ms. Tagawa, is there a comm relay platform that we can send to from our current position?"

"No, sir. All ancillary comm and sensor platforms were seeded near or at the approaches to planet two, where the fleet engaged the Arat Kur. Nothing's been deployed out here yet."

And why should there be? We plan on leaving Arat Kur space as soon as possible. But that meant there was no one to alert, no one to call for help. SS *Arbitrage* was all alone. With one chilling exception. "Ms. Tagawa, please hail the contact. All frequencies, all languages and codes. Don't forget to include the Accord code."

As she did so, Piet turned from the helm. "Jorge, whoever is on that ship is not interested in talking with us."

Velho nodded. "I agree."

"Then why try?"

"Because we know nothing about them. So any reply gives us more knowledge than we have now." He turned toward Ayana. "Response?"

"No response, sir. And I don't think we're going to get one. The contact's telemetry suggests intentions that, as Mr. Brackman speculates, preclude communication."

Jorge felt his heavy brows bunching against each other as he frowned. "What is its telemetry?"

"Range, closing; bearing, constant."

It took a moment for Velho to recall what that crisp definition actually meant. "It's going to *ram* us?"

Tagawa shrugged her narrow shoulders. "Or board us."

"That's impossible." He hesitated, remembering some of the stories that had come out of the Epsilon Indi system just after the war. "Well, it's *nearly* impossible."

Ayana nodded. "Yes, sir, that is the conventional wisdom." She pointed into the plot again. "But this craft is wholly unconventional. I am not sure the same rules apply. And it is difficult to conjecture why a ship that can withstand immersion in the upper stratosphere of a gas giant and capable of such extraordinary thrust would expend itself in a ramming attack. Which leaves one logical alternative: she is attempting a rendezvous. And if we refuse to let her dock..." Tagawa's voice trailed off; the conclusion of her analysis was inescapable.

Piet cleared his throat. "So: what do we do? I'd like to suggest running like hell, but we don't have ten percent of that hull's acceleration."

"First," Velho announced at the end of a sigh, "we start screaming for help."

Tagawa raised one eyebrow. "We *are* in the communications shadow of the gas giant, sir."

"Yes, our lascom is useless, but if we start broadcasting a wide-dispersal distress signal now, we could reach any covert patrols or classified microsensors that might be lurking out here. In the meantime, we'll give our visitors something to worry about."

"Such as?" Piet sounded doubtful.

"Such as having to work to catch us, even if we can't outrun them. Max burn on the main drive, Piet."

"Sir," began Piet, whose sudden formality meant he was getting seriously scared, "as per your orders when we cut thrust to effect retrieval of the tankers and skimmers, our plants are now in power-saving mode. We can't reach full thrust until we get to eighty-five percent of maximum power plant output, and that will take at least fifteen minutes."

"I am aware. Maximum means you get me as much thrust as you can, as fast as you can. Also, accelerate the skimmers and put them into a close slingshot orbit, the closest they'll take without being pulled in. And Ayana, I want them running their transponders in distress mode, nonstop."

She nodded, understanding. "So that the intruder must choose between chasing us or catching the skimmers before they get around the gas giant's far terminator and beyond its broadcast shadow."

"Yes, and in the meantime, I want the point-defense fire mounts brought to bear. At the intruder's rate of closure, we'll be able to use them as ship-to-ship weapons in about eight minutes. Now, where's Mr. Kozakowski?"

"Just arrived, sir," came the corporate factotum's voice from the hatchway.

Jorge turned, nodded tightly and wondered how long the unctuous owl of a man had been listening just beyond the hatchway. "You received an update on our situation?"

"Which situation do you mean, Captain? The umbilical hoses or the unidentified intruder?"

"For now, our concern is solely with the latter. Your technicians are to meet ours back at the cargo freight module, just forward of the cargo cradles."

"Very well. What is their task?"

Kozakowski is the last human I want to reveal this to, but now I have no choice. "When we commandeered the ship, we took the precaution of not just refitting it as a tanker. We added some cargo modules of our own."

"I have noticed."

Snide bastard. "Did you also notice that one of them is auto-deployable?"

Kozakowski frowned. "You mean it is a cargo module that can be triggered to release its payload into free space? That is usually a military variant, is it not?"

"It most certainly is. As a precaution, we were tasked to carry a small number of ship-to-ship drones in the autodeployable module. But it needs to be powered up and patched into our command system, first."

"So we have some real weapons?" Piet almost shouted.

Velho smiled. "As soon as we activate the module's integral subsystems, we can send out a little fleet of our own."

Kozakowski's smile was dim: he was clearly unhappy that this information had been withheld from him. "I shall get right on it, sir." He nodded and moved toward the hatchway that led off the bridge and into the keel-following transport tube.

"Mr. Kozakowski, can't you coordinate your technicians from up here?"

"Perhaps, but many of them are, well, suspicious of your prize crew. And although your personnel are obviously the experts when it comes to an autodeployable cargo module, mine are familiar with the particulars, and idiosyncrasies, of the *Arbitrage*. So I think it wisest that I be present to ensure that my crewpersons cooperate smoothly with yours, given that our lives are at stake. Wouldn't you agree?"

"Absolutely. Go at once."

His smile still wooden, Kozakowski left the bridge.

—Just as Ayana's unflappably calm voice cracked under the stress of an urgent report: "Intruder's energy levels are spiking. Our hull sensors detect a low-power laser painting us: they're acquiring ladar target lock, sir. And probably readying a beam weapon of some kind. I recommend—"

And then the world wrenched violently sideways.

Chapter Ten

"Results?" demanded Nezdeh, glancing at Sehtrek.

"UV laser blisters one and two have eliminated *Arbitrage*'s facing point defense fire batteries. Marginal damage to surrounding structures of the command section."

"Was the bridge hit?" Nezdeh's tone was sharp. As she'd intended.

"N-no...Srina Perekmeres," Sehtrek assured her hurriedly.

Tegrese hovered eagerly over her weapons panels. "If the Aboriginals tumbled their ship, they could bring their navigational laser to bear. Is it advisable for us to—?"

"We will need the *Arbitrage*'s nav laser ourselves. Besides, it bears upon too limited an arc to be of any danger to us. It is designed to engage targets at ranges of multiple light-seconds, but also within a very narrow forward cone. What of *Arbitrage*'s communications arrays?"

"Both primary and auxiliary arrays have been eliminated by blisters three and four. Blisters five and six remain ready in PDF mode."

"Excellent. Time to intercept?"

"Eight minutes, Nezdeh. We will be tumbling for four-gee counterboost in ninety seconds."

"Understood. Pass the word. Sehtrek, I require a magnified image of the Aboriginal ship."

A highly detailed 2-D visual of the *Arbitrage* replaced the navigational view. Nezdeh sought, and saw, the damage inflicted by her lasers. As she inspected the enemy's wounded hull, she peripherally noticed activity at the head of the cargo cradles, where the two tanker-tenders were moored and several conventional cargo modules were secured. "Sehtrek, I cannot tell what the Aboriginals are endeavoring to accomplish near their cargo modules. What do the sensors tell you?"

"Several things, Srina Perekmeres. The most obvious is that they seem to be attempting to resolve some sort of malfunction involving the first tanker-tender transfer's umbilicus and its connection to the fuel intake port."

"You are sure this is a malfunction, not the opening gambit of some defensive ploy?"

"I see no evidence of the latter, Srina."

"Very well. It also appears that there is some reconfiguration occurring near one of the wedge-shaped cargo modules just forward of the main tanks."

"Yes, Srina Perekmeres. I believe they are attempting to open one of the cargo modules presently, but are encountering difficulties. However, I suspect—"

"Yes, it is almost certainly a weapons pod of some kind." Nezdeh leaned back, rubbed her chin, measured the benefits and risks of the alternatives for addressing this new challenge. Destroying the cargo pod before it opened was simplicity itself: two of her UV laser blisters could reduce it to glowing tatters and strips of metal and composites. But any weapons inside the module—indeed any and all assets on board the *Arbitrage*—were worth their weight in gold to a small, independent, and desperate group such as hers. Perhaps, if they were careful enough...

No. I cannot risk it. "Blisters one and two, target the opening cargo pod. Fire until it is destroyed. Keep your aimpoint away from the keel and adjoining pods and structures."

Tegrese muttered, "Yes, Nezdeh," even as she worked to follow her orders.

On the screen, the weapons module flew apart as if being savaged by an invisible flail. A moment later, two bright flashes obscured the view of the *Arbitrage*, and, fading, revealed that significant damage had been done to two nearby cargo modules, as well as the already struggling tanker, which had now been half torn out of its docking cradle and was floating at an acute angle relative to the keel.

"Nezdeh," began Tegrese carefully, "I—"

"It was no fault of yours," Nezdeh interrupted. "The damage was caused by the secondary explosions from the weapons the Aboriginals had stored in that module. It was a risk, but one we had to take. *Lurker* is too small to be safe from even such rudimentary drones and missiles as Earth produces. If our PDF arrays had failed to intercept any one of those munitions—" Nezdeh left the comment uncompleted. *Red Lurker* might enjoy many extraordinary technological advantages over her immense, lumbering foe, but this much was true: size was a value unto itself. More specifically, *Arbitrage* was large enough to carry munitions so powerful that even a near miss could cripple a small hull such as the Ktoran patrol hunter. *Even when fighting hobbled kine, one must still avoid the horns.*

Sehtrek's tone was perplexed. "Srina Perekmeres, the Aboriginals' active sensor array is gimballing away from us."

Nezdeh stared, thought, smiled when she realized what the Aboriginals were attempting. *They are clever, not readily cowed or dismayed. One day, their genelines will refresh ours most productively.* "Tegrese, eliminate their primary and auxiliary arrays, immediately."

"As you order, Nezdeh." She complied without a pause, realigning her weapons. "But what are they attempting?"

"They mean to use their active sensors to send messages. It is a crude broadcast signal, at best, but, pulsed, they could send a simple report in their species' distress code." As she watched, two of the long, narrow masts of the *Arbitrage*'s dispersed array shuddered, then almost jumped away from the shift-carrier as if an invisible scythe had severed them. "Maintain fire until their systems are eliminated."

"Yes, Nezdeh. The Aboriginal ship is slightly faster than we anticipated, more responsive to her attitude and plasma thrusters."

"That is to be expected. The *Arbitrage* has only completed half of her refueling requirements. She has less mass to push than when she's fully loaded."

Tegrese glanced up. "What shall we do with the Aboriginals themselves?"

"That will be determined by their reactions to us. Ulpreln, prepare for terminal intercept." Nezdeh secured her straps: four gees of counterthrust was nothing about which to be cavalier.

"What do you mean, 'how they react to us'? We are dominant!" Tegrese held tightly to her gunnery console as Ulpreln slowly tumbled *Lurker* so that her engines now pointed at *Arbitrage*, the correct position for terminal braking.

"Tegrese, except for a few of the Aboriginals' leaders, they all believe our charade: that the Ktor are a nonhumanoid species indigenous to some frigid world, with body chemistries based on ammonia or hydrogen fluoride. Once we have boarded them, and they quickly discern that we know little of Earth, they will just as quickly conjecture that we must either be the Ktor or their servants—which, for all intents and purposes, has the same effect upon our charade: it will be over. At that moment, their fates are bound to ours, for they may not return to their own kind to tell our secret. Ulpreln, attend the mission clock: commence our counterboost as scheduled."

Three seconds later, Ulpreln engaged the thrusters once again; the counteracceleration crushed Nezdeh back into her couch.

Jorge Velho released his white-knuckle grasp on the arms of his command couch. "They've destroyed both arrays?"

"Yes, sir." Ayana Tagawa's reply was eerily calm.

"Probably because they realized that we meant to try signaling with them. As you feared."

She half turned, so that their eyes could meet. "Sir, I meant no disrespect or criticism with that warning. Despite the risks, it was the only reasonable course left to you. Many civilian commanders would not have conceived of it."

Velho noticed the slight emphasis she put on the word *civilian*. Why would she even phrase her comment with that adjective, unless her dossier was somehow incomplete—?

But there was no time to pursue that thought; the attackers were not wasting time. "The intruder has tumbled and is counterboosting." Ayana paused, checking her data. "At four gees."

Piet glanced up at the navplot, assessing. "They're going to shoot past us."

"Why do you say that?" asked Jorge, who had piloting credentials but nothing like his helmsman's experienced, instinctive surety.

"Because unless they mean to maintain that counterboost right up until they kiss our hull, they won't have killed all their forward momentum, relative to making an intercept."

Ayana stared at the plot. "But that is exactly what they mean to do. Look at their telemetry: at their current rate of relative deceleration, they are going to match our vector and achieve an approach velocity of zero at exactly twenty-one meters from *Arbitrage*. And they are making for a logical boarding point: the EVA hatches in the lading and remote engineering sections, just forward of the tanker cradles and cargo racks."

Piet shook his head. "That's madness. No one can take four gees of sustained deceleration and then be ready to un-ass their couches and conduct an assault. One or the other maybe, but not both."

"And yet," Ayana pointed out calmly, "there is no other explanation for the intruder's course of action. They mean to board us."

Velho accepted that the impossible was becoming the inevitable and sought for a way to reverse that trend. "Piet, give me full portside roll from the emergency attitude control system."

Ayana looked around with a smile. "Excellent, sir. They will not be able to dock with a rolling ship, not until they have rematched relative vectors. That will delay them considerably. And using the compressed gas of the emergency ACS will not give them a ready thermal target, as would the plasma thrusters."

Jorge smiled, but feared the expression was as crooked as he felt. "That's the idea. Now, let's see if it works. In the meantime, get me an updated damage report, and get Kozakowski back on the bridge."

"Srina Pere—Perekmeres," Sehtrek grunted out past the lung compression of the sustained four-gee counterthrust.

Impressive; not many low-bred, even Intendants, have that much willpower. "No need to speak," Nezdeh said with considerably less effort. "I see it. A faint roll in the target. Tegrese, thrust signatures?"

"No new thermal signature," she replied.

So. The Aboriginals are not using their heavy plasma thrusters, then. Which logically meant compressed gas thrusters. "Sehtrek, give me a particulate density scan of the space immediately proximal to *Arbitrage*."

"Plumes of p-parti-ticles on the port side—"

"Track those plumes back to the hull of *Arbitrage*. Relay those coordinates to Tegrese. As soon as you have them, Tegrese, fire one UV laser blister at each."

Sehtrek gasped out, "Relaying."

Tegrese nodded. "Firing."

"Report," Nezdeh demanded as, at three points along its port side, the Aboriginal craft spat out showers of violently spinning debris.

Sehtrek coughed. "Plumes dissipating. No new particulate emissions from compressed gas thrusters."

"Roll rate of target?"

"One tenth of an RPM."

"Ulpreln?"

"Commencing correction." *Lurker* bucked slightly as a new, inward-spiraling vector was added to her course.

"Time to intercept?"

"Revised ETA is five minutes."

Nezdeh toggled her beltcom. "Brenlor?"

"Here."

"Stand by for boarding. In five minutes, the rehabilitation of our House begins in earnest."

Chapter Eleven

FAR ORBIT
SIGMA DRACONIS TWO

By the time Caine and Downing reached the secure conference room on board the Commonwealth shift-carrier *Lincoln*, the rest of their delegation workgroup was present: Sukhinin, Gray Rinehart, and biological expert Ben Hwang. The Marine guards started to close the door—

Flashing a clearance card at the guards and breezing past them into the compartment, Etienne Gaspard continued toward the head of the table. Once there, he took the chair that the other five had left unoccupied, so as to avoid the appearance of taking charge. "Good," Gaspard said, "we are gathered."

Caine and Downing exchanged looks. "Why, yes," Downing murmured, "we are gathered."

Caine resisted the impulse to close his eyes. *Really? I'm going to have to babysit this jackass across God knows how many light-years?*

Sukhinin had the rank, both military and political, to bring Gaspard to heel. Or at least, to try: "*Gospodin* Gaspard, while it is good of you to come, it is also a mystery. You were not summoned, to my knowledge."

"An understandable oversight. Fortunately, upon debarking from *Doppelganger*, I requested an update on all top clearance communiqués. When I saw the topic of this meeting, I realized that I would have to be involved. It is only logical that we are sending a consul to the Slaasriithi, is it not?"

"Yes," Sukhinin said slowly, "it is."

"Then let me be the first to congratulate you on this extraordinary assignment, Admiral Sukhinin. I'm sure you will be—"

"I'm not going," Vassily said with all the animation of a slab of granite. "You are."

Gaspard smiled, then looked at Vassily and the other people in the room. The smile fell away from his face. "Gentlemen, this jest is in very poor taste."

"It is not a jest, *gospodin* Gaspard. Consul Visser must return to Earth. I must remain here, due to relationships already forged with the Arat Kur. You are the only available consul."

"But—but I have prepared for this assignment to Homenest assiduously, constantly, for many months! It is an outrage that I should be asked to—"

"*Gospodin* Gaspard, you are not being asked. You are being told. Am I clear?"

Gaspard finished sputtering, remembered the poise he had lost about two sentences earlier. "What is *not* clear to me, Admiral Sukhinin, is whether you have the authority to make this decision."

Sukhinin smiled. It was not a pleasant expression. "Computer," he spoke at the ceiling, "secure communication protocol Borodino Five. Raise UCS *Trafalgar.*"

Within two seconds, a new voice boomed out of the speakers: Admiral Lord Thomas Halifax, C-in-C of the Republic Expeditionary Fleet. "Vassily, to what do I owe the pleasure?"

"Thomas, I am sorry to disturb you, but I require a confirmation of one of today's earlier decisions. You are comfortable designating Consul Gaspard as Ambassador Plenipotentiary to the Slaasriithi, yes?"

"Comfortable? Completely! Right man for the job, I'd say. And we can't have *you* gallivanting off to parts unknown, you old war-dog." He paused. "Problems, Vassily?"

Sukhinin's narrowed eyes and mirthless grin were aimed at Gaspard. "No, I think not. Thank you, Thomas. Tea, sometime?"

"Of course. Your way or mine, Vassily?"

Sukhinin sighed. "I am a good host. We shall spoil the tea with clotted cream and serve it in dainty cups."

"Right, then. I'll have my orderly set it up. Halifax out."

"Computer," Sukhinin spoke to the ceiling, "close channel." He lowered his gaze back to Gaspard. "Consul Visser solicited Admiral

Lord Halifax's recommendation on this matter. He witnessed, and seconded, her appointment of me as her replacement. Therefore, it has the approval of both military and civilian authorities. Now, are there any further questions about my *orders*?"

Gaspard's chin was desperately high. "No, Admiral. I am satisfied as to their legality, but must question their advisability. Specifically, what background materials do we have on the Slaasriithi?"

Downing leaned forward. "Only the 'child's primer' that they gave to us at the Convocation, of which I believe you received a copy."

"Yes...but, *mon Dieu*, that document is so general as to be worthless. Have you not requested more details?"

"We have," Caine explained. "When we asked for a more extensive history of their species, we got a response that boils down to 'come meet us; then you will understand.'"

Gaspard stared at the others in the room. "Gentlemen, must we truly accept such an enigmatic invitation? This is all most irregular."

"Yes, it is irregular," agreed Downing. "But yes, you must go. This is not just a matter of seeking a conventional, *realpolitik* alliance, but a unique opportunity to initiate a technical intelligence pipeline that could furnish us with paradigm-shifting advances. Bloody hell, if the Slaasriithi don't keep you bottled up in your own modules the whole time, just touring their ship could be an engineering gold mine."

Riordan took up the thread. "The Dornaani have told us, point-blank, that the Slaasriithi are significantly more advanced than the Arat Kur, whose technology we've now inspected in detail. The Arat Kur fusion plants are smaller and more efficient than ours, as are their antimatter production and retention systems. The Slaasriithi are an order of magnitude more advanced."

"Gentlemen," Gaspard sighed, "your enthusiasm for machinery is understandable. But are there no other objectives? No cultural initiatives? That, after all, is my area of expertise."

Caine leaned forward. "Frankly, I think the cultural benefits of a meeting with the Slaasriithi could be the most significant, in the long view."

Gaspard, finding some ground on which he was comfortable, leaned into Caine's comment. "Go on, Mr. Riordan."

"The Slaasriithi are a conduit into the deeper history of this part of space and of the exosapient races we've discovered within it. They might be able to answer key strategic questions, such as: why are so many intelligent races contained in a one-hundred-light-year-diameter sphere? Why is there no Convocation record of making contact with other intelligences beyond that range? Why are so many green worlds readily inhabitable by the majority of the races of the Accord?"

Gaspard's eyebrows had risen high on his forehead. "I understand that these are crucial questions, but they speak more to cosmology than strategy, *non*?"

"Not entirely," Riordan responded. "Getting those answers helps us understand the larger political and astrographic environment in which we're operating."

"Have we not had analysts studying these ramifications?"

"Mr. Gaspard, as I understand it, every single analyst we have has been working overtime for the past year and then at triple-speed when we were invaded. This is really the first opportunity we've had to lean back and look at the bigger picture. There have been too many impending catastrophes to spend time pondering the deepest implications of the marble and granite bones of the twenty-thousand-year-old human ruin—and conundrum—we found on Delta Pavonis Three."

Gaspard nodded. "Yes, I have thought this too. Even now, too many strategists and statespersons are flushed with the euphoria of victory and the relief of deliverance. They are not speculating upon the mysteries behind us, only upon the possibilities before us."

Caine nodded. Well, Gaspard had frequently been an asshole, but he was proving to be a fairly insightful asshole. "Mr. Gaspard, I couldn't have said that better myself."

Gaspard frowned, considered. "No, you probably could not have."

So he's not just an asshole: he's a total *asshole.* Aloud: "I just hope the Slaasriithi are going to be as productive as we'd like them to be in answering these questions."

Downing leaned forward. "Why do you think they wouldn't be?"

Caine shrugged. "I don't mean they'd be uncooperative, but so far, their self-representation suggests that they might not record or even think of history the way we do."

Gaspard shook his head. "History is history. How can it be different?"

Ben Hwang folded his hands as he took up the explanation. "The Slaasriithi are polytaxic. The integration and interaction between their different subspecies—or, more properly, taxae—may necessitate a tendency toward what we would think of as self-effacing consensualism. There are hints, in the primer they relayed to us, that in their society, pride of self and cult of personality are not merely morally egregious but might be considered dangerous psychopathologies."

"What you are suggesting," Gaspard summarized over steepled fingers, "is that they might not keep a history, but merely a chronicle of the past events."

Downing nodded. "I think that's possible."

Gaspard gaze slid away from Downing, settled upon Caine. "And you concur with that conclusion?"

"Frankly, I don't know enough to concur or demur, Mr. Gaspard."

"Yet it was you who brought up the possible limits of their historical perspective. Do you doubt your own assertion?"

"Mr. Gaspard, I presented a possibility, not an assertion. As for doubts—well, we've spoken to a grand total of *one* Slaasriithi, and we have their primer." Caine shrugged. "I know it's human nature to want to draw conclusions, but I distrust straight-line projections when we only have two data points."

Gaspard nodded sharply. "I quite agree. All these hypotheses follow logically from the data we do have, but we do not have very much. Well, when the time comes for me to be awakened, I will ask you to apprise me of any new information you have acquired from our Slaasriithi hosts."

Caine frowned. "You intend to travel in cold sleep?"

"Of course I do."

"Mr. Consul," Downing began cautiously—Caine could not tell if he was being cautious about arousing Gaspard's temper or his own—"it was presumed that you would logically wish to spend all available time preparing for your meeting with the Slaasriithi."

Gaspard stared at Downing. "I am pained to point out that there is nothing logical about that presumption at all, *Monsieur* Downing. Here, instead, is what is logical: that this mission, too, may be cancelled. And if it is, I much prefer not having burdened my mind with yet another encyclopedia of facts that I shall never use, and having lost a further four months of my waking life needlessly committing them to memory. After all, if the Slaasriithi decide to strictly enforce their statement to Mr. Riordan, that we must 'meet them to understand them,' they may not even allow us access to their vessel or provide us with additional preparatory materials during our journey to their homeworld. In which case, I would have remained awake for the singularly productive pleasure of staring at the dull walls of one of our habitation modules. Of course, I insist on being awakened should we face a crisis or emergency."

Caine smiled. *Well, you clearly don't know much about the real practicalities of cold sleep. Not if you think being roused for an unfolding crisis is a good idea. Awakening cold sleepers into a crisis is like dragging a boozehound out of bed to rescue his family when he's still sleeping off a binge. Accelerated reanims are more trouble than they're worth.*

Sukhinin's voice interrupted with a toneless imperative: "Ambassador Gaspard, for that is your primary title for the duration of this assignment, let us be clear on one further matter. Although you are our senior envoy and a consul of the Republic, do not presume that you may issue orders to Captain Riordan in all matters."

Caine's surprised sputter did not allow him to get out the question before Gaspard did: "*Captain* Riordan?"

Sukhinin stared at Gaspard, then glanced at the other faces ringing the table. "Was I unclear?"

Downing leaned forward. "Ambassador, it is necessary that we send along a person of appropriate rank, both to advise you on the military ramifications of any agreements you might make with the Slaasriithi, and as your legation's security and intelligence overseer. Riordan's former rank of commander was deemed insufficient for this role. He is thereby being promoted to captain, although that is as much in recognition of his actions in the recent war as it is an administrative necessity."

Caine looked from Downing to Sukhinin. "Thanks. I think."

Sukhinin fixed him with a look that said, *You poor young fellow,* and held up a hand to stop Gaspard's imminent protestations. "This is not open to debate or discussion," Vassily declared. "Firstly, although you are a consul, and so carry plenipotentiary powers for entering into treaties with the Slaasriithi, you have been a politician, not an ambassador, up until this point in time. *Nyet?*"

"I trained as a diplomat, in the most prestigious—"

"I was at the Parthenon Dialogues with you, *gospodin* Gaspard, and so have heard of your credentials from the Sorbonne. From your own lips. Repeatedly. But in point of fact, while you have served on numerous international councils and commissions, you have never worked as an ambassador between two human nations, nor have you ever been on a first contact mission. Correct?"

Gaspard had no ready response.

Sukhinin ploughed ahead ruthlessly. "Even more marked is your lack of specialization in military and intelligence matters. In short, Captain Riordan has exactly the experience and skills to assist you in assessing the full implications of any agreements you might make with the Slaasriithi. Actually, if I had the authority to promote him further, I would: protocol implies that a flag officer should be charged with these responsibilities. The rank above captain—commodore—at least occupies a gray zone between command and flag ranks."

"So, Riordan may contravene my orders?"

Downing shook his head. "No, you have different spheres of authority. In matters pertaining to the security of the delegation and its operations, he makes the final decisions, although he must solicit and consider your input. Conversely, in diplomatic activities, you hold full authority, although, once again, Captain Riordan is obligated to offer his opinion on the military implications of your decisions, and you are obligated to take those into consideration."

Gaspard stared at Caine. "Well then, Captain, I shall look forward to your military assessment of whatever information is conveyed to us by the Slaasriithi—or not—during my slumbers." He rose. "I shall be preparing for relocation to the Slaasriithi shift-carrier and the commencement of my cryogenic suspension. As I understand it, you will make the final arrangements for the transfer of my staff, who are already in cold sleep. Good day." Gaspard was out the door without a glance behind or even a nod of farewell.

Gray Rinehart looked at Downing. "So, does Caine get combat pay while traveling with that jackass?"

Downing sighed, smiled ruefully at Riordan. "If there was any justice in this universe, he would."

Chapter Twelve

IN CLOSE ORBIT
V 1581 FOUR

Kozakowski had rolled back the blast covers on the *Arbitrage*'s portside bridge windows to watch the intruder approach. It was no longer obscured by the wispy edges of V 1581.4's cream-and-ochre atmosphere. "My God, they *must* mean to ram us."

Ayana shook her head and glanced over Kozakowski's round shoulders at the brilliant blue exhaust flares of the intruder. "No, Mr. Kozakowski, but they do not mean to give us much time to prepare or fire at them."

"As if we had anything left to fire," Jorge Velho amended. He finished activating the automated anti-intruder systems, then turned to the intercom, collecting himself to give an order that he never wanted, and never thought he'd need, to give: "All hands, this is the captain. The intruder is confirmed to be on an intercept course, with the evident intent of boarding us. They do not respond to hails. All security teams: confirm your readiness with the XO and secure for vacuum operations."

"Vacuum operations?" echoed Kozakowski.

"Yes," confirmed Ayana. "Although contested boardings are extremely rare, one of the most common tactics by a boarder is to create conditions of explosive or at least dislocating decompression. That is why we have sealed the bulkheads communicating with the hull-proximal sections and reduced them to zero point two atmospheres. Fortunately, even though we've cut rotation, we still have some gravity, due to the proximity of the gas giant beneath us. Combat in true zero-gee is extremely unforgiving to the untrained."

Kozakowski nodded. "Some of my crew is trained for both low- and zero-gee operations. Let them help."

Velho did not turn to look at Kozakowski. *Yes, your crew was trained by the same megacorporation which sold us out to invaders just half a year ago. And with you in charge of that crew, we might have the same mysterious "difficulties" that kept us from getting the drones released from the autodeployable module in time. What should have been a twenty-second operation took over a minute—which was too long.* But instead, Velho said: "Mr. Kozakowski, we have taken heavy damage to a number of key systems, systems with which your personnel have far greater expertise. We are going to need that expertise if, after this action, we hope to effect repairs. By holding back those experts, that reduces your available crew complement to twenty. Those remaining twenty are currently manning the essential systems in engineering and staffing damage control parties.

"Conversely, most of my prize crew are reasonably proficient with weapons and antiboarding tactics, and more than a hundred are defending the EVA ingress points in the engineering and cargo oversight modules. In short, we have the right assets in the right places." *Which also means I don't have to worry about any megacorporate turncoats shooting my people in their backs.*

"And if you really want to help," Piet muttered, "you could decant a few dozen of those clone-soldiers riding in the freezer section."

Kozakowski did not deign to face the pilot as he rebutted. "CoDevCo's Optigene clones are not superhuman. Just like anyone else, they cannot be roused straight from cold sleep into operations. The biochemical reanimation requirements take forty-eight hours alone. It would require another thirty-six to forty-eight hours for full restoration of autonomic and voluntary muscular function, and perhaps yet another day for full mental function. I hope it is enough that I have granted you full access to their equipment lockers. And I am still willing to take my place among the defenders, even if you do not permit any of my crew to accompany me."

Jorge considered the offer: it was too measured to be fully convincing. *So, Kozakowski, the first time you're eager to help us is when you could be killed doing so? Or rather, so you can sabotage our defensive preparations and curry favor with your true masters? Or am I just being overly suspicious?* "No, Mr. Koza-kowski, as the original master of the ship, I think it important that you remain here on the bridge." Velho picked up one of the autoshotguns that had been liberated from the Optigene clones' combat stores. "I will oversee the defenses personally." *As if I really know what the hell I'm doing. This was not part of the job description when the government came looking for civilian prize crews.* "Now, before I go, let's see if we can give our attackers at least one nasty surprise. Is Mr. Vindar off Deal Two?"

"Yes, sir. Remote piloting protocols are engaged."

"Are the thrusters still hot?"

"Enough for one good burst, sir."

Kozakowski looked from one face to the other among the three bridge crew.

Jorge suppressed a smile at the CoDevCo factotum's perplexity. "Piet, do you have the controls routed through to your board?"

"Aye, sir."

Jorge eyeballed the trajectory of the intruder in relation to where Deal Two was dangling, only half in its docking cradle. "She might not come out of the clamps cleanly," he warned.

Piet shrugged. "We knew that from the moment we came up with this harebrained scheme. But it's the only shot we have, Jorge."

"It is as you say, my friend. And we will let your instruments and eyes determine when to—"

"Engaging now!" Piet interrupted.

He triggered Deal Two's emergency umbilical release, slammed the thrust relays on his remote operations board to maximum, yanked the tanker's flight controls up and then savagely over.

In the screens, Deal Two's thrusters blasted out a glowing wave of plasma. They propelled her up out of the docking cradles and then, gimballing, began to swing her in a scalded-cat hop toward the oncoming intruder—

But something unexpected was trailing behind Deal Two as Piet tried to effect his own, unorthodox ramming attempt: the tanker-tender's umbilical was still attached to the *Arbitrage*, probably due to the prior damage—

Although the resistance only caused a mild jerk and delay in Deal Two's half-Immelman attempt at smashing itself into the oncoming ship, that was time enough for the attackers to react. Two of the low, black, lusterless mini-domes near the prow of the enemy ship spun in the direction of the tanker—

—which was abruptly ripped end to end by invisible, crisscrossing beams which left glowing slices along Deal Two's fuselage. One of those beams triggered an explosion which converted the whole boat into a tumbling storm of debris. The intruder jinked slightly to avoid a spinning, savaged bay door, and kept coming on.

No one said anything. Jorge Velho hefted the autoshotgun, reflected that he hoped his experience with semiautomatic sporting versions on his uncle's sugar and silviculture plantation near Belém would stand him in good stead. "Ms. Tagawa has the con. And she will assume command in the event that I am—incapacitated."

Ayana started. "Captain Velho, as the XO, I am expendable and should be—"

"Ms. Tagawa, the matter is not open to discussion. Ignoring my command prerogative for a moment, it is quite obvious that you are more familiar with the best protocols to employ in this scenario." *You seem to be* much *more familiar with them. Indeed, suspiciously so* ... "*Arbitrage* needs that expertise, whether in escaping, or negotiating a settlement with the intruders." He told himself that only a tiny part of his motivation stemmed from male protective instincts that had been drilled into his genome through uncounted millennia. "Piet, keep a firm hand on the tiller."

"Aye, sir," said the South African ruefully.

Velho exited the bridge, pointedly resisting the urge to glance back.

At Ayana.

Nezdeh watched the external monitors as Ulpreln counted off the last ten meters to the *Arbitrage*. "Ten, nine..."

"Slow us."

"Obeyed. Eight, seven." The pause lengthened. "Six. And..."

"Now: final retroboost."

"Boosting—and we are at relative-velocity all-stop, Nezdeh."

"Still no countermeasures deployed by the target?"

Sehtrek glanced up. "None observable, Srina Perekmeres."

She nodded and switched channels. *Action: at last.* "Primary EVA team?"

"We are ready."

"Commence assault."

"Complying."

In the external monitors, Nezdeh watched the main EVA hatch, just aft of midship, open. A line of spacesuited figures emerged. Organized as three separate teams, they traversed the four remaining meters to a double-sized EVA portal in the *Arbitrage*'s hull, a small access bay for loading ship's stores. Each team's lead figure used active maneuver jets to reach the Aboriginal ship, towing three more figures behind. As two of the team leaders produced tools consistent with forced ingress procedures, the third team leader floated to the side, weapon ready.

"Secondary EVA team?"

Brenlor's impatience was audible. "Here. And still waiting."

Nezdeh almost rolled her eyes. *And you shall continue to do so. For one more minute.*

On the bridge of the *Arbitrage*, Emil Kozakowski was tempted to shove Tagawa out of the way to get a better look at the small external monitor that showed the would-be boarders who had gathered forward of Deal Two's empty docking cradle.

"Yes," Tagawa was telling Velho over the intercom, "a dozen boarders at bay Foxtrot-Twelve. I do not recognize their weapons or suits."

Velho's voice, Lilliputian as it escaped Tagawa's earbud, began shouting for more personnel to deploy to the bay, drawing them from the teams watching other access points and from the reserves being held further in-hull. Kozakowski estimated that the defenders would outnumber their dozen attackers by better than six to one, once the repositioning was completed. He leaned toward the screen and Ayana. "What are the raiders doing at the bay, do you think?"

Tagawa did not even move her eyes toward him. "They seem to be attempting some kind of external electronic bypass."

"Odd. How could they hope to understand the electronics of our ships?"

Now she did turn toward him. "I was wondering if you might be the very person to answer such a question, Mr. Kozakowski." Her gaze was level. It was no more emotional than usual, but somehow, it conveyed a startling degree of animus.

Kozakowski felt his face grow hot. "I do not appreciate your insinuation, Ms. Tagawa."

"And I do not appreciate your presence, Mr. Kozakowski. But, as to the matter of their boarding attempts: you will notice the large cases carried by two of the waiting team members on each of the boarding strings. I suspect that if they cannot bypass our electronics, they shall use explosives. I expect, given the technology we have witnessed so far, they would breach the hull easily."

"Wonder why they didn't just use charges in the first place, then," commented Piet sourly.

"The mere fact that they are boarding us suggests that they value either the ship, or something on it," Ayana replied, without glancing at Piet.

She was studying the actions of the breaching team so closely that she did not notice new motion in another screen, half-obscured by Kozakowski's pear shaped body. It offered a wide-angle view that, while reprising the boarding attempt in miniature, showed the entirety of the raider—

—From behind which, four more space-suited figures emerged. Unlike the first twelve, these boarders were wearing large maneuver packs, carrying sizeable weapons, and seemed, if anything, overburdened. As soon as they had regrouped just beyond the far aft quarter of their own hull, they fired their maneuver jets and moved rapidly forward, angling toward the keel of the *Arbitrage*.

Kozakowski glanced at Ayana, who was not allowing her gaze to drift in his direction—or, therefore, toward the monitor containing the wide-angle view of the intruder.

Kozakowski watched the four new figures jet out of the side of the frame. They would soon be between the stilled rotational armatures of the *Arbitrage's* twin toruses, heading toward the bow.

He said nothing.

Nezdeh watched the four members of Brenlor's Team Two, all wearing heavily armored EVA suits, cut a straight line through the radial arms of the *Arbitrage's* two rotational habitats. "Is there any sign they've been detected?"

"None, Srina Perekmeres," Sehtrek replied.

Nezdeh shook her head. "Still, they will spot Team Two any moment." But every additional moment that Brenlor's men remained undetected meant less warning for the defenders. And given the diversion that Team One was staging near the more logical entry point—the bay door—the Aboriginals might, even now, be concentrating their forces away from Brenlor's actual point of entry.

Nezdeh activated her beltcom. "Brenlor, ETA?"

"Thirty seconds. Radiation dose-rate from this gas giant is tolerable."

"Is it interfering with your electronics?"

"No. They are sufficiently hardened. Heads-up display and map schematics are reading clearly. How kind of the Aboriginals to provide us with deck plans of their ship."

"That is the point of suborning an opponent, rather than attacking or conquering them outright." *A distinction which the other Perekmeres males would have been wise to appreciate before they hatched the ridiculous plots that ultimately led to our House's Extirpation.* In the monitor, she saw the four figures of Team Two arrive near a small, personnel-sized airlock door, just forward of the leading rotational habitat. "Activate your helmet cameras."

Brenlor's reply was sardonic. "Activating—and enjoy the spectacle. Idrem, enter the ship's secure code into the manual access keypad."

Ayana Tagawa frowned. For a military boarding party, the dozen figures at the threshold of bay door F-12 seemed to be taking their time, most of them hanging patiently on their lead-strings.

Too patiently, she suddenly realized.

Tagawa leaned forward to inspect the nine non-team-leaders closely. What she saw was not consistent with techniques for conserving life support: rather, it was a complete lack of motion.

Which instantly changed her perception of what she was seeing. This was no longer an oddly casual boarding attempt by twelve personnel, nine of whom were remaining admirably motionless. It was a ruse, in which only three persons were showing any signs of activity, urgent or otherwise. Which meant—

Ayana leaned forward to peer around Kozakowski, who was still staring out the windows like an utter idiot—and, in the portside bow monitor, she saw four figures gliding to a halt near the outer hatch of airlock C-2. Each wore a heavier, bulkier spacesuit, the torso covered by armored plates. And their weapons—"Captain Velho, the primary boarding attempt is taking place now at airlock Charlie-Two. I repeat, primary boarding attempt is under way at Charlie-Two, not Foxtrot-Twelve." She stared into Kozakowski's almost-surprised eyes. "You weren't watching the monitors?"

"The monitors?" He sounded puzzled. "I wanted to make sure they didn't come near us here on the bridge."

"You—?" *Can Kozakowski really be that stupid, that—?* Ayana leaned away from the man before she was conscious of doing so: *no, he can't be that stupid. No one can. I should shoot him now—but I have no proof.*

In her earbud, Ayana heard Jorge shouting for several fire-teams to double back to Charlie Two. But Ayana knew those reinforcements were already too late: one of the four boarders was entering a code into the external control panel. And there wasn't enough time to crash the computer or override the systems.

Not anymore.

Brenlor's voice was harsh. "Idrem, what is delaying you?"

If you had a genuine interest in anything other than weaponcraft, you might know. "Brenlor, simultaneously opening both the outer and inner hatches of an airlock is a difficult override to achieve, even if one has the codes. There are built-in safety constraints that preclude—"

"Just be swift in your task, Idrem."

"I shall." *And I shall not title you Srin or any of the other obeisances you especially want from* me, *since you know I am your superior in every way but one: I lack the Blood of the First Line of the First Family. Although, given the failures of that Line's Extirpated Hegemons, I suspect their geneline had already been corrupted—*

The airlock's external panel began flashing red, along with all the lights ringing the outer hatch. "Brenlor, we are ready."

"Assault positions," Brenlor ordered over the tactical channel. "Vranut, you enter. I shall cover, then follow. Idrem, you and Jesel secure the inner hatch behind us."

Vranut was already in position when Idrem warned, "The hatch will open very quickly. I am invoking an emergency protocol for rapidly expelling contaminants or extinguishing a fire."

"I am ready," Vranut replied, setting his needler to low power and maximum rate of fire.

"On three. One, two—"

On "three," Idrem hit the entry tab; the outer hatch flung itself aside. Vranut was halfway in the doorway, started, and with catlike speed and grace, rolled himself back out—just in time to avoid a flailing human as he tumbled out into space. The Aboriginal was wearing a light duty suit, trailing a snapped lanyard. The garment was already beginning to balloon. Unrated for full vacuum, the occupant would not live long enough to deplete the small life-support unit strapped across his shoulders.

Vranut peeked back into the airlock cautiously, then entered low and fast against the diminishing outrush of atmosphere and detritus. Sparks and chips marked where defensive fire began seeking him.

Brenlor extended his weapon around the rim of the outer airlock hatch. "I see them," he muttered, playing his coil gun about slightly so that it transferred the whole interior picture to his HUD. "Transmitting."

The view from his weapon's scope was now on each of the four boarders' HUDs. Idrem studied the tactical situation: three defenders just recovering from the outdraft of the explosive decompression, half concealed in doorways on the entry corridor. Further on, at a tee intersection, there was what appeared to be a barricade behind which several indistinct figures lurked.

"We've surprised them," Brenlor shouted. "Vranut, prepare to advance. We will fire high-power bursts to clear the near doorways. You are to take cover in the furthest one you can reach."

"And Vranut," added Idrem, "I will follow up with a grenade down the hall." He stare-selected a spot just behind and beneath the barricade, letting his eye remain fixed until a crosshair appeared at the desired point. "Wait until it discharges. It should interrupt their fire for several seconds." *Or perhaps permanently.*

Brenlor grunted something that sounded like consent, then yelled. "All fire!"

Without exposing any part of themselves other than their weapons, Brenlor and the 'sul named Jesel set their needlers on maximum propulsive power and began firing four-round bursts. In the HUD, Idrem could see the four-point-two-millimeter projectiles go through defenders and the doorjambs behind which they hid.

Idrem did not wait for the bodies to begin their slow slump to the deck. He leaned his grenade launcher around the corner, depressed the trigger that showed the thirty-eight-millimeter self-seeking rocket grenade the aim point he had stare-selected, and then squeezed the firing trigger. The grenade sped towards its target, self-correcting for any post-firing motion of the launch tube with micro thrusters while the grenade launcher itself selectively counter-vented the propulsive gases to eliminate muzzle jump and recoil.

The grenade exploded—noiselessly in the air-evacuated corridor—sending obstacles and bodies spinning away from its point of detonation.

Vranut did not wait for Brenlor's "Advance!" Consistent with training and reflexes ingrained since he first sprouted facial hair, the Evolved maintained a low posture as he glide-sprinted forward, making it to the furthest doorway along the corridor. He turned to wave the other three boarders inside with one hand, keeping his weapon pointed back toward the ruined barricade with the other. His weapon's scope evidently showed him a defender rising up from the blast, wielding an archaic assault rifle. Without turning, Vranut used the HUD to aim at the figure behind him, squeezed off a low-power five-round burst. Three of the rounds were stopped by the tangled remains of the barricade; the other two made pinhole puncture marks in the defender's chest. The four-point-two-millimeter flechettes' biosensitive nanites instantly registered contact with living tissue. The stabilizing fins snapped backward and perpendicular to the axis of the penetrator core, inducing wild cavitation before they emerged, corkscrewing, from just beneath the Aboriginal's scapula. In contrast to the modest entry trauma, the exit wounds were marked by broad gouts of blood.

"Corridor cleared," Vranut reported as the others took shelter in the doorways.

Except Idrem, who remained at the control panel alongside the interior airlock hatch. He entered the codes for full override authority, triggered both doors to close—and then the illuminated keypad grew dark. The roaring cyclone of the automated repressurization system died down to an anemic wheeze, and amber hazard lights began glowing along the junctures of the deck and the bulkheads.

"What is it? What's happened?" Brenlor demanded.

"I believe the Aboriginals have performed an abrupt termination of their computer's function. They have 'crashed' it, in their parlance."

"So they no longer have control of the ship?" Brenlor's voice was not merely eager, but malicious.

"No, but nor do we." *Although I was about to secure it.*

"Then they are helpless."

"They have fewer options. But now, so do we. I can no longer terminate their life support, nor can I secure tactical advantages by controlling bulkheads, lighting, and other on-board systems."

"They are not needed." Brenlor rolled out of from behind the cover of a doorway and into the corridor. "And I suspect they won't have many defenders left." He slid a thick tube off his back and began undoing one tightly sealed end. "Jesel, check for thermal blooms at the intersection."

Jesel complied, moving forward and turning up the sensitivity of his faceplate's built-in thermal imaging sensor. He stopped about three meters away from the corner. "Faint signatures to the left; none to the right."

"We might miss some of the defenders, particularly if their duty suits are sealed and fitted with cold cans," Vranut pointed out.

"It is unlikely that they are taking precautions to conceal their body heat," Brenlor countered. "Look at these." He toed a dead Aboriginal. "They've left their helmets unsealed. Probably to conserve the pittance of air they have in their tanks. But today, that conservation of resources will prove their undoing."

"How?" Jesel asked.

"Because today they are going to meet these." Brenlor smiled as the lid of the canister came off with a depressurizing hiss. The open mouth was a honeycomb of twenty-two hexes in two concentric rings around one central hex. A hideous head, somewhat larger than that of the animal that the Aboriginals called a weasel, popped out of one of the cells of the honeycomb.

Three similar heads followed shortly. In the thin air, the creatures emitted coarse, clattering whines, akin to sand being tossed into a desk fan. "These are upt'theel," Brenlor explained with a smile. "They are old friends of our Family, used for boarding or other assaults where a well-prepared defender has taken refuge in tunnels and similar close structures."

More upt'theel heads emerged from the canister. Idrem had only seen the diminutive monsters twice before, had only used them once, and did not relish the memory. The upt'theel was a long-bodied octoped with chitinous legs that were even sharper than they looked. Its almost neckless head was liberally and evenly speckled with light sensors, with two genuine eyes directly above the mouth. Its wide-hinged jaw hung open to pull in as much of the thin air as possible, revealing a serrated ridge in place of teeth. The ridge was the color of obsidian and, by repute, harder than basalt.

"Should we not be moving?" Vranut asked from the corner of the intersection.

Brenlor watched the other creatures emerge, with the same rapt fascination of the Evolved who patronized helot death-arenas. "We do not need to rush. Their slow movements tell us that no enemies are near."

"They are... Awakened?" Jesel asked.

Brenlor laughed aloud. "Idiot. No, of course not. But their sense of smell is acute. They will detect a carbon-based animal, or its decaying flesh, quite readily."

"So the other defenders of this ingress point have fled?" Jesel sounded dubious.

Idrem looked at Vranut, who ran a thermal imaging sweep down either branch of the tee intersection.

Vranut shook his head. "No; they are edging closer again."

Brenlor actually smiled. "Then let us welcome them back." Taking an opaque vial off his light cuirass's left load-strap, he walked to Vranut's position, the canister of upt'theel in his other hand. "They are unique creatures." He spoke with the didactic detachment of an aficionado. "Their world was at the inner edge of the habitable zone—such as it is—of a blue-white giant. Not many species can evolve, much less thrive, under the gaze of such a punishing furnace of heat and radioactivity. Yet this species did." Brenlor laid the canister down. "It is always gratifying to watch them do their work." He slung the opaque vial around the left-hand corner, ending the toss with a sharp twist of his wrist. The glass container smacked into a wall: its shattering elicited one or two cries of caution from the Aboriginals who had apparently been trying to sneak up on the boarders.

The sand-and-fan whine of several of the upt'theel suddenly rose to a full chorus of pebbles-into-a-turboprop screeching. Like a horde of perverse lemmings mutated into pangolin-centipede-gila monster hybrids, the strange beasts flowed out of the honeycomb cells of the container with serpentine fluidity, snuffling as they sped around the corner. Not one bothered to look down the other, right-hand extension of the corridor.

Idrem nodded in that direction. "Apparently, the right-hand turn is clear." Meaning that the most direct path to the bridge was open.

Brenlor was unconcerned. "By the time the upt'theel reach the rotting bait I've thrown down the hall, they will smell the Aboriginals who are approaching."

"And this is why we remain with suits sealed?" Jesel asked.

"Yes. As long as the upt'theel cannot smell us, we are of no more interest to them than the bulkheads."

Stony, screeching disputes—probably over Brenlor's morsel of bait—rose, and then were suddenly still.

"Ah," said Brenlor, "they have the new scent."

Jesel made toward the corner aggressively, his needler coming up.

Brenlor put a restraining hand upon his arm. "Give them a moment to get started. It's easier for us. And more gratifying for them."

Around the corner, a fusillade of panicked gunfire erupted, followed closely by high-pitched human screams.

Ayana could not breathe as she watched the monitors displaying the approaches to airlock C-2. A swarm of small creatures akin to crustacean weasels had emerged from one of the attackers' containers and were now flowing like a low, rolling tide toward a half dozen defenders preparing an ambush in the corridor beyond the ruined barricade.

The creatures' sinuous, serpentine advance ensured that only a few were hit by the crew's gunfire, mostly by their one auto-shotgun. Then, as the strange animals neared the defenders, they launched into what appeared to be a somersault.

But the somersault did not end. With their eight liberally jointed legs rolling them forward, their exoskeletal back plates worked like the rim of a wheel. The defenders, apparently perplexed as much as unnerved, fired wildly. The duty-suited humans splattered a few more of the attacking beasts into chunks just before discovering that they had emptied their magazines. The rolling creatures bore in among them like a herd of animate hoops.

The small predators used the speed they had accumulated by uncoiling straight out of their final revolution into a mouth-first leap at their prey. Even before the creatures' claws and legs started slicing at and embedding in the flesh of the defenders, their sawlike jaws were at work, burrowing into viscera. Ayana felt bile jet up into her mouth as the killer weasel-crustaceans became more akin to gut-burrowing worms, their progress marked by intermittent spurts of blood and ruined intestines. Their screaming victims tried yanking them out, only to slice their hands open on the knifelike edges of the beasts' bodies and legs.

"Jorge—Captain!" Ayana cried, knowing she could not regain full vocal composure. "The boarders have eliminated both layers of defense for airlock Charlie-Two. Repeat: the—"

As if being progressively drowned by an advancing wave of darkness, the screens in the bridge went blank, one after the other. The carrier signal in her earbud died as well.

Piet spread his hands upon the bridge controls. "What just happened? How did—?"

Ayana interrupted, looking at the sensor logs. "We were just swept, from the docking cradles to the bridge, with some kind of focused EMP wave. Our less robust electronics have been disabled. The rest seem compromised."

Piet leaned aggressively over his console. "That's not possible."

"Apparently, it is," Kozakowski muttered.

Ayana turned on him, her sidearm out of its holster with considerable speed. "Tell us what you know about this weapon. Now."

"Kn-know?" Kozakowski stammered, his hands rising in a mix of haplessness and tentative surrender. "I don't know anything. There are rumors that the Ktor might be capable of such things, but I have had no contact with them or their technology." He blinked rapidly. "Now, put up that pistol, Ms. Tagawa. I am not the enemy."

"That," she said, "remains to be seen." She turned away from Kozakowski, but did not reholster the gun. "Mr. Brackman?"

"Yeh, Ms. Tagawa?"

"Since you no longer have a bridge station to run, concentrate on trying to raise the captain through one of the hardwired emergency intercom sets."

Piet frowned. "This megacorporate econobucket doesn't have an extensive intercom system, sir."

"Do your best. We must inform the captain that the boarders are not attacking toward the bridge, as we anticipated. They are heading straight toward him."

Chapter Thirteen

IN CLOSE ORBIT
V 1581 FOUR

As Team Two moved by leapfrog toward the Aboriginal defenders in the cargo and docking modules, Idrem's helmet comm buzzed: a private channel from Nezdeh. He toggled it with a push of his chin. "It is Idrem."

"The deck plans indicate you are approaching the defenders' primary concentration. Do you expect that Brenlor will be able to defeat the Aboriginals with only minor damage to the facilities?"

Idrem wondered at the directness of her question and what it implied: that she was depending upon him, Idrem, to attempt to limit the operational excesses of their mission's nominal commander. "Yes, I can see to it," Idrem replied.

Nezdeh was apparently not expecting that answer: she was silent a moment before asking, "How?"

"Before leaving *Ferocious Monolith*, I purloined several canisters of antipersonnel heat-seekers and marker nanites. I have already convinced Brenlor that this would be the most expeditious, and least damaging, means of securing the ship."

"That could be a risky operation, Idrem."

"Do you trust my competence, Nezdeh?"

Another pause. "Yes."

"Then I shall not do anything to risk the success of this mission, nor shall I fail you."

"Very well. I must coordinate with Brenlor now."

"Acknowledged."

The circuit closed at the same moment that Brenlor paused to shoo some of the upt'theel away from an Aboriginal corpse. After he used a spray bottle to douse the body with chemicals that the creatures found aversive, they came wriggling up out of the thoracic cavity, dripping gore and whining irritably. He herded the remaining dozen beasts forward to break up another knot of defenders who had been too late to help their comrades at airlock C-2.

Judging from the flags on the sleeves of the corpses, and from snatches of their panicked exclamations, they were all from the human political entity known as the Trans Oceanic Commercial and Industrial Organization bloc. Usually referred to as TOCIO, its acronym was neither a subtle nor coy referent to the capitol of the nation state that was its dominant power. Many of the bloc's nationalities were represented among the casualties inflicted thus far. Other than the red ball of Japan itself, Idrem had identified national patches indicating that their wearers were from Brazil, India, Myanmar, and Chile.

Even without control of the ship's command systems, defeating the ill-equipped Aboriginals had not posed much difficulty and even less threat. Only the Japanese nationals had been carrying truly dangerous weapons: dustmix battle rifles which, at these ranges, were certainly just as deadly as the Ktor's own needlers. However, they did not have the muzzle velocity that made it possible to penetrate almost every wall or floor in the ship except for vacuum-rated bulkheads and hatches. But for the Ktor, constrained to wearing only the light armor augmentations that were standard issue for the crew of a patrol hunter such as *Red Lurker*, there was still risk involved if they rounded a corner into a torrent of automatic fire from the Japanese rifles.

The other firearms were not particularly dangerous. The majority were caseless assault rifles that had been furnished to the Optigene clones by their Indonesian hosts. These serviceable weapons, named Pindads, were unable to penetrate the Ktoran light armor at all. And while the hailstorms of slugs fired by the enemy's autoshotguns could batter one of the Evolved to the ground, their penetrative power was even lower, and their raw kinetic impact was easily distributable through the smart armor fabrics of the Ktor.

"Idrem, are you ready?"

"I am." He inspected the corridor ahead. "The Aboriginals are around the far corner?"

"Yes," Brenlor confirmed. "According to the deck plans, it is a double-width passageway that opens out into a wide marshalling area with multiple egress routes. That is where their main body has deployed itself. And if the engagement goes against the humans, they have various retreat options that lead to regrouping points."

"In that case," Idrem replied, "we must ensure that they are unable to make use of those options. Please load the nanite marker grenades into your launcher."

Brenlor took the three thirty-eight-millimeter grenades that Idrem proffered, none of which were fitted with rockets, and loaded them into the left-hand cassette that fed his needler's underslung launch tube. "I have not had the occasion to employ this system, nor this tactic," Brenlor admitted in a low voice.

"It is not difficult, and it is most effective against lightly armored targets, such as our present adversaries."

Vranut and Jesel continued to guard the corner screening Team Two from the mass of Aboriginal defenders. As Idrem loaded three miniature signal-seeking submunitions into his needler's side-by-side grenade cassettes, he watched Brenlor guide three of the remaining upt'theel back into their carrier. "If we lose the rest in this assault, these will enable repopulation," he explained, almost defensively.

Idrem ignored the gruesome images that Brenlor's comment invoked. "Whenever you are ready."

Brenlor nodded and, using the right combination of attractant and repellent scents, prompted the nine remaining upt'theel around the corner.

They lifted their noses, catching the fresh prey scent—just before two of them were blasted to slimy mauve and gray bits by the hammering of an autoshotgun. As if they had been one creature, the survivors sped in that direction. The volume of gunfire rose precipitously. The Aboriginals were now busy enough for the Evolved to commence their actual attack.

Idrem nodded at Brenlor, who lifted his needler, stepped forward so he could see partly down the corridor at a very shallow angle, and discharged his grenade launcher at a distant point along the opposite wall.

The round struck the bulkhead, caromed off as per Brenlor's

intent. Abruptly, through the many awakened eyes of the warhead's submunitions, Idrem could see the casing split off, freeing a flock of small gray balls that flew in a wide arc, and then rolled as Idrem directed through his HUD. As these devices drew near to the defenders, he activated their proximity deployment systems. Nanites sprayed out into the spaces occupied by the enemy.

Idrem nodded to Brenlor. "The next two, now. In rapid sequence."

When Brenlor's second nanite-dispersing grenade landed nearby, the Aboriginals attempted to assess what nature of weapon was being fired at them. But seeing no explosion or gas or other aversive effect, they returned their attention to the onrushing upt'theel, and the raiders they presumed to follow shortly behind them.

When the third canister ricocheted down toward the defenders and broke open, a few of them discerned that the small rolling balls were something other than debris and shot at them without effect. That last swarm of rolling nanite dispensers made it into the deepest reaches of the defender's positions, thereby also providing Idrem with extensive advance reconnaissance of their enemy's deployment. Not that it would be required.

Idrem stepped forward, watching the munitions-cued timer tick down in his HUD, measuring the elapsed seconds since Brenlor's third round had deployed its spherical submunitions.

"How long—?" Brenlor began impatiently.

Idrem stepped in front of Brenlor and fired the first of his signal-seeking cluster munitions on a similar, wall-glancing trajectory. A moment later, Idrem patched the streaming recon-view that the nanite dispensers fed to his HUD through to the other members of his team.

The first cluster munition was angling off the wall when its seeker head emitted a brief, powerful microwave pulse. Instantly, human silhouettes glowed into existence on the Ktor's HUDs. The nanites, primed by settling on warm moving objects, responded to the microwave wash by absorbing and then reradiating it, albeit much more gradually.

In the same moment, the round's flechette warhead discharged. Over a hundred of the small darts whined forward like mosquitos, jetting into the same cone that the microwave pulse had illuminated. But each flechette was equipped with a seeker-head that detected the now-radiant bodies of the nanite-dusted humans. The flechettes twitched their tail fins slightly; each altered its flight path to intercept one of those glowing silhouettes.

The effect was gratifying. The defenders in the corridor went down in windrows. The micro-tine neographene penetrator points breached their suits easily, and the fins of each flechette stripped off upon contact with flesh. Consequently, whereas the entry wounds appeared like sudden sweeps of tiny stigmata, the exit wounds were akin to those made by a tight pattern of pistol slugs, pulping whatever they had passed through. The Aboriginals fell, their clutching fingers attempting to staunch wounds that could not be staunched.

"Impressive," Brenlor allowed. "The corridor is clear."

It was, except for one terrified Aboriginal who had been out of the signal-seeker's line of sight at the moment the flechettes were discharged. Idrem changed the next round's setting—spherical dispersal—and laser-painted its discharge point at the entry to the cargo marshalling area. He fired again.

This round glanced off the wall at roughly the same spot but bounded until it reached the discharge point. The sharp flash momentarily hid the sudden sprawling of almost a dozen bodies all around the warhead, including the hapless Aboriginal that the first round had been unable to "see."

Idrem changed the next aimpoint to a spot deeper in the marshalling area, stepped out into the body-littered passageway, fired it, set a fourth and final round for a still further discharge, fired. He waited for the glowing, thrashing bodies to settle as the two rounds went off in quick succession. Six figures, two only partially dusted by the nanites, were running toward the exits. Most were limping or staggering. "Vranut, Jesel; follow those six and eliminate them. Brenlor and I will dispatch the enemy wounded, unless we find useful survivors."

"And who among these slaughtered sheep would be useful, now or even beforehand?"

Idrem suppressed three Progenitor axioms that seemed to have been written expressly as rebukes for Brenlor Perekmeres' impetuosity. Instead, Idrem merely countered with, "One may always be surprised by advantages arising from unexpected sources."

"I suppose so," Brenlor allowed. "Let us eliminate the unexpected sources." He led the way.

Too eagerly, Idrem thought.

✧   ✧   ✧

Nezdeh made sure that she arrived on the bridge of the *Arbitrage* while Brenlor was still securing the rest of the ship. Thankfully, Idrem remained with him; the Progenitors only knew what he might have done without some tactful supervision.

There were three Aboriginals on the bridge, already deprived of their weapons. "Who is in command here?"

All three of them made to speak, but, seeing each others' motions, held back.

The first to recover was the tall, spindly male. "I am in command. Piet Brackman, First Officer and pilot."

Nezdeh glanced at the others. The female—a small, distinctly Asian subtype from what Earth experts called "the Pacific Rim"— had no reaction to the statement. The other, a Eurogenic specimen who was small for his sex and flabby, seemed to become thoughtful at the ostensible first officer's claim. It was not credible that command succession was unclear after the death of their captain, whose body and station were conspicuous among the fifty-two Aboriginal corpses in the cargo marshalling module. Consequently, something was being withheld. That was unacceptable, both in terms of gathering intelligence and in establishing dominion.

Nezdeh drew her liquimix pistol slowly. "I was born and bred to command. I will not tolerate lies or disobedience." She raised the weapon, aimed it at the tall human male's forehead. "Of the three persons on this bridge, I know you will lie to me. A true commander would have spoken quickly and assertively regarding his or her place in the chain of command. And there would have been no uncertain glances." She snapped the safety off. "Because it would be useful to have your cooperation, and because you are ignorant of our ways, you have one opportunity to redeem yourself: identify the actual commander."

The human named Brackman swallowed—*piteous,* she thought, *how openly they display their anxiety*—and explained, "There was a...a disagreement about command."

"How so?"

"I was the XO. Not common for a pilot, but I have seniority. But when Captain Velho left the bridge, he put Ms. Tagawa—" the tall Aboriginal glanced at the small Asian female—"in charge of negotiating a surrender in the event that we lost control of the *Arbitrage.* But he didn't change the chain of command."

"I see. So he did not trust your judgment?"

"I get angry. Easily. So I guess he didn't think I'd be a good negotiator."

"Interesting." The main lights reilluminated suddenly, as did the external monitors. The life-support system sighed into renewed activity. "We have restored your electronics and restarted your computer. We have also accounted for the entirety of your armed crew, who seem to be wearing national uniforms, not those of the Colonial Development Combine. Explain."

The tall Aboriginal's stare suggested that he had only heard the first phrase in Nezdeh's second sentence. "You have 'accounted' for the—my—prize crew? What does that mean?"

"It means precisely what you conjecture. They have been eliminated."

"All of them?"

Nezdeh closed the distance between them so fast that the low-breed male blinked—*good; it is time to acquaint them with our innate superiority*—and she slashed the pistol barrel across his face. The Aboriginal staggered, almost fell, but caught himself on the helm console. "You answer questions; you do not ask them. I am patient because it has been several centuries since any of your cultures have embraced the truth of the will to power, as does ours. But you shall learn. Or die. Now, I ask you again: why is this crew comprised of two distinct groups, one national, one megacorporate?" Peripherally, she noted that the other male's eyes had widened slightly when the blow fell. The small Asian female had not reacted at all. *Excellent training and possibly excellent genelines, but that could also be problematic. Time will tell.*

Brackman was rubbing his jaw. But what the Aboriginals lacked in readiness, they made up for in spirit: although at the wrong end of a gun barrel, the male's eyes were wide, bright, furious. "This ship, the *Arbitrage*, is a megacorporate hull. Which means it belonged to traitors." He glanced at the other male, and the look in his eyes changed from fury to hatred. "When we kicked their invader cronies off Earth, we took over their shift carriers, but we had to crew them with loyal personnel from the merchant or colonization services. Like me and Ms. Tagawa. But we had to keep a core staff of the CoDevCo crew; they know the ship best."

"Very well. Now, why is this ship in this system?"

The human frowned. "We're just refueling to—"

Nezdeh had to repress a sigh. "You will find that while I do not relish violence for its own sake, I am ready to embrace it where it is an effective tool. Now, I will ask again, for you know the intent of my question: how is it that a shift-carrier from Earth, which cannot reach this system directly, is here at all?"

The male shrugged. "We had help." Nezdeh made sure her move to strike him again began at an inordinately slow pace; Brackman stepped back, hands raised. "The Dornaani. They gave us what we needed to make a shift to deep space."

"Gave it to you? Their modification is presently integrated with your drives?"

"No. They came aboard, modified our guidance systems. Added things to it—I don't know. I'm not sure they let anyone know exactly what they did, including the officers who came on board with them. Then, right after we arrived here, they removed it."

"And your ship acted as a tanker, carrying the fuel for the rest of the fleet that moved directly on from deep space to carry out the attack against this system, and then Homenest?"

"I guess so, yes. Look: they didn't tell me—us—much."

Which made unfortunate sense. The information in the *Arbitrage*'s databanks—the first thing she had accessed when the system started rebooting—had some small but important gaps, particularly in the recent navigational and operational archives. "So, what orders are you carrying out now?"

"We're refueling."

"Do not be obtuse. I refer to your current, and your contingency, orders."

"We're to shift to join the fleet in Sigma Draconis."

"When? You no doubt have a projected departure window."

Brackman glanced away, looked as though he might throw up. "Forty to forty-two days, depending upon skimming conditions."

"And how soon will there be an inquiry if you do not arrive at Sigma Draconis?"

"Well, we—Immediately."

"Immediately?"

"Yes."

Nezdeh smiled. "Thank you. You have been very helpful. Unfortunately for you, you are not at all a convincing liar." She raised the pistol and fired twice.

The first round hit Brackman square in the forehead, but had barely enough energy to make an exit wound. The second popped open a dark red hole just to the left of his sternum; that round did not emerge from his back. Nezdeh had reduced the propellant not only to reduce the recoil to zero, but to prevent overpenetrations, and hence, damage to important ship's systems.

Brackman hit the deck with the odd gentleness of all limp bodies that fell in low gee. Blood spread out slowly from the back of his head, giving him a round red martyr's nimbus that shone in the overhead lights.

Nezdeh turned to the two remaining Aboriginals. "A commander would not have a moment's uncertainty regarding the response protocols to be observed if his ship was overdue. Besides, a search would not be 'immediate'; this hull adds no appreciable combat capability to your counterinvasion fleet. It is an auxiliary, and an increasingly redundant one."

"Which makes it perfect for our purposes," added Brenlor as he entered the bridge with Vranut and Idrem. "If there was one ship your fleet could afford to lose, it was this one."

Nezdeh smiled tightly, kept her eyes on the Aboriginals. "I trust you understand now that I will not tolerate liars." She turned to the male. "You are Kozakowski, are you not?"

He blinked in surprise. "I am. How do you—?"

"Do not question me. Besides, the answer to your question is obvious. Our agents aided your megacorporation in the recent war. Do you think we did not acquire complete information on your assets and personnel? And you, having been a direct liaison to one of us at Barnard's Star, should certainly know better."

The Asian female glanced sideways at Kozakowski; had she possessed a knife, Nezdeh had no doubt that the diminutive woman would have gutted the collaborator. Kozakowski swallowed tightly, looked imploringly at the Ktor. "I kept your secrets. I have not failed you. I compromised and delayed the defense of this ship. Why would you expose me?"

"To bind your fate to ours. Irrevocably." Nezdeh was annoyed that the Aboriginal did not see it for himself. "Now, there is no path back for you. Your secret is revealed. You cannot return to your own primitive peoples; they will be happy to execute you. And some of the nations of your planet have retained suitably agonizing forms of capital punishment."

"But if he kills me first, his secret remains safe," the Asian female murmured.

Nezdeh turned, surprised. *She saw that far, that quickly. Let's see what else she has deduced*: "So, do you presume I wish you dead?"

"No," said the female. "The opposite. Now that I am aware of Kozakowski's treason, if anything befalls me, you will look to him as the architect of that misfortune. And so, I am the means whereby you ensure that his fate is sealed, if he should abandon you. In that event, you would return me to my people, who would have every reason to believe my accusations. So, logically, you intend to keep both of us alive for the foreseeable future, or you would not be using us as means of leverage against each other."

"You are correct. We need you alive to oversee the operations of this ship and its megacorporate crew. But be warned: the crew's continued survival is contingent upon your cooperation, Tagawa. That includes whatever persons may be in your cryogenic suspension modules." She turned to Kozakowski. "In your case, you may hope for a richly rewarded future with us."

Brenlor leaned forward. "But should you displease us—" He let the statement hang unfinished.

"You can count upon my loyalty," Kozakowski hurried to assure them.

Nezdeh turned toward Tagawa. "And you?"

"I am compelled to comply and shall do so."

Idrem raised a single eyebrow. "Will you?"

The Aboriginal female stared but did not say anything.

Nezdeh glanced at Idrem. "You have additional information on her? What have you learned?"

"It is not what I learned, but what I *found*. We were searching all bunks and staterooms for undisclosed weapons or communicators. I discovered this in a hidden safe beneath her bunk." He produced a long wooden box, closed with an old bronze latch.

Nezdeh frowned, took the box, and opened the lid. Inside was a long knife with a broad, oddly angled blade that came to a slanted, off-center point. The blade itself was half wrapped in a length of white cloth. She removed and unwrapped the knife; the blade shone and winked wickedly. "This is not primarily a weapon, I think," Nezdeh speculated. She stared at the Asian female. "Tagawa, what is this?"

For the fifth time in as many minutes, Ayana Tagawa prepared herself to die unflinching and with honor. "It is a *tanto*."

The female Ktor—for she could not be a representative of any
other power; the Ktor were the only alien species that humanity had not yet been seen in the flesh—frowned at the blade. "I
know this term from studying one of your warrior cultures. It
is, and you are, Japanese?"

"It is. I am."

The Ktor named Nezdeh tested the edge with practiced care,
touched the ceremonial cloth that had been bound around the
center of the blade. "This is used for ritual suicides, is it not?"

"It was." Ayana left out the fact that although that use was
now quite rare, it had not disappeared entirely.

Nezdeh fixed red-flecked hazel eyes upon hers. "Do not attempt
to lie to me, low-breed. You would now be as dead as Brackman
if you did not interest me."

Untrue. Brackman was extraneous to your plans. But you need
me *to ensure your hold over Kozakowski.* "I misspoke. The *tanto*
is still used in this fashion, but very infrequently."

This seemed to partially mollify the Ktor, but only partially.
"It is a warrior's means of preserving honor, I recall. So tell
me—warrior—did you intend to use it on yourself?"

Not before I used it on as many of you as I could catch by
surprise. "No, it is not mine," she lied. "In my culture, a woman's
honor is not that of a warrior, and her failures are not effaced
in this fashion." Which was no longer uniformly true in Japan's
changing culture. "This *tanto* was my father's and those of my
family's many fathers before him. He was a warrior, as were
they." Which was true.

Nezdeh stared at her for a long time. Ayana had the sense that
her life depended upon the Ktor being unable to read anything
in her face, her eyes.

Apparently, she succeeded at remaining expressionless. Nezdeh
passed the box to the most junior of the four Ktor. "You may not
have this weapon, of course," she commented casually, "but we
shall retain it, undefaced. On this you have my word." The other
two senior Ktor glanced at her in what might have been surprise.

"In the meantime," Nezdeh continued, "both you and Kozakowski shall acquaint our logistics officer, Sehtrek, with the
contents of your ship, its lading manifest, and most particularly,
any pertinent facts or contents which do not appear in your data
files. And unless you wish to lose appendages, do not think you

will conceal anything from us. Nor should you think that we will be so gullible as to believe that you have no hidden caches or off-manifest items. Sehtrek will be here within the minute: attend him when he comes." She turned to the two other Ktor who had spoken. "We should confer on our next steps." Then, with a final glance at Ayana, the Ktor woman exited.

Ayana, half-surprised to still be alive, wondered if she should be grateful or dismayed that she was.

Chapter Fourteen

FAR ORBIT
SIGMA DRACONIS TWO

Caine Riordan watched as a crab-armed cargo tug grabbed a habitation module from the *Lincoln*'s forward cargo racks, leaving a gap in the serried ranks of its fellows. The tug's operator was quite accomplished: even as its manipulator arms half rotated the hab mod, the tug was already boosting away from the human shift-carrier and angling into a trajectory that would take it toward the nearby Slaasriithi ship.

Downing approached the gallery window, nodded at the tug as it overtook their shuttle on a roughly parallel course. "I believe that hab mod is your new home. It should be in place by the time we rendezvous with the Slaasriithi."

The deck moved slightly under their feet. Their own craft had cut thrust, probably to let the tug get farther ahead. Riordan reached out for a handle, steadied his body against a slow drift up from the deck. "So where are the other warm bodies who'll be going down the rabbit's hole with me?"

As if in answer to his question, Ben Hwang drifted into the room. "I'm here. Can't say I'm enjoying the ride, though." He moved slowly toward the gallery window, carefully towing himself from one hand hold to the next.

Downing watched the Nobel prize winner's cautious progress. "Rulaine and O'Garran are coming out on the next shuttle, along with this Tsaami fellow who ferried you to and from your meeting with the Slaasriithi ambassador."

"A second shuttle, just for the three of them?"

"No, they're just tagging along with all the kit we've scratched together for you. I'm not sure you appreciate the challenges this has posed, Caine. This fleet came out here to fight a war, not explore new biospheres. This mission has half a dozen logistics staffs scrambling to find compact, pioneer-grade biosensors, microlabs, an automed, and more Dornaani translators."

"Hah," said Vassily Sukhinin from the doorway, "those bean counters have it easy."

"Oh?" smiled Riordan. "And you've come along to say farewell, too?"

"*Da*," Sukhinin grinned back as he glided, quite professionally, to join the other three at the wide expanse of triple-layered glass. "Anything to get away from the staff officers who have been pestering me about finding personnel for your legation. The Fleet doesn't have enough of the civilian-grade specialties and is also struggling with an incomplete database."

"Incomplete?" Hwang echoed.

Sukhinin nodded. "Yes. It was just luck that *Doppelganger* is carrying most of the needed specialists. Along with *gospodin* Gaspard and his staff, she brought hundreds of civilian personnel, many with credentials that are rare among military ranks. But each of them must be added into the Fleet's database. And only after trickling through *Doppelganger*'s Arat Kur communication systems. It is not a smooth operation."

Downing stared at the distant speck that was *Doppelganger*'s sister ship, *Changeling*. "And I won't even be here to see the end of it."

"You are leaving already?" Hwang sounded as surprised as Caine felt. "I thought you were staying until Visser formally hands the reins over to Vassily."

Downing shook his head. "The secure pouch that came on board *Doppelganger* carried new orders. Due to Wasserman's discoveries, I have to catch up with the outbound *Changeling* and oversee his security, all the way back to Earth. Lemuel Wasserman is now the pearl of great price, so we can't let anything happen to him. The wanker."

As Hwang pushed himself further down the expanse of window to get a better vantage point as they approached the Slaasriithi shift-carrier, Riordan's took advantage of the comparative privacy. "So Richard, once you've left Sigma Draconis, who's going to run the on-site intelligence operations?"

It was Sukhinin who responded, elliptically. Or so it seemed, at first. "Originally, I was concerned that it would be intolerable to remain here, working alongside that arrogant upstart, Gaspard." The Russian's smiling eyes became sharp. "But now, he is traveling to have tea with aliens. And I have determined, after speaking with Richard, that there are additional interesting activities that want my attention while I am in this system."

Caine looked from Downing to Sukhinin and back again. He nodded thoughtfully at Richard. "So. Vassily is replacing you."

"Yes."

Caine waited a moment. "In every relevant regard."

"Yes."

Caine glanced at Sukhinin. "So you know."

Vassily smiled. "Yes, I know about your clandestine Institute for Research, Intelligence, and Security."

"For how long?"

Vassily's smile widened as he checked his watch. "About five hours, now, I estimate. But its existence was no surprise to me."

Caine nodded. "Did Nolan drop some broad hints?"

Sukhinin straightened. "Nolan Corcoran and I were friends, but you must also remember that the admiral was a consummate professional. I understand your supposition: that given our coordination before the Parthenon Dialogs, and our prior friendship, he might have . . . well, 'encouraged' me to speculate that there was an undisclosed international intelligence group assessing Earth's vulnerability to exosapients. But he did not do so. And he did not need to. I had my own suspicions."

Downing, surprised, glanced at Sukhinin. "I didn't know you guessed at the existence of IRIS before the Parthenon Dialogs. I doubt Nolan did either. He was very fond of you and certainly would not have wanted you to feel excluded."

Sukhinin waved a dismissive hand. "Nolan did not exclude me; he *spared* me. I see very well how this IRIS has tied all of you in knots, has ruled your lives. Besides, at the Parthenon Dialogs, it was crucial that I had no knowledge of the secrets he kept. That way, no collusion between us—either as individuals or as representatives of our respective blocs—could be asserted."

Riordan's nodded. "But you suspected that IRIS existed."

Sukhinin grinned. "Caine, *parnishka*, I *knew* it existed. I just did not know what it was called or precisely what it did. Years before, several of Moscow's most gifted intelligence analysts had been reassigned to a secretive transnational cooperative which put them above my clearance level." He wagged a finger. "Above *my* level. But I was satisfied that whatever this mysterious organization was, it posed no threat to the Federation or to Russia."

One of Downing's eyebrows rose. "You don't strike me as the trusting sort, Vassily."

"Well," the Russian replied, scratching at his ear, "my superiors assured me that the unusual clearance elevations were proper and necessary. And you can imagine how much confidence that instilled in my cautious soul." He had inserted his small finger halfway into his ear; he grinned meaningfully. But his expression became serious, even melancholy, when he removed it. "However, I deduced that Nolan was at the center of this star-chamber. And I had trusted him ever since he risked a court martial by helping my men during the Belt War. I knew who Nolan was, in here." He thumped his chest faintly. "So I reasoned that, eventually, he and I would have a private chat, and my questions would be answered. However, I did not foresee that he would be assassinated, any more than I foresaw that I would *become* the answer to my own questions. As is the case now."

Downing's collarcom toned softly. He cupped a hand over his earbud, responded with a resigned, "Very well," tapped out.

"Problems?" asked Hwang, who was drifting back into earshot.

"What else? The Euro armored cargo shuttle that was scheduled to transport the second half of the cold-sleepers has had an engine failure. Not serious, but it can't be fixed in time."

"And what was so special about this cargo shuttle?"

Sukhinin smiled slowly. "I suspect that it was not the shuttle, but certain members of her crew, that were special."

Downing nodded. "Secure personnel, one of whom is an IRIS operative. Now we have to make do with a set of routine boat jockeys. The closest available is a TOCIO lighter."

Hwang shrugged. "Well, it's not as though some enemy agent would just happen to be assigned to the TOCIO shuttle that just happens to be filling in for the EU craft that just happened to break at the wrong moment." Hwang grinned. "Rather implausible, wouldn't you say?"

Downing's answering smile was faint. "I suppose so."

❖   ❖   ❖

Agnata Manolescu brushed a bang of fine, dark brown hair out of her eyes, visually confirmed what her dataslate told her: all eleven cryogenic suspension pods flagged for transfer to the Slaasriithi shift-carrier had been scanned, data-tagged, and were now awaiting pickup by the TOCIO lighter that was due in—

—*That is due right now!* Agnata realized with a gulp. It was a rushed transfer, one which she'd been pulled out of her bunk to expedite. And, expected or not, she insisted that her work be invariably perfect, which is probably why the duty officer of the RFS *Ladoga* had interrupted her dreams of hiking in the Carpathian Mountains to handle it.

Well, that and her security clearance, which was evidently why the D.O. had sent her down here without even one deck-hand to provide assistance. She glanced at two of the cryopods, the ones that could not have been released without her direct electronic countersign. Clearly, this was not just any shuffling of near-frozen personnel.

The lights in the cargo bay's control room strobed at the same moment that orange tabs began flashing on the main control panel: the TOCIO lighter had arrived in the approach envelope for docking at her bay. She toggled the secure circuit: "This is RFS *Ladoga*, bay control D-8, awaiting authorization code."

"This is TOCIO lighter, B-114. I am in your envelope and transmitting the code."

Agnata's computer recognized the code. "Accepted. Stand by to commence hard dock."

"Standing by."

Agnata hit the autodocking touchpad, split her attention between monitoring the actual process through the glass panel of her control booth and scanning the telemetry data on her overwatch monitor. The flashing red lights in the outer bay—the part of the loading platform that could open directly unto space—doubled in speed as the muted rush of evacuating air diminished. The relatively small bulkhead doors retracted, revealing a slowly widening rectangle of star-strewn space, the center of which was dominated by a roll-on/roll-off TOCIO lighter. A brief nimbus of thrust limned its stern and the craft drifted forward slowly, the pilot counting down the meters over the comm channel. When the pilot reached the one meter mark, she pulsed the forward attitude control rockets: terminal braking. The craft drifted to a halt a few centimeters away from the cargo bay's outer coaming, from which four articulated clasps reached out and snugged the lighter against the docking sleeve. As the sleeve started inflating and the so-called "hard rim" clutched the nose of the lighter, the pilot signaled the end of the process: "My instruments show hard dock."

"Mine also," Agnata replied. "I shall meet you at the inner bay door."

"We'll be there within the minute."

The pilot had not lied: she and her sizeable, silent cargo-handler were waiting by the time Agnata arrived to check their clearances and cycle them into the actual lading spaces of the *Ladoga*. She indicated the three loaded standard robopallets and then the partially loaded secure robopallet, which was framed in red and yellow stripes. The pilot strolled past the lashed-down cryopods, aiming her data-slate at each until the inventory numbers matched and showed green. However, at the secure robopallet, the screen of her dataslate flashed red. "This is incorrect," she muttered, removing her space helmet.

Although protocols dictated that full vacuum gear be worn and sealed at all times in both inner and outer bays, it was traditional courtesy to remove helmets and converse in real air if an exchange was going to be anything other than perfunctory. Agnata removed her own helmet. "What seems to be the problem?"

"Inventory number mismatch. These two secure cryocells: they're the wrong ones."

Agnata shook her head. "That is not possible. I checked the physical labels against the inventory code, and then against the order tear sheet that came in from Lord Admiral Halifax."

"Well, the chips in both of those cryocells are not recognizing their inventory code. Unless—could the physical labels have been switched?"

Agnata started. "It is unlikely—but it is possible." She moved forward, bending over to inspect the top surface of the first cryocell more closely. "Wait a moment. I shall check to see if the labels have been rebonded to the surface of the—"

Lightning exploded between her temples, froze her, overrode the grinding of her own teeth—

The pilot nodded to her assistant. After he removed the livestock stunner from the back of the Russlavic cargo-chief's reddening neck, she tossed her head toward the mass of stacked containers. "Find the two cryocells we need."

The hulking cargo-handler nodded, started to move off with the secure robopallet. "Do I refile these, or—?"

"Not where they belong. Put them in the holding cage for damaged cargo and pull their lading chips."

"But then the manifest updating system won't read them, will show them missing."

"That's the idea. Now hurry."

The pilot ran an implant scanner over the pale, unmoving cargo chief, detected the Russlavic-standard transponder-biorelay in her left tricep. She zipped down that sleeve, then removed a small gray container and a circular scalpel from her own breast pocket. She swiftly scooped out the device located in Agnata's arm, and dropped it into the container, which was half filled with a nutrient medium surrounding a pulsing EM emitter. It was a sophisticated underworld method for keeping a biomonitor from signaling complete failure—until the emitter's battery ran out, at least.

Agnata moaned softly, one hand rising toward the red hole that had been cut into her arm.

The pilot's assistant returned with two new cryocells on the secure robopallet. "I'll load those," she said, "you take care of her."

"Take care—?" He stopped, probably comprehending, but not wanting to.

"Yes. We're going to take her with us. But it would be needlessly cruel to dump her into vacuum while she's still alive. Take care of her with that." The pilot nodded at the livestock stunner, started guiding the robopallet toward the outer bay, their lighter, and their rendezvous at the Slaasriithi ship.

"But I—I've never killed a woman." The assistant's massive shoulders were slumped.

The pilot rolled her eyes. "You'll get used to it. Now get going; we don't have a lot of time."

When their armored shuttle came about for nose-first docking, Caine was not immediately certain he was looking at the Slaasriithi shift-carrier. Although it was clearly formed from metals and composites, it did not look mechanical. "It's so smooth," he wondered aloud. "It almost appears as though—"

"—as though it was grown, not built or manufactured," Ben Hwang finished, nodding.

Sukhinin stared sidelong at the two of them. "Gentlemen, I do not pretend to have much grounding in the life sciences, but of this I may assure you: that vehicle is not some great space-plant."

Downing grinned. "No, but I suspect Slaasriithi metallurgy—probably material sciences in general—employs entirely different processes than ours. Hopefully," he finished, glancing at Caine and Hwang, "that's part of the information you'll bring back home."

Caine nodded, looked for the complicated and diverse structures found at the bow of any human shift carrier but saw none of them. Instead, a large silver sphere capped the keel: almost certainly the command and control section. Starting just behind it was a stack of toruses which resembled a keel-enclosing sleeve of immense, brushed-chrome donuts. They were set off at points by symmetrically arrayed metallic or composite bubbles, and even smaller bean-shaped objects.

As they watched, one of the donuts split into two half-rings. Each half was pushed outward slowly from the keel by what appeared to be self-extruding composite-filament shafts. Once at full extension, the donut halves started rotating around the keel.

Downing shook his head. "Well, that's a different way to create a gravity-equivalent environment."

"Look at their cargo containers," Hwang added, pointing back toward the waist of the craft. "Like something bees would build."

Instead of the heavily built cargo frames and docking cradles of human shift carriers, the Slaasriithi craft used various permutations upon honeycombs and hexagons. The keel was, itself, a cluster of hexagonal shafts: it was as if the Giant's Causeway of Ireland had been reformed into a kilometer-long pole. Shorter hexagonal sections, probably cargo containers, were affixed along its length, reprising the keel's own shape. The sections were subdivided into segments, each juncture joined and reinforced by a substance akin to the composite, which had extruded from the hull to deploy the half-donut rotational habitats. And aft, where a human ships' drives, power plants and even fuel tanks tended to accrue in boxy agglomerations, the Slaasriithi ship was distinguished by symmetric clusters of spheres, all seamless and perfect.

"It doesn't look real," Riordan murmured.

"Yes," Downing agreed. "It has a rather impressionist feel to it. Something Magritte might have imagined."

Hwang was smiling. "I wonder what our ships must look like to them?"

"Great angular monstrosities," Sukhinin pronounced, then pointed. "This should be interesting."

Caine and the others followed the vector implied by his index finger. The tug carrying Caine's and Ben's hab mod was approaching the bow of the Slaasriithi ship, cruising slowly past the fat silver toruses.

Halfway toward the large silver sphere at the bow, one of the smaller spheres began moving out from the keel. The tug angled sharply towards it, maneuvered so that the human hab mod—a comparatively inelegant tin can—was poised next to the aft surface of the sphere. It held that position.

Caine scanned the rest of the Slaasriithi ship: no other motion. No ROVs or other craft were on their way to help with the attachment of the module—which was looking damned near impossible.

Until Ben Hwang chuckled. "Well, that's an odd way to dock a module." He pointed.

Six small, equally spaced extrusions were emerging from the rear of the sphere, reaching to make contact with the hab mod.

Caine stared. "Is it *growing* the docking interface?"

Hwang frowned. "I don't think it's growing, at least not the way we'd mean it. But it seems the Slaasriithi have materials that synergize mechanical and biological properties. Look: those extrusions resemble the racks holding their cargo tubes in place: six parallel ribs projecting backward from the vertices of a hexagon, with secondary extrusions stretching between them. When they're done, they will have woven a basket around our hab mod."

Sukhinin nodded, stood away from the gallery window. "We are nearing the point where we shall release your transfer module to a Slaasriithi tug, and I am thirty minutes overdue for my final conference with Consul Visser. Doctor, Caine: I wish you the best of luck and safe travels. Richard, you shall continue to brief me on local intelligence matters during our return trip?"

"I'll be right behind you, Vassily." As Sukhinin exited, Downing turned to Riordan and Hwang. "Well, chaps, I can't say I envy you."

Caine hooked a thumb over his shoulder. "You mean because we're sailing off into the great unknown on the SS *Magritte*?"

Richard smiled. "Well, that too. But truth be told, I was thinking of traveling with Gaspard. Beastly duty, that."

Hwang smiled. "I'm sure we shall manage." He put out a hand. "Safe travels home, Richard."

As Downing shook Hwang's hand, Caine found himself unable to keep thoughts of "home" under the tight control he had exerted since being roused from cold sleep only seventy-two hours earlier. Images of Elena Corcoran—and their son, Connor—displaced what his eyes were showing him. "I'd like to get home, too. Pick up where I left off with Elena. Start being a father to Connor." Pushing aside the sudden homesickness, Caine stuck out his hand as well, did not care, at least momentarily, that Richard Downing hardly deserved a fond farewell from him.

But when Caine mentioned the lover and son he had left behind, Richard glanced away quickly, feigned interest in the now fully loaded—or would that be encysted?—habitation module. "They'll be ready to launch your transfer module any minute now." He let his eyes graze briefly across Riordan's. "Safe travels, Caine."

If Downing had left the room any more quickly, his stroll would have qualified as a trot.

"Odd," observed Ben Hwang. "I wonder what troubled him?"

Caine shrugged. "His conscience, probably."

"Yes, but why just now?"

Caine said nothing, but silently agreed: *yes, why just now?*

The almost mythological outlines of the Slaasriithi shift carrier loomed before them as they awaited the two-minute warning to board the transfer module that would convey them to the alien ship.

PART TWO

June–September 2120

Chapter Fifteen

The bridge of the *Arbitrage* was packed tight with the *Lurkers'* crew. Only the two low-breed aspirants to Elevation, Jesel and Suzruzh, were absent, ensuring that the Aboriginals remained locked in their quarters. Nezdeh rose into the microgravity. "We have finalized our plans." She nodded toward Idrem.

He activated his beltcom's projector: eight wire-thin arms emerged from the top of the unit. A moment later, a crude, semi-flat holograph was floating a meter above it. The image was a stylized Aboriginal graphic depicting the refueling operations of the *Arbitrage*. "Attend. This ship was to conduct two to three more days of fuel harvesting here at V 1581.4. It was then scheduled to break orbit and head for its prearranged shift point to Sigma Draconis, here." Idrem gestured toward a pulsing cross-hairs symbol, far beyond the heliopause. "It would have taken them five weeks to reach this point at an approximate velocity of zero point two cee: a total of thirty-eight days from now. Keeping to that schedule would prevent the Aboriginals in this system from suspecting that the *Arbitrage* has been seized.

"However, we may no longer do so." Idrem brought up a schematic of the shift-carrier. "In addition to minor damage that our attacks inflicted upon this hull's fuel handling capacity, we also destroyed one of the tanker/tenders when the Aboriginals attempted to ram us with it."

Tegrese frowned. "So the Aboriginals back at the second planet will detect and inspect this refueling delay."

"They would notice it eventually, but we will be sure to report it before then."

Zurur Deosketer sounded skeptical. "Will the Aboriginals trust a report that does not come from the captain of record?"

Brenlor smiled. "No, but fortunately, the Aboriginal captain *will* make the report."

"The Aboriginal captain is dead."

"His voice is not."

Idrem expanded upon Brenlor's response. "The Aboriginals record all communiqués. So, once we have recalibrated the comm array on the *Red Lurker* to emulate the *Arbitrage*'s, we shall send a damage report and revised mission timeline using edited clips of the voice of the dead captain. The Aboriginal force back at Planet Two will have questions. But given the transmission delay of almost twenty minutes, it will not seem unusual that some other member of the command staff would answer. Accordingly, Kozakowski will reply as we instruct."

"Consequently, the *Arbitrage* shall resume her current timetable with a four- or five-day delay. But she shall never arrive at Sigma Draconis." Idrem waved his hand over his beltcom: a glittering three-dimensional array of the stars within fifteen light-years floated before them. He pointed toward one incarnadine chip: it pulsed as his finger neared it. "Our present location." He moved his finger until it rested on an orange-yellow dot, which also bloomed. "Sigma Draconis; just under eight point three light-years. But our actual destination is here"—he pointed at a more distant, dual-lobed red spot—"GJ 1230. It has other names as well, all equally uninspiring."

Tegrese squinted, frowned. "It is almost twelve light-years from this system. How shall we reach it? This wretched hull can barely shift two-thirds of that distance."

"That is true, presuming it is unaided." Brenlor smiled. "I told you at the outset that six other Aspirants, soon to be Evolved, would join us. What I neglected to mention is what they would be bringing with them." He swept his hand over Idrem's beltcom.

A new image appeared next to the three-dimensional star map: a blocklike spacecraft, as uninspiring to the eye as the Aboriginal star names were to the ear. But the Ktor reacted as if it was an object of surpassing beauty, just as Nezdeh had known they would.

"A shift-tug!" Ulpreln almost laughed. "An old one—almost

two centuries, from the look of the thermionic radiator grid—but still, that should give us ample shift range."

"Almost twelve and a half light-years," Brenlor confirmed. "She and the six huscarls manning her are in this system already. She will rendezvous with us in four weeks."

Vranut folded his arms. "And how is it that a Ktor tug happens to be in such a convenient location, Brenlor?"

Brenlor seemed to approve of Vranut's cynicism. "An excellent question. And here is the excellent answer: it was part of our Earth-related operations more than a century ago."

Vranut's eyebrows elevated slightly. "It helped position the Doomsday Rock?"

"No, it was not part of our own House's covert forces. The Autarchs ordered this tug to support the Dornaani Custodians in their monitoring of the Aboriginals. It was listed as lost due to shift-drive failure."

Nezdeh waved a hand at the fuel skimmers in their berths. "Our one irremediable operational weakness is the *Arbitrage*'s damaged, and primitive, refueling technologies. We will expend considerable time taking on hydrogen between shifts."

"Yes," Vranut countered carefully, "but we will also require less time to preaccelerate, once we have rendezvoused with our tug and its antimatter drives."

Nezdeh nodded. "Our per-system turnaround time will shrink to approximately ten days. Technical intelligence estimates that the Slaasriithi turn around is twelve days. With that two-day advantage, we should be able to overtake our target and so, begin to both restore and avenge our Extirpated House."

Tegrese pointed back at the red speck that was GJ 1230. "We shall restore our House by traveling *there*? An uninhabited system? And in pursuit of what target?"

Nezdeh chose to ignore Tegrese's borderline insolence. "The target is a Slaasriithi shift-carrier carrying human envoys to Beta Aquilae. Destroying that ship will simultaneously derail any rapid alliance between those two polities while also creating an incident which shall provoke open war."

Vranut's eyes had remained on Nezdeh. "I have a question that I hope you will not consider impertinent."

I hope so, too. "Proceed," she said.

"So: I understand that destroying this Slaasriithi ship will damage or at least delay an alliance between two of our adversaries. But how does that facilitate the resurgence of House Perekmeres?"

Nezdeh nodded. "Your question is perceptive, not impertinent. Bluntly, we have patrons back in the House Moot who have assured us that such an event would be a political disaster for House Shethkador, which has been entrusted with managing affairs in this salient. A significant decrease in the fortunes of House Shethkador will create an opening for the restoration of House Perekmeres.

"You may have been too young at the time of our Extirpation to know just how tirelessly House Shethkador schemed to effect our downfall. They are now the dominant voice in the House Moot. But their preeminence is built upon their supposed skill at destroying enemies from within rather than upon battlefields, and for reclaiming clandestine operations which threatened to spin out of control or become politically injurious." *Such as the folly of our own Hegemons' Doomsday Rock scheme, unfortunately.* "House Shethkador's support in the House Moot would diminish if it stumbled in its current efforts to control the war's political backlash. Logically, it is in their interest to calm the postwar waters by lulling the other species of the Accord back into apathy and indecision. So, conversely, it is in our interest to stir those waters as violently as possible.

"Moreover, if a small band such as ourselves can successfully ruin House Shethkador's tortuously subtle plans by striking directly against our collective foes, it not only proves the tenuousness of Shethkador's control over this salient of operations, but will solidify support for us and our boldness. The Houses that now aid us covertly will become our overt champions. Houses that are currently undecided will decide in our favor. It will not mean the downfall of House Shethkador, but it would at least cost them their preeminence and a few sacrificial scapegoats. Conversely, the value of our Perekmeres genelines will soar, and we may be allowed to fully reconstitute our House. If not, then at least as a First Family within another House. And from there—well, we Perekmeres have never had a paucity of ambition."

The group's feral smiles dimmed as Idrem introduced a sobering note. "Our patrons, most of whose identities we cannot confirm, assert that it would be advantageous if the elimination of the Slaasriithi ship and the Aboriginal envoys could be carried out in such a way that the cause of their destruction was a mystery, or, better yet, appear to have been caused by each other."

"The latter scenario is preposterous," Vranut objected. "There is no reason for the two species to betray each other, and every reason for them to become allies. Quickly."

Idrem nodded. "This is true. But it is in the nature of inferior species to become distracted and indecisive when confronted by unanticipated and unexplained events. While they investigate and remain at arm's length from each other, months and years shall pass. That alone will disrupt House Shethkador's plans and reveal both their incompetence and ill-advised preference for guile over direct action."

Brenlor expanded the starfield display. "And so, our target is GJ 1230. You will observe that almost all the routes from Sigma Draconis to the Slaasriithi homeworld pass through it."

Vranut's frown had not diminished. "You seem to have known ahead of time that the Slaasriithi would invite a human envoy to their homeworld. How? Informers?"

Nezdeh smiled. "No: logic. Once the Aboriginals defeated the Arat Kur, the Slaasriithi would have been fools not to ally with them. This conjecture led us to be watchful for signs that the Slaasriithi would make just such overtures. Those signs were detected and confirmed just before *Ferocious Monolith* shifted to Sigma Draconis."

Ulpreln frowned. "How could *Ferocious Monolith* have learned what had transpired in the Sigma Draconis system before she shifted there? Was there an Awakened on board?"

"No Reification was required to vouchsafe us this information," Brenlor explained. "Half a day before *Monolith* shifted out, an Aboriginal craft shifted in near Planet Two. It was an Arat Kur prize they seized during the fleet actions in Sigma Draconis. Our servitors on board the TOCIO shift-carrier already orbiting Planet Two—the *Gyananakashu*—learned of the Slaasriithi invitation from that prize ship. They relayed the news to us using a trickle code protocol: single, seemingly random signals sent over the course of several hours." He pointed to GJ 1230. "So, knowing that these envoys are making for Beta Aquilae, we can be relatively certain that they must pass through this system, or one slightly further along their path. Where we shall intercept them."

Idrem deactivated his beltcom. "But we must do so swiftly.

Our projection of their path could be in error. Accordingly, we must be ready to leapfrog ahead if we miss their ship in GJ 1230. Now, return to your stations."

Brenlor's tone and expression changed as soon as he was alone with Idrem and Nezdeh; he glanced at her sharply. "You should tell them you are capable of Reification. It would increase their confidence in our mission and would boost morale."

Nezdeh shook her head. "It might also undercut their sense of urgency, of the magnitude of the challenges before us. Besides, I am only recently Awakened and have but two Catalysites remaining. No, it is best that the crew assumes we have no special assets and that we are totally alone. Because, quite frankly, we are. Should we succeed, we shall become the symbol and proof of our patrons' arguments against the lethargy of the Older Houses. On the other hand, if we do not succeed, we shall be glad that I was never in Reified contact with our patrons and that, therefore, they do not know where to find us."

Brenlor stared through the bridge windows at the small ruby that was V 1581. "Caution and prudence; prudence and caution. It sorely tasks a warrior to think like a fugitive."

"It does," Nezdeh soothed. "It surely does."

Brenlor stared at her. "I return to my quarters. You have the con, Nezdeh." He stalked out the hatchway.

Nezdeh glanced at Idrem, thought, *between the two of us, we shall be able to manage Brenlor.* But she only said, "We work well together, Idrem."

Idrem stared at her. "It seems so, Nezdeh."

Standing at the same viewports after completing their shift six weeks later, Idrem observed that GJ 1230 was an even smaller ruby than V 1581 had been.

However, that was merely what the eye could show. GJ 1230 was a flare star, and the variations in its luminosity were minimal compared to its sudden tsunamis of radiation. The crew sections of the Aboriginal ship were lined by meter-thick water tankage, sandwiched between a comparatively soft outer hull and an armored inner hull: proof against this star's maximum REM spikes.

Even so, the *Arbitrage* remained in the shadow of one of the system's gas giants, but not due to the hazards of radiation. Rather, it was endeavoring to avoid the dangers of detection.

Because the Slaasriithi ship had arrived at GJ 1230 ahead of them. It was already preaccelerating toward its next shift, a dimming particle trail indicating it had refueled at the same gas giant around which the Ktor were now entering a stealthy, unpowered orbit.

Brenlor glanced at Idrem. "Intercept is impossible, then?"

Idrem nodded. "If we pursued them at maximum acceleration, we would still be many light-minutes out of range when they shift again."

Brenlor's next question did not rise above a faint grumble. "And how soon until we can commence our refueling operations?"

"Their sensor activity is intermittent and, at this range, weak. We would be relatively safe today, completely safe tomorrow."

"Then we send out the skimmers tomorrow." Brenlor turned to examine the nav plot. "We will continue to presume their next shift shall be to AC+20 1463-148, and we shall follow their lead."

Idrem nodded. "The charts for AC+20 1463-148 indicates that if we arrive in the lee of an outer gas giant, we may remain unseen, even during most of our refueling. We may then shift out ahead of them; the gas giant and the photosphere of the primary will be positioned so as to distort and obscure the signature of our preacceleration."

"Excellent," Brenlor decided. "That is our plan, then."

But it did not work out that way. Early on their fifth day in the AC+20 1463-148 system, Idrem heard Nezdeh enter the bridge behind him. "You are up early," she said. Her tone had become more familiar.

"I want to be present the moment these accursed Slaasriithi disappear from our sensors," Idrem responded, not turning toward her. "We must commence antimatter production as soon as possible."

Nezdeh came to stand beside him. "It has been frustrating, being delayed this way."

Idrem managed not to scoff. Brenlor had been on the bridge when they shifted into the system. He had taken one look at the readouts and stalked off to his quarters: a blip denoting the Slaasriithi ship had loomed unexpectedly large in their sensors. Evidently, its refueling in the previous system had taken much longer than predicted. Consequently, the ship arrived at AC+20 1463-148 later and would be in a position to spot them for much longer. And that meant more delay before the Ktor could jump ahead to GJ 1236.

Brenlor had returned to the bridge, asking about the possibility of changing plans and intercepting the enemy craft in this system. Idrem was at pains to point out that the *Arbie*'s tanks were dry and her antimatter reserves low. And since the replenishment of those reserves required full output from all the available fusion plants, the skimmers would have to harvest even more hydrogen than usual. Brenlor had stalked back off the bridge. The ensuing five days had not been pleasant.

Nezdeh pointed at the sensors. "A power spike from the Slaas-riithi."

Idrem nodded. "Without question, they are preparing—"

The radiant energy level peaked asymptotically and then dropped to zero. The green blip disappeared.

Idrem immediately brought the fusion plants on both the *Arbitrage* and the tug up to full power, leaned over to summon the necessary technicians—fuel processors, flight personnel, bridge staff—to their stations. He stopped when he felt something gentle touch his arm.

Nezdeh's hand. He looked up from it into her eyes.

"You are a great asset to this House, Idrem Perekmeres."

"My apologies, but you forget, Nezdeh: I am twice removed from the main geneline. Technically, I am Perekmeres*uum*."

"I do not need your correction, Idrem," she said firmly, but not sternly. "Besides, that distinction is now nonsense. There are so few of our lines left, we must salvage everything we can." She looked out into space. "In which task you are tireless. Now: get some sleep."

"I shall. As soon as the second bridge crew reports, I will be returning to my quarters."

"Your quarters on *Lurker*, or here on the *Arbitrage*?"

Idrem was rarely confused, but this question disoriented him. "Eh . . . here. Does it matter?"

Her gaze was unblinking. "It does. I shall see you. Very soon."

She turned and left the bridge, with Idrem speechless at the center of it.

Brenlor tapped one finger against his bicep as, ten days later, the *Arbitrage* approached the shift point to their next destination: system GJ 1236. "All systems nominal?"

"Yes, Evolved," answered Ayana Tagawa, whom they had trained as the second pilot for the *Arbitrage*. She had good basic skills and very high inherent aptitudes. "Terminal preacceleration energy state has been attained."

Nezdeh noted the lack of affect in her voice. Brenlor thought she had become the most compliant of all the Aboriginals. Nezdeh wondered if her constrained demeanor and minimal expressions and speech might not indicate the exact opposite.

Brenlor nodded to Ulpreln. "Deactivate the space-normal helm. Tagawa, you are dismissed. Go with the guard." One of the two dozen Optigene paramilitary clones that they had awakened from cold sleep took a step toward her, waited. She nodded to the Evolved on the bridge and exited with the slow dignity that was her wont.

"Ulpreln, is the shift-drive charged?"

"Completing charge...now."

"Engage."

The universe seemed to flutter unpleasantly, as though consciousness threatened to blink off, and every muscle in Nezdeh's body was preparing to spasm...And then it was over.

"Sensors, confirm destination," Brenlor ordered.

The Aboriginal crewman glanced at his instruments. "Stellar type: M3 dwarf, main sequence. Emission bands match target star precisely. Stellar field parallax assessment confirms we are in system GJ 1236."

"Position?"

"Two hundred sixty-two light-seconds from the primary, absolute bearing of 167 by 14."

"Position of nearest planet and target planet?"

"Nearest planet: small gas giant, absolute bearing 187 by 3, two hundred ninety-three light-seconds from the primary..."

So a bit behind us on the port quarter—

"...Target planet: absolute bearing 84 by 2, ninety-nine light-seconds from the primary."

Brenlor turned to Ulpreln. "Plot course for the gas giant. Second sensor operator: contact report."

"No proximal contacts. Several structures in orbit around the target planet. Two, possibly three, sensors in orbit around the gas giant. Very small. Unpowered."

"Time to refuel?"

"Five days, presuming typical meteorological patterns."

Brenlor turned from the forward view ports, drew closer to Nezdeh. "You have confidence in Idrem's estimate?"

"That we may be able to refuel before the Slaasriithi arrive? Yes. Their shorter range compelled them to shift to another system— GJ 1232—before they were able to continue on to this one. But remember Idrem's caveat: GJ 1232 is reserved for Slaasriithi use. It is unlikely but possible that they have a fuel depot here."

"And so, they could be here in half the time we expect," Brenlor concluded sourly. He moved to the hatchway and ducked under the coaming as if dodging the possibility that, once again, his quarry might unwittingly frustrate his plans.

Except the Slaasriithi arrived in much *less time,* Nezdeh thought forty hours later, recalling and amending her prior cautionary caveat.

Idrem was on hand, having heard the news of the Slaasriithi's appearance near the other gas giant halfway across the system. And, she realized with a start, her gaze kept returning to Idrem's broad back.

She wrenched her eyes away. Tender sentiments were vulnerabilities, even among those who had become intimate. Many of the Progenitors had authored axioms warning against them, and she had always heeded them. *But now—*

When Brenlor entered the bridge, the Aboriginals and Evolveds all straightened in unison. He looked directly at Idrem. "Do we have a reasonable chance of making a stealthy approach to the target?"

Idrem shook his head. "Even if we court the shadows of the other planets and the primary, and coast on battery power when we are not concealed, we will not reach them unobserved before they commence preacceleration."

Brenlor stalked to the front view ports. He was silent for several moments, looking toward the primary. "Apparently they had access to a fuel depot at GJ 1232."

Nezdeh was surprised by how calm he sounded. "Almost certainly."

Brenlor nodded. "Can we continue our own refueling?"

"Slowly," answered Idrem, "and only when this gas giant is between us and them."

"So, when we have finished refueling, they will still require four to five days of further preacceleration, correct?"

"Correct."

"And from that same moment, we too require approximately four and a half days of preacceleration also, yes?"

Idrem nodded. "Yes. So we could be shifting within hours of each other."

Brenlor actually smiled. "Very suspenseful." His smile widened. "I like that."

Nezdeh glanced at the mission clock located between the two forward view ports: the *Arbitrage* was in the last thirty seconds of the countdown to her own transit to the system Aboriginals labeled GJ 1248.

As the bridge crew finished calling out the readiness marks, Brenlor leaned forward eagerly: "Engage!" Nezdeh's stomach sunk as the world shimmered at the edge of annihilation and then, just as speedily, reasserted—but with a new starfield peering in at them through the view ports. "Sensors, report: proximal contacts?"

A tense second before the Aboriginal reported. "No proximal contacts."

"Expand passive scan footprint. Report all contacts. Ulpreln, shift accuracy?"

"Within eighteen light-seconds of the target gas giant, Brenlor. We are behind it, but are situated to rise into clear line-of-sight for observation of the main planet in orbit one."

Perfect, Nezdeh thought. *Now if only—*

The oddly strident Aboriginal klaxons began hooting over the senior sensor operator's report: "Asymptotic energy spike sixteen light-seconds out from the main planet." At the same moment, the green blip denoting the Slaasriithi shift carrier appeared in the navplot.

Nezdeh frowned. *They shifted in next to the* main *planet? Logically, that must mean—*

"They have a base at that world, or some other fueling facility," Brenlor announced quietly. "Sensors, any orbital facilities?"

"Unable to confirm at this range."

Brenlor thought for a moment. "Sensors, narrow sweep of target planet: inferential spectroscopic analysis of atmosphere. Also, maximum enhanced image."

The sensor operator's compliance was swift. "Spectroscopic analysis returns high confidence of oxygen-nitrogen atmosphere. Image confirms that the planet is gravitationally locked in a one-to-one resonance with the primary, and that it has a habitable band following the approximate terminator line."

Brenlor leaned back, resigned. "This is precisely the kind of planet that the Slaasriithi would develop. And so, construct a fuel depot." He shook his head. "We will not be able to surprise them."

Ulpreln looked sideways at his commander. "But if we do not intercept them here—"

Brenlor nodded. "Yes, I know: they can reach Beta Aquilae in one shift. And so our chase is over and we have failed."

Nezdeh glanced back over the screens which displayed the Slaasriithi's prior path. "They might not shift directly to Beta Aquilae, though." Seeing Brenlor's surprised stare, she added, "I have no concrete evidence for my speculation; it is pure conjecture."

Brenlor folded his arms. "Your speculative insights have often been correct, Nezdeh. For the good of our House, employ that skill now."

"Very well. We know the Slaasriithi are, of all the species of the Accord, the ones most deeply involved in biological development. And we know that they have made all haste to arrive at this place. Yet, look at their progress toward the main planet"—she gestured at the navplot—"an unusually slow pace, almost casual."

Ulpreln frowned. "And what do you infer from that?"

"That they are in no hurry to get to the fuel there because they are in no hurry to move onward. Not this time. I suspect they mean to visit the surface of this world, possibly to acclimatize the humans to their biota."

Brenlor nodded. "By pausing here, do you think they will become vulnerable to attack?"

Nezdeh shook her head. "Probably not. But they are giving us the opportunity to refuel and shift much sooner than they do."

"Are you suggesting that we precede them into their home system and ambush them there?"

"No. That would be utter and immediate suicide. But there is also the possibility that this world is only the first stage in their acclimatization of the Aboriginals. If it is, they might shift here, next." She extended her finger toward the navplot, put her finger on the orange speck that denoted BD +02 4076. "Their own self-reference indicates that they have been transforming this world for at least eight hundred years. Logically, it might be an intermediary acclimatizing step between this newly shaped world"—she nodded outward toward the unseen planet in this system—"and Beta Aquilae itself. Consequently, if we cannot intercept them here, we might have an opportunity to ambush them in BD +02 4076."

Brenlor squinted up into the glittering star map. "And if they do not detour there at all, but go on directly to Beta Aquilae?"

"Then we have lost nothing that is not already lost at this moment."

Brenlor nodded. "Agreed. So we shall refuel and watch. And wait."

Chapter Sixteen

Caine Riordan rose after checking on the reanimation progress of one of the legation's coldslept security personnel: an Australian SAAS officer by the improbable name of Christopher Robin who had helped rescue him in Jakarta. Ben Hwang exited the cryobank module as Riordan turned back toward Karam Tsaami. "You okay on your own?"

Karam waved him out. "Yeah, yeah: I've got these sleeping beauties." He glanced at the two rows of cryocell bays behind him. Most had a unit in them, all of which showed green status lights. A few were blinking, the rest were steady. One unit was dark and unoccupied. "I've done this more times than I can count, on colony ships. You'd just be slowing me down."

Caine nodded, resisting the urge to stay: he'd never seen anyone other than himself going through the slow process of reanimation. Two days ago, he had helped start it, but other than the automated reswap of nonglycerinated plasma and associated cellular purging, there had been nothing to do other than taking a preanimation reading, pressing a button, watching each unit's steady blue light become a steady green light. He suspected that a chimpanzee could be trained to do it as well as he had, possibly better. He nodded at the slightly inclined cryocells. "You know, given the number of times I've been in cryosleep, you'd think I'd have more skill managing it."

Karam cocked a rueful grin at Riordan. "Being in a cryocell

doesn't teach you anything about how to operate one, Caine. Now scoot: you're cramping my style."

To Caine's eyes, Karam—reading a book on his dataslate as he waited to start transferring the awakening cold sleepers to cocoonlike warming couches, IVs at the ready—didn't seem to be doing anything he could possibly obstruct, but he nodded a farewell and gave the pilot-turned-EMT his requested privacy.

Ben Hwang had strolled halfway back to their hab mod. The featureless metal corridor was the only part of the Slaasriithi ship they'd been allowed to access during the twelve long weeks of hopping from one star system to the next. "Hard to believe we're finally going to get out of these tin cans," Hwang murmured.

Caine caught up with him at the entry hatch. "If I never have to travel on a shift-carrier again, that will be fine with me. But it's given me some time to catch up."

Hwang looked back. "On recent history?" Riordan, having slept through the years 2105 to 2118 thanks to a hypervigilant Taiwanese security operative, still had gaps in contemporary references.

Caine shrugged as they moved through the antechamber that was also an airlock. "Some history, but mostly, well, personal matters. This is the first chance I've had to find out what happened to my family, and to Elena and Connor, when I was out of circulation."

Hwang nodded, did not inquire further into the matter. Which was odd, since Hwang had been the most personable of his fellow travelers on the voyage into Slaasriithi space.

The compartment beyond the airlock was configured to function as a combination living room, work room, gathering space. The outfitters had attempted to make it look homey. Instead, they had achieved a dismal parody of that effect. Reclining in an incongruously stylish easy chair, Bannor Rulaine looked up from the pulp-and-ink book he was reading. Hwang tossed a jocose question toward Riordan's security XO: "Catching up on your military theory?"

"Catching up on my Milton," Rulaine replied. And, with a nod at Caine, went back to his reading.

Caine crossed over toward the Special Forces major turned IRIS striker, sat and glanced at the cover of his companion's dense tome: *Milton: Collected Works*. Riordan grinned: "So, passing some time with a ripping yarn?"

"Yeah. Brought it along to read on the beach."

"Or the fiery lakes of brimstone?"

Bannor looked up. "Are you casting me as Lucifer?"

"Hell, no—to coin a phrase. How could I do that to someone who's been my guardian angel?"

Rulaine's lips crinkled; for him, that was a broad smile. "I'm not reading *Paradise Lost*, anyway."

"Oh? Which one, then?"

"*Comus.*"

"So, a journey into a mysterious forest where temptation lurks. Thinking of our current travels?"

"No, thinking of how the title character reminds me of the Ktor." Bannor settled back, a gentle, if clear, message that his interest in banter had waned beside his interest in the verse.

Caine settled back in his own chair. Ben Hwang might be the chattier and more intimate of the two men, but Bannor was calmer and well-grounded. And a walking contradiction. His dossier was as filled with combat commendations as it was with examples of how, despite his academic brilliance, he was a poor fit for conventional learning environments. Rulaine's brief Ivy-League career began its final, precipitous decline on the last day of what had been his favorite class, an advanced Shakespeare seminar. When asked what he had done instead of showing up for the final exam, Rulaine calmly reported that he had elected to spend the time rock-climbing. Alone. When pressed to explain this choice, he responded that while he found great pleasure and value in both the substance and form of the Bard's plays, he simply could not abide rote memorization of passages, which had been a required component of the final exam. When the academic review board suggested that perhaps he shouldn't presume to judge the pedagogy of his august and much-published professors, Bannor shrugged and replied that while his instructors might be excellent scholars they were poor educators. After offering a further, provocative enlargement upon that opinion, his absences mounted, his GPA plummeted, and he was summarily dismissed. But Bannor's fateful, final words had even made it into his Army dossier (although they were buried deep): "most of my professors can't see the wider forest of meaning because they've become obsessed with a few mostly meaningless trees."

Peter Wu poked his head into the common room. "O'Garran tells me that Gaspard is awake and asking questions. Imperiously."

Bannor shut his book: an annoyed thunderclap. "Does he ask questions any other way?"

"Occasionally." Ben's tone was noncommittal. He rose. "Let's go see the Great Man."

Bannor grimaced. "I'd rather spend another few hours on the flight simulator." He did not rise.

"C'mon, let's go," coaxed Caine. "It'll be more fun than crashing during an unpowered landing. Again and again. Bannor."

Bannor glared at Riordan. "That's a low blow. If accurate."

Caine smiled. Of all the distractions that he and his five conscious fellow travelers had shared during their journey, the flight simulator had been the most useful and the most frustrating. An actual training sim used by the Commonwealth space forces, it was realistic in all regards but one: feel. Karam Tsaami, an accomplished transatmospheric pilot, had tried his hand at it early on. He crashed twice, landed in a heap three times, and then finally put the delta-shaped lander on the ground with only a few nicks and scratches. "It's bullshit," he'd pronounced as he pushed away from the controls.

"Why? Because you crashed it?" Hwang's tone had been almost impish.

"No, Mr. Nobel-Winner Wiseass, not because I crashed it. It's because you can't feel anything."

"You mean, like the crushing impact when you stick it nose-first into the ground?" Peter Wu's deadpan rejoinders were becoming his trademark.

Tsaami glared at the Taiwanese tunnel rat whose cool competence and valor in Jakarta had ensured that he, too, would be recruited into IRIS. "Wu, has anyone ever told you that you are one hell of a funny guy? Because if they have, they're liars. Look: this simulator isn't even a good approximation of instrument flying. This is like—like flying a drone. But drones have all sorts of expert systems, which uneducated idiots call 'AI,' to compensate for minor stability issues. This thing"—he jerked a thumb at the console—"is the worst of both worlds. You're flying an authentically unstable platform but without the real 'feel' of being in it. And you're relying on controls that are less sensitive than a drone's."

Caine had been curious. "Then why do they use it as a trainer?"

Karam shrugged. "Look, there's a lot of details to flying, particularly in a lander. This sim is fine for most spaceside maneuvers.

They're a piece of cake if you can do some basic math or know how to tell the computer to do it for you. Atmospheric flight is trickier, but, unless you're in dirty weather, it's still pretty straightforward as long as you don't try to pull any fancy moves. But reentry? Or fast climb to low orbit? That's where the job gets a lot harder because that's where things go wrong most frequently, and you don't get a lot of warning when they do."

"Odd, then, how all those quaint twentieth-century space capsules managed to land without computer control. Or without any controls at all." Hwang couldn't keep the bait-happy smile off his face.

"Yeah, real odd," Karam retorted, "since reentry and landing was all they were designed to do. Put them in the right place, at the right angle and speed, and they'll land. But a platform with lifting surfaces and designed to be capable of launch, landing, and flight in both space and in atmospheres? Those increased capabilities mean increased complexity."

Bannor had put a hand on Karam's shoulder. "Ben's baiting you. He knows all that."

"Yeah?" Karam sounded dubious. "He's just annoyed that I like Wu's food better. Sound about right to you, Pete?"

"Peter," corrected Peter Wu.

"Yeah, yeah, sure—*Pete*. But Ben's just jealous of your cooking, don't you think, *Pete*?"

Wu sighed. "Yes, I'm sure that's it."

That had been another welcome distraction during the outbound trip: the dueling regional cuisines of China. Wu was Taiwanese. Ben Hwang had dual citizenship, China and Canada, and had grown up eating authentic Szechuan in Vancouver, before living in Canton as a student. The cooking wars between the two men had become twice-weekly events. But before long, it was obvious that while Ben Hwang was more knowledgeable in the different nuances of the many regional cuisines and use of ingredients, Peter Wu had that unquantifiable gift for knowing—just *knowing*—the moment when the meat had been seared enough, the leeks wilted enough, the peppers sliced finely enough. The final, almost pitiable, conferral of victory upon Wu had come when Ben Hwang had been discovered making a midnight raid on the leftovers of Peter's cooking, even though the refrigerator was still well-stocked with his own.

Caine rose to his feet to respond, along with the others, to O'Garran's summons.

Bannor remained seated. Kept reading. Conspicuously.

Ben motioned. "C'mon."

"You can't make me go."

Caine had the sudden impression of Bannor as a quietly intransigent four-year-old. "I can make you go."

"Yeah? How?"

"Miles O'Garran, your brother-in-arms, is in there with Gaspard. Alone. And you won't do your part to rescue him?"

Bannor glared at Riordan, sighed, put down his book, and rose. "That wasn't fair. Lead on."

It took Gaspard a moment to notice that Caine and the others had entered the room.

Miles O'Garran came over quickly. "So, am I off-duty, now?"

"Uh...yes. Sure."

O'Garran nodded tightly. "Good. I've got to get out of here." He shouldered past the others, several of whom had seen him stand unflinching in the face of alien invaders almost twice his size.

"*Monsieur*—ah, pardon, Captain Riordan?"

Lead from the front. Caine approached Gaspard's bed. "Yes, it's me."

"I am sorry I did not recognize you. My vision is...blurry. Is it possible that the cryogenic suspension has damaged my optic nerve or—?"

Riordan went closer. "Nothing to worry about, Ambassador. That is completely normal." He knew he shouldn't, but he added, "Didn't you read the briefing on cryogenic suspension?"

"No. There was no time."

—*Unlikely*, Caine observed silently—

"I must confess: the less I knew about what was going to happen to my body, the less I worried about being frozen as solid as an icicle."

"Well, Ambassador, had you read the briefing materials, you would probably have worried a lot less. To begin with, you were not frozen."

"Then why was I just removed from a cocoon originally designed to aid victims of hypothermia?"

"Because your core temperature was lowered to approximately

zero point one to zero point five degrees centigrade. And to ensure against any control fluctuations, your blood plasma was replaced with an artificial surrogate containing a limited amount of glycol, genetically adapted from what Arctic cod produce when the surrounding waters drop below freezing."

"Well, that would certainly explain the taste in my mouth."

"Yes, that will persist for at least three or four days. Before your own blood was pumped back into you, a glycol cleanser replaced the surrogate to leach the glycol out of your cells. That takes a while, and even so, it's not perfect. The glycol residue is what causes your blurred vision, as well as dulled sense of taste, numbness in the extremities, loss of short-term memories, and easy disorientation."

"How long will I be so incapacitated?"

"We began your reanimation two days ago, so the symptoms will be gone the day after tomorrow. You'll experience marginal sequelae and that lousy aftertaste for another half a week."

Gaspard sighed. "Delightful." He looked down his nose at the group of them, but this time, it was probably not arrogance but visual impairment which caused him to adopt what looked like a haughty posture. Actually, Caine reflected, the ambassador was behaving better than he had expected, particularly given O'Garran's desperate dash for freedom.

The ambassador waved a hand at his other visitors. "I had expected to see you when I awoke, Captain Riordan, and of course your good self as well, Dr. Hwang. But I am not acquainted with these other gentlemen."

Caine made the necessary introductions, made mention of Karam as Gaspard's awakener. The ambassador took it in silently. "And with the exception of Mr. Tsaami, they are our legation's security detachment?"

"They are, along with a few more who, like you, shipped out with us in cryogenic suspension."

"And, how may I ask, were they selected? Unless I am much mistaken, they are all from nations of the Commonwealth bloc."

"They are, but that was not what drove their selection. Not directly, at any rate."

Gaspard shook his head; it looked more like a semi-conscious lolling. "That is a riddle, and I am too befuddled to solve riddles today, Captain."

For Gaspard, that objection was positively gracious. *Maybe we should stick him in a cryocell more often.* "Apologies, Ambassador. The security personnel were chosen because they had prior contact with exosapients. By including them on this mission, Mr. Downing not only took them off the intelligence grid, but was assured that they had no latent xenophobic pathologies."

"I see. However, I suspect that the short, annoying fellow who had such an aversion to my questions—and my needs"—he gestured to a soiled bedpan—"may have an aversion to humans. He did mention that it has been eighty-three days since we departed Sigma Draconis." Gaspard stared at them unsteadily. "I should have thought you could no longer stand to be in the same room together."

"We can't," Rulaine lied. "But we're professionals. These are the sacrifices we make."

For a moment, Gaspard seemed uncertain if he had heard Bannor correctly. Then he smiled. "And you still have a sense of humor. Excellent."

"Yes, well, Karam doesn't have a sense of humor," Wu corrected. "Not anymore."

Gaspard frowned. "Why not?"

"Because Bannor beat him at the small craft gunnery sim. Every time."

Gaspard looked baffled. Caine felt a flash of pity, provided the missing context. "I'm sorry, Ambassador. We passed a lot of time reading, in the gym, and acquainting ourselves with xenobiology and other pertinent topics, but we also spent lot of our time in training sims."

"Such as?"

"Flight, remote vehicle operations, nav plotting, and Bannor's favorite, small ship gunnery."

"I didn't actually like it all that much," Bannor corrected.

"Maybe not," Hwang commented, "but it sure liked you."

Gaspard did not attempt to keep the exasperation out of his voice. "And did you not meet with the Slaasriithi, see their ship, learn their ways?"

Caine shook his head. "No, Ambassador, your premonition about them not providing us with any new information was sadly accurate. We have seen their ambassador, Yiithrii'ah'aash, three times and then only for purely functional matters. The first time was to welcome us on board and acquaint us with the parts of the ship we were allowed to visit."

"And how much of their ship did you see?"

Hwang's answer was solemn. "The twenty meters of corridor that separate our hab mod from the cryobank module. They also took us to our cargo module once in an enclosed hovercraft."

"And that is all?"

Bannor shrugged. "They allowed us to perform two routine maintenance checks on our lander and our corvette. One of the Slaasriithi went with us, observed, said nothing either time."

"Well, I do not think much of their hospitality," Gaspard sniffed. "And they gave you no other information?"

Caine shrugged. "They told us which systems we were in, when we were shifting, when we'd arrived, when they began acceleration, when they were going to end or start rotation. The bare minimum."

"And did you ever ask them why they were not more forthcoming?"

I wasn't that rude, you ass. "I invited Yiithrii'ah'aash to stay and converse. He was very polite, expressed his regrets, but insisted that words were not the right way to start our relationship. However, three days ago, he announced that we would soon be arriving at a Slaasriithi system. He chose a sparsely inhabited planet because it is the best way to begin what he called 'the showing that leads to knowing.'"

"*Mon Dieu*, even their apothegms are uncongenial to finer sensibilities."

Well, evidently Gaspard has begun his recovery to full-bore asshole . . .

The ambassador glanced beyond the knot of them in the doorway. "And where are the others whom you have awakened?"

Caine shook his head. "At this point, there are no others awake."

Gaspard blinked. "You have awakened me first?"

Caine nodded. "We commenced your reanimation thirty-six hours before the others. It seemed best to brief you first, to discuss and strategize before awakening the rest of the staff."

Gaspard's frown was one of intense concentration. "This precaution, and personal consideration, was well-conceived, Captain. Thank you."

"*Thank you?*" *Well, there's a first time for everything.*

"But I will learn the details of our situation with the rest of the group."

Caine felt the others looking at him. They had discussed the various surprises, all unpleasant, that Gaspard might spring upon them when he was reanimated, but this had not been among the expectations. "Ambassador," Caine said slowly, "perhaps I was not clear. There *are* a few official conjectures, based on classified analysis, which cannot be shared with the group. Only I, you, Dr. Hwang, and Major Rulaine have sufficient clearance levels to access them."

Gaspard seemed entirely unimpressed by this information. "Are these speculations of a biological or political nature?"

Riordan shook his head. "When dealing with first contact, the line between physical differences and social differences from human norm is often murky. Behavior follows biology the way form follows function."

Gaspard smiled, nodded. "I keep forgetting you were a writer. An excellent point excellently presented. But I deduce that these speculations are essentially strategic in nature, and that their purpose is to inform my objectives when we come to the stage of negotiation, yes?"

"Well, yes."

"Very well. Then I shall hear these after the unclassified briefing materials have been shared with the rest of the legation. Now, let us rouse the others."

Chapter Seventeen

Two days later, once Riordan and the rest of the legation had gathered for their first collective meal in the overcrowded main room, Gaspard rose to formally announce where they were bound and why: a necessity, since many of the legation's members had been loaded into their cryocells before leaving Earth. Expecting to be roused for either the counterattack on or policing of Sigma Draconis, they were startled to find those scenarios already outdated. Adapting to the new one took a little getting used to.

After being handed some notes by his administrative assistant Dieter, Gaspard segued into introducing Morgan Lymbery, who had originally been sent along to seek out and investigate technologies that the Arat Kur might not have risked bringing to Earth. His naval designs had made him the war's least known and most decisive innovator, and Gaspard apparently wanted the gathering to understand that they had a genuine, if unfamiliar, celebrity in their midst.

Caine had taken a seat to the side of the impromptu head table, an unobtrusive spot from which to survey the entirety of the legation. Some predictable professional affinities were already emerging. Karam had made the acquaintance of the mission's two other designated pilots: Qin Lijuan, a much-decorated Chinese sloop jockey who had been one of the few to survive the Second Battle of Jupiter, and a Russian veteran by the improbable name of Raskolnikov who was renowned for his ability to fly without instruments in the most adverse conditions. Another such pairing had occurred in the form of NCO bonding between ex-tunnel rat chief Miles O'Garran and towering Kiwi master sergeant Trent Howarth, who was as uniformly amiable as he was silent.

Gaspard finished eulogizing the increasingly uncomfortable Morgan Lymbery and introduced another member of the senior staff, the multiply-accomplished Dr. Melissa Sleeman.

As Gaspard began his overwrought panegyrics, Bannor found a chair next to Caine's. SAAS Lieutenant Christopher "Tygg" Robin trailed after, eventually perching on a footrest, his knees almost as high as his chin. He looked like a naughty adult who'd been punished with a "time-out."

"Hello, Caine," Tygg whispered. "Glad to catch up with you finally. So why isn't Trevor on this mission? Is he back home minding—?"

A sharp look may have shot from Bannor to Tygg. Who abruptly shut up.

Caine frowned. "Is Trevor 'at home minding' what?"

"Minding the store?" finished Tygg, almost smoothly. "I figured Mr. Downing might make him chief overseer of IRIS' strike teams."

The response was reasonable, but it still had the sound of a hasty invention to replace whatever the Aussie had planned to ask before Bannor shot him the look. "You sure that's the question you meant to ask, Tygg?"

But Tygg's eyes were no longer on Caine; they were focused over and past his shoulder. "Who's that?" he muttered.

Caine turned. Gaspard was concluding Sleeman's introduction. "That's Melissa Sleeman. The Wasserman replacement."

Bannor raised a quizzical eyebrow. "I didn't read that in the dossier."

"It's there between the lines." Caine dug around for the last chunks of meat in his almost empty bowl of excellent lamb madras. "When the Earthside brain trust realized they had to call Wasserman back home, they started casting around for another all-purpose scientific genius. That's who they came up with."

"Well, she sure is easier on the eyes," Bannor commented quietly. "Probably more useful to a mission like this one, too."

Caine nodded. "She might not have Wasserman's depth of insight, but she's less narrowly focused—a genuine broad-spectrum expert." He noticed that Tygg was still staring at Sleeman, whose features were a dramatic blend of her Indonesian, Dutch, Canadian, and Sierra Leonian heritage. "Lieutenant Robin, you seem very impressed by Dr. Sleeman's, er, credentials."

Tygg nodded. He might or might not have heard what Caine had said.

Bannor pointed across the room with a flick of his eyes. "Well, there's a familiar face."

Caine did not recognize anyone. "Who? The big guy hunkered over his curry?"

Bannor nodded. "Yeah. Keith Macmillan. One of the Commonwealth strikers who was providing security for Downing's classified forward ops center in Perth at the end of the war. Saw him there after we rotated out of Jakarta."

Caine shrugged. "News to me. I have no idea about what happened after Shethkador shot me in the back with his bogus mechanical arm."

"Didn't Downing catch you up on what followed?"

Caine shook his head. "Nope. When they yanked me out of cold sleep in Sigma Draconis, I had one night to get myself briefed on why the Arat Kur weren't talking to us and why we might have to slaughter them all with a plague. A day later, the Ktor showed up. No time for small talk."

"Ah. Right." Bannor returned his attention to his curry. And he avoided Caine's inquisitive gaze.

Caine kept looking at him, and Bannor kept on not noticing. *Now what the hell was* that *about? That's more chatty than Bannor has been since, well, since I've known him. Why is he—?*

Gaspard gestured toward Riordan. "And there, to my distant right, is Caine Riordan, now Captain Riordan, who needs no introduction. He is my deputy on this mission and in charge of security. So, if you are not feeling secure, I commend you to his services." The weak witticism received a few equally weak laughs, but Gaspard was obviously eager to move on. Caine simply smiled, waved, and went back to his meal. No reason to extend the formalities. He'd already been in touch with half of the new team members. He'd get to the other half tomorrow.

Gaspard began to enumerate Ben Hwang's many scientific achievements, which was probably unnecessary, since the high points of his career both before and after his Nobel prize were common knowledge.

Tygg leaned over toward Caine. "Hsst. You've got an admirer."

Riordan, surprised, glanced up just in time to see Dora Veriden looking away from him, quite bored. "That's Ms. Veriden, Gaspard's private security."

"More like bodyguard," grumbled Bannor.

"And I'm certainly not getting a come-hither vibe from her, Tygg," Riordan added quietly.

The Aussie frowned, still looking at Veriden. "Took an eyeful of you just a second ago, though."

Yeah, if she's memorizing my face, it's probably because her boss has told her to bump me off if I become troublesome. "She's been a pretty closed book, so far," Riordan observed.

"What's her story, then?"

Bannor put down his very empty bowl. "Trinidadian native. More or less. Has lived in almost a dozen countries, most of them former French colonies. Any degrees she has are from the school of hard knocks and the college of dirty tricks. There's no record of her in any of our databases, and the dossier Gaspard forwarded for her has more blank spaces than details. My guess? She's a DGSE street recruit. Probably a jack of all trades, sharp as a tack, and hard as nails. And if you want more tired colloquialisms, I charge by the word."

Caine almost choked on his last bite of food.

Ben Hwang rose before Gaspard could attempt to summon a round of applause. "Allow me to overview what we know about the Slaasriithi. I assure you it will be brief, because we know very little. The most distinctive feature of the Slaasriithi is that they are polytaxic."

Joe Buckley, a Chicagoan who was the legation's combination purser, quartermaster, and logistician, squinted at the unfamiliar word. "Poly-what?"

Hwang smiled. "The Slaasriithi are a single species, but are divided into specialized subspecies distinguished by significant physiological differences. However, according to the one source we have on them, all these subspecies have consistently evolved to be cooperative parts of their larger, stable social matrix and remain universally interfertile."

"This one source you referred to: is that the child's primer we've read about?" The question came from a heavy-set young Ukrainian who was the legation's physicist and primary assistant to Sleeman.

As Ben Hwang confirmed that this simple text was, in fact, the only speciate information the Slaasriithi had provided, Caine leaned toward Rulaine. "That physicist is a relative of one of the other members of the team that went to the Convocation, Natalia Durniak. His name's Oleg Danysh. A second cousin."

"You think he pulled family strings to get shipped out to Sigma Draconis?"

"I think that anything is possible."

Hwang had resumed his overview of the Slaasriithi. "Their eyes are not arranged for binocular vision like ours. Instead, they have dispersed eyes and light sensors which evidently give them a field of vision that is almost two hundred seventy degrees in all directions from their front facing."

"What kind of neural bandwidth does that require, I wonder?" Nasr Eid, the Egyptian computer and cryptology specialist, had clearly meant it as a rhetorical inquiry, but Hwang elected to address it.

"An excellent question, but we lack direct biological data to answer it. However, we do have some fruit and vegetable samples they sent to a reception our delegation hosted at the Convocation. Although their xenogenetic structures do not mimic our double-stranded DNA helix in the least, they are biochemically compatible, or at least benign. Additionally, we found indications that one of the vegetables can express a latent chimaerism that manifests as inverted chirality."

Esiankiki Salunke, the legation's arrestingly tall Indian-Kenyan linguist, blinked. "So it can mutate?"

Hwang's assistant, Hirano Mizuki, and the mission's ranking expert in planetology and biome studies, explained that chimaerism was distinct from mutation. Specifically, the vegetable's exogenome was capable of evolving a variant in which the chirality of the plant's amino acids—their right- or left-handedness—would be reversed.

"Would that threaten us?" asked Xue Heng, the team's EMT, assistant quartermaster, and a long-service army veteran.

Ben shrugged. "Unknown, but the Slaasriithi biosphere clearly contains organisms which follow a very different genetic and chemical map than our own. That's consistent with what we've discovered about much of the biota on Delta Pavonis Three. Which brings us to a point that few of you have been briefed on.

"As I'm sure you all know, it was Captain Riordan who reported that there was a species of primitive exosapients on Delta Pavonis Three at last year's Parthenon Dialogs. What we did not know until recently was that those primitive beings and the Slaasriithi have common origins. As their ambassador Yiithrii'ah'aash put it, the Pavonians are related to the Slaasriithi the way Neanderthal is related to Cro-Magnon."

"Just when was that learned?" asked Rena Mizrahi, the surgeon and neurology specialist from Tel Aviv.

Caine smiled ruefully. "The same day we got the invitation."

Phillip Friel, an engineer who'd imbibed engineering theory at Trinity in Dublin before an extended tour with the EU navy, looked up from under dark bangs. "This all happened rather suddenly, it seems." The group's other engineer, Tina Melah, was sitting alongside him and nodding vigorously.

"It did come together suddenly," Caine agreed. "Particularly once the Ktor showed up to retrieve their ambassador. That made the Slaasriithi extremely uneasy. So they accelerated the process of inviting us for a visit." *And here's the part where we have to stay very, very vague; if they start asking about the Ktor role in this, one slip could pop the intel lid off the fact that the Ktor are humans, too, rather than the methane-dwelling ice worms they implied they were . . .*

But instead, the legation's official recorder and archivist, Qwara Betul, grumbled. "I must say I am not happy about such a hastily organized mission."

"None of us were, but it was either go now or not within the foreseeable future," Caine said sympathetically—just before the external airlock page double-chimed.

Riordan stood. "I think we have company."

After remaining in the airlock for three minutes so that those humans unaccustomed to his appearance could absorb it, Ambassador Yiithrii'ah'aash entered the module. "Greetings, honored guests. I thank you for allowing me to intrude."

Gaspard glanced at Caine as if to say, *so liaise, liaison.* Caine obliged: "Your arrival is a gift, not an intrusion, Yiithrii'ah'aash. And I have the pleasure of presenting the entirety of our legation to you, but most especially, our ambassador, Etienne Gaspard, Consul of the Consolidated Terran Republic." The last phrase caused a few starts among the lately awakened team members, who had entered their cryocells when Earth's fledgling polity was still called the World Confederation.

Gaspard approached his Slaasriithi counterpart. Who extended his many-tendrilled "hand," adding, "If the form of my appendage troubles you, we may forego this ritual. I offer it in recognition of your traditions."

Gaspard took the alien hand. If he felt any repugnance, he did not show it, although he withdrew his hand promptly. "Ambassador Yiithrii'ah'aash, what is your customary manner of greeting? I would assay it."

Yiithrii'ah'aash burbled spasmodically—laughter? "You could not do so. You lack the correct pheromones. However, we are eager to share our ways with you. Accordingly, I have come to invite you to visit this system's world tomorrow."

Those who were enthusiastic about this news, including Caine's five cabin-fevered fellow travelers, made sounds of approval. Those who were not so ready to debark upon an alien world were markedly silent.

Riordan made note of the most reluctant faces, asked, "How large a party should we prepare?"

The Slaasriithi's finger-furlings and -unfurlings paused. "All may visit."

"That is most generous, Ambassador, but our security policy prohibits full attendance. Some must remain behind with the hab module." *Not that you'd go rummaging through our drawers, but protocols are protocols.*

Yiithrii'ah'aash's frozen digits came to life in a sudden roiling motion. "Understood. However, those who do not make this first journey may not leave this module for subsequent journeys."

"They will be restricted to this ship?"

"They will be restricted to this habitation module. To be safe in our places, you must visit them. So we cannot guarantee the safety of those who do not visit. This is the requirement for access to our worlds. We regret if it is inconvenient and we accept that some of your legation may not be able to comply."

Yeah, but, we didn't come out here to leave any of our experts corked up like genies in a lamp. Caine glanced at Gaspard—

—who nodded his approval.

Riordan flashed him a grateful smile—*he does have his moments*—and nodded at Yiithrii'ah'aash. "I am happy to say that all will go."

"And we are happy to hear it. In preparation for your journey, we will allow free access to your two ships, as well as protected access to your cargo module, so that you may retrieve any equipment that you consider prudent. We have automated transportation waiting to carry the entirety of your legation there and back. However, be warned: it would not be safe to return there unescorted, so be sure to collect all the supplies you require before we depart."

Hwang bowed slightly, waited until Yiithrii'ah'aash had turned his "face" toward him. "Ambassador, every time you mention entering your ship, you speak of these dangers. Do you have guards that would harm unauthorized visitors?"

The exosapient's ostrich neck pulsed through a quick set of peristaltic ripples. "Not such as you mean. It is simply that our ship would not recognize you."

"And so its systems would attack us?" Tygg asked.

"No, but they would not know to *avoid* you. Which could be just as bad. They would not desist from functions that might be injurious to bystanders. Before we reach our next stop, you will have been added to their recognition template. In your parlance, it is a biochemical database in which your genotype can be coded as being a friend."

"Or a foe?" Caine inquired.

Yiithrii'ah'aash turned back toward him. "Yes. That, too. Now, let us go."

Chapter Eighteen

IN TRANSIT
GJ 1248'S INNER SYSTEM

Exiting the habitation module at the head of the humans, Yiith-rii'ah'aash gestured toward four waiting conveyances. Unlike the small, sealed eggs that had carried Caine and his fellow conscious travelers on their earlier trip to the cargo module, these vehicles were fitted with clear canopies that emerged seamlessly from their ellipsoidal chassis.

However, "vehicles" didn't seem an apt word for these objects. They had no protrusions or lines that betrayed the presence of maintenance housings or weld points. The only component reminiscent of human machinery was a panel behind which an operator might sit. But it was impossible to be certain of its exact function; the curved black-glass surface was inert.

It also fronted the eighth seat in the lozenge-shaped craft, into which Melissa Sleeman gleefully slid as she began inspecting the shining ebon arc. Behind her, Morgan Lymbery peered closely at the seamless juncture of the glass canopy and the vehicle's body. His concentration was as monofocal and unblinking as that often associated with the autistic.

Tygg managed to get into the same pod-car, trailing just behind Peter Wu and Rena Mizrahi. The tall Aussie stole a furtive glance at Melissa as he slung himself into the seat next to Bannor. Unaware of his attention, she continued inspecting her novel surroundings—until the vehicles rose in unison. Gimballing their rotor-cans, they started toward the cargo mod at a reasonable rate.

"Shouldn't we be starting to feel a loss of gravity equivalent?" wondered Tygg.

"It will take a little longer, and only if we're moving inward toward the keel," Caine answered.

"And we're not," put in Melissa, "We're moving at about a twenty-five-degree angle to it right now."

"How do you know?" Tygg's voice was wonderstruck and completely incongruent emerging from one of the most blooded veterans of the recent war.

"Oh, well, I just counted the bends we've navigated."

Riordan, who prided himself on being observant, wondered: *bends?* What *bends?*

The pod-bus veered into a side tunnel, sped forward a short distance and then slowed as it emerged into an open area. The high-domed space reminded Caine of a small, trackless turning yard: wide oval bulkhead doors were inset upon each of the other five sides of the hexagonal chamber. The pod-buses all landed in a row before the door opposite the tunnel mouth.

After Melissa had exited in an exuberant rush, Bannor asked, "Did anyone else see those bends she mentioned?"

"Not me," Caine confessed.

"I didn't see anything," Tygg breathed, his gaze following Melissa.

"That's because you had something in your eye," commented Rena over her shoulder as she exited.

"Something in my eye?" Tygg repeated, baffled.

"Yes, as in Dr. Sleeman." Wu managed not to smile.

"It's that obvious?" Tygg asked.

Bannor rolled his eyes. Caine laughed, then the mirth suddenly inverted into sharp longing for Elena. He exited the pod-bus quickly.

Caine and the others who had been conscious for the trip helped the rest of the legation unload their scant belongings from the personal luggage antechamber of the cargo module. Finished, they gathered before the large doors into the main lading section, waiting for their hosts.

"Unloading should be easy," commented Esiankiki Salunke, who moved gracefully in the slightly reduced gravity. "Everything weighs less."

"Yeah," commented Joe Buckley, "just remember that mass is unchanged. People who forget that often get squished."

Esiankiki raised an eyebrow. "My, you are a most cheery person."

"Comes from seeing newb cargo handlers get smashed as flat as a surfboard. Gives me a sunny outlook on this job."

Caine heard a soft hum, turned to see another vehicle gliding to a halt in the turning yard. As soon as the craft had settled to the deck, Yiithrii'ah'aash emerged from it, followed by a pair of Slaasriithi whose matching physiognomies differed slightly from his. Their necks were shorter, thicker, more like a giraffe's than an ostrich's. However, their bodies and limbs were longer and thinner. Their fingers were wraithlike tapers, as were their bifurcated prehensile tails. And instead of having Yiithrii'ah'aash's stunted, toelike protrusions, they had what appeared to be another set of full grasping tendrils in contact with the deck. Overall, whereas a quick glance at the ambassador's odd-hipped torso produced the impression of a lean gibbon, his two associates' bodies recalled lemurs on the edge of emaciation.

"What's wrong with them?" Buckley muttered.

"Nothing. I think they're part of a different taxon," answered Ben Hwang.

Buckley stared blankly at the word "taxon."

Well, it's clear who doesn't *pay close attention during briefings.*

Ben moved forward to greet the new arrivals. "Ambassador Yiithrii'ah'aash, I wonder if I might ask you a question about your companions: are they members of a different taxon?"

Yiithrii'ah'aash's purr was long and continued beneath the first half of his reply. "Your perception is excellent, Doctor. They are members of a specialized subtaxon, to be exact." He turned to one of them.

Which bobbed its head once, and spoke through a translator hanging beneath its arm. "I am a"—at which point the translator fumbled and spat random syllables. "We were induced to serve in environments where gravity is low or nonexistent. It was deemed prudent to encourage a return of certain features from our arboreal origins"—he/she/it wriggled the deck-splayed toe-fingers meaningfully—"to provide us with better grasping and maneuvering capabilities in zero-gee environments. I am incompletely informed, but I understand that in your own species, some of the same attenuations of skeleton and musculature are observed after several generations of low-gravity breeding."

Gaspard, who had moved forward more slowly than Hwang, nodded. "Yes, this is so. However, we discourage this. It problematizes our social coherence."

"The inducement of a useful new subform tends the group toward disharmony?" The low-gee Slaasriithi's neck seemed to quiver faintly, like a tuning fork losing the last vibrations of a tone. "I do not understand."

Yiithrii'ah'aash intervened, several finger-tendrils uncoiling toward Gaspard. "You will appreciate that for those of us not well acquainted with humanity, your disapproval regarding a physical alteration in your species sounds contradictory. For us, social harmony is not physically dependent upon, nor a product of, homogeneity of form. To the contrary, our harmony arises from the diverse capabilities enabled by carefully selected variations in our forms. As you shall see more completely tomorrow. Now, allow me to enable access to your supplies."

Yiithrii'ah'aash raised his "hand," which, Caine saw, was now sleeved in something that looked like a form-fitting glove moored by nonornamental rings and covered irregularly by studs. The ambassador's prehensile fingers went through a set of impossible contortions, apparently bringing several of the rings and studs into rapid contact with each other. The heavy doors into the main cargo compartment clunked heavily: unlocked.

Bannor, eyes still on Yiithrii'ah'aash's glove and rings, raised an eyebrow. "That is one strange control device."

"Strange but effective," Hwang murmured. "I bet they can get more combinations drummed out faster than we can with our touch screens. And it's obviously versatile enough to interface with our own systems." He followed Yiithrii'ah'aash into the cargo mod. Caine trailed after.

It was, on first impression, like entering the belly of an industrial age Leviathan. They stood at the threshold of a cavernous hexagonal tunnel, fifty meters long and twenty meters high. Two elevated gantries ran its length, the first one perched eight meters over the deck, the second at sixteen. Spools of zero-gee guide wires and their mooring points dotted the metal gridwork of ladders, decks, and stalls. And stacked upon or jammed against every available surface except the ground-level's central walkway were universal lading containers of several different shapes.

Nasr Eid smiled up into the cubist cave. "A toy box for a giant infant."

"Yeah, just don't let any of those blocks fall on ya," Tina Melah chuckled as she moved past with easy familiarity. "Buckley's not the only one who's spent some time in these death-traps." She saw Nasr's fearful look. "Now, now, no reason to get your jammies in a twist, Nasr. We've got steady rotation to keep everything where it's already locked in place. But, if you go to zero gee, take a few hits, and have a few restraint bars break and lashings tear—well, then you've got some serious anvil-dodging fun on your hands!" She strode ahead into the dim bowels of the mod. Most of the others followed as motion-activated lights popped on, marking Tina's progress down the length of the module. Caine strolled after them.

Coming around a massive cargo pod, he discovered Joe Buckley seated on a small container, his hands covering his face. Keith Macmillan was standing nearby, saw Caine approach, shrugged.

"Damn, it all looked fine at first," Joe lamented, "but—oh, Jesus H. Christ!" Buckley groaned as if he'd been bayoneted in the gut.

"What's wrong?"

"What's wrong? Christ, just look at it!"

As Tygg and Oleg Danysh walked up, Caine looked around for the wrongness that so afflicted Joe. "Okay. And . . . what am I supposed to be seeing?"

Tygg frowned, glanced at the hard-copy lading list attached to the cargo pod, checked it against the chip-coded inventory on his palmcomp. "Oh, they've bollixed all this right enough. Everything they sent with us is smart-tagged, but they split up most of the individual lots between the different containers."

Danysh grimaced. "Please, in words we all understand."

Buckley, sitting with his head in his hands, shouted. "Everything is all mixed up. Food packed in with electronics. Medical supplies layered into survival gear. And the damned index is chock full of errors, too. It's like some workgang and their robots just pushed every container into the first empty space they could find, going as fast as they could and the hell with anything else."

Caine nodded. "Joe, this mission was put together in less than twenty-four hours. They pulled equipment and team members from all around the fleet. That may have something to do with it."

"Probably has everything to do with it," Buckley muttered. He looked up. "Captain, this is going to take days to untangle. Maybe weeks."

"I'll see what I can do about getting you semi-regular access, Joe."

"But, Captain—"

"Joe, we're here to open diplomatic relations with the Slaasriithi.

Who might be the only species in the Accord willing to be our allies. And they want us all down planetside tomorrow. I don't know what they might want after that. But here's what I do know: *those* jobs come before *this* job." Caine waved a hand at the mélange of mismatched bulk containers around them. "And here's the first part of *this* job: you are to locate and data-tag all the defense and emergency stores."

"Well, I can get locator numbers out of the database pretty quickly. But I can't verify that—"

"We'll work with whatever data you give us and I'll provide the backs to move the gear. Get that list compiled and give it to Mr. Rulaine."

"Yes, sir. When do you need it done?"

Caine stared at Buckley. "Five minutes ago. Any more questions?"

Buckley blinked, shook his head. "No, sir." He turned and jogged off into the deeper recesses of the cargo mod.

Bannor had just arrived alongside Caine. "Did anyone ever mention that you have a really icy stare, sometimes?"

"Not that I can remember."

"Well, then I'm the first. No wonder they made you an officer. What next?"

"Next we gather all the security personnel and start moving our gear to the corvette and the lander."

Danysh started. "Are you expecting trouble, Captain?"

"No, Dr. Danysh, but if it arises, I want to have our defense and emergency gear where we need it and ready to go. It won't do us much good otherwise."

"Very well, I shall not intrude upon your preparations."

Or volunteer to help, Caine thought as the physicist made himself scarce. Riordan took a few steps away from Buckley toward the comparative privacy of a corner. He glanced at Macmillan, who strolled over.

"Yes, Captain?"

"I notice from your dossier that you and I have an acquaintance in common."

"Oh? And who would that be, sir?"

"Richard Downing."

Keith smiled a big, congenial, shit-eating smile. "Richard Downing? Never heard of him. Or of you, Mr. Riordan. Or of your walkabout on Dee Pee Three which indirectly brought us to where we're standing right now. No—never heard of any of that." Macmillan's Scottish burr was so faint as to be almost unnoticeable.

Like a ghost emerging from shadows, Bannor drew up from the other side, jerked his head toward Keith. "Told you," he muttered at Caine.

Caine ignored him. "Mr. Macmillan, what was your mission after providing security for Spookshow Prime?"

Macmillan kept smiling but stood a little straighter. "I have no knowledge of any missions relevant to your inquiry, sir, and would not be disposed to discuss them if I had."

Okay, so his responses were as genuine as the IRIS ID codes in his dossier. No reason to belabor the point. "I presume you had special orders embedded in the personal effects they shipped with you?"

"Yes, sir. From this same Mr. Downing I've never heard of."

"And those orders are—?"

"I'm to be your eyes and ears within the group, sir."

So, internal security. Prudent, although it was hard to imagine how even the Ktor could have managed to infiltrate the delegation with less than twenty-four hours' notice. "Very well, Mr. Macmillan. What's your cover role in the legation, then?"

"As far as the personnel roster goes, I'm just a warrant officer from the integrated Commonwealth task force. Jack of all trades, master of none. In terms of command structure, I'd be below Miles O'Garran, and on a par with Trent Howarth."

Caine smiled. "Well, then"—he raised his voice—"Mr. Buckley, do you have a list yet? Mr. Macmillan is still waiting around for something heavy to carry."

Buckley came over with his palmcomp, transferred the defense and emergency stores inventory to Caine, Macmillan, and Bannor. "I don't envy you guys. You've got a lot of ground to cover."

Bannor scanned the list. "We're not going to get this done today."

"No, we're not. So let's get going on the priority items. Bannor, you find Tygg, Wu, O'Garran, and Howarth. We're going to need all hands for this. Macmillan, you go with Buckley and have him electronically tag all the containers so they show up on our smartmaps." Caine started to move off.

Bannor held up his hand. "Whoa, Boss. Don't take off until you tell us where to find you. What will *you* be doing?"

Caine shrugged. "Moving the boxes. Like I said, 'all hands.' Let's get going."

Chapter Nineteen

Caine stepped back, hands on his hips and shirt clinging to his sweaty back, as Yiithrii'ah'aash's two helpers sealed the cargo mod once again. Bannor nodded at the dull gray door, moved past Riordan. "Let's get a beer. Sir." He continued on to the pod-bus.

Caine followed, discovering most of the passengers they traveled with on the previous ride. Sleeman and Lymbery had tarried to examine the quasi-biological extrusions that had extended into the module's interior, up its sides and, after seamlessly merging with the docking sleeve, reportedly reemerged out in space, fusing into the mooring arms.

As the pod-bus began the short run back to their hab mod, Sleeman, still staring at the strange, grainy growths, leaned toward Lymbery. "That extrusion is not just a reinforcing structure. Through it, they're extending their power and data grids to mesh with the ones in our cargo module. And I'll bet it didn't break any seals when it pushed out into free space; it just resumed growing in the vacuum. Probably completed the encystment of the cargo mod."

Lymbery may have nodded.

"But what's really interesting is that the extrusions are not homogenic. They're comprised of diverse strands, some of which seem to be evolving into power conduits, judging from the havoc they played with my magnetometer. It looks like the parts that are now in contact with our electrical and data junctures began as probes, gel cysts that contact, sample, and assess the interface. They measure and learn to replicate its electromagnetic 'flavor,' so to speak. Then, about an hour later, I saw what looked like a custom-grown interface biot being budded off from the end of that bioelectric vein. By the time we come back here again, I'll bet that biot has evolved into a power transformer which converts Slaasriithi data and electric current into Terran equivalents and vice versa." She waited, unaware that the entirety of the pod-bus was staring at her. Tygg's face was a mix of awe and wonder. When Lymbery failed to react to her hypotheses, Melissa leaned in closer. "Well, whaddya think, Morgan?"

Morgan Lymbery blinked as if roused from a waking dream, winced in annoyance. "All possible but excessively speculative. I remain focused on first matters."

"What first matters?" pursued Melissa, undeterred by Lymbery's snappish response.

"The chemical nature of the primary extrusions. I posit supramolecular liquid crystal templating or thermoplastic elastomers."

"Elastomers?" Melissa echoed skeptically. "Natural rubber and polypropylene isn't likely to be biogenically organic. Its softening temperature is too high and its glass transition temperature is still not rugged enough for—"

"That analysis is unrealistically constrained to current human standards. Theoretical limits and permutations point toward lower temperature production ranges and broader operational durability limits. There are—"

Melissa interrupted: Caine had the impression her focus on the topic was so intense that she wasn't even aware she was being rude. "Yeah, but polypropylene is really nasty stuff. Even if its reliability regime could be expanded, how would an organism that's carbon based not find that lethally toxic?"

"Analysis flawed at root. Example: hydrochloric acid in the human stomach would be lethal to the parent organism if it escaped containment. Directly analogous internal safe containment systems possible. Also, capability for polypropylene extrusion does not require the storage of propylene itself. Raw stock for combination could be stored as separate constituent parts. Conversion into propylene occurs in peripheral organ or sac, which then immediately expels the compound as extrusions."

"And how—?"

"Storage mediums could include ethylene and other compounds, exploiting olefin metathesis to reverse the necessary—"

"Can someone translate?" Bannor grumbled. "Or get them to stop?"

Caine smiled. "Melissa, Morgan, you might want to save the rest of your debate for the ride down to the planet tomorrow. We're home."

"Home?" said Lymbery, rousing out of what had sounded like demonic possession by a chemistry computer. His wistful reaction to the word "home" hardened into adult resignation when he saw the entry to their hab module. Perhaps, Caine speculated, he had expected to see the quaint roofs of the small Cotswold village from which he had revolutionized human naval architecture. "Oh. Here." Lymbery sighed, exited the pod-bus.

Caine was the last to step down from it, and was immediately set upon by Joe Buckley. "Captain," Buckley began without the courtesy of a preamble, "I didn't have enough time to get a full inventory of the contents of our individual survival packs."

Caine hadn't minded being made an officer—until now. "Uh, Joe, if you have the standard allotments of each item in each pack, and you have the total number of packs, then you just multiply and you have your inventory totals, right?"

Joe shook his head. "Except the pack allotment data is bad. Most of the kits were upgraded after the fleet left Earth. So a lot of them have outdated content descriptions. The only way to get an accurate inventory is by checking each one."

"Can't we get by with an estimate, instead of a precise accounting?"

Buckley looked away. "Only if you're willing to accept a pretty wide margin of error."

Caine couldn't tell if he was hearing a tone of frustrated professionalism or innate anal retentiveness. "Joe, for now, take your best guess at the standard contents of the upgraded packs, and flag the result as 'estimated.'"

Joe looked away, someplace between disappointed and sullen. "Yeah. Okay. Captain." He started into the hab module.

"Joe?"

"Yes, sir?"

"Don't get stubborn and do something stupid."

Joe's voice was now thoroughly respectful, if no less disappointed. "I won't, sir. I understand the situation."

Caine almost believed that he did. "Good night, Joe."

"Good night, sir."

Caine sealed the hatch of the hab module behind them, watched Joe slouch away toward his stateroom. Given Yiithrii'ah'aash's warnings about the dangers of moving around the Slaasriithi ship unescorted, Riordan assured himself that *no one* was stubborn—or stupid—enough to take that kind of risk just to sort out some cargo. Not even Joe Buckley.

Joe Buckley was that stupid.

Unfortunately, he was also suspiciously proficient at bypassing electronics. He avoided triggering the exit alarm slaved to the inner airlock door. He anticipated and deactivated the touch-sensitive sensors lining every surface within the airlock itself, did the same with the laser tripwires crisscrossing both the inner and outer hatch coamings, and overrode the lock and disabled the alarm on the outer hatch.

All of which Caine realized in the jarring moment between being awakened by the sound of a repetitive warning tone and the approach of pounding feet. Riordan was already pulling on his duty-suit by the time Ben Hwang, still in shorts and tee shirt, opened his door and panted: "Buckley's biomonitor in the dispensary just started coding. And he's not in his cabin."

Damnit! I should have set a live guard, Caine hammered at himself as he yanked on his shoes and raced past Hwang. "Where does his transponder say he is?"

"He's off our structure; somewhere on theirs."

Oh, for Christ's sake—

Bannor nearly collided with Caine as he charged out of his own stateroom. "What's up?"

"Buckley. On the Slaasriithi hull. Alone. His biomonitor has spiked."

"Just great. I'll assemble a team."

Caine held Bannor's considerable bicep a moment. "No. You keep Wu and Tygg back here with you. You're the CO in my absence, and you keep everyone except my response team here in this module. You pulled the firearms from the security packs?"

"As we discussed on the second day."

"Excellent. You're to keep them hidden unless someone tries to leave. Then you use them to enforce the no-trespass rule that Buckley ignored."

"And now you're going to ignore it, too? Bad plan, boss."

"Yes, a bad plan. Problem is that doing nothing could be worse. We don't know what Buckley has done to set off his biomonitor. He could have damaged the ship, hurt a Slaasriithi. He's our—he's *my*—responsibility. I've got to get him back. I'll take Miles, Trent, Keith, and . . . and the guy from Peking, the vet who's an EMT?"

"That would be me," announced Xue Heng, who came striding up the hall. "I will get a med kit, Captain."

"Excellent. I'll meet you at the hatch."

"Keep your collarcom open, Caine," Bannor called after him.

"We all will. No way to know what we're going to run into. Also, get me an earcam. I want you to see what we're seeing."

"I'm on it." Bannor peeled off into the hab mod's combination dress-out compartment and ship's locker.

Caine got two steps closer to the commons room when Gaspard's voice emerged from his outsize quarters. "Captain Riordan, what has happened?" Caine told him. Gaspard nodded. "I will ready a team to follow yours just as soon as—"

"No. You will sit tight. This is a security matter and those are my orders. I've already spoken with Major Rulaine, who has instructions in case something happens to me. We discussed contingencies extensively on the trip out here. Now, I've got to go."

Gaspard was still trying to say something, but Caine didn't have time to listen. According to Ben's distant, rolling updates, whatever was happening to Buckley was getting more severe. His heart rate was dangerously high and his bloodstream was awash with endorphins and a number of unknown substances.

By the time Riordan reached the commons room, Miles, Trent, and Keith were there. All had guns. Caine shook his head.

"But—" began Miles.

"No. We can't. It's not our ship. The Slaasriithi warned us against this. We can't inflict any damage on them, or their ship, to save Buckley or even ourselves. Besides, guns are likely to exacerbate any misunderstandings that already exist among our hosts." None of them looked happy as Xue arrived with a medkit and Bannor showed up with an earcam.

Caine snugged the loop of the tiny device over his ear and added, "Look, this is my screwup: it was on me to ensure that this didn't happen. So although I asked you to report here, this is strictly a volunteer mission."

Keith looked at the open hatch. "We're wasting time."

Trent smiled his big, easy smile. "After you, sir."

Caine, feeling very much that he did not deserve the loyalty of such fine persons, led the way.

Halfway to the cargo mod, underneath the sounds of the team's sprinting progress, Riordan heard other footfalls. He turned. Swift and stealthy, Dora Veriden was following them. *Damn it, what's she doing here? But no time to stop now: her choice, her fate.*

As they rounded the second of the corridor's slight bends, differences in speed began to stretch the group out. Trent—tall, athletic, in his twenties—was outpacing all of them. Miles and Xue, short legs pumping quickly, lost their early lead and started to drop behind, particularly Xue who, although a veteran, was not an active-duty SEAL like O'Garran. Keith had originally outpaced Caine slightly, but age and a heavy, if muscular, build were wearing him down. Meanwhile, Dora Veriden, despite a much later start, had almost caught up to Xue.

Trent looked back. Caine waved him on. The big Kiwi showed his real speed and started pulling far ahead.

"You shouldn't be out here." The voice from over Caine's shoulder was guttural, strained: Dora Veriden.

Caine didn't waste the breath on responding, saved it to try to keep pace with Trent.

Veriden uttered an annoyed grunt, and, with a surprising burst of speed, pulled ahead of Riordan and started closing on the Kiwi. *Good God, is she enhanced? Does Gaspard know? Would he have brought along an illegal—?*

Up ahead, Trent sprawled headlong just before the turn that led into the turning yard chamber. Veriden veered toward him—and went down an eyeblink later. They both tried to rise, but a mist seemed to be surging intermittently about them, battering them down. *Damn it; what the hell—?* "Are you seeing this, Ben? Any guesses?" Caine muttered into his collarcom.

No response. Not even a carrier tone. Probably jammed by the Slaasriithi ship's on-board electronic countermeasures.

Caine veered toward the right-hand wall, the one that led into the turn, kept running while he tried to make out whatever had hit Trent and Dora. But as far as he could tell, they were unharmed, unmarked, except they were covered in what looked like cobwebs—

Webs—?

Caine glanced up. Where the walls met the ceiling, there was a dark seam, rimmed by the same substance which had extruded itself across the cargo mod. Could it also conceal something like spinnerets?

Caine hadn't realized he'd slowed so much and was surprised when both O'Garran and Macmillan raced past him to help Trent and Dora. As they did, vapor-fine filaments jetted downward, so thick that they created the impression of fog.

Within half a second, the strands that had landed on Macmillan stiffened, and the increased resistance brought him down. However, O'Garran managed to dance out of the spray pattern—or had he? Given its density and dispersion, that seemed impossible, unless—

Had the filaments only hit O'Garran because he was close to Macmillan? *No time to observe or think: those spinnerets are still spraying. If there's a better chance to be had by rushing through while they're busy with Macmillan—*

Caine sprinted toward the corner, felt some of the filaments land on him, felt them change consistency; one moment they were as loose as a strand of hair, the next they were steel thread. But the few that hit him were just nuisances; they had evidently been aimed at Macmillan.

As Riordan and O'Garran rounded the corner, they also detected the first whiffs of an astringent, medicinal smell.

"Gas?" O'Garran panted, struggling to run. The fibers across the front of his duty suit had hardened into a mostly immobile cast.

"Probably," gasped Caine. "The others—they alive?"

"Think so. Breathing."

"Good."

O'Garran started lagging as the scent of the gas rose behind them. "Go," he said.

Riordan nodded. There was nothing else to do, although helping Joe Buckley—whose skills evidently included those possessed by accomplished felons—had now become a rather ironic objective.

As Caine rounded the final corner into the turning yard, he heard a thump well behind him; O'Garran had gone down. Pushing back against a surge of vomit, Riordan sprinted across the chamber's circular expanse, came up short when he confronted the cargo mod's still-open doors. The fibrous extrusions now resembled a mahogany lava flow that ran from the bay of the Slaasriithi vessel into the cargo mod as one seamless mass. And from beyond that resinous cavern mouth, Riordan heard a single, child-high shriek.

Riordan's plunge through the doorway was reflexive, but not incautious. Uncertain of what he'd find, he went in low and straight toward cover. But there was no fight in progress, no torture, not even any Slaasriithi or intruders to be seen. Just Joe Buckley's distant torso, squirming irregularly beyond one of the motion-activated lights, halfway along the length of the cargo mod.

Caine jumped up, sprinted those twenty yards, scanning for tools as he went, preparing to help Buckley however he could— but stopped when he saw Joe's predicament. And thought: *what the hell is that?—And what the hell can I do?*

Vac-suited Joe Buckley seemed to be pinned to the wall next to one of the cargo mod's primary power mains. But in the next moment, Caine realized that the extrusions which had snaked down the wall toward the mains were holding Joe up. But no, that wasn't quite right, either—

They had transfixed Joe, and were growing, even now, toward the cargo mod's power mains, burrowing through his body to do so. In the one paralyzed second that it took for Riordan to understand what he was seeing, more of Buckley's abdomen sagged. The hole in it widened, the extrusions leaking a slow but constant secretion that was, from the smell of it, highly alkaline. Joe seemed to rouse out of a stupor, yelled incoherently, sobbed back into quasi-consciousness.

Caine looked around: a power-saw. Hand-sized, the kind used to cut off locks or through simple sheet steel. He grabbed it off the deck, jumped next to Buckley to get to the power mains— and discovered what had probably initiated the horrific scenario.

The power mains were covered by a luminescent polyp that emerged from the extrusion burrowing through Buckley's body. Another such polyp, lifeless and dull, lay on the deck, evidently torn aside by Buckley when he attempted to connect the saw to the mains and scorched his hands trying. Beyond the burnt meat smell, the air was thick with the medicinal tang of the gas from the corridor, but it was stale, had probably been used at the outset. Apparently, the gas had also kept Joe senseless as the extrusion burrowed through his body in its unswerving purpose: to get to the power mains.

Caine spent one moment looking at the situation, waiting for a solution—any solution—to come to him. But the only course of action that he could think of was the same that would have occurred to his Cro-Magnon ancestors. Without attempting to plug it in, and using his left hand to cover his nose and mouth, Riordan slammed the hand saw down across the conductive polyp attached to the mains.

A blast of heat and energy sent him backwards. The extrusion transfixing Buckley, which had seemed as solid as a stalagmite a moment ago, writhed. Buckley's eyes opened into panic and pain as the spasms of the extrusion widened the wound, his weight slamming back and forth against the dark rootlike protrusion upon which he was impaled. He shrieked. Blood spattered. A fresh wave of the astringent smell preceded a glistening rush of the corrosive fluid which had already eaten a hole through Buckley's torso. The edges of that gore-rimmed gap widened more rapidly. Fumes arose as tissue and fluids bubbled.

As Caine rose, groggy but resolved to try again, Joe's screams became more desperate, his writhing wilder—which brought him fractionally closer to the mains. Apparently, the once-luminous fluid that splattered on him when he'd smashed the first polyp remained a powerful conductor. Actinic, blue-white charges danced out of the mains' sockets and along vaporous trails leading to Buckley's chest and shoulders. The smell of charring flesh increased along with the of the gas. Caine staggered forward, fell to his knees. The scene began doubling, the sounds blurry and indistinct as Buckley's desperate struggles transformed into spasmodic convulsions—

Chapter Twenty

Caine started awake. He tried to get off his back, get to Buckley—

Hands he hadn't noticed were holding him down. And he wasn't in the cargo mod anymore.

"That was fast," commented Bannor's voice, just behind him.

"The effects of the gas are immediately dispelled by the antidote," Yiithrii'ah'aash's voice answered.

Riordan tried to rise up on his elbows. "Buckley is—"

Rena Mizrahi's face was over his; she was wielding a diagnostic stylus. A light stabbed into his left eye briefly and went away. "Let's worry about you for now, Captain. Contraction and dilation already normal. Vitals normal."

"As I assured you," Yiithrii'ah'aash said. His tone was not impatient or even disappointed; it was sad.

"Thank you, Doctor. And you as well, Ambassador." Gaspard's voice was more distant. Caine's voluntary nerve functions finally began catching up with the restoration of his senses and involuntary reflexes; he rolled his head to the right, saw Gaspard standing in the doorway to the dispensary. Closer, almost out of his field of view at the head of the bed, were the edges of one human torso and one alien torso: Bannor and Yiithrii'ah'aash, respectively. Now realizing that Joe Buckley would have been found and assisted long before he was, Riordan simply asked: "Buckley?"

Bannor moved into Caine's field of vision, shook his head.

Riordan had expected that answer, but it felt like a physical blow to his stomach, even so. He swallowed. "Ambassador Yiithrii'ah'aash, I take full responsibility for—"

Gaspard interrupted. "Captain, I have already reviewed the events with Ambassador Yiithrii'ah'aash, whose surveillance systems recorded everything. He knows you are blameless."

Blameless? Bullshit: my man, my fault. "Ambassador, with all due respect—"

"Caine Riordan." Somehow, Yiithrii'ah'aash's interruption didn't feel like one; it sounded like a gentle but firm request for attention. "I am aware of the scope of your duties. I am also aware that no being may fully anticipate the actions of another, particularly one so briefly and incompletely known to you as Mr. Buckley."

"I—"

"Please allow me one further statement. Mr. Gaspard has also acquainted me with the contents of Mr. Buckley's dossier. There is nothing within it to suggest that he might behave in such a way. Furthermore, none of his prior actions or statements validated taking any abnormal precautions. Indeed, your newly awakened legation members might have construed such precautions as signifying that you distrusted us, or them, or both. In short, you made the best decision, given all the variables and available data."

"Yes, but it was the wrong decision, nonetheless," Riordan insisted. "I am the head of security. Even if you—dubiously—insist that I didn't make any bad decisions, it's still my command. That makes it my responsibility, and my fault." Caine saw a slight wrinkle quirk the corner of Bannor's mouth: a rueful smile which translated as, *they're not going to understand. Ever.*

Yiithrii'ah'aash's tendril fingers straightened into columns, were still. "I am only slightly familiar with this human predilection for elevating an individual's level of responsibility above their ability to assure desired outcomes. I note that it is a particularly strong tradition in your human militaries. Am I correct?"

Before Riordan could fashion a reply, Gaspard rolled his eyes and sighed. "You are quite correct, Ambassador. And you are not the only sentient being that finds these superhuman expectations absurd."

Two of Yiithrii'ah'aash's tendrils rose: a motion calling for a pause. "I am not suggesting it is absurd. Indeed, given the relationship between your species' sociology and expressions of authority in crises, it is probably inevitable."

Bannor raised an eyebrow. "Ambassador, would you care to explain what you mean?"

"Certainly. Most simply, it is inarguable that there are events for which no individual has sufficient agency to affect the outcome. Yet, those members of your species who are assigned to confront extreme challenges are, by rituals of ranks and oaths, made 'accountable' for just such outcomes. This is inherently illogical."

"Precisely," Gaspard agreed.

"However," Yiithrii'ah'aash continued, "this absolute account-ability is required in order to overcome your species' powerful self-preservation instinct. Only because there is no acceptable excuse for failure will an individual court certain death in the discharge of a crucial duty."

Caine swung his legs over the side of the bed. "And the Slaas-riithi have no such instinct toward self-preservation?"

"We do not have it in your measure."

"And why is that?"

Yiithrii'ah'aash emitted a short, faint purr. "The answer to that is best seen, not explained."

Well, that's certainly a convenient all-purpose deferral. "I welcome the opportunity to see and understand. In the meantime, I assure you that there will be no further unauthorized human presences on your ship. This module's access airlock will be secure-coded, locked, and guarded at all times." He glanced up at Bannor. "I suspect it already is." Rulaine's nod was as faint as his smile. "However, I doubt those precautions will be as effective as the legation's detailed knowledge of just how Buckley paid for his trespass."

"Caine Riordan, Mr. Buckley's death was not a consequence of his trespass. Our ship's security systems only immobilize intruders, as demonstrated with the others in your own group. Mr. Buckley's death was simply the result of blocking our power interface extrusion. As I warned you, our systems have not yet been coded to recognize humans as a higher life-form."

Rachel leaned back sharply. "Then what did 'your systems' think Buckley was?"

"They identified him as a collection of biological resources that also happened to be obstructing them. So they harvested needful compounds from his body as they pushed through it to their objective. They regrettably achieved both all too completely."

Caine glanced at Gaspard. "Has a burial detail been assembled?" Gaspard became pale. "None is required."

Damn. "Ambassador Yiithrii'ah'aash, why didn't your anti-trespass systems stop Buckley? Or me, or Chief O'Garran?"

The Slaasriithi's fingers unfurled into what looked like an appeal. "We presumed that no intruder interested in stealth would slow or encumber themselves by wearing a vacuum suit. However, because Mr. Buckley did, and because it was sealed, our trespass monitors did not detect a bioform. Consequently, their coding instructed them to act as if the intrusion was being carried out by a mechanism. They attempted to disable Mr. Buckley with localized electromagnetic pulses. They were, naturally, ineffective."

Bannor folded his arms. "Naturally." And he didn't say what Riordan presumed he was thinking: *you Slaasriithi have pretty lousy autonomous security systems if they can't figure out and handle something as simple as an intruder in a vac suit.*

Yiithrii'ah'aash's tendrils writhed without apparent pattern. "I am puzzled, however, by Mr. Buckley's reason for risking unauthorized entry to our ship. I have heard several of your legation speculate that he may have been motivated by larceny. However, to the extent I understand that concept at all, I cannot see what he hoped to gain. He is extremely distant from any markets where he might liquidate stolen property."

Caine stood, found his balance unimpaired. "Given how Joe tried to press me for increased access to the cargo module, I suspect he meant to retrieve something incriminating that was mixed in with our shared gear, something he couldn't get to without raising suspicion."

Gaspard nodded. "That would explain his power-saw, also. If Buckley wished to remove some object that would bring his checkered past to light, then it would not only be worth the risk of trespassing, but his use of the saw. Once the incriminating object was gone, we might still suspect him of the trespass, but would lack definitive proof."

"As likely an explanation as any other," Bannor agreed.

But Riordan's focus remained on the one failure of the Slaasriithi security system that remained unexplained. "Yiithrii'ah'aash, you still haven't explained how Chief O'Garran and I slipped through."

Yiithrii'ah'aash emitted more of a hum than a purr: *perhaps he was hoping we wouldn't return to this topic?* "You and Chief

O'Garran have been aboard for many weeks. And we met several times. During that time, you were pheromonally marked." His head angled slightly toward Bannor. "As were you, Major, along with the rest of the conscious travelers. Indeed, your party would not have been gassed at all, had the sensors not detected a weapon."

Caine shook his head. "That's not possible. None of my personnel were armed."

"That is true. But you and your personnel were not alone in responding."

Gaspard's pallor became a flush. "Ms. Veriden. Without doubt."

Yiithrii'ah'aash's ostrich neck bobbed. "As you say. Usually, our defenses would only physically immobilize intruders. But if a weapon is detected, it activates suppressive gas biots."

Well, that explains their reaction to Buckley's handsaw, too. "Ambassador, I offer my personal apologies that a human brought a weapon on board your ship. I am—"

Gaspard shook his head sharply. "No, Captain; this is not your responsibility, even by the letter of the often-absurd laws of military accountability. The culpability is mine." He turned to Yiithrii'ah'aash. "Ms. Veriden is not part of the legation's security team; she is my personal, er, assistant. As such, I am to answer for her indiscretions."

The Slaasriithi's small head inclined slightly. "We thank both of you gentlemen for your forthrightness. It is, as your saying has it, the silver lining to this dark event. However, your protestations of responsibility are as unnecessary as they are illogical. My concern is solely with ensuring that there are no recurrences." He shifted slightly. "I am also constrained to point out that we must now descend as planned to the planet below us."

Caine, Bannor, and Gaspard exchanged baffled glances. "We have to leave right now?" Caine asked.

"Yes."

"With all due respect for our itinerary, Ambassador, we should first ensure that there are no other—well, loose cannons—in our legation."

"I do not know what unsecured artillery pieces have to do with our current situation, but we may not delay. Various activities have been scheduled to coincide with your visit. But, more importantly, we cannot loiter because we dare not presume that this region of space is secure, even though it is well within our borders. Experience has shown us that all borders are porous. The Arat Kur have occasionally proven it to us in this very system."

"But the Arat Kur are defeated. Word must have reached even their most far-flung units, by now."

"Agreed. I invoke the Arat Kur only as an example." Yiithrii'ah'aash's ostrich neck seemed to shorten slightly. "The Ktor are much more advanced than the Arat Kur, and if they have the ability to enter Arat Kur space as a surprise to all other powers, including the Dornaani, then our safety is not absolute until we reach Beta Aquilae."

Gaspard had blanched again. "Do you really think we could be pursued by the Ktor? Here?"

"I think that is extremely unlikely. I also think that very few things in this universe are impossible. Let us make haste to the planet."

Chapter Twenty-One

Karam Tsaami was in the pilot's seat of the delta-shaped lander and was not at all happy. He hadn't been since the slightly smaller, but more versatile and rugged Euro model had been stricken from the legation's inventory just hours before their departure from Sigma Draconis Two. Two small maintenance glitches and subpar thrust measurements resulted in the mission planners going to the second vehicle on the roster. The TOCIO-manufactured Embra-Mitsu lander was capacious, but also more lightly built, and if push came to shove, simply didn't have the thrust-to-mass ratio of the EU model, despite its responsiveness.

Karam's displeasure was increased when the Slaasriithi prohibited the legation's Wolfe-class corvette from serving as the lander, citing its paucity of passenger couches. Karam had argued the milspec advantages of the craft's speed, agility, toughness, and systems redundancy. Yiithrii'ah'aash had patiently heard him out and then explained that the humans had to land in their own craft, and only one, if possible. So the Embra-Mitsu would suffice. The career pilot had muttered imprecations and suspicions about the Slaasriithi just finding a convenient excuse to keep them from landing in a warship. Caine observed that this might be true, but given the nasty surprise that Joe Buckley had dealt to everyone's easy confidence in the safety of the mission, Yiithrii'ah'aash certainly had the right to err to the side of caution. Tsaami's dark grumblings did not cease, but they did subside.

Karam put his hand on the hard-dock release lever, and called out, "I need a vocal confirm that you are strapped in. All the green lights on my board are not good enough."

A confirming chorus came from the passenger compartment. The three other persons in the cockpit—copilot Qin Lijuan, planetologist Hirano Mizuki, and Riordan, whose ostensible job was security overwatch of flight operations—murmured their own assent.

Karam pulled the handle; he preferred manual controls for some functions. "Okay, everyone, we've got some odd descent telemetry on this ride, so be prepared for a few sharper-than-average turns. Here we go." He puffed the attitude control thrusters to put the nose down and in line with the trajectory guidons and waypoint boxes painted on his HUD visor. The world beneath them rose into view—and revealed itself to be a world like no human had ever seen before.

Riordan stared at the faintly ovate planet. Scientists and planetologists had speculated that such worlds would—indeed, must—exist. Its primary, a red dwarf labeled GJ 1248, was just thirty-nine million kilometers away. Consequently, the planet was not only face-locked to the star, but had been structurally deformed by it.

Qin Lijuan's eyes were wide. "Is it slightly egg-shaped?"

Hirano Mizuki nodded. "The inner pole, the part of the planet always closest to the star, was constantly stretched in that direction throughout its formation."

"Which is one of the two things that makes landing here so challenging." Karam was fussing with his instruments, particularly his navigational sensors. "I've never had to put down on a world which isn't functionally a sphere. Orbit tracks are messed up. The relationship between altitude and gravity are skewed."

Qin Lijuan was studying the instruments carefully. "Because in a sphere, a constant orbital altitude means constant distance from the center of gravity."

"Right. But here, not so much."

"Would a polar orbit be better? If you remain consistently over the meridian, you will be able to follow a roughly circular orbit with roughly consistent gravity."

Karam nodded. "That's what I'm shooting for. But it's easier said than done, lacking a full planetary survey and nav charts.

The Slaasriithi relayed the relevant astrophysical data, but the software on this barge doesn't have a preset template for a non-spherical planet."

Riordan glanced at Karam. "So you're running the nav numbers in real time?"

"No other way, Captain. Couldn't run a simulation since I didn't have the time to write a custom subroutine. So we'll still need some adjustments on the way in. You ready to help with that, Lieutenant Qin?"

Her hands rested confidently, lightly upon the controls. Qin Lijuan didn't even bother to nod; she simply glanced at him.

Karam rolled the shuttle, boosted so that its approach to the planet became oblique. Riordan watched as GJ 1248 One's sun-blasted surface swam across to the right-hand side of the cockpit windows, sinking as it went.

Qin's left eyebrow raised. "We're going down there? Without hard suits?"

Hirano Mizuki's answering smile was almost invisible. "We won't need anything more than filter masks."

Qin's other eyebrow rose to join the first. "How is that possible?" She tracked a raging, twister-pocked dust storm as it scoured its way across the ochre flatlands over which they were passing. "The temperature down there must be over two hundred degrees centigrade."

Hirano nodded. "More, in places."

Riordan glimpsed the terminator, the line marking the border where the perpetually sun-scorched side of the planet gave way to its perpetually lightless hemisphere, and noted that it was peculiarly smudged—not at all like the hard, crisp demarcation that he had seen while orbiting comparably featureless moons and planets. "Is that a lifezone lying along the terminator?"

Karam nodded. "Yeah. Yiithrii'ah'aash briefed me on this for a grand total of two minutes while you were sleeping off the gas. The Slaasriithi call this kind of world a meridiate. A face-locked world that is large enough to retain both an atmosphere and some water can develop what they call a bioband, which follows the terminator's meridian."

The bioband was only a few hundred kilometers wide, and the sunward margin of it still showed no sign of water or plant life. But whereas the far wastes of the sunward face were flat and uniform in both color and reflectivity, the margins where it abutted the bioband shaded into darker patches. There were also more geological irregularities along that fringe. Glacial deformations resembling dried finger lakes, hillocks and successive ridgelines paralleled the edge of the zone that human planetologists that speculatively labeled the "life-belt." The ridges became higher and more frequent as they receded toward the more shadowed center of the zone.

"Terminal moraines," Hirano commented.

Caine nodded, watching them accumulate and stacking into a washboard collection of faint, meridian-following ribs. "The limits of a glacial advance?"

Hirano nodded. "Yes. We can't see the darkside glacier yet—most of it will be well-shadowed—but it won't be a perfectly stable formation. Stellar flares and libration will change the temperatures in the bioband. With those changes will come glacial advances and retreats. And every time the glacier retreats, it will leave behind one of those." She gestured down at one of the ridges paralleling the further, darker reaches of the bioband.

Riordan watched Karam align the shuttle to follow the same meridian-riding track of the terminal moraine. "Assuming that there is any periodicity to temperature change, there should be some spot where the glacier is most likely to halt, right?"

"Yes," Hirano confirmed with an eager nod. "That moraine should be the highest, being a compound of multiple terminal deposits. It would logically function as a kind of sunside 'wall,' according to some of the planetological predictions."

Karam glanced at Hirano Mizuki. "I'm not unfamiliar with planetology, given my job, but I've never even heard of speculations about a world like this—uh, 'meridiate.'"

"Such work is rare," Hirano admitted in a small voice.

Caine smiled. "You wouldn't happen to be one of those rare researchers, would you, Mizuki?"

Her answering smile was also small. "I have shared my opinions in one or two papers."

Karam snorted, but it was not a derisive sound. "Figures." He boosted the craft slightly. "Pretty lively air here where the hotside drafts are zooming across to equalize the subzero soup on the dark side. We've just started biting into the atmosphere and I can already feel the buffeting."

"You can?"

"Sure," Karam answered as Qin Lijuan nodded her confirmation.

"I can't," Hirano confessed.

"That's because it's not your job," Karam observed. "And that's why we're landing this barge in a hands-on mode. We're depending as much on the feel of this bird and the nav-sensor readings as we are on the avionics and the flight computer." Karam put his palm on the manual throttle and pushed the thrust higher, along with the shuttle's nose.

Riordan felt the increased, thready vibration through his seat. "Isn't this when we would normally be backing off the thrusters?"

Karam didn't turn away from his instruments, but Caine could see a smile quirk the rearmost corner of his mouth. "So, you *have* been paying attention during the sims."

"Weeks of running them again and again will even help a newb like me," Riordan replied.

Karam nodded tightly as the shuttle jounced, settled, seemed to float upward on a giant palm before dropping down sharply. "To answer your question: yeah, at this point, we'd normally be backing off the thrust, letting the belly soak up the energy of our descent as we serpentine in to dump velocity. But here, that protocol would get us killed. We've got to get through the turbulence of the air masses moving from the brightside to the darkside. We need powered flight for that. And our glide path, even from this altitude, is fundamentally perpendicular to the plane of the equator."

"Because we are making a longitudinal, not latitudinal, approach?"

"Correct, Captain," Qin Lijuan answered, who was now in control of the shuttle as Karam plotted telemetry changes to compensate for new meteorological data. "However, it will not be convenient to answer further questions at this time."

Riordan reflected that he really didn't have any more flight-related questions, now that the life-sustaining sections of the bioband were in plain view. It was a meandering valley cut with swathes of mauve, maroon, teal and aqua foliage, and they were slowly angling down into it from the hotside.

The thermals came in layers, the faint shuddering of the calm belts alternating with teeth-rattling surges from the more superheated currents. At times, Karam and Lijuan had to fight to keep the shuttle from rolling by nosing slightly into the drafts, being pushed sideways as they maintained dynamic equilibrium against the lateral forces until they could get underneath each successive current.

After almost a quarter hour of jostling alongside and against the cyclonic winds rushing toward the distant glacial wall of the darkside, Lijuan was finally able to bring the nose back down. The shuttle slipped beneath the level of the terminal moraine which rose up like a long, high ridgeline interspersed with hillocks. As the craft did so, the orange-red light coming in the cockpit windows dimmed, the shielding ridge blocking the line of sight to the sun. The wide valley beneath them swum into sharper focus with the loss of the glare: patches of spongy aquamarine plant canopy snugged against the backside of the ridge. Swards of dusky maroon and vibrant violet flora reached out from its foot, shot through with occasion streaks and patches of white-washed ultramarine and teal. The sharply separated colors chased up and down faint bowl-shaped depressions, in and out of faint hollows where thin water courses glimmered in the indirect lighting.

"Damn," muttered Karam, "I've been to at least half the green worlds out beyond Epsilon Indi. Half of the brown ones, too. But this—"

"Different?" Caine asked.

"And then some."

Hirano, her nose pushed up against the cockpit glass, nodded in eager agreement.

Lijuan, who had transitioned back to dynamic controls, initiated the landing sequence. Two of the thrusters slowly rotated into a vertical attitude as the landing gear began groaning out of their wheel-wells.

"How long, Lieutenant?" Riordan asked.

"Four minutes, sir."

"Then it's time to have the rest of the mission break out the filter masks. We've got a planet to visit."

With the entirety of the legation sheltering under the still-warm belly of the lander, Gaspard approached Caine and flipped open the speaking port beneath the filters of his mask. "Your security personnel seem pensive, Captain. Have you passed them any warnings of which I should be aware?"

Riordan squinted into the strangely diffuse light, saw that

Yiithrii'ah'aash had now debarked from his own craft. Two significantly shorter but stockier Slaasriithi were approaching from the edge of the landing pad, carrying what appeared to be boxes. Caine shook his head. "No, I haven't issued any special orders, Ambassador. My personnel just don't like being tasked to protect against threats if they don't have weapons."

"And you have similar feelings?"

Riordan shrugged. "After what happened with Buckley, I can hardly blame our hosts for not allowing us to carry devices which could turn a simple misunderstanding into a massacre. Besides, I think the last thing the Slaasriithi want to do is to harm us."

"I find it refreshing, if surprising, that you agree with our hosts, and with me, in this matter."

"I do," affirmed Caine, "but that's not the same thing as saying that I don't understand how my security team feels or that I don't share their sentiments. I simply concur that, in this place and at this time, it's best for us to leave our weapons behind. Besides, I don't think Yiithrii'ah'aash was going to brook any debate on the topic."

Gaspard's voice conveyed what sounded like a rueful smile. "On that point we are in complete agreement, my good Riordan."

As Yiithrii'ah'aash and his attendants drew close, the ambassador unfurled several long fingers into an undulating greeting.

Tygg's *sotto voce* comment rose up from the rear of the ragged cluster of humans. "We wave hands; they wave fingers."

That prompted a few chuckles and giggles, one of which came from Melissa Sleeman. *Which means that Tygg is wearing a big, stupid smile right now.* As Riordan raised a hand to return Yiithrii'ah'aash's greeting, he stole a quick look at the ambassador's new companions. These Slaasriithi were not only smaller and stocky, but had lightly furred, symmetrical protrusions where a hominid's short ribs would be located. Yiithrii'ah'aash noted Caine's curious stare. "They are not neoplasms, as you might conjecture if you relied upon visual parallels from your own physiology."

Rena Mizrahi answered before Riordan could formulate an adequate response. "I can see that: the protrusions are too regular, both in their own shape, and in their bilateral placement." She pulled in a deep, air-testing breath as she continued to assess the two protrusions on each of the new Slaasriithi. "The air here is somewhat thin. Are those bulges, uh, symbiotic—living—air compressors?"

Yiithrii'ah'aash's purr rose in a surprised surge. "You are quite correct, Doctor. We rarely induce special subtaxae to caretake xenobiomes during their transitional phases. Rather, we provide the most suitable extant subtaxae with symbiots that allow them to adjust to the local environment without resorting to intrusive devices." He paused, his sensor-cluster head swiveling more directly toward Riordan, who realized he had blinked several times during Yiithrii'ah'aash's explanation. "You are perplexed, Caine Riordan?"

"No," Caine confessed, "but your explanation left me with about a dozen questions. And I can't figure out where to begin."

Yiithrii'ah'aash's purr modulated into a subaudial hum. "We will have time for all those questions after today. By then, I expect some of those queries will have been answered, others will have changed, and many, many more will have arisen. For now, let us walk into this world we call—well, in the dead language you use for attaching scientific classifications to objects, it would roughly translate as Adumbratus. But before our journey, we ask that you spray yourself with the contents of these canisters."

Responding without any overt summons, Yiithrii'ah'aash's two companions brought forth the boxes that actually proved to be semi-rigid angular bags. They dispensed the canisters.

"What does this do?" asked Morgan Lymbery, squinting at the container suspiciously. It appeared to be made of a very fine-grained version of the same material which comprised the extrusions that secured their cargo-mod—and that had burrowed straight through Joe Buckley.

Yiithrii'ah'aash was already dousing himself with a mist from one of the containers. "The contents are scent markers, adapted from both our own pheromones and local spores. The latter ensures that the local biota will find you wholly uninteresting, and the former ensures that our own transplanted biota will be affined to you."

"Affined?" asked Tina Melah. "Is that still a word?"

"Was it ever?" echoed Trent Howarth.

"Actually," answered Esiankiki, "it is the past-tense verb form of 'to have affinity for.'" She turned to Yiithrii'ah'aash. "So your own flora and fauna will identify us as living beings who are nonthreatening?"

"That is a most adequate summation, Ms. Salunke."

"How easily does it come off?" asked Dora Veriden darkly from the back of the group.

"The markers are not readily soluble. They do not simply remain on your skin, but will, by osmosis, vest in the outermost cells of your epidermis. This contact with your own fluids enhances their duration and eliminates the risk of dissolution."

"That's not what I was concerned about," Veriden muttered.

As the group applied the spray, Yiithrii'ah'aash continued. "We will be near hard shelter at all times. You must follow me, or our guides, to that cover quickly in the event of a solar flare. This is a low-activity period for GJ 1248, but no star has fully predictable cycles and red dwarfs have the greatest proclivity to deviate from their own patterns.

"Lastly, while there are few bioforms on this planet that would intentionally threaten you, no environment is without risks. This is why you are wearing filter masks in addition to the scent markers. Various airborne spores are present here, and since no humans have visited this environment before, we cannot be certain of their effect upon your respiratory tract. However, we have been able to ascertain that, if you keep your duty-suits sealed and your masks on, you need fear no exposure hazards for several weeks, at least. Now, please follow me."

As the legation trailed Yiithrii'ah'aash across the tarmac, Riordan realized that the surface was comprised of neither macadam nor tar, but, from the look of it, was some kind of finely threaded plant that had hardened into a chitinous mass.

Bannor drew alongside Riordan. "Moment of your time?"

"Take as many as you'd like."

The landing pad underfoot smoothed into what seemed like a vast plastic expanse. "After what happened with Buckley, I think we have to assume that some of our team members may be, well, infiltrated."

Caine made sure that neither his face nor his gait changed. "Hard to see how. No one knew this trip was coming, and Downing, Sukhinin, and Rinehart reviewed the final candidates with very fine-toothed combs."

"Agreed, but still we've got Buckley dead trying to break into his own, or maybe someone else's, gear. And we won't get a chance to learn anything more until the Slaasriithi give us access to the cargo mod again. But in the meantime—"

Caine suppressed a nod. "In the meantime, we have to pre-sume that where there's one inexplicable wildcard, there could be others. I just don't see what an enemy agent would hope to achieve, or how."

"Neither do I. And Buckley could simply have awakened into this gig knowing that he had to get rid of some incriminating black-market goods that were sent along with his gear. But we can't rely on that supposition."

"Agreed. But since we can't confirm that or some other motive, we'd just be spinning our wheels when it comes to internal security protocols. So, we'll have to be on constant watch for anything suspicious. Which means we won't be watching any-thing very well."

"No argument, sir. But one suggestion, if you don't mind."

"Look, Bannor: I'm not a professional soldier or a covert opera-tive, so I'm glad for any advice you care to give."

"First, don't beat yourself up because you didn't put safeguards in place after Buckley started acting hinky. Everyone makes mistakes in this business. And although you started as an amateur, you're losing rookie status pretty quickly. Second, and more important, make sure you keep some distance from Keith Macmillan."

"Do you think he could be suborned?"

Bannor clucked his tongue. "If I thought that, I'd tell you to stick to him like a tick. Never let your enemies out of sight. No, I'm thinking he's your best bet for sniffing out if something is brewing in the legation."

"You mean sabotage?"

"I don't think that's likely, but as you've said, we've got no leads and no hypothesis, only nonspecific worries. In that situa-tion, the most valuable asset you can have is a pair of eyes and ears that no one knows is a member of IRIS. So if you chat with Keith too often, or act as though you have innate trust of him, then any plants in the group will notice. That means you lose Macmillan as the one trump card that you've got mixed into the deck but can pull out at any moment. Keep him as a secret asset that might either tweak to a plot in the making, or who can be in the right place to reverse a—well, an unfortunate incident." Rulaine squinted ahead, toward a cluster of low, squat conelike trees. "You would not believe how often problems arise in the most unlikely places and for the most unlikely reasons."

Caine remembered narrowly avoided assassination attempts on Delta Pavonis Three, in deep space, in Washington DC, in Greece, at the Convocation, on Barney Deucy. "Bannor, that is one bit of tactical wisdom of which I do not need to be convinced."

Rulaine grinned crookedly at him. "No, I don't suppose you do."

They reached the edge of the pseudo-tarmac as Yiithrii'ah'aash led the legation to join with a cluster of Slaasriithi from the same subtaxon as his new attendants. Continuing onward, the ambassador began gesturing and explaining something about the grove of bush-trees which they were entering.

"Come on," urged Caine. "Let's not miss the tour."

Chapter Twenty-Two

As Caine worked his way to the head of the legation, Yiithrii'ah'aash continued on into a grove of immense, hypertrophied bushes which were simultaneously reminiscent of pointy mushrooms and very squat Christmas trees. "These are one of our most effective organisms for inducing xenobiots to become receptive to our own flora. And ultimately, to our settlers and other fauna."

Trent Howarth looked around, puzzled. "Isn't this planet already inhabited by Slaasriithi?" He glanced meaningfully at the ambassador's shorter, thicker assistants.

"What you see, Mr. Howarth, are pioneer inducers of change, not colonists. Their life work is to shape the environment by fostering symbiotic or cooperative relationships between the indigenous biota and our own. Where that is not possible, we will establish preserves of our own biota by crowding out the native ones. These plants excel at that task." Yiithrii'ah'aash gestured toward what Riordan was already thinking of as a cone tree. "By using their canopy to capture all the light and water that would normally find its way down to the ground, and by selectively sharing the resulting resources with our own—or receptive indigenous—biota, the trees claim the area beneath them for our exploitation. We introduce our own biota into it, and then work at inducing further mutations to maximize the harmony between the two families of bioforms."

Phil Friel's soft voice rose from the rear of the group. "You

195

keep using the word 'induce' when you speak about changing an organism. Since you seem to have a wide command of our language, I'm wondering if that repetition is not merely intentional, but important." Tina Melah glanced at the quiet Irishman with unveiled admiration. Of course, Tina didn't seem to bother with veils of any type.

Yiithrii'ah'aash purred. "Indeed, we use the word 'induce' quite purposefully. It describes how we prefer to transform biota: to provide the correct environmental circumstances and monitoring to encourage natural change in a desired direction. Creating change by using sudden force, whether by traumatic stimuli or mechanistic alteration, rarely produces stable environmental blending."

They left the grove of cone trees along a path that straddled an irregular border between day-glo green lichens struggling out from beneath the Slaasriithi plants on one side and a diffuse violet moss pierced by intermittent black spikes on the other side. Caine tried to recall an analog for the latter flora, but the only image that came to mind was of sea urchins trying to push up through a carpet of violet cotton candy. The ground between the two masses of plants was a tangle of runners from both, many of which were brown and lank: die-off where the two families of vegetation met, fought, and died.

Oleg Danysh squinted along their probable path, which remained in the shade of the brightside wall: the high terminal moraine that sheltered both the indigenous and exogenous biota from the steady red-gold light of GJ 1248. "It seems, Ambassador, that you mean to follow the contact margin between your own imported species, and those native to this planet."

"Very astute, Dr. Danysh. In addition to keeping us in the shade of the ridgeline, it allows us to visit where we are making our greatest progress to transform the native life. And so, it offers you the best opportunities to learn about us."

"Well, about your work as planet-changers, at least," Tina Melah drawled.

Yiithrii'ah'aash's head turned back in her direction; he did not slow his forward progress. "You may find, Ms. Melah, that the latter reveals the former more profoundly than any other behavior of ours. What we do here is no different from what we do everywhere."

"Even on your homeworld?" she wondered.

"Especially on our homeworld," Yiithrii'ah'aash emphasized. "We seek to reconcile and blend different species, taxae, individuals. It is the great challenge and conundrum of life, wherever it exists, that stability is only achieved by acknowledging the inevitability of change, and is only preserved by working with the forces of entropy to create a dynamic equilibrium in the natural order."

Gaspard aimed his chin toward the rose-tinted cream sky. "And if those endeavors reveal the nature of the Slaasriithi best, which behaviors would you say reveal humanity's nature most clearly to you?"

"We have not known you for that long." Yiithrii'ah'aash might have sounded evasive.

"True, but you have had reports on us from the Custodians while we were a protected species, and you have had access to a full compendium of our history and media for almost a year now. Surely you have some sense of which endeavors reveal the most about us."

"I do," Yiithrii'ah'aash admitted slowly. "Human nature, we find, is best revealed in endeavors characterized by uncertainty, innovation and crisis. So, we find depictions of your exploration, and of rescue operations, particularly informing."

Caine waited for the third category of activity and, when he did not hear it, asked outright. "And war?"

Yiithrii'ah'aash slowed slightly, swiveled his head back at Riordan. "Yes. Most especially, war."

They continued up the rough trail in silence.

As the legation descended into a shallow, bowl-like declivity, a number of indigenous creatures—akin to eyeless, arthropod-legged horned toads—leaped up from the native sward. Their coloration changed rapidly from an almost pixelated purple-magenta pattern that blended into the violet of the cotton-candy moss, to a cream gray. They hop-sprinted on their stick-pole legs to a pond fed by the small watercourse that burbled down from the rear lip of the hollow. Leaping into the pond, they remained in the shallows—and promptly disappeared, their cream coloration now blending with that of the sky-mirroring surface.

Hirano Mizuki lagged behind to observe the arthropod-toads. "How do they see where they are going? Sonar?"

Yiithrii'ah'aash's tendrils switched downward, stayed there. "No.

That creature's eyes, while individually rudimentary, are distributed across the trunk of its body. Our analysis of its ocular neurology suggests it has full three-hundred-sixty-by-three-hundred-sixty-degree vision: not as acute as yours, but highly sensitive to changes in its visual field. It is very difficult to surprise them. Which is no doubt why they evolved their visual arrangement. It is their only defense against most of the local predators. That and their numbers."

"Their numbers?" Nasr Eid echoed. "I do not understand."

"A predator can only concentrate on, and eliminate, one creature at a time, Mr. Eid. The ubiquity of this species is an integral part of its evolutionary survival adaptation: it can easily absorb casualties which sate its predators."

"Like rabbits," Phil Friel observed.

"Sure don't look like bunnies, though," Tina Melah said quietly, using her confidential tone as an apparent justification for leaning in toward him.

"There are predators?" Gaspard's assistant Dieter sounded more worried than curious.

"Most assuredly. Here at the contact zone between our exogenous biota and the planet's indigenous species, we have particular need for the protection of our biological markers. The prey species learn quickly enough that the predators and larger creatures are perturbed by the scents and fauna of our transplanted ecozones. So the local prey species tend to gather at the margins of our ecozone, and may even flee into it to disincline predators from sustaining pursuit. This, of course, induces the indigenous prey species to form positive associations with our ecozone."

Hirano Mizuki had not taken her eyes away from where the eye-gouging arthropod-toads remained motionless in the shallows. "It seems that you have done this many times before. Have you not, therefore, identified any of your own pheromones, or spores, which have the desired effect upon the local fauna?"

Yiithrii'ah'aash emitted a two-toned buzz-purr. "That is indeed a suitable question from an environmental planetologist. And yes, we have identified such species among our own flora. But unfortunately, the method whereby our plants transmit the desired compounds does not have acceptable latency in this environment."

"You mean, they die off?" asked Miles O'Garran.

"Eventually, but that is not the primary drawback. The difficulty is in how quickly our compounds are carried out of this sheltered spot of the bioband, which we call its valland. Obviously, during your descent, you encountered the winds that blow constantly from the bright face to the dark face of this world."

"Hardly noticed them," Karam grumbled. Qin Lijuan hid a smile behind a hastily raised hand.

"Those winds create downdrafts as they reach the rear, glacier-wall of the valland. The lowest air currents are cooled as they pass over bioband and sink. However, the speed of the wind also creates a following draft, and the combination of the two exerts mild suction upon the air of the valland, creating a faint updraft. This updraft picks up any light airborne materials, such as our spores and pollens, and carries most of them over the glacier into the dark side wastes."

Karam nodded. "Yeah, that kind of meteorology doesn't sound ideal for airborne seeds that developed on a world where they could spread around easily."

Yiithrii'ah'aash nodded. "There is a second challenge that is almost as great for seeds that evolved in an environment where they might, as you said, 'spread around easily.'" The Slaasriithi gestured to the panorama of the valland: distant white glacial walls toward the darkside, the tall, shadowing moraine beneath which they walked, and an irregular and light-dappled postglacial terrain that stretched and rolled between them. "This biome is as long as Adumbratus' equator. With the exception of some areas where the valland is disrupted by longitudinal, and thus transverse, mountain ranges, the vigorously biogenic part of this world averages less than one hundred kilometers in width. However, on most planets, plants evolve in an environment where there is global circulation of air and water; it is an ecosystem based upon *radial* patterns of expansion. Here, life exists within a narrow trench. Consequently, our species, which lack highly motile reproductory cells, are slow to spread, slow to take hold, slow to thrive. But even so, this world will thrive more profoundly because of them."

"How so?"

Yiithrii'ah'aash's fingers wriggled without specific direction. "Our flora is increasingly dominating this shaded lee of the terminal shielding moraine. This increases the amount of water retained in the valland, since our flora is more hydrophilic than the local plants. This has increased the density of indigenous fauna, particularly here along the margins of the two different biota. The creatures which thrive on water tend to be more prolific breeders when they are more lavishly hydrated, and so, improve their own biome. Ultimately, this new, positive survival trait for local species—the ability to tolerate the presence of ours—will dramatically enrich the entirety of this biosphere. That is in the nature of all biota: it changes its planet to become more suitable to its own procreative impulse."

Riordan smiled. "When you put it that way, your process of biosphere transformation sounds almost mystical."

"Does it? I wonder if something is simply being lost in translation. There is nothing mystic in this process. Life's mission is to expand itself, to bring existence to where there was nothingness. And so, life is the great conundrum of the universe: it is a lever which lifts itself up. Its presence in the organic molecules of deep space, and what you label their interstellar panspermiate diffusion, is evidence of just how pervasive and powerful that impulse is."

"So, one of the defining impulses of the physical universe is the creation of life?"

"It is, to use your own apt idiom, a force of nature." Yiith-rii'ah'aash ascended to the rim of the bowl, pointed down the opposite side. "Come; let us see this force at work."

The lip of the bowl opened on to a flat expanse where the native "forest"—stacks of vine-bound cream-teal tumbleweeds— were embroiled in a war of econiche flanking maneuvers against the cone trees and giant ferns of Slaasriithi origin. Arrayed just in front of that latter mass of Kelly- and lime-green vegetation, Slaasriithi were patiently watching some of their own fauna roll what looked like unripe grapefruits toward a waiting clutch of indigenous animals. The Slaasriithi creatures, which resembled a nutria-flying squirrel hybrid with far too many eyes, deposited the fruits in the midground between the two groups, then backed off a few steps and waited.

Their local counterparts—smooth, leather-backed creatures with six squat legs, four small eyes, and a head that resembled an armor-plated badger crossbred with a catfish—waited, watched, and began side-winding forward. Several emitted a crackling hiss as they approached. In response to those which hissed, the surprisingly swift Slaasriithi nutria-squirrels scuttled forward and grabbed their fruits back to safety. In the case of the local creatures that approached more placidly, the flap-legged nutrias edged forward slightly. In most cases, the local creatures retreated. In several cases, they tolerated the modest advance of the alien animals until they could grab the fruit and scramble away. When the more truculent catfish-badgers then tried to muscle in and get some of the water-rich fruits retrieved by their fellows, the Slaasriithi summoned an almost invisible drone, which made a quick pass between the contending local creatures. The drone was noiseless and did not visibly discharge any payload, but it must have released a marker spore which repulsed the less cooperative local creature: in each case, the would-be fruit hijacker scuttled away empty-handed.

Another group of Slaasriithi, a taxon subtly different in physiology, unobtrusively followed the more cooperative local creatures. When they began tearing into their fruit, the Slaasriithi released insects which quickly caught the familiar scent. They hovered over the backs of the greedily feeding indigenous creatures until they abandoned the stripped rind. Then the insects descended to scavenge the remains.

"Let me guess," Ben Hwang muttered, his arms folded. "By hovering over the local animals, these insects inadvertently 'marked' them. That allows you to follow the individuals which grabbed the fruit and to encourage their propagation."

Yiithrii'ah'aash seemed pleased. "You are an exceptionally quick study, Doctor Hwang. Your surmise is correct. The rest is, I trust, obvious."

Hirano Mizuki nodded. "The indigenous creatures which have tolerated greater proximity with your own species, being better fed and hydrated, now have better survival and breeding odds. In that way, you are increasing the prevalence of whatever combination of predisposition and learned behaviors made them more tolerant. Conversely, by ensuring that the aggressive ones cannot hijack the fruit, you reduce their breeding odds and, consequently, their ability to impart the unwanted traits to subsequent generations. Over time, you will provide the changed species with additional training opportunities and consequent survival and breeding advantages. And the final step will be to increase their toleration for your own fauna until they are comfortable mingling, and even sharing the fruit."

Dora Veriden was watching the flapped nutria-squirrels. "Must be handy to have those trained muskrats ready to work for you. How long does it take to bribe them into submission?"

Yiithrii'ah'aash turned, as did several of the legation, at the facetiousness of Dora's tone. "The species you refer to, Ms. Veriden, has several of our own traits, which we find not only useful but crucial. Specifically, Slaasriithi intelligence arose not so much from tool use, but from our reflex to establish relationships with other species, and thereby increase our social sophistication, specialization, and survival strategies."

The ambassador gestured back toward the nutria-squirrels. "We did not *train* these creatures to apply a crude version of operant conditioning upon these indigenous species. It is a reflex, coded into their genetic matrix. This is how they, and we, survive and ultimately thrive in new environments."

Ben Hwang nodded thoughtfully. "It sounds like a very gradual process, however."

"'Gradual' is an extremely subjective concept, Doctor." Yiithrii'ah'aash began leading them into rougher terrain that was centered around a drumlin in the lee of the terminal moraine. "Time cost is strongly influenced by how one perceives time itself. And that perception, in turn, is strongly influenced by one's concept of self and mortality."

Gaspard eagerly snapped at the discursive bait Yiithrii'ah'aash had left trailing in the wake of his last statement. "And how would you say Slaasriithi perception of self, and mortality, differs from human?"

Yiithrii'ah'aash purred low and long. "Our individualism and self-worth derive from the role we play in the polytaxic matrix that is our community. Conversely, in human cultures, community is the outgrowth of a consensus between individuals. Which is to say, the individual is the foundation of your society, not the community.

"And so, when you label our bioforming a 'gradual' process, I believe you are measuring it according to the life-costs *you* would associate such an enterprise: lost experiences, socialization, resources, additional accomplishments. It is, according to your species' natural scales of value, a 'bad deal.' However, for my species, one's role is innate to one's taxon, so our instincts and aptitudes lead inexorably to the tasks that are our sources of fulfillment."

Gaspard cleared his throat. "And which, er, taxae, are working here on Adumbratus?"

"My assistants are hortatorae. The trainers you saw are gerulorae. Only one other taxon is present, and very few of those: the novitorae. They are responsible for researching innovations in biota."

Caine, on Yiithrii'ah'aash's other side, asked quietly. "And what of you, Yiithrii'ah'aash? To what taxon do you belong?"

The ambassador swung his sensor cluster slowly toward Caine. "I belong to a taxon that is much, much less populous than the others. In your language, the closest approximation would be ratiocinatorae."

Caine smiled to himself: *And why am I not surprised?*

They made their way down into the rougher terrain.

Gaspard was gasping as the legation, now strung out, paused to regather in a wide, rocky wadi. "I must confess, I am astounded at what you have achieved in the modification of this planet. I admit enough envy to wonder if these are skills you might teach us?"

And so begins the prenegotiation process. Riordan hopped up on a rock, waved for the stragglers to catch up. Macmillan and Wu, now at the rear of the group, waved their acknowledgement. Collarcoms had very limited range on Adumbratus.

Yiithrii'ah'aash responded to Gaspard with a lazy roll of his fingers. "Our bioforming processes are not difficult if one does not proceed in haste."

Caine wondered if that caveat would remain audible over the cascade of imaginary gold ringing in CEOs' ears. With Slaasriithi methods, marginal planetary environments could be made shirtsleeve, and brown worlds could be made at least marginally green.

If those long-term prospects were not a sufficient hook with which to snag the attention of human avarice, Yiithrii'ah'aash's next offer was sure to irresistibly harpoon it. "A selective application of the processes you have seen here, and on board our ship, might also help you in other ways. For instance, what if your spacecraft were able to reduce their environmental resupply needs by ninety percent?"

Morgan Lymbery broke his long silence abruptly. "That would mean achieving a ninety-eight percent efficient bioloop compared to the eighty percent that is our current best."

"Yes," Yiithrii'ah'aash answered simply.

"You could do that?" It was no longer shortness of breath which made Gaspard sound like he was on the verge of panting.

Yiithrii'ah'aash's neck oscillated diffidently. "Your ships, being mechanical, have intrinsic efficiency limits. But they could be dramatically improved, with the right biota and symbiots."

"The right biota and symbiots"? Caine hopped down from his perch. *And what pheromones or spores might they start releasing, either on our ships or our new shirtsleeve worlds, to make sure that* we *don't hiss or growl when grabbing the next piece of fruit you offer to us? I just wonder if—*

"Caine, come in." Bannor's collarcom-distorted voice was sharp, no-nonsense. "We've got trouble."

Riordan saw a plume of dust at the midpoint of their slowly recompacting column. *Damn it*—He started sprinting in that direction. "Sitrep, Major."

"Something charged out from the shadows of the shield moraine. Didn't seem affected by the scent markers; went straight at its target."

"Which was?"

"Dora Veriden. And she's running like hell in your general direction."

Chapter Twenty-Three

BIOBAND'S VALLAND and IN ORBIT
GJ 1248 ONE ("ADUMBRATUS")

Caine started shouting instructions into his collarcom. "Tygg, did you hear Bannor's report?"

"Most of it. I think. Commo's scratchy."

"Stay close to the ambassadors. You and O'Garran set up a defensive perimeter with the others. If Yiithrii'ah'aash can do something about the situation, have him do it quickly. Without weapons, all we can do is throw sticks and shout. Doubt that's going to do very much."

"I'm on it."

Riordan changed the com channel. "Bannor, is Wu with you?"

"No, back with Macmillan."

Damn it. "So who's closest to Veriden?"

"Me and you. But I'm just topping the rise that she got chased off of. Karam took off after the critter that rushed her. More guts than brains, that guy. But he's dropping behind pretty quickly."

Caine swerved off the path they'd followed, headed out into the alien undergrowth. "Can you still see Veriden and the—the creature?"

"Yeah, but—"

"Then stay right where you are. You're the only one with eyes on both objectives. Can you see me yet? I'm coming around the northern spur of the drumlin."

"No, I—yes: you just came into sight."

"Good. I can't see Dora or the creature, so talk me into an intercept. And talk Veriden toward me."

205

"Yeah, but what the hell are you going to do?"

"Find a handy rock and hope to hell it doesn't want to tackle two of us. Talk Karam toward us also, and Howarth. Have Wu and Macmillan watch our backs for more critters. They might not hunt alone."

"I'm on it. For now, angle a little to your left. You've got about a minute of running ahead of you. Well, maybe more." The carrier wave snicked off.

Riordan heard yelling behind him, then multiple pages to his collarcom from random team members. He ignored it all. Bannor would either intervene and play switchboard or delegate it to Tygg, but either way, combat experience had taught Caine that when you are at the tip of the spear, you cannot see and coordinate the big picture. His only job was to keep closing, stay alert, and listen for updates.

Which came in fast enough. "Caine," Bannor shouted, "swerve into that gulch you're approaching on the right. I got Dora to duck in there. She'll be coming straight toward you. With company right behind."

"Roger that. Where's Karam?"

"Bringing up the rear. Probably wishing he'd spent a few more hours in the gym."

"You get a look at the thing chasing Dora?"

"Nope. Just saw its dust."

"Veriden tell you anything?"

"She's too busy sprinting, breathing, and cursing."

Can't say I blame her. "Any sign of other predators?"

"Nope. Yiithrii'ah'aash's signal is bad, but he made it clear that this creature is not a pack predator."

Well, some good news at last. "Send Macmillan and Wu after me once the rest of the legation has regrouped under Tygg's protection. And send out the ex-military EMT from Peking, Xue."

"You've got it—and you should have a visual any moment now."

"Maybe, but I've got a big boulder in my way. I'm going to have to go arou—"

Riordan dodged a blur that shot out from the blind side of the boulder: Dora Veriden. She detected Caine just before colliding with him: her sidestepping dodge morphed effortlessly into the karate move known as a back-stepping shuto, or knife-hand block. *Damn. Bodyguard, indeed.*

"Shit, Riordan: are you trying to kill me with a body block?"

"Hello yourself. Find a weapon. How far behind you is it?"

"We have three seconds. Fan out."

Which seemed the only thing to do. Caine spotted and scooped up a hand-sized stone the same moment he saw a new blur come around the boulder. He went into a sideways ready stance, stone cocked back—

And stared. The creature halted abruptly, might have been staring back. But Riordan couldn't tell because he could not discern any obvious eyes. Hell, nothing was obvious about this critter.

Clearly one of Adumbratus' indigenous species, it was a chitinous triped standing—crouching?—over two meters tall. Its smooth legs swept upward into curved, articulated joints. Its ovate thorax was topped by a tapering, swaying neck sheathed in reticulated plates. The head resembled a hyper-streamlined ball peen hammer, black specks chasing down either side of it like a dotted line. The underside of the hammer's head snapped up and down once; not a typical predator's jaws—no fangs or decisively sharp teeth—but the force of that surprised bite at empty air would have put a grizzly bear to shame.

The creature—a blend of dark cerulean and cyan with black-violet racing stripes—started toward Caine but then flinched toward Dora again. *Wait: did it feint at me before attacking her? Or was it jumping* away *from me? One way to find out—*

Riordan leapt into the space between the creature and Dora.

The blue tripod-nightmare drew up short, rattled ominously from someplace in the rear of its ball peen head, but finally jerked back. It swayed from side to side.

Caine swayed with it.

More annoyed rattling. It feinted as though it might try to slip through the gap between Riordan and the boulder, and thereby get to Dora, but Caine had the measure of the creature: its aversion to him precluded its use of that excessively narrow space. Anticipating its ploy, Caine jumped to the other side.

The tripod, leaping to exploit what it clearly hoped would be a widened hole in Caine's other flank, thrashed in midair, screeching like china plates in a woodchipper as it collapsed into an abortive tangle of limbs.

Veriden moved to stand just behind Caine. "*Coño,*" she muttered.

"Yeah," Riordan agreed. He took a step forward.

The blue and black monster, having just regained its tripedal footing, skittered backward. It quivered, as if at the end of an invisible leash. Caine had no knowledge of the fauna of GJ 1248, and damn little of any other planet besides Earth's, but the creature's intents were unmistakable. It desperately wanted to leap forward, to trample and gut Riordan. But a countervailing impulse was holding it back: not mere uncertainty or fear, but a shuddering aversion akin to a human resisting immersion in bleach.

From the direction of the trail and from beyond the boulder, distant cries were growing rapidly louder.

With a swiftness that Riordan had never seen in a quadruped—possibly because this creature's body didn't turn; its thorax simply rotated—the tripedal attacker skittered off, raising up a considerable cloud of dust.

Caine, duty suit sticking to his sweat-covered body, shouted into the collarcom, "Bannor, call off Karam. Make sure that thing's got an unobstructed route of retreat."

"Already done. And Jesus, is that monster fast. So much for 'no predators worth worrying about.' I'm really interested to hear how Yiithrii'ah'aash is going to explain *that* one."

"Yeah," Caine agreed. *And I'm going to be even more interested to learn why it avoided me like the plague—and hunted Veriden like she was dinner.*

Caine's hair was still damp from showering when his stateroom's privacy chime rang. "Computer: permit entry." Then, louder: "Come in."

Ben Hwang and Bannor Rulaine stepped through the opening hatchway. "Got a minute?" asked the major.

"Probably just about that. We haven't heard from Yiithrii'ah'aash since getting back to the ship, but he'll want to chat with us pretty soon."

Hwang nodded. "Undoubtedly. Gaspard is concerned that today's events could derail what he calls the 'relationship fundament of initial diplomatic overtures.'"

"Do you think Gaspard spoke that way before he attended the Sorbonne?"

Hwang sighed. "Bannor, I suspect he came out of the womb speaking that way. But he may be right. Yiithrii'ah'aash cut the tour a lot shorter than he intended and has been very reticent since."

Caine shrugged. "Yes, but I'm not sure that's indicative of disappointment or anger with us."

Ben folded his arms. "No? Why not?"

"Look, we don't know why that creature didn't avoid Veriden's scent marker, but the bottom line is that our visit to Yiithrii'ah'aash's 'safe' planet went to hell in a handbasket. It was like going to a new friend's house who tells you that his dog doesn't bite, and then looking down to find its jaws locked on your leg. So Yiithrii'ah'aash may be as embarrassed as he is upset."

"Yes, but Gaspard is still worried that Yiithrii'ah'aash will reassess whether the Slaasriithi should ally with us."

Which might be a blessing in disguise. But what Riordan said was: "That's a reasonable trepidation." He sat, looked at Bannor. "So, you were going to speak with Dora."

Bannor nodded. "I did."

"She didn't know why that thing might have attacked her?"

"We didn't get that far. She pulled rank and clammed up."

Hwang stared. "She pulled *rank*? How? She's part of our security detachment, right?"

Riordan shook his head. "Technically, she is Gaspard's personal security asset. She doesn't have to coordinate with, or report to, me at all. Unless she wants to. Or Gaspard instructs her to do so."

Bannor nodded. "Which was the line she took with me."

Hwang's stare had grown wider. "So we can't get her to answer questions about the incident until he, or she, says so?"

Bannor's nod seemed to trigger the privacy chime. Caine raised his voice. "Come in."

Dora Veriden entered, looking more sullen than usual. Caine stood, resisted the urge to comment on her extraordinary timing. "Hello, Ms. Veriden. How are you feeling?"

Her incongruously elfin features went from dour to vinegary. "You keep asking me that: why?"

"I only asked you one other time: right after the creature ran away. I'm checking that you're doing okay."

"Listen: when it was chasing me, I wasn't so okay. That's over. So now I'm okay. Is that so hard to understand?"

Riordan suppressed a sigh. "I understand that, Ms. Veriden. But I don't understand your attitude. You're part of the legation, and I'm concerned with your welfare, both professional and personal. That's all." He gestured toward a seat as he resumed his own.

Dora ignored the gesture. "Look, I don't need your personal concern. And professionally, the only person who has any reason, or right, to inquire after my status is my employer: Ambassador Gaspard."

Riordan shook his head. "That's not quite accurate, Ms. Veriden. He is certainly the only person who can give you security-related directives." *Which is a bad arrangement, but that's a different topic.* "However, as a member of this legation, your moment-to-moment personal safety is my responsibility. Whether you like it or not."

"Not," Dora answered. And finally took a seat.

Well, I've got to give her points for bluntness. "Ms. Veriden, while I'd have been glad for you to stop by on your own initiative, I doubt that's what brought you here."

Veriden nodded. "Yeah. Gaspard sent me."

Caine waited. He didn't want to make Dora any more uncomfortable than she had to be, but on the other hand, she tended to nip and snarl when others initiated conversation. Better to let her proceed in whatever manner she chose.

She looked Riordan in the eye. "That animal came at me because I didn't put on the biomarkers."

Bannor leaned forward sharply. *"What?"*

She leaned right back at him. "Are you deaf? I said I didn't put on the markers."

Bannor's posture did not change, but his color did; flushing, Rulaine's jaw muscles clenched as he struggled to suppress a presumably blistering reply—

"Ms. Veriden." Riordan kept his voice professional, but sharp. "I assure you, Major Rulaine's hearing is unimpaired. You may not be a part of my security team, but I will insist upon a modicum of respect when you interact with its members. Now: why didn't you apply the protective biomarkers?"

"I—I thought it would be best if one of us didn't."

Caine leaned back, considered. The tone of her voice suggested that the explanation wasn't a complete fabrication, but he could tell it wasn't the whole truth, either. But right now, he had a concrete explanation, and that was enough to start with. "Why did you think it prudent that one of the legation remain unmarked?"

She looked at Caine quizzically. "You really want to know?"

"If I didn't, I wouldn't ask."

She stared at him sidelong for a moment before replying. "Okay.

So, these Slaasriithi seem to have reversed the importance of machinery and biology. That makes me wonder: shouldn't we be as careful of their sprays and markers and gifts as they should be of accepting our bugged ID badges and presents? How would we know if they're marking us for their own purposes? And how can we be sure that they won't include biochemicals that can be used to influence or control *us*?"

Hwang was shaking his head, but Caine jumped in before he could start enumerating the many ways in which this was unlikely or impossible. "Ms. Veriden, I admire your attention to our more subtle security challenges. Be assured, the same thoughts have occurred to us."

She was surprised by that response but rallied rapidly and went on the offensive: "Yeah? Then why didn't you dump *your* container on the ground when no one was looking?"

Caine smiled. "Firstly, I was in the front rank. It's not as though I had the opportunity to do so surreptitiously. But the real reason is this: have you also considered that part of our legation's role is to function like a canary in a coal mine?"

Dora Veriden's mouth closed and then opened; she spent a moment waiting for a retort that never materialized. "No," she said flatly. "I'm not even sure what you mean." Hwang and Bannor looked equally flummoxed.

Riordan steepled his fingers. "Ms. Veriden, it seems you've spent most of your life on the sharp end, so this won't be news to you: any probe into a new area is somewhat like a recon mission. The main objective is to get in, look around, then return to report. But even if the mission is lost, even if it disappears without a trace, that's still valuable intel. It warns the people who sent the recon team that the region is not completely safe and that any further entry should be handled with caution. And if even a few survivors make it back? More valuable still: not only can you debrief them, but scan them for pathogens, nanites, any other contaminants or suspicious substances."

Riordan leaned forward. "We're a diplomatic mission, Ms. Veriden, but we're also performing that recon function. Part of our job is to take risks, to gather information, even if it means making ourselves vulnerable to possible ploys and bugs and viruses by which our hosts might influence us. Because when we get back home, we'll be quarantined and examined like few humans ever have been. Consequently, our apparently uncritical trust in the Slaasriithi is not a sign of incompetence. So, in the future, when our diplomatic host makes a request of the entire legation, you will do two things."

Dora's jaw set. "And those are?"

"You will inform me if you intend not to follow that request, and you will get express permission from Ambassador Gaspard before you refuse to do so, which he will relay to me. Because he is the head of our legation, and because you are his personal employee, you alone of all persons even have that right. But you will keep us in the loop." *Because you sure as hell didn't clear today's noncompliance with Gaspard first, or he'd never have ordered you to come talk to me like a truant child sent to the principal's office. Which he surely knows is worse than any other punitive action or reprimand he could impose on you.*

Veriden's teeth might have been clenched as she muttered, "Agreed." She rose to leave.

"Ms. Veriden, one other matter."

She turned back toward Riordan. "Yes?"

"I'd like to combine your professional efforts with those of my team, when and if the ambassador permits it and circumstances dispose you to be willing to do so. This legation will be strongest when all its security assets are pulling in the same direction."

Her expression was equal parts incredulous and amused. "Are you serious?"

"You might say I'm deadly serious, Ms. Veriden, since it is our shared responsibility to deal with matters of life and death. And frankly, I know high ability and intelligence when I see them."

She folded her arms. "You've probably figured out that I'm not much of a team player. And I don't like taking orders."

"I've noticed. I also observe that you *do* take orders even if you don't enjoy it, and that you have skills which make you a valuable addition to any team, even if you are mostly working on your own."

Veriden opened the door, paused on the threshold. Her mumbled response sounded more like a confession. "I'll think about it."

Once the door closed behind her, Bannor shook his head. "Caine, you're the boss—but her? Really?"

"She's difficult, yes. But she's damned good." Bannor rubbed his chin briskly. Caine had learned what that gesture meant: the ex-Green Beanie didn't want to be insubordinate, but there was some issue he really wanted to raise. "You're worried about something besides her sunny disposition?"

"Yeah," Rulaine admitted. "Gaspard's assistant Dieter got nervous and talkative after today's mishap with the local wildlife. Seems this isn't the first time that Ms. Veriden went off cowboying on her own and became an embarrassment to her employer."

"So she's ruined operations that got in the way of her own special brand of problem-solving?"

"Oh, that too, but I was thinking more about her political, er, forthrightness."

Caine nodded. "Go on."

"One of the reasons she never finished college or even a certificate program was because she always took the administration to task and made herself persona non grata in record time. Maintained a few vlogs—some directly, some via aliases—that are about as inflammatory as you can get before becoming a 'person of interest' to security agencies."

"Whose security agencies, specifically?"

"Take your pick. She's pretty much an equal-opportunity anarchist."

Hwang's eyebrows went high. "She's a genuine anarchist?"

Rulaine waved a dismissive hand. "A figure of speech, but apt. Can't find a single bloc or nation that she trusts or even considers acceptable. All her sympathies are with resistance movements, underground organizations, and what activists dub 'post-national collectives.' And you know what that means."

Hwang looked from Bannor to Caine and back to Bannor. "Well, *I* don't know what that means. So please add a caption."

Rulaine shrugged. "The megacorporations have a long history of mining antigovernment organizations for support. They throw a lot of money at them: sometimes directly, sometimes through plausibly deniable proxies."

Hwang screwed up his face. "And do these groups really join forces with the megacorporations? They're far more autocratic than nation-states."

Caine shook his head. "It's not a direct alliance. But the megas aren't really looking for cocombatants against 'the tyranny of nations.' They're just funding grassroots resistance to national authority." He turned back toward Bannor. "But do you really think Dora's been a megacorporation's *agent provocateur*?"

Rulaine shrugged. "No way to know. Dieter tells me that Gaspard has complained to DGSE that even her classified dossier is threadbare. Lots of gaps in her timeline. Lots of arrows pointing to sealed case files and intelligence summaries."

Ben Hwang's palmcomp buzzed. He glanced at it, rolled his eyes. "The Great Man has summoned the two of us. He wants that classified summary he put off."

"And he wants it right now, I'll bet."

"No. He wants it an hour ago. When should I tell him we'll be there?"

"An hour ago," Caine sighed. "Let's go."

Chapter Twenty-Four

Karam Tsaami, his head half into the avionics interface bay on the bridge of the TOCIO shuttle, nearly knocked off the top of his skull when a female voice murmured, "Hey," not half a meter behind him. The resulting occipital thwack literally made his vision swim—and made his uninvited visitor chuckle.

Determined to show just how little enthusiasm he had for being a source of slapstick humor, Karam yanked his torso out of the bay, ready to tear the head off whatever damn fool had—

He discovered Dora Veriden watching him with a sardonic smile. "You always that graceful?"

"No," Karam grumbled, rubbing the back of his head and unsuccessfully trying to remember what choice cascade of insults he had been preparing to unleash. "Sometimes I'm *really* clumsy."

Veriden grinned, flopped down into the copilot's couch, avoiding the various screens and protuberances of the half glass/half "steam" cockpit. And Tsaami realized, *she knows her way around flight controls.*

"Yeah," she agreed, "you are clumsy. And sometimes you're really stupid, too."

Karam stared at her. "You're welcome."

"Huh?" she replied.

"Well, I figure that tracking me down on the shuttle so you can insult me is your own special way of saying thanks for my chasing after the monster that was trying to eat you earlier today."

He had intended his tone to indicate that his comment was as ironic as hers. But Dora's considerable brows met in a descending vee. "Didn't ask for your help, and didn't want it. Which is part of why I'm here: you were damned stupid chasing after that thing. It could've eviscerated you."

"Yeah, well, it seemed like you could use a hand. Or at least a diversion. So I—"

"That's exactly what I'm talking about: that was really stupid. If I need your help, I'll ask for it. But your macho button got pressed and out you charged, making just that much more trouble for *me*. Because then I had your safety to worry about, too."

"Hey, I was safe enough. You were its only target, and I've heard through the grapevine why that was. But secondly, I didn't charge out there because of machismo," he asserted half-truthfully. "I've been shuttling people back and forth to new planets and new colonies for ten years now. When they run into trouble, I go help. It's that simple. It's reflex: not duty, not machismo. Get it?" Karam almost believed the whole spiel himself. *Damn, I'm good.*

Dora Veriden frowned. "Okay, fair enough. Because you'd have been pretty disappointed if you were motivated by hopeful chivalry."

"You mean because of the peculiar way you show gratitude?"

"No: I mean because I don't usually walk on your side of the sexual street."

Karam felt his eyebrows come down, then jump up. "Oh." He shrugged: not like that was a big deal, or would have influenced his actions one bit.

"Oh," he repeated and felt like an idiot. They sat in the pilot and copilot couches in silence for almost half a minute. It felt like half an hour.

"Look," Dora started as suddenly as their semi-conversation had stopped, "I came here to explain something to you. And only to you."

"Are you asking me to keep it a secret?"

She thought for a moment. "No. I just don't feel I owe anyone else the real explanation for why I didn't put on the marker spray."

Karam cocked his head. "Really? Not Cai—Captain Riordan? Hell, he got in the critter's way."

Dora had made a face. "First, that was his job, right? And second, I'm not in the habit of thanking the people who've made a career out of using me."

"Whoa, whoa: Riordan has made a career out of *using* you?"

Dora rolled her eyes. "Hey, figurative language alert. Not him, personally, no, but people like him." When she saw the unrelieved perplexity in Karam's face she threw up her hands. "Government types. Our Illustrious Leaders. Protectors of the Social Contract."

Karam found he really didn't want to argue with Dora—which was odd because he had a natural gift for contrarianism—so he frowned and shook his head. "I think you may want to revisit your assumptions about Caine."

"You mean, *Captain* Caine Riordan? The guy who was sent by *governments* to find exosapients on Delta Pavonis Three? Who then made his report at the *interbloc* Parthenon Dialogs? Who was then appointed as the primary liaison for the *international* delegation to the Convocation of the Accord, and who then fought in the war we just finished? You mean *that* dedicated antigovernment figure?"

Karam kept his voice level. "Seems you've filled your own pockets with more than a few kings' coins, over time." Seeing Dora's dark olive-toned skin darkening even further, he hastened to add, "All I'm saying is that what people do isn't always a reliable indicator of their sympathies, of why they did those things."

"Are you saying that Riordan is antigovernment? He sure doesn't seem like it to me. His current uniform and titles fit him like a glove."

Karam shrugged. "Yeah, but Caine hasn't been very popular in the halls of government, either."

"No? He charge too much?"

"No: he has a bad habit of telling the truth. Including the truths that governments don't like hearing."

Dora slouched back, arms crossed, but she didn't follow up with a new gibe.

Karam leaned back as well. "We got to know each other pretty well on the way out here. All the other guys knew him from before."

"Yeah; all servitors of the state."

"Yeah, servitors of states which protected Caine, but weren't always comfortable with him or what he might do. Of which those protectors were apprised."

Dora nodded faintly. "So they were really his warders."

Karam tilted his head from side to side, not disagreeing, but not wholly agreeing either. "It's more nuanced than that."

"Oh, it always is. Naked oppression is never naked oppression. Except when it is. But then the victims deserve it."

Karam couldn't keep himself from rolling his eyes. "Look, I'm sure you've got a boatload of witty barbs and comebacks for every occasion and this one in particular. But the bottom line is this: from what I can tell, Caine has considerable reservations about how much anyone can trust government. But he usually takes the side of government against any of the megacorporations which are trying to become more powerful than nations because he doesn't trust those at all. And given how CoDevCo tried selling our whole species into Ktoran slavery just a year ago, I can't say that he was too far off."

Dora frowned, looked out the cockpit windows; the shields were mostly closed, so only a narrow slit of starfield was visible. When she spoke again, her voice wasn't as hard, had a musical flow rather than a staccato edge. "I grew up in Trinidad, mostly. My grandmama was one of the refugees during the Megadeath famines. She was tough as nails. Had my Mom even before she married my grandad, who died during one of the anti-refugee riots of the Fifties. So grandad's mother took in my grandma and helped raise my infant mother, whose health was never good. Might have been one of the immune viruses that came along with the refugees. Might have been years of malnutrition before the richer countries decided to help the ones they abandoned during the Megadeath.

"Anyhow, I remember when the big countries started coming back. And when they did—even before they brought food, even before they started reopening our hospitals—they sent 'health workers.' And do you know what those health workers did first?"

Karam, who had grown up in Toronto and hadn't the faintest idea of the conditions which had been prevalent in poorer countries after the Megadeath, shook his head.

Dora grimaced, and if her expression usually fluctuated between sardonic and angry, it now slid toward bitter and sad. "The health workers—*health* workers—from the big countries came in and dusted us with poisons. Poisons to kill lice, poisons to kill bed bugs, poisons to kill chiggers. And then our own governments dusted us with poisons to kill fungi, because they knew that any new clothes we received we'd try to save for good. We'd hide them away in a closet, where they would get filthy with mold in a month."

She scratched her shoulder-length hair distractedly. "Dusted, dusted, dusted. You could always smell it; you could always feel it. The health workers claimed that, in order to be effective, it had to be everywhere. And it was. Everywhere. I had only two sets of clothes: torn pants and an old shirt for work and a faded, fraying dress for 'good.' And it didn't matter how much you washed them; the dust was always on them, in the seams, inside the fabric. It got inside of us, too, I guess. Sure got inside of my mom. Killed her."

Karam hadn't intended it, but his voice came out as a whisper. "Your mom died of poisoning?"

"I'm pretty sure that's what caused her leukemia, or myeloma, or whatever cancer killed her." Dora's voice grew distant, distracted. "There was a big surge in toxin-related cancers at that time. But after the famine and epidemic death-counts of the Megadeath, no one much worried about what might kill you ten years later. Everyone was still worried about staying alive for the next week, the next month." Her eyes and voice resharpened. "Until, of course, our old colonial masters returned in the guise of megacorporations who employed us for pennies on the dollar to work in conditions that wouldn't have passed the health codes of any developed nation."

"I'm sorry," mumbled Karam.

If Dora heard, she didn't give any sign of it. "So I don't like getting dusted or sprayed with anything. Not then, not now, not ever." She turned to him. "It wasn't your job to help me. And you don't know me from Eve. But you seem like a decent enough guy. So I wanted you to know why today's attack occurred. It was on me, and only on me. I endangered myself, and that was my business. Maybe I endangered others, too, which wasn't my business, but that only makes it all the more stupid that you were trying to help *me*. Of anyone out there on that alien grassland today, I was the person *no one* should have been helping."

"But you were the one who needed the help."

"Damn, Karam, you are one thick-skulled moron, aren't you?"

"I like you, too."

She rolled her eyes. "Look, didn't your mother or someone tell you to stay away from trouble? Well, I'm that trouble."

"Yeah, well, I didn't much listen to Mom."

"Well, this time you probably should. I'm not safe to get too close to. Hell, that's why they named me Dora."

"Um...Dora isn't exactly a name that says, 'danger! danger!'"

She shook her head. "You wouldn't think so, would you? Hell, even I didn't get it until I was older. Growing up, I just thought I was named after Dora the Explorer."

"Named after *who*?"

Dora smiled ruefully. "Dora the Explorer. It was an old, old video show for kids. But we still had it because—well, because my grandmama hoarded crap. We had six different computers stashed away, and we used them up, starting with the oldest first. But damn, grandmama was one shrewd lady: she could patch together kluges of software that should never have worked, and videos, and songs, and, well, you get the picture. So there was this show, *Dora the Explorer*. She was this girl adventurer who looked a little like me, and was Latina like me—kind of. I watched it a lot. I knew my mom had, too, so I thought she had named me after Dora.

"But my mom died when I was only five, so I never thought to ask her. I just assumed it, and I kept assuming it until my grandmama was dying and called me by my real name, the name my mom had actually given me: Pandora. The mystery box that should not be opened." She rose from the couch. "So you might want to think about who you go saving, or trying to become friends with."

Karam shrugged. "If I had to do it again, I would. Because it doesn't matter who you are, or who you aren't." *Well, mostly.*

Dora threw up her hands. "I just can't beat the stupid out of you, can I?"

"Not now, you can't," Karam muttered as a message scrolled across his comms monitor. "Yiithrii'ah'aash is about to arrive."

Chapter Twenty-Five

As Caine entered Gaspard's otherwise empty quarters, he ignored the chair toward which the Frenchman waved an inviting hand. "Ambassador, we just heard that Yiithrii'ah'aash is on his way."

Gaspard nodded. "I have been alerted, as well."

"Then we need to settle something before we get down to what will probably be the swiftest, and most insufficient, strategic briefing in the annals of diplomacy. I need to know that, as we go forward, you can either ensure Ms. Veriden's compliance with the protocols you yourself have approved, or that you put her under my direct command for the duration of this mission. I can't do my job, otherwise."

Riordan had expected an argument, possibly a brief tantrum. Instead, Gaspard simply nodded. "You have my apologies, Captain Riordan, and my thanks for salvaging today's unfortunate situation on the planet. You and the entire legation were placed at risk. As was its chance of success. I have spoken with Ms. Veriden and she will follow the protocols I set for her, or she will spend the remainder of this mission confined to her quarters."

Caine managed not to reveal his surprise at Gaspard's frank and eminently sane response. "Thank you, Ambassador." He took the indicated seat. "Actually, what concerns me most is that she didn't inform us of her intent to avoid the Slaasriithi markers, and then did not alert us to that fact immediately afterward."

Gaspard held helpless hands aloft. "I am often at a loss to explain her behavior. She is an intrinsically suspicious and cautious

221

person, and so, she does not say much. Which I usually find quite agreeable in a guard."

"But not so much, today?" Hwang added with a rueful smile.

Gaspard returned the expression. "It is as you say, Doctor. Today, I could have wished for her to be more communicative, more informative. Which is a natural segue to the business before us: in the matter of the experts' xenosociological projections about the Slaasriithi, did they advance any theories about—?" The privacy chime sounded. Gaspard sighed. "Reality has preempted theorizing, it seems." He rose. "Please enter."

Yiithrii'ah'aash entered the room. He did so slowly, almost cautiously.

He stopped when Ben Hwang rose. "I mean no offense, Dr. Hwang, but you do not have sufficient clearance to remain for this particular meeting. My sincere regrets."

Gaspard's chin came up slightly. "Captain Riordan does not have my diplomatic rating, either, yet you are evidently prepared to allow him to stay."

"Ambassador, Captain Riordan may remain because his standing with *us* is commensurate with the clearance assigned to you by your government."

"In what way?"

"Allow me to ask you a question, Ambassador Gaspard. From what authority does your position as ambassador-plenipotentiary derive?"

"The political will of the Consolidated Terran Republic. Through that authority, I am empowered to make decisions for my species."

"Yes. And Captain Riordan has an oft-demonstrated gift for *understanding* other species. This makes him a necessary part of our communication and so my race extends him recognition and standing equal to your own. We are pleased to have him remain, just as we were pleased to request him for our first contact in the Sigma Draconis system."

Ben nodded and started toward the door. "If you'll excuse me."

Yiithrii'ah'aash made one deep, slow neck-bob and held it until Hwang had left. "I would very much regret if the doctor was affronted by my insistence upon protocols."

"I doubt he was," Gaspard commented diffidently, gesturing for the ambassador to sit. Which he did, although that posture more resembled a well-supported squat.

Yiithrii'ah'aash swiveled his head to focus directly upon Gaspard. "Ambassador, I must regrettably begin our meeting by insisting that you take whatever steps are necessary to exert greater control over your personnel."

Caine interrupted. "I take full responsibility for Ms. Veriden's actions—"

Yiithrii'ah'aash raised an objecting pair of finger-tendrils. "It has already been established that Ms. Veriden is not your responsibility. The matter lies with Ambassador Gaspard. It is his personal security assistant who has, within the space of one day, twice violated our requirements."

Gaspard nodded noncommittally. "Yes, although I suspect the second incident might not have occurred had I been given time to confer with her regarding the full significance of her first violation. But our immediate departure after Captain Riordan recovered from the anti-intruder gas precluded that discussion. Similarly, with more time and warning, we could have better coordinated our visit to Adumbratus, or least selected the right persons for inclusion."

Yiithrii'ah'aash's tendrils drooped. "While your analysis is no doubt accurate, it ignores our initial stipulation: that every member of your legation must visit these introductory planets. This prepares you to move about freely upon our homeworld, to help you understand and distinguish between the various taxae of my species and how best to interact with them."

Riordan folded his arms. "While we're on the topic of interacting with the locals, I noticed that the creature which pursued Ms. Veriden had a marked aversion to me. What did you do to ensure that my biomarkers were so much more effective than the others'?"

Yiithrii'ah'aash waved languorous tendrils. "Your preparation was no different from the others."

Caine heard the evasive tone. "But that's not the same thing as saying you don't know why the creature had a stronger reaction to me." He waited.

After several seconds, Yiithrii'ah'aash buzz-purred. "No, it is not the same statement. But I only possess conjectures on this matter, not knowledge. And there is no way to conclusively test my hypotheses."

Gaspard leaned his fine-boned chin into his long-fingered hand. "Even so, I am most interested in your speculations."

Yiithrii'ah'aash tilted his sensor-cluster in Caine's direction. "This is not Captain Riordan's first contact with our biota."

Caine was stunned that he had not thought of this before. "Of course. The natives on Delta Pavonis Three. They probably still mark fauna, and visitors, with pheromones."

Yiithrii'ah'aash raised attention-commanding digits from either pseudo-hand. "Since the primitives there have not entirely reverted, and since interspeciate pheromone-marking predates our tool-use, I suspect that you were multiply and powerfully marked on Delta Pavonis Three. But after at least twenty millennia of genetic recidivism and drift, that planet's primitives may have marked you with pheromones that we no longer recognize."

"But how would *any* pheromones remain active so long?" Gaspard wondered, frowning. "The captain visited Delta Pavonis Three over two years ago. Since then, he has twice been purged in preparation for extended periods of cryogenic suspension. How could a marking persist through all that?"

Yiithrii'ah'aash's fingers writhed in apparent uncertainty. "I cannot say. However, markings have different depths. Most are superficial and can be removed by several meticulous bathings. However, some are not merely external but internal. They introduce microorganisms that produce the needed pheromones for excretion through fluids, perspiration, even wastes. Such markings could persist for years. Perhaps decades. Perhaps longer."

Caine nodded, forced himself to sit calmly as his mind shouted: *And our best decontamination procedures and most advanced biological screening didn't detect anything? So how the hell do we know what they might choose to put in us now, and which we might be carrying back to the fleet? And then Earth? How do we know these microbes only mark us? And how can we be sure they won't replicate and spread? Yes, the Slaasriithi have been amicable and helped us against the Arat Kur, but how do we* really *know they can be trusted? Because they told us so themselves?* At the end of Yiithrii'ah'aash's explanation, Riordan nodded one last time. "That's very interesting. Thank you for explaining."

Yiithrii'ah'aash's neck seemed to collapse, even retract slightly into his torso. "It is we who must thank you for your patience. We not only regret the haste with which this mission was conceived and launched, but we deeply appreciate your willingness to adapt to our means of communication."

Riordan shook his head. "I do not understand. Your English is flawless, Ambassador Yiithrii'ah'aash."

"I do not refer to language. I refer to our insistence that you 'see' us rather than 'read about' us."

Gaspard's smile was gracious, if brittle. "It has been challenging, yes."

"More than challenging, Ambassador Gaspard. It has been the source of Ms. Veriden's infractions and the cause of Mr. Buckley's death. And I am sure it has thwarted your efforts to plan for our negotiations, since your species invariably strategizes how to gain objects you strongly value in exchange for objects you value less."

Hearing it broken down that way, the legation's sober diplomatic intents suddenly sounded like well-heeled con artistry.

Gaspard cleared his throat. "These are concerns to us, yes. Are they not also to you?"

Yiithrii'ah'aash's tendrils seemed to spin for a moment: intense frustration? "Not as you mean it. We too hope to create bonds through exchange. We too hope that these exchanges are materially beneficial to us. And, like you, we will not disclose all our future plans or certain details of our deep history. But our concepts of 'negotiation' and 'gain' are qualitatively different, and the number of secrets we keep is very, very small."

Caine experienced both a surge of shame and a stab of wariness. If Yiithrii'ah'aash's depiction of Slaasriithi negotiations and exchange was even partially accurate, it made humanity look like a bunch of grifters and frauds, by comparison. On the other hand, although the Slaasriithi kept few secrets, they did, by Yiithrii'ah'aash's admission, keep *some* secrets. Which suggested, by inverse deduction, that those secrets would be very important. Perhaps important, and problematic, enough to necessitate reappraising an alliance with the Slaasriithi.

"We find similar distinctions between ourselves and almost every other species," Yiithrii'ah'aash hastened to add. "Less so with the Dornaani, but even they record material exchanges the way you do, as well as the passage of events."

Gaspard frowned. "So your recording of history is fundamentally different from ours?"

Yiithrii'ah'aash bobbed. "What you call 'history' is not a useful concept to us. We notice with interest the linguistic fluke latent in the term you use for narratives of your past: 'his-story.' At every level, the focus of your chronicles is upon egocentric personalities: who did what, which group of combatants won and gained specific resources, and how contending philosophies of different peoples sparked both intercultural debates and religious wars." His neck contracted sharply. "We lack internecine analogs for these events; they only arise when we deal with other races."

Gaspard raised his hands in appeal. "But in order to deal with the other races of the Accord, you must have kept records of your negotiations, what transpired when you sent or received diplomatic and trade delegations."

"We welcome such contact, Ambassador Gaspard, but we have experienced much less of it than you might suppose. Only the Dornaani ever displayed much interest in our society. And if you are using 'trade' as a synonym for commerce, you must understand that this is not our way."

Gaspard was silent for a long moment before responding. "I would like to understand what you mean. But I do not."

"To us, 'trade' means exactly that: an exchange. Among ourselves, we do not buy and sell but rather—what is your word for it?—ah yes; we 'swap' things. We do not 'manufacture' for 'markets,' or maintain competing accounts of personal assets, or track what you call 'balance of trade.' There are many reasons for this. Arguably, the most prominent is the absence of your universal tradition of attaching the possession of material goods to narrow genetic lineages."

Caine felt, rather than saw, the consequences. "So, you have no social unit akin to our nuclear family?"

"Correct. Biologically, our reproductive process is considerably different from yours, as is the manner in which we raise our young. It follows, then, that our species' individual affiliations and social patterns are equally distinct. For example, because of the innate differences between our taxae, there are no 'class struggles.' Our individuals are born to their tasks, and evolved to find them more gratifying than any others."

Good grief; their evolution has made them the ultimate communists. "I can see that there might be no basis for commerce among your own people, but is there no way for our respective societies to accommodate each other in the matter of material exchanges? If only to facilitate cultural and political connections?"

Yiithrii'ah'aash emitted a slow clicking noise from his tightly furred thorax. "I am certain we may find ways to do so, but I suspect we will seek very different ends from those exchanges. It is in the nature of your species to use commerce as a means of consolidating power. It is in our nature to see exchange as an opportunity to create further harmonies and interdependencies among all biota, in the interest of establishing a peaceful and stable macroecology."

Gaspard seemed to be grasping for words. "And what sort of—of trade item would be of interest to you, in that context?"

Yiithrii'ah'aash's answer rode over the top of his eager buzz. "We have read much about your honey bees, particularly the variety you label the 'bumble-bee.' We do not know if we would find their sugar-intensive byproduct palatable, but there are other species that surely would. Logically, it would be a powerful 'reward object' with which to accelerate behavioral modification in those species. Another byproduct—the pure wax they generate in constructing their shelters—would be useful in various material processes. Lastly, the bee's selfless communal defense instincts interest those of us who are tasked with refining the security response templates for our various autonomous drones and missiles."

Caine's train of thought staggered to a halt, spun about, began inexpertly down a path he had never considered before. "Are you saying that your computers are partly biological?"

"Yes, although some would be more accurately described as partly mechanical. Those systems, which we call OverWatchlings, are rare but also more crucial to us."

Riordan was careful not to look at Gaspard. Who, he sensed, was pointedly not looking at him. No matter how friendly the Slaasriithi seemed, it would be imprudent to give any outward sign of how pivotal Yiithrii'ah'aash's last revelation was, and how decisively it might figure in any future negotiations or possible alliance. Caine shifted the topic slightly. "How extensive are your defense needs?"

"Until now, fairly minimal, but we project that the recent hostilities are merely precursors of more to follow. The war resolved very little. The Arat Kur have been temporarily neutralized. The Hkh'Rkh have been contained, but will not remain so for long. The Ktor are stalemated. The Dornaani were not sufficiently alarmed to pay closer heed to the warnings of the Custodians. Your own species has already begun to capitalize upon the technological insights derived from your attackers' equipment, and is entering its characteristic postcrisis phase: spatial expansion combined with political consolidation. This postwar environment is inherently unstable; there will be further conflicts. We must prepare."

Yiithrii'ah'aash's summary was breathtaking in its ruthless and egoless accuracy. "So how large a defense increase will you require? How extensively have you settled this region of space?"

The Slaasriithi's tendrils waved languidly. "Where life has arisen, there we have remained. And we have had a long time, even by our standards, to nurture biota on even the most inhospitable worlds."

So, pretty extensive settlement. "I take it, then, that you are well-furnished with shift-carriers, to serve so many systems."

"Not so well-furnished as you might expect, Caine Riordan. The great majority of our expansion has been effected by slower-than-light ships, many of which are directed by semiautonomous machine biots."

Gaspard's question was slow, calm, careful. "You have living, self-directed ships?"

"That characterization would imply a greater degree of awareness than is possessed by these craft. Each ship's semiautonomous system resembles a highly advanced hive-mind. Its task is simply to deliver its payload from one known place to another known place."

"I understand," Gaspard replied in a tone that suggested he might not. "But why do you not prefer to use a crew of intelligent beings? We have seen at least one subtaxon which you specially evol—er, induced, to meet the challenges of working in space. Why not create an even more narrowly specialized subtaxon to live upon your STL ships?"

"Because we eschew generating more subtaxae than is absolutely necessary. The capability to induce a new subspecies or subtaxae does not mean that one should do so whenever it would be most convenient. So, instead of complicating our polytaxic society with yet another subtaxon, we attain our objectives by relying upon the universe's most underappreciated and yet greatest force."

Gaspard leaned forward. "And what force might that be?"

Yiithrii'ah'aash purred faintly. "Time, Ambassador. As your own aphorism has it, time changes all things. It wears down mountains, moves continents, even exhausts stars. Perhaps this is one of the reasons we do not record history similarly to other species: our relationship to time itself is different. Your species and the others manipulate time to your own ends, your own pleasure, and even to assure that you will, for at least a while, transcend its limits."

"You mean, that we perform deeds or create objects that will be associated with us, even after we are dead."

"Precisely. We do not have these motivations. Indeed, understanding what they truly mean to you remains our greatest interspeciate challenge, since we lack any serviceable analog. We imagine them as a hypertrophied amplification of our self-preservation instinct. But even our self-preservation instinct, while strong, is not so overpowering as your own."

"Do you mean that you don't fear death?"

Yiithrii'ah'aash purred again. "That question is the one we hoped you humans would ask. It is worth all the mishaps this mission has stumbled through thus far, if it has prompted you to ask it so soon."

Gaspard's eyes were wide. "So you do *not* fear death?"

Yiithrii'ah'aash's purr diminished. "I did not say that. But our attitude towards it is so different from yours that you cannot understand us without understanding that difference. We are not defined—even in our diplomatic exchanges—by the number of ships, or planets, or weapons that are at our disposal. We are defined by our macroecological impulse. And no force shapes that impulse more than patience and its corollary: an egoless conceptualization of time. Which, in turn, also shapes our perception of death."

Caine smiled. "I suspect this is only the first of many conversations we shall have on this topic."

Yiithrii'ah'aash's purr grew along with Caine's smile. "Understanding another race is not something that happens swiftly. But for your species to identify, and to question, this signal difference between us is the beginning of the process of knowing."

Gaspard rested his chin in his palm. "So this is why your primer mentions no historical figures, cites no earlier Slaasriithi by name."

"Correct."

Caine frowned. "But if you have no history of conflict, and

your leaders must now deal with it, what models do they have for emulation?"

Yiithrii'ah'aash's head turned slowly back in Caine's direction. "This is a matter of deep concern to us. As you have no doubt discerned, we are happy to appease, just as we are willing to be appeased, when disagreements arise. To do so, to compromise, is our preferred method of interaction where harmony has not yet been established. However, we lack a taxon which is inherently capable of conflict, what you might call a warrior caste. If members of such a taxon had existed any time in the last ten millennia, they would have encountered no challenges, no need for their skills. Indeed, they would have been counterproductive to our harmony. According to apocryphal tales of the last such taxon, they devolved into hermits, whose once valuable decisiveness ultimately became disruptive impulsivity."

Caine tried to tame his leaping speculations to follow only the most pertinent track. "You had other taxae, at one time?"

Yiithrii'ah'aash's head bobbed. "We have had many for which our need diminished, and ultimately disappeared. But in some cases, that disappearance need not be permanent."

"You mean you can reverse the process?"

"It is not a simple matter, genetically or socially, to reintroduce a taxon. Sometimes it is impossible if it was lost too long ago or too completely. Our polytaxic structure has many strengths but its complexities can make it especially vulnerable to disasters. If either our social or reproductory matrices are shattered, we are likely to revert, to become a different and devolved species."

"Like on Delta Pavonis Three," Caine murmured.

"Just so. As I once said, the natives of that planet are *of* us, but are not *us*, not today's Slaasriithi. They are a genetic throwback to when we had fewer taxae. Consequently, you have already seen a Slaasriithi community that has been shattered. Today you saw one in its infancy, facing an uncertain future: we cannot know if the changes we mean to induce on Adumbratus will become strong enough to create an equilibrium between our biota and the indigenous life. Finally, in a little more than a week, we will show you a Slaasriithi community on the cusp of becoming one of our primary colonies." Yiithrii'ah'aash stood. "Speaking of which, refueling will soon be complete, and we will begin preacceleration for our next shift. The members of your legation will be permitted to have free access to your ships and your cargo until then. Prepare for a longer sojourn: we shall examine the next planet more closely, as there is much more to see."

Gaspard smiled. "And fewer untamed dangers to encounter?"

Yiithrii'ah'aash's voice was grave. "We find that an environment's dangers do not reside in any of its creatures."

"No? Then where does the danger reside?"

"In the mind of any visitor who makes the mistake of believing that any environment is ever without danger. Good day, Ambassador, and you as well, Caine Riordan. Please prepare your people for departure."

Chapter Twenty-Six

CLOSE ORBIT, GJ 1248 THREE
and FAR ORBIT, SIGMA DRACONIS TWO

"Nezdeh," Sehtrek called over his shoulder, "the Slaasriithi ship is breaking from orbit. At full acceleration."

Nezdeh Srina Perekmeres had not yet crossed from the *Arbitrage*'s bridge hatchway to the con. "Did they detect us?" Refueling out at GJ 1248's gas giant, she and *Red Lurker* had been shielded from the Slaasriithi shift-carrier's active sensors. Also, there was no sign that the outer planets had been seeded with passive trespass monitors. Nonetheless...

"No indication of detection, Nezdeh. But the target has acted with considerable dispatch ever since the two interface craft returned from the surface of the planet."

Nezdeh fastened the top clasp of her tunic when no one was looking. Over the past three days, she and Idrem had only had a few intermittent hours when their off-duty cycles overlapped, and this had been one of them—until she had been summoned to the bridge two minutes ago.

Brenlor ducked through the hatchway, waved off Sehtrek's attempt to update him. He had been aboard *Red Lurker* when its superior sensor suite had alerted them to the first signs that the target might be preparing to move. "Your assessment, Nezdeh?"

"They mean to make best speed to their shift point."

"Then we must break off our own refueling immediately and commence preacceleration. That way, we will arrive before them in BD +02 4076 with enough lead time to take on fuel and seek a suitable position from which to ambush them."

"Assuming they are heading to that system at all," added Sehtrek.

"And if they are not," Nezdeh amended, "then we will refuel and seek our fortunes elsewhere. And elsewise."

Brenlor was able to hear this disappointing possibility with almost complete equanimity now. "We would have little choice. Sehtrek, commence preacceleration for the shift point to BD +02 4076 as soon as our skimmers have returned to their berths." Leaning over, he asked Nezdeh in a lower voice, "Has Idrem determined the likelihood that the Slaasriithi will see our tug's antimatter drive, this time?"

Nezdeh nodded. "If we stay in the shadow of the gas giant, and if the target continues to maintain its current course, that will put the star directly between us. They have, at best, a twenty percent chance of detecting us as we accelerate."

Brenlor did not take his eyes away from the starfield. "I do not like those odds."

Nezdeh decided to take a chance: changing into the ancient dialect used only among the Srinu of the Creche worlds, she observed, "Twelve weeks ago, you would have found those odds exhilarating."

Brenlor nodded tightly, answered in the same tongue. "Twelve weeks ago, I was still thinking like an angry Srin, and a prodigal to boot. Now that the die is cast, I think like a man who may one day be a Hegemon." He turned to face her. "Before our Extirpation, I had no such hopes. I was rash during my first years outside the precinct walls. I resented the Breedmistresses' prediction that I would never rise high enough to even guard a Hegemon's dais. Now?" He shrugged. "I may be the last of our line left to ascend that platform myself. And so I school myself to think appropriately."

Nezdeh put a hand on her cousin's arm. "And have done so admirably." She looked at the virtual instruments showing their telemetry and other transit data. "How long?" she asked Sehtrek.

"One hundred and fifty hours."

Nezdeh rose, relinquishing the con to Brenlor. "Only six days to wait, now."

His smile was both rueful and feral as he slid into the captain's chair. "I would not mind if it was a bit longer, this time."

"Really? Why?"

Brenlor's smile was now wholly feral. "So I have enough time to prepare our ambush."

✧   ✧   ✧

One hundred and forty-nine hours later, when the *Arbitrage* reached her shift point, Nezdeh and Brenlor were back on its bridge. In the faux-holograph of the navplot, the green blip of the preaccelerating Slaasriithi ship was headed directly away from them.

"Threshold energy state attained," the Aboriginal pilot announced. "Shift drive ready."

"Engage," Brenlor ordered.

Reality seemed to swim through a hole in itself and emerge on the far side, unchanged—except for the star field and the nearby mass of a gas giant.

The communications officer put a hand to her ear. "Idrem with a sensor report; multiple small objects orbiting the main planet."

"Size of objects?"

"Initial densitometer readings are imprecise, but they seem to vary between seventy and four-hundred fifty cubic meters. All are spherical."

Brenlor nodded. "Surveillance satellites and automated craft. Any sign of weapons?"

"Given the distance and our reliance upon passive sensors, Idrem reports that we are unable to discern any. He remarks, however, that the trojan point asteroid fields of the main planet are both highly attenuated and quite dense."

Brenlor nodded. "We will approach the spinward trojan point carefully and ensure that it has no dormant trespass sensors. If it doesn't, then we shall spring our ambush from there."

Nezdeh nodded. "In the meantime, let us fill our tanks at the gas giant so that, if the Slaasriithi shift-carrier does make this its next—and final—destination, we are in readiness." *And then quickly move on, before Tlerek Srin Shethkador catches our scent and sends some stealthy hounds to track us down...*

As soon as Tlerek Srin Shethkador heard Olsirkos enter his spin-chambers, he asked, "You have completed your review of both the general ship's log and the communications log?"

"Yes, Fearsome Srin. As I reported, *Ferocious Monolith*'s journey to Sigma Draconis was largely uneventful. In fact, the senior annalist recorded statistically low mortality among the unshielded low-gee helots, of which all deaths were, happily, cull-worthy. As one often encounters on an Aegis ship, there were several disputes that required intervention and summary discipline. One evolved into a formal duel."

"What do you know about that duel?"

"Very little, Honored Srin. After it was reported to me, I had the senior lictor investigate to ensure there were no security or operational consequences. The senior annalist collected the particulars to make his report. That was the end of the matter."

"I see. When did the duel occur?"

"Several days before departing the V 1581 system, the last shift on our journey here. The duel involved the second bridge crew's communications officer and one of his journeyman-trainees. There was no indication that House rivalry was the cause of the duel."

Shethkador waited for further explication. None came. "The loss of the second communications officer affected crewing, did it not?"

Olsirkos shrugged. "Slightly. The second communications officer was scheduled to transfer to *Red Lurker*, which we left behind in V 1581 three days later. The first alternate communications specialist was tasked to take his place aboard *Lurker*. The second alternate, the trainee who won the duel, became the second crew's communications officer here aboard *Monolith*."

"So, as the new secondary comm officer, the trainee's duties now include maintaining the communications logs, running readiness checks, and monitoring enemy communications, correct?"

"That is correct."

And still Olsirkos does not see the connection. "Has your new second communications officer brought any unusual enemy communications to your attention?"

Olsirkos frowned. "No, Fearsome Srin." This time, Olsirkos put extra emphasis upon the word "fearsome."

"So, shall we presume that he failed to notice this?" Shethkador pressed a stud on his belt-com. Behind him, communications records from twelve days prior rose up as a holoflat. Shethkador had flagged one of the entries in red.

Olsirkos scanned it: a footnote appended to the report of an informer aboard an Aboriginal cargo ship, the RFS *Ladoga*. Her master, Captain Ludmilla Privek, had hurriedly submitted an exhaustive report concerning the last known whereabouts of a senior-grade cargo worker. This worker, Agnata Manolescu, had been officially missing for ten weeks. However, it seemed probable that her disappearance occurred earlier and that Privek had avoided drawing attention to it, hoping to resolve the matter independently and save face.

Olsirkos' frown deepened. "Potent Srin, I fail to see—"

"Read every word, seek every nuance. Why, after the worker had been officially missing for over two months, was the master of the ship suddenly compelled—*compelled*—to submit a complete report, at the direct and confidential order of Lord Admiral Halifax himself?"

Olsirkos scrolled back through the Aboriginal communications traffic. He stopped at an entry dated five days prior to the submission of Privek's report. "This must be it. The Aboriginals found the cargo worker's body adrift in space." His frown returned. "It was not discovered near any currently used orbital track. Why did they even think to look for it?"

Shethkador wondered if Olsirkos' future might not merely include demotion but an appointment with the cull-master. "Logic dictates that we must return to the beginning of the incident: the first, internal record of Manolescu's disappearance. Her last known location on the *Ladoga* was in a cargo bay during a high-priority transfer of cold cells, and you will note their destination."

Olsirkos' voice was dry—or possibly strangled with anxiety: "The cold cells were being transferred to the Slaasriithi vessel."

"Yes. This tells us how the Aboriginals found Agnata Manolescu's body. Logically, since she disappeared from the bay where the transfer took place, the Aboriginals determined which lighter effected that cargo transfer and then checked its flight recorder data. They performed close sensor sweeps radiating out from its flight telemetries and discovered Manolescu's corpse spinning slowly away from the lighter's prior path. The subsequent question is, obviously, why would the person overseeing the transfer of the cargo from the *Ladoga* be killed?"

Olsirkos' frown was replaced by wide-eyed revelation. "The cryocells loaded on the lighter were not the ones it had been sent to transfer. Some of the cargo was switched."

Well, there is some hope for you after all. "Correct. According to our informers in the Aboriginal military structure, two of the coldslept personnel chosen to accompany the legation into Slaasriithi space were never removed from the *Ladoga*. Their cold cells were later found 'misfiled' in the same cargo bay."

"So, the two coldsleepers who went in their place are infiltrators, sent to sabotage the Aboriginal envoy to the Slaasriithi?"

"Likely, but impossible to determine without investigating. Which we should have been doing for the past ten weeks."

Olsirkos sounded like he wanted the change the topic. Desperately. "It is strange that the Aboriginals have not detained the crew of the lighter and questioned them."

"More persistence in reviewing the data would have shown you that they tried and failed." Shethkador changed the file displayed on the holoflat to a secure bulletin calling for the apprehension of two missing persons of interest: the Aboriginal female and male who had crewed the lighter.

"It is not conceivable that they could remain undetected on one of the fleet's hulls," Olsirkos asserted. "So where are they?"

Shethkador brought up a holograph of the interstellar region surrounding Sigma Draconis. He pointed into it: the red star closest to Sigma Draconis flared in response. "The two renegades are almost certainly here: system V 1581. We know that Visser, one of the human Consuls, and a significant intelligence chief named Richard Downing commenced transit to Earth aboard the prize ship *Changeling* the same day that the Slaasriithi departed. I suspect that the two fugitives, furnished with false identities, were already aboard *Changeling* when she shifted out to V 1581. So, we must journey there and intercept them before they can flee to Earth: they are the only remaining clues to the rest of the plot."

Olsirkos was lost again. "The rest of the plot?"

Shethkador rose. "I must recontact the Autarchs. They require an update." He stared hard at Olsirkos. "The rest of the plot is obvious, or should be. The two who operated the lighter could not have had longstanding orders to switch the cold cells on the *Ladoga*. Only three days earlier, the Slaasriithi had not even arrived in Sigma Draconis, much less invited the Aboriginals to visit their homeworld. So if you find the persons who signaled the lighter's crew to switch the cold cells, you will ultimately find the persons who *were* ready to launch this plot in a matter of hours." Shethkador brought up the communications logs. One entry was flagged in red. "The day that the Slaasriithi departed, there was a routine communications test, to assess mechanical readiness. Read who oversaw the test."

Olsirkos stared, swallowed, managed to get out the words: "It was the recently promoted trainee, the one who killed the former second communications officer in a duel."

Shethkador nodded, walked to the hatchway, exited, made briskly for the Sensorium, Olsirkos trailing behind. "I will make my Reification to contact the Autarchs swift. I will explain that we must return to V 1581 to recover *Red Lurker*. In actuality, we shall be following the path of the crew of the lighter and whoever contacted them and is behind this plot. You have half an hour to quietly detain and interrogate the communications trainee who won the duel. In the interrogation, presume that you will have to use drugs and extreme measures. Presume that the subject is not a knowledgeable part of the greater plot. Discover how he used the communications testing routines to send the necessary message to the lighter crew, who gave him that message, how he knew where to send it and when." Shethkador paused before the threshold of the Sensorium. "Impress me by succeeding in this, and I shall overlook your signal failures in detecting this plot from the outset," he lied.

"I am my Srin's right hand," Olsirkos breathed with a low bow.

"Yes," Shethkador muttered. *Which would make me half a cripple, if it were true.*

Chapter Twenty-Seven

Shethkador wasted no time entering the Sensorium and only partially infusing the essence of one Catalysite. Left undrained, it would hopefully regenerate: they were a finite resource, so far from home. Once on the cushions, he brusquely pushed himself into the entangled particularities of time and space that defined the symbiot's natural state of sensory awareness. The Autarchs felt the summons and responded with extraordinary speed. Tlerek Srin Shethkador smiled: he might not be well liked, but he was evidently well respected. Or feared.

The formalities and obligatory obeisances were quickly performed and Tlerek informed them of his impending departure to system V 1581. His given reason, to reclaim *Red Lurker*, was accepted as a matter of course. The small craft could not be left behind indefinitely, and if its limited endurance compelled it to rise up out of the gas giant in which it had been hidden, the possibility of its discovery increased dramatically.

Beren Tval Jerapthere's question came with a peremptory edge. "What about reestablished communications with the Arat Kur? What progress have you made?"

"For three weeks after our last Reified contact, I endeavored to achieve that daily. I received no response. I believe the Arat Kur are convinced that we, not the so-called 'Terrans,' are responsible for the cataclysm that nearly destroyed their society approximately fifteen millennia ago." *A conclusion which was, frankly, inevitable and uncontestable.*

"So you believe the Arat Kur are lost to us?"

"Yes. Which is not the same thing as saying that they will become allied with the Terrans. Many of them remain suspicious of all humans. Some are amenable to contact with the Aboriginals. However, the contentious nature of the current negotiations will serve to poison the well of amity for some time to come. And even if the Arat Kur were to put aside their reservations and make common cause against us with the Aboriginals, they would contribute very little to such an effort. The humans are bleeding them dry of ships and industrial output."

"I did not suspect the Aboriginals would be so materially rapacious." Ulsor Tval Vasarkas' comment was slow, measured.

"Most of them are not, but they are divided both between and within their blocs. There are still strong and insistent voices calling for xenocide. To balance against this, moderate factions support the aggressive dismantling of the Arat Kur's military capabilities, thereby reducing the popular fears upon which the xenocidalists prey."

"And weakening the Arat Kur so profoundly that they will probably be of no use to our enemies in the next war. Excellent."

"Yes, but the Aboriginals may make better use of these arrogated ships and resources than the Arat Kur would have. It is difficult to foresee which would have been the better alternative, in light of our future plans. However, a more immediate threat to those plans has arisen: the Slaasriithi invited an Aboriginal envoy to their homeworld mere hours after my last Contact with you."

"And did the Aboriginals accept?"

"Immediately. They departed that same day."

Beren Tval Jerapthere's response was unpleasantly barbed. "This is unacceptable, Srin Shethkador. How did you allow this to occur?"

"Esteemed Autarch, had my advice been followed, it would never have occurred at all. Instead, heavy-handed initiatives have characterized our operations in this entire region of space. This is why the provocative arrival of *Ferocious Monolith* was ill-conceived. Without the alarm it caused, the Slaasriithi might have maintained their typically glacial pace of cultural contact and exchange. But instead, they pressed for and obtained an immediate diplomatic mission from the Aboriginals."

"You must contrive a way to stop them from realizing their objectives."

"What method do you propose?"

"The most reliable: follow their ship and destroy it."

"I reply with as much deference as I may muster, and more respect than such a plan is due: nothing could be more injurious to our plans. Our willingness to destroy such a mission will signal to both powers that we fear nothing so much as the possibility of a swift alliance between them. And so, they will be quick to conclude one."

Tlerek could almost hear Beren's teeth grinding across the many parsecs. "I do not propose the elimination of the envoy be done openly."

"I do not suppose you did, but we cannot ensure secrecy if we undertake the ambush you so blithely suggest. We are not familiar with Slaasriithi space. They have been the most reticent of all the races and have been most effective patrolling their borders against our covert surveys, despite their lower technological level."

Ruurun's confirmation was patient, studied. "The Srin is correct. We would be proceeding blindly and without any plausible pretext."

"Precisely," Shethkador agreed, grateful that House Tharexere did not have as much vigor as it had wisdom. "And if such a trespass is detected, the probable loss of the ship would be a paltry matter compared to the diplomatic damage. We will have pushed two races together into an alliance against us, whereas, unprompted, they might require years of diplomatic exchange before concluding such a pact."

Davros' contact was cautious. "Agreed, but is detection so likely? The Slaasriithi are most decidedly our technological inferiors."

"The Slaasriithi are well behind us in military and space technology, but their sensors are subtle, small, predominantly nonmetallic. And the Slaasriithi are patient. Their seeming lethargy conceals an extraordinary unity of action and fixity of purpose. Unlike the Aboriginals, who will bicker over plans incessantly and change them midcourse, the Slaasriithi are doubtless responding to the late war by increasing the sophistication, precision, and quantities of their remote sensor platforms."

"Not active, crewed defenses?"

"Not at first, and not primarily. The Slaasriithi will, rightly, be more concerned about furnishing the Custodians with incontrovertible evidence of any violations of their space."

Ulsor's contact was grim. "And so, they would have the Custodians do their fighting for them."

"Yes, which is also the path of action stipulated by the Accords.

So, in reporting our intrusion, they would both have the legal right of the matter, and also awaken the one foe that might still defeat us if sufficiently aroused and committed: the Dornaani. That is an eventuality we must avoid at all costs."

"Your contact grows weak, Tlerek Srin Shethkador," Davros sent with extra strength.

"My gratitude for your counsel and attention, Autarchs." Shethkador let the link slip away—and suddenly he was back in the Sensorium, fixed in one time and one place, perceiving no greater connections to the universe around him than those which could be established by the reach of his eyes, ears, nose. His nose might be particularly useful, now, he reflected: he wondered if he could smell the stink of Olsirkos' fear, who was no doubt waiting just beyond the well-guarded iris valve.

Shethkador was not disappointed in half of his prediction; his executive officer was waiting there, but without any discernible odor of fear. "I have news, Fearsome Srin."

I'm sure you do. "Inform me."

"There is, as you suspected, a deeper plot that connects the murder of the cargo worker aboard the *Ladoga*, and the outcome of the duel fought aboard *Ferocious Monolith*. The communications trainee had no quarrel with the second communications officer. He was paid to instigate the duel, and then send one of several prearranged signals to the lighter's mother ship. What is most interesting is that the person who secured his services in exchange for this assistance—"

"—was the first alternate communications officer, the one who ultimately replaced the dead officer aboard *Red Lurker*."

Olsirkos dropped behind; he had stopped walking. "You knew."

Shethkador managed to repress a smile. *Mostly.* "The interrogation of the duelist was simply a matter of confirming the obvious. Is he still alive, by the way?"

"Yes, Fearsome Srin. Shall I vac him?"

"Imbecile! This is not deep space, back home. We must protect our genelines from Aboriginal analysis for as long as possible."

"Then how do you wish me to dispose of him?"

Shethkador considered: there was no value to retaining the traitor. His employers would doubtless have understood—far, far better than he—just how likely this outcome was. He would not possess any evidentiary or informational value. "Send a summons to all autarchons and lictors who came into Aegis service because their Houses or Families were Extirpated. Have them gather in the observation gallery of the after docking bay. Place the traitor in the bay and evacuate the atmosphere slowly, without opening the doors. Let them watch his death and be reminded that this is what befalls those who would help to restore genelines upon which Extirpation has been decreed."

Olsirkos frowned. "As you order, it shall be, Fearsome Srin, but…"

"Yes?"

"Why such emphasis upon Extirpated Houses and Families?"

"Because that was the root of all these crimes. Have you examined the background of the communications officer you ultimately assigned to *Red Lurker*?"

"I am ashamed to say that I completed the interrogation mere minutes before arriving at the Sensorium."

Probably true. "Here is what you will find: her name is Nezdeh, a former Srina of House Perekmeres. She was behind much, if not all, of the planning and collusion and bribery that we have now uncovered. You will also find, if you research deeply enough, that many of the Undreaming who were awakened to round out the crew of the *Lurker* were not who they were purported to be. They were more renegades from House Perekmeres."

Olsirkos shook his head. "But to what end would they fashion such a strange plot? If they seize *Red Lurker*, where may they go? Without us, they will remain stranded in system V 1581."

"Will they? They are too adept at overcoming obstacles for me to rely upon that assumption. They have suborned human agents among the civilian auxiliaries of the Aboriginal fleet. They were able to infiltrate cryocelled Terran collaborators into a diplomatic mission with only twenty-four hours notice. So I am unwilling to make any presumptions regarding what capabilities they do and do not have. We may only be sure of this: as renegades, they will take every possible precaution to remain undetected. And also, having no House left to support them, they must have sponsors among either the Autarchs, the Hegemons of the Great Houses, or both."

"Yes, Fearsome Srin"—and Olsirkos did genuinely seem to be awestruck at Shethkador's calm, confident unfolding of the conspiracy—"but I still do not understand how the architect of this plot could be located in V 1581 and yet be influencing events that were taking place here."

"That mystery is not solved by a single answer, but rather two. The first part is that the Slaasriithi invitation to the Aboriginals was not *wholly* unforeseeable. Therefore, it is possible, if unlikely, that the duelist you just interrogated was left with a complex flow-chart of contingency orders to execute, as dictated by subsequent occurrences. This alone could have produced the chain of events we have uncovered. But I suspect there is a second, more likely, answer to how these renegades managed to influence events in another star system.

"Only hours after *Monolith* left V 1581, another preaccelerated Arat Kur prize hull—*Mimic*—shifted into that system from Sigma Draconis, probably carrying a warning of our sudden appearance there. It seems likely that the ex-Srina Perekmeres—or her sponsors—had agents aboard *Mimic*, who reported the Slaasriithi's diplomatic overtures to the Aboriginals. The ex-Srina then contacted the new second communications officer."

"So she is Awakened?"

"Almost certainly."

"But what are these traitors hoping to accomplish?"

"That we cannot know until we track them down. But they clearly intend to compromise the Aboriginal legation to the Slaasriithi homeworld."

"So our travel to V 1581 to retrieve *Red Lurker* is but a stalking horse to conceal our investigation into the connections between this plot and rogue elements of the former House Perekmeres."

"Exactly."

They had returned to Shethkador's spin quarters. "Dominant Srin," Olsirkos breathed, "you have been inconceivably kind to show me the workings of your mind, that I may be inspired and educated by them."

Shethkador resisted the urge to rub his eyes. "Yes, of course. Now, commence preacceleration for shift to V 1581. I had expected to depart this wretched region of space as soon as I was repatriated. Now I must investigate a pack of meddlesome renegades who should have been culled with the rest of their scrofulous breed."

"At least, being renegades, they are desperate and possess little real power. After all, how much damage could they do?"

Shethkador fixed Olsirkos with a brutal stare, compelling his irises to contract into pinpricks of contempt and dismissal. "Since they have nothing to lose, what *won't* they do?"

PART THREE

September 2120

Chapter Twenty-Eight

"They call the planet 'Disparity'?" Tygg stared at Riordan, who had conveyed the information. "What the hell kind of name is that? What's it mean?"

"Wish I knew," Riordan confessed, "but I don't. Got the name from Yiithrii'ah'aash just a few minutes before we started shuffling gear around for tomorrow's landing."

Keith Macmillan, hearing the exchange as he went to get another load from the cargo mod, grunted. "I guess we're going to be staying here a little longer than on Adumbratus."

"Why do you say that?" Melissa Sleeman asked over her shoulder. She was helping—well, more like directing—Tygg as he relocated her test gear to the corvette.

"Because they're having us pack for a bloody camping trip, and landing us in two boats," Macmillan answered as he disappeared around the bend.

Which Caine knew to be only part of the reason for tomorrow's two-vehicle planetfall. After Adumbratus, the Slaasriithi had sheepishly admitted to overestimating the avionics automation of the TOCIO shuttle and had been alarmed when neither their shift carrier nor Adumbratus' ground station had been able to achieve a solid lascom lock to relay telemetry and meteorological data to it during the unexpectedly rough descent. This time, the Slaasriithi had urged a "buddy-system" landing. The concept was to let the far more robust and cutting-edge Wolfe-class corvette, the UCS

247

Puller, lead the way down, relaying both its own sensor readings and any transmitted data to the shuttle following on its heels.

Few of the legation noticed the change: they were eager to begin the visit, particularly since getting their first look at Disparity yesterday. Easing into near orbit, they had watched as, due to the rotation of their habitation module, the green and blue planet slid swiftly in from the top of their view ports and dropped just as swiftly out again every forty-eight seconds. Unlike the outré appearance of Adumbratus, the second planet of BD +02 4076 conformed to the image invoked by the term "green world."

It was indeed the greenest planet Riordan had ever seen. Only fifty-four percent water-covered, Disparity's seas followed the equatorial belt, dividing the planet into pole-centered landmasses. There were a few land bridges joining the two ragged collections of top and bottom continents and one seasonally-migrating ice cap. But those land bridges were apparently eroding: coastal archipelagos flanked the remaining spines of once-wide isthmuses.

Disparity's other unusual feature was the bright blue of its seas, which were much shallower than Earth's oceans and were reportedly well-populated by analogs of cyan-colored algae and plankton.

But even those colors were faint when compared to the vast verdant swathes extending away from the water on both the north and south continents. Whether light grasslands or dark forests, the rich, saturated hues indicated that the vegetation was not interspersed with many badlands or scrub-plains. With the exception of a few dramatic mountain ranges and small wind-shadow deserts that clung to their upland skirts here and there, the green of Disparity's landmasses did not suffer interruption or preemption until it grudgingly mixed in with the tans and browns that rimmed the seasonal icecap.

Caine reached the corvette's portside hatchway and passed his load to Peter Wu, who glanced at the other people approaching with similar burdens. "Captain, don't the Slaasriithi have robots?"

"Some." Riordan considered reminding Wu that there was no reason to revert to addressing him by rank again, but thought the better of it. The career military personnel had their own very practical instincts about such matters. In this case, while exchanges remained informal within their own circle, they stuck with the basic formalities of ranks and titles when mixing in with the civilians. Caine had spent as much time as a grass-roots insurgent as he had in true military formations—which was to say, not much of either—but accepted the wisdom of their unspoken but unanimous choice in the matter.

Peter was still looking grimly at the approaching bucket-brigade of packages to be passed through the hatchway. "So where *are* the robots, sir?"

Caine shrugged. "Far away from us. After the debacle with Buckley, the Slaasriithi have become extremely cautious about bringing any systems into contact with us. However, I am told that stops tomorrow."

"What happens tomorrow?"

"We get hit with another dose of markers."

Trent Howarth stooped through the airlock to take the load from Peter. "Yeah, magic dust with mucho mojo, according to Major Rulaine."

Riordan smiled. "According to Yiithrii'ah'aash, he'll shower us with a super-strength mix just before we start planetside. The markers will provide us with up to a week of affinity and even influence over the local wildlife. Well, the Slaasriithi biota, that is; not all of Disparity's flora and fauna have 'harmonized' just yet."

"So why not put the magic dust on us now?" Peter passed the package to Howarth, eyed the next, larger one being carried jointly by Phil Friel and Tina Melah.

Riordan stepped back out of their way. "Gaspard and I wanted it checked out, first. So Ben Hwang has been looking at it from the bio side, Rena Mizrahi from the medical angle, and Oleg Danysh has been pulling apart its atomic structure." He turned to head back for another load.

Wu sagged under the crate that Tina and Phil passed to him. "How unfortunate for them, having to work so hard."

Caine smiled, waved, turned the corner around which Mac-millan had disappeared and which led to the shuttle and the other modules that comprised their restricted domain aboard the Slaasriithi shift-carrier.

As he went further along the gently curving stretch of corridor, he encountered more of the legation's sweaty geniuses-become-stevedores, mostly carrying survival packs toward the shuttle. Riordan was considering lending a hand there, as well, when his collarcom emitted a flute-and-wind-chime tone: an incoming signal from Yiithrii'ah'aash. Caine tapped the collarcom. "Hello, Ambassador. How may I help you?"

"Caine Riordan, I trust the relocation of your supplies is proceeding well?"

"Yes. Not without a few mishaps, of course." *But you're not contacting me to check on our box-juggling follies.* "Are our activities causing you any concern, Ambassador?"

"No, but we are experiencing an unexplained malfunction at the berth where your shuttle is docked."

Caine hardly realized that his pace had slowed. "What kind of malfunction, Ambassador?"

"Power loss. However, it is only affecting the securing clamps and the hatch seals, which have released."

Riordan came to a stop. "Is there a danger of separation? Do we need to evacuate the bay?"

"That would be precipitous, Caine Riordan. I am sure that we shall have isolated the problem in a few minut—"

The circuit cut out; the lights flickered once and died. The hallway was plunged into darkness, except for the bobbing blue collarcom lights of a few distant team members. One fell with a curse; something she'd been carrying broke with a sound like smashed crockery.

Damn it. Caine tapped his collarcom, tried to recontact the ambassador. The corridor's emergency lights flashed on—amber, low, calming—and went out again, just as fast.

Riordan began feeling his way forward in the darkness and hammered at his collarcom—which emitted an affronted chirp; the wireless power supply was off, too. Batteries only, now. He switched over to the legation channel. "Everyone, this is Captain Riordan. Get to the nearest wall so you can feel your way along. Move with all haste to whichever of our two boats are closest. Hold your collarcom over your head with your other hand, so people can see where you are."

"Captain Riordan." It was Gaspard. "What is happening?"

"I don't know, but the Slaasriithi are as surprised as we are. I was on a channel with Ambassador Yiithrii'ah'aash when—"

"Then why should we move to our ships, before we even know what is happening?"

You shouldn't be doing this on an open channel, Gaspard; I don't have the time to save face for you. "If something does go wrong, those ships are our only assured means of escape." Riordan heard Dora Veriden mutter something about prudent action and no reason to take any chances.

"Very well, Captain; we shall do as you say. Do you have any recommendations regar—?"

A fierce quake sent Riordan to his knees. *Shit.*

"Mon Dieu!" Gaspard's voice was more surprised than it was panicked: better than what Caine would have anticipated three months ago. "What is happening?"

Caine scrabbled back to his feet, double-timed forward. "Ambassador, absent other data, I would say we are under attack."

"Under attack? But I thought it was merely a power failure of some kind—"

Bannor began snarling at panicked team members to stay off the line and keep moving to the closest boat. Caine hoped the legation would be able to make out his words through the cross talk: it was unlikely that there'd be time to repeat anything. "The power outage was probably sabotage, since the emergency power went out as well. We've lost mobility, which makes us an easy target, particularly with the ship's point defense systems and sensors off-line. Whoever is out there shooting at us, almost certainly with a laser, lined us up and hit us as soon as their sensors confirmed that all our active systems had gone dark. Which they seemed to waiting for. The hit we felt was pretty far away from us, though. Probably up near the bow."

"Concur," Bannor said sharply. And then his voice was on the secure tactical channel. "Caine, how long until you get back to *Puller*?"

"I'm not heading toward *Puller.*" Up ahead, a male member of the legation fell, cursed, fell again, his voice getting more shrill and panicked. Caine moved in that direction.

"Sir, with all due respect, we're your ride. Civilians go planetside on the shuttle; security forces go on the—"

"Bannor. It's now twice as far for me to get to *Puller.* Besides, your top priority is to pull in all the people who are closest to you, lock down, and get away."

"Can't. Power outage has frozen our berthing cradles in place."

"And you've got shipboard lasers at murderously close range. Keep your plants at low output: enough power to cut yourself free, but not enough to give the threat force an easy lock on you.

And if you can't release the airlock's mating rings, blow the outer coaming with the embedded explosive bolts."

"Okay, sir, but not until we see you and the shuttle safely away."

"Don't be insubordinate."

"I'm not, Captain. I'm obeying orders."

"Whose?"

"Mr. Downing, sir. He thought it was possible that something like this might happen."

"Target damage assessment?" demanded Nezdeh.

Tegrese's reply sounded as though it was coming through clenched teeth. "Modest. I did not hit the presumed command and control section. Given the light debris and heavy outgassing, I project we hit a large access tube."

"Our railgun projectiles?"

"Estimating impact in eighty seconds."

If the Slaasriithi ship hadn't been paralyzed by sabotage, it was doubtful that those staged composite penetrators would have hit her at all; the range was too great and the large ship's PDF batteries were too numerous and powerful. Apparently, the Slaasriithi did not have separate high power offensive lasers, and smaller, weaker point defense batteries. In keeping with the species' decidedly nonwarlike nature, they folded the two roles into a single system. The result was a significantly weaker offensive laser threat, but a significantly greater defensive intercept capability: more beams, with higher power, greater effective range, and lavish targeting arrays.

But right now, the Slaasriithi shift-carrier's lasers were as cold as her power plants and her fusion drive, and they would hopefully stay that way long enough for Nezdeh to finish her off.

Something in Sehtrek's voice told her that she might have less time to deliver a *coup de grace* than she wished. "Nezdeh, the first enemy 'cannonball' has risen above the planetary horizon."

Right on time. She waved a hand through the distance-hazed close-up of the Slaasriithi ship in the holosphere: it disappeared. "Tactical navplot," she ordered the computer.

The ship's outline was replaced by a three-dimensional overview of nearby space, where a threat-coded orange ball was rising over the rim of the blue planetary sphere. On the other side of the sphere, a larger orange spindle—the stricken enemy shift-carrier—floated haplessly. As she watched, several orange pinpricks in the vicinity of approaching orange ball flickered into existence, pulsing. "Microsensor phased array?" she asked.

"Correct," Sehtrek replied. "As small and undetectable as our own. They are almost certainly relying upon broadcast power from the planet's many orbital solar collectors. I detect seven active sensors. They are striving for target lock."

"That is their only reason for illuminating them," Nezdeh muttered, assessing the distribution of the enemy sensors and the respectable rate at which the orange ball was approaching.

Tegrese's voice was tense, eager. "Shall I target their sensors?"

Nezdeh shook her head sharply. "No." *Tegrese, at this moment you are a fool asking to play a fool's game.* "We haven't the time to spare. Besides, we are seeing only the first tier of their detection assets. They doubtless have many replacements seeded in various orbital positions, still floating inert. Resume firing upon the Slaasriithi ship as soon as you have corrected your locational lock."

"Which lock, Nezdeh? The one guiding our laser strikes against the bow, or for the railgun lock upon the stern?"

"Correct both, but the stern is the most critical. If we can cripple its main power plant before our saboteur's work is undone, we can easily destroy the target, despite the size difference." Which was why *Lurker* had a self-guiding tactical nuclear missile in its recessed bay; once targeting was assured and either the Slaasriithi's PDF batteries were inert or the flight time was brief, that single hammer blow would finish the job. But the Slaasriithi's present power loss would not be permanent, and the range was still too great. *And since we have but one sure way to kill our foe...* "Ulpreln, both fusion and plasma drives to full on my mark. Zurur, send word to the rest of the crew to secure themselves for sustained four-gee thrust." She saw Ulpreln's head start to turn. "When we activated our own dispersed array of microsensors, they had an indefinite warning, at best. But when we fired, we revealed our precise coordinates. There is no longer any advantage to hiding among the debris from the asteroid collision we caused. Tegrese, illuminate all active sensors. Ulpreln, plot the most direct course toward the target and accelerate to full."

Ulpreln nodded, turned to his console—and the universe slammed Nezdeh back into her acceleration couch.

In the viewscreen, the last few widely spaced rocks drifting between *Red Lurker* and her target rushed past them. Nezdeh was sorry to see them disappear astern. The asteroids had been helpful, obscuring companions ever since the *Arbitrage* and her Ktoran tug had edged in toward the spinward trojan point after finishing a hasty and incomplete refueling. They had counterboosted into the midst of the drifting rocks using a retrograde approach effected solely by the Aboriginal ship's magnetically accelerated plasma thrusters, thereby minimizing all chances of detection.

Once hidden, Brenlor had exhibited admirable patience as they determined their best ambush point and observed what little they could from that extreme distance. He even accepted that his role in the coming attack would be to remain hidden with the *Arbitrage* and the tug. This had happily obviated any need to underscore that Brenlor's personal mastery was in hand-to-hand, not ship-to-ship combat. As one of the least patient of the young Evolved in his House, he had not possessed the precision and cool calculation that made for excellent ship captains. Fortunately, other matters had precluded his participation in the strike. Preserving his geneline, the closest to the progenitorial core of House Perekmeres, was first among these, followed closely by maintaining the reign of terror he had established over the Aboriginals aboard the *Arbitrage*. Given its size, the human ship had to remain hidden and distant from the engagement since, along with the tug, it was their only means of exiting the system, whatever might transpire.

Nezdeh's more difficult, and tedious, problem had been to make a sufficiently stealthy and close approach to the target zone. Coasting, running off minimum batteries, and often tarrying in the shadow of one or more of the rocky fragments of the asteroid collision they had caused, Nezdeh approached their ambush point on a retrograde vector, sending a cluster of disposable microsensors on ahead. Functioning as a passive phased array, they immediately detected the orbiting, spherelike vehicles the Ktor had observed upon arriving in the system. The larger ones, which they dubbed cannonballs due to their occasional bursts of astounding five-point-five-gee acceleration, were evidently the most sophisticated of the objects and also the most likely to be defense systems. They changed their telemetry without any regular period: in short, no firing solution calculated from their orbital path remained viable for more than seven or eight hours.

The planet's scores of smaller spheres were, presumably, communications and sensor platforms. Although the cannonballs were the greatest direct threat, these smaller spheres, as well as any undetectable devices comprising a phased array, had commanded Nezdeh's attention. Would they scan the new, slowly diffusing spray of gargantuan boulders behind which *Lurker* was approaching?

But the orbital array's passive sensor results apparently did not alarm either its live or expert system controllers: no active scan had been initiated. The collision *Red Lurker* had engineered resembled the sequelae of a natural event, and since none of the ejecta was heading directly toward the planet, its denizens had evidently concluded that it was unnecessary to inspect the debris more closely. Besides, in order to do so, they would have had to illuminate and thereby reveal the active sensors kept in the region for detecting enemy craft. Reassured by the Slaasrii-this' complacency, *Red Lurker* concluded her approach, drifting along behind the largest rock chunk that would pass within sixty thousand kilometers of the planet.

Tegrese's voice roused Nezdeh out of the momentary reverie that had arisen even as she continued to assess the data streams floating next to the holographic navplot. "New firing solutions are ready, Nezdeh. Using both phased array and on-board sensors, confidence of laser solution is absolute. Railgun targeting confidence is ninety-five percent, with mean point of impact variance of up to ten meters."

"Continue to refine railgun targeting. Sehtrek, how long before the cannonballs are in range, presuming they are capable of six gees?"

"Uncertain. At their current rate of acceleration, the first one will be in our laser's effective range in four minutes. Our railgun—"

"The railgun is useless against the cannonballs under these conditions. The flight time of our projectiles makes hits improbable until the enemy craft are much closer. Any sign of the other cannonballs?"

"None have appeared above the planetary horizon yet. We conjectured that they would be profiling themselves against open space by now."

Nezdeh looked in the holotank, read the data. "And the one approaching us is only accelerating at four gees." She shook her head. "Unpromising. If they were all closing at six gees, we would know they are not taking the time to measure our actions. Instead, the lead cannonball has slowed itself so that the others can accelerate and catch up while it observes us." She drew in breath against the push of *Lurker*'s acceleration. "We must expect that the last two targets will come over the horizon together." *So much for defeating an amateurish enemy in detail. The lead cannonball is their sacrifice: they will use it to see how we fight, our capabilities, and our limits. And the latter two will rush in to take advantage of that knowledge by attempting to overwhelm our defenses. Ruthlessly efficient, for an ostensibly nonviolent species.*

Tegrese's voice was tight with resisting the four-gee compression. "First flight of railgun munitions are about to hit their shift-carrier. Targeting update: laser mean point of impact certain to the limits of sensor accuracy. Confidence of new railgun firing solution: ninety-eight percent with seven-meter MPI variance. Am I to keep all lasers on the primary target?"

Nezdeh nodded. "We have several minutes before the first cannonball can threaten us." *I think.* "We must keep the Slaasriithi vessel powerless. To do that, we must concentrate our fire upon her." *Unfortunately, at this range, our lasers lack the coherence to inflict maximum damage, and if she manages to change course, our railgun may miss.* "We shall cripple her now so that we may kill her later."

"While hoping that the cannonballs don't kill us in the meantime," Tegrese murmured.

"True," replied Nezdeh. "Now: fire all."

Chapter Twenty-Nine

Caine Riordan had just finished helping up the man who had fallen ahead of him in the darkness—Nasr Eid—when the world shook again. But much harder.

Riordan hit the far wall of the corridor like a rag doll slung across a room. He bounced off, the wind driven out of him, but was glad for the reflexes that brought up his left arm to cover his head and turned his fall into a crude roll. Finally, the long hours of intermittent martial arts practice were paying a muscle memory dividend.

As he rose, a sudden forward-suction draft pulled the air from behind him, the force against his back building swiftly toward hurricane intensity. *Goddamn, explosive decompression up ahead? Nothing to grab on to, no way to—*

The growing maelstrom diminished quickly, then stopped. His collarcom, still in his right hand, emitted a wind-chime and flutes tone. He tapped it. "Ambassador?"

Yiithrii'ah'aash's connection was very poor. "Caine Riordan, can you hear my words?"

"Yes, but not well. Can you give me a sitrep—uh, a situation report?"

"I can, but it must be brief. I am using a personal communicator with low batteries."

I doubt we have much time to talk, anyhow. "Ambassador, do you know who's attacking us?"

"We have no sensors, and so cannot tell. You must board your ships and descend to the planet at once."

257

"Already under way."

"Excellent. Do not stop to draw supplies from your cargo module."

"We're not. Was it hit? Was that what caused the explosive decompression?"

"It was. Our extrusions have sealed the breach. But the module was not the attacker's target. Its rotation simply brought it into the path of a beam locked upon the main spin-armature. You must evacuate at once; without power, we cannot stop the rotator arm. The damage and postexplosion vibrations will cause it to tear apart and fly away from the ship."

Caine, panting, had been sprinting since he'd answered the page and now he could feel that the rotator arm was, in fact, wobbling: the irregular Coriolis effect made the deck swim unsteadily under his feet. "Ambassador, our corvette is still in hard-dock and the power is out. Will your biosystems resist our attempts to override your locks or clamps?"

"They will, but— Do any of your personnel have access to the samples of the new markers? If your crew coated themselves with those, that would allow you to—"

"Negative; all the samples are in the hab mod. They'd never make it there and back to the corvette in time."

The bulkhead disappeared from under Caine's trailing palm; an intersection. *Damn it, which way—? Right!* He scrabbled in the dark, found the right-hand bulkhead, ran onward, staggering as the deck undulated beneath his feet.

Yiithrii'ah'aash's next suggestion was hurried. "I have sent a disabling command through the chemistry of the ship's biota; it may or may not reach the correct docking ports. But use whatever means you must to break or blast yourself free."

Yeah; that's the plan. Caine heard what sounded like a flurry of gunshots up ahead. *What the—?* "Ambassador, is there any chance that you will be able to get your ship's power back on-line?"

"Unknown. Hull breaches have restricted our access, and because our ships are far more self-repairing and self-monitoring than yours, our crew is much smaller."

Although that's not working out so well for you right now, is it? "Were the power plants hit or—?"

"It was sabotage, Captain."

"But I assumed that no Slaasriithi would ever—"

"You are correct, Caine Riordan: we do not have traitors. It was one of your people, Dr. Danysh. We do not know how, but he entered the keel access tube and deployed a feedback device that caused cascading overloads. It did not disable our power plant, but has blocked all electrical current to the bow of the ship, including the bridge and its command circuitry. The engines shifted into standby mode the moment they were no longer under positive control. Now hurry; you have little time left. When you commence planetfall, inform me of—"

The channel crackled and died as Caine rounded the last bend, saw that the shuttle's forward and dorsal boarding tubes were sealed. However, a dim light shone from the doglegged passageway that connected to the aft airlock nestled between its drives. He reattached his collarcom. "Bannor, do you read me?"

"Five by five, Skipper. Where are you?"

"In the shuttle's aft boarding tube. Get going."

"I leave when the shuttle's flight crew tells me the hatch is closed. But be careful; there's been comchatter about shots fired in the after compartments."

"Yeah, I heard them."

"Then don't waste time talking to me when—" Bannor's voice was suddenly muffled; he'd leaned away from his audio pickup. "Dr. Lymbery, I need a green light on that cluster-munition drone. Dr. Sleeman, sensor status?"

As Caine rounded the corridor's final bend, he heard metal groaning behind him: the rotational arm was starting to deform. It almost drowned out Sleeman's response to Bannor: "Passive sensors are tracking back along the attacker's firing vectors. We can—" A surge of static obscured the rest, broke the circuit.

Riordan ducked through the hatch of the shuttle's rear airlock—and stumbled over something.

Caine threw his hands out to break his fall, discovered that whatever had tripped him was soft, warm, and wet. At the same instant, his collarcom crackled back to life on a new channel. "Captain Riordan, you are on board, yes?" Humanity's premier crash-lander, Raskolnikov, sounded impatient.

"Yes, I'm—"

"Excellent. We are leaving. Strap in."

But Caine, seeing what he had fallen on—or into—almost recoiled back out the autoclosing hatch as it bumped against his spine and pushed him closer to—

A tangle of bodies. And blood.

"Captain Riordan: strap in!"

"Go—go; I'll...I'll be there. Soon. Undock and go." It wasn't a prudent order, but Riordan needed five more seconds to memorize the forensic details of the murders he'd discovered:

—Rena Mizrahi, body twisted, eyes open, arrestingly pale, three bullet-holes in her torso, one center-lined on the sternum through which blood had flowed freely. A dated Steyr-Aug ten-millimeter caseless pistol lay just beyond her limp fingers.

—Gaspard's assistant Dieter, crumpled in a heap, like a marionette with all its strings cut. He had been killed by a single round to the back of his head which had exited at the top of his left eye's orbital ridge. A gory red and maroon hole revealed brain tissue.

—Oleg Danysh, lying his length across the deck, an Embra-Mitsu dustmix pistol still locked in his hand. He had been hit four times in a pattern stretching from the base of his neck to his right upper chest. The other entry wounds—arm, leg, hip—were equally wide, almost certainly the handiwork of ten-millimeter fast-expanding hollow points from the gun beside the late Dr. Mizrahi's hand.

Riordan jumped up, sprinted toward the combination ship's locker and main cabin access foyer. The drives behind the bulkheads on either side of him shrieked with sudden, deafening urgency. He yanked open the hatch to the foyer/locker, dove through—

The shuttle pulled sharply to port, away from the crippled Slaas-riithi ship, and then upward, rearing like a horse and twisting as it did. Caine's body went sideways as he entered the foyer. His gut and floating rib slammed into the coaming, bent him like a pretzel just before tossing him aside, rather than back down the passage toward the airlock. "I'm in," he grunted into his collarcom.

The hatch behind him rammed shut as the shuttle's next maneuver threatened to throw him across the foyer.

But having been in enough desperately maneuvering vehicles to distinguish sudden engine thrust from a hit, Riordan was able to ride the wave of motion. He rolled sideways as he neared the door into the cabin and hung there until the shuttle righted. He slammed his palm at the door release, then tumble-crawled through the opening door—

Just as the shuttle dove sharply. He bounced off the ceiling. The craft veered briskly to port. He crashed into an acceleration couch.

Riordan struggled to hold on to the couch, the world indistinct and gray as he swam up out of the successive blows and shocks. Far away, his collarcom crackled: "Captain, strap yourself in. I must resume evasive actions in three seconds." The new voice—calm, unflappable, and deadly serious—was Qin Lijuan's, who was now handling the shuttle as though it were a stunt plane. This was Qin's *forte*, was why she'd been multiply decorated after the Second Battle of Jupiter.

Caine clambered into the couch and was just securing the straps when she resumed her corkscrewing evasive maneuvers. He looked out his passenger window—its cover had frozen in the half-closed position—and saw the rotational arm begin to flop like a limb with multiple fractures. Its crippled contortions carried *Puller* into view. One of the corvette's laser-focusing blisters emerged and swiveled toward the berthing arms. Each docking clamp flared as if an invisible brace of gigantic arc welders were cutting at it. The claw-like protrusions flew back in pieces, tumbling end over end—and directly toward the shuttle. Closer. And closer—

—and missed the shuttle by five meters. The tube connecting *Puller*'s ventral airlock to the shift carrier exploded outward in a sharp orange flash: explosive bolts had blasted its hatch and outer coaming away from the vehicle, freeing it from the rapidly disintegrating rotational arm. *Puller* was dense enough that the rapid unmooring didn't sling it off like a spinning top, but Karam was going to have his hands full correcting the significant three-axis tumble.

The chaos at the bow of the Slaasriithi ship fell away as Lijuan tumbled the shuttle and boosted back along the shift-carrier's keel, getting distance from the tangle of flying debris and thrashing rotational arms.

Caine had just started to become aware of his immediate surroundings—the whimpering of at least two passengers, his own rank sweat, his blood-splattered duty suit—when a flurry of bright flashes speckled the shift-carrier's aft-mounted spheres, the ones which housed both fuel tanks and power plants. Riordan knew what he had seen: impacts by a dispersing pattern of railgun sub-projectiles.

Two of the globes exploded in silent, self-shredding fury, sending a wave front of small debris racing outward.

Straight toward the shuttle.

Chapter Thirty

Nezdeh stared at the holotank and the view screens and reflected how aptly the changes of the last twenty seconds illustrated the tired Progenitor axiom, *Good fortune arrives in bits and pieces, but bad luck comes all at once.*

Moments after the target had finally been dealt a solid blow—two of her fuel tanks destroyed and her primary rotational armature coming apart in a roiling litter of modules and debris—the last two Slaasriithi cannonballs emerged from behind the planet. As they did, the third, closer cannonball commenced a six-gee counterboost, slowing it at the same moment that Sehtrek reported it was now targeting *Lurker* with active sensors. Nezdeh ordered Tegrese to bring the starboard laser blisters to bear upon the enemy craft. It was not yet at optimal range, but there was nothing to be lost by trying to destroy or disable it, particularly before it initiated its own attacks.

But then Sehtrek called Nezdeh's attention to two new drive signatures that had sprung into existence near the Slaasriithi hull: smaller vessels, drawing rapidly away from her. One staggered through a hail of debris, and, trailing hydrogen, dove straight into the planet's gravity well. The other seemed to emerge straight out of the debris cloud, accelerating rapidly. Two seconds later, it illuminated active sensors and acquired target lock with extraordinary speed. The engine signatures of both craft were primitive—first-generation magnetically accelerated heavy-plasma thrusters—and the radar and ladar emissions were crude. So: these were not Slaasriithi craft, clearly. Aboriginal, therefore. But the one meant to fight and the other meant to make planetfall, both of which complicated her mission.

"Nezdeh, I await your orders," Tegrese said urgently.

"I am waiting—for that." Nezdeh pointed in the holotank; the orange delta signifying the human warship spat out an identically-hued spark at *Red Lurker*. "The humans have launched a missile. No, correction: given its size and complexity, it is a drone."

"It is not homing."

"It does not need to, not yet. We have an active sensor lock on the Slaasriithi ship, so they have simply established a reciprocal lock along our emission. We are doing the drone's work for it. And as for the Aboriginals' other weapons—"

Red Lurker shuddered. Sehtrek looked up. "Lasers. Two hits. Low power beams, visible wavelength. Highly diffused at this range."

Tegrese had apparently forgotten she was speaking to a Srina. "What are you waiting for, Nezdeh? They could destroy—!"

Nezdeh turned, fixed her with a stare, regretted taking the seconds to deal with Tegrese. But the loss of some additional paint and laser-ablative layering was nothing compared to losing even one iota of dominion. "The Aboriginals cannot destroy us with their laser at this range. Which you would know if you had the proper mastery of your station. We have exhaustive data on their technology. Or had you forgotten that, along with your deference?"

Tegrese's eyes widened, then tightened and grew tense crow's-feet at their corners, but finally, her gaze lowered. "My apologies for both transgressions, Srina Perekmeres."

"I shall forgive them both, this one time. Now: adjust railgun targeting to correct mean point of impact to the engines on the Slaasriithi shift cruiser."

Sehtrek leaned closely over his readouts. "Nezdeh, the forward sections of the Slaasriithi craft are beginning to receive power again. She has just illuminated active sensors."

Keeping the tactical initiative was looking ever-more questionable. "Portside lasers are to target the Aboriginal corvette. Commence fire as soon as you have an eighty percent confidence solution."

"And their drone?"

"Shift one of our starboard laser blisters to PDF mode and

commence streaming interception fire immediately. Inform me when it is neutralized."

Tegrese's voice was careful. "I mean no disrespect, but I must confirm: do you intend to dedicate only two starboard laser blisters to the closest cannonball?"

"Yes. Regaining control of this engagement means reducing the number of opposing threats. The human corvette will be the easiest to eliminate, and in so doing, we also complete part of our mission. We will then be able to reconcentrate on the more difficult targets."

"And the human shuttle?"

Nezdeh resisted the urge to close her eyes in frustration. "The debris, range, and other threats are too great for us to engage it now."

"We could use our own missiles to—"

"No: we must launch a full spread of missiles at the Slaasriithi before she is able to reemploy her own lasers in the point-defense fire mode. Once her PDF systems are active, we will be as power-less to damage her as the humans are powerless to damage us." She glanced at the lead cannonball; it still had not fired. Which bothered her. "Commence all attacks," she ordered.

As soon as the shuttle's rapid acceleration down toward Dis-parity settled into a consistent trajectory, Caine unbuckled and struggled forward against the two gees to reach the bridge's iris valve. He triggered it, pushed into one of the two support seats, nodded to Raskolnikov and Qin, who spared one precious second to nod back at him. "I understand there was gunfire back in the rear airlock, Captain."

"There was. And three bodies."

"Do you have any idea what happened?"

"Not yet," Riordan admitted as he strapped into his new seat. "Except that I don't believe the setup."

"The setup?" Qin echoed.

"The way the bodies are set up to make it appear as if they all killed each other. It looks plausible enough forensically, but I don't buy the scenario. It's extremely rare that *everyone* in a gunfight winds up dead. But we'll figure that out later. If we get the chance."

Raskolnikov turned a rueful smile back at him. "So you have seen top side of our lifting surface?"

Riordan nodded. "Took some hits from that debris you dodged."

"Not me. That was Lieutenant Qin. She got us out of that mess."

"Not entirely," Qin grumbled. "My apologies, Commander Raskolnikov. I am afraid I have made your job much harder."

"This?" Raskolnikov smiled broadly as he tilted his head at the pockmarked portside "wing" of the shuttle. It was one of those "so we die? so what?" smiles that Caine had seen on the faces of too many fatalistic Russians over the past two years. "This is not so bad," Raskolnikov asserted. "We will keep nose up and minimize atmospheric heating on damaged area. You will see: all shall be well."

And if it isn't, who'll be left to call you a bullshitter? But what Caine said was: "How soon before the ride gets rough?"

"Soon, Captain. You should return to seat."

Caine shook his head. "I need the radio for a minute."

Both pilots shrugged, scanned their mostly-green system monitors, began checking for ground beacons or automated telemetry feeds guiding them toward approach paths: neither one was showing up on their instruments.

Caine snagged a thin-line headset, activated a secure channel to *Puller*, scanned the black vault above them. Well away from the Slaasriithi ship, the corvette's twin, blue-white thrusters brightened—just as its hull seemed to flare. One engine went dark and *Puller* started to lose way, veering closer to the planet. "Bannor!"

A moment of paralyzing silence was supplanted by static and then an open channel. "Caine? Glad to hear you guys are okay. Heading planetside?"

"Screw the small talk. What the hell are you doing?"

"Helping our hosts, sir."

"Damn it; you are to go dark, break contact, and run like hell."

"Sir, with all due respect, mounting a covering attack was within my prerogatives. It ensures that they don't shoot at *you*. A logical extension of Mr. Downing's orders, sir."

You goddamned barracks-house lawyer. "We'll argue that some other time. For now, you've taken your best shot and given them something to shoot at until Yiithrii'ah'aash got his ship running again. Now, get *Puller* and your crew out of that battlespace. You've already lost one thruster—"

"That's coming back on line. They didn't tag us too hard. And now that the Slaasriithi ship is powering up again—"

"Major, before her power comes back, she could take another burst of railgun penetrators to her power plants or engine. Or bridge. And then you'd be stuck facing the attacker on your own." Riordan dropped his voice. "Bannor, someone has *got* to live to report this. This shuttle is going down hard and I don't know how many—if any—of us are going to walk away from it. And remember: this is happening just one system away from the Slaasriithi homeworld."

Bannor's reply was not immediate. "Sir, are you thinking that this might be a prelude to a general attack?"

"No. If it was, our first warning would have been an enemy battle cruiser showing up and converting us all into subatomic particles. But it's equally alarming that someone is playing this kind of hardball deep inside Slaasriithi space for a *lesser* reason. The Custodians have to be informed, as well as both our government and that of our hosts. And *Puller* is the only hardened target on this shooting range which just might get out in one piece. You're small enough and fast enough to hide and survive to tell the tale. So get going. Now."

"But Downing said—"

"Major Rulaine, you've discharged Downing's orders. Now you're taking mine. Log it as my responsibility, and contest the order later, if you like, but right now, you *go!*"

"Yes, sir."

Caine had never heard Bannor sound glum before. High overhead, the darkened thruster of the *Puller* flickered back into life as the haze of the atmosphere began increasing, diffusing the twin pinpricks of the corvette's drives. Within the space of two heartbeats, they vanished.

For the first time since the attack had begun, Riordan had a scant moment to pull back from immediate events and consider the bigger picture. Whoever was behind this attack had infiltrated one or more saboteurs into the legation within twenty-four hours of its being announced and had sent an assault force unthinkably far into Slaasriithi space. The enemy was, by any conceivable measure, incredibly resourceful, bold, and dangerous.

Riordan found he was still looking at the spot of thickening sky where *Puller* had disappeared. *I hope they make it. But if they don't*—Riordan activated the preset comm link for the Slaasriithi ship, asked over his shoulder: "Is the channel for Ambassador Yiithrii'ah'aash's ship secure?"

"Scrambled and encrypted," Raskolnikov confirmed. "Your two minutes are up, Captain. Things become interesting, now."

"Acknowledged," Riordan replied, activating the link and listening for a reply. As he waited, he glanced out the cockpit.

They had descended far enough that Disparity's planetary curve had leveled out into a horizon line. The clouds were coming up at them, along with stratified drifts of faint green dust. Yiithrii'ah'aash had mentioned atmospheric spore layers, many of which soaked up and reflected UV, thereby adding to the planet's surreal green-blue appearance. Auroras flickered high above: BD +02 4076, being at the approximate peak of its nine-year solar activity cycle, was emitting a growing wave of solar particles. Which meant sensor degradation and a better chance for *Puller* to get away. Conversely, it portended radio problems, possibly an impending blackout—

The channel opened to Yiithrii'ah'aash's ship; it sounded like a stonecutter's saw accompanied by a chorus of banshees being boiled in oil. "Caine Riordan?"

"Yes, Ambassador. Auroras are degrading our communications, I think."

"They are. Have you made planetfall? I do not have enough sensor assets available to track your progress."

"Negative, Ambassador. We are approaching the highest cloud layers. Since this may be our last communication until the solar activity fades, I wanted to confer on a course of action."

"I agree. In order to ensure your survival on the planet, I recommend—"

"I'm sorry to interrupt, Ambassador, but frankly, I'm more concerned about *your* survival."

"That is welcome, Caine Riordan, but we must first see to your safety. It is our responsibility that such dangers have befallen you."

"Ambassador, with all due respect, that cannot be the first priority for either one of us. We have to ensure that this incursion on your space, and the attempted assassination of the entire legation, is reported with all possible speed. So, first things first: is your ship still capable of making shift?"

"Caine—Captain Riordan: we will not leave you behind. We must exert all efforts to—"

"Ambassador, we're running out of time. Given that you are arguing *against* shifting, I deduce that you are still capable of doing so. And you must. As quickly as possible."

"We have offensive systems aboard our ship which are perfectly capable of—"

"Ambassador, your ship only has dual-purpose lasers that fulfill both offensive and point defense requirements, correct?"

"Correct." The reply was reluctant.

"So, they don't have the distance or power of purely offensive systems. And from what I can see, your ship does not have a spinal main weapon, does it?"

"It does not."

"Then it would be reckless for you to stay and fight. You've already suffered significant damage. The next hit could destroy your ability to shift. On the other hand, if you preaccelerate immediately, you will be sure to shift, report, and bring back a rescue mission."

The two-second pause seemed to last two minutes. "Your logic is unassailable. I shall undertake actions that allow us to shift more promptly than usual." A new form of static started encroaching on the channel. It was like bagpipes playing through a thickening blanket of white noise.

"Ambassador, your signal is degrading."

"That is the planetary defense system," Yiithrii'ah'aash explained. "Since your ship has crossed the security threshold of the planet without being expressly cleared to do so, the defense system has begun to jam all signals."

"You mean, all legation signals?"

"No: *all* signals. When the planetary defense system perceives an unauthorized entry, it initiates what you would call a communications 'lockdown.' This way, reconnaissance landings cannot relay any intelligence or targeting data to enemies in orbit or beyond." Yiithrii'ah'aash's words were beginning to bleed into each other as the signal continued to erode.

"Ambassador, what special methods are you employing to achieve shift more rapidly than usual?"

"We will make for this system's automated port facilities."

"They are not here, near Disparity?"

"No. They are in the leading trojan point of the first orbit. We have a solar array there, constantly fabricating antimatter."

Yes, but if the enemy has learned about it... "Do you have sufficient antimatter for a shift?"

"Yes, although not enough to shift with minimal preacceleration.

We would require an extra three days of preacceleration to make up for the partial insufficiency of antimatter."

"Then that's what you must do."

"Caine Riordan, that would delay our return by three additional days. And if these attackers attempt to follow you planetside, that could mean the difference between life and death."

"It could mean life or death for a lot more people, humans and Slaasriithi alike, if you don't bypass the automated station. If you travel there, you could discover that the enemy has more ships in-system, possibly waiting to ambush you as you approach the facility. And if they seize its antimatter reserves, they will be able to swiftly refuel whatever ship brought them here, and undertake whatever energy-expensive operations they need to overcome this planet's defenses. And then exterminate us." Riordan paused; the channel was degrading even more rapidly. "There's only one way you can prevent that."

"How?"

"I presume that your communication net allows you to interface directly with the refueling station's controls?"

"It does."

Caine drew a deep breath. "Then here is what you have to do."

Chapter Thirty-One

In the portside extremity of *Lurker*'s holosphere, Nezdeh watched her spread of missiles draw within twenty thousand kilometers of the Slaasriithi ship—and then flare like a string of firecrackers. As she feared, her opponent's PDF systems had repowered before she could strike her most decisive blow. But, with any luck, the Slaasriithi defenses had been so riveted upon that primary threat that they would be unable to quickly retarget and achieve the more concentrated, intensive fire that was required to spall, and thereby deflect, the railgun projectiles that Nezdeh had sent racing in behind her missiles.

At the starboard extreme of the plot, the three enemy cannonballs approached *Lurker* in an elongated triangle, the first cannonball leading from the point, the other two back at the base. The first had been lightly damaged by a single laser hit. Its immediate return fire had been surprisingly powerful for such a small craft. However, whether it was the limitations of fitting adequate focusing equipment into such a compact hull, or a consequence of the damage that the cannonball had received from *Red Lurker*, the enemy beam had been highly diffuse when it struck. A mild shock had trembled through the patrol hunter, and some lower ablative layers had fumed off the hull, but fortunately, that was the extent of the damage.

"She means to bring her laser into more effective range," Tegrese commented.

270

"Or to ram us," Idrem commented over the intercom from his position in engineering.

Nezdeh started. "Explain?"

"Consider the first cannonball's vector in light of its prior operation and the changing course of the other two cannonballs. Their delta formation is beginning to spread out. I suspect the two rear ones mean to bracket and ultimately move behind us, to force us to evade and so, curtail our rate of closure with our primary target. Ultimately, retargeting our railgun will require that we do not merely change our current heading but tumble the ship."

"Yes—but ramming?"

"I do not suggest it is the lead cannonball's primary or preferred attack option, but consider the way it has eschewed evasion since we hit it. Having the measure of us, and of our superior beam weapon, it is now rushing in for the kill. And disabling it will not be enough: if we do not destroy its drives soon, we will have to reduce it to junk to be sure of avoiding a collision that would be catastrophic."

Nezdeh nodded to no one but herself. *That is why their tactical maneuver is so odd. Despite their size, they are not ships; they are drones. And the Slaasriithi are willing to spend them freely in order to destroy us.* "I believe you are correct, Idrem. And if you are, we must consider—"

"Nezdeh!" interrupted Sehtrek. "The enemy corvette is under full power again. It is coming about."

"To resume attacking?"

"No, it is tumbling. Facing to the rear. Its new course would take it behind the planet."

"Well, that is one less problem," Tegrese muttered.

Yes, you would see it that way. "No, it has become a *larger* problem. There are now three ships which can report this attack and we cannot track down all of them. However, we *must* destroy the human warcraft first." *And we must strike before it swings behind the world's far, night-cloaked horizon and makes good its escape.* "Tegrese, bring all weapons to bear on the Aboriginal corvette. Given her current course and rate of acceleration, we will have one last firing opportunity before the curve of the atmosphere comes between us."

At well under a light-second, the *Lurker*'s lasers accessed the new target almost instantly. The railgun's firing solution lagged significantly behind, given the Aboriginal vessel's smaller size and greater agility.

"Laser lock on the enemy corvette has been reacquired," reported Tegrese.

"Confidence of railgun solution?" Nezdeh demanded.

"If we use a maximum dispersion submunition, just over fifty percent."

"Estimate: will longer aim time increase or decrease confidence?"

"Impossible to calculate; the corvette is undertaking evasive maneuvers."

Nezdeh frowned. *Shoot now? Or wait to improve the railgun's targeting?* The time had come to choose between a bad option—*I can probably cripple the craft now*—or a worse option: *to wait for a slightly better shot might mean missing it entirely.* It was no choice at all. "Fire all, immediately."

At this range, the results were quick in coming. The lasers achieved two hits, one of which was fleeting, at best. Moments later, the viewscreen showed that one, maybe two of the railgun's flurry of thirty-by-ten centimeter penetrator rods struck the corvette along her ventral surface; small bits of debris fluttered outward from the hull and her drives went dark. She began to tumble slowly as she disappeared over the planetary horizon: a lightless spot disappearing behind an ink-black crescent.

Lying further out from the planet, the Slaasriithi ship was also showing the effect of the penetrator rounds that had followed closely in the wake of the Ktoran missiles. Guttering, oxygen-starved flames flickered about one of the shift-carrier's main power plants. Gashes in her long, hexagonal cargo sections bled trails of ruin and debris, and several of her combination thermionic-radiator arrays looked like broken windows that opened unto deep space.

Nezdeh leaned back, considered the holosphere. "Tegrese, reacquire laser lock on the lead cannonball. Sehtrek, damage assessment on Slaasriithi ship."

Sehtrek almost sounded apologetic. "Her power generation has dropped by twenty-five percent, but she is maintaining full thrust." He paused, looked back at her. "She is tumbling."

"She is running," amended Nezdeh with a grim nod. "And why would the Slaasriithi do otherwise? If they can flee and make shift—"

"We must not let them!" Tegrese cried from her station. "They must still break out of orbit. If we resume full acceleration, we can—"

"We can ensure our own destruction at the slim possibility of hers. Look at the plot, Tegrese, and improve your insight. If we resume full acceleration, the cannonballs will have our rear flank. So if we must then constantly tumble—first to attack the shift carrier before us, and then the cannonballs behind us—we will do both jobs poorly. And to what effect? The cannonballs are much faster and nimbler than we are. The shift carrier has the use of her PDF batteries once again. Even if we launched all our missiles in one immense salvo, preceded and followed by as many railgun submunitions as we might launch, we are unlikely to inflict any damage that would prevent her from making shift. And to launch such an attack, we would need to get closer and concentrate fire on her for several minutes, ignoring the cannonballs. Which will be breathing down our necks. We, not the shift carrier, are much more likely to be destroyed by such a strategy." Nezdeh moved her stern gaze away from Tegrese before it could become a look of contempt. "Do you have a lock on the lead cannonball, yet?"

"Just this moment, Nezdeh."

"Fire all lasers."

"Shall I reacquire railgun lock on the enemy shift carrier?"

Nezdeh weighed reflex—to strike at her enemy however, whenever, she might—against reason: not many of this salvo of railgun munitions would avoid the PDF beams that, spalling a fraction of their dense matter upon contact, would thus impart the nudge that would cause the warheads to miss the Slaasriithi by dozens of kilometers. And those few that might get through were increasingly unlikely to inflict decisive damage. "No," she decided with a sigh. "If we do not have a reasonable chance of rendering the Slaasriithi ship incapable of shift, then we are wasting ammunition. Of which we might have urgent want, later on."

Ulpreln turned. His voice was careful, respectful. "Can we be so sure that the Slaasriithi ship is still capable of shift? Or that it even has enough antimatter aboard? Or enough fuel for preacceleration after we destroyed two of their tanks?"

"We may be nearly certain of all those things," Nezdeh answered. "We have no evidence that we inflicted any damage upon their shift drive, so it would be irresponsible to base any plans on such a hope. Next, they have made only one shift since taking on supplies at the meridiate world they last visited. It is inconceivable that they would not have replenished their antimatter stocks there. Lastly, even with the loss of two fuel tanks—"

"Nezdeh," Tegrese interrupted. "All lasers have struck the closest cannonball. But—"

Nezdeh looked in the plot, glanced at the sensors and then the viewscreen: although trailing debris, and no longer firing, the cannonball was still boring in on them.

Sehtrek was hoarse. "Range closing, bearing constant."

"Ulpreln, evasive maneuvers! Time until impact?"

Sehtrek had trouble finding his voice. "Ninety seconds."

Nezdeh wondered at the cannonball's design, that it could absorb that kind of punishment and still function. "Tegrese, maintain firing."

"I am. Continuing to degrade target."

But not fast enough. "Ulpreln, discontinue evasive. Release bearing control to gunnery station. Tegrese—"

She was already yawing the ship hard to starboard to face the oncoming cannonball; they leaned with the maneuver. "Target telemetry constant. Acquiring lock. Seventy percent confidence, seventy-five—"

Nezdeh interrupted. "At eighty-five percent, commence firing. Single penetrator rods, one every three seconds, maximum power."

"And—firing!"

The tremendous energies being discharged pulsed the deck under their feet like the slow heart of a great beast. In the plot, thin tines of green jetted toward the onrushing orange globe—

The fifth rod struck the cannonball dead center. Nezdeh almost sighed out her relief—then remembered to look in the plot:

Orange specks tumbled toward the green delta that marked the position of *Red Lurker*. "Brace for impact!" Nezdeh shouted at the same moment that Sehtrek yelled, "Debris still on intercept vector. Secure for—"

Red Lurker shuddered, pitched, then was righted to her prior orientation by her automatic attitude control system.

Nezdeh had managed to stay in her acceleration couch, glanced at the holosphere. "Sehtrek—damage?"

"Not critical. Report follows—"

"No time." Nezdeh jabbed a finger at the plot: the two remaining cannonballs were now speeding directly toward *Red Lurker* at a separation of over one hundred and forty degrees and widening quickly. She remembered her war tutor's wisdom: *Evading flanking pursuers is a difficult task that often ends in disaster.* "Ulpreln, reverse course, full thrust. Tegrese, acquire aft-facing lock as possible. If you have a shot, take it."

"I cannot promise hits, Nezdeh."

"I just want them to take evasive maneuvers and give us more time."

"They will catch us." Sehtrek commented. It was not a criticism, just a statement of fact.

"If they are so instructed," Nezdeh replied, and settled in to watch the pursuit.

At precisely four light-seconds from the planet, the two surviving cannonballs began counterboosting at the same blistering six-gee acceleration they had maintained during their pursuit.

"They're breaking off?" Tegrese wondered.

"Given the distance, I suspect it is an automated protocol," Nezdeh observed, hearing the iris valve open behind her. "It is consistent with what we know of the Slaasriithi. They intrinsically focus on defense. Beyond a certain limit, and probably influenced by whether or not they are still taking fire, the intelligence or expert system controlling these cannonballs informs them that the fleeing target is no longer a credible threat. And so the cannonballs break off to resume their orbital defense duties. Otherwise, feints could easily pull them too far off their patrol circuits and leave the planet unprotected."

The voice from the iris valve was Idrem's. "And I suspect there is another reason for their constant proximity to the world they defend."

Nezdeh turned. "What do you conjecture, Idrem?" She had come to love hearing her own voice say his name. It was not a sign of which the Progenitors—or her own Breedmothers—would have approved. But she did not care.

"There is the problem of control range," Idrem answered. He nodded toward the holosphere. "At four light-seconds, it is reasonable to suspect that the cannonballs' reaction time to new events is ten seconds. Four seconds to communicate the event to the planetary defense planner, two seconds for that planner to decide upon and transmit a response, and four more seconds for the response to reach the cannonball. All too often," he concluded, "that would result in a destroyed cannonball. Even assuming they have excellent on-board expert systems, a battlefield is Fate's laboratory for crafting novel challenges and unexpected conditions. The Slaasriithi will not be sanguine sending these drone-ships beyond the limit of optimal control."

"Yes, they *must* be centrally controlled." Nezdeh called up a holosphere image from earlier in the battle. "Notice how the two cannonballs were held back while our advance upon the Slaasriithi shift carrier increasingly put us on a predictable trajectory. They did not attack until we were as firmly set on our course as a fly is affixed to flypaper."

Sehtrek leaned back from his console, frowning. "Srina Perekhmeres, I must point out the dire situation in which we now find ourselves."

"Speak," she said.

"*Arbitrage* and the tug did not have time to fully refuel, and have been unable to produce antimatter for want of that fuel, as well as the need to avoid generating high-energy emissions. If the Slaasriithi ship can still effect shift, then they will have carried news of this attack to their homeworld at Beta Aquilae within nine days. Logically, we must assume that within three to four weeks, they will return here with a force over which we shall have—excuse me—no hope of acheiving dominion."

"This is well spoken, and true besides," Nezdeh acknowledged with a nod. "What do you recommend?"

Sehtrek folded his hands. "We must send *Arbitrage* and the tug to the gas giant to commence fueling and antimatter production immediately. If we are very lucky, that will have furnished us with enough antimatter to shift before the enemy relief forces arrive. We must then refuel and produce more antimatter in the next system as quickly as possible and shift again. Otherwise, the enemy ships shall surely expand their search radius faster than we may escape it. And they will have access to various prepositioned caches of fuel and antimatter." He sighed. "At the best, I consider our chances of survival uncertain."

Nezdeh nodded. "Your reasoning and your plan are both sound. But they are uninformed by one crucial datum." Nezdeh activated one of the bridge's hardware screens; it showed a bright red dot mixed into the sparse trojan point debris preceding the first planet.

"What is that?" Tegrese's curiosity was childlike, unguarded.

In every regard, she has poor control. "That is an automated base," Nezdeh said with a disarming smile. "It was identified by sensor operators on board the *Arbitrage*, shortly before we commenced our attack. Judging from the thermal and radioactive output, it is also an antimatter manufactory. Its stores of fuel and antimatter will not only allow us to expend energy lavishly in resuming our attacks upon the cannonballs and any humans who survived this combat, but will ensure our escape from Slaasriithi space. Within thirty hours, we should have fully loaded—"

Sehtrek's panel flashed: a prominent new source of emissions—thermal, radioactive, photonic—had just been detected. He glanced at the coordinates, and then at the viewscreen.

In the spinward trojan point of the first orbit, exactly where the small red marker was placed, a tiny white star winked briefly into existence, just off the orange-yellow shoulder of BD +02 4076. The pinprick sized star was gone as quickly as it had flared.

In the holosphere, the marker designating the Slaasriithi's automated fuel base faded away.

It was Sehtrek's duty to report the obvious to the suddenly still bridge. "The Slaasriithi base is gone."

Idrem nodded, no emotion in his face or voice: "Of course."

"How?" Tegrese asked.

Nezdeh suppressed a sigh. "The Slaasriithi no doubt had remote system commands that allowed them to terminate the flow of power to the magnetic bottles in which the stocks of antimatter were stored. The resulting annihilation would be absolute."

Idrem checked the mission clock over the central viewscreen. "Judging from the time delay, if the shift carrier sent such a command when she started withdrawing, it would have arrived at the station just in time for us to see its results now."

Tegrese's voice was gruff, grim. "This makes things much more difficult."

"Which was the enemy's intent, obviously." Nezdeh turned back to Sehtrek. "We must now follow your plan. However uncertain it is, however close a pursuit it may entail, it is our only remaining option. *Arbitrage* and the tug will return to the gas giant, and as they go, they will commence converting their current fuel load into antimatter."

Sehtrek's shrug looked more like a wince. "It is a slow process, Srina."

"All the more important that we commence now, even as we shape our new plan."

"Our new plan?" echoed Tegrese.

"Of course. Before the *Arbitrage* departs for the gas giant, she must furnish us with sufficient assets to complete the elimination of the Aboriginals. This will mean fighting past the cannonballs, then locating and exterminating our targets on the surface of the planet. Happily, we have an agent in place among the survivors."

"How do you know?"

"I know," Nezdeh answered, accepting that it was now essential that she reveal herself to be Awakened. To make sure of her claim, she extended her awareness—and immediately sensed the saboteurs' sole remaining Devolysite dwindling along with the insignificant thickening of time and space that was the planet behind them.

She nodded slowly at the faces ringing her. "Yes. I know."

Chapter Thirty-Two

The battered TOCIO shuttle started down through the bank of clouds that threatened to obscure the coastal river valley toward which they had been descending. The cottony whiteness that swallowed them quickly became an ugly gray. "Heavy weather," Raskolnikov muttered.

Caine gripped the edge of his seat as a cross current buffeted them, caught a glimpse of the instrument board. Three new orange lights had appeared among the ones monitoring the port side fuselage. "Have we lost airframe integrity?"

"Not yet," Qin Lijuan said calmly. "However, stress alerts are increasing. No matter how high I keep the nose, those portside breaches are catching air, increasing drag. It does not help that some of the largest debris went in the variable-thruster intake."

"Hard to keep her flying straight?"

"Yes, but the larger problem is that we are no longer capable of making a vertical landing. Also, the heat shielding there is no longer uniform. Even though the damage is on the dorsal surface, and even though we leveled out into a slow reentry slalom once we descended through the thirty-kilometer mark, there is no way to stop the drag from widening the breaches."

"My esteemed colleague is saying that our shuttle wants to shake apart and she is not letting it do so." Raskolnikov punctuated his sardonic synopsis with a wide grin.

Caine mustered a smile. "Thanks: I got that. Any idea how far down this cloud cover goes?"

279

Raskolnikov, all business again, shook his head. "No. It may go right down—what is your expression?—to the deck. Variable wave sensing suggests it begins to thin out at eight hundred meters, but beyond that, who knows? It might be fog, mist, mixed, raining, or clear."

"Eight hundred meters?" Caine's stomach tightened and descended. "That doesn't give you a lot of time to find a good landing zone."

"You are right, Captain: it does not. But the river beneath us had many straight stretches."

"So: a water landing."

Raskolnikov grinned that crazy grin again. "If we are lucky. Now, Captain, you must return to seat." He paused. "One at midsection, please."

Caine nodded. "I'll make sure the others get out. I've memorized the emergency exits, in case the hatches are jammed."

"*Horosho,*" Raskolnikov smiled. He glanced over at Qin Lijuan. "Perhaps I shall take it from here, yes?"

Egoless, Lijuan ceded him the controls. Nodding to the two of them, Caine cycled through the iris valve and moved quickly to the midsection of the craft.

He passed Ben Hwang, who opened his mouth to speak—

Caine shook his head, got into a couch across the aisle from Gaspard, who seemed to be concentrating on a deep-breathing exercise, his eyes closed.

As the three jammed windows in the passenger section darkened even more and rain began hammering down on the shuttle, Caine finished belting in—and started when Gaspard's voice announced, so calm as to be eerie: "For the record, Captain Riordan, I consider this crisis to be the province of security management. I shall not gainsay your orders."

Caine glanced over at Gaspard. Other than his reclosing lips, the ambassador was completely motionless, as if in a meditative state. "Thank you, Ambassador." If Gaspard responded, Caine missed it.

His collarcom buzzed. "Riordan here."

"Captain, this is Qin. You are strapped in?"

"Yes."

"Good. Please push your seat's paging button." Riordan did. "I am activating your seat's data link. Please put on the viewing monocle you will find in the seat pouch." Riordan had the small video-display device settled over his ear and in front of his left eye before she had finished the sentence. The small eyepiece flickered, then showed him the ground rushing up swiftly: a jungle cut in two by a meandering ribbon of rain-speckled river. "We will make our final descent soon."

But in the meantime, you're trying to preemptively kill me with terror? But Caine understood the real reason the pilots were showing him the view from the nose of the shuttle: "I'll call out the steps back here."

"And keep watch for the best way to exit the shuttle. If we are fortunate, there will be an option other than the dorsal hatch."

"Understood. There are three window covers jammed half-open back here. Can you unfreeze them?"

"We tried several times when we undocked. We have tried at least once a minute since then. We suspect that the sabotage created a power surge which disabled those circuits. However, those windows would only shatter if hit directly. I advise you not to worry about them." Which was a nice way of saying: *if that glass breaks, it will be the very least of your problems.* "We will be down within the minute. Please prepare the passengers."

In the data monocle, the river rose closer; in the distance, it seemed to narrow and bend. "Everyone," Riordan said loudly. "We are making a water landing."

"What?" shrieked Nasr. Ben Hwang released a long shuddering sigh—just before the two-toned crash landing alert started blaring.

Caine raised his voice over it. "This vehicle's tilt-thrusters are disabled, so we are landing runway-style. But we haven't seen any airfields or received any communications from the ground. Fortunately, we've got the best pilots in the business up in the cockpit and they've found a good stretch of river to put down on."

"Are there rafts? Are there life-pre—?"

"You'll find flotation packs under your seat. They clip on to your duty suits' shoulder clasps and will autodeploy the moment you hit water. Rafts will too." *I hope.* In his left eye, the river loomed large, and then suddenly glistened: the shuttle had passed beyond the shadowing storm clouds. Faint stretches of foggy silt and rocks shone up through the translucent water. This river was shallow: maybe *too* shallow. The camera crept closer to the rippling water, the strange foliage speeding past on either bank. "Everyone: crash positions. I will count us down. Five meters, four, three—"

Caine didn't see the long mass of subsurface rock at first; just the rapidly lapping wavelets it threw up as the current skimmed over its flat expanse. His mouth was open to shout a warning to Raskolnikov—

Who obviously saw it. The shuttle banked quickly to the left, rose up to hop over the rock—and inadvertently dipped the leading corner of its left wing into the river.

The sudden drag pulled the shuttle sharply to port. The engines roared as Raskolnikov fought its nose back to centerline, powering it upward. But as the wing pulled out of the water, Caine felt a transverse shiver run from the left side of the fuselage and pass under his seat. He glanced out his half-sealed window in time to see the pock-marked section of the wing buckle and then shred.

Freed of that drag, the shuttle suddenly pulled in the direction of the intact starboard wing, even as it jerked down toward the water. The starboard thruster screamed again; Raskolnikov had pulsed it to recenter the nose. Which dropped swiftly as soon as he eased off the thrust: the vehicle's ability to glide was wholly gone. Caine had a split-second monocle view of the rushing water leaping up at him—

The impact both threw him forward against the straps and the couch-back in front of him. And then—nothing: a surreal moment as the craft skipped off the river's surface like a stone. The fiber-optic bow camera sent a static-littered image of the nose rising, then falling again—

Toward a long, flat, wave-crested rock.

The second impact was so hard that Caine's teeth snapped together painfully, and his whole abdomen spasmed, his viscera jumping forward against his stomach muscles. Several shrieks cut through sounds of shearing metal, splintering composites, shattering glass—all of which was loudest from the bridge and the belly of the shuttle.

Which was still skipping forward along the river, yawing as it went. Sharp jolts hammered up through Caine's body, as if he was riding a sled down jagged marble stairs. There was a final dull thump—and then, stillness.

"Survival packs out; filter masks on!" Caine shouted. He

struggled free of the straps and stepped down into rising water. *Shit.* "By names; sound off!"

Voices shouted back: "Hwang!" "Betul!" "Gaspard!" "Xue!" "Veriden!" "Hirano!" "Eid!" "Macmillan!" "Salunke!"

The still-intact window showed water lapping along the half-amputated portside lifting surface. The remains of the wing were canted slightly backward; the tail section was in deeper water. Xue splashed forward, glanced at the emergency airlock door just aft of the bridge's now severely deformed iris valve. Caine nodded: "Go."

Macmillan, the farthest in the back, calmly announced, "Smoke coming out of the engineering spaces, Captain."

Caine, who was helping Gaspard to yank his survival pack out of the cubby under his acceleration couch, paused, sniffed. "That's not a fire. That's steam."

"Not so bad then." Eid smiled hopefully through chattering teeth.

"No, it's bad," Dora corrected. "This shuttle is a long-range model. That means a small nuke plant for powering the MAP thrusters."

Hirano frowned. "But if there is no leak, then—"

Caine gently pushed her toward the airlock Xue had opened; the air pushing in was pungent, thick. "Ms. Hirano, we're not worried about radiation. If the plant is hot and immersed in water, the temperature differential could cause it to shatter. Violently."

Hirano Mizuki's eyes were wide and her gait swift as she went through the forward exit. Ben Hwang, favoring his right side, approached. "Any word from the bridge?"

Caine met his eyes. "I don't think there is any bridge. Not anymore." He glanced at the iris-valve. Something had struck the other side hard enough to buckle the overlapping plates in toward the passenger compartment.

Hwang nodded and followed after Hirano.

Macmillan was the last out, carrying two extra packs. "Rations," he explained. "I could go back to the locker and—"

Looking over the IRIS agent's shoulder, Riordan saw that the water was waist deep around the shivered door into the aft compartment, and wisps of steam were rising up from it. "No time for that. And you'd parboil yourself." Caine bringing up the rear, they hurried out the exit.

It was a short jump down into shallows sloping up toward a marshy bank. Which was actually part of a riverhead: a stream meandered out of the frond-and-tube-weed fen in which the shuttle had buried its nose.

Or rather, what was left of its nose. The entire starboard side of the cockpit was in shreds, much of it missing. The port side had been squashed, accordioned up and back against the passenger compartment.

Macmillan put a hand on Caine's shoulder. "We were lucky to get out. Let's not stick around to get blown up."

Nodding, he followed Macmillan and the others up the narrow bank and into the tangle of alien vegetation that it was tempting, but altogether wrong, to call a jungle.

The column of steam that rose up from the shuttle became thickest approximately thirty minutes after they had put a kilometer between themselves and the wreck. An hour after that, it had shrunk back to its original size. A further thirty minutes reduced it to a wispy curlicue.

Caine turned off his collarcom, gestured for the others to do the same. There was no detectable signal other than the band-spanning white noise, so calling for help was pointless. Besides, preserving the remaining battery power meant retaining the ability to communicate with each other in emergencies, albeit over very short ranges.

"So now what do we do?" asked Nasr Eid.

Riordan stared directly at Nasr. "Now, we protect ourselves and take a fast inventory of our gear."

As the rest of the group started opening their packs, Hirano Mizuki stared around at the foliage. "Protect ourselves? From what?"

Riordan's unvoiced reaction—*Good grief: civilians!*—brought him to a startled mental halt: what had happened to his self-identity as a "civilian"? He wasn't sure where it had fallen away—and it hadn't fully. He wasn't enamored of imposing military discipline or having it imposed upon him. But then again, discipline and its trappings—ranks, protocols, traditions—did not define the difference between a soldier and a civilian. The difference was in outlook. Brilliant civilian researcher Hirano Mizuki stared into the shadowy reaches of alien underbrush and saw no reason for caution. Caine, on the other hand, saw an unguarded perimeter in unexplored terrain that might conceal unknown threats.

Riordan smiled gently at Mizuki. "Ms. Hirano, I hope that there is nothing to fear in this brave new world. And we shall not go looking for any trouble while we're here. But until we know we are safe, we will take precautions to deal with trouble, should it come looking for us. Am I clear?"

Hirano nodded, opened her pack, started checking its contents. Caine popped open his own, mostly for the theater of it: *always obey your own orders.*

Arguably they were already wearing their most important piece of gear: multipurpose, reconfigurable duty suits. Each pack contained important enhancements for them: a light raingear attachment, as well as a half parka with a reflective liner. There was a pony tank (he'd have preferred the Commonwealth tank/ rebreather combo), as well as a short duration EVA/SCUBA shell that integrated with the exterior of the duty suit. The comestibles satchel contained four days of fifteen-hundred-kilocalorie rations and supplements, three liters of water, and a dubiously diminutive solar still that doubled as a mess kit. The signaling kit included a flasher, a flare, transponder, dye, glow sticks, and various fire-starting options. The medkit was a densely stuffed cornucopia that, once opened, could not be repacked by mere mortals.

Consigned to the bottom of the pack were both its most and least useful components. The most useful was the lightweight but very robust multitool: knife, wire cutter, saw, screwdriver, vise; you name it. The least useful was its larger cousin, the so-called combopioneer tool. Ostensibly combining the features of a mountaineer's pick, hammer, a sleeve-over hatchet head, attach-able shovel blade, and handle extender, it managed to succeed at none of its designated roles, but instead, failed spectacularly at all of them. Furthermore, despite its much ballyhooed nano-bonded composite carbon-fiber construction, it had the strength and durability of an origami butterfly.

Caine's pack did not contain a firearm, but that was no sur-prise: only the Commonwealth and Federation packs included one in every kit. One in three of the TOCIO kits provided a break-down rifle which was designed so that both the barrel and receiver fit inside its hollow stock. Included in lieu of the com-bopioneer tool, the weapon was chambered for the venerable—not to say decrepit or feeble—nine-millimeter parabellum cartridge. A wonderful round in its day, but that "day" had begun in the early twentieth century and had ended by the middle of the next. But evidently, all that overstocked ammunition still had to be used somewhere, and each TOCIO survival rifle provided one such venue of terminal consumption, at a rate of forty rounds per weapon.

All in all, the survival pack contained about fifteen kilograms of gear and four more of garments and footwear, all of it so light-weight and flimsy that it was a wonder any of it held together long enough to be useful. Assuming that it did.

Everyone reported that their kits were complete. Four of the ten had the nine-millimeter break-down rifles. So, slightly better than average. Caine glanced in the direction of the wreck. The last wisps of steam had disappeared.

He rose. "Okay, everyone, we're heading back to the shuttle. Not because we're expecting a rescue to team to find us there," Caine added, seeing the hopeful look in Eid's eyes, "but to see if it's safe to salvage more gear. After that, we'll set a watch and survey our surroundings."

"Surveying the unknown always entails risk." They were the first words Gaspard had uttered since the crash.

"That's true, Ambassador, but total ignorance is an even greater risk. The only thing Yiithrii'ah'aash told us about Disparity is that our filter masks are the only environmental protection we need. We don't know the length of day, the mean temperatures at this latitude and in this season, or what kind of wildlife we might encounter. However, since we needed markers for this world, it's a safe bet that some of the wildlife might be unfriendly.

"So, first rule: when we travel, we travel in a secure formation. And everyone is going to take a turn walking point. With two exceptions: Mr. Gaspard and Dr. Hwang."

Hwang was already glaring at Caine when Gaspard looked up slowly. "It is not right that I do not share in the risk, Captain."

Damn it, I could come to like you. "Mr. Gaspard, you are ambassador plenipotentiary to the Slaasriithi. You are the package that must be delivered to them, and then back home, safely. That is my primary mission. I will not jeopardize it by putting you on guard duty. And Ben, before you torque up, let me ask you a question: how's your gut feel?"

Ben's glare faltered. "It's—I'm fine."

"Ben, you are a noble liar. But a liar just the same. You took that landing hard. Judging from the way you're moving, you may have sustained some internal injuries from rapid deceleration. Or are you saying that's impossible?"

"I—I cannot tell. But—"

"No buts, Ben. Lieutenant Xue, given your EMT and physician's assistant certification, you are now the party medic. You will stay by Dr. Hwang's side for the next twenty-four hours. Should our stoic Nobel laureate experience trauma symptoms that he tries to hide from us, you are to report them to me immediately. Mr. Gaspard, you will remain with them as well, and the three of you will travel at the center of our formation.

"In layman's terms, we will be traveling in a delta formation. The three persons tasked to keep watch will be armed and occupy the points of a moving triangle. The foot of the triangle will actually be out to our front. Our rearguard occupies the single point behind us. The fourth rifle will be carried by one of the persons at the center of the group. Now, who wants to stand the first patrol?"

Keith pointedly did not take this as a cue to step forward. *Good: if you're too eager to help me, that would blow your cover.* "Okay; no volunteers, then. First security detail will be Ms. Salunke on right point, Mr. Macmillan on left point, and Ms. Veriden on rearguard." Riordan saw Dora roll her eyes. "You have a comment, Ms. Veriden?"

"No. Just wondering if you feel safe with me at the back of the formation."

Caine frowned. "Elaborate, please."

"C'mon, when do we talk about the elephant that's not just in the center of the room, but bursting its walls? We heard the gunshots in the rear section; we see the people who are missing. But no one knows what happened back there; no one saw. Raskolnikov sealed the after-compartments the moment the firing started, kept it locked down until Rulaine called to tell him you were about to come aboard."

Caine folded his arms. "There were three bodies just inside the aft hatchway: Mizrahi, Dieter, and Danysh. The arrangement of their bodies makes it forensically possible that the murderer was killed by one of his victims. It is also likely that the murderer was the same person who sabotaged the Slaasriithi shift cruiser. During our evacuation, Yiithrii'ah'aash informed me that Oleg Danysh caused the power loss that exposed us to what was obviously a carefully staged ambush."

"It's possible that Danysh and the other two killed each other, but it's not likely," Veriden insisted, staring hard at Caine.

"No, it's not," Riordan agreed, motioning her toward the rear of the gathering group. "But right now, Ms. Veriden, whatever happened on the Slaasriithi ship is not of primary importance. Figuring out how to survive on this world is. Part of that process means traveling safely. So get to your position in the formation. We are moving out."

High in the neoaerie of Disparity's Third Silver Tower, Senior Ratiocinator Mriif'vaal considered the speakers of both the cerdor and convector taxae who had come to deliver their reports in person. Their pheromones were an olfactory cacophony of uncertainty, anxiety, dismay. "The first alert of the alien craft came from the spore-shields, correct?"

"That is correct, Mriif'vaal," asserted the cerdor, whose individual specialty was in overseeing the data interfaces and transfers between biota and mechanisms. "But the alien craft was not marked as an intruder."

"Truly? Why not?"

"That is unclear, Mriif'vaal. The high-air spores are too simple to discern anything other than whether an object has been marked with Recognition, or not."

"Yes, but you only said it was not marked as an intruder. Did it therefore carry the mark of Recognition, or did it somehow pass through the spore-shield without triggering either categorization?"

"I—I do not know, Mriif'vaal. The spore-shield did not dust a Recognition confirmation upon the regional ground biota, but nor did it signal an absence of Recognition marking. I suppose," the cerdor mused, "that it must have detected a Recognition but did not transmit it."

"That would be a dangerously uncertain supposition," Mriif'vaal said mildly. "Besides, there is no precedent for such a mixed result. But let us turn to the reports of the convectorae. What did your foragers encounter, Unsymaajh? Did they observe the descent of the craft?"

The unusually large convector's neck contracted slightly. "No, Mriif'vaal. They only detected the breaking of the sound barrier as it descended."

"Did any of them send Affined *sloohavs* to fly in search of the place it where it came to ground and to sample the spore-change in that locale?"

"There were no *sloohavs* on hand to summon to that task."

The cerdor's eager interjection sounded like an extended chirp. "Would it not be prudent to send a rotoflyer to explore the alien's projected region of terminal descent?"

Mriif'vaal raised a temporizing tendril. "That is an excellent idea, which we will hold in reserve." The Senior Ratiocinator smiled within: *and which you are eager to enact, given your taxon's love of complicated machines.* "But for now, we shall pursue subtler means of detection and, if deemed prudent, contact. We do not know these aliens' capabilities or their intentions. Any machines we might deploy, particularly aircraft, will be easily discerned. They are particularly susceptible to detection by orbital sensors."

Alongside Mriif'vaal, his designated respondent and Third Ratiocinator, Hsaefyrr, stirred from her meditative absorption— and thus, recording—of the discourse. "The defense spheres are no longer actively engaged. Is it likely that hostile or unpermitted objects remain in orbit?"

Mriif'vaal's tendrils switched once. "The absence of detectable orbital objects only means that nothing anomalous remains within the range of our sensor-cloud or the action range of the defense spheres. This descended craft might have a homing beacon. Its crew could thus establish lascom lock with extraorbital allies and transmit information. Or perhaps the forces which attacked Yiithrii'ah'aash's ship may have seeded the space above us with sensors as undetectable as our own. So, while the current circumstances *might* signify that we may act without fear of report, they do not guarantee it. We may simply be unable to detect all the elements that might bring us under observation."

Hsaefyrr swiveled her head toward the bantam cerdor. "Did you detect any radio emissions from the craft?"

"We were uninformed of its initial descent, and so were not attentive to any signaling at that time. Since it made planetfall, we have detected a few transmissions, but all are low power and very short range."

Mriif'vaal released a few Appreciation pheromones in elderly Hsaefyrr's direction before resuming his inquiries. "Cerdor, tell me: are any of these radio signals known to us, either in their cyphers or physical characteristics?"

The cerdor emitted a rattle of chagrin. "I regret to say that I have little expertise in such matters. However, I may assure you that the signals are not ours, nor the Arat Kur's, nor the Hkh' Rkh's."

Mriif'vaal mused a moment. "So it may be that this ship carried the visitors that Yiithrii'ah'aash informed us he was bringing planetside tomorrow. About whose species I have some conjectures. But it is just as likely that this ship was part of the force that attacked them, and whose origins are equally unclear."

The cerdor's hip joints flexed anxiously. "Then what shall we do?"

"We shall send three overseers to manage this matter as it unfolds: one cerdor, one convector, and one ratiocinator. The two of you shall fulfill those roles I have thusly designated for your respective taxae. I shall find a suitable midlife ratiocinator within the hour. You shall approach, observe, and report upon the aliens, aided by biota only. You shall make direct contact with me if the ratiocinator and at least one of you two deem it wise. You may employ whatever subtaxae you require to locate and keep track of these arrivals to our planet. In the meantime, our rotoflyers and other relevant mechanisms shall remain ready and preloaded with defense automata. Lastly, we will see to the distribution of spores that alert all our taxae to evacuate the area that lies along the projected route of the aliens' advance." Mriif'vaal stared at the luminous holograph which floated before them, offering an unusually precise view of the region in which the alien craft was thought to have descended. "Do you have any sense of their progress, yet?"

"No, but it seems likely they will follow the river downstream," answered Unsymaajh.

Mriif'vaal bobbed agreeably. "Which will make them easy to find and follow."

Hsaefyrr's observation was typically sour. "Which, in turn, will make them easy to kill for any pursuers that might hunt them."

"Yes," Mriif'vaal agreed sadly. "This is also true."

Chapter Thirty-Three

SOUTHERN EXTENTS OF THE THIRD SILVER TOWER
BD +02 4076 TWO ("DISPARITY")

Caine glanced up at the murky golden star in the teal sky. It didn't seem to race through the hours much faster than Earth's did, so in all likelihood, and allowing for the current latitude and season, Disparity's rotational period was probably not much shorter.

The survivors were moving carefully into and out of the wrecked shuttle, its nose having settled even further into the marshy bank. Higher up the shore, Ben Hwang sat checking for anything of value in the salvage that the team members brought to him, but that didn't amount to much other than the tools and the sealed rations from extra survival kits. Anything made of fabric had already been inundated with a fine, algaelike slime that had entered wherever the shuttle's hull had been warped, sprung, or ripped open by the force of the crash.

Macmillan emerged, carrying several packets that had not come from survival kits. "What are those?" Caine called to him.

He shook his head. "Don't know. Dora found them in the ship's locker before she headed back into the engineering crawlspace."

"They look like extra filters for our masks."

Hwang held up the dripping bag, kept it back from him. "That's what they *were*. Who knows what they've been saturated with now? Probably some of the fast-growing slime we've found on everything else." He glanced at Dora's own mask farther up on the bank, picked it up. "I don't think these are safe to leave around. We just don't know how quickly the mold and algae can ruin them in this environment."

Far in the distance, Caine heard what sounded like the hoarse hoot of a foghorn. He turned in the direction of the sound, saw nothing that might have made it. However, looking in the other direction, he noticed a constellation of large, orange water lily analogs that extended all the way to an upriver bend. Beyond that, all visual details were swallowed by the humid haze.

Xue, sitting between his charges, nodded in the same direction. "I heard it earlier, while you were all recovering items from the ship."

"Mechanical or biological?" Caine wondered aloud.

Hirano Mizuki, whose duty suit was wet up to her small waist, shook her head. "Unquestionably biological."

"Unquestionably?" Ben repeated.

"Well, almost unquestionably," she amended testily. "But this call lacks any of the patterns of machine sounds, which tend to repeat or to be comprised of remixed sub-patterns."

Qwara Betul, who was resting a moment, nodded at Mizuki. "Yes. She is right. Before I became a multimedia recordist, I worked in audio simulation. A machine, even one trying to mimic animals, can only mix, match, and modify what is in its catalog. That sound"—the distant, soft, and sonorous foghorn was back—"is an original utterance, every time. Or it is the best imitation of an animal I have ever heard."

Caine nodded. "Okay. Well, if you have any guesses about the creature that might be making it, please share them."

"Of course. Why?"

"Because that sound is coming from downstream. Which is the direction we are ultimately headed."

Mizuki nodded sagely. "Logical. Rivers tend to lead to social aggregations, whether the species in question is intelligent or not. Of course if we are presently in higher altitudes, rivers will not be so reliably correlated with settlements."

Caine started making his way toward the shuttle. "Fortunately, from what I saw as we descended, we're not in a highland flood-plain. This quasi-jungle is part of a long carpet of foliage that runs toward the northern shore of a southern continent. The longer we follow a major watercourse, the more likely we are to have the kind of encounters that Ms. Hirano mentioned."

"And," added Macmillan, "since we don't have maps, nav satellites, or any other means of knowing where the blazes we are, following a river at least keeps us from walking in circles without knowing it."

Caine smiled. "Yeah, there's that, too." He side-shuffled down the soggy bank, waded out to the forward hatchway; the water was now knee-level, there. As he ducked in, he almost collided with Nasr Eid, who was lugging more salvaged rations in one of the ruined packs they'd pressed into service as carry-sacks. "Nothing else of value," he panted, his voice muffled and warped by his filter mask. "Everything is smashed in the back."

"Where is Ms. Veriden?"

"She is a fish!" Nasr's voice was admiring and aghast, all at once. "She fitted her duty-suit with the underwater attachments, connected a pony-tank, and dove into the engineering companionway." He shook his head. "I would not go there. It is dark."

"Is she using one of the glow-sticks from a signal kit?"

Eid stopped in the exit, looking back at Caine. "Perhaps. Yes. Perhaps she is." Clearly, the thought had not crossed his mind before.

Caine moved further back along the flooded passenger aisle. Each time he waded through the shuttle, it looked more devastated than before, partly because all the compartments had been yanked open in search of useful objects, and partly because as the shuttle settled, the fuselage's cracks and split seams were sagging ever-wider.

There was movement in the water at the rear of the passenger compartment; Caine hefted his hatchet-headed combopioneer tool slightly higher.

Dora Veriden's head popped out of the water with a splash, her dark brown shoulder-length hair plastered to her scalp, neck, cheeks. "Shit," she announced. "I'm done back there."

"I recommended against going in the first place."

"No, Captain; you recommended that *you* go in my place. Then we compared how many times we've each been on, er, underwater operations. Added to the fact that I can fit into tight spaces easier than you can."

"Evidently, whatever caused you to decide against further dives has not diminished your propensity to argue. Find anything?"

Veriden cut an annoyed glance at Riordan but said nothing; he suspected that even she saw the irony in starting an argument over whether she was argumentative. "The engineering section is pulling itself free of the fuselage. We must have taken a hell of a whack back there. Besides, I think I've seen everything there is to see."

"Any updates, forensically speaking?"

She nodded. "Yeh. I haven't been able to find the pistols you mentioned, but the after section is a mess: gaps in the bulkheads and the deck where they could have washed out, or they could still be mixed in with the heavier debris. But I got a look at the bodies." She shook her head. "Between the wound patterns and the tight quarters, I just can't make a picture of a gunfight that would produce those results. If Danysh was discovered trying to tamper with the engines or the hatchway, then how did he get shot from hip to neck from about a meter's range? And why would he tamper with the engines at all? That would have killed him, too. And if he was simply trying to close the hatch before you got on, then why did that turn into a gunfight at all? He could have acted like it was all a misunderstanding until the other two let their guard was down. *Then* he could have shot them. And what the hell was Mizrahi doing with a gun?"

Caine shrugged. "I wish I knew the answer to any of those questions. In large part, because they are exactly the ones I've been turning over in my mind since I saw those three bodies. Now, let's get out of here before—"

"There's one more thing you should see. And probably only *you* should see it, for now." She held something out in her hand. It was a small vial of unusual manufacture, almost as if it were handmade.

"What's this?" Riordan held it up, saw what looked like a large, cubical tissue sample lumped at the bottom.

"Don't know," Veriden admitted. "But it was in Danysh's pocket." She waded past Caine, glanced upward as the top of the fuselage groaned faintly. "We'd better get out of here."

Ben Hwang, who seemed to be moving more easily, gestured at the collected salvage. "It's mostly food and combopioneer tools. Have you found any of the inflatable rafts?"

Caine shrugged. "What was left of them. They were stored ventrally, for easy deployment. They didn't handle that belly landing too well."

"Maybe we could make use of the plastic, though," Qwara Betul mused.

Caine nodded. "It's a good thought, but without those rafts, we're on foot. That means we're going to be leaving behind a lot of potentially useful objects. First priority is food and water, and stocking up on it is going to slow us down."

Hwang nodded. "And, dividing the ration packs ten ways, that still only gives us about five days. Less water, though: a lot of the containers didn't handle the shaking too well."

Salunke stared at the rear of the shuttle, where a sizable rent had caused the majority of the on-board flooding. "That hole, back near the ship's locker. We lost a lot of stores from there." A few of the darker orange lily pads had drifted up against the aforementioned wound in the hull; the wreck looked like it had thrown off vermilion clots before dying.

"That is probably where the extra food supplies were kept," Xue agreed.

Dora shook her head. "There's nothing there. I dove and checked."

Esiankiki Salunke was still looking at the water and the lily pads. "No. I mean that the ration packs might have fallen out of the shuttle. Into the surrounding water."

"Which might have any number of dangerous species in it," Ben Hwang pointed out.

The voice that rose in polite dissent was that of his assistant, Hirano Mizuki. "We have not seen any so far, and we have been wading to and from the shuttle for over an hour. If any local fauna was going to be attracted by our movement, or by what little of our scent enters the water around the cuffs of our duty-suits, I believe it would have appeared by now."

Dora screwed up her almost elfin features. "Yeah, but even if you're right about the food being lost through that hole in the fuselage, that means it could have fallen out at any point along the two kilometers over which we bumped and skittered before coming to a stop."

"I must disagree." Nasr Eid looked around the impromptu group which had been attracted by the discussion. "If that hole in the fuselage had been inflicted during the initial impacts, the subsequent shocks should have torn off the shuttle's entire tail, no?" He glanced around the group.

After some delay, Keith Macmillan agreed. "Almost certainly."

"And either way, it does no harm to look in the shallows around the wreck," Hirano finished. "Does it, Captain?"

Caine had let the debate continue because he himself was of two minds on the matter. On the one hand, the armpit-deep water into which the tail of the shuttle had sagged was a complete unknown, and in new environments, the unknown was to be presumed hazardous until proven otherwise. On the other hand, moving on foot with only five days of food meant they were not going to get very far on their own rations. And there was simply no way to know and no reason to presume that any of the local flora or fauna was safe for human consumption. They could cut rations, sure, but that would cut their rate of progress. So if there was any reasonable chance of locating some additional food—"Let's be clear about this: there is one excellent reason *not* to search the surrounding water for ration packs. All hypothesizing aside, we just don't know what might be lurking in there." Hirano seemed ready to pout. "But our ability to survive and keep moving is determined by our caloric intake. So we'll take the risk to search for the ration packs but on a volunteer basis only." Caine removed his filter mask, handed it to Ben Hwang: the air smelled of musk, marsh, and loam, with hints of something akin to a mix of cloves and cinnamon. "Who else will go?" Xue started to put up his hand; Caine shook his head. "Sorry, Mr. Xue. I appreciate your eagerness, but you are not eligible. You are both anchor watch and, for the time being, Dr. Hwang's attending physician."

Macmillan kicked at the lichen streaked shore. "I never have gone swimming on an alien world," he observed. "Might as well go home being able to say that I did, though."

Salunke, Hirano, and Betul signaled their willingness also.

"Okay," said Caine, "let's go fishing."

"Let's hope you're not the bait," Veriden muttered from her seat on the bank. Just before she frowned and rose to join them as they waded back into the water.

Caine slogged up the bank, blowing out water that smelled, perversely, akin to fresh cut grass with a hint of coffee.

Ben Hwang squinted at him. "You realize, of course, that you could be killing yourself. The microbes in that water—"

"May finish me, and the rest of us, more quickly than starvation. Yes. But unless we want to trust in fate and an early rescue, I don't see that we have much choice."

Xue, glancing at Hwang, nodded faintly. "I have been having that very debate with the honored doctor from the first time you submerged."

Hwang huffed diffidently. "I very much hope I am wrong. In the meantime, I thank your for your services, Mr. Xue." Caine did not hear the tone of polite dismissal, but evidently Xue did. With a shallow nod, he rose, walked the short distance to the line of packs that were being restocked according to the group's most urgent needs, and set about removing most of the useless elements of each combopioneer set. Even when communicating in English, the Chinese retained subtle social and rhetorical codes which allowed persons of different—or the same—station to send a variety of cues. In this case, Hwang's message had obviously been: "Please leave me alone with Captain Riordan."

Caine waited until Xue was fully involved in his task. "What's up, Ben?"

"You asked me to look at the vial Ms. Veriden ostensibly recovered from Danysh's body. I did."

Caine glanced at Gaspard. "Have you shared your findings with the ambassador?"

Gaspard continued to watch the heads of various team members rising and sinking beneath the water at the midpoint of the craft. "This is the first moment that we have had any privacy. Please update us, Doctor." Having found nothing immediately alongside the jagged gash in the vehicle's side, the searchers were moving further aft, examining the lily pads before resuming their search.

Hwang nodded, winced as he reached into his pocket. "This is what happened when I tried to take a sample." He produced the vial. The vaguely cubical, fleshy mass at the bottom had been replaced with a brown ooze. "As soon as I uncapped the container, it deliquesced. With extraordinary speed. Gave off a nasty smell; like rotting patchouli. I recapped the vial as quickly as I could."

"And did that stop the reaction?"

"Not immediately. It slowed, but continued for as long as there was air left in the container."

Riordan kept his voice low. "That's what happened to the organism they took out of Nolan Corcoran's body during his autopsy, just a little more than a year ago."

Gaspard started but said nothing.

Hwang nodded. "So I recalled. But you reported that the

Dornaani—well, Alnduul—told you that they had put that organism in his body. To help his heart."

That and possibly other things, as well. "Correct."

Gaspard stared hard at the slime in the vial. "Are you suggesting that the Dornaani might be behind this sabotage? And the attack?"

Caine shook his head firmly. "No. If the Dornaani wanted us dead—which makes no sense—we'd be dead. Most of our sensors can't even see their ships if they don't want to be seen. So whatever attacked the Slaasriithi shift-carrier wasn't their technology. And Danysh's security screening indicated that he could not have been contacted by the Dornaani beforehand, so I can't see how they could possibly be behind his sabotage."

"So is it just a coincidence, then?" Gaspard wondered. "Or could someone else have the ability to geneer an organism that destroys itself after it has been used?"

"It certainly is a possibility, so we can't conclusively assign this biotechnology to any one of our neighbors' flags. We only know that something analogous has been employed by the Dornaani. Ben, do you have any idea how this thing"—Riordan aimed his chin at the vial—"manages to deliquesce so quickly? It was already looking pretty sloppy when Veriden found it."

"*If* Veriden 'found' it," Hwang corrected with signal emphasis. "Actually, if one's xenogenetic science is advanced enough, and one chooses the right organism, it would not be so difficult to build a failsafe switch into its basic biology. You could create a hormone or protein that activates when the creature's autonomous functions stop. Those hormones could work like triggers to initiate changes in the membranes that protect the life-form from its own digestive juices." He shrugged. "That's only one possible method of achieving this outcome." They both looked into the vial; faint misty wisps rose up from the formless goo.

Gaspard cleared his throat. "The question is, how did Mr. Danysh come to have it in his possession?"

Hwang's tone was deferential but firm. "I must once again point out, Ambassador, that it is impossible to verify Ms. Veriden's account of how she came to possess this vial. It is possible that she, not Danysh, was in possession of this vial."

Gaspard nodded impatiently. "So, lacking any concrete evidence, Captain do you suspect that other saboteurs are involved, or is it possible that Danysh was working alone?"

"Let me answer your last question first, Ambassador. Since we can't *know* that Danysh was working alone, then we have to presume he *wasn't*—and so we have to remain alert for further sabotage. Beyond that, too many details at the crime scene almost shout 'set up.' For instance, those two handguns I discovered along with the bodies: we're *presuming* they were the weapons used. Just as we're presuming that any of those three people used them. It's entirely possible that there was a fourth person—the real shooter—who killed them all and staged it to look otherwise. And it does make operational sense that there would be a second saboteur, one unknown to Danysh."

Hwang nodded. "That way, the second agent could kill Danysh and thereby prevent us from acquiring any knowledge about how he crippled the shift-carrier, how he received the orders to do it, or from whom. The other two victims might just have been convenient means of misdirecting us, of allowing us to presume that Danysh had been working alone."

Whether by spoken or silent consensus, the searchers were now returning, their duty suits soaked. One person remained in the water, as far to the rear of the wreck as the encroaching lily pads allowed: Hirano Mizuki. *Of course.* Despite her mild demeanor, she had a stubborn streak a mile wide. She wasn't about to give up on her notion of finding the missing food, not until someone made her do so, Caine realized. He stood up: "Ms. Hirano!" She either could not, or chose not, to hear him.

Riordan walked down to the water's edge. "Ms. Hirano, you've done everything you can. There's nothing to find."

She half-turned. "I think I feel something, just down here." She had made the same claim three times in the past ten minutes. She pointed further aft. "I am going to take one last look." The others on the shore had stripped out of their duty suits; they'd dry faster that way, and the air was warm.

Caine put his hands on his hips. Although tempted to order her out of the water, he held back. He'd get compliance, but that might also start stratifying this overwhelmingly civilian group into sharply defined leaders and followers, and to disincline spontaneous sharing of ideas while simultaneously stirring up resentment. No reason to go that route until and unless it was absolutely necessary. "Ms. Hirano, we're going to—"

But she didn't hear him as she ducked under the water. The

vermillion lily pads bobbed in unison with the ripples made as she passed under them in an effort to get further back along the hull. And they continued to bob. Even once the ripples had subsided.

Before he knew why he was doing it, Caine was sprinting into the water: "Ms. Hirano!"

A meter beyond where Hirano had ducked under, her head burst through the lily pads, sending up a spray of water and a piercing scream. The water around her churned in fine, ferocious agitation, as if a pot teeming with minnows had been brought to a sudden boil.

Riordan hardly heard the shouts from the shore—"Mizuki!" "No, Caine!"—as he ploughed through the water, saw red blood on the orange water-lilies. Covering her head and her hands, small wormlike fish writhed and burrowed in desperate, ravenous delight. She flailed to break free of the twitching, clutching water plants, went under—

Just as Caine got close enough to plunge his arm under the surface, and—careful to keep the neckline of his duty-suit out of the water—grab for her. He got a handful of hair and pulled upward as more of the ferocious creatures swarmed out from under the water-lilies with which they evidently had some kind of symbiotic relationship.

Hirano Mizuki came up, shrieking, sputtering, gagging. Riordan felt the flutter of the small fish all along his body, felt them pressing and gnashing at his duty suit. He got an arm under hers, started to haul her toward the shore, felt the first stinging nips breach the legs of his suit. Macmillan, Salunke, and Xue were splashing out to meet him, arms outstretched for Hirano, whose face and neck were still speckled with the quivering, fry-sized carnivores, but it was unclear if they would get her to shore in time. Or if he would, either: Riordan could feel more of the piranhalike minnows sawing through the legs and waist of his suit—

On the far shore, a dim form rose up in the mists, sending a swift, powerful ripple across the river's central currents. It was five; no, eight; damn, maybe ten meters tall—and it emitted a strident, higher-pitched version of the same hoot the group had heard earlier.

The piranha-minnows immediately sprang off Mizuki Hirano's

savaged flesh and dove deep into the water. Riordan let the rest of the team take her from him, as the strange shape, a gargantuan badger on heavy stilts, hooted again, even more stridently. Riordan felt the insistent rippling of the worm-fish against his duty suit diminish rapidly; the sensation was gone by the time he had reached the knee-depth shallows. The lily pads, their coordinated undulations working like a wave-generation machine, began to back away from the wreck and push out into the downsteam current. As they did, the immense silhouette across the river sunk down and disappeared back into the mists.

As Caine staggered up the bank, Gaspard was there to take his arm and help him up the slight slope. "*Mon Dieu*, you are mad, brave, or both, Riordan. But heroics are not your place; you cannot lead us to safety if you are dead. What were you thinking?"

Caine stared at Gaspard, shook off his hand. "I was thinking of saving my team member's life." And he stalked up the silt to where Hirano Mizuki was screaming in agony.

Chapter Thirty-Four

Unable to move Mizuki, the group had to stay put for the rest of that day. Her screams diminished into sobs by dinner, and then soft moans when she began drifting off to sleep and losing conscious control over the pain. Besides widespread wounds that looked like horribly pulped flesh, one of the piranha-minnows—or, now, pirhannows—had bored partway into her left eye, breaching the sclera.

During the night, they rested in shifts, each armed watch staring out into dark brush that blinked, waved, and rippled with bioluminescence, particularly at dusk and dawn. Just as dim light began brightening the sky, and the presunrise bioluminescence began to subside, Ben Hwang sat down beside Caine. "Ms. Hirano's eye could become necrotic if it is not removed."

Sitting only two meters away, Xue leaned toward them and whispered. "How could that be done? Such a surgery would require anesthetics."

"Or she would need to be restrained," Hwang murmured.

Caine looked out at the river. The sky was beginning to reflect in it as a light gray-green-blue. "Mr. Xue, can you give us another option?"

"I can attempt to pack the wound in between irrigations, but I am still unable to determine if the blood supply remains intact throughout the sclera."

"Let's say you do that. How much warning will you have if you ultimately need to operate?"

302

"I will know in two days from now, at the most."

"Okay, then. You will continue to irrigate and change the dressings on the wound while you monitor it."

Hwang frowned. "It is kind that you wish to preserve her eye, but it might be better to—"

"Ben, I am not just preserving her eye. I'm trying to preserve our morale, too. Holding someone down to exenterate the entire eye without benefit of anesthesia would shake up any group, but civilians more than most. And how long do you figure it would take for her to recover from what will almost certainly have to be a midday surgery, so that Mr. Xue can adequately see what he is doing?" *Which is to say, "conduct an intrinsically difficult surgery for which he is totally untrained."*

Xue lowered his eyes. "I would not want to ask Ms. Hirano to become ambulatory for at least three hours."

Caine nodded. "And that means more lost time. As it is, we lost the end of yesterday. At least now we've got our kits repacked and can make some progress. If our enemies come down here to search for us, we've already taken a terrible risk by remaining at this site for twenty-two hours. Let's get moving." He started reaching for his pack.

Nasr Eid stood quickly. "Captain Riordan, how can we travel safely when there might still be a saboteur among us?"

Caine lifted his pack, settled it on one shoulder. "Mr. Eid, you make an excellent point. But every minute we delay here is a much greater danger. If any enemies are out there to strike at us, the worst thing we can do is remain at the crash site."

"Yes, but we are traveling as an armed party." Nasr eyed the rifles waiting to be picked up by the three persons who would be assigned to the first security patrol. "If there is still a saboteur, we are arming them, enabling them to finish their job."

Riordan shook his head. "Most saboteurs are not suicidal, which is exactly the kind of pathology that attempting a one-versus-nine attack requires. It would also require a world-class assassin to ensure that none of us would escape during their attempt. And if there was such an assassin among us, he or she would have attacked at dusk last night, when most of us were trying to help Ms. Hirano, distribute food, set up perimeter watches, arrange basic challenges and passwords, and dig a privy pit." *Which was why I felt like I needed an additional eye in the back of my head when dusk came on, and why I slept with one open all night long.*

"So," said Mizuki, her voice hoarse and a bit brittle, "you think it unlikely there is still a saboteur amongst us?"

Riordan heard the hopeful, rising note at the end of her question: it was an unconscious plea for him to make at least one of her fears go away. But Caine couldn't do so, not at the expense of the truth and the vigilance that the group had to maintain. "No, I'm not saying that, Ms. Hirano. But if our spaceside enemies intend to finish us off, then a saboteur's logical objective is to guide them to us, not mount a solo attack. That's also the only way for a saboteur to get home, because they're certainly not leaving Disparity in that"—he hooked a thumb over his shoulder at the ruined shuttle—"or getting out-system without a shift-carrier."

Caine put his other arm through the pack's other strap. "We're moving out. First security patrol is Mr. Macmillan, Ms. Betul, and Mr. Eid on rearguard. Second patrol will be Ms. Salunke, myself, and Ms. Veriden on rearguard. Questions?" There were none.

Wordlessly, the group began following the narrow shore toward the downriver bend.

Shortly after turning that bend, the river became increasingly constricted between tough volcanic formations which refused to submit to the wear of the water. Instead, its currents had backed up and scalloped out a turbulent pool, framed by basaltic outcroppings which split the outflow into several different watercourses. Judging from what they could see in the distant mists, these various streams all ran between low, rocky ridges, each channel becoming a rock-strewn flume. The one exception was a wide-mouthed outflow which was also the shallowest. Its relatively broad, clear shores were covered with tightly thatched mini-ferns that were the local equivalent of meadow and marsh grass. Various narrow points promised easy fording: swathes of modest white ripples stretched between the two shores. Without even stopping to confer, the group began working around the pool toward the wider, shallower stream.

Caine, who only nine months ago had been leading Indonesian guerillas in the West Java jungles, dropped back a few steps to walk alongside Ben Hwang. "I must be out of shape from shipboard living. I never used to notice the humidity. How are you holding up?"

"About the same. But I'm not so sure that it's just the humidity we're feeling. The filter masks significantly dehumidify the air. I'm worried about inhaled microbes."

Caine frowned. "The filter mask should be even more effective at screening those out."

Ben nodded. "Yes, assuming we are wearing them all the time."

Riordan heard the veiled accusation. "I know you think that those of us who went dunking for food rations yesterday were idiots for for taking off our masks. But since you didn't, how do you explain your own shortness of breath?"

Hwang smiled. "Last night, when I woke up for my half-watch, I saw that three people had removed their masks in their sleep. Then I realized that I had also."

"They are pretty uncomfortable when you're trying to rest," Caine agreed. "I wonder if there's a way to rig them so they are harder to get off?"

"I've been thinking about a modification to the straps that might help with that. I'll try making the adjustments when we stop for lunch."

"If we do stop for lunch," Caine amended.

Hwang glanced at him. "I know that you're in a hurry to put some distance between us and the wreck, but—"

"Ben, it's possible that Mizuki is never going to be any stronger than she is right now. Not if her eye infects and requires exenteration. And if our respiratory problems are the onset of a microbe, once again, our ability to make progress is never going to be any better than it is right now. So today, we eat on the move. Because we can." Caine picked up the pace again, heading for the rocks that stretched across the one narrow watercourse that lay between them and the wider, shallower one that was their ultimate objective.

Not knowing what other dangers might lurk in the shallow water or beyond the far margins of the shore, Caine kept the group to the center of the riverbank, which turned into an impromptu walking tour of the disparate flora and fauna that might have inspired Disparity's name. The plants varied from cactus-analogs with feeler-laden twigs instead of needles, brain coral spongiforms that could open into four equal parts and lure in a variety of quickly flitting creatures, and a thick tangle of black-maroon ground cover that resembled brittle, self-climbing kelp. These plants and their permutations tended to occur together, either in clumps, or as extensive, shore-lining swards.

The other, wholly distinct class of flora was more reminiscent of terrestrial forms, and the further they moved downriver, the more of it Caine noticed, particularly along the water's edge. The most dramatic exemplar was what the group came to call bumbershoots. Their tops, vaguely reminiscent of palms, were immense, pouting petals: in the daytime, the tree resembled a ridiculously tall umbrella. The tops of the petals were a dark, rich violet, whereas the undersides shone as if they had been brushed with a thin coating of silver-gold. But as the first day's march came to an end and the light began to fade, these petal-fronds drooped until they lay flat against the bole of the tree, which was comprised of an immense cluster of millimeter-gauged tubules with an almost lacquered exterior. Around the bumbershoot was an entirely different form of ground cover: the tiny spatulate fern-grass that they had seen near the crash site. Beneath that, almost invisible, was a substrata of ground-following fungi and lichen.

It was among these plants that the group witnessed much of the second night's bioluminescent light show, which winked and flashed as creatures occulted the glowing foliage during their silent dashes through it. Caine started keeping count and timing the eclipses of three particularly bright plants. By dawn, he had concluded that either there was quite a bit of nocturnal fauna roving about, or that, if it was sparse, it was also quite hyperactive. He mentioned it to Hwang.

The biologist nodded slowly. "There is, of course, another explanation."

"Several. We could be attracting curiosity because we're different. Or some of the local wildlife is shadowing us before they decide to attack."

Ben nodded. "I'll pass that word, if you like."

Caine considered. It might panic a few of the team, but the others were shaping up well enough that the possibility of an impending encounter might give them the extra edge of alertness they needed to detect and foil an ambush. It would also give everyone a bit of an adrenal boost and help them march a little faster and a little longer. "Thanks, Ben. By the way, how are you holding up?"

Hwang rubbed the right side of his torso, just a few centimeters lower than the pectoral. "Sore, but no more sharp pains. Xue and I agree that I'm healing from whatever internal dance my viscera did during the crash."

"Has he looked at Mizuki yet this morning?"

Ben nodded. "So far, so good. That means we probably don't need to worry about trauma-induced necrosis. But an infection could bring us back to the same point."

"So we keep irrigating and using the disinfectant from the medkits."

"Yes, but at this rate, we're not going to have much left if anyone else needs treatment."

"Necessary risk. We can't afford to have Mizuki slow down, and I'm not going to leave her or anyone else behind. So we use the resources we have to keep going now." Caine rose. "Ready to move?"

Ben smiled as he rose. "Not really, but let's go."

About an hour further into their march, the large stream split into two meandering courses, and the foliage became more dense, largely because of a profusion of trees that were more akin to immense bushes with high ground clearance. Their broad leaves, each a collage of green and orange, rose into a domed canopy that reached as high as fifteen meters, crowning the plant like the head of an immense mushroom sagging down to conceal its own stalk. The smaller, younger specimens did not have rounded canopies; their foliage was akin to a broad cone—

A cone.

Riordan dropped back to where Ben was helping Mizuki; her compromised depth perception made her susceptible to falls. "Ben, look: cone trees. The same species we saw on Adumbratus."

Ben dashed Caine's momentary hope that he had been the first to notice them. "Yes. It's clear now that we are on a battle line. Walking right along it, in fact."

"You mean, the battle line between the different biota."

"Yes. The self-climbing kelp and related plants are clearly the native species. The others, including the cone trees, have been introduced by the Slaasriithi."

Caine felt a quick pulse of hope. "Which they must watch over. To track the changes that they are trying to induce."

"True, but they might not visit here more than once or twice a year. If that. As Yiithrii'ah'aash pointed out, they are not in a rush to effect change."

They were drawing close to a copse of cone trees that had tall bumbershoots mixed among them. Mizuki looked up along their trunks, murmured, "Fascinating. And elegant."

Caine looked, saw how the underside of the palmate fronds sent back whatever light was reflected upward by the leaves of the cone trees. "You mean the way the bumbershoots make sure that the cone trees get all the light they can, even bouncing back what they don't capture on first exposure?"

Mizuki's good eye rotated toward Riordan. "You are a quick study, Captain, but I was referring to the bumbershoot's trunk."

"The trunk?" Caine echoed. He had gone from feeling botanically perceptive to utterly stupid in the space of a single second.

"Look closely: do you see how it shines? That is water, from condensation, which trickles down and feeds the ground around the cone tree. Which, because of its own dense canopy, catches almost all the light that falls upon it, yet sheds almost all the water."

Gaspard, who had drifted closer to them as they walked, shook his head. "And how is that elegant? It sounds quite the contrary. The cone trees would be strangling themselves out of existence if the bumbershoots didn't supply them with water."

"But that is not coincidence, Mr. Ambassador," Mizuki retorted. She pointed at one of the largest cone trees, located near the center of the copse. Its impressive wide-spreading canopy sheltered low thickets of ferns, mosses and fluffy crabgrass nestled between the roots that radiated out from its gnarled trunk. Day-glo yellow lichens were growing up into the lower shoots of the tree, and apparently, beginning to strangle it. "What do you see?" Mizuki asked.

"Lichen choking a bush imitating a tree," Gaspard replied.

Hwang smiled. "Yes, to our eyes. But the undergrowth that's killing off the tree is all exogenous, is part of the new biota."

"Yes. So now I see fratricide, as well."

Caine understood. "The canopy of the cone trees kills off the indigenous ground cover by cutting off the light and water. While it's doing so, it still gets the water that runs down the trunk of the bumbershoot overnight. The bigger the cone tree grows, the more free space it's making for its related flora to start seeding under it."

"Which those plants pay back by destroying the cone tree that gave them life," Gaspard concluded ironically.

"No," Caine contradicted, gathering confidence from Ben's encouraging stare. "By dying, the cone tree becomes the compost for the next stage of Slaasriithi plant life. Its canopy has outlived its purpose once the soil under it will receive the new plants."

Gaspard raised one eyebrow, lifted the other when Hwang nodded. "Exactly. What we are looking at is not permanent flora, but a collection of plants which are orchestrated to convert the indigenous biome into the new, exogenous biome. In larger copses, I have noticed a smaller subvariety of the cone tree; they are more widely spaced and not so thickly leafed. And although they are shorter, I suspect that they are actually the permanent form of the species. These large ones"—he gestured toward the mushroom-shaped tree which now had small bioluminescent seed-pods shining like lanterns high up in the underside of its canopy—"they are the advance guard of their species. They exist only so that they may die in the fight to expand their biome."

Mizuki waved a hand which followed the borders of the two warring biota as they roved back and forth across the two streams. "They are locked in a slow-motion struggle for dominance."

Just like we seem to be, ever since we discovered we're not alone in the cosmos, Riordan reflected as he resumed his position behind the point-walkers, Macmillan and Betul.

Chapter Thirty-Five

As the day wore on, Disparity's flora continued to command Riordan's attention—not because of what it displayed, but rather, because of what it might conceal.

Disparity's foliage was worse than the Javanese jungle. Here, the mists and humidity not only reduced visibility, but often painted halos around the numerous reflective surfaces. The supersaturated air also grayed-out objects very rapidly, obscuring even nearby silhouettes or terrain features. In short, Disparity conspired to reduce the visual acuity upon which effective security watches depended: an unnerving factor that soon evolved into a dangerous one.

Caine had just come off point when Macmillan held up a large, thick hand and crouched. The entire team took a knee; those without rifles hefted their axe-headed combotools. Caine crept a few steps closer to the burly IRIS operative. "Report."

"Movement there." Macmillan jerked his now red-furred chin at the narrow band of low land that separated the stream's split courses; they had taken to calling it the median. "I think something from the far bank forded over to the median when our line of sight was blocked a hundred meters back."

Riordan nodded. "Whatever they are, they're paralleling us, using cover to get closer." He scanned ahead and behind. "But if they are predators, and they have any brains whatsoever, they won't charge at us from the median. If they can, they're going to get across the river and approach our opposite flank before they attack us."

Macmillan glanced at the gentle wooded slope behind them. "You mean, they'll either get ahead or behind us by crossing the near stream when we can't see them, and then press us so that our backs are to the water?"

Caine nodded. "Where they'd plan to run us down along the shore or in the shallows."

Qwara Betul had drifted in far enough from the right point position to overhear. She hefted her rifle anxiously. "So what do we do?" She claimed to be a good shot, and Caine believed her, but hitting stationary targets on a range was a lot different than hitting moving creatures in combat. Particularly when the creatures wanted to kill you.

"We're changing formation." He waved Dora forward; she arrived with startling speed.

Before he could update her, she nodded. "I thought I saw something over to our left, just as Macmillan called for a halt. I've been checking the slope to our right. I don't think anything has made it across and worked behind us, yet."

Damn, she's good. "And we've got to keep it that way. The three of you on watch are going to walk beside the stream. The rest of us are going to push away from the water a little bit, higher up the slope. That means we're giving up the delta formation. We'll be moving as two columns; the unarmed folks up higher on the bank, you three down closer to the water. That way, if the creatures try to cross the stream either in front of us or behind us, we've got a better chance of seeing them. And putting a bullet into one of them."

Betul's eyes widened. "Will that not just anger them?"

Macmillan looked thoughtful. "These aren't big critters, Qwara. Pretty light-footed from the way they move, and their haunches don't make a long flash when they pass between the fronds." He shook his head. "Besides, most predators run from the sound of a gun. And if one goes down, the others tend to flee."

"Sharks don't," Dora argued. "They don't give a damn about what happens to other sharks. If they aren't hurt, they don't run. And the creatures here may not be any smarter."

"Maybe not, but fish don't work as cooperative hunters." Caine pointed across the stream. "The group trailing us does. So, the same bonds that make the group work together can be used to collectively scare them into running." *Theoretically.*

Dora shrugged. "Hell, it's our best shot, anyhow." She turned and scooted back, shooing the unarmed persons at the center of the delta up the slope and into a column paralleling the tree line. Macmillan started to move toward the point position on the stream-hugging patrol column, saw that Riordan wasn't moving. "What about you, Captain?"

Caine rubbed his chin. "I'm going to play free safety in the center, between your column and the upslope group. Can't really be an effective commander from back there." He gestured toward the jungle to their right, where the first bioluminescent lures and attractors were warming to the approach of dusk. "We'd better get going, see if we can find a defensible rock outcropping or something similar before nightfall."

Macmillan shrugged. "You're the boss, boss," he said, but Caine could read the real meaning in Keith's tone easily enough: *please don't be stupid and get yourself killed.*

The lower the sun sank, the more frequently the group saw movement. But their change in formation seemed to discourage the creatures paralleling them. They kept their distance, which probably signified that if the humans were considered prey, they were not deemed unaware nor easily frightened prey.

As more of the bioluminescent plants began speckling the undergrowth with orange, yellow, magenta, and indigo glows, the movement of the trackers became easier to follow. Although it was impossible to make out a flashing flank or leg, swift occultations of the glowing dots in the underbrush revealed the direction and speed of the creatures' movements. Most of them had now crossed the far stream and were on the median. A few minutes after Keith Macmillan quietly reported he didn't have enough visibility left to reliably hit a target at forty meters, the river's northerly course bent slightly to the west and the narrow band of salmon and teal sky that had been visible between the trees on either bank suddenly widened.

"Watercourses rejoin up ahead," he reported. "The median runs out."

"Any rock formations?"

"Not that I can see from he—yes. About one hundred meters

beyond where the river comes together again. There's an angled bluff that juts into the current. Naked rock. If we get to the top of it, we'll be in a defensible position."

Caine stopped, scanned the terrain. The creatures knew this land, which meant that they knew they were coming to the end of the easily fordable part of the river and were coming to the end of the median, too. Which meant that they were running out of areas where there was enough cover to screen a crossing. In fact, they had already run out of opportunities for crossing the stream ahead of the group, as shown by the widening space between the trees downriver. Which meant they only had one option left: "Keith, double-time forward!"

"Forward?"

"Yes: watch for critters trying to cut you off from that bluff. Ambassador," he called over his shoulder, "everyone in the upslope column runs after Macmillan. If he stops to shoot, you go past him. Lead our people up the rocky bluff you're going to see in a few meters. Dora," he shouted, moving to the rear. "Form up on Qwara, and watch the stream behind—"

Up ahead, Macmillan's rifle spat three times as something started splashing across a rocky shallow where the streams began to reconverge. Whatever it was went down, thrashed, went down again. As it struggled, it made a sound like a soprano screaming over a fast rattle of deep-toned castanets. Another of the creatures, a thin-limbed and nimble quadruped with a heavy body, was sprinting past its feebly kicking packmate. Two more shots from Macmillan's nine-millimeter had no effect. The animal started up the shallows toward the now sprinting group—then Macmillan's weapon fired twice again, rapidly.

The creature, a bulldog body perched on whippet legs, spun away from the impact of a hit. Its broad, blunt head tossed— upward jutting fangs flashed as its jaws snapped irritably—and then it charged back into the water, fleeing for the median and the far stream beyond it.

Behind, Dora was approaching Betul—just as the median vomited out a handful of the same creatures, splashing across the shallow water. Dora shouldered her rifle, fired twice—the second bullet elicited a brief castanet-shriek—and then she ran. Caine sprinted toward Betul, who had drilled on what to do in this situation: aim, fire twice herself, turn, and run past Dora, who would then repeat the process. A simple leapfrog retreat. Riordan should have been retreating as well, but hung back to make sure that nothing went wrong. Because when even the simplest maneuvers had to be executed in combat—

This day was no exception. Betul fired once, tried again: nothing. But Riordan had heard the incomplete cycling of the bolt, knew what had happened: "Jam! Cycle the action, Qwara!"

Qwara Betul was either too terrified, too surprised, or too unfamiliar with the terms to react quickly enough. Instead, she tried firing again, to no avail.

Caine ran past her. "Just run. Now!" He brandished his combo-axe at the scattered creatures just coming up the shore, and shouted at them. But the words of his shout were also a signal: "Dora! Cover fire!"

The creatures stopped for a moment.

"Dora!"

But she was gone, was too fast. And the creatures were edging forward.

Damn it: if they charge Qwara now—

Riordan yelled at the ugly predators again: no words, just an animal howl. They froze in midstride; Caine jumped into the stream and made for the end of the median, finding the footing on the rocks swift, but dangerous. If he slipped or tripped just once—but he didn't and evidently, that was the last direction the creatures had expected their prey to go.

The barrel-chested predators spent a moment in indecision, and then the largest ones went after the main group: more meat in that direction. A trio of smaller specimens, probably having learned that they did not get much of the kill when they competed with their bigger pack mates, veered after Riordan.

Who was already charging up the far shore. Far behind, he heard his name being shouted: *no time for that now.* He just hoped that Qwara had been able to use the momentary distraction to break out of her panic and run like hell. Riordan scanned the median: there wasn't even a tree large enough for him to climb. He could always try his risky backup plan: to push out into the reunited currents of the river and swim over to the rocky outcropping—

But beyond the further, narrower stream, he spotted the distinctive shape of a large cone tree, alone among indigenous vegetation. It almost came down to the water's edge, and was cinched close against a rock face on the downstream side. The clearance under the lower margin of its canopy was less than a meter.

Riordan's decision was as much instinct as tactical insight: under that tree, his rear flank was protected by a sheer rock face. Along the rest of its perimeter, enemies would have to hunker down to get at him and so, lose their speed and leaping advantages. He sprinted into the stream on the other side of the median, discovered the light was failing.

As he waded through the midcourse currents and heard the creatures skitter to a stop on the bank he'd just left, his collarcom paged. Again, no time. With one hand clutching the pseudo-axe and the other out before him to maintain balance, Riordan sloshed through the accelerating, groin-deep current. Behind him, the predators jumped into the water and started picking their comparatively hesitant way after him.

Caine came up on the far shore, raced along the dark ribbon of muddy silt that led all the way to the cone tree. It would be close; he had a decent head start and had gained on them during the crossing, but once on the shore they were much faster. As he neared the tree's canopy, he saw hints of light under it, hoped he wasn't jumping from a frying pan into a fire, and, hearing the pattering of speedy pursuers behind him, dove forward at an angle. His sideways roll carried him under the lowest branches and sent him banging over a washboard of crisscrossing roots.

The first of his three pursuers fetched up outside the canopy, ducked its head under to get a look—

Riordan, axe cocked as he came up from his roll, swung hard.

The creature saw the movement, flinched its head back, scream-clattered as a glancing blow tore a divot out of a cartilaginous flap that might have been an ear. Furious, ravening, the other two angled apart with the innate tactical insight of all predators; any prey can be brought down if it can be flanked. Caine cocked the axe back again, wondered how long this could go on—

A monstrous, outraged foghorn roar froze him and the predators midaction: a savage tableau illuminated by pink and violet seedpod-lanterns now brightening in the cone tree's undercanopy. A great rush of water swept under its low boughs from the direction of the riverbank, where something large, terribly large, was rising up, torrents of water pouring off the sides of its shadowy bulk, obscured by the leaves of the tree.

The predators inched back, muted castanet-clatters vying with shrill warbles and yelps as they made a show of standing their ground. But the foghorn-hooting—the same made by the dimly seen gargantua which had ended the pirhannows' attack upon Hirano—sounded again, and a broad, spatulate foot thudded down into the shore-silt so hard that gouts of the sandy black sludge sprayed under the tree and toward the predators.

All of which promptly ran, making sounds akin to fighting tomcats as, scalded by terror, they leaped off into the underbrush.

The foot in the silt remained planted there for a long moment, then, wavering, turned, moved back out toward the water. But the creature did not seem to be leaving. Instead, it seemed to be brushing along the riverside periphery of the cone tree's canopy, searching—

With a blast of musk and mist, two immense legs forced open a gap in the cone tree's shoots and branches. The legs bent and with one surprisingly deft dipping motion, the blunt body of the river-striding behemoth was crouching under the ten-meter canopy of the tree. Its head, not much more than a trough-jawed protrusion of its body, swiveled toward Caine, a pair of round, wide eyes both above and below the gaping maw. Jaw-lining light sensors pulsed and bulged in his direction as well. The gigantic animal staggered toward him, a grumble rising up out of its gut like a chorus of bears waking up from hibernation.

Riordan, panting, looked up at the creature, hefted his ax ironically, and wondered: *so does he stomp me or bite me?*

Chapter Thirty-Six

The water-strider stared down at Caine, leaned slightly closer. Riordan watched the extraordinarily wide mouth of the creature, held the futile axe ready, but did not move it.

The water-strider snuffled at him, then blew out a great, surprisingly sweet, breath—a mélange of lilies and ginger—and swayed unevenly away.

Caine forgot his fear as the creature's unsteadiness caught his attention: *is it weak or—*?

And then Riordan noticed that the ground around the creature was not just wet from its steadily dripping pelt; there was a faintly iridescent maroon spattering that did not readily mix with the water. Caine traced it, found that it was streaming down one of the water-strider's immense, bowed legs, which was quivering. Riordan looked more closely—

Pirhannows, by the scores, had worked themselves into the creature's short fur. And now that he knew what to look for, Riordan saw them everywhere, writhing along the water-strider's belly, around its mouth, up near its haunches, and at a few points on the strange, almost antennalike protrusions that lay along its back to either side of its spine.

The water-strider took two more staggering steps away from Caine, revealing the pulverized remains of several orange water lilies stuck to its far flank. The strider crouched low and slowly slid on to its side, where it preceded to roll fretfully to and fro, apparently trying to cake dirt on its innumerable wounds.

Unfortunately, the soil under the cone tree was too sparse and too dry to stick. The protuberant roots gave the strider surfaces against which it could squash a few tormentors, but the main infestations were not concentrated where the rolling routinely crushed them. Some did fall off, though—

Caine leaped closer to the water-strider and smashed a handful of the pirhannows into mush with the back of the axe head. The sight, and the smell, was not unlike stamping on corpse-bloated maggots.

The water-strider started, stopped its rolling, focused all four eyes on Caine, snuffled lightly—then seemed to catch the whiff of its dead tormentors. It stopped, stared at Caine again, and then began rubbing its broad flat face along the roots that radiated out from the trunk of the cone tree. A dozen of the worm-fish were scraped off, still squirming. The strider leaned back its head—and out of pure instinct, Caine pulped them with the back of the axe. Savagely. He didn't know if it was for Mizuki, or out of gratitude for being twice-saved by water-striders, or something more primal. *Or possibly*, he wondered, standing back, *this is an example of the Slaasriithi process of Affining one species to another*. But despite the chilling implications of that possibility, Caine Riordan realized that there was simply no arguing that he had become, well, *fond*, of this powerful yet gentle creature.

Riordan resumed his strange partnership with the water-strider, lethally grooming the pirhannows from its pelt for another fifteen minutes. By then, the remaining wormlike tormentors were located in anatomical regions that the creature could not reach, and which Caine had no way of approaching without seeming like a new threat. The water-strider looked at him—it recalled the patient, steady stare of a grateful horse or dog—and rolled its mass a bit further away, the margins of its mouth not only caked with its own blood, but dry and cracked.

Caine rocked back upon his buttocks, sat, reflected on the surreal circumstances in which he found himself—and, for the first time, heard his collarcom paging steadily. Clearly, Gaspard had used his command-level authority to unlock the devices. Riordan tapped it. "Riordan."

"Captain Riordan! We had given you up for—never mind. We are delighted that you have answered. But where are you?"

"I believe I'm directly across the river from you, Ambassador. Can you see a large cone tree on the opposite bank, the only one for hundreds of meters in either direction?" As they spoke, dusk was making its final surrender to night.

"I do not see—" Eager exclamations behind him suggested that others had better awareness of their surroundings. "Ah—yes, yes. Your position is known. But—"

"Ambassador, first things first: is everyone all right?"

"Happily, and improbably, yes. Ms. Veriden and Ms. Betul covered our retreat up the rocky outcropping by greeting our pursuers with a flurry of bullets. One was killed, two were wounded. That was enough to convince them to flee. But you have found shelter? Even though we saw you pursued? And you are safe?"

Caine stared at the water-strider; it may have been sleeping fitfully. That, or it was an awfully noisy breather. "Frankly, Ambassador, I doubt I've been safer since I stepped foot on this planet."

"I am confused, Captain: how could you be—?"

"Ambassador, it would take far too long to explain. For now, let's concentrate on arranging the safest way for me to rejoin you tomorrow. Have Mr. Xue and Ms. Veriden make their way over here to escort me back one hour after dawn. They should both be armed with rifles. After last night, if those predators are still in the area, they will hightail it the other direction if they take more fire. Other than that, I think we should save the batteries of our collarcoms."

"Very well, Captain. You seem to lead a charmed existence."

Caine looked at the strider. "A very unusual one, at least. Good night, Ambassador. Signal me when Xue and Veriden leave tomorrow."

"Very well. *Bon nuit*, Captain."

"Likewise." Riordan turned off the collarcom.

The water-strider fell into a restless slumber, judging from its phlegmy susurrations, but its bleeding increased steadily. Riordan wondered if—following the apparent intent of the water-strider— he might have more success at making mud to cake its wounds. But the pirhannows had pulped the large animal's hide in so many places that it was difficult to discern the worst sources of the bleeding.

The other problem—beyond Riordan's innate reluctance to

touch the large creature without its express toleration for such contact—was the lack of mud or suitable soil. Caine searched around the sub-biome that existed beneath the cone tree's canopy, but the ground cover was thick and the dirt somewhat sandy: it crumbled when he tried to pick it up.

So maybe the answer was to make one's own mud, or, better yet, to bring it in from the shore that crept right up to the margins of the tree. Armed with one of the tree's large, spatulate leaves, Riordan moved through the arch the strider had used to enter under the canopy—

And recoiled: the riverside shallows were choked with orange lily pads. Well, that answered why the gargantua had not returned to its natural environment after confronting the predators. It had probably been run ashore by this immense colony of lily pads and its attendant swarms of pirhannows. Which also made it impossible to get enough river water to make mud. Walking back into the microecology under the canopy, and into what seemed like a growing mélange of sickly-sweet scents, Riordan looked for other sources of water.

The search was made easier by the bioluminescent clusters that were nestled in the high reaches of the undercanopy. One of the clusters, a helix of puffballs interlaced by tubules filled with a lighter-than-air gas, had detached from its bud and was descending in a slow spiral. As the glowing lavender and violet lei rotated and the play of light changed, Riordan noticed a glistening, sloped root that ran in under the canopy from outside.

As Caine guessed, the root emanated from the cone tree's invariable botanical partner, an adjacent bumbershoot. Early evening condensation was accumulating on its bole, which sent the runoff trickling down microgrooves that ran onto this angled root. *It's a tiny natural aqueduct*, Caine realized, tracing how the runoff spread slowly throughout the microecology huddled beneath the cone tree and was further distributed by the capillary actions of ground mosses and day-glo lichens. Along with a thick, mown-grass smell, the flow increased as he watched. With any luck, there would be enough water to make a mud plaster for the water-strider. But even if he was able to create a serviceable mass of the slop, he was still confronted by the initial, troublesome questions: where should he apply it? And was that really what the water-strider had been trying to accomplish? All of which begged the question: would the water-strider allow him to do so? *One way to find out.*

Riordan approached the behemoth carefully. After two complete orbits of its side-slumped form, he remained uncertain about where to treat it. Almost a quarter of the its body and legs were covered in bloody bore-holes, and no spot seemed any worse or better than another. Ultimately, Caine's attempt at veterinary assessment yielded only one useful result: a better understanding of the water-strider's physiology.

In addition to the four eyes that bracketed its wide mouth like corner-points on a rectangle, the creature was dotted with a vast array of light sensors that had no eyelids, no irises, no protective bone ridges. They were simple, possibly expendable, and probably essential to the animal's safety. Whereas terrestrial herbivores tended toward opposed ocular arrangements—one eye on each side of the head, often furnished with fish-eyed lenses—to increase the total field of vision and hence watchfulness, this creature had evolved a different solution to the same challenge: more eyes. The quality of vision was probably vastly inferior, but the increased awareness was likely to be a good trade; the long-legged quadruped had a lot of potential blind spots. Audial sensing seemed to be more rudimentary, probably because the water-strider spent much of its time submerged: two small bony tufts at the front of its membranous backsails answered for ears.

Its four primary eyes still closed, the creature uttered a sharp, startled snort-hoot that sent Caine back upon his haunches. The water-strider was suddenly awake, its many eyes open and roving fitfully. It worked its mouth; the dried edges cracked anew and bled freely. Several of what looked like feelers split away, fell off in gory clumps. Ignoring Riordan, the strider worked its legs feebly against the ground, trying to push its body in the direction of the water running in from the neighboring bumbershoot's root-aqueduct. After several heavy shoves, the creature gave up and seemed to deflate, a low, rolling groan coming out of its dorsal respiration ducts.

Caine rose, went over to where the runoff was now audibly trickling along the root: maybe not enough to make mud, but certainly enough to drink. Riordan harvested one of the cone-trees' spatulate leaves, curved it into a crude basin, and pushed it against the current of water washing close along the surface of the bumbershoot's root. Slowly, like holding a cup beneath a dripping faucet, the hollow of the leaf began to fill. As it did, Riordan noticed that, in addition to the cloying scents being emitted by the cone-tree, the runoff was strongly aromatic as well. Probably from airborne spores and pollens that stuck to the wet bumbershoot and were then carried along by the runoff, which apparently seeded as well as irrigated the area under the cone tree.

It took ten minutes for Riordan to collect the one-and-a-half liters of water he carried back to the water-strider, moving cautiously as he reentered its field of vision. The creature's eyes focused, swiveled towards him—it was unnerving to be the center of attention for four eyes—and the behemoth snuffled tentatively. Then eagerly. Its tongue—an immense, blue-gray anaconda covered with slowly waving polyps—slipped outward, moved toward the water like a blind man's arm extending toward an expected door handle.

Caine brought the water closer, shielding it with his body so that the strider's tongue wouldn't slap at the leaf and inadvertently knock it apart. The strider's tongue retracted, Riordan brought the water to the edge of its mouth and the animal drank, partly slurping at it, partly allowing the human pour it in.

When the water was done, the tongue explored the leaf carefully, being equally careful not to touch its human bearer. The strider sighed: a deep, bellows grumble of relief and comfort. Riordan almost reached out to pat the great stricken beast, thought the better of it, and instead returned to the root-aqueduct for another leaf-full of water.

Caine became quite adept at the process over the ensuing hour. Five more times he gathered the runoff; five more times the strider consumed it. By the end, they had it down to a cooperative pour-slurp-pour routine that wasted a minimal amount of water.

But when Caine returned with the seventh leaf-full, the water-strider closed its eyes and turned its body so that its wide face nestled into the soft mosses and lichens of the ground cover. It emitted a long sigh and was still. *Well, if the poor critter can get some rest despite all those wounds—* Caine crept away, trying to ignore the queasiness brought on by the growing riot of aromas under the cone tree. It was easy to imagine that he was locked in a closet with thousands of scented candles, each one different, each overpowering odor vying with all the others.

Resolved to get some sleep himself, Riordan found a soft, rootless patch of ground a few meters away from where the glowing puff-lantern had finally landed, near the edge of the canopy. As he watched, a small, scurrying creature edged under the leaves and tore it apart, devouring the tubules and puffballs before darting away again. Caine smiled: so that was how the cone trees' oppressive canopies managed not to prevent their own repopulation. Their fragrant, glowing fruit baited in small raiders who also worked as seed dispersers. Keeping an equal distance from the edge of the canopy, and the hulking mass of the water-strider, Riordan lay down on the soft spot he had found. If he could just rest a bit—

Riordan awoke from a sound sleep, startled by the strider's sounds of distress. The hoarse elephantine bleating increased, along with a thick odor that cut through the cone tree's own olfactory chaos: it was the strider's musk, but amplified. Caine moved quickly to where the creature's head was still mostly embedded in the moss. Its eyes were roving blindly. It snuffled when he came closer: not an aggressive sound, but one of recognition, maybe need. Riordan jumped away to get more water, returned with less than a liter. The water-strider closed its eyes allowed him to pour a little in between the great grinding ridges that were its version of teeth, and then stopped, as if something was confusing it. It lifted its head slightly, quaking, and two of its eyes opened, focusing on Riordan as it inched toward him. Caine anticipated that it was going to vomit on him, but instead, it released a great, musk-reeking breath: a surprisingly sweet smell that was part grassland breeze and part old leather.

When the creature had finished that unusually long exhalation, it laid its head down close to Caine, who knew death signs, even alien ones, when he saw them. Taking a chance, he moved closer to it, which the water-strider rewarded by shifting its head to rub three times against his knee. Then it breathed out and was still.

It was impossible to tell exactly when the water-strider died. There was no death rictus or dramatic eye-rolling or sudden gush of fluids. But sometime over the next half hour, the breathing became faint, then undetectable, and then was no more.

Caine stared at the great, gentle beast, wondered if their mutual accord had simply been the artifact of a mortally wounded animal's desperate toleration, or whether it was indicative of a genuine congeniality intrinsic to water-striders. Whichever it had been, the rest of the night passed in melancholy silence, lit faintly by the violet and fuchsia puff-lanterns.

After having goggled wordlessly at the fallen water-strider, Veriden and Xue reclaimed Riordan shortly after dawn and the group set out into the early morning mists. They made good time, but despite his filter mask, Caine found it slightly harder to breathe.

Just before midday, and just as Riordan was preparing to take his turn walking patrol on the left point, Dora Veriden pointed out into the river. "Could be more trouble."

The group followed her gesture and saw three humps in the strong central current, paralleling them. Xue and Salunke raised their rifles—

"No," said Caine. "Don't fire. I don't think they'll harm us." He walked down to the river's edge, washed his hands, and then washed his arms. Behind him, the group stirred restively. *They probably think I've gone nuts. But unless I'm much mistaken, I am truly a "marked" man.*

"Er, Captain—?" began Gaspard.

"Let's just wait a moment," Riordan urged.

The group was already quiet, but became utterly silent when one of the humps rose out of the water: a smaller strider, only about seven meters in height. Its two back-faring bat-wings rose slightly and a soft bass tone stretched out over the rushing current toward them.

Caine stood. After a few moments, the other two humps rose up into similarly-sized striders and, together, they began approaching the shore. They waded forward slowly, cautiously, but also gently, their long, gangling legs moving through the currents with ease, barely raising any bubbles as they came.

As they entered the shallows, towering higher and higher over the group, Riordan heard Keith Macmillan swallow and mutter, "And now what do we do?"

"And now," Caine answered, turning toward his fellow IRIS operative with a smile, "we travel with an escort."

Chapter Thirty-Seven

Bannor Rulaine ate the last bite of his cold tilapia burger *sans* bun and wished they could heat food whenever they wanted to. But life on the stricken UCS *Puller* made unscheduled cooking a death sentence.

"Enjoying every last bit of *faux* beef, eh?" "Tygg" Robin asked as he entered their shared compartment.

"Am I ever." Bannor chewed and decided several things: that raw fish was arguably better than cold cooked fish; that the beef stock in which they marinated the tilapia really didn't work worth a damn as a flavoring agent; and that although none of them were going to starve to death as they tumbled ass-over-elbow around Disparity, gustatory boredom might do them in just as well. "Any news?"

"Yeh. Morgan's ready to give the damage assessment."

"Good. I'm coming." What Bannor did not add is that he was not sure why, after yesterday's eight man-hours of EVA hull survey, it had taken design whiz Morgan Lymbery a whole day to decide he was ready to report the obvious. Rulaine followed Tygg to the bridge.

When Bannor entered, there were respectful nods, but no salutes or stands to attention. Rulaine had followed Riordan's example when maintaining discipline amongst this mixed crew: respect for the rank, yes, but no formalities. Hell, as it was, there were more officers—Bannor, Tygg, Wu, and ostensibly Karam—than there were enlisted personnel. And both of the enlisted men were high-ranked NCOs, one of whom had served longer than everyone but Bannor.

Rulaine turned to Morgan. "Mr. Lymbery, I hear you have the final word for us."

"I do," said the bantam Englishman. Following their current precaution of minimizing power use, Lymbery brought out hard-copy blueprints of the Wolfe-class corvette. "We took two significant hits on the starboard side, both from railgun submunitions. We took another hit from a laser on our stern, and another on our dorsal surface.

"The dorsal laser hit was at a shallow angle of incidence, and therefore did nothing beyond leaving some heat-scoring on the hull. The second one seemed like it was going to be harmless at first: the beam itself did not breach the hull, but did generate internal heat spalling. The fragments narrowly missed the portside MAP thruster's reactor."

"Okay, but I worry when I hear about hits that 'seem' harmless," Karam grumbled.

"I'll come back to it," Morgan promised glumly. "Moving on. One of the two penetrator hits was a nonevent; it clipped off a secondary sensor mast. The other penetrator did the damage that Mssrs. Rulaine and Robin spent most of yesterday surveying. The submunition impacted us on a trajectory that was almost parallel with our keel, so it cut a short trough along our ventral hull before it penetrated and skewered all our portside fuel baffles. As it exited the hull, it sent some high-speed debris forward into our ladar masts and our secondary avionics suite. We can trim the remaining stubs of the masts to normalize airflow, but those systems are now heavily compromised, meaning significant reductions in both range and acuity. And obviously, we're going to have to make some hull repairs before this craft can conduct atmospheric reentry or flight."

"Mr. Lymbery," Peter Wu intruded.

"Yes?"

"We are very far from any repair facility, sir."

"I didn't say we needed a repair facility; I said we needed to make repairs. Not the same thing. I'll explain later. Now, about that harmless-looking laser hit on our stern. The larger fragments from the spalling took out a control board and a coolant conduit. The former was redundant and we had spares to replace the latter. Even so, we had to shut down, and Mr. Friel would be dead if he hadn't been wearing a duty suit with both a hazardous environment shell and armored liner: he was right on the edge of the spalling's ejecta pattern."

Phil Friel, leaning against the portside observation window, turned a little more pale than usual. "Damn it all, that's twice now. Hardly fair, I'd say."

"'Twice now'?" Melissa Sleeman echoed.

Phil shrugged. "I was in the first echelon under Halifax at the Battle of Earth. I was on a corvette like this one, playing bait-the-battlewagon with the Arat Kur when one of their UV lasers opened us up like a rusty sardine can. Lost two friends that day because they were standing half a meter closer to the preheating cores that got vented. And the plasma that half-vaporized them gave me a good scare and a lasting scar."

Lymbery waited to be sure that the exchange was over. "We were lucky in terms of our crew—Mr. Friel missed being hit by mere centimeters—but not in terms of the effects on our machinery. We did not initially detect the damage done by the smaller, needle-sized fragments. They riddled the coolant supply distributor adjacent to the conduit. Makeshift repairs are possible. It's a simple job for the hand-welder in the ship's locker, but since we do not dare bring the engines back on line, we have no way to test if the repairs will hold. Which I rather doubt."

And so there it was again: more problems arising from the possibility that they were still being observed. In this case, because *Puller* had to keep her reactors and drives dark, there was no way to assess the durability of the repairs. "So let's assume the repairs don't hold. What happens?"

Lymbery held up one bird-thin hand. "That depends upon how and when the failure occurs. If the distributor goes completely pear-shaped, the thruster will shut down automatically. You could override, but in that case, you shall blow out the drive in minutes, perhaps seconds. It depends entirely upon your operating temperature and the amount of residual coolant in the system at the time. Luck of the draw, I'm afraid.

"If the line is compromised but still functioning, one might extend the operating time by pumping smaller amounts of coolant through it at lower pressure. The engine heat will build, but the decreased coolant flow reduces stress on the distributor and also reduces the rate of leakage, since the contents are not under as much pressure. You get a drip, not a spray, if you take my meaning. Finally, I have had a few ideas about how to best repair the hull damage."

Bannor crossed his arms, leaned back. This was going to be very good, very insane, or both. Having spent a few weeks around Lymbery, he was willing to wager on "both."

The Englishman steepled his fingers and began emitting a stream of nongrammatical phrases: he sounded more like a victim of adult aphasia than a genius. "We scout around for rusty bits throughout the hull. Or rig a catalyzer. To create ferrous oxide, of course. The hand grinder should work. And also Ms. Sleeman's biosample centrifuge. But how much aluminium do we have on hand?"

Eight of the other nine persons aboard *Puller* stared blankly at each other. But Melissa Sleeman's face was curving to accommodate a slow, crafty smile. "Thermite," she said.

"Yes, of course," Lymbery replied, looking about the group in as much confusion as they were looking at him. "It's obvious, isn't it?"

Bannor unfolded his arms, putting the pieces together now, but saw that most of the others were no closer to seeing where the mad genius Englishman was trying to lead them. "Maybe it's not quite as obvious as it seems, Mr. Lymbery. Why don't you break it down for us?"

While Lymbery was still frowning and blinking in consternation—Rulaine could almost see a thought bubble above his head that read, "surely I made it all perfectly clear"—Melissa launched into the explanation. "Thermite burns at twenty-five hundred degrees centigrade and is a welding compound that doesn't require an oxidizer. If we can rig a work cover over the damaged section of *Puller*'s belly, we can use thermite to repair the hull. It won't be pretty or precise, but it will get the job done."

"Yes—but where do we *get* the thermite?" asked Trent Howarth, who had to bend at the waist to fit into the hatchway where he was floating.

"Oh. Yes. Sorry. Thermite is just a mixture of rust and aluminum. So we scavenge rust from around the ship, or make it by reverse-catalyzing iron into ferrous oxide. Then we collect whatever aluminum we can find."

"Plenty in the kitchen," Wu offered. His culinary skills had elevated him to lord of the galley for those thirty minutes per orbit when they could risk enough power output for him to cook.

"Right," Sleeman picked up. "So you grind down the rust and

the aluminum into powders. Then you use the mini-centrifuge in my bio sampling kit to separate the grain size of the powders into the tolerances you need, and then you make the final mix."

"Um, can't we just use the hand-welder in the ship's locker for this job?" Howarth looked hopefully around the group.

"Impossible," Lymbery pronounced. "Working temperature insufficient. Fuel too limited. Unsuitable for vacuum operations."

Peter Wu put up a finger. "What about an arc-welder? We certainly have enough electricity."

Sleeman shook her head. "We'd have to fashion an arc-welder that will hold up in hard, EVA conditions. Also, the job would take much longer and we can't afford to run the welder for more than thirty minutes per orbit. Not if we want to be sure we stay hidden."

Which brought them all back face-to-face with the single most crucial uncertainty in their day-to-day existence; after a moment's silence, Tina Melah wondered aloud, "Are we really so sure that we *are* being watched?"

Rulaine shrugged. "Ms. Melah, we could get a definitive answer to that question quickly enough: we could power up our drives, charge our capacitors, illuminate our active arrays, and wait to see what happens. If nothing, great. But if there's still someone out there to see it, their ship will also be the last thing we ever see—as they come charging in to polish us off. That's why we're using only solar cells to recharge our batteries, and that's why we keep our power generation to a few hundred watts during the thirty minutes we spend in the safe zone of our orbit."

Howarth scratched his head. "So, if someone might still be out there"—he waved widely at space in general—"what makes any spot of our orbit 'safe'?"

Karam took up the explanation; his experience had led them to adopt their near-absolute doggo running conditions. "Reason one: the attackers came out of the rocks in the leading trojan point. Probably retreated back there as well. And no, the Slaasriithi shift carrier didn't eliminate them, because if Yiithrii'ah'aash had accomplished that, his first order of business would have been to rescue us and then go looking for the shuttle, and the other half of the legation, on Disparity.

"But instead, he hightailed it out of the battlespace, pushing straight into preacceleration. We can still see him burning for shift as hard as he can, every time we come around to that part of our orbit that has us directly opposed to the sun. Which is why I suspect that that area of space is clear: if our attackers followed Yiithrii'ah'aash, we'd have seen their exhausts. And there's no cover for them to exploit out in that direction; no moon, no trojan asteroids, nothing.

"Reason two: that part of our orbit also takes us through latitudes where there are a lot of auroras. If we have to give off any electromagnetic emissions at all, I want us to be backdropped, or better yet foregrounded, by those pretty shimmering ribbons of charged particles. I'll take any interference I can get, right now."

Phil Friel nodded. "So, that's when we'll do our thermite welding: in intervals, whenever we pass through the safe zone."

Rulaine nodded. "Yes."

"How soon do we start? Mr. Tsaami mentioned that we'll begin to deorbit in two weeks. Maybe less."

Bannor didn't stop nodding. "The sooner we start the repairs, the better. Because if our attackers are still out there, they'll need to move pretty soon themselves."

Karam nodded. "Yeah, they've got their own countdown clock ticking. Specifically, when Yiithrii'ah'aash eventually shifts out-system and his taillights wink out, it will be less than two weeks before they wink back in. Along with a whole lot of his friends from Beta Aquilae."

"It makes me wonder what our enemies are waiting for." Wu's mutter was as dark as it was low.

Rulaine shrugged. "They may be repairing damage to their own ship. And they have to figure out their next move."

"Such as, coming in and wiping us out?" O'Garran proposed sardonically.

"If it was that easy for them, they'd have already done it," Karam retorted.

Bannor nodded. "The game has changed. They've lost the element of surprise and have a lot more unknowns to deal with. Like this ship: we look to be dead in space, no one left alive, but they can't be sure. Same with the shuttle: it could have been lost with all hands, but it's just as likely that some survivors made it to the ground and are looking for help while hiding as best they can. And the attackers probably didn't destroy all the Slaasriithi defense spheres.

"So the bad guys have got a lot of work left to do and not a lot of time in which to do it. They have the same operational countdown on Yiithrii'ah'aash's ship that we do. Except for us, when that clock runs out, the cavalry comes over the hill and we're saved. For them, it means 'game over.'"

Tina Melah rose. "So we'd better get on the repairs right away."

"You just can't wait to get your hands on some thermite," Phil murmured at her with a small smile.

She returned a wide grin.

Rulaine leaned forward, holding himself in place with three fingers he had hooked under the rim of the sensor console. "Before we get to work, you should be aware of the different tactical scenarios we might face and our planned responses to each one."

The growing buzz of side conversations stilled.

"The happiest scenario is the one in which it turns out that the attackers are gone, the Slaasriithi come back, the rest of the legation is rescued, and we go on as before. A variant of that scenario is that the Slaasriithi come back, which is what triggers our hidden attackers into action again. In that scenario, we have to be ready to help fight them, or to run like hell."

"Or to help retrieve the rest of the legation," Trent added.

"No," Rulaine countered immediately. "That's not an option for this ship." He held up a hand in response to the suddenly erect spines and opening mouths. "I'll come back to that point. The next scenario is that nothing happens until we are about to deorbit. In that event, we wait until we're in our safe window and boost outward from the planet." He rode over the top of the growing frowns. "But the final scenario is the one that's most likely and that I'm most worried about: that our attackers resume their operations before either of those conditions are met. Now, if they come in supported by whatever shift carrier brought them here, we have no choice but to run. Again. Captain's orders, actually. But if the attackers only bring the same small ship they used the first time, and if they bypass us to search the planet, that will force us to descend and try to help the rest of the legation."

Melissa Sleeman started. "Major, that—I'm sorry. That's crazy. No matter the scenario, we should be heading planetside to find the rest of the legation as soon as we can."

Rulaine leaned back. "And then what?"

Sleeman blinked. "Why, we boost back up to orbit, or find whoever's in charge on Disparity, or—"

But Karam was shaking his head. "That won't happen." Seeing the growing outrage on her face, he rephrased: "That can't happen."

She frowned. "Why not?"

It was Phil Friel who answered her. "The hull damage. Specifically, the gouge that damned penetrator rod carved into our belly."

"But we—you—can weld that, right?" Rulaine had never heard Melissa sound confused before this moment.

This time Tina answered. "Oh, we can weld it. And it will hold air and be fine for spaceside operations. But reentry? Phew." She shook her head dubiously. "I don't know. I just don't know."

"Unfortunately, that's only half the problem," Karam sighed. "I might—*might*—be able to get this bird down. Mostly because she's a solid military hull, tough as nails, and has plenty of redundancy. But even if we go in turned turtle, it's a one-way trip. If we go down, we're not getting back up without full repairs."

Morgan Lymbery nodded. "It is due to the coolant line damage," he explained. "During routine descents, and even more so during ascents, the engines are frequently at maximum thrust. But with a damaged craft, the pilot"—he nodded respectfully at Karam—"will have to push the engines and power plants beyond their rated limits.

"*Puller*'s hull damage and compromised aerodynamics ruin her airflow characteristics. That requires compensatory and corrective thrust. Each time Mr. Tsaami applies that extra thrust, we will be living on borrowed time, hoping the coolant pressures don't cause the distributor to finally give out." He threw up one hopeless hand. "Once that happens, we're done. We'd be lucky to get to the ground in one piece before the engine dies. Or explodes."

The bridge was silent for several long seconds before Peter Wu cleared his throat. "I grew up speaking English as well as Mandarin, but"—he turned toward Karam—"what do you mean by saying that the ship would descend while it was 'turned turtle'?"

Karam smiled ruefully. "'Turned turtle' means 'on your back.'" When he saw confused, and some disbelieving, looks around the bridge, he explicated. "That belly weld won't take the brunt of reentry superheating. If it splits, or even flakes a bit, the underplating will burn through in less than a minute and we'll come apart like a model airplane hit with a sledgehammer." Several of the surrounding faces grew pale. "But our dorsal surface is pretty much pristine. So we'll go in on our backs."

Whereas many others looked pale, Phil Friel looked intrigued. "Can it take that? I thought that there were special alloys layered into the ventral surface to absorb and diffuse reentry heat."

The answer came from Lymbery. "Not to worry, lad. *Puller* is up to the task."

"With respect, Mr. Lymbery, why are you so sure?" Friel smiled. "You didn't design this ship too, did you?"

Lymbery did not smile. "No, I didn't. I was merely the independent inspector who signed off on the design."

Friel's mouth made a round, soundless, "Oh."

Rulaine smothered his own incipient grin and, pulling against his finger-hold on the sensor console, tugged himself back into a fully upright position. "So we can fix this ship, but not like new. If we head planetside, it's a one-way trip. And we only take that trip if it looks like the bad guys have decided to go hunting our friends. Then, we're the equalizers."

"If we make it down alive," Karam grumbled.

"Always the optimist," drawled Tina Melah.

"Bah humbug," Karam replied. "I'll have you know that I am optimist enough to have already run multiple computer simulations of how to get *Puller* out of her three-axis tumble when the time comes for us to straighten out and get moving."

"Is our tumble really that bad?" asked Melissa Sleeman, who'd spent most of her days manning the passive sensors, both those observing the planet beneath them and the dangerous vastness of space behind them.

Tygg leaned toward her; she leaned towards him. "Have you looked out a window?" he asked gently.

She frowned slightly. "No."

"Don't," he urged her.

"Make you puke, fer sure," Tina added.

Bannor nodded at Karam's piloting console. "How long from the time you start firing the attitude control thrusters until we're out of the tumble?"

"Thirty-one seconds."

"That's impossible. No one could do that." O'Garran's blunt assertion bordered on truculence.

"Watch your tongue, Stretch," Karam countered. "And I didn't say *I* was doing it." He patted the console. "The computer will handle it. I ran the sims until I got it optimized, then recorded the sequence. When it comes time for us to move, I hit the right button and the show begins. But, fair warning: be strapped in. And try not to eat anything heavy beforehand; correcting this tumble in thirty seconds means a lot of hard thrusting along sharply opposed vectors. It will not be a pleasant ride."

"Damn," answered O'Garran with nod and a frown. "That's pretty impressive."

"Yeah," Trent agreed. "But why wait? If you did it now, it would make the welders' EVAs a lot less disorienting, wouldn't it?"

Karam nodded. "Yes. But it would also get us killed." He pointed out beyond the bulkhead. "Remember all that talk about the bad people who might be out there? The ones who've already tried to kill us?"

Trent shrugged. "Yeah, but we know they're not running active sensors, so they can't know what our tumble-pattern is, not enough to determine that it's changed."

Karam sighed, his eyes were shuttered. "Listen, greenhorn. A lot of space combat is nothing but our computers and sensors dueling with their computers and sensors. But there's also a common-sense side. First, anyone watching us from a passive posture will measure our reflected light: how much, which wavelengths, and most important, when do we shine and how long? Variations in the first two variables can be altered by other elements: the position and angle of the ship relative to the sun, a solar flare, or if any dust is moving in or out of the radiant path from the primary to Disparity.

"But any alteration in the latter two variables—the timing of our reflection—tells them that we've changed our tumble. And that means they'll come after us. So we stay as we are until we're ready to fire up the engines."

"Can't happen soon enough," O'Garran opined brusquely, turned to Bannor to look for the "dismissed" nod.

"Actually," Rulaine commented, "we need every calm minute we can get, Miles."

"That may be, Major, but I doubt those minutes are being very friendly to the captain and the others. I'm just worried that Disparity might be finishing the job that the enemy started. Sir."

Bannor nodded sadly. O'Garran was correct in all but one particular. The force that had brought all this misery to pass wasn't simply "the enemy," wasn't simply "the threat force." They were assassins.

And I am going to send them all to hell.

Chapter Thirty-Eight

SPINWARD TROJANS, BD +02 4076 TWO ("DISPARITY")
and CLOSE ORBIT, V 1581 FOUR

Nezdeh purposely seated herself next to Sehtrek, which put her directly across the table from Idrem. She did not want to manage the distraction of sitting alongside Idrem, or the possibility that she might absentmindedly reach out toward him. *This is one of the reasons the Progenitors warn that romantic love is the seed of all weakness. It creates reflexes that we must control, and that, therefore, distract us from optimizing the realization of our individual will to dominion.* "Let us begin," she said.

Sehtrek raised an eyebrow. "Shall we not wait for the others, Nezdeh?"

"I have not informed others of this discussion. It would not be prudent to pull them away from their stations." Which was, she knew, a pretext so threadbare that Sehtrek would see straight through it to her real reason: to eliminate the ultimately unproductive output of the lesser intellects among her crew. But that could not be admitted openly. To do so would be to imply that Sehtrek, an Intendant who was not even designated for Elevation, was more intelligent and capable than many of Nezdeh's fellow Evolved.

Tegrese chose that moment to enter the small briefing and ready room. "So, here you are." She sat. "I was told by Ulpreln that he suspected there was a meeting in progress."

Nezdeh looked at her.

Tegrese returned the stare. Her puzzlement transformed into a frown. "I *am* off duty," she explained.

*Of course you are. And of course this had to be the one time
you did not sleep or mate or train during your off-hours.* She
repressed a sigh. "I saw no reason to disturb you. And you need
not remain."

Tegrese shrugged. "But I shall do so. I am eager to learn of
our next steps."

"This is to be a quick meeting. There will be little time for
any input."

Tegrese's frown was short-lived. "Understandable."

Nezdeh turned to Sehtrek. "You have accumulated one hundred
hours of data on the planet and the objects orbiting it. What
recommendations do you make?"

"That we make a carefully timed ground attack within the week,
presuming that there are no further changes to the battlespace."

"There have already been changes?" Tegrese had not been at
the table for a minute and was already beginning to burden
the process. Nezdeh glanced at Idrem, who was attempting to
suppress—a smile? Yes, there was an amusing irony to Tegrese's
arrival, Nezdeh allowed, despite the annoyance.

Sehtrek touched his beltcom. Between the silver spider-leg tines
of its holographic projector, a representation of the Slaasriithi planet
rotated, three small dots keeping pace at equidistant points along
a shared orbit. "A new defense sphere was launched. It occupies
the same orbital spot as the one we destroyed four days ago."

"Meaning there could be more."

"Almost certainly so, Idrem. Although I am surprised that it
took them this long to launch a replacement."

Nezdeh shook her head. "The Slaasriithi are not at all dominion-
oriented and, so far as we can determine, do not have wars. This
far within their domain, a prompt defense replenishment system
may be an afterthought. But they are not stupid; if they have
more defense spheres in their local inventory, we must expect
that they will now be ready to deploy them more rapidly."

Sehtrek nodded. "Agreed. Which means that the harder of the
two targets we must engage are the Aboriginals who landed on
the planet. We must penetrate the cannonball defense, find the
targets, neutralize them, and then return to orbit."

Idrem nodded. "Brenlor sent us a tight-beam update half an
hour ago. He estimates that the additional landers we require for
the assault will arrive here in eight days."

"The sooner the better. The Slaasriithi shift carrier is probably no more than four days away from making shift. Consequently, a response force from Beta Aquilae could arrive here within two weeks. We need to have concluded our operations and be well into our preacceleration phase by then."

Tegrese gestured at the cannonballs orbiting the image of the planet. "It would be helpful to have the *Arbitrage*'s navigational laser array on hand when we confront the cannonballs again. It would make short work of them, even at extreme range."

Sehtrek nodded patiently. "Helpful, yes, but the enemy sensors, of which there seem to be an almost inexhaustible number, would detect the approach of *Arbitrage* days before we could include it in an attack. That would prompt the Slaasriithi to launch more cannonballs, or undertake different strategies that could complicate our primary objective: to find and eliminate the planetside Aboriginals."

Nezdeh steepled her fingers. "So, we will watch the cannonballs' orbital patterns, crack a hole in those defenses using *Lurker*'s firepower, and then send one of our landers through that hole to locate and neutralize the Aboriginals on the surface."

Idrem's eyes drifted to a yellow triangle that was closer to the image of the planet, looping around it in an uneven, wobbling orbit. "So, when do you envision eliminating the other Aboriginal craft?"

Sehtrek had evidently thought the question to be addressed to him. "I do not know that we must, Idrem. It has shown no power output and its orbit continues to decay. As an added precaution, I have projected attack times during which it would be on the other side of the planet, should it retain some combat capability."

Idrem folded his arms. "Although it shows no power that we can discern at this range, the ship in question—a Commonwealth Wolfe-class corvette—has reasonable capacitors."

"Capacitors are useless without a working power plant," Tegrese asserted. "There is never even residual heat to suggest that they powered up while out of the field of our sensors."

Idrem stared at her near-insolence. "Most versions of the Wolfe-class are fitted with retractable solar panels. They can maintain minimal power by recharging the ship's batteries."

"As it might be doing now," Nezdeh concluded.

"Or it may simply be the lifeless wreck it seems to be." Tegrese's comment doubled Nezdeh's annoyance.

Idrem intervened. "We know the craft was significantly damaged. Time will help us further determine its status. And if their
orbit decays to the point where they start entering the atmosphere,
they are finished, even if there are survivors aboard."

Nezdeh nodded her agreement. "Happily, we need not confirm
the status of the Aboriginal craft before we commence our operations. Once we have removed a cannonball to open a landing
window, *Red Lurker* will continue to track both the remaining
two cannonballs and the Aboriginal wreck whenever their orbit
puts them within sight of our sensors. If the wreck attempts to
challenge *Lurker* in any way, we will be able to destroy it, even
from our standoff position."

Tegrese shrugged. "If you are so fearful of it, then why not
strike now and eliminate this troublesome variable?"

Sehtrek's tone was careful and very patient as he pointed out
what should have been obvious. "The present range of engagement
is far too great for us to be assured of success, and a renewed
attack may bring more cannonballs after us. At any rate, it would
not only reveal our presence but our position, depriving us of
the surprise we need for our planetary assault."

"Very well. But what of the ground target? Isn't it possible that
the shuttle crashed? That all the Aboriginals are dead?" Tegrese
was asking the questions Nezdeh had feared she'd ask: questions
that she, Idrem, and Sehtrek had already considered and answered.

"There are survivors. My Reifications confirm that there is
at least one Devolysite still extant on the surface. Furthermore,
our sensors showed no thermal blooms consistent with either a
catastrophic reentry or a crash."

"So," said Tegrese with a sardonic smile as she leaned away
from the table. "The impossible task of eliminating the escaped
Aboriginals is now merely improbable." She became serious. "We
shall need many of the frozen clones, and all four of the *Arbitrage*'s landers, if we are to—"

Idrem shook his head. "That will not answer our needs. Firstly,
several of the *Arbitrage*'s landers have been converted into refueling auxiliaries. Secondly, any clones which are still in cryogenic
suspension will be of no use. They take too long to revivify and
longer to indoctrinate to our dominion. The Slaasriithi response
from Beta Aquilae will be here before they are ready."

Tegrese seemed almost abashed. "Then what are your plans?"

"We shall dedicate all our revivified clones to the project, who are currently aboard one of the two landers that are en route to us. The other one, a paramilitary version, will be our landing and assault craft."

Tegrese nodded, seemed to be searching for some worthwhile point to raise. "Will the other cannonballs not simply follow our lander planetside and destroy it?"

Sehtrek pulled up a holographic report on what they knew about the cannonballs. "I do not have complete technical intelligence on the devices, but their shape and performance indicates that they are intended for extraatmospheric work. Without wings, all their flight must be powered. So, given their very limited atmospheric duration compared to craft with lifting surfaces, it seems unlikely that they would descend to pursue our lander."

Tegrese finally asked Nezdeh a pertinent question: "So, given the planetary communications blackout, how will you find the Aboriginals?"

"Our agent has a Devolysite that will deliquesce when I send the appropriate Reified command. As it dies, it emits a strong return wave through the Reification, which shall guide our initial point of descent. Its deliquescence also signals our saboteur to begin providing us with terminal guidance, that we may more narrowly locate the Aboriginals and kill them."

Sehtrek nodded at Nezdeh's synopsis. "Is there anything else we need to consider?"

"We will need patience," she answered. She considered Tegrese from the corner of her eye. *A great deal of patience.*

Tlerek Srin Shethkador allowed the iris valve to remain open for several seconds before he entered the isolation cell in *Ferocious Monolith's* brig. It had already been determined that the subject was susceptible to the will-eroding power of fearful anticipation. So it would be now.

The Aboriginal woman was sitting well away from the door. But since the cell was round, there was no corner in which to shelter her back and gain some sense of defensibility, of security. Her clothes were still wet from the hourly drenchings of cold water he had ordered. Every sixty minutes, one autarchon entered to hold her down, another brought in a container of cold water which he poured over her slowly. Then they left, never having said a word, never having met her eyes. She was an object they were watering: nothing more.

Shethkador stared at her slim, shivering legs. Some Aboriginals— they were rare, but they existed—were able to immediately discern the true purpose of such treatment: to unnerve and defocus the subject by demonstrating that they were alone, helpless, and of no urgent interest to their captors. Questions and direct engagement sent a message to most subjects that they were important, and that was a form of power, a slender bit of nourishment for their own aspirations to regain dominion. The rare captives who were able to distance themselves from their fears intrinsically understood that there was no act of cooperation or placation that would serve to appease or please their captors, because their captors desired neither. The captor-captive relationship was not, ultimately, social: it was simply manipulation exercised by the dominant to extract compliance from the subordinate.

So taught the Progenitors; Tlerek silently recited, *such is the truth of the universe.* To which this sodden Aboriginal female was as senseless and deaf as the rocks floating around them, here in the trailing trojan point of the fourth planet out from V 1581.

She looked up; her shivering redoubled. Shethkador was pleased. In his youth, he had spent some effort perfecting the disinterested stare with which he regarded her now. "Stand," he said.

She did, slowly. The reluctance with which she complied was not indicative of defiance, but uncertainty over what actions might displease him. *Excellent.* "You may ask questions, now," he told her.

"Where am—?"

"When you are given the privilege to speak to me, you are to address me as Fearsome Srin. If you fail, you shall be immediately punished. If you fail repeatedly, you shall be terminated. Now, try again."

"Fearsome Srin, where am I?"

"Aboard my ship. What do you last remember?"

She frowned. "I was being sedated for cryogenic sleep procedures on Jam."

"What is Jam?"

"That's what we call the second planet in V 1581."

"You call it 'Jam'? As in, a sweetened fruit spread?"

"No, as in a traffic jam." When she saw that Shethkador's

expression did not change, she tried a different approach. "Like a big guy trying to crawl in a small space; he gets jammed, stuck—"

"So the name refers to all the fleet traffic that is passing through the orbital facilities there. Continue."

She nodded with tolerable deference. "My partner and I were able to get away from our original ship in Sigma Draconis Two and stow away on the *Changeling*, just after we did the job for you."

"You did a job for *me*?"

She blinked, fearful. "Yes. You—you're a representative of CoDevCo, right? Fearsome Srin?"

Now it becomes clear. "I am not a member of the Colonial Development Combine. I, along with others, compelled that megacorporation to do our bidding during the recent invasion of Earth."

The Aboriginal was now too confused to remember to be fearful. "You compelled CoDevCo to—?"

"Attend," Shethkador ordered. "The Colonial Development Combine was suborned by Ktor to facilitate our invasion of Earth. CoDevCo may have retained your services as a confidential agent and saboteur, but it was ultimately acting at our behest."

"But the Ktor are—are creatures with pseudopods, that live in liquid methane, or—"

"Female, assess me; do you see any pseudopods?"

"No."

"That is because there are none. The description of our appearance was a ruse, so that no other power would be aware that we, too, are humans. However, our breed last dwelt upon Earth over twenty millennia ago, before the harvesting."

The woman's face was expressionless: Shethkador knew the symptoms of information excess when he saw them. "This is of no concern. You were hired as servitors of the legitimate leaders of the Ktor. But those who ordered you to change the cold cells you delivered to the Slaasriithi ship were impostors."

"How do you know about—?"

Shethkador crossed the distance between them in a single long step and swung the back of his hand against the side of her face. It was a mild blow, compared to what he was capable of, but it spun her head, sent her against the wall. She slid down, stunned, and then started to weep. "When you address me directly, you use my title." He waited. "What is my title?"

She choked out the words. "Fearsome. Srin."

"Correct. Now: you must provide every detail of what you were to do after you switched the cold cells."

"Yes; I—yes, Fearsome Srin." She waited for his dismissive nod of approval before continuing. "Our employers arranged for a purser's assistant on *Changeling* to sneak us on board. After it shifted here, we debarked as soon as we could and took on identities as ordinary dock workers."

"So that you would not attract attention?"

"Yes, Fearsome Srin. Also, anyone looking for us would presume that we were trying to get out of Arat Kur space as quickly as possible and would concentrate their search on the shift-carrier."

"So it was your intent to remain in your unassuming roles until you believed that you were no longer being sought?"

"Actually, Fearsome Srin, our employers told us to await a coded signal which meant that they had completed fabricating two new identities for us. Which they did six days after we arrived at Jam, Fearsome Srin."

Shethkador did the math. The *Arbitrage* had still been in-system, then. *So someone aboard her had purloined the false identities for them and was also the source of their "employer's signal."* "And I presume your employers instructed you to travel onward in cryogenic stasis, since officials would not rouse you to confirm your identity." *Ingenious, and just what I would have done.*

She nodded. "Yes, Fearsome Srin, but—what happened? Why am I here? Did you seize the ship that was carrying our cold cells to Earth?"

Aboriginals: always presuming that ends are attained by battle, rather than deception—or a knife in the back. "We used tight-beam relay to contact our own servitors in orbit at Jam and instructed them to do to your cryocells what you did to the cryocells bound for the Slaasriithi ship: they made a switch. Once your cells had been removed from the waiting list of pending cold-freight, they were shipped out by small craft to the gas giant in orbit four. Your cryocells were set adrift in a vacuum-rated cargo container. We waited for an auspicious moment and sent a stealthed patrol hunter to reclaim you."

She looked around. "Where is Manuel, the man I worked with, Fearsome Srin?"

"He was extraneous."

She shivered; she may have held back a sob. "We—I didn't mean to fail. We did what we were asked to do. We had no way of knowing it was not authorized."

"That is true. It is also irrelevant. But we could not allow you to remain among your own kind. Upon returning to Earth, the counterintelligence agencies would have apprehended you."

"So," she shuddered, clutching her arms tightly, "are you going to kill me?"

Such an amateur; as if I would not have done so already, had that been my intent. "I should," Shethkador lied, and let the pause draw on, "but no: you may prove valuable as bait."

She blinked. "As bait?"

"Of course. Whoever hijacked our assets and acted without authorization must be located and punished. So far, the pawns have been easy enough to eliminate. We found and executed the person on my ship who sent you your initial messages in Sigma Draconis. We uncovered the parties that hired him and shall have them soon enough, too. But they did not have enough power or information to undertake this ambitious scheme on their own. To that end, I will ensure that news of your capture and interrogation 'slips out,' and so, touches a wider circle of ears than it should. And then we shall see what responses those rumors generate."

"I do not understand: what kind of responses do you expect them to generate, Fearsome Srin?"

"Attempts against your life, of course."

She blanched.

"Surely you understood this is what I meant by keeping you as 'bait.' We shall also intimate that you are not the mere informant you seem to be but are one of our most prized, deep-cover Aboriginal agents. Our adversaries will not know, or be able to retroactively ascertain, the truth of this claim. Earth was chaotic enough prior to the invasion and our networks there are now in utter disarray. So, in order for the guilty parties to be sure that they have concealed their involvement, they will have no choice but to kill you. If they can."

"But you won't let them—will you, Fearsome Srin?"

"I will prevent it." Which, for the moment, was true. But Shethkador could anticipate many reasons for changing his mind later on, not the least of which was to prevent his enemies from discovering how very little the Aboriginal female actually knew.

Indeed, the only way to perpetuate their uncertainty would be to allow his adversaries to assassinate her and thereby eliminate their only hope of determining what she did and did not reveal to him.

"And, Fearsome Srin, what assurance do I have that you'll keep that promise?"

He smiled. "That is an amusingly ironic question, coming from someone who has not only broken her oath of service, but has become a meretricious traitor." He turned to exit, but stopped on the threshold of the iris valve. "Your people have a customary good night wish: 'pleasant dreams.'"

As the portal squealed shut behind him, he discovered Olsirkos Shethkador-vah waiting just beyond the entry to the brig. Tlerek motioned that he should walk alongside. "Has the patrol hunter finished its survey of the gas giant?"

"Yes, Fearsome Srin. *Doom Herald* just submitted its tightbeam report."

"And?"

"As you suspected, *Red Lurker* did not leave a camouflaged data cache at either of the covert drop sites. Also, there was sign of a combat just above the gas giant's exosphere: light debris, including parts of a communication mast and a length of refueling hose. All Aboriginal."

"Of course. No sign of debris consistent with *Red Lurker*, I presume."

"None, Srin Shethkador."

"Have our collaborators on the second planet relayed the logs of the port authority's preshift communications with the *Arbitrage*?"

"The logs show no irregular reports, Honored Srin. However, several days after refueling, the *Arbitrage*'s transmission characteristics altered slightly. It was presumed to be the result of changes in the gas giant's magnetosphere and local ionization."

Shethkador shook his head. "But that was not what caused the discrepancy. Those postrefueling messages had to be sent by *Red Lurker*'s array, since the debris found by *Doom Herald* included pieces of the Aboriginal ship's communications mast."

"So the crew of *Red Lurker* commandeered the *Arbitrage* and used it to shift out of the system."

"It is the logical conclusion from the evidence before us."

They had arrived in the commander's oversight compartment, just off the bridge. One of the two holographs on display was a rendering of the local stellar group. Olsirkos stared into it. "But where would they go? None of these destinations are useful to them, assuming, as we must, that whoever is now in control of *Lurker* was also behind switching the cryocells that were delivered to the Slaasriithi shift carrier."

"That, too, is a logical conclusion."

Olsirkos seemed to be grinding his molars. "But how is the hijacking of an Aboriginal shift-carrier that can barely reach Sigma Draconis useful to a group that has introduced saboteurs or confidential agents into the Terran legation to Beta Aquilae?"

"That is an excellent question. But there may be other elements in play, Olsirkos, and assets of which we have no knowledge. After all, the Srina who we must now presume to be in command of *Red Lurker* carries one of the last viable genelines of House Perekmeres."

"A dead house, Honored Srin."

"Yes, it is dead—now. But for many decades prior to its Extirpation, House Perekmeres supported our observation of human space in their guise as the Custodians' assistants. It is possible they cached assets in this region of space, and that knowledge of them was snuffed out of existence along with the geneline. Except, perhaps, for a few clever Evolved, who formulated plans to reunite here, far away from the direct oversight of the Great Houses and the Autarchs."

Olsirkos reexamined the star chart. "If that is true, then their shift range could be much greater than that of the *Arbitrage*."

"Exactly. And with such range, they might hope to intercept the legation on its way to Beta Aquilae, or, failing that, on its return. Either way, it is such an inspired and insanely bold ploy that it is all but unthinkable. As is their hijacking of Aboriginals we suborned during our infiltration of Earth's megacorporations and governments. Brilliant. But they could not have done so without the aid of a sponsor."

Olsirkos nodded. "These Perekmeres dogs knew which persons in Aboriginal cold cells were our suborned agents. They had the confirmation codes that identified them as legitimate authorities. They probably knew of collaborators aboard the *Arbitrage*."

"Yes, megacorporate collaborators who were suborned at *my* orders." Shethkador took a moment to ensure that the annoyance did not manifest outwardly. "A scattered remnant of an

Extirpated House does not have access to such secrets. They had a sponsor with access to the relevant intelligence, inventories, and code-words."

"Meaning that one of the other Houses—"

"Has elected to support the resurgence of House Perekmeres covertly, or has at least promised to do so. I suspect the sponsor ultimately intends to dispose of these renegades to eliminate any evidence that this plot was orchestrated at a higher level. But I suspect that the Perekmeres' expect that."

"But who among the Houses would wish to undermine our operations here?"

"Whoever is not happy with them."

"Or with House Shethkador," Olsirkos ventured.

Tlerek nodded approval at Olsirkos' insight, frowned at its content, and thought, *All too likely.*

Chapter Thirty-Nine

SOUTHERN EXTENTS OF THE THIRD SILVER TOWER
BD +02 4076 TWO ("DISPARITY")

Five days after the water-striders began paralleling the group—
or, as Hwang quipped, "following Captain Riordan like tame
ponies"—Caine pulled wearily to the top of the first significant
slope they'd encountered since commencing their downriver trek.
The trees parted, revealing that the river's course straightened
as it followed along the floor of a shallow valley. The flanking hills ultimately rose up into higher peaks, which pinched
the river tightly between them in the far distance. Beyond
which, if Riordan recalled his brief glimpses from the shuttle's
cockpit, it was only a short march to the shores of a long
inlet that led ultimately to the southern reaches of Disparity's
equatorial seas.

Salunke, a few meters ahead, shaded her eyes, then pointed
toward the peak-lined gateway through which the valley had to
squeeze. "There, do you see it?"

Caine, vision blurry from the effort of the sustained march,
squinted, saw a vertical spark of metal down near the base of
the nearest left-hand peak. "What is it?" he panted.

Nasr Eid's voice was excited. "It is a silver object, a tower of
some kind."

The rest of the group moved to his vantage point. An eager
conversational buzz rose up. The decision to head downriver,
conceded to be the best path in the absence of other information
but never embraced with particular confidence, was suddenly

hailed as just short of oracular in its insight. Riordan started to chuckle, but coughed instead.

Macmillan drew close, glanced down. "How are you holding up?"

Caine, head hanging as he caught his breath, nodded.

"You don't look, or sound, so good," the Scotsman added.

"Might be bronchitis," Riordan offered, straightening.

Xue shook his head as he passed. "That is not bronchitis, Captain. It sounds more akin to asthma."

"I'm not asthmatic."

Xue shrugged. "No undiagnosed adult is ever asthmatic. Until they are."

"Yes, well—let's just keep focused on making progress."

Xue paused, scanning Riordan's face. "We will make no progress if you collapse, Captain. We should rest."

Riordan's first impulse was to insist that he was fine, damn it, but that would be a lie. The shortness of breath he'd experienced the day after the crash had seemed to improve at first, but was now growing steadily. If he lied about it, he'd not only set a bad example, but be seen as unreasonable, as requiring forced rest. And if anyone started to force a leader to do anything, it usually spelled doom to their authority. *But if I slow down the very people I am honor-bound to save, then what the hell am I—?*

Dora Veriden had drifted forward, out of her rearguard position. Macmillan frowned. "Hey, if you're up here, who's watching our—?"

Caine waved him to silence, looked at Dora. "Something?"

She nodded faintly. "Our new friends are back. And as shy as ever."

Macmillan lifted his rifle slightly. "Where?"

"Other side of the river this time. At about our eight o'clock. But there are more of them now. I think."

Gaspard strolled over. "A problem?"

Macmillan nodded tightly. "The same beasties that started following us three days ago. Same sounds, same motions."

"And you remain convinced that they are not the same creatures that chased us at the end of the second full day on planet?" He looked directly at Riordan.

"I remain *doubtful*, Ambassador. We haven't seen them or any of their tracks, so it's impossible to assert anything definitively. But they keep greater distance and they move differently."

Veriden nodded. "These critters are not as fast as that pack of predators when they're moving in a straight line. But what they lack in speed they make up for with agility."

The ambassador nodded at Dora's confirmation but never took his eyes off Riordan. "Very well, but what do you propose to do about them, Captain?"

Etienne Gaspard had greatly improved as a human being in Riordan's eyes, but sometimes the diplomat still said things that made him sound like an utter prig. "Well, since they're not coming forward to be recognized, I propose we just spend a few moments ignoring them and taking in the view."

Gaspard raised an eyebrow. "Do you really think—?"

"He means," Dora muttered into her employer's ear, "that right now, we should allow most of our group to rest—and stay the hell out of our way."

Riordan couldn't repress a smile: Veriden was a pain in the ass, but she was an extremely competent and insightful pain in the ass. "Meanwhile, Mr. Macmillan and Ms. Veriden will drift toward the forest behind us, because they are bored bored bored by all our chatter."

"Right," said Veriden and loped back off toward the rear of the column, looking pretty bored already.

Macmillan's brow beetled, then rose. "Oh, yes," he said, "I'm turribly, turribly bored."

"Off you go, Keith. I'll give you two the signal when one of them has come close enough for you to flank it and get a good look."

"I'll be waiting." Macmillan wandered off, angling to the front of the column.

"Now, Ambassador, why don't you join me over here, where we have a great view of the valley?"

Gaspard did. They gazed at the many shades of green and no small amount of orange, violet, yellow, and black. After half a minute, the ambassador commented, almost casually, "Your breathing is becoming worse, Captain."

"I am fi—"

"Spare me your brave denials. A blind man could see it with a cane. The question is, what are we to do about it?"

"Frankly, Ambassador, we have bigger problems than my respiratory infection. We are down to our last food and water.

Two days from now, most everyone in this party is going to be staggering around from the lack of both. In five days, all but a few of us will be immobile. Once we solve the food and water problem, then we can worry about my ability to keep up."

Gaspard nodded tightly. "I cannot argue the logic of that, but—"

"Ambassador." Riordan waited for Gaspard to make eye contact. "I'm going to keep doing my job. I'm going to get us to safety."

Gaspard glanced away, then nodded.

Riordan looked out over the valley, keeping an ear and an eye on the situation developing behind them. Veriden and Macmillan were drifting further apart, and closer to the tree-line.

As the river descended toward the valley, it was marked by intermittent but gentle rapids. Each bank's flood margin had become meadows dotted with rushes resembling uptwisting orange helixes. Among those bright, motionless spirals flitted examples of the region's most common animal: a wiry creature that recalled a flying squirrel crossed with a newt. They pursued and ate various insects that hovered near the boundary between the exogenous species and their indigenous rivals.

Most species of the two biota did not interact; they ignored each other if they came close to their own borders and rarely crossed over. But in a few noteworthy cases, the rivalry became competition and ultimately violence. In the past few days, Riordan had seen a smaller variety of the predators he'd fended off circling a multieyed arboreal marsupial that was vaguely reminiscent of the Slaasriithi themselves. Hissing, clattering, screeching, the two species marked their respective territories until, as if by mutual agreement, they rushed together in a sudden tangle of bodies and flashing teeth—and then sped apart just as fast, neither appearing any worse for the wear.

Having now witnessed many similar scenes, Riordan understood why Yiithrii'ah'aash insisted that the story of the Slaasriithi had to be seen, not read. The legation would have certainly understood logical explanations of what they were witnessing: slow-motion terraforming that replaced the human tactic of supplantation with cooption. But they would not have realized that they were also witnessing the core truths of the Slaasriithi in action. This terraforming was not driven by economics or grand strategy or population pressures. It was an affirmation: of life, of death, of limitless time, of integration with a reality that transcended any one species or epoch. Consequently, there were no endless committee meetings over budgetary or procedural problems, there was no desperate concern about maintaining the political will to see projects to completion, there was no perpetual need to reinform, reexcite and reassure a voting populace that today's path was, indeed, the right path. And above all, there was no conflation of the Slaasriithi's objectives with the egos of those who were charged with attaining them over the course of decades, centuries, even millennia.

Riordan, relaxing from the exertions of the trail, enjoyed a slightly deeper breath and stared out across the increasingly misty valley: a planet so superficially similar to the green worlds of the Consolidated Terran Republic, yet strikingly different from its monocellular foundations up to its most complex organisms.

Some of which were apparently still tracking them. Riordan glanced over his shoulder, saw that Veriden had retraced the last one hundred meters covered by the group. Macmillan had made equivalent progress in the other direction. That separation would be sufficient for an effective flanking move. Riordan turned to Gaspard. "Ambassador, if you will be so good to run toward the woods when I do so—"

"*Me*?"

"Yes, you."

"You mean, *toward* the animals following us?"

"That is exactly what I mean. Trackers as cautious as these will tend to scatter if confronted swiftly and by surprise. And if Keith or Dora manages to bring one or two down, that will dissuade these creatures even further."

Gaspard stared wide-eyed into the foliage. "But I—"

"Etienne: this is not a matter for debate. Just do it—*now*!"

Veriden and Macmillan reacted to Riordan's shout by turning and sprinting straight into the tree line. Caine and Gaspard, closer to where the group had halted, and further from the foliage, were longer in reaching its shadowy outer fringes. By which time, Macmillan was shouting:

"I've flushed them; they're heading your way."

"Dora?" yelled Caine through wracking gasps for air.

No report came from her.

But up ahead in the bush and in the trees, there was a surprising amount of motion. Most of it was withdrawing toward the taller, inland stands of bumbershoots and cone trees, but there was also some crisscrossing confusion as creatures fled from one human flanker, only to find themselves confronted by the other. Through a gap between two sapling-sized ferns, Caine saw one of these trapped creatures leap from the ground into the lower branches of a frond-tree, its long-limbed torso a blur of motion— and Riordan stopped, paralyzed by a memory:

Delta Pavonis Three. He was suddenly reliving the first moment he encountered the regressed Slaasriithi of that planet, glimpsed their gibbonlike leaps into the trees— *Those motions were the same as* these *motions, right here*—

"Macmillan, Veriden, stop! Stay where you are! Don't move! And for Christ's sake, don't shoot!"

"What?" Macmillan shouted back at Caine; he sounded slightly annoyed.

"Why?" cried Veriden; she sounded downright pissed.

"These aren't animals."

"Then what are they?" asked Macmillan.

But Veriden had obviously had an epiphany of her own. "Shit," she said.

Deeper in the forest and overhead, the sounds—a panicked rout in the face of an unexpected charge—diminished, the noises quieting more rapidly than could be explained by dwindling into the distance.

"Now what?" Veriden hissed from almost fifteen meters away.

"Now we wait," Caine answered with no more volume than was necessary.

Chapter Forty

Akin to Riordan's initial encounter with the regressed Slaasriithi on Delta Pavonis Three, the passage of time seemed impossibly dilatory. And when Veriden shifted impatiently, Riordan was gratified to see Gaspard make a savage gesture of cessation in her direction.

A faint movement stirred in the bush, well ahead of Caine.

"Something coming," Macmillan muttered.

Riordan nodded. "Let it come. Lower your rifle. And stay where you are." Caine was about to suggest that the Scotsman should also try to relax when a great wave of calm flowed through not just his mind, but his body—which Riordan reflexively resisted, much the same way he would shake off drowsiness when driving at night.

"It is not necessary that you use friendship spores on us," he said calmly into the underbrush ahead.

The brush parted. A Slaasriithi of Yiithrii'ah'aash's general physiology and size appeared. Its pelt was somewhat darker, it wore a backpack, and its finger-tendrils were festooned with numerous control rings akin to those the legation had seen used on the shift-carrier. "I believe you mean amity spores," said a pleasant but machine-generated voice from the Slaasriithi's backpack, "although the meaning is similar. However, I did not project amity spores upon you. That would compromise your freedom of action and will."

353

"Then what did you use?"

"A combination of relief and rapport spores."

"Rapport sounds as though it might influence one's will, as well," Gaspard pointed out as Veriden and Macmillan drew closer.

"It does not. It maximizes"—the computer-generated voice uttered a set of meaningless twitters and squawks—"between species which otherwise lack a shared medium of communication. Such as our two species."

"Yiithrii'ah'aash seems to understand us just fine without a magic box." Veriden's voice was sharp, cautious.

"Yiithrii'ah'aash? Is he the Prime Ratiocinator who directs the actions of the *Tidal-Drift*"—more unintelligible squeaks and yowls from the backpack—"*to-Shore-of-Stars*?"

"Eh?" grunted Macmillan.

Caine understood. "Is that the name of Yiithrii'ah'aash's shift-carrier?"

"Yes. I am not well informed in the matter of Yiithrii'ah'aash's mission here or your identities, other than that you are humans who have been invited to travel on to our homeworld."

"And that someone is trying to kill us all."

"Yes. This also we have deduced."

"Have *deduced*?" Veriden shouted. "What, wasn't it obvious enough when ships are getting blown to pieces right over your heads?"

The Slaasriithi seemed to start backwards slightly. "Your tone is one of agitation. I am unsure what I have—"

"It has been a very trying time for us," Caine interrupted. "Several of us who crashed in our shuttle were killed, several others wounded."

The Slaasriithi's tetrahedral head turned slightly, as if he might be considering Caine more closely. "You are not well, either."

Caine waved off the concern. "It's nothing. We have more immediate concerns. We are running out of both food and water. I am sorry to ask for help even before we have exchanged names and learned more of each other, but it is imperative that we see to the needs of our group."

"The water in the river is safe for your species to drink—"

—which we would have discovered, out of desperation, in the next few days—

"—but the matter of food that is both palatable and nourishing will require the labor of several taxae. To initiate that process, I must coordinate with my partners. Will it alarm you if I bring them here to join us?"

"Not at all," Gaspard jumped in eagerly. "We have hoped to meet you, to meet anyone. How fortunate that you have found us at last!"

"In actuality," the Slaasriithi responded slowly, "we have been following your movements for three days now. I just arrived yesterday, however."

"For three days—?" Gaspard blinked rapidly. "Then why did you not offer help? Why did we have to beat the bushes to discover you? This is most inconsiderate."

The Slaasriithi reeled in its neck a bit. "We were instructed only to observe and, when feasible, report. But that has been difficult, due to the OverWatchling's general elimination of broadcast signals."

"OverWatchling?" Macmillan echoed.

"A planetary, uh, guardian?" Caine guessed. "But not actually part of a taxon?"

The Slaasriithi turned towards him. "Yes, it is as you say. It has been coordinating all activities."

"Are there no ratiocinatorae on Disparity to temper this Over-Watchling's actions, then?" Gaspard pressed.

The Slaasriithi's "head" hovered a bit more erect. "I am a ratiocinator, but even Seniors of my taxon rarely, if ever, challenge the instincts of an OverWatchling."

Gaspard considered that. "May we know your name, ratiocinator?"

"I am W'th'vaathi. Allow me to summon the others who speak for their taxae, here."

"Please do."

W'th'vaathi slid swiftly and noiselessly back into the brush.

Riordan turned to Macmillan. "Go back to the group, tell them what's going on, and that they should sit tight. This is not, I repeat *not*, a threat scenario."

Moments after Keith had left, the brush parted more widely; two other Slaasriithi were with W'th'vaathi, both wearing similar backpacks. One was slightly taller, but proportionally similar in build. The other was considerably smaller and had rings on its toe-analogs as well as its fingers. It was of lighter build, but had a proportionally longer neck. The sensor cluster capping it jerked to attention. "Humans," a slightly different voice announced from its backpack. It was, from the tone, a self-confirmation, not an attempt to summon their attention. "I am Thnessfiirm. I have the honor of speaking for the cerdorae, here."

Gaspard frowned in an apparent effort to focus his recollections. "Cerdorae," the ambassador mused. Then, turning to W'th'vaathi, "That taxon is the one that is machine- or device-focused in their activities, correct?"

"You might see it that way, yes."

"And so he is that taxon's local spokesman?"

"In a manner of speaking," W'th'vaathi allowed, "but Thness-fiirm is not, to use your term, a spokes*man*. He is a she. As I am. Technically."

"'Technically'?" Dora's tough-as-nails demeanor lapsed just long enough for her to sound completely baffled.

"Distinctions of gender, or sex, are mostly meaningless to us. We adopt the sexed pronoun appropriate to our last reproductive role, since any of us may perform any of the roles."

Gaspard and Dora looked at Caine, who looked at both of them. "That's, um, a new concept for us," he confessed.

"We presumed that it might be. And the Slaasriithi to my right is Unsymaajh."

The largest of the Slaasriithi bobbed. "I have the honor of speaking for all convectorae. The smallest and fleetest of my taxic family have been watching you for the past several days. You will appreciate, I hope, that, lacking any concrete information of what transpired in space, we had no way to be certain that you were the guests of Yiithrii'ah'aash, rather than those who attacked him. We are glad to learn that you are friends and that our paths may be joined, now."

"So are we," Riordan affirmed as Macmillan returned. "And speaking of joining our paths, we should resume our journey and get as far away from the wreckage of our shuttle as possible. And if that silver object at the north end of the valley is a construct of yours, it would be best to—"

"I regret interrupting." W'th'vaathi had risen up again; her hip joints seemed tense. "However, you must abandon your current path. The Silver Tower you have seen is not the place that Yiithrii'ah'aash and Disparity's Prime Ratiocinator, T'suu'shvah, determined that you should be received and housed."

Riordan paused. Was W'th'vaathi reluctant to continue on to this Silver Tower because that might attract hostile attention to it, or was she simply determined to follow the letter of the law? "W'th'vaathi, but is our current path not the *best* one?"

W'th'vaathi's pause was halting, puzzled. "We should not travel there because it is not where you are to be received." W'th'vaathi said it slowly, as if she presumed that Riordan had not heard what she said the first time.

Okay, so W'th'vaathi just doesn't like, or isn't accustomed to, thinking outside the box. "But there's no reason we shouldn't go there, then?"

W'th'vaathi paused again, but this time, as though she was having to consider an entirely new concept. "No. But it lacks adequate preparation."

Gaspard leaned into that explanation. "Adequate preparation?"

"We have not sent appropriate provisions or furnishings there. Nor have Yiithrii'ah'aash's picked taxae spokespersons convened there. Also, is it not a likely site for the attackers to destroy, if they penetrate our defenses?"

"It might be," Caine admitted. "But is it not fortified, or equipped with defenses of its own? Is it not a comparatively safe place?"

W'th'vaathi thought again, but more briefly. "It is, but we find that safety in such situations is better achieved by being difficult to find, rather than hard to destroy."

"Normally, I would agree, W'th'vaathi. But I fear that there is no way that we can be made as difficult to find as you would be on your own."

"Indeed? Why do you so conjecture?"

"Sensors will pick us out," Macmillan asserted with confidence. "If the attackers come after us, their sensors would easily discriminate our thermals and outlines from yours. Our own arrays could manage that, and the enemy technology seems to be well ahead of ours."

W'th'vaathi considered this new information carefully. "It seems, then, that we must go to the Silver Tower. It is one of three such places on Disparity, a place where our spokespersons convene and where we store artifactures."

Veriden frowned at the strange word that had emerged from W'th'vaathi's backpack. "'Artifactures'? I think your translator needs a programming update."

W'th'vaathi's tendrils made a wavelike motion that Caine read as easy agreement. "It may be as you say. Our translating artif—no, I perceive now: our translators are what you would call 'complex machines,' not merely 'tools.' So: these translating *machines* were last updated before the most recent Convocation. I suspect they are deficient in many of the nuances of your various languages. Specifically, we label all nonliving creations as 'artifactures.' This is a crude approximation of our actual term, which contains more embedded allusions than may be conveniently referenced during a conversation."

"So, you store all your machines—and tools and gadgets—in the silver towers?" Dora seemed all at once surprised and doubtful.

"All those we deem complex. We keep unpowered tools and very simple machines, such as vises and gliders and winches, in our arboria, but nothing that would be efficacious in defense."

Upon hearing the word "defense," Caine nodded. "But the Silver Towers *are* equipped with defense technologies?"

"Some," W'th'vaathi answered tentatively.

"Yes," asserted Thnessfiirm. "They are mostly of a remote-operated nature. And the towers have reinforced subterranean layers. They provide shelter and are constructed so that occupants may withdraw from the structure without being observed."

Well, the cerdorae certainly seem to be the go-to taxon for military needs. Caine nodded. "Then the Silver Tower is precisely where we must go."

W'th'vaathi's long neck wobbled from side to side. Her tone was uncertain. "It is not in our nature to give visitors access to our complex machines. I have instructions to observe and to render aid. But bringing you to a Silver Tower that has not been adequately prepared—"

Or do you mean, "adequately sanitized?"

"—contravenes prior guidelines."

"Can't your Senior Ratiocinators be contacted to vouch for us, to confirm that it is safe to bring us to this closest Silver Tower?"

"We cannot contact them directly. The OverWatchling prevents all long-range communication during any incident where invaders may be in or near orbit."

"Then how the hell do you coordinate counterattacks, ambushes, supply disruption, jamming, observation?" Keith Macmillan's voice was relatively calm, but his face was becoming a bright red.

Thnessfiirm seemed to have the best implicit sense of the humans' frustrations with Slaasriithi defensive preparations and infrastructure. "You will understand that the circumstances occasioned by your arrival are unknown to us, except as mentioned in the chronicles of our distant past."

"We do understand," Riordan assured the smaller Slaasriithi, cutting a sharp look at Keith. "But those of us who are charged with ensuring the safety of our group find it worrying that we will not have access to, er, complex machines with which to protect ourselves."

"I comprehend their worry and share it," W'th'vaathi asserted. "And I am decided: your party is other than we thought it to be. And it is not credible that you are attackers masquerading as victims. This was a possibility which my taxon's seniors warned me to guard against, but I am satisfied that you are not dissembling. We shall travel to the Third Silver Tower. On the way there, your need of food can be answered by the efforts of the convectorae. However," she looked at Caine directly, "your illness is a more difficult matter. Did you spend any extended time sheltering under one of these trees?" She gestured to a cone tree.

"I did."

"Was the olfactory experience not...aversive?"

"Yes, but the predators that had me ringed in were even more aversive."

Riordan had the sense of a dire silence as the Slaasriithi looked at each other with unseen eyes. "We comprehend. We will make all haste. We shall invite these water-striders to summon others of their kind and we shall go downriver as swiftly as we may."

"Um, we were expecting help from those complex machines you mentioned," Veriden intruded brusquely.

W'th'vaathi's tendril-fingers drooped. "I regret to say that the Third Silver Tower lacks many of the assets of our other two. It is equipped to receive and launch our cargo craft, but they are all hypervelocity ballistic systems. They are unable to land without special facilities. Besides, they would attract the attention of your attackers."

"Do you know if the attackers are still near Disparity?"

"We suspect so. There is no indication that they have left the system."

Macmillan now sounded distinctly annoyed. "Then why haven't you hunted them down, chased them off?"

"I reemphasize that Disparity is a transitioning colony world. We have no such defense-in-depth, and cannot risk losing more of our assets."

Gaspard threw up his hands. "But this system is adjacent to your homeworld."

W'th'vaathi's sensor cluster fixed on him. If the Slaasriithi had been a human, Riordan had the impression she would simply have shrugged and asked, "And what's your point?"

The ratiocinator's silence seemed to increase Gaspard's exasperation. "How can you *not* have more developed defenses at such a close approach, such a key access point, to your homeworld?"

"Why should we?"

"*Mon Dieu*, because this might be the system from which an invader would stage an attack to *destroy* your homeworld!"

"But the destruction of any race's homeworld is directly prohibited by the Twenty-First Accord. And there are many defenses at the system you call Beta Aquilae. But even if it was to succumb to an attacker, we would simply shift our emphasis to a new homeworld."

Caine goggled. "A new homeworld? Can't there only be one?"

"Yes. One at a time."

"No, no. I mean, how can you come from more than one world?"

"Ah. You have confused the word 'homeworld' with 'world of origin.' They are explicitly not the same."

"Not to you, perhaps."

"I commend you to consider that you should not consider these terms synonymous, either, and that other races use these as we do, rather than in the context you have presumed."

Wait: so when the Dornaani, or other races, refer to their "homeworlds," they do not mean—?

But W'th'vaathi was expanding upon her comment. "Once a race has been changing biospheres for millennia, the planet of its origin becomes more a matter of curiosity than urgent information. Now, we must resume the journey at once. The others of Unsymaajh's subtaxae shall forage for your nutritive needs as we travel, and any newly summoned water-striders should join us before midday."

As they walked out of the trees and met the stares of the rest of the survivors, W'th'vaathi stopped and studied the three water-striders waiting patiently in the river. She turned to Riordan. "The convector subtaxae who have observed you reported that you had been traveling with the water-striders. Were they in error?"

Caine shook his head. "No." He gestured toward the striders. "They've been keeping us safe for the past several days."

Unsymaajh's head moved forward slightly, as if he were trying to get a better look at something between Riordan's eyes. "They have been keeping you safe? How?"

"By escorting us downriver."

Unsymaajh and W'th'vaathi exchanged glances with their undetectable eyes. W'th'vaathi turned back to Riordan. "Did you not summon them?"

Caine looked at the rest of the group, who were all looking at him: every human face was a study in perplexity. "Did I *summon* them?" Caine repeated, feeling stupid. "No: I don't know how to do that. They just—showed up."

Another set of looks were exchanged among the Slaasriithi, more of whom were drifting toward the shore, and toward the humans, all the time. "So," W'th'vaathi said slowly, "Yiithrii'ah'aash did not brief you on the flora and fauna that our race brought to this world, even though you are so strongly marked—and with the musk of the water-striders most strongly of all?"

Riordan shook his head. "No. Besides, that marking wasn't conferred by Yiithrii'ah'aash. A water-strider did that, just before it died." W'th'vaathi folded her tendril-fingers patiently, and settled into a hip-stabilized crouch. The expectation of hearing the story behind the death of the water-strider was obvious. Caine imparted an extremely truncated version.

At the end, W'th'vaathi extended her neck a little further and said, "Come."

Riordan followed her down to the water. W'th'vaathi turned. "Wade toward the largest of the water-striders. You have nothing to fear. Truly."

Caine moved out into the water, and, after a few steps, the largest of the water-striders seemed to be bending its—well, its "knees"—to get a better look at him. The further out Caine waded, the further down the water-strider bent, its legs spreading sideways and its joints allowing the heavy body to lower toward the river. For a moment, it resembled a four-legged mammalian tarantula, the joints of its legs higher than the trunk of its body.

By the time Caine had waded hip-deep into the current, he was only a few meters from the creature, which was almost eyeball-to-eyeball with him. And in those alien eyes, Caine read—what? Nothing? Perplexity? Curiosity? Or even—expectation?

"She is waiting," W'th'vaathi called from the shore, as one of the water-strider's legs began stretching out, lowering into the water at a more gentle angle.

"For what?"

"For you to take your place."

Caine hated feeling stupid and he'd spent most of the last five minutes doing exactly that. "To take my place where?"

"Upon her back."

"You mean, we're supposed to—*ride* them?"

"Of course." W'th'vaathi's reply was mild, too mild to conceal a hint of ironic amusement.

Or so Caine told himself.

Chapter Forty-One

By the time noon was past, the group had made as much progress downriver as they normally made in a full day. Also, Riordan no longer felt like one of the water-striders was standing on his chest every time he inhaled.

W'th'vaathi, who had not noticed how Ben Hwang and Caine surreptitiously arranged to be on the same water-strider as she, remarked, "Your respiration seems less labored, Caine Riordan."

Riordan smiled. "Yes, thanks to you and the water-striders."

"It is a great misfortune that you were unable to obey your instincts to leave the area under what you call the cone tree. You may have become more deeply infested with the defense spores than we believed possible."

Caine tried to remain calm. Being super-saturated with defense spores did not sound particularly promising.

"Without your filter masks," W'th'vaathi continued, "you would be affected. However, even with them, you would eventually succumb. Uptake also occurs through mucous membranes, albeit more gradually."

Great. In addition to my eyes, I have a vented suit, courtesy of those damn pirhannows. "Can I be cured?" Caine asked when he was sure he could keep his voice level and calm.

"Yes," W'th'vaathi replied. "But my knowledge in such matters is incomplete. I was not even aware of these defense spores until Senior Ratiocinator Mriif'vaal informed me about them."

Ben Hwang was frowning deeply. "W'th'vaathi, did Mriif'vaal happen to mention whether these defense spores would impact *all* biota that are not Slaasriithi in origin?"

"They do not. For instance, they do not affect the indigenous biota of Disparity. If they did, we could not build symbiotic relationships and ecological synergies with it."

Ben nodded. "Of course. But that's not what I'm referring to. I'm talking about, well, *unwelcome* xenobiologies."

"I do not know. Why do you inquire?"

Caine saw the implications as Ben replied. "Well, it's somewhat peculiar that, even before we arrived here, both Yiithrii'ah'aash and Mriif'vaal knew that these spores would be dangerous to humans. And evidently they also knew that you possess an antidote or cure for afflicted humans. I find that curious."

W'th'vaathi's "head" turned toward Ben, wobbled a bit as the water-strider moved into slightly shallower water and cast about for better footing. "Yes. That is curious."

"It makes me wonder if you've had human visitors before," Caine speculated in a casual tone that, he realized, was probably lost on the Slaasriithi.

"I believe so," W'th'vaathi affirmed. "Of course, you have been long known as a protected species, watched over by the Custodians of the Accord. But it seems you must have been known before that, even before we started receiving your broadcast signals more than a century ago."

"What makes you think that?"

W'th'vaathi's neck wiggled a bit. "Because there is no mention of your ever being 'discovered' or 'assessed' by the Custodians, as were the Hkh'Rkh, and even the Arat Kur. From the earliest Custodial records, knowledge of your homeworld and the systems reserved for your expansion have always existed. Logically, our species may have had earlier contact. At that time, perhaps it was deemed prudent to create spores that are particularly inimical to your biochemistry. Otherwise, how would our Senior Ratiocinatorae know to preemptively provide for your safety during your visit, and indicate that there was a cure in the event of an accidental exposure?"

"How indeed?" murmured Ben Hwang with a quick glance at Riordan. Once again, getting a better picture of what had been going on in this particular stellar cluster twenty millennia ago rose up as a significant, even urgent, intelligence objective. "Tell me, how do the spores work?"

"There are many different spores: a novitor or hortator would be able to provide a comprehensive explanation. My understanding is that when human secretions are detected in our environment, the small but persistent production of defense spores is triggered to enter a hyper-production stage. Some of the defense spores cause our fauna to avoid humans, some will agitate suitable species to attack, instead. But the most common variety of spores simply lodge in your mucous membranes and generate a pronounced histaminic response, as well as respiratory swelling. The sequelae include decreased cognitive clarity and mobility, thereby rendering the subject—"

"—extremely tractable," finished Hwang.

"You perceive, then."

"All too completely," Hwang murmured.

"And what of you, Caine Riordan? Do you understand how very profoundly you were marked by the dying water-strider, and why?"

"I probably don't fully understand either," Caine confessed.

"Then I shall elucidate. The water-strider marked you more deeply and broadly than is typical outside the limits of its own species. To simplify, it marked you with powerful rapport and affinity spores when it last breathed upon you. When it rubbed you, it saturated you with compliance pheromones. That is why the water-striders are waiting to aid you."

"And it imparted these gifts because I was kind to it when it died?"

"That is part of it, certainly, but there is something else: you have been marked before. That other mark is deep and strong, but it is also unfamiliar. I believe it is very old."

"Yes. It happened about two years ago."

"I do not mean that the marking occurred long ago. I mean that the marker itself is unfamiliar to today's taxae. It seems ancient, even primal. It is—most striking."

Ben nodded slowly. "So, you feel it yourself."

"Yes. It is peculiar to find glimmers and scents of our unrecorded past wafting about an xenosapient such as yourself, Caine Riordan. It elicits many questions."

I'll bet it does. Caine was wondering whether he should let the topic slide when a flapping sound and a rising shadow distracted him. The water-strider upon which he was riding had raised the two membranous fins that had been lying folded to either side of its back-perched passengers. "Is everything all right?"

W'th'vaathi's bifurcated prehensile tail flicked dismissively. "Our herd has detected the presence of another, downstream. Although none of us are masters of water-strider communications, I presume it is alerting the others that our approach is not a challenge or a purposive territorial encroachment." Her tone changed. "Or they could be sending premating signals."

"Mating signals?" Caine suddenly wanted to be off the water-strider's back, far away from having to witness, let alone dodge, the amorous frolics of these ungainly giants.

W'th'vaathi may have been amused: one of her tails shimmied irregularly. "Allow me to be more precise. They might be exchanging expressions of interest and receptivity. For later."

From further back on the creature's back, Macmillan snorted. "Hey, baby, here's my number. Call me." If W'th'vaathi understood Macmillan's truly alien quip, she gave no sign of it.

Caine glanced at the two ribbed and leathery fins rising up on either side; fully extended, they were more akin to long, triangular pennants. "These extensions must serve a purpose other than imparting mating signals. Stability while swimming, perhaps?"

W'th'vaathi's head swayed gently from side-to-side: a gesture that Riordan had come to associate with tentative agreement. "Fossil records suggest that this may have been their original purpose. But that was probably before their large flippers elongated and evolved into legs. However, the force of evolution does not waste useful resources. Study the tips of the spines which raise and spread the fins."

Caine did so and noticed that the spines protruded beyond the membrane of the fins and did not end in tapering points, but were angle-cut, akin to the nub of a quill pen. It took several moments of scrutiny before Riordan realized what he was looking at: "Are those breathing tubes?"

"Yes. When a water-strider submerges and seals the row of large respiration ducts on either side of its spine, the fins function as snorkels."

Hwang nodded. "So, the fins' courtship use is secondary. Tell me: do fin differences signal sex differences?"

W'th'vaathi turned from her position just behind the head of the water-strider. "As with us, and many other species that we brought to the stars, the water-striders are not gendered or sexed as is your species. Rather, among striders, there are two different reproductory variants, the impregnator and the depositor."

"Those sound like the same things," Macmillan murmured.

"In your heterosexual dyads, yes, but not among this species. The impregnator chooses which of the depositors it shall fertilize, as well as the kind of offspring: either a depositor or, far more rarely, another impregnator. In this way, the herd's fertile and dominant impregnator determines the demographics of the herd, and even its genetic characteristics."

"So why are the impregnated water-striders called depositors?" Hwang asked, hanging on to a fistful of their mount's fur as it dipped back out into the deeper water.

"Because they do not retain the fertilized egg. It is immediately passed back to the impregnator and embeds in its womb."

Macmillan stared. "So the impregnator is also the...the mother?"

W'th'vaathi's left tail-half flicked once. "As I mentioned, terrestrial sexual dyadism offers few productive analogs for understanding water-strider reproduction. Caretaking and postbirth nutrition are the province of the depositor which was impregnated, not the impregnator. Also, any attempt to apply the sex-associated dominance and behavior templates common among your planet's social mammals will be quite futile. For instance, genetic selection is not established through external forces, such as you biota's male aggression contests, but by the impregnator's detection of desired traits in a depositor's pheromones."

Riordan nodded, seeing the paradigm of Slaasriithi consensuality reprised in the water-striders. "So the evolutionary rule is not survival of the fittest, but selection of the fittest, according to the changing needs of the herd."

W'th'vaathi's tendrils straightened with a pop. "An apt adaptation of one of your own axioms, if I am not mistaken. And, as you may perceive, not wholly inapplicable to we Slaasriithi. Water-strider reproduction resembles ours in many particulars."

"Och, here we go," Keith exclaimed, "the alien 'birds and bees' talk. Damn, how I wish I'd stayed home in Dundee." Caine raised an eyebrow at Macmillan who simply shrugged and smiled.

W'th'vaathi had, once again, shown no understanding of the

big Scotsman's comments. "These words baffle me, although we know of your terrestrial bee and admire many of its features."

Ben glared at Keith who smiled sweetly in return. "Mr. Macmillan was using an idiom that refers to the—the details of mating."

"I understand. Although I must offer an initial correction; one could not characterize any stage of Slaasriithi reproduction as mating. What humans refer to as sex—and the consequent emotional phenomena you label longing, romance, and passion—are anathema to us. Our reproductory process is partly instinctual, and partly guided by Senior Ratiocinatorae, much the way that a water-strider impregnator determines which depositor shall be fertilized."

Hwang stared dubiously at W'th'vaathi. "So you have a womb?"

"No, not presently. As I mentioned, all Slaasriithi are capable of all reproductory roles. The ratiocinator that guides the process will, itself, not receive a quickened egg. However, in conjunction with communally informed instinct, it determines the demographic mix that shall arise from a gathering of Slaasriithi who are to be quickened."

"And how does the ratiocinator accomplish that?"

W'th'vaathi's tendrils swayed in time with the rolling gait of the water-strider. "Pheromonic emissions from the entire community determine what proportion of each caste should be quickened, which is achieved in a communal pool. Each individual who is to become gravid both releases and receives genetic material from all the others."

Caine tried to rise above the bizarre images W'th'vaathi's description was prompting. "Then how do the taxae remain, er, coherent subspecies? Doesn't the free exchange of"—*the mind reels*—"genetic material create hybrids?"

"This is, again, an expectation that would be logical in your genetic template, but not ours. Fragments of each Slaasriithi subspecies are present in every individual's genome, regardless of their taxon. Therefore, all taxae are repositories of genetic diversity for all taxae.

"Once the genetic exchange is complete, the ratiocinator releases a second pheromone that triggers the chemical process which determines how each pregravid Slaasriithi's host gamete will select and become receptive to the various genetic material that surrounds it. In this way, the community maximizes genetic diversity while also producing demographic outcomes optimal to its changing needs."

"But then . . . you have no families?" Macmillan's voice had become serious, now. Haunted, even.

"Not such as you mean. Our young are far more self-sufficient upon birth; the genomes of the respective taxae prespecialize its members for their predetermined tasks and predilections. Consequently, the genetic complexity that enables humanity's variability and versatility is not necessary. Our young aggregate in groups maintained by older and less mobile members of their taxae, who control them through pheromones and redirection."

"It all sounds very . . . logical." Ben's nod was emphatic, but his voice was carefully controlled.

"Logic is often overrated, Doctor," Macmillan countered quickly. His face was pale and his freckles stood out more profoundly than before. "And do these, eh, OverWatchlings also oversee your breeding, prodding the ratiocinators here and there, where needed? That would be logical too. Why let anyone make a choice for themselves?"

Riordan turned toward the Scotsman, who matched stares at first, but then looked away, jaw muscles bunching. *What's got into you, Keith?*

If W'th'vaathi had detected Macmillan's sarcasm, he nonetheless elected to treat the question as serious. "I have failed to make clear the role of the OverWatchlings. They are not, strictly speaking, intelligent. To use the closest terrestrial analog, imagine a queen bee who sleeps until the nest is disturbed. Awakened, she instinctively sets about sending pheromone commands to alert and marshal the hive's defenses."

"Given its reactions so far," Macmillan grumbled, "Disparity's OverWatchling doesn't seem very versatile. Or bright."

"If by 'bright' you mean perspicacious, this is a non sequitur. The OverWatchling does not yet have enough experience for that assessment to be made. But it is quite ignorant."

"Because it hasn't dealt with crises before?" Caine asked.

"In part. But being new, it has also benefited from very few Absorptions."

Riordan heard the emphasis. "What are Absorptions?"

"The primary way the OverWatchling learns and how we pass on knowledge to subsequent generations."

Ben Hwang's deepening frown opened into something approaching alarm. "You mean you absorb each other's thoughts? But how?

Yiithrii'ah'aash explicitly indicated on several occasions that the Slaasriithi are not a hive mind."

"And so we are not, Doctor Hwang. But this does not prevent us from passing on our life experiences when we expire. As does your own brain, ours chemically encodes and stores our life's many lessons and discoveries. The most dramatic of these are passed along at the time of our demise."

"Physically?"

"Yes. Strong emotional or cognitive reactions are not only retained in our active memory, but in crystalline structures produced by that part of our brain which is located in our trunk."

The concepts were so novel, and came in such a cascade, that Caine could already feel them slipping away. "Wait. So firstly, your major, uh, life events, are recorded in crystal form? And that's stored in your brain—which is actually not all in one place?"

"Correct. The decentralization of our brain was evolutionarily essential, given our arboreal origins and the smaller sensor and reaction clusters which you have identified as our 'heads.'"

Hwang nodded. "Of course. Your head, er, sensor cluster was too small to develop a large enough brain for cognition. But once that seat of protointelligence was sited in the trunk of your body, the neurological lag time was too long for it to coordinate your arboreal acrobatics. So your brain evolved along a distributed processing model. Your conscious decisions are sited in your 'body-brain,' but your physical coordination is at least partially sited in your sensor-cluster."

"Yes."

Caine resisted the impulse to shake his head. "All right, but let's get back to these, er, memory crystals. When you die, how do they get transferred?"

"They are released from the brain stem and become encysted near the top of our spine. When the cyst ruptures, it releases the crystals in a liquid medium which we call Past Water, for it is how we pass along the collective insights and taxon-specific knowledge of our species."

Too weird: cerebral kidney stones with a purpose. "So the Over-Watchling is somehow, uh, upgraded by exposing it to Past Water?"

"Yes. Crystals with fundamentally similar encoding do not get absorbed by other members of a taxon, and so, are passed on to the OverWatchling. It does not so much understand the data as its behaviors are shaped by it, much as the way you would train a dog to perform certain tasks or tricks." W'th'vaathi's neck shimmied slightly. "But since there have been few crises on Disparity, our Senior Ratiocinatorae have had little to add to the defense instincts of the OverWatchling. This partly explains what you perceive to be its tepid response to the current threats."

"There's another reason?"

"Yes. The recent war depleted Disparity's defense systems. When our ships were dispatched to conduct raids along the border between the Arat Kur and the Hkh'Rkh, they expanded their stocks of defense spheres and related systems by appropriating one or two from every planet they passed on their way to engaging the enemy. Those depletions have not yet been restituted."

"So that's why you don't have much defensive gear to help us on the ground here, either?" Macmillan sounded like he was trying to come up with an excuse for the Slaasriithi insufficiencies of the moment.

"No, our engagements with the Arat Kur and Hkh'Rkh were limited to space. Ground systems were not required. We have not released any ground systems because this situation has not yet evolved to that point where the OverWatchling deems it necessary to set aside our primary constraint protocol."

Caine frowned. "And what, exactly, is that protocol?"

W'th'vaathi's tendril-toes writhed slightly. "It is deemed unwise to send advanced technology into an environment where aggressive species are involved, and in which it is possible that we might lose control over the machines in question. We consider this protocol particularly urgent to maintain in regard to your species, Captain."

Riordan kept his voice calm. "Are we deemed less reliable than other species?"

"No, Captain. We simply acknowledge that humanity is extremely inquisitive, and thus, by examining our machines, it may acquire technical insights that do not arise from its own experimental efforts. This could be highly destabilizing."

It is also the history of our race, W'th'vaathi. Stealing loot was never more than a penny-ante pickup game for chumps. The big players have always known that the big stakes are in stealing information. "I suspect that destabilization is normative for us, then."

W'th'vaathi considered that for a moment. "That may be true.

But it would be irresponsible for us to act differently. It is not our place to be a change-agent in the evolution of your race."

If only I could believe that you felt that way about influencing us biologically, as well. "So is that why you are reluctant to incorporate much technology into your environment? To ensure that it doesn't destabilize you, too?"

"Correct. For our species, complex machinery distracts, and ultimately conditions, individuals away from the processes and temporality of a natural environment. We are not reluctant to employ technology. We use it freely and gladly where natural processes offer no reasonable alternative. Space travel is one example. Rapid long-range communications is another."

W'th'vaathi's tendrils drifted lazily in the wind. "Each evolutionary path has its advantages. We have many worlds, and balance in each. But now we live in an age where military capability is needed. In that domain, we have no skill and little appropriate technology. The price of living in unvarying peace and balance is that, in the face of war and chaos, one is ill-suited to answer the challenges they pose."

Riordan nodded respectfully. "You are uncommonly honest."

"If one would be in harmony with one's environment, one must be. We do not have your varying belief systems, no theories which attempt to promote some of our characteristics or traits above others." She reflected a moment. "Of course, if your species was any less contentious and turbulent, you would not be the soldiers you are, and so, would not be the pivotal species of this moment."

After several seconds passed, W'th'vaathi obviously sensed the humans' dumbfounded silence. "Surely, you have seen that, in the wake of the late war, you are nothing less than the fulcrum point which shall determine the tilt of subsequent interstellar events. Even though you are not a very advanced race, humans are the great variable."

"Why do you believe that?" Riordan asked.

"The versatility and innovation of your species determines what you may accomplish, how swiftly you may change and act. That, not the starting differences in technological or biological mastery, will shape the course of imminent events. Surely, you have seen this."

Without a further word, W'th'vaathi turned to study the shining ribbon of river ahead.

PART FOUR

October 2120

Chapter Forty-Two

APPROACHING ORBIT, CLOSE ORBIT, and
SOUTHERN EXTENTS OF THE THIRD SILVER TOWER
BD +02 4076 TWO ("DISPARITY")

Sehtrek confirmed *Red Lurker*'s passive sensor scan of the Slaas-riithi orbital defenses. "The sequence and intervals of the enemy craft are optimal, Nezdeh."

Nezdeh Srina Perekmeres assessed the scrolling telemetry of the cannonball they had tentatively identified as their target six hours before. The spherical craft all varied their speed, vector, interval on each orbit. The variations were, at most, of marginal tactical significance, but this time, the interval between the currently approaching cannonball and the next in sequence was wider than usual, thanks to whatever randomizing or optimizing algorithm determined the gaps in their orbits. It was only an eleven-minute difference, but it was the largest the crew of *Lurker* had seen. Additionally, measurement of the derelict Aboriginal corvette suggested that it would begin to enter the atmosphere within the next two or three orbits: clearly, if the craft was either operable or still crewed, it would have saved itself by now.

"Commence the attack," muttered Nezdeh. "And inform Pehth-rum to ready his assault team in the armored shuttle. They will be landing within the half hour."

Sehtrek nodded and tapped one of the dynamic tabs on his control panel.

✧　　✧　　✧

Less than half a light-second away, the lascom signal sent by Sehtrek's tap hit a sensor no bigger than a dessert plate, embedded in a shed-sized asteroid fragment. That sensor sent a brief electrical pulse along a wire that led to a self-seeking missile loosely moored on the lee side of the rock. The clamps holding the missile in place fell away, and a small spring mechanism uncoiled against its fuselage, imparting enough momentum and slow spin so that the missile moved out of the concealing shadow of the boulder. The missile's nose swung toward the cannonball rising up over the planetary horizon. Dozens of primarily plastic passive microsensors, scattered by *Lurker* during the first engagement, detected the oncoming sphere's reflection and captured its telemetry and image. When polled by another lascom squeak from *Lurker*, each sensor relayed its data on the object by physically vibrating a reflective plate in code.

The remote targeting computer aboard *Lurker* correlated the data from this almost invisible phased array and transmitted an intercept footprint. However, it did not instruct the hidden missile to illuminate the active sensors in its seeker head to acquire a lock. Instead, it simply noted the missile's status: ready to engage.

Tegrese glanced up at Nezdeh. "The missile acknowledges receipt of primary guidance to the intercept envelope."

Nezdeh nodded. "Ulpreln: set our thrust to two-gee constant. Jesel?"

Jesel's voice crackled out of the intership speaker. "Here, Nezdeh."

"Have your pilot keep your armored shuttle fifty kilometers behind us and match velocity until you receive the deployment order." She closed the ship-to-ship channel. "Tegrese: commence railgun salvoes of area denial munitions into pretargeted orbital paths. And launch the remote missile." She rose, pushed herself toward the ready room.

Tegrese was too surprised to sound deferential. "Nezdeh, why are you leaving the con?"

"To locate our agent on the planet." She slipped the vial holding her last Catalysite out of her pocket. "I shall not be long."

Bannor Rulaine was staring at the countdown clock: thirty-seven minutes until they were compelled to boost in order to sustain orbit, which would almost certainly bring the attackers down on them.

But better a fighting chance than a crash landing—or immolation, if the deorbit heat undid the hull welds first.

Karam was glowering at the clock. "I just hope our numbers are right," he muttered.

Bannor kept his own voice low; no reason to alarm the rest of the bridge crew. "I thought you were sure about the timing."

"Yeah, well, because I couldn't illuminate the active arrays to double-check the passive spectroscopy, I had to guess at Disparity's atmospheric composition and the rate at which its density increases. And my best guesses may not have been good enough."

"And if we start the burn early—?"

Karam gestured to the holotank. A pulsing red plane rested alongside the image of the planet and projected out into the spinward reaches of nearby space. "An early burn is like sending up a signal flare for anyone who might be lurking closer than that detection limit. Because if they are on our side of the planetary horizon, watching for us to go active, they'll jump us the moment we—Wait: what's that?"

A red blip appeared well behind them in the plot; it was just barely in that part of space delimited by the red plane. The passive sensors registered an immense thermal bloom in that same spot.

"What, they've seen us *now*?" Melissa Sleeman wailed at her sensor console.

Bannor leaned back, watched the blip for a moment. "Let me know when you've got telemetry."

"Shouldn't we be fleeing, rather than staring at the sensors?" Morgan Lymbery asked through chattering teeth, clutching the gunnery console.

Bannor shook his head. "Not yet." He turned toward Tygg. "Go gather the troops, Lieutenant. If I'm right—"

Sleeman interrupted with a surprised shout. "The bogey—it's not making for us. Wide telemetry divergence."

"Unless they are trying to flush us toward a ship they have coming around the other side of the planet," Lymbery added.

Melissa shook her head. "Not unless the other ship is pulling five gees. They couldn't get around to catch us before we could break orbit. No, I think they're—"

"Now reading a second thrust signature in the wake of the first." Karam jabbed a finger at the thermal readouts a moment before a second red mote appeared riding piggyback on its leader.

"And it's on precisely the same heading," Melissa added.

Bannor looked at the vector of the bogeys and then scanned the other elements in the plot: the defense spheres, the planet, the geosynchronous marker positioned over the patch of the south continent where the first engagement had taken place. "They're making planetfall."

Karam arrived at the same conclusion a moment later, having run the numbers rather than analyzing the tactical picture. "Absolutely. And they're headed toward the landing footprint we projected for the TOCIO shuttle." He leaned back, a bitter smile growing as he said: "They're not after us at all."

Lymbery nodded, his voice pitched a whole octave lower. "They've written us off as dead. Unpowered, we'd go down before our orbit brings us back to their descent vector."

"And they are moving to intercept the defensive sphere that's got a larger-than-usual interval between itself and the one following," Sleeman added.

Tygg nodded, looked at Rulaine. "Yeah, they've got business planetside, all right. They're moving to clear both the orbital- and air-space for a dirtside operation."

Bannor nodded back. "I'd bet dollars to donuts that the first blip is the hull that did the shooting last time and the second is carrying in the assault team."

Lymbery frowned. "But how do the attackers know where our people are located or that they are even alive?"

Bannor shook his head. "I don't know that, but I don't need to, right now." He pointed at the arrow-straight path of the blips, a path which was going to carry them through the prior-engagement orbital marker as if it was a bull's-eye. "*They* know where our people are, and that's all *we* need to know." He glanced at the countdown clock, then at Tygg. "I'll meet you in the ship's locker in five minutes. Break out the packs and get the ground team suited up." Tygg nodded, remembered to add a salute, turned to carry out his orders.

He hadn't taken half a gliding step toward the hatchway when Melissa jumped up out of her seat into the growing micro-gee. "Be careful," she blurted nervously at Tygg's receding back.

Lieutenant Christopher Robin turned to face the petite genius. Bannor waited for the witty or poignant reply that he presumed Tygg had prepared for just such an occasion. The tall Aussie smiled his big wide smile, and said, "I will. Be careful, I mean." And then he was heading through the hatchway, as Bannor thought: *Really? Really? That was the best you could do?*

But Melissa Sleeman was smiling as Tygg left—and then, just as suddenly, was frowning. And clearly scared.

Well, we'll all be scared before this is over—"Karam, let's think this through—fast. Looks like those blips are going to disappear behind the planetary horizon in about nine minutes."

"I'd call it ten, but go on."

"Once there's no longer a clear line of sight to them, do you think it's safe to light up our own drives?"

Karam frowned and shook his head. "Sorry, but no. We still haven't seen whatever shift-carrier brought them into this system, which could still be watching us. Or they could have dumped a remote sensor when they were lurking out there, allowing them to peer around the horizon."

"I agree. So we're still in a scenario where any spaceside maneuver or thrust could reveal us to our enemies almost instantaneously."

"I think until we're on the far side, we've got to assume that."

"So that tells us what we have to do: get to the far side."

Karam looked at Lymbery and Melissa, and then all of them looked at Bannor, almost timidly. "Boss," Karam said in an almost gentle voice, "you do remember that we'll be burning up in the atmosphere by that time, right?"

"That assumes we aren't already committed to a reentry."

Karam blinked. "Well, yes, but—" Then his eyes opened wide: "Oh." Then they opened wider. "No way."

"No choice."

Melissa Sleeman broke in loudly. "What the hell are you two talking about?"

Karam leaned back, his face settling into a customary frown. "Well, *he's* talking about suicide. Or damn close to it."

Bannor decided it was time to put their exchange on a military footing. "What Senior Flight Officer Tsaami is trying to say is that he lacks the nerve to attempt a maneuver that I thought was well within his skill set."

Karam sat up straight. "Now, hold on, Ban—"

"Our backs are against it, now. So 'Major' or 'sir,' will do, Flight Officer."

"Well—uh, yes Major. So, Ms. Sleeman, here's the implications of the major's various and decidedly dangerous inquiries. Rather than boosting for orbit, or hanging on until the very bitter end to do so, he's suggesting we initiate a descent. Unpowered except for the secondary attitude control thrusters, I'm guessing."

Bannor nodded. "They use compressed gas, so no thermal signature."

Sleeman saw the rest. "Sure: I get it. So we're inside the atmosphere in a landing mode when we get to the far side. Then we burn for high-altitude controlled flight, swing around the planet, land, and intercept them. Hell, we've already got their descent trajectory plotted to within a reasonable approach sleeve, so when we come back around the planetary horizon, we just look for their exhausts and follow them in. We won't even have to light up our own active arrays to find them."

Karam leaned forward. "Yes, but all that assumes *Puller* holds together and that the threat force stays on their current heading."

"I don't think there's much worry about them staying on course." Bannor hitched a thumb at the holoplot: the two blips were holding a perfectly straight line. "They are wasting no time. And if their planetary assault doctrine is anything like ours, as soon as their lead ship takes out the defense sphere that's crossing their descent sleeve, the second ship will continue to bore in for a high-speed, high-angle descent. Then the other one will boost back out a bit and hold position to cover the assault lander's return to orbit."

Karam nodded. "I agree. Sir. That's probably SOP whenever flesh-and-fluid critters of any type decide to send a raiding team down to a planet. Been on a few of those myself. But we shouldn't be making any easy assumptions about *Puller*'s ability to survive the maneuver you're suggesting. Those belly welds won't hold, and we'll be so far into the descent when we reach the farside that I'm going to have to redline the power plants and engines to keep us from falling like a brick. Except that I wouldn't bet a counterfeit uni on how long any of those systems will last, given our wounded coolant system. Which is all a bit of a problem, since we need to get halfway around this damn planet before landing, and somehow get you and the rest of our ground-pounders into the fight. Regarding which: on what prepared landing strip would you like me to deposit you, sir?"

Bannor shook his head. "That's not how it's going to go, Flight

Officer—and watch your sass. You are not landing to deploy us. Instead, you will maintain altitude, which should make it easier for you to maintain speed. At least until we're over the drop zone."

Karam's jaw sagged. "'Drop zone?' Are you mad—sir?"

Bannor shook his head. "No; desperate. Look, Karam, we have a grand total of one operational option that gets us into the fight when, and where, we need to be. The five of us grunts do a HALO drop—"

"A HALO drop? Bann—sir, in order to keep this hull airborne that long, I'm probably going to have to run in sprint mode."

Lymbery went pale. "The engines and the coolant lines will never take that. Not now."

"Will they suffer catastrophic failure?"

Lymbery frowned. "Well, no—probably not."

"Then I will trust our flight officer, ably assisted by you, Mr. Lymbery, to land this stricken bird after we deploy."

Karam shook his head. "Land where? And deploy at—well, at way too high a speed. Bannor, this *is* suicide."

Rulaine leaned back, folded his arms. "The odds are that three or four of us will land and remain combat effective. The alternative is to boost away from this planet and be destroyed while our friends are hunted down like rabbits by an enemy strike team." He stared at them all.

Karam looked away, mumbled, "Well, when you put it that way—"

Sleeman stared up at Rulaine, her eyes bright, sharp. "Okay, Major; I'm in. How do I help?"

Her bravery melted the last hints of reluctance on the faces of the other two, and Bannor thought, *You just did help me, Miss Sleeman. More than you know.*

Caine tried to eat another bite of the food proffered to him by one of the Slaasriithi who specialized in harvesting and tending the environment: the pastorae. But Riordan's shortness of breath made him susceptible to nausea when he tried to eat or drink anything substantial.

Besides, while the food wasn't exactly bad, it was very strange. The Slaasriithi seemed to have modest nest-raiding privileges with a variety of species: eggs were always on the menu as the protein component. That, and a kind of sardine paste mixed with something that tasted like peppery pickled plums, had started out as the party's favorite, but soon became cloying. It was a strong, wholly unfamiliar taste and one for which the human palate, and stomach, seemed to have limited toleration.

The easiest foodstuff was a standing tuber that, when boiled, fell into strands not unlike spaghetti squash. It was mild and, if uninteresting, was utterly agreeable to the human stomach. But today, even the smell of that bland dish brought on a wave of queasiness, followed by concerned looks from what Riordan had come to think of as the Three Almost-Wise Slaasriithi: W'th'vaathi, Unsymaajh, and Thnessfiirm.

Seeing Caine's distress, W'th'vaathi pulled her water-strider alongside his as they began making for the shore. "We are concerned for your health, Caine Riordan. We were unaware that this malady would affect you so severely. If you did not have a filter mask, it might be conceivable. But never having had human visitors to Disparity, we could not anticipate, and still cannot explain, the severity of your affliction."

Caine looked downriver. "Nothing to worry about. I'm sure we'll get to the tower in time." Since the Slaasriithi had joined them four days ago, the group had closed the distance to the Silver Tower by more than two hundred kilometers, which had required about three hundred kilometers of actual travel. W'th'vaathi estimated that their journey would take another two days, which meant that this gleaming edifice was much, much larger than the humans had originally conjectured.

"We are making excellent speed," agreed Thnessfiirm, "but within the hour, we will reach a section of the river where the shore drops off sharply to a very deep bottom. We will need to move by boat from that point on."

"You have boats?"

"Simple ones with sails. We have them secreted at forty-kilometer intervals from this point onward."

"So won't our travel be faster, then?"

"For some of us, yes. But we have only one boat hidden in each riverside cache, and none of them are large. Most of the party must remain with the subtaxae and water-striders as they make a circuitous detour. This concerns us, since you have insisted upon personally ensuring the security of your entire group." Thnessfiirm's tendrils writhed fitfully. "That will no longer be possible."

Nice to tell me about this now. "The water-striders are endangered if they enter this deeper part of the river?"

"No, but because of the depth, they must travel submerged." Thnessfiirm's sensor-cluster-head wobbled meaningfully in the direction of two of the other water-striders with riders perched upon their backs. "Clearly, that would not be suitable for you."

Clearly. "Then I suppose I must—"

Thnessfiirm's neck snapped rigidly erect; so had W'th'vaathi's. Unsymaajh, whose water-strider had already deposited his passengers on the shore, was not in sight. The rest of the Slaasriithi ceased whatever they were doing, gazed skyward slowly, uncertainly.

Caine frowned. "What is—?"

But Thnessfiirm was grabbing handfuls of the water-strider's pelt and pulling it in the direction of the shore. "Caine Riordan, we must hide."

"Why?"

"Sporefall. The defense spheres have sent a warning packet that caused the spore layers above us to rain—well, sleet—down warning microbes."

The other humans on the strider with him—Xue, Salunke, and Eid—sat upright. Salunke unslung a rifle; technically, it was her watch.

"Hiding will not help us, or you," Caine started to explain.

"Perhaps, but being trapped in the middle of the river is not how we should face this threat."

Well, there was no arguing that. As the water-striders made their way up the bank in close formation, Riordan was near enough to call over to W'th'vaathi. "You must contact the Silver Tower. We will not be able to flee from these attackers."

"How can you be certain of this, Caine Riordan?" she asked as the various passengers began dismounting from the lowering backs of the striders.

"Because the attackers will quickly discern where to commence their search. Given the scarcity of metal objects on your surface, our wrecked shuttle will show them the start of our trail."

"But you left no initial tracks that could have endured the rains of the two prior days. And in the river, we leave no tracks at all."

Thnessfiirm retracted his neck. "Our own sensors would be able to discern the humans' thermal signatures and outlines as being different from ours. As Keith Macmillan asserted, we must expect no less of the attackers' sensors. Rather, we must expect them to be markedly superior. Consequently, the humans would leave distinctive signatures unless huddled with us. Nor would such a tactic impede the actions of these attackers."

W'th'vaathi was silent for several seconds. "You are correct. The attackers showed no interest in distinguishing between Slaasriithi and human targets in space, so we must also presume that they would be equally indifferent to such distinctions planetside. Thnessfiirm, dispatch a *sloohav* to ask the Third Silver Tower to convey helpful technology to us here."

"What helpful technology it might have is another concern," Thnessfiirm answered. "And I hope the *sloohav* reaches it in time."

"We may only do what we may do," W'th'vaathi replied with a grass-in-the-wind wave of her finger-tendrils. "Now, we must gather the persons who will be going downstream on the boat. Ambassador Gaspard must be evacuated, and Ms. Hirano's injuries require that she departs also. Caine Riordan, your condition makes it clear that you should be the final human passenger aboard the—"

"No. I'm staying here."

The three Slaasriithi exchanged another set of unseen glances before W'th'vaathi reaimed her sensor cluster at Riordan. "You are the second most senior person in the legation, were requested specifically by Yiithrii'ah'aash, and are barely able to move. You must travel with the boat, Captain."

"And the last word of your argument—my title—tells you why I won't and why I can't go with you."

"You mean the word 'Captain?'"

"That is exactly what I mean. My primary responsibility on this mission is as the head of security. That means protecting these people, however I can, whenever and wherever that is needed. That's what I'm going to do."

Unsymaajh reached out an appealing appendage. "Caine Riordan, you cannot do so effectively. Your breathing is labored, your vitality low."

Riordan nodded. "I am aware of that." *You have no idea how aware I am of that.* "But there are ways to compensate. For a little while." He lifted his head, raised his voice. "Mr. Xue?"

Maybe it was something in his tone that announced the change in relationships, but Xue responded, "Yes, Captain Riordan?"

"You gathered together half of the meds we each had in our medkits, correct?"

"That is correct, sir."

"Then I want half of the amphetamines." The antihistamines had been exhausted, without effect, almost a week ago.

"Sir?"

"I need to keep going for another few hours, so I'm going to need those pills. Give me the fast-acting formulation with the adrenal stimulant."

Xue, staring, nodded and hastened to comply.

"You plan on modifying your metabolism to function at a higher level?" W'th'vaathi asked.

I'm taking the pills to keep functioning at all, Riordan thought. But he said: "Yes, as needed. Now, instead of me on the boat, you're going to take Dr. Hwang."

Ben was close enough to hear and to shout a negation.

Which Riordan did not let him complete. "Dr. Hwang, this is an order, not a suggestion. In my role as head of legation security, I am instructing you to accompany W'th'vaathi downriver in the boat. You will not turn back, you will not delay the journey. You will do only one thing: make best time for the Third Silver Tower."

Hwang's face seemed to be crumbling. "Riordan—Caine—don't do—"

"Ben, my order is not based on sentiment, but cold-blooded logic. Gaspard is going to need your xenobiological insights during his conversations and negotiations with the Slaasriithi. We suspected as much from the start. Now it's a clear imperative. And you are still nursing visceral trauma from the crash. The decision is made: you're going."

Gaspard passed by, glancing at both men. "No cause for regret, Dr. Hwang. We will not last much longer than Captain Riordan. We shall be in a boat upon a river—the only manufactured object in hundreds of kilometers and leaving a wide wake." Gaspard snorted his grim resolve. "As soon as the attackers are done here, they will see and come for us." He shrugged. "That is why I have granted Ms. Veriden's request to remain behind. Not only is the boat already full, but she is a fighter by nature. She no doubt prefers to meet her end on this battlefield."

Riordan shook his head. "Not if I can help it."

"Captain, your courage does you credit, but the stand you mean to make here—"

"Is the lesser half of my overall plan, Ambassador." Again, Riordan called over his shoulder. "Qwara?"

"Yes, Captain?"

"When we were lightening our load a week ago, how many of the pony-tanks did we keep?"

"Uh, three—no: four, sir."

Caine smiled. "Good. We're set, then."

Gaspard shook his head. "And those tanks will magically ensure that our plans are 'set'?"

Caine smiled wider. "They most certainly will. Now, here's what we do—"

Chapter Forty-Three

The Slaasriithi cannonball did exactly what Nezdeh and Idrem had predicted. As it swung around the planetary horizon, it boosted into a shallow slingshot assist that helped it hurtle straight toward *Red Lurker* and the armored shuttle behind it.

"The Slaasriithi are predictable, if nothing else," Idrem observed. He and Tegrese had exchanged positions; she was now the ranking Evolved in engineering, whereas Idrem was manning the gunnery station on the bridge.

Nezdeh nodded, watching her first volley of missiles burn hot and hard toward the oncoming cannonball in the holosphere. "Have they spotted the missile we launched from behind the asteroid fragment?"

"Unknown," Sehtrek answered. "The Slaasriithi craft has not activated its own arrays, and we have no way of ascertaining how many passive or dormant dual-function assets they have in orbit."

Which meant that the two minutes of low thrust that had sent their hidden missile into an intercept footprint might have been missed (unlikely) or was deemed to be of secondary importance. There were certainly more immediate threats to occupy the Slaasriithi's attention. *Lurker*'s relentless salvos of railgun-propelled flechette canisters kept the oncoming enemy craft bracketed in an ever-more constricted approach trajectory. Nezdeh's current flight of missiles were rushing along that trajectory toward a head-on intercept. "Idrem, illuminate one seeker head among our missiles."

"In order to acquire a remote lock on the cannonball for our lasers and railgun?"

Nezdeh smiled: what a relief to have Idrem at gunnery. "Exactly. Fire a full flight of penetrators on that lock."

"So I presumed: to sneak in behind the missiles' sensor signatures. The lasers?"

"Hold them: I do not want them to point back to our precise position." Beams, more than any other weapons, had the unfortunate consequence of providing their targets with a reciprocal lock on their attackers.

"Understood. Railgun firing."

"Has the cannonball fired upon the lead, seeking missile?"

"Not yet. The enemy will probably deny us a reciprocal lock upon its own lasers until the last possible second, in order to close the range."

"Of course. The cannonball presumes only brief survival, so it will endeavor to remain out of lock until it is close enough to inflict significant damage."

Idrem nodded, highlighted the position of their formerly concealed missile; it was now coasting into the projected engagement envelope. "There is still no indication that the enemy has targeted our first missile, either. It may be that their sensor assets are so limited that they cannot establish an active lock on that target. Or, if the system is entirely automated, it may have dropped our missile from high priority tracking."

Sehtrek nodded. "Such a system might also be foolish enough to dismiss its lack of further thrust as indicative of a malfunction."

Ulpreln turned to look at Sehtrek. "Could they be so imbecilic, to think that a remote weapon fired from stealth has failed simply because it does not bear straight in upon its target?"

Sehtrek shrugged. "It is quite obvious that the Slaasriithi are not adept at, nor familiar with, war. It is possible, I suppose, that they—" He stared at his board, suddenly silent. Then: "Two small orbital arrays have just illuminated our coasting missile."

"Respond as we have practiced," Nezdeh ordered. "Idrem, fire portside laser blisters at the cannonball, starboard side blisters at the active sensors. Ulpreln, evasive maneuvers: the Slaasriithi droneship will begin firing soon. Activate all remaining seeker heads in our flight of missiles; set them to relay targeting data to us. Zurur, tightbeam relay that targeting data to our coasting missile."

It happened with the swift, casual precision characteristic of Evolved professionals.

"One of the enemy's small orbital arrays has been eliminated, the other damaged," Idrem reported. "The damaged one continues to scan our coasting missile, but seems unable to acquire lock."

"The cannonball's lasers are operating in defensive mode, eliminating our missiles," Sehtrek reported. "Nezdeh, we are losing redundant targeting data from those seeker heads—"

Which is acceptable because I will not need it for much longer—

"Cannonball now activating its own arrays, targeting our coasting missile—Wait; it is now retasking them to quick forward sweeps."

"It has seen the railgun projectiles behind the missile volley," Nezdeh muttered with a smile. "Idrem, stand ready. Intercept time for our coasting missile?"

"Twenty seconds."

The thin green tines that denoted *Lurker*'s railgun rounds began deviating or, in a few cases, winking out of existence. "Cannonball lasers remain in defensive mode against our penetrator rods. It is also launching a missile—no; two missiles."

"Does it have lock on us?"

"It is trying to acquire, Nezdeh." Sehtrek's voice was admirably calm.

Trying will not be good enough—"Now, Idrem: relay our target lock on the cannonball to our coasting missile and activate both its stages."

"Complying..."

Out in space, the drifting missile suddenly blazed to life, far brighter than any of the others. A brace of solid-rocket boosters ignited along with its main motor, propelling it forward at half again its unmodified maximum speed.

The cannonball quickly swung some of its sensor assets over to establish a lock on this new threat, which was approaching much, much faster than the Slaasriithi had any reason to expect, based on prior encounters.

"Increase laser fire on the cannonball," Nezdeh ordered, "and initiate direct fire by the railgun, one penetrator per second. We must maximize hit possibilities, not damage potential."

Idrem nodded, his fingers playing across the dynamic control panel like a concert pianist at his instrument.

In the plot, several of the railgun's first wave of green tines were still bearing down upon the orange sphere denoting the cannonball. The alien craft jittered and jumped as it strove to remain within its flechette-constricted safe vectors while also evading the steady fire from its primary target; it narrowly avoided hits, but did not manage to fix a lock on the ambushing Ktor missile until it was within a kilometer. One of the cannonball's lasers finally found and destroyed it; in the holosphere, the dissipating green-dust remains of the rocket overlapped the orange cannonball for a moment—

"Enemy craft has sustained light damage from the rocket's fragmentation warhead. It is attempting to compensate—"

But the cannonball's attempt to compensate made it vulnerable to other attacks: a laser hit by Idrem's constant peppering damaged it further, and as it struggled to correct, one of the railgun penetrators hit it almost dead center. The orange sphere in the holosphere dissolved. A moment later, *Lurker*'s lasers, retasked to the PDF role, eliminated the two missiles the cannonball had launched.

"All targets destroyed," Sehtrek said calmly, almost contemptuously.

Nezdeh did not release her breath quickly, did not lean back in relief. Her demeanor had to affirm that victory was never in doubt, not now, not ever. Because if her crew were to dwell upon the full consequences of failure, those dire imaginings would erode their confidence and performance. Anything less than complete success would turn their House's faceless sponsors into executioners, eager to conceal their conspiracy against the dominant powers of the Ktoran Sphere.

And yet, without the enthusiastic support of those potentially faithless sponsors, House Perekmeres could not be restored, either in full or in part. She and her crew would remain rootless renegades in a universe where every hand was against them. *But now, perhaps, we are nearing the moment when we may put such grim forebodings behind us.*

Turning to Zurur, Nezdeh nodded and said, "Tell Jesel to commence his assault."

Jesel sul-Perekmeres glanced at the armored shuttle's pilot, Pehthrum. "Intendant, start the descent."

"Do you not wish to strap in, Jesel?"

Perhaps if Jesel had been Pehthrum's superior in anything but birth-determined rank, the young Aspirant to Evolved status would not have been sensitive to the Intendant's simple, practical question. But Pehthrum was older and more accomplished in every particular that could possibly bear upon the mission, and self-conscious Jesel heard his question as an oblique critique. "I do not wish to strap in, Intendant. Fly this shuttle. For now, that is all I require of you."

Pehthrum lowered his head in compliance and then lowered the nose of the shuttle, angling it toward the planet's atmosphere.

Jesel had been expecting the maneuver, swayed with it, used his wrist muscles to keep his feet on the deck. He felt the strain and cursed his geneline—or rather, his lack of one. The son of a jur-huscarl, Jesel had been a child at the time of House Perekmeres' Extirpation. Under any but those desperate circumstances, his genecode would not have been deemed sufficient to groom for eventual inclusion in the ranks of the Evolved.

But harsh fate had compelled the remaining leadership of House Perekmeres to confer the possibility of Elevation upon him. And what he lacked in genecode, he made up for with boldness and an instinct for dominion. Or so he told himself.

As the armored shuttle leveled into its new course and the fuselage shuddered under increased thrust, Jesel surveyed the personnel of his first combat command. His fellow 'sul, Suzruzh, was strapped in at the rear, ready to lead team three; the assault's main contact and harrying element, it would locate and engage the Aboriginals. Team two, under Pehthrum, was designated to carry out a flanking maneuver once the target was fixed in place by team three. And Jesel's team one would be the command and final assault element, ostensibly screened by Suzruzh's harriers.

The only significant drawback was that all the teams were comprised of CoDevCo's Optigene troops. The clones were not even Aboriginals, really. They were simply Wildings: the pristine genelines from which their template was drawn had been artificially constrained and culled, but without the refining, expert touch of a Breedmistress. Unfortunately, the clones had deficits beyond the typical low-born decrements in speed, agility, strength, senses, autonomic muscle control, heightened vascular trauma resiliency, and secretion modulation. They were also utterly without the capacity for innovation, at least so far. Having been recently awakened, they had not acquired any significant diversity of experience, much less consequent skills in problem solving.

According to the fear-reeking low-born Kozakowski, these clones were in fact less responsive due to the tight controls that the Ktor had put upon their training and exposure to unplanned stimuli. The clones knew little beyond obedience yet, but all data suggested that this would change rapidly, and it was unlikely that any of this first group would be safe to leave uneuthanized. The perversities of their early training would scar them, leave them asking too many questions and resentful of the narrow limits of their existence.

That concept, the narrow limits of one's existence, struck home as Jesel's gaze drifted back across Suzruzh, whose face suggested that he was waiting for his fellow 'sul to commence the pre-deployment briefing. The two of them had narrow existences, as well. Although no direct mention had been made of it, all of the Ktor knew precisely why such an important mission was being entrusted to a pair of 'suls whose sires had been low-breed jur-huscarls. It eliminated the risk of a postmortem analysis of an Evolved genecode. Although both Brenlor and Nezdeh asserted that failure was impossible and that the Aboriginals would not inflict any significant casualties upon the strike force, the two Srinu had clearly not deemed such outcomes wholly unthinkable. Consequently, if the entire strike team was lost, no Elevated cell samples would fall into Aboriginal hands: hands that might, given time and sufficient resources, begin to understand the genetic changes that ensured the innate superiority of the Ktor.

The same kind of precaution had informed the combat team's equippage. Rather than being issued the vastly superior Ktor weapons which had decimated the Aboriginal resistance aboard the *Arbitrage*, Brenlor Srin Perekmeres had decreed that the only weapons, armor, and support systems to be used in the assault were those from the Terrans' own stocks.

This was not merely disappointing; it was utterly depressing. The best weapons in the *Arbitrage*'s original armory, nine-point-two-millimeter Jufeng dust-mix battle rifles manufactured by the Developing World Coalition, were among the most rudimentary of their kind. There were only four available, and the three Ktor leaders of the raid were grim in their gratitude to have at least that much offensive firepower. The clones themselves were armed with either their ubiquitous Indonesian Pindad caseless assault rifles, or TOCIO's copy of a widely licensed automatic shotgun designed by a firm called Heckler and Koch. Jesel wished he could have jettisoned every single one of the primitive firearms out the nearest airlock. They would not have been satisfactory as reserve training arms, back home in the Creche Worlds.

Well, Jesel accepted as he once again became aware of the twenty-six duty-suited troopers sitting in the fuselage of the shuttle, *there's nothing to be gained by putting off the briefing.* "Attend my words."

It was a largely unnecessary call for their attention; none of the clones had been speaking or looking anywhere other than directly at Jesel.

"We shall enter the atmosphere of the target planet within twenty minutes. We should be over the target zone within forty minutes. Our first pass will be to seed quadrotor sensor platforms that will scan the surrounding area for vehicles the enemy might be using to leave the target zone."

Suzruzh frowned. "I thought we had acquired a fix upon the targets' position."

Jesel shrugged. "Nezdeh received a signal from our agent among them. However, this signal carried no data regarding the composition, status, or numbers of the target low-borns. So it does not necessarily follow that all the targets will be in one location. However, during our final approach, there will be a radio signal upon which we shall orient and so, find an optimal landing zone."

Suzruzh lifted one shoulder in a resigned shrug.

Jesel nodded toward the pilot.. "Pehthrum, you shall seek to flank whatever positions the Aboriginals have adopted. Once Suzruzh's skirmishers have pinned them down, you shall release the upt'theel."

The most freshly reanimated clone, a replacement for one among the first batch that had proven dangerously intractable, cleared his throat. "Commander, I am unfamiliar with this term, *upt'theel.*"

"The upt'theel is a sinuous and unrelenting carnivore that is not strictly a carbon-based life-form: it is incredibly rugged due to various silicate hardenings. It has highly alkaline body chemistry and is perpetually ravenous in our environment in order to maintain a body temperature in excess of forty-five degrees centigrade."

"And how does it know to distinguish us from our enemies?"

"Your equipment, and you, have been liberally doped with a chemical which the upt'theel find unappetizing. Also, since they have rudimentary intelligence, they associate that scent with handlers." Jesel smiled. "However, that loyalty association does not endure beyond the first unsatisfied growlings of an upt'theel's stomach. So, while you have no reason to fear the upt'theel, you should not be careless about them, either.

"Many of you will recall training with light armor. That is not available to us." *True.* "But nor is it desirable in this environment." *More lie than not.* "Although the plant growth in the target area is not uniformly thick enough to be called a jungle, areas of it are. We must expect the targets to take refuge in those areas. Consequently, matching their speed and elusiveness is better protection than full composite armor. Your ballistic cloth chest and groin protectors are optimal for this operation.

"We must also operate without remote tactical communications. The entirety of the radio bandwidth is being jammed. We must rely upon hand and voice signals. So, in order to maneuver effectively, we shall remain close."

"Very close, when we enter the areas that resemble jungles," Suzruzh added.

Jesel nodded, not overly annoyed at his distant cousin's timely addition. "However, we are more prepared to meet the challenge than most of our targets. From what data we have of them, they overwhelmingly lack any military training or wilderness experience. Their lack of radio communications will be far more detrimental to them than it will be to us. Lastly, our *in situ* agent's signal duration indicated that either steps have been taken to ensure that any military gear aboard the shuttle was compromised or that no such gear was present."

The clone labeled Gamma-Twelve stirred slightly. "Leader, what if the Slaasriithi have provided the targets with better weapons?"

Jesel shook his head. "From what we know of Slaasriithi physiology, it would be surprising, almost inconceivable, that humans could operate their weapons. It is equally improbable that the Slaasriithi would take the risk of providing them: they are an overly cautious species, more so than the Arat Kur when it comes to sharing technology. Are there other questions?" No responses. The deck tilted and shuddered slightly: Pehthrum was easing the armored shuttle into the outer reaches of the atmosphere. He glanced at Suzruzh. "Any additions?"

From the absurdly primitive cockpit just behind him, Pehthrum's voice inquired, "With your permission, Jesel sul-Perekmeres?"

Well, it was a respectful request, so—"Permission granted, Pehthrum."

"It is more legend than data, but accounts dating from the Progenitors' time strongly suggest that the Slaasriithi shaped their worlds in such a way that they were inimical to all varieties of our species. It seems that spores and other air- and water-borne microbes may, after a short exposure, begin to cause shortness of breath and general disability. So it is imperative that you wear your filter masks at all times."

Jesel nodded. "And our stay must be brief. The longer we are planetside, the more likely that the Slaasriithi defenses will effectively contest our planetfall and that our orbital window might be compromised. So the faster we move, the more likely we will safely achieve the most important objective of our attack."

Clone Gamma-Fourteen frowned. "And which is that?"

"To kill all the Aboriginals. Naturally."

Chapter Forty-Four

Caine tossed back another of the amphetamines, listened and glanced up at the light teal sky: a distant sound of thunder that he knew was not thunder. It was their attackers' final descent. But how quickly would they detect the group and land? Both humans and Slaasriithi were already near their positions, so that was not an issue. However, what was more challenging and uncertain was when he should begin staging his pills. *I have to get the timing just right, can't afford to peak the effects before, or after, I need them.*

Thnessfiirm jogged up to Riordan with the fast, rolling gait of her kind. "I have offloaded the autonomous munitions platform from the rotoflyer."

"Excellent. Send the rotoflyer back to the Silver Tower. It will only help the enemy locate us if we keep it here. Any update from the pilot on how soon we might expect the supersonic defense drones to enter our airspace?"

Thnessfiirm's upraised tendrils went over sideways like dead toy soldiers. "I am sorry, but no. There are only a few ground wire communication links, and the atmospheric defense drones are clustered in the more advanced facilities on the northern continent. When the rotoflyers left the Third Silver Tower to convey the munitions platform here, Prime Ratiocinator T'suu'shvah had still not sent her approval for the supersonic drones, much less their estimated time of arrival."

A drooping equilateral triangle, hovering on one central and three corner fans, whined into view behind Thnessfiirm, trailing her like a lazy dog. Its upper surface was scored by a hexagon pattern, two sensor masts rising up from either side of the central rotor. "Where are the weapons?" Riordan asked, suddenly concerned that the Slaasriithi had misinterpreted his request for a combat platform: the local lack of personal firearms made this munitions dispenser their only option.

Thnessfiirm trailed three of her tendrils over one of the hexagons. "The weapons are stored in these bays."

Caine stared at the platform's three-meter sides. "They must be pretty small weapons."

Thnessfiirm's neck retracted slightly. "Do not presume that their size indicates insufficient power. In this environment"—she gestured to the patches of daylight coming through the loose forest canopy—"we cannot employ the larger platforms that carry longer-range weapons. The platform's maneuverability and stealth characteristics are more important, if the system is to survive the first few minutes of engagement."

If the bad guys have any airborne weapons or observation systems, that's undoubtedly true. "What kind of weapons does this platform carry?"

"Mostly conventional high-explosive rockets with enhanced fragmentation. There are also several clusters of miniature antipersonnel heat-seeking rockets and a few surface-to-air missiles." Apparently, the Slaasriithi were becoming increasingly adept at reading human facial expressions: in this case, Riordan's surprise and dubiety. "They are *extremely* short-range surface-to-air missiles," Thnessfiirm qualified.

"How short?"

"Only four hundred meters of active thrust, with small warheads but extremely rapid flight times. All the munitions are independently deployable."

Riordan knew an insufficient translation when he heard one. "I am uncertain what you mean by 'independently deployable.' I presume they can be launched individually?"

"That too, but what I refer to is this." Thnessfiirm clicked several new ringlike adornments on her toe-tendrils in rapid sequence. The lines delineating one of the hexagons suddenly became deep grooves, and that part of the platform's—chassis?—dropped down to the ground: a six-sided tube akin to a single cell from a honey-comb. It swayed as it landed; prehensile actuators whipped out of its base, righted it, retracted until they became a short-legged stand for the object. "An excellent feature." The way Thnessfiirm said it, Riordan had the distinct impression that she was immensely proud of this novel stabilizer but was unsure about its usefulness.

"An excellent feature," Caine agreed. "If we use it properly, we should be able to minimize—"

The thunder, having diminished somewhat, began a swift crescendo.

"Cover!" Caine shouted. "Now!"

As arranged, the humans darted under cone trees and huddled into the midst of waiting groups of convectorae, thereby blend-ing the two species' thermal signatures. Smaller clusters of the Slaasriithi, those without any humans in them, moved toward the edges of other, scattered cone-tree canopies; slightly more exposed, they'd present more pronounced thermal silhouettes. Caine glanced at the sky again: *Now sort us out, you bastards. If you can.*

The thunder became an oncoming, rocket-propelled freight train, up-dopplering sharply. The Slaasriithi shied closer into their cover. The four humans who were carrying the pathetic survival rifles—Keith, Dora, Xue, and Salunke—glanced at Riordan. He shook his head, waved his hand from upriver to downriver—

Just as a TOCIO-manufactured armored shuttle roared overhead at an altitude of five hundred meters, following the trajectory Caine had indicated with his wave.

"How did you know it would be flying toward—?" Thnessfiirm began.

"No big trick." Veriden checked that the action of her weapon cycled smoothly. "They clearly found our wreck, started river-following. And by the time we heard them, they were moving too fast to slow down and drop in on us here."

"So what do they mean to do, then?"

"Sweep downriver," Caine answered. "They'll double back when they find that this area had the only large collection of biothermal signatures gathered in one place."

"Should we not have spread out more?"

Riordan shook his head. "Wouldn't have mattered. For us to be able to defend ourselves, we have to be relatively close together.

And once you cluster up that way, there are too many bodies in one grid for them to mistake us for anything other than their target. They can't be sure until they sweep the whole of the river, but once they have, they'll be back." He turned to Unsymaajh. "What did your subtaxae see? Did the craft drop anything off?"

"My convectorae saw nothing separate from the vehicle."

"It couldn't have, moving at that speed," Keith murmured.

Riordan nodded. "Only milspec ROVs hardened for high-speed deployment could have survived getting dumped out at that velocity, and those systems are too big to miss. Okay; we've got thirty minutes, forty at most. Let's get into positions."

Thnessfiirm was staring northward, downriver. "I am confused," she admitted finally. "The craft resembled images of your own crashed shuttle."

Riordan nodded. "It's a variant of that design."

"But—are your own people trying to kill you?"

Caine shrugged. "The people in that armored shuttle might or might not be from Earth. But they are certainly using our tools. Which might be good news: if all their tools and weapons are ours, we understand what they have and are not at a technological disadvantage."

"But how could it be your people? You humans cannot shift this far, cannot reach our space on your own—can you?"

"We cannot," Riordan admitted.

"Then what other species would have access to, and be able to use, your equipment?"

Caine selected a carefully worded, technical truth. "I can't be sure. But we are certainly going to find out."

Thnessfiirm's sensor cluster swung back northward. "They will see the boat. And destroy it."

Riordan did not answer. There was no point in confirming what was now an inescapable conclusion. "Let's get into position."

Pehthrum called to Jesel. "A lateen-rigged sailboat on the river up ahead. In a river gorge. Trying to stay in the lee of overhanging rocks."

Jesel pulled himself forward into the cockpit, looked out the starboard window. "Is there any way we can get close enough to take it under effective small arms fire?"

Pehthrum slowed the shuttle, spun up the ducted tilt-fans to slow their approach into a gradual forward hover. He glanced at the walls of the gorge. "Not without coming down between these rock faces. And if they have any rockets—"

Jesel nodded. "An unacceptable risk. Maintain altitude and maneuver to a position directly adjacent to the boat, but keep the overhang between us."

Pehthrum swung the shuttle, now in VTOL mode, toward the right side of the river. "Complying. Our visibility of the boat is very limited from this angle, though."

"We only need to know where it is," Jesel tossed over his shoulder as he returned to the passenger compartment. "Suzruzh, ready the package."

His distant cousin was out of his seat, four of the clones following him back to the access hatch just aft of the shuttle's waist and just forward of its engineering section. Following the drill they had practiced a dozen times before, one pair of the identical soldiers opened the hatch and extended a small aluminum ramp, adapted from a freight-moving kit. The other two manhandled a container out of the largest of the ship's lockers.

Suzruzh bent over the container, opened it, adjusted a single control on a detonator slaved to the two ship-to-ship missile warheads bolted to the plastic bottom. "Primed," he shouted as he closed the lid and locked it. At his nod, the two clones who had removed the container from the locker now positioned it at the top of the aluminum ramp.

Suzruzh stood sideways in the wind-buffeted open hatchway, his hand gestures telling Jesel how to shift the position of the shuttle. Jesel relayed the appropriate piloting commands to Pehthrum. "Three meters more to the right. Wait—correct for the prop-wash coming back off the rocks. Now, another meter to the right..."

Suzruzh held his fist upright: Jesel motioned for Pehthrum to hold the shuttle in precisely that spot. As soon as the craft stabilized, Suzruzh nodded to the two clones holding the container on the slide. They released it.

Where he was, Jesel knew he would not be able to see or hear the splash as the container hit the water almost thirty meters beneath them, and a few meters to the left of the boat as it hung tight against the side of the gorge. Suzruzh, on the other hand, watched the container's descent, and after what seemed like several long seconds, pressed the remote activation stud on his belt-com.

At such a short range, the signal got through the radio interdiction easily, and the detonator went off, triggering the two warheads not more than two meters beneath the surface of the swift current. A blast came up from the river. Jesel gestured for Pehthrum to spin the shuttle, which had passed the drop point. Pehthrum did so, just in time for them to see the lateen mast reach the peak of its upward course atop the explosion's white-frothed plume. It began tumbling back down toward the wreckage-strewn waters.

"Any sign of bodies?" Jesel shouted at Suzruzh over the whine of the VTOL fans.

"No sign of anything," he answered. "Except that mast and a few shreds of hull."

Jesel nodded, turned back to Pehthrum. "You have performed adequately, Intendant. Now return us to the coordinates where we detected the biosignatures upriver." He moved back into the passenger compartment, affixing the straps of the ridiculously primitive Aboriginal helmet. "We have a job to finish."

Karam Tsaami peeked overhead—the direction in which he would be falling, if he wasn't being held upside down by the straps of the pilot's chair. Through the sliver he'd opened in the cockpit's sliding covers, he saw greens and teals and violets streak past in a psychedelic rush of formless color. He looked away: if he'd withdrawn all the blast-shields at this point, he wouldn't even have trusted his own well-honed instincts of spatial orientation. Flying upside down, for this long, at this speed, and this altitude, was for stunt fliers and test pilots, not boat jockeys.

The intercom crackled. "Karam?" Bannor's voice.

"Yeah, Major, what is it? Kind of busy up here."

"I figured as much. Now that all the bumping is over, give me a report on the ship's systems."

"Not much to report. Coming in belly-up should have protected the weld points in the hull, but with our hard aerobraking attitude on the way in, I suspect all of our surfaces still got baked somewhat. So I'm going to fly *Puller* inverted until after you jump."

There was a long pause. "Say again, bridge. Sounded like you said you were maintaining inverted attitude until after you clear the drop zone."

"You heard right, Major. If I were to roll over now, we could find ourselves with a hole in the hull catching the air in excess of fifteen hundred kph. That could tear us to pieces in seconds. So we're going to get you where you're going first, which also means we'll be down to about four hundred kph, give or take. Once you're out, I'll roll her and we'll see what happens."

Behind Karam, Morgan Lymbery may have choked back a curse or a whimper or both.

"You've still got a location on the enemy craft?"

"Sure do. They are clearly not worried about being spotted. Going in straight lines, leaving a thermal trail as wide as the Strait of Gibraltar and running active sensors. And moving from objective to objective like they don't have to do a lot of searching."

Melissa Sleeman, although pale-faced and white-knuckled, had evidently been following the conversation closely. "So the attackers have a fix on the ground team already? How could they?"

Karam sighed. "Either there is a still a traitor among them or the bad buys have miracle sensors. And I don't believe in miracles. I particularly don't believe in miracles coming from a lander that is throwing off the thrust signatures of a TOCIO-made shuttle."

Bannor's voice was quiet. "You've confirmed that?"

"Can't confirm anything at this range, and I'm running passive sensors only. But if I was a betting man—well, I'd say we've got some interesting questions to ask whoever's flying that lander. Like, where'd they get it?"

"I agree." Rulaine sounded excessively composed. "Give me a two-minute warning. I'll be back at the aft hatchway preparing for the jump."

"You've got it, Major." *And better you than me, you poor bastard.*

Caine heard the roar of the returning shuttle diminish into a thready whine: it was crawling forward in hover mode. *Damn it, they know right where we are.* "Unsymaajh, Thnessfiirm. Keep your subtaxae watching the skies carefully. We need to see where the attackers come down." He turned to the armed persons in his party. "They are finding us too quickly. No way the cavalry is going to get here in time, even if it's coming. So this is up to us."

Nasr Eid's voice quavered. "And Ms. Betul and I are just to watch?"

"No: you are to maintain *a watch*. Very different." *As I've already explained, but you're too jittery to process and remember. So: one more time*—"We need you to watch our flanks. If you detect any movement there, you sneak back and report it so we can try to adjust our positions to deal with that new threat. Qwara, you're going to be down near our revetment by the river. Nasr, you're going to be positioned near a large clearing that is on our other flank, and you'll have some special local help. And of course, if any additional weapons become available"—*or if any of the survival rifles suddenly and sadly find themselves without their original wielders*—"we'll want you ready to join us on the line."

Qwara nodded calmly. "I—we understand, Captain."

Unsymaajh ducked back under the canopy of the cone tree without noticeably breaking his stride; his flanged hips seemed to allow him to dip, swerve, and rise up again in one fluid motion, even at speed. "My subtaxae have seen flying machines leaving the belly of the attacker's shuttle, which approaches slowly."

Caine nodded. "Are these flying machines flat and mostly square, with rotors at all four corners?"

"They are as you say."

"Those are recon ROVs. Again, probably of our own manufacture. The enemy is trying to find exactly where we are before they land and attack." He turned toward the edge of the cone tree's canopy, called "Thnessfiirm!"

Salunke frowned. "So: they will find and reach us quickly by using their aerial sensors. What should we do?"

Caine rose into a crouch. "We need to slow them down, make them land further away. Which means we need to put out their airborne eyes."

"But how?"

The answer to Salunke's question materialized in the form of Thnessfiirm, who swooped under the canopy with almost the same swift facility as Unsymaajh had. "You summoned me?"

"I did. I need the autonomous munitions platform. Let's call it the AMP."

"Very well. It is close by."

"Excellent. How many of those SAMs—er, surface-to-air missiles—does it have?"

"Four."

Well, we'd better make this first volley count. "Okay. That's how many targets we've got. But I want you to move the AMP into the zone I designated as Salvo Point Three. Once it's there, drop the launcher cells for all four missiles, then scoot it over to Salvo Point Two and activate its reactive camouflage systems."

"It shall be as you say, Caine Riordan." She left in a smooth rush of gangly limbs.

Salunke's mouth had curved into a small, almost hopeful smile. "So: 'putting out their eyes.' Now I see."

"And hopefully, now they won't. At least not very long."

Nasr was the one frowning now. "If we have these missiles, should we not use them against the shuttle itself?"

Riordan shrugged. "That's good thinking, but I doubt they'd do much. The missiles have small warheads, and with only four hundred meters reliable range, I doubt the shuttle will become a target for them. The attackers will stand off, wait for their ROVs to bracket us, and then force us to either take potshots at those quadrotors or hunker down where we can't be seen and can't defend ourselves. However, if we take down their sensor platforms, they can't see how we're positioned, or any munitions we might have. And when they see rockets take out their ROVs, they're going to realize that we're not as poorly armed as they suspected."

Keith looked up. "The problem is that they suspected anything about us at all."

Riordan did not nod, did not want to dive back into their most gnawing problem: that they certainly did have a traitor in their midst. Who had waited until now to strike. *Textbook sabotage: never act until there's no time left to uncover your identity.* "Unsymaajh, any more word from your treetop convectorae?"

"Yes, Caine Riordan. The small hovering objects are approaching in a diamond formation which shrinks as it approaches us."

"They're putting a detection net around our clustered thermal signatures," Dora summarized. "Tightening it as they see the limits of our dispersal."

Riordan nodded. "Range, Unsymaajh?"

"The lead sensor is now within five hundred meters of our closest cluster. The tail of the diamond is approximately two hundred and fifty meters further away."

Caine did the math. "Send a runner to get Thnessfiirm; I'm going to need her by my side from now on. Tell the convectorae I need to know when the rearmost ROV is within three hundred meters of our closest position. And as soon as our missiles launch, all positions within one hundred meters of the lead ROV are to be evacuated. Everyone goes to their first designated fallback. Except the flank-watch near the river; they have to hold in place."

"It is fortunate they are not close to the ROVs, then."

"Very fortunate," Caine agreed. *But also a bit predictable; the team by the river is outside the primary footprint of our dispersal.*

Caine glanced at his watch, popped two more pills, checked his breathing, found it tolerable. *Although that's going to change as soon as I have to start moving. Which will be any second now.*

Thnessfiirm reappeared. "How may I assist you, Caine Riordan?"

"You must be my, well, we humans would call it a 'technical expert.' You did an excellent job familiarizing me with the controls for the AMP right after it arrived, but I might forget some of your instructions. I need you with me so that I won't make any mistakes."

Thnessfiirm's response was interwoven with a rich, gratified purr. "I am happy to serve as your technical expert, Caine Riordan. How may I assist at this moment?"

"For now, you hold on to the controls. And I'll take the laser-designator."

"Very well." Thnessfiirm handed Caine what looked more like a titanium wand than a laser-designator. "Do you require anything else?"

"Yes. I want you to choose two of your fastest, smartest assistants. We need them to be ready to move more swiftly and silently, carrying messages when and where we instruct."

"I understand. I also predicted this. Three such assistants await us just beyond the fringe of the canopy."

Well, son of a—"That is very well predicted, Thnessfiirm. You are an excellent assistant."

Unsymaajh turned from a hasty consultation with the convectorae on the other side of the cone tree's canopy. "The furthest ROV is at three hundred seventy-five meters. The leading ROV is only one hundred ninety meters away."

"Thnessfiirm, how are the missiles targeted?"

"We have multiple options: thermal, object designation, object characteristics—"

"That: characteristics. Now, can you combine targeting options? Such as, both speed and altitude characteristics?"

"I am not sure what you are requesting."

"Can you instruct the targeting system to select all objects that are traveling above the treetops, at a rate exceeding ten kilometers per hour, and within the missiles' primary intercept envelope?"

"Yes, but—ah: these characteristics eliminate all other possible targets except the ROVs. I see now, and—"

"Thnessfiirm."

"Yes?"

"Just do it. Quickly."

As Thnessfiirm turned to comply, Unsymaajh announced, "The trailing ROV is now at a range of three hundred and thirty meters, lead ROV at—"

"Thnessfiirm?"

"Ready."

"Fire. Unsymaajh, evacuate the closest positions. Dora, Keith, heads up: they're going to show us their playbook in the next minute or so."

From a clearing slightly beyond the area the ROVs were searching, the four Slaasriithi SAMs leaped skyward and then snapped over into head-on intercept modes. It took a moment for the ROVs to detect the incredibly swift missiles, to begin to react—

Four explosions rippled across the treetops; four sharp flashes became dirty gray blossoms of airborne smoke and shimmering showers of debris.

"Four targets confirmed destroyed," Thnessfiirm reported proudly—and needlessly.

Riordan nodded, pointed at Unsymaajh. "In the next few minutes, our enemies will decide where they are going to land troops to move against us. Their choice of landing site will reveal much about the tactics they plan to employ. Your watchers must keep us informed—constantly—of where their shuttle flies, where it lands, how many persons come out, where they go. Our survival depends upon this."

Unsymaajh's sensor cluster bobbed sharply. "We shall not fail." He was beyond the cone tree's canopy issuing instructions before Riordan had turned on his collarcom.

"What are you doing?" Nasr Eid gasped in alarm.

"Not sending. Just listening."

"Still—"

But in the time it took for Nasr to renew his protests against activating even a tiny a power source in such close proximity to the enemy, Riordan heard what he had expected: one of the group's other collarcoms was on and dial-sweeping. Every five seconds, it was sending out a signal that essentially tumbled through the bandwidth, like a beacon to any other receiver that might be looking to connect to it. Except, in this situation, it was working as a homing device for whoever was listening for it aboard the enemy shuttle. Given the interference, the collarcoms' ranges were reduced to less than four hundred meters, but that would be all their adversaries needed.

"What have you found?" Xue asked quietly. There was a pensive undertone in his voice.

Is he the traitor, or does he simply suspect what I've discovered? Caine shook his head, tasked his collarcom to identify which of its networked siblings was sending the signal. Mizuki's. Which meant that, when their half-blind and wounded fellow-survivor had left for the boat, someone had nicked her collarcom, set it to dial-sweep and had ditched it somewhere nearby.

Caine carefully considered the ramifications of his next action, then reactivated his collarcom's transmission capability.

Eid's eyes grew wide. "No! Don't—!"

Riordan, along with Gaspard, had one of the two collarcoms that were network administrators for all the others. He chose one of the executive overrides, entered his code, gave the command, turned off his collarcom.

As he pocketed it, Veriden frowned deeply. "What did you just do?"

"I shut down our comm net. Completely."

Xue nodded. "So, someone has been helping them locate us by sending a signal."

Riordan nodded. "And there was no way to be safe eliminating just one collarcom. If one gets shut down, our turncoat might have access to another, or might use his or her own." Caine stood. "Now, the bastards have to hunt us down fair and square."

Unsymaajh swept back under the canopy. "The shuttle has kept its distance, is landing in a small clearing three hundred and fifty meters south of our fallback position."

"Inland, or close to the riverbank?"

"Within sixty meters of the river."

Keith nodded. "So they are in a hurry."

Qwara frowned. "Why do you say so?"

Veriden answered. "The shore is flat and hard-packed right up to where the captain put our flank against it. It's marshy there, but up to that point, they can approach us at a good trot."

Xue rose into a crouch, cradled his rifle. "So do we follow Plan Gamma and flank them for an ambush?"

Caine shook his head. "Tempting, but no. I don't think we're up against amateurs. They may move a force down the shore, but they'll keep another force paralleling them in the bush. Our own ambushers would get hit in the flank that way."

Keith looked at Riordan. "So what's our plan?"

Caine suddenly discovered he was not so much thinking about the tactics as he was about how much of them he could share. Someone listening to him now was a traitor who might try to subvert their plans. Ironically, the only persons he could trust were the Slaasriithi. "We go with Plan Beta. We pivot our positions so that our backs are no longer to the river, but face upriver, toward their landing site."

"They'll try to get around us."

"I know. With the river on our left, they're going to try to find the limit of our lines to the right. They probably know they have more personnel. So they'll believe they can win a flanking game."

"And you think they're wrong?" Veriden sounded doubtful.

Riordan shrugged. "We have some tricks they don't know about. But here's what I'm expecting: they'll use their superior numbers and firepower to press us all along the line. They'll find our center and fix it. And then they're going to threaten us from either flank. Whatever they plan for the right, inland flank—well, we'll have to evolve a response as we see what they do. But we can be certain that they'll send a probe down along the river, expecting us to swing to prevent it."

Keith shrugged. "Aye, and they'll rush us there if we don't react. The riverbank gives them better visibility, and solid footing except for the silted stream upon which you've anchored our, well, 'line.' But once they're past that obstacle, they can turn that flank. And they'll move to do so."

Riordan nodded. "I'm counting on it."

Veriden frowned. "Oh? And how do plan on stopping them?"

Caine smiled. "Well, since you ask—"

Chapter Forty-Five

Bannor Rulaine surveyed his combat team: Tygg Robin, Trent Howarth, Peter Wu, and Miles O'Garran. The Wolfe-class corvette's standard load of six full EVA-rated combat kits had just barely been enough. Although they had no use for the extra suit of light combat armor, or the CoBro eight-millimeter liquimix battle rifle, they had been glad for the extra ammo, the extra cans of "hot sauce"—liquid propellant—and spare rounds for each rifle's underslung launch tube. Sitting on what was normally the ceiling of the aft airlock, the century that had elapsed during the past ten minutes had been bumpy, twisty, and frankly, terrifying. A high altitude jump into a hot landing zone with no support and no means of extraction would be a positive relief.

Or maybe not, as Tygg's question pointed out all too clearly: "Major, given that the aft hatch will barely admit two persons going sideways, just how do you mean for us to deploy?"

"Tygg, you and O'Garran jump first—a big guy jumping with a little guy will give you some extra space." He glanced at the SEAL almost everyone called Little Guy. "No offense, O'Garran."

"Major, if I got offended every time somebody implied that I could use a pair of platform shoes, there would be a lot of black eyes in the crowd running after me, I'd be in jail, or both."

Rulaine almost grinned. "Same strategy applies for the next pair: me and Wu. Trent, you bring up the rear; you're big enough to need that whole damned hatchway for yourself."

"Mom always said I was larger than life."

"And she was right. So: the exit. It's going to be too fast, and there's nothing we can do about it. We don't have sufficiently reliable flight control to slow, make the drop zone, and then get the ship clear for some hope of a safe landing. We can do any two of those things, but not all three."

Peter Wu rubbed his hands together very slowly. "So just how fast are we going to exit?"

"Probably about three hundred seventy kilometers per hour."

Trent looked at his own and then everyone else's armor and double load of ammo. "We're pretty heavy for that fast an exit. Hope the lines and straps all hold when the chutes deploy."

Rulaine nodded. "That's the worry. You've got to work to reduce your airspeed as much as possible before you pull the cord. How many times have you jumped from this altitude before?"

Tygg and O'Garran held up three fingers, Trent one. Wu just sat, stared, and commented, "And as I understand it, we're jumping into a jungle?"

"More like scattered woods. There'll be places to put down, and these HALO rigs have maneuver packs. And don't forget the attitude control rockets we scavenged from the emergency reentry kits. You've got a lot of resources for correcting your landing point."

"We may need those same resource just to hit the LZ," Tygg pointed out. "Since Karam can't take a chance banking and spending thrust, we won't be following up along the river, but flying across it at a right angle. That, plus our speed, is going to make it difficult to come down close enough to each other *and* close enough to the bad guys to get in the fight effectively. Or at all."

Rulaine nodded. "Which we've gone over plenty of times. So remember: keep an eye on everyone else and the key terrain features of the drop zone." *Which we could use about now, Karam.* "If you don't land within a few klicks of that site, you won't be able to—"

The intercom crackled before Karam's voice blared out of it. "Major, guys, listen up: you are at the two-minute mark."

"My chrono is running." Rulaine motioned for the others to rise. For sake of irony, he added. "Flight Officer, I'm waiting for a visual in my HUD, marked with a drop-zone guidon."

"Sure, and I'll make sure tac-air is standing by, thirty seconds out, along with a squadron of winged unicorns. Now that we've got those delusions behind us, here's what I *can* give you: when you straighten out from your exit, you want to look for the river. Once you've sighted that, look for a silted-up tributary that winds into the river from the west. The opposition just put down a little upstream, or south, of that position. If you can't see the old streambed right away, look north for a downriver section where rocky ridges start to hem in the river. Track back upriver five clicks from there and you'll see the dried-up tributary. It's the only contiguous clear path in the foliage other than the river itself."

"Thanks, Karam. Just count down—"

"I'm not done. I didn't want to have to do this, but I'm going to dip the thrusters to near zero right before you jump. That means I have to engage sprint mode about fifteen seconds after you clear the hull."

"Gotta make up for the lost altitude and speed?"

"Afraid so, Major. You'll be clear of the thruster wash, but everyone on the ground is going to know something just passed overhead. Sorry, but if I don't hit that juice—"

"Then you go nose first into the turf and vaporize: I get it." Sprint mode, the equivalent of afterburners on amphetamines, was the desperate move that they'd been trying to avoid. Not only would it attract unwanted attention, but it dramatically increased the chances of the power plant or cooling system burning out. And because it was unsafe to maneuver the corvette at all with the hull damage, Karam had been unable to use a tight serpentine deorbit to shed velocity, which also could have increased *Puller*'s nonexistent loiter time over the drop zone. In short, it would require extreme precision to both avoid scattering the five jumping grunts across the landscape and to prevent the ship from coming apart.

Rulaine motioned for Tygg and O'Garran to stand in front of the hatch. "Lanyards," he ordered. They all secured themselves to mooring points on the interior of the airlock. "You detach when you go. Karam, how are we doing on time?"

"We're fresh out, Major. Counting down from eleven, ten, nine—"

"Hatch open, Flight Officer."

The aft airlock's outer hatch, an iris valve, cycled open. The howling roar of the air and the scalloping in-draft staggered them. Between the twin plumes of air-shimmer trailed by *Puller*'s super-heated thruster bells, they spied dense vegetation, clouds, and flat, drifting sheets of airborne spores.

"—four, three—"

"First pair: detach."

"—one, and mark!"

"Go!"

And so they did.

Jesel waved his arm in a circle. Suzruzh and Pehthrum detached from their squads, joined him behind a low rise formed by several fallen trunks, most of which were markedly different from those of the more common trees shaped like cones and umbrellas. "Any contacts reported?"

His two lieutenants shook their heads. "Visibility worsens fifty meters ahead. The scouts did not probe too far into the forested thickets, there," Suzruzh explained. "As per your orders."

"How much further to that old streambed, beyond?"

Pehthrum checked the extremely basic Aboriginal data monocle that was furnished with each Jufeng battle rifle. "Another two hundred meters, Jesel."

Suzruzh shrugged. "We must expect that they will make their primary defense from the other side of that open terrain."

"Yes," Jesel agreed, "but they may site snipers in the thickets we must traverse before arriving there."

"If they have persons trained in combat," Suzruzh amended, "that could slow us further, inflict a few casualties. But they cannot stand long before our numbers. I predict they would inflict a casualty or two and flee. Back across the former riverbed."

Jesel nodded. "I concur. Now, what of the scout you sent to examine the launch site of the enemy missiles?"

"He returned, reported that the area seemed to be under enemy observation, or possibly, that it was a habitation for arboreal creatures. He could not determine which."

Pehthrum shrugged. "That is because the Slaasriithi hardly seem different from half of the animals we have glimpsed swinging between the trees: same basic size and shape, same biothermals."

Suzruzh nodded. "The scout did report finding four stationary launcher stands in the small clearing. He describes their manufacture as being unfamiliar, very possibly Slaasriithi."

"Which makes sense," Jesel concluded. "It is extremely unlikely that such missiles were sent along with this group of mewling Aboriginal diplomats." He rose. "We have no need to change our strategy, simply to accelerate it. I will, however, not bring my triads along right behind yours, Suzruzh. I shall be offset inland, to your rear left flank."

"You are thinking of sweeping around their probable center by going through that remote launch zone?"

"I wish to be in the position to exploit such an opportunity, but also to follow in behind you. Pehthrum, you shall move swiftly along the river until you make contact. If you believe you have the possibility of breaking through quickly, use everything at your disposal to do so. Suzruzh, when you hear gunfire or Aboriginal screaming from the riverbank, probe your front briskly."

Suzruzh nodded. "That is probably where they will have the bulk of their defense: right in front of me."

"Yes, and I will need to know as soon as you have confirmed or disproved that conjecture. The clone Gamma Fourteen seems to be a particularly swift runner, for some reason. Use him to alert me when you contact the enemy defenses and have fixed them in place. That will be my cue to either turn their inland flank, or support you. Return to your—"

In the high distance they heard a roar of thrusters and then a rolling boom. They stared at the sky, then at each other.

"I thought it was determined that the cannonballs are unable to conduct operations inside the atmosphere." Suzruzh's tone was wry, rueful.

"You are correct," Pehthrum countered, frowning. "That is something else."

One of Suzruzh's eyebrows elevated. "Such as?"

Jesel shook his head. "There is no way of knowing. But we may be sure of this: it is not a craft of ours. Therefore, it is an enemy."

"An airborne counterforce?" Suzruzh grumbled. "How does this change our plans?"

"We press forward even faster than before." Jesel pointed in the direction of the Aboriginals. "Move to contact and engage. Now."

As the sound of the aircraft dwindled into the western horizon, Macmillan cut a worried glance at Riordan. Caine shook his head. "I don't think that was an enemy craft. Those were dual-phase thrusters—not jets—which means whatever it was shot past this area too quickly to pull a fast turn and come back at us."

Veriden's voice was uncharacteristically tense. "So was that one of the Slaasriithis' supersonic defense drones?"

Thnessfiirm retracted his neck sharply. "Those were not the engines of any of our craft."

Veriden scowled. "Then what the hell—?"

"We'll find out when we find out. Now get under cover." Riordan waved the primary fire-team—Macmillan, Veriden, and Salunke—down into their forward positions, which were slightly inland from the narrowest point of the old streambed. Turning on his heel, he sprinted after Qwara, and Xue, who he'd sent ahead to the river, where Unsymaajh was waiting for them. After only ten strides, his lungs burned and his throat threatened to close. *I can't pop another pill, not yet. Just don't pay attention to the pain.* Which was easier said than done, particularly as he tried to keep pace with Thnessfiirm.

By the time he arrived at the concealed river-facing revetment the subtaxae had fashioned from downed trees, he was covered in sweat. Again. Xue frowned as Riordan jogged up, unable to disguise his ragged panting. "Captain—" the team's medic began.

"Not now. No time. They'll be. Coming soon." Caine bent over forward, then quickly back to fend off the imminent stomach cramp. He threw himself down against the back of the revetment, which the subtaxae had packed with dirt, as he had hastily shown them.

Unsymaajh called from overhead, where he hung easily from one of the indigenous trees. "The captain is correct; the attackers are moving swiftly along the shore."

"How many?"

"Nine. No, ten."

"Are any equipped differently than the others?"

"There is only one whose equipment, or even appearance, is distinct."

Caine waited, remembered that Unsymaajh might not intuit what information a human, or a warfighter, might be looking for. "How is he different?"

"He is taller, has slightly thicker clothing. He carries a longer weapon."

"You say the others are all similar?"

"With the exception that some carry heavier weapons that almost look like boxes, they are not merely similar: they are identical."

"Identical?" As in "clones?" Could they be from—? Riordan smothered curiosity in favor of immediate tactical response: "Thnessfiirm, instruct the AMP to drop the next set of weapon pods."

"Caine Riordan, I do not wish to question your judgment, but nor do I wish you to place excessive confidence in the miniature heat-seekers—"

"Thnessfiirm, we can't use any of the AMP's main rockets here. We have to save them."

Unsymaajh swung easily down from the tree, gestured at the tall ferns to the downstream side of the revetment. "You have other means to defeat your foes."

Riordan frowned. "I don't understand."

Unsymaajh clicked two of his own control-rings together in an intricate pattern. A flight of what looked like newt-bats—Affined *sloohavs*—glided down from the trees, made what looked like a crop-dusting run just beyond the tree-high ferns. As they swept away, the brush shook.

A water-strider rose up. It was one of the younger ones, and it seemed eager to join Unsymaajh. Others moved restlessly in the brush behind it.

Riordan realized he was staring and they had maybe a minute left before the enemy charged up the shore and either turned to follow the old streambed—which would bring them face to face with the revetment—or they would not see it and continue on, which would put Caine's forces on their left flank. "They will follow you into combat?"

"No; they will follow, or protect, *you*."

"Me? Why me?"

"Because of your marking. You are of them."

Caine looked up the long legs to the flanks of the creature, which turned to regard him with its four front eyes. Patiently. Even contentedly.

"How would they be able to help us?"

"Many ways. We shall see which option is best soon enough."

Riordan swallowed, horrified at the thought that now, in addition to scores of Slaasriithi, he might give orders that would lead to the deaths of these usually gentle creatures. "Xue," he croaked.

"Yes, Captain?"

"Go back. Help hold the center."

"But then you will have no rifle here."

"That's okay. Qwara, stay with me. I may need someone to run back to Fallback Point One with a message."

Qwara nodded. "We have strange allies," she murmured.

Caine nodded. "Yes," but thought: *I think our identical enemies may prove to be even stranger...*

Karam Tsaami had drilled and then reminded his so-called bridge crew to exhale as he threw the thrusters into sprint mode, but Morgan Lymbery had apparently forgotten: he gasped and gargled as *Puller* leaped forward, its shallow, declining arc suddenly straightening, then rising. At least they were flying right-side-up again. Which probably helped Lymbery keep his lunch in his stomach. "Tina," Karam grunted into his collarcom, "I can see the engine and power plant readouts, but tell me what you see and feel back there in the drive room."

Tina Melah, slightly senior to her fellow-engineer Phil Friel, sounded improbably chipper. "Nothing that worries me yet. But if these fixes don't hold, we probably won't have a lot of warning."

"Roger that," Karam agreed grimly. "Leave your circuit open. Melissa, what are you seeing on the aft scope?"

"Nothing, yet, but I—no, I see a chute! No, chutes. They're—"

"Melissa: count the chutes."

The pause was longer than it should have been: "Four. Only four chutes." Her voice sounded like her throat was closing, choking off the words. "Is there any way to—?"

"No way to know who drew the short straw, Melissa." *And shit, they beat the odds: four out of five was the best success ratio Rulaine could validate. But now we've got to focus on beating our odds—*

Sleeman had not stopped staring into the scope. "But can't we check—?"

Jeez, she must really like Tygg. Well, no accounting for taste— "Dr. Sleeman, you need to take a deep breath and think. We can't send radio messages through the Slaasriithi jamming. If we tried, the only thing we might accomplish is giving our enemies a lock on our position. And right now, we have to—"

The comm channel from the drive room was suddenly alive with sounds of chaos and shredding metal. "Shit! Karam?"

"Yeah; talk, Tina."

"Coolant line just blew out. And I mean blew; sprayed shards into the control panel and cut some cables. It's a friggin' mess down—"

Karam stole a glance at the engine readouts. One showed steady with the power plant temperature rapidly climbing into the red. The other readout on the dynamic display had gone dark; its relay had probably been in one of the cut cables.

"Karam, what do we do?"

"Tina, you hold tight. I'm going to need you and Phil back there when I try to land this thing."

"Yeah, well hurry up about it."

Karam couldn't help smiling at Melah's salt-encrusted truculence as he triggered the canopy covers. They retracted quickly, revealing—

Green, black and violet expanses rolling further and further away until they ended at a thin blue line that rimmed the horizon: the straits separating the north and south continents.

"Will we make it?" Lymbery asked.

"Don't know," Karam grumbled as he studied the gauges. The power plants and engines were both spiking their temperatures toward the red line. But even without doing the math, he knew what would happen if he nursed those systems along at lower power levels: they'd remain only moderately compromised—until they disintegrated under the impact of their crash, at least one hundred kilometers short of the sea. Karam sighed, resolved to take the only action that might save them. And to do so before he could consider it in detail, because then he would probably soil himself. "Everyone: hold on."

"Why?" chorused Lymbery and Sleeman.

There wasn't enough time to explain. But apparently Phil Friel knew what was coming: over the engineering circuit, the Irishman shouted for Tina to strap in, for the love of God—

Just as Karam pushed the engine and power plant gains to maximum.

Bucking, shuddering, *Puller*'s nose rose back up into a faintly skyward arc, the red limit indicators of the ship's thrusters and power plants rising even more quickly.

Melissa Sleeman's voice was uncharacteristically small. "Will this save us, or blow us to pieces?"

Karam shrugged. "Damned if I know."

Chapter Forty-Six

The Aboriginal binoculars were quaint, but Pehthrum discovered them to be reasonably effective. Although they lacked the sophisticated analytical electronics of the models he was used to, these purely optical systems had one immense advantage: simplicity. There was no possibility of malfunction or misreading. The lenses magnified what your eyes could already see. And these did so quite well; they had revealed the tell-tale signs of a revetment on the far side of the silted streambed.

The clone Pehthrum had chosen as the assistant squad leader—Beta-Three—raised his Pindad caseless assault rifle to his shoulder. Pehthrum pushed it back down. "No. If we rush this position directly, we could take significant casualties. We have to clear almost sixty meters of soft open ground. If they have any modern weapons, they could cripple us."

"Leader, I understand. But if we lay down suppressive fire with our rifles while the shotgunners charge across—"

"Be still. There is a better way." Pehthrum motioned to Xi-Two, who passed forward two long cases.

Beta-Three shrank back. "Will that work—here?"

"Most assuredly, given that we know the biochemistry of our Aboriginal targets." Pehthrum opened the two containers. After a moment, upt'theel started streaming out, noses questing desperately: they had been in food-deprived hibernation for more than a month now. Pehthrum palmed a piece of bait and waved

418

it in their direction—briefly—before throwing it as far as he could toward the revetment.

The milling brood of weasel-pangolin monsters had just caught the scent—ominously—as the rotting meat described an arc that ended with a sloppy thump only twenty-five meters in front of the revetment. As if controlled by one ravenous mind, the upt'theel spun in that direction and swarmed over the ground toward the bait.

Beta-Three started to rise. Pehthrum cuffed him with the back of his gauntleted hand. Not enough to inflict a concussion: just a love tap that partially severed the top of his ear. "You wait for my order. And for our pets to do their work."

The upt'theel certainly seemed eager to do just that. They flowed over the lumpy, partially marshy ground like a clattering, squealing carpet. When the first few reached the bait, they struggled, rolled in furious arabesques of mortal competition—until one put up a sharp nose and detected the scent of more sustenance. Its head swiveled, others following, toward the revetment. With a renewed cacophony of clacks and shrieks, the majority of the horde swept toward it.

Unsymaajh looked at Riordan, who was keenly aware of the many, massive eyes watching him from behind the fronds, straining to either run or protect—

Caine waved his hand, spoke one of the commands the humans had used in directing the water-striders: "Go."

The gigantic creatures trampled out of the brush with a chorus of ululating hoots, like enraged foghorns testing their vocal range. In three strides they were into the wave front of the startled upt'theel, which, true to their nature, launched themselves at the striders' lower legs.

However, for every one that managed that feat in time, half a dozen were smashed into screaming, writhing pulp.

Caine saw one of the loathsome octopedal monsters begin burrowing into a water-strider's lower leg—just as another strider grazed its own wide leg across that of its afflicted herdmate. The upt'theel's rear half was kicked away like a writhing rag, the front half screeching starved outrage at the immense animals towering over it.

Caine swallowed, discovered his throat was as dry as sun-baked leather. "Thnessfiirm."

"Yes, Caine Riordan?"

"Has the AMP relocated?"

"Yes, and it has self-stealthed again."

"Arm the launch pods."

"It would be best to prepare to designate the targets. And you will need to keep the targets in the designator's line of sight until—"

"I understand. We have a similar guidance system: we call it fire-and-forget." Riordan raised the wandlike designator. "I'm just waiting for our real enemies to show themselves."

Qwara had been silent beside him the whole time. "They are rising up, now. Look—wait, is that—are they—?"

"Those are Optigene clones, Ms. Betul."

The same kind that were sent to kill me just last year.

Pehthrum did not understand what he was seeing, at first. The tall stands of ferns and frond-trees on the downstream side of the Aboriginal revetment had vomited out large, impossible quadrupeds. Some as high as ten meters, sounding like a collection of war-trumpets and bone *krexyes* horns, they charged the flank of the upt'theel swarm, stomping as they came. The small creatures, ferocity undiminished, were no match for the close-furred colossi: bright spatters and sudden smears marked the carnivores' demise beneath the massive feet of the counterattackers.

Beta-Three stared at him. "Respected Intendant, what do we—?"

"Rifles of triad one and two; suppress the revetment. Rifles of triad three; engage the—the creatures. Shotgunners: charge to thirty meters range and engage the creatures with single slug rounds. Full automatic. Now!"

Pehthrum's clones rose up from the tall, spiky thickets in which they had been hiding, started firing at the revetment. But that withering fusillade did not generate the multidirectional spray of wood that the Intendant had been expecting. So: an earthen redoubt behind it. Clever.

The two riflemen firing at the tall creatures were passable marksmen, but only passable: most of their hits did more to enrage the long-legged behemoths than incapacitate them. Concentrating most of their fire on the largest specimen, they did inflict some wounds that looked mortal, but in the sense that they would kill in minutes or hours, not before the infuriated animal completed its charge.

And still the riflemen of triads one and two were dutifully and futilely peppering away at the revetment. *By the Progenitors' scrofulous testicles, have these accursed clones no greater sense than this?* "All rifles on the creatures; shotguns hold your ground and fire, point blank!"

As his men started to follow these orders and the first of the charging quadrupeds stumbled under the more intense fire, Pehthrum, hanging back, took the Jufeng dustmix rifle off safety, snapped over the trigger selector so that it would fire the underslung launch tube, and selected a conventional high-explosive grenade from the rotary cassette just in front of the trigger guard. He shouldered the weapon, braced it by wrapping its sling around his arm, raised the barrel slightly in the direction of the revetment—and noticed a small, color-changing dot on his sleeve, which vanished in the same instant he saw it. *A laser designator? Dung and submission!* "Get down!" he tried to scream over the clones' chattering rifles and shotguns. "Concentrate your fire on—!"

Caine nodded to Thnessfiirm. "Fire the first five MAPHs."

Thnessfiirm bobbed her compliance and tapped a thick control rod with several of her rings.

From a clearing thirty meters behind the revetment, angry sibilant hisses up-dopplered and materialized in the form of miniature antipersonnel heat-seekers, each only fifteen millimeters in diameter. They sped through the dwindling melee between the water-striders and weasel-monsters, bypassed the shotgun and rifle wielding clones that had closed with the one charging strider, and disappeared, fire-tailed, into the bodies of the rearmost enemy troops. The one who had held the long weapon was hit first. His torso exploded from inside, clumps of flesh and bone bursting outward as the lower half of his body swayed, and then toppled. Before it hit the river's silty shore, three of the riflemen who had remained behind to provide a base of fire were also hit, two with similar results. The third shrieked as his left arm was blown off at the shoulder.

Riordan saw this and, peripherally, the slow fall of the much-mauled water-strider. He moved the laser designator from one clone to the next, starting with the rearmost and moving forward. "Launch the next three," he ordered Thnessfiirm.

But the fairly neat arrangement of targets was rapidly becoming chaotic. Some of the water-striders were hooting and stomping at the attackers in what seemed to be threat displays. Several of the clones swerved away from the huge creatures, two of whom, finding themselves only twenty meters from the revetment, charged it. Caine quickly cancelled the primary designations for the next flight of MAPHs, painted these two new, rapidly approaching threats, ducked, saw Qwara crouching, watching, aghast at the speed with which the carnage had taken place. He stabbed an arm out to grab her: "Get dow—!"

A jackhammer stutter. The top of Qwara Betul's head smeared away under a shower of shotgun slugs—just as three of the MAPHs raced over her falling corpse. An eyeblink later, three small, sharp explosions beat a nearby, percussive tattoo. Caine leaned down to look out the observation slit they'd built into the revetment: there wasn't much left of the two charging clones, and it was difficult to determine where their remains ended and those of the pulped upt'theel began. But the rifleman's weapon was apparently intact...

Rifle rounds peppered the top of the revetment, the treetops: one of the convector subtaxae tumbled from a frond tree, emitting a sound that was part chirp, part bleat.

Unsymaajh appeared, swinging downward from behind the canopy of the cone-tree that stood at the juncture of the revetment and the fronds that had hidden the water-striders. The big convector's long arm stretched down to scoop up his fallen taxonmate—

A flurry of fire from back near the river: Unsymaajh seemed to writhe upward in midglide and then collapsed, blood trails marking his descent like dotted lines.

Caine rolled to the other side of the vision slit, ducked back and then out to get a quick look. The four surviving clones had doubled back and discovered their dead commander. One had found the Jufeng, was lowering it; that weapon was probably what had killed Unsymaajh. Of the other two, the one who was armed with a shotgun had put it aside, was inspecting which of the fallen riflemen's weapons was still serviceable. Caine called to Thnessfiirm, who had retreated into the far corner of the revetment and was shivering as if she had been dropped in ice water. When the traumatized cerdor failed to respond, Riordan scrambled over, gently helped her raise the control rod into their shared field of vision. "Thnessfiirm, I need you to launch two MAPHs. I need you to do it now."

Thnessfiirm's head bobbed and weaved erratically, and she was emitting a wheezing buzz, but her rings clacked against the rod with shuddering purpose.

Caine rolled back to the vision slit, aimed the designator, painted the clone with the Jufeng—and ducked back as an improbably loud roar of weapons-fire accompanied a hailstorm of high-velocity rounds that clawed and ripped at the edges of the slit. *Now that they've spotted me, they are likely to—*

Only then did Riordan realize that the gunfire hadn't merely come from the enemy rifles; that thundering crescendo had been caused by the simultaneously launching Slaasriithi MAPHs.

But not just the two Caine had called for: Thnessfiirm had fired all of them.

A flock of the bright-tailed missiles sped over the bodies of clones and upt'theel and water-striders and streaked to a ruinous convergence upon the wielder of the Jufeng. He disappeared in a set of overlapping explosions that left no trace of him, and very little of his weapon.

But with the miniature antipersonnel heat-seekers gone, the rest of Riordan's strategy was in ruins. Fatal ruins. Caine turned to Thnessfiirm, about to ask why the cerdor had launched all of them: had she misheard? Had it been a command error? Had she been panicked? But the answer was obvious at first glance: Thnessfiirm was still quaking, still sitting folded into the back corner of the revetment, her own wastes pooling out from beneath her.

Unsymaajh dead, Qwara dead, Thnessfiirm in shock: Riordan crawled to the other end of the revetment, risked a peek around that leaf-shrouded corner.

The three surviving clones were advancing at a trot, weapons at the ready. The water-striders, not under immediate attack, hooted their challenges, stood their ground, but wavered, uncertain what they should do as the soldiers gave them a wide berth.

One chance. And it almost certainly means my death to try: to roll out, grab the Pindad just a few yards away and get back behind the revetment. It's not much of a plan, but short of running and leaving Thnessfiirm to die and our rear undefended, it's the only plan I've got. Caine gathered his legs under him, felt his overtaxed heart hammering in his chest, heard his own wheezing breath—

And heard a startled cry from the corpse-strewn field. Hoping that anything which surprised the clones would give him a moment of safe observation, he popped his head back around the corner of the revetment.

One of the clones was down, the other two staring wildly about—just as, faint as the echo of a distant dog's bark, they all heard a rifle report. And having carried that model of rifle, Caine knew exactly what it was, and exactly what it meant.

The distant CoBro eight-millimeter liquimix battle rifle—the new standard of Earth's Commonwealth forces—fired again: another of the clones went down, two puffs of dark mist jetting from his chest. The dying echo of the blended reports confirmed the direction and the range of the fire: it had come from well beyond the far side of the river. And it meant friendlies were on their way. The last clone dropped to a knee, scanned quickly for cover—

Caine sprinted out around the corner of the revetment, grabbed the blood-slick Pindad on the move, rolled into a prone position, his heart hammering so hard he knew he would never be accurate enough to hit his enemy—

Who, hearing the noise, had spun around, his own Pindad coming up—the same moment that three rapid maroon vapor jets erupted from his torso. He fell over and did not move.

Caine resolved to take three seconds to rest and think and listen.

And the first sound he heard made him cancel the last two seconds: more Pindads firing, back near Fallback Point One. *Damn it.* The attack here, which he'd guessed might be a feint or merely an opportunity attack, had obviously been the signal for another, possibly larger force to hit his main line.

So, how best to help? What will hit our enemies the hardest? Caine's eyes strayed out over the bloody silted riverbed—probably a handful of firearms, but it would take time to find them, time to get the ammo, and all the while, he'd be getting shorter and shorter of breath.

Which reminded him: time to pop another pill. He did.

The alternative? See if Thnessfiirm could move now. If she could, and was able to operate the AMP, that would bring a far more powerful weapon to bear far more rapidly.

Caine snagged the Pindad's bandoliers from the dead clone's torso, jogged around the corner of the revetment—

—and almost ran headlong into Thnessfiirm. The Slaasriithi's very pale neck and tendrils looked like they were now covered with sagging, old skin. "Thnessfiirm, are you—?"

"I am able to function. I believe." Her sensor cluster wobbled uncertainly in the direction of the distant gunfire. "They are attacking where you expected."

"I think so. Can you travel?"

"I must. I shall lead the way." And Thnessfiirm was moving into the bush, gaining speed as she went.

Riordan started after her, stopped. He turned to face across the river, put up the arm holding the Pindad and waved it wide, three times. *Thanks.*

He turned and plunged into the foliage after Thnessfiirm.

Eight hundred and seventy meters beyond the river to the east, and cinched between the bole of a bumbershoot and the canopy of a cone-tree, First Lieutenant Christopher "Tygg" Robin lowered the eight-millimeter Colt Browning's scope from his right eye. He smiled sadly. "You're welcome, Caine. Just sorry I didn't hit the drop zone."

Tygg nestled into the upper branches of the cone-tree. Having no way to get across the river, his best option was to remain in his present perch, which provided a commanding view of the opposite bank of the river for over a kilometer in either direction. Now that he knew what the bad guys looked like, he could pick off any that might come back near the river. He nodded reassuringly to himself; *even from here, I can help, I can turn the—*

But then Tygg heard distant stutters of assault rifles, the crump of a grenade, and once again he damned his distance, damned his reluctance to use the boosters Rulaine had scavenged from the emergency reentry kits. Uncertain of how hard the rockets would kick, Tygg worried he might overshoot the drop zone. And ironically, because of that caution, he had come in a kilometer short of it.

Tygg stared at the far bank and felt quite keenly that, despite his best efforts and best guesses, he'd let his friends down. "Good luck, mates," he whispered at the distant trees where God-only-knew-what was transpiring.

Chapter Forty-Seven

Dripping sweat again, and tossing away his last, drained water bottle, Riordan staggered into Fallback Two, expecting to find it empty—but Veriden, Macmillan, and Xue were already there. Not good. "Report," Caine gasped.

Macmillan, whose beefy strength apparently came at the expense of endurance, gasped back at him. "We were in our positions, caught them in the flank. Bunch of hits. But nine-millimeter wasn't enough to drop them, usually."

Veriden took over as Macmillan sucked in a deep breath; the filters in his mask whined as that volume of air rushed through them. "We killed or incapacitated one. Wounded two, maybe three." Veriden hardly seemed winded. Riordan had known that she was lithe and tough, but hadn't realized just how lithe and how tough she was until now.

"Where's Esiankiki?"

Xue shook his head. "I do not know what became of Ms. Salunke. She was firing until the attackers used their grenade launcher. I think it is the model built into the Jufeng."

"I heard it. And yes, it is."

"So our own people are attacking us?"

Riordan shook his head at Macmillan. "I doubt it's anything that straightforward. But we've gotta move."

Veriden frowned, looked around. "Yeah, but where?"

"Fallback Three."

Xue looked at him carefully. "Captain, that is our last fallback point."

Caine motioned for them to follow him. "Yes, but since you're already here at Fallback Two, and they can't be far behind, that's our last option. Just get to your fighting positions." He saw glances go back and forth between the three of them. "What is it?"

"Ammo." Veriden shook her rifle; the bolt was back and the breech was open. "I'm dry."

Caine considered, then held out his Pindad and its magazines. "Here." As Dora took it, Macmillan looked up as if he'd been given a mild rebuke. "Keith, she's a good shot and she's not winded. Only one of us can say that, right now. So mobility gets the firepower. Now keep moving." Macmillan shrugged then nodded at the logic. Veriden checked the weapon with professional surety and ease.

"Where's Thnessfiirm? And Qwara?" Xue asked as they exited the thick brush and began crossing the silted streambed at the narrowest point.

Hunching to keep his head below the level of the spike-grass and tuber-saplings that dotted the soft irregular ground, Riordan gestured to the stands of trees and ten-meter fronds lining what had once been the stream's far bank. "Thnessfiirm is just behind Fallback Three with the AMP. Qwara...Qwara didn't make it." He thought to order Xue and Keith to equalize their remaining ammo, but saw that they were already in the process of doing so.

Back among the tangle of copses and thickets they had just exited, sharp whistles and trilling calls arose from the treetops. A brace of Pindads sent up a furious counterchorus, then silence.

Macmillan hunched a little lower, jogged a little faster as they neared the tall growth on the far side of the silted streambed. "Seems like the convectorae positioned around Fallback Two spotted some enemy scouts."

Probably a few paid for that with their lives, too. Riordan nodded. "That puts the bad guys about three minutes behind us, maybe four. Get to your positions." He pulled out one of the pop-flares that had been in their emergency signaling kits. "If they don't attack where or as we expect, commence firing on my signal."

"Yeah, but—"

"What is it, Dora?"

"Captain"—it was the first time she had used his title—"what then? We don't have any dance steps beyond this part of the song."

Riordan nodded, pulled himself up the bank toward his own position, which was built more for concealment than protection. "That's because this is the end of the choreography. After this, you split up and try to survive. I'm guessing we've already hit them harder than they expected. If we take out some more of them, they may be too thin on the ground to find us all. I suspect they never had a long operational window. And since that wasn't one of their boats roaring overhead, and we've got some help on the ground now, I'll bet the window is closing even faster than they expected. So, once we abandon these positions, our only objective is to stay alive by staying lost."

Riordan slumped down into his position; the three were still standing nearby, watching—waiting? "You've done a great job," he told them. "Do it just a little longer. Now, get moving. They'll be here soon." They silently went to their shallow holes, Xue near Caine in the center, Macmillan and Veriden to either flank.

Thnessfiirm's voice was tremulous behind him. "I do not understand the ways of making war well, but—"

"Yes?"

"I have observed the power of the weapon you gave to Ms. Veriden. Would that not be better placed in the center, where it can bear upon more of the streambed?"

Riordan smiled. "That's an excellent question." He rose, stood behind the crook of a tuber tree, laid the targeting wand in it, peered down its surprisingly good scope. "And normally, you would be right. But that tactic would be best if we actually wanted to cover the most ground and inflict the most casualties with her assault rifle."

"Is that not what you wish to accomplish?"

"No: this time, I want the attackers to avoid it." Riordan, satisfied with the scope's placement, held out a hand. "May I have the activation rings for the remaining rockets on the AMP?"

Thnessfiirm handed them over. "You want your enemies to avoid your best weapon? I do not understand."

"Sometimes," Riordan explained, "the best use of a weapon is to influence your enemy's behavior. In this case, where they decide to charge us. I am fairly sure they would prefer to go through Dora's position: it's the furthest from the river, and the driest. But when they probe our line, they will discover that the center and the flank closest to the river will have the weakest defensive fire."

Thnessfiirm's neck oscillated slightly. "And so you anticipate they will change their point of attack to those less daunting areas."

Riordan shrugged. "I sure hope so." Xue, whose position was slightly forward of Caine's, waved twice. "And I think we're about to find out."

On the opposite side of the streambed, there was faint movement in the lowest levels of the fronds. Thnessfiirm pointed to a flight of smaller *sloohavs* which rose up in pairs: released by the convectorae, it confirmed that the enemy had reached the old streambed at that point. More pairs rose skyward farther up the dead watercourse; none appeared from the stretch where it neared the river.

"As you projected," Thnessfiirm purred.

Riordan shook his head. "No real surprise. They're on foot, so they are going to want the most solid and most narrow stretch of open ground to cross. Once they are in the trees on our side of the streambed, they know we've lost the battle. Their shotguns will then be at optimum range, and they'd overrun us. It would be suicide for us to even put up our heads, and certain death to remain in our positions while their riflemen flank us." He adjusted the sighting of the targeting wand. "The convectorae did an excellent job of concealing our positions. If the attackers don't have thermal goggles, I doubt they will pick us out before we start firing."

"Hiding," Thnessfiirm explained with a tremor in her neck, "is our accustomed means of dealing with threats."

Riordan nodded, reflected that this would have been an excellent place to begin an important cross-species discussion, but there were far more important matters at hand—

From the brush line where the flights of *sloohavs* had risen up, a few fleeting figures—clones—darted into the old streambed. They vanished into the patchy, shoulder-high mix of tuber-saplings and fronds, riddled with the spiky marsh grass. Their initial rush slowed rapidly; the ground underfoot was no longer a fen, but it was not fully solid, either.

Caine made his observations in a quiet voice aimed at Xue's back. "Looks like two scouts probing further up the streambed, two more coming straight across."

Xue turned his head a few degrees, nodded. "Yes, sir."

The intermittent growth in the otherwise open ground forced the enemy's scouts to advance in leaps and starts, rushing from one covered position to another. When the upstream group got within fifty meters of Dora's position, her Pindad spat forcefully. Bits of vegetation flew up as one of the figures fell; he hit the ground, groaning. The other disappeared but the tops of the stiff grass trembled on a reverse course that led back toward a thick clump of ferns: the closest available heavy cover.

The two scouts in front of Caine's position paused, then continued forward. "Prepare to fire," he ordered Xue.

Whose back straightened in surprise. "At this range, sir? With the nine-millimeter, I won't be—"

"Just do as I say, Mr. Xue. We want them to think we're weak here."

And the anemic performance of the nine-millimeter slugs, fired at about fifty yards, accomplished just that. Of four rounds fired at a brisk pace, only one hit; the target fell but remained capable of cursing and counterfiring. Xue ducked back down.

Thnessfiirm's necked goggled at the strange silence that settled over the streambed. "And now what?"

"And now, we wait."

"How long?"

"Thirty seconds, maybe a minute. They are not going to want to give us a chance to change positions."

"Why?"

"Because right now, they know where most of our shooters are and they will want to hit those positions with suppressive fire while the bulk of their forces charge across the streambed. That's why they probed us first; to determine where—"

The distinctive stutters of Pindads snapped at them from the far side of the streambed. Nearby tree trunks spat out splinters; fronds bowed and fell; leaves fluttered in colorful swirls of agitation. Caine, hunkering a bit lower, peered towards Dora's position: she was getting her fair share of suppressive fire as well, but far less that Xue was taking. "They've made their choice," Riordan reported to Thnessfiirm. "Get back to the AMP. If there is any malfunction with this control, you will need to fire the rockets manually."

"How many?" Thnessfiirm asked.

The throaty clatter of an automatic shotgun preceded a shredding of the vegetation around both Xue and Riordan. The clones were spraying and praying, but at ranges under one hundred meters, it was effective enough to prompt Caine to think about saying a few prayers of his own. He lifted his head up after the wave of devastation had passed, asked, "What do you mean, 'how many'?"

"I mean, how many rockets should I launch if I must do so manually?"

Caine answered—"All of them"—but did not have the time to look at Thnessfiirm; six, no seven more of the attackers had leaped out of the far brush line. They were sprinting unevenly across the streambed, the two scouts rising to join them. *There; that's the attack. They're committed.*

Xue fired at the onrushing squad, the magazine of his survival rifle emptying when they were halfway across, just as Macmillan joined in. But, being even further from the enemy's route of attack, the big Scotsman's rounds were either not finding their mark, or simply not stopping the targets they hit.

Thnessfiirm's voice was hushed. "You wish me to launch all of the rockets?"

Christ: are you still here? "Yes. All the rockets. Go."

At which point, Riordan suspected that Thnessfiirm would not get to the AMP in time if the control rings failed to work. Caine glanced in Veriden's direction; her position was being constantly peppered with counterfire, pinning her down.

Xue finished reloading, rolled to the other end of his fighting position, popped up—and was drummed back down by a storm of suppressive fire.

Caine moved slightly, so that he could peer down the targeting wand's scope again. Its frequency sampling protocol allowed him to see what no one else could: the three-laser aimpoint arranged in a wide triangle just twenty meters in front of Xue's position. He glanced at the closest of the clones—closing on thirty meters distance as they ducked and weaved through the brush—and was satisfied by their approach formation: a wedge, about fifteen meters wide and twenty-five deep.

It's not going to get any better than this, Riordan decided. He made sure that the targeting wand was snugged firmly in place so that it would continue to paint the target zone and clicked the control rings together. Caine rolled out of his position, yelled "Fall back" at Xue's spine, spun into a rising sprint that carried him through the curtain of fronds behind them. Bullets—not aimed at Riordan, just in his general direction—buzzed and snipped at the frond tops half a meter over his ducked head.

From one hundred meters to the rear, a rippling roar washed out toward him: a sudden, strident burst of massed rocketry.

Caine glanced behind, saw Xue clear his position, then clutch at a mortal spatter of torso hits. He went down, bloody and limp.

The roar grew, up-dopplered sharply and became a chorus of screams rushing overhead—

Caine sprinted hard, felt his chest burn, then constrict, then harden. But he needed to get more distance. Not being familiar with these rockets, there was no way of knowing how large their blast pattern was—

The overhead screams down-dopplered crisply into roars plunging toward the dried streambed. Or more precisely, the phased-laser triangle painted on an open expanse of water-smoothed rocks and scrub brush—

The stuttering cacophony of blasts didn't just assault Riordan's ears, it sent an overpressure wave bumping against his back. He staggered but did not fall. Pushing between closely spaced cone-trees, Caine realized that he was no longer hot, but cold, his palms clammy, his lungs no longer able to rise or expand without conscious effort. As debris from the explosions began fluttering down around him, and Dora's Pindad resumed its duel far more decisively with whomever still had her pinned down, Caine stumbled forward, acutely aware that his field of vision was narrowing.

He broke out of the brush into the smoking clearing from which the AMP had launched its last rockets. Thnessfiirm edged out from behind a bush as Riordan, world swimming unsteadily, staggered forward to catch his balance against the bole of a bumbershoot. The Slaasriithi's neck stretched toward him.

"Caine Riordan, you are not well."

Caine almost laughed—*you think?*—but even the mild expulsion of air from the first chuckle was so painful that it smothered any momentary amusement. "Thnessfiirm, you and I need to stay together, to operate the AMP."

"But it has no weapons left."

"No, but. It can . . . distract the enemy. Make them . . . chase after . . . it. We have to—"

Dora's distant Pindad was answered by a much closer automatic shotgun. Thnessfiirm started, jumped back toward the bushes.

Caine shook his head. "No, they won't find us . . . right away. We can . . ."

But Thnessfiirm was continuing to back into the bush. Away from the sound of the guns. Away from Caine. "No, Caine Riordan. I am sorry you are so afflicted, but we cannot remain together. Humans are already slow in our forests, being unable to travel in the trees. You are now almost immobile. I would die if I stayed here with you."

"You—you're abandoning me?" Despite all the contingencies Caine had considered, despite all the unlikely events he had foreseen, this had not been among them.

"Caine Riordan, my species is not like yours. Individually, we avoid needless death."

"So you're just leaving me here?"

"I am saddened to say it, but you are sure to die. What good is it that both of us should perish?"

Riordan stumbled away from the tree. "We humans—it is our way to stand by each other. Even when it puts more of us at risk."

Thnessfiirm's sensor cluster oscillated slowly, "And it is our way to survive individually, and so be most numerous when we regather." Thnessfiirm bobbed briefly and was gone.

Riordan looked after the disappeared Slaasriithi. *And there, in two sentences, is why our races will never fully understand each other. Evolution has taught us lessons so radically different that a species-positive trait for us humans—sticking together as a team—is a species-negative trait for you.*

Caine heard the shotgun's stuttering cough close at hand, turned, and stumbled into the brush that stretched inland, away from the river.

Jesel bounded through the bush toward Suzruzh when he saw his distant cousin approaching, nursing his left arm and favoring his left leg. "Report! Immediately!"

Suzruzh waved an arm—prickled with red puncture wounds—back toward the streambed. "You heard the rockets. They waited until our assault, knew where we were coming."

"And did you not pin down one flank, find their weak spot, and then—?"

"That is exactly what we did, *cousin*." Suzruzh's eyes narrowed. "I am not an imbecile. I know how to conduct a simple attack, arguably better than you do. But they must have eliminated Pehthrum's flank attack—there were sounds of a pitched firefight there—and brought whatever resources they had left to cover against any move we might make across the streambed. One of them had an assault rifle. Two of my men pinned that one down, the rest charged across the flat ground. They were within ten meters of the other tree-line—" He shut his mouth abruptly.

"And?"

"And they were annihilated. It was comparable to a barrage from one of our own tactical support launchers. If I had not hung back, according the Nezdeh's orders—"

"Yes, but now you are here and we must achieve our objective."

Suzruzh looked at the one scout that had survived out of all of his men, then at Jesel's reduced squad of six: one of his triads had been sent to join Suzruzh's forces, to bolster the charge across the riverbed. "We have few tools left with which we may achieve anything, Jesel."

"That is true, but our duty and our survival require our success. We must first know how many Aboriginals we are still hunting. How many did you kill?"

Suzruzh shook his head. "I am unsure. We could not search their abandoned positions thoroughly since one of the Aboriginals had us under fire. We did find their launcher, some kind of autonomous platform, hovering in a glade. It was no more than a frame. I suspect all its munitions cells were expended. We destroyed it, but we had no time to search for Aboriginal bodies. We had to see to our own wounded and hasten here."

"And have you indeed seen to all your wounded? I heard no shots."

Suzruzh shrugged. "That would have revealed our position after the enemy broke contact. A knife sufficed—and there wasn't much work to be done, it turned out."

Jesel nodded, looked west, away from the river. "They will flee in that direction. They will not run back to the river; they can be trapped against its banks. I will take five of my men. I will leave one to remain with you and your survivor."

Suzruzh flinched in surprise. "I am to stay here? To what purpose?"

"To return to our landing zone and secure our shuttle."

"But we locked it against all—"

"Suzruzh, shake off the ear-ringing of the rockets; it is addling your wits. When we left our security-locked shuttle, we had clear superiority over our targets. We numbered twenty-nine, with superior weapons, and faced a proximal foe. Now we are down to two Evolved and seven clones, and have no idea where our enemies might have gone. It is entirely possible that they could slip behind us and compromise our craft. Also, whatever went overhead just before we commenced this battle is not ours. It is not impossible that some Slaasriithi craft could be searching for us, which they will do by scanning for the dense metals of our shuttle."

Suzruzh glanced away, annoyed, but said. "It is wisdom. I shall secure the shuttle."

Jesel nodded curtly. "And I shall hunt down these Aboriginal mongrels." He hefted his rifle, gestured for one of his men to join Suzruzh, and nodded to the others. "We shall cut over the streambed farther inland from the river and seek their tracks or trails leading away from the point of assault." He tossed two orders over his shoulder: "Staggered delta formation. Advance at the double quick." He nodded to his cousin, then turned and pushed into the shoulder high growth, his men at his back.

Suzruzh stared after them, rubbing his left arm. "We shall travel in a staggered triad. I shall take the second position. We move slowly, carefully, and ten meters off the trail we used when advancing from our landing site. There have been enough surprises this day."

The clones nodded and complied, falling into the ordered formation. Traveling swiftly, they became increasingly wary of every dense clump and impenetrable thicket. It took them ten minutes to make good their return to the shuttle, which, observed from the edge of the clearing in which it had landed, seemed unmolested. But Suzruzh, never a trusting sort, was even less so this day.

"Alpha-Six," he ordered the clone that Jesel had assigned to him, "advance to the waist hatchway and examine it for any signs of tampering or attempts at forced entry."

The clone barely nodded before rising and advancing, weapon to eye, in a fast crouch to the side of the shuttle. He inspected the hatch for several seconds, then waved an all-clear.

Suzruzh rose, led the sole surviving scout from the streambed attack toward the craft. "We will make ready for immediate take-off," he ordered as they crossed the fern-spotted clearing. "We must be ready to return to orbit the moment that Jesel and his—"

Suzruzh heard three sharp reports: a high velocity weapon, very nearby—

At that same instant, three projectiles cut through him like hot pokers: one vented his left lung, another pulped his liver, and the last sliced through his descending colon—before they all emerged from his back. He staggered, tried to initiate the venous and arterial constricture reflexes that might keep him conscious, but realized within the same second that the damage was too widespread, too serious for those disciplines to save him.

As he fell, the reports continued as a steady tattoo that dropped his two clones with multiple mortal wounds; unlike an Evolved, they had no way to mitigate or delay either shock or blood loss. As Suzruzh's vision began to constrict, to become a view through a closing pipe, he had an impression of two armored figures advancing cautiously toward him—

—before the pipe was sealed by unremitting darkness.

Bannor Rulaine took cover next to the shuttle, sweeping the tree-line as Peter Wu crouch-ran forward to check the target who'd had the better equipment and had clearly been in charge.

Wu reached the bloody figure, turned and shook his head. "Gone. What now, Major?"

Rulaine looked at the figure slumped by the hatch. "Well, given that the leader didn't let his lead trooper open the hatch, I'm guessing this shuttle is either code-locked or booby-trapped. Either way, we move on and find our people."

"How? Backtrack where these three came from?"

"That's a start, but we've got to stay off whatever trail they followed here. I doubt they took time to set traps, but this isn't the time to guess wrong."

Wu had already risen, entered the span of brush from which their opponents had emerged, found the faint trail they had left. "You think the others in this raiding team have finished their mission? And sent this group on ahead to prepare the craft for launch?"

Rulaine shrugged as he joined Wu. "Don't know. There's too much craziness here, as it is: a TOCIO armored shuttle and Optigene clones being used by the same attackers who pounded the crap out of us two weeks ago and knocked a cannonball aside a few hours ago? It doesn't add up, so I'm not about to make any tactical assumptions. We just move forward and try to get in the game to save our people. That's all the plan I've got right now."

Wu nodded, looked at the wounds on the dead leader's arm. "Looks like our people are putting up a fight, too."

"That's to be expected." Rulaine checked his weapon, started toward the trail. "I just wish I knew if they're still alive."

Chapter Forty-Eight

SOUTHERN EXTENTS OF THE THIRD SILVER TOWER
BD +02 4076 TWO ("DISPARITY")

The water frothed and fumed above Ben Hwang before he broke the surface of the river. The streamlined compressor he held clenched in his teeth pulled free as the chop of the water buffeted him.

But a moment later, that turbulence was behind—or rather, beneath—Hwang and his three companions. The water-strider on whose back they had ridden rose up quickly, ascending toward the cone-trees clustered tightly along the eastern shore of the river.

W'th'vaathi, whose torso was adorned with four flat, multieyed fish that had affixed themselves to her respiratory ducts, gestured toward the stand of trees with a dripping tendril. "There we shall find the next boat that we have positioned for use along the river. With it, we shall reach the Silver Tower swiftly."

Gaspard spat out the air line from his own pony tank. "How quickly?"

"Half a day, several hours: it depends upon the wind as well as the current."

Ben shook his head. "Escaping interstellar pursuers by sailboat; this is madness. Do you truly think machines are so dangerous that it is better to live, and die, like this?"

W'th'vaathi's tendrils rolled in a waving fan that indicated the world around them. "We do not fear complex machines, but we only use them where necessary. As I explained, they are disruptive to our society."

"Technology is not evil," Mizuki murmured, shaking. Although

437

they had only traveled underwater for ten kilometers, it had felt much longer and the currents and cold had obviously bothered her wounds, particularly her reddened eye.

W'th'vaathi signaled agreement. "Indeed, objects cannot be evil. But they have an inducing power of their own, and for us, anything that circumvents natural processes and their tempos threatens to unravel biological balance. But let us turn to practical matters: we will resume travel most swiftly if you help me ready the boat."

Hwang strapped on his filter mask and followed W'th'vaathi beneath the canopy of a particularly large cone tree. A boat, its stepped mast affixed to the deck with some form of elbow joint, was hidden under what looked like a cross between cobwebs and Spanish moss. Several of the fibrous "boxes" that they had first encountered on Adumbratus were stacked next to it. "Equipment and provisions," W'th'vaathi explained as she set about removing the covering from the boat.

Gaspard looked at the slim hull, hands on hips. "You are sure we shall be safe, now?"

W'th'vaathi's neck oscillated. "Captain Riordan's plan did not merely allow us to escape, but should have convinced the attackers that we are dead. They did destroy the first boat which we were towing, and did not seek further along the river."

Hwang worked his pinky into a waterlogged and sound-deadened ear. Although they had towed the first boat almost two hundred meters behind them, the concussive and audial aftershocks had been painful, had staggered the water-strider beneath them. "We were underwater. How do we know they did not search further?"

"There are no alert or distress spores in this area, Benjamin Hwang. Had there been an intrusion by an unmarked foreign object, biological or otherwise, the sign would be thick around us." She waved two dismissive tendrils up beyond the canopy. "The local biota is unperturbed."

Gaspard still stood motionless. W'th'vaathi stopped unfastening the lashings which held the mast down. "You are disturbed, Ambassador."

Gaspard's fine jaw worked. "Can your spores, or any of your biota, tell you what happened further upriver?"

W'th'vaathi's tendrils wilted. "I have no way to ascertain the fate of your friends. Or of my people. I may only hope for the best."

"And what of the ship we heard overhead? You say your spores perceived it as marked, so it must have been our corvette. Is there any way to project its fate, based on its speed, or angle of descent?"

"Sadly, our spores do not register such information. Now: we must ready our boat."

Karam Tsaami glanced at the engineering board: a solid bank of red glared back at him. Not unexpected, but still depressing.

He looked out the canopy: the blue line on the horizon had become a white-flecked azure band, widening with every passing second.

Melissa Sleeman must have been watching his eyes. "Will we make it?"

"To the water? I think so, but that's no guarantee that we'll be able to slow this bucket enough to make a safe—"

"Karam, this is Tina. The reaction preheating chamber is going to go any second."

But, without any gauges left—? "How do you know?"

"It's starting to glow dull red."

Oh. "All right. Then here's what you and Phil are going to do with the severed coolant line. You've got to snug it into the engine trusses so that it's aiming straight at the chamber, and it's got to be secure enough to hold that position under pressure."

Tina's question arrived as a screech. "Under pressure from what?"

Phil Friel evidently saw where Karam was headed. "From coolant flow. Karam is going to open the registers again."

Tina did not become less shrill. "And flood the whole chamber with the remaining coolant?"

Karam didn't bother to keep his tone civil. "That's exactly what I'm going to do. Seal your suits; it's going to be pretty unpleasant"— *well, lethal*—"in there. Let me know when you've got it rigged."

"Harebrained scheme if I ever heard one," Tina grumbled as she worked.

"Might be," Karam admitted. "But we've got to cool that chamber down for just another minute, enough so that we can maintain thrust and not explode. You done yet?"

"Working."

"Damn, you two are slow."

"Shut up. There: we're finished."

"Good. Get in the equipment locker."

"Why?"

"Because I don't want you in the compartment when I uncork the remaining coolant on that line. The steam could melt straight through your gear."

"Okay, we're in the closet. Sort of."

"Tight fit," Phil agreed.

"Well, you two lovebirds make the most of it." Karam was gratified by what he presumed was their embarrassed silence. "Releasing the coolant in three, two, one; now—"

There was a slight tremor on the bridge. Evidently, the effect was much more noticeable back in the drive room. "Holy shit!" screamed Tina. "Sounds like a tornado out there."

"Banshees on steroids," Phil agreed. "But it's dying down already. Figure it will be safe to reenter in about four or five seconds?"

"Make it ten. But we'll reach the coast, now. Just strap in and stay handy."

"To do what?" Tina asked.

"Can't say just yet," Karam lied. *Because hopefully I won't have to ask one of you to take an even more insane risk before this is over.*

Sleeman breathed a sigh of relief as *Puller* cleared the coast-hugging foliage at one hundred meters altitude—then gasped as she was thrown forward against her straps. "What the hell—?"

"Just shifted one third of our thrust to our VTOL fans," Karam grunted. "They're in forward attitude to brake us. With any luck—"

But the onrushing blue horizon revealed that their luck had run out. Undetectable from their prior angle, the initial drop-off of the tidal shallows reversed itself, climbed up again to give birth to spray-wreathed rocks and a few small islands. Dragons teeth waiting to tear *Puller* apart. "Shit," announced Karam calmly.

Lymbery had seen it. "P-pivot on your fans," he stammered.

Damn it, the guy has good ideas when he's too busy to be scared. "Pivoting," Karam confirmed, reaching down and cutting the starboard fans back to ten percent. *Puller* groaned, lost altitude crookedly, but heeled starboard as she continued forward at a widening angle, her nose swinging away from the rocks. "Great idea, Morgan. We just might—"

"Critical overheat," Phil Friel's voice shouted at him. First time the calm Irishman had ever shouted, so Karam accepted his report as gospel: he shut the engines down.

"We're going in," he announced in as calm a voice as he could manage. "Strap in. Stay calm." The mandatory platitudes common to all imminent crashes.

Karam snapped on the bow's emergency attitude control thrusters—compressed gas canisters usually used spaceside when the main engines were off-line—and blew what little was left in them in one long, concentrated burst. That brought *Puller*'s nose up a bit, which gave her a little more glide, a little more time to dump airspeed.

The blue beneath them began lightening: shallows. That was good for getting out of *Puller* safely, but not good for putting her down in one piece: if they hit the bottom with any appreciable force—"Call out our final descent, Ms. Sleeman. Tongues away from your teeth, folks."

"Four meters, three, two—"

Melissa never got to "one," but Karam had expected that. With *Puller*'s nose still slightly raised, her stern hit first, creating a momentary sense of drag, as if someone had half depressed the emergency brake. Then a stomach jarring slam as the tortured ship's belly swung down flat against the water. *Come on*, thought Karam, *rise up*—

And for just a fraction of a second, they were seemingly weightless again. The view in the canopy showed the water drop away for a moment—

—and then they dug in hard, metal screeching and squealing and half of the secured objects coming loose and flying about the bridge. Karam heard the air come out of his lungs like a bellows as he slammed forward against the straps—but he was smiling, even as he felt his sternum wiggle uncomfortably: *made it. Hit the right contact angle and skipped the hull like a stone on a lake. Only one hop, but that's all we needed to surviv—*

"Karam." It was Phil Friel. Hushed but strident.

"Talk," Karam answered; *Puller* was now drifting through the water, listing to starboard, with waves lapping up its long narrow nose toward the bridge windows.

Friel's voice was low. "I've seen one wet ditch like this, with a hot power plant. I know what happens if this chamber floods all at once."

Shit. Just what I was afraid of. "Tina?"

"I shifted to a private circuit. This is you and me."

Jeez. Calm, unassuming Phil Friel can get all business when he has to. "I get it. But you can gradually flood the compartment if the inflow vents are still functioning—"

"They're not. I checked them as soon as I got out of my couch. I'm guessing that during the fight, the hit on our fuel tankage warped the valve housing. So I don't have any way to gradually cool the plant. Which will eventually blow on its own."

"Or shred itself and us if it's suddenly immersed in a rush of cold ocean water." *Damn it, I didn't want to have to ask this.* "Phil, I don't know how to say—"

"You don't have to say anything. Get Tina out of here. I can crank open the emergency depressurization vents. That will let the water in a bit at a time."

"Yeah, but don't stay a second longer than you have to."

"I have no intention of being parboiled, Karam. Now, get Tina out of here so I can get to work."

Karam watched the water edge up over the cockpit canopy, switched to the open circuit. "Tina?"

"Yeah?"

"We have to evacuate through the dorsal hatchway. You're closest; check it, make sure it's full-function, and pull the water-landing kits."

"I'm on it."

Lymbery and Sleeman were already at the bridge hatchway. Karam unstrapped, rose. His rueful and sardonic "Abandon ship" did not diminish the alacrity with which they entered the aft-leading corridor.

As they made their way back to the dorsal hatchway, *Puller* showed herself much worse for the wear. Lockers had sprung open, freshers were running and overflowing, access panels hung and swayed from both ceilings and bulkheads. But they reached the hatchway swiftly, helped Tina open it into a stiff breeze that mixed the smell of salt with that of musk.

"Where's Phil?" Tina asked as she handed up one of the inflatable rafts.

Karam handed the raft down to Sleeman. "He's coming." *Puller* had settled on the bottom just after the water had risen up over the top of the bridge windows. Lymbery was standing on the hull, just beyond the reach of the lapping wavelets.

Tina Melah frowned. "He should be here by now. What's he doing?"

"I asked him to secure the electronics," Karam lied. "If we're going to have any chance of raising this craft and flying her again, I can't have a systemwide shortout. We'll inflate a second raft, leave it behind for him."

Tina nodded as Sleeman and Lymbery avoided her eyes and inflated the second raft. As they clambered into their own slightly larger one, she glanced behind at the dorsal hatch.

Karam and Sleeman began paddling toward a small chip of rock that was almost an island. It actually had a single, wind-bent cone-tree on it. "I make that land about four hundred meters off," Karam commented conversationally, hoping to distract Tina.

But her eyes never left the stricken *Puller*. "Something's wrong," she murmured. "We should go ba—"

She was interrupted by a sudden plume of steam hissing up from *Puller*'s stern, like the spout of a gigantic, superheated whale. Except that this spout did not relent; it grew in volume and intensity as the water around the back of the ship growled and hissed.

Tina's eyes widened. She rounded on Karam. "You bastard. You left him behind to cool the plant—and die. You lying bastard."

Karam looked away. "Phil is a top hand at his job. If anyone can get himself out in time, it's him."

"Fuck you, you lying bastard. You made him—"

"Tina. He called me. He asked. He didn't want you to be in there. He—" Karam stopped: if she didn't already know that Friel was as quietly smitten with her as she was almost comically smitten with him, there was no point bringing it up now.

But Tina had turned from Karam to glare at the steam-spewing wreck of the *Puller*. "Well, Phil's a lying bastard, too." A single tear ran the length of her gracefully curved cheek. "A damned lying bastard."

Caine Riordan stumbled into the small glade he'd designated as Point Bug Out: the place where the survivors had stored their gear before dispersing to their various defensive positions. There was water here, and he'd need it if he was going to . . . to . . .

Suddenly, the sun was glinting directly down through the trees. Riordan discovered he was on his back, gasping. Couldn't breathe, despite the filter mask. He'd obviously lost consciousness and fallen, but couldn't remember it. And still couldn't breathe: his lungs worked, but his mask wasn't allowing in any air—

He pulled off the mask, drew in a breath: ragged, tight, insufficient, but he could feel his ability to reason returning. The smell of the environment rushed in at him as he sat up, turned the mask over to inspect the filter warning indicator: had the filters failed, clogged?

The indicator's small panel was still green. But whatever else was happening, it wasn't allowing air into his lungs. Protocol was to never crack the hermetic seal on the filter compartment, but the resulting contamination wasn't going to kill him any faster than outright suffocation and he had to get moving. No time for a better plan: he popped open the filter compartment.

The first thing he noticed was that the wires leading from the filter sensor to the indicator had been cut and reattached so that the sensor had no power and the indicator would always read green. In the next moment, he saw that the filters were resting low in the compartment, almost as if—

He pulled out the filters: they had been shaved to half thickness, and the back side of them, the part that was in contact with the native air, was caked with green mold. Riordan shuddered, tossed the mask away, felt nauseous: *there are a lot of ways to die, but betrayal by a friend, a teammate, may be the worst.*

So: the traitor had gotten hold of his filter mask at some point, sabotaged it. But when, and who? Caine tried to think back along the events of the past two weeks—

But couldn't. Possibly because he was still bleary from the pain and near-asphyxiation, but also because he was unable to still the contest between his most primitive impulse—*screw this; you've got to run now!*—and his rational impulse—*take a few seconds, because if you run into the traitor, you'd better know it.*

He closed his eyes, tried to push his mind past the fog that kept him from disciplining it.

But nothing. And even when he abandoned trying to figure out who had done this to him, he was too tired to think of any course of action, any plan, other than running as far and as fast as he could. The mind that had always been ready with options and alternatives was now just a froth of disorganized facts and memories. He kept trying to pull up a stratagem, a new approach to the current crisis, but it was like trying to draw water from a well that you could see was dry: no matter how many times you lowered the bucket, that repetitive act just didn't bring up any water. He tried to rise, discovered that his limbs were all at once heavy but somewhat insensate, wondered how long he'd been sitting, dazed.

The southern edge of the glade rustled. He turned in that direction, tried rising again, fell on his side, wheezing—as Keith Macmillan came bounding out of the bush, florid, shiny with sweat. He saw Caine, froze, then rushed over. "What the hell—? Where's your mask, Riordan? Are yuh daft? You'll—"

"It was killing me." Caine gestured toward where it lay in the low fronds. Macmillan stared, frowned; his teeth gritted. "Right. We've got to get you out of here, Caine."

"No. You can still run. Better if. We split. Up."

"Nonsense." Macmillan rushed over to the packs. "I'm traveling pretty light, now. Fired the rifle dry. Tossed it. Only weapons we have left are these bloody combitools." He grabbed one, snagged some rations as well. "Now let's get you moving."

Riordan knew he should reject the offer, order Keith to go on his own, but whatever part of his mind elevated rationality and duty by suppressing primal self-interest, failed. He tried to rise, did, then staggered and fell flat on his ass. *How dignified.*

Keith strode over quickly. "Here, I can help." He reached out a hand—but before Riordan could clasp it, Macmillan's thick paw grabbed his duty suit. His other arm slammed the combitool down into Caine's left tibia.

Pain shot up and outward from the shattered bone. Riordan vomited as he fell backward, the treetops spinning around his narrowed field of vision.

"Wh-why?" he asked the sky, since he could not see Macmillan and was sure that if he moved his head, he would vomit again.

Macmillan sounded like he might cry. "Because they might want you alive, damn it."

Caine seemed to dip down into and then rise up out of a heavy, hot fog; he wondered if he had blacked out momentarily. "No—why, why betray us? Betray Earth? You're—you're IRIS."

"I'm a father before I'm anything else, Caine. And I wish it was me lying there. I surely, bitterly do." His voice was choked, may have stifled a sob.

Riordan rolled his head around, fought through the pain to frame a question. "What do you mean, a father?"

Macmillan rose, listened for something in the bush, then crouched back down. "This time last year, I was just a highly trained grunt from Dundee with a wife and a daughter in Aberdeen. I'd been sent to Australia during the war. I was security for where the Dornaani were being stashed; we called it Spookshow Prime. That was where I met Downing and Rinehart, heard about you, was recruited into IRIS to be backup security to Sigma Draconis. But I was granted leave, first."

Macmillan's voice became thick. "There were no external communications at Spookshow Prime, so the first I knew of my daughter's leukemia was when I walked through the door to surprise my family." He choked, went on. "Quite a surprise. She'd been a solid little tomboy when I left; less than half a year later, she was a wee ghost of a thing. 'A highly aggressive and unusual subvariety,' they said of the leukemia."

He spat. "It was their way of saying they'd never seen its like before. And I found out soon enough why they hadn't. First time I took Katie for one of her follow-ups and treatments, some unctuous bastard of a suit sidled up to me in the waiting room. 'It's a shame so many of the children here don't have a chance,' he says. 'How fortunate that your daughter does.' I stared at him, because it was the only alternative to beating him senseless. And that's when he put the hook in: he had a treatment. Highly effective, he said. Almost miraculously so."

Macmillan ground his fingers together until they were white on the handle of the combitool. "I knew what I was agreeing to. But I would have done anything for my little Katie. Anything. And by the time I left, she was running around the house like a wild thing, once again." He smiled and tears ran down his face. "Complete remission, they said. A miracle, they called it." He looked at Riordan. "These people—whoever or whatever has infiltrated and infected CoDevCo and other megacorporations—are bloody monsters. There's nothing they won't do." He stood, wielded the combitool, stared at Caine for several seconds. "Since the regret of a damned man isn't worth a pin, I can only offer you one thing you might value."

"What's that?"

"I can kill you, make it look like I had no choice. Better that than—"

The ferns on the southern side of the glade whispered apart: Pandora Veriden emerged from between the leaves, frowning. "You bastard. You fucking bastard," she whispered. Riordan wasn't sure whether she was cursing at Macmillan's perfidy, or annoyance at her own inability to sneak up on him silently.

Macmillan stood. "Guilty as charged, Ms. Veriden." He studied her, saw what Caine had noticed immediately as well: she no longer had her rifle. The flaps of her bandolier were all open; she too, had shot her weapon dry. Without turning back toward Caine, he strode steadily, even grimly in her direction.

And stopped when a water strider crashed into the clearing from the east, evidently having followed Caine's path. The huge creature surveyed the tableau, snuffled in Caine's direction, emitted a vaguely distressed grunt.

Riordan knew that Veriden was fast but had never realized just how fast: before Macmillan had recovered from his surprise, she had sprinted to the strider, bumped into its leg. It was startled but did not flinch away as Dora remained in contact with, and seemed to rub herself against, that faintly shaggy leg. Then she darted toward the survival packs.

But Macmillan jumped to interpose himself between that source of combitools and Dora. She shied back, tried circling around to get at them; he shifted with her, slipped the hammer covering off his tool. Now he had an axe.

Dora glanced at it. "You're crazy if you think they're going to let you live."

"Who?"

"Whoever bought you, asshole. You think you can get rid of us and return home as the sole survivor of the legation? That you alone, Ishmael, have lived to tell the tale? Bullshit: you're a loose end. They're going to snip you off."

"Maybe so, maybe not. They may have other uses for me. Hardly matters, though. My Katie is cured. Nothing else—"

Veriden feinted left, lunged right toward the handle of the closest combitool. But Macmillan was quicker than he looked, too; the axe head swept around so fast that it whistled. Veriden had to bend back sharply at the waist to avoid it. She danced away; he sidestepped warily forward.

Veriden studied Macmillan carefully, then glanced at Riordan, who saw that, in a split second of partial distraction, she was computing odds, making a decision. She dodged in toward Macmillan, who swung at her again, but missed more widely. Eyes narrowed, calculating, she studied the big Scotsman closely. Then she glanced over at Caine, nodded briefly, and darted for the tree line on the west side of the glade.

Whatever Macmillan had been expecting, it obviously had not been that. Looking quickly from the leaves shuddering where Veriden had plunged through them, and where Caine lay wheezing and bloody, he grimaced. "Bollocks," he muttered and turned to sprint after Dora.

Riordan felt as though he might vomit again, pushed that feeling away, looked around. What could he do? He had no weapons and he couldn't flee anymore. Maybe he could hide—?

He turned toward the northeast edge of the glade. The group had scouted this site quickly—they'd had little chance to do otherwise—but there were two bumbershoots which had fallen, side by side, just inside that tree line, with a sizable depression between them. Riordan frowned: the chance that an enemy would fail to detect him there was next to zero—

He angrily dismissed that thought: there was no other plan. *And odds that are* slightly *better than zero are, well, better than zero.*

Gritting his teeth against the pain of dragging his broken left tibia behind him, Riordan began to crawl the ten meters toward the fallen bumbershoots.

Chapter Forty-Nine

Dora Veriden sprinted hard for the far inland clearing where Riordan had sent Nasr Eid to stand watch on that flank. *Most likely to keep him out of the way of people who can stand up in a fight.* But now, Eid—and what he was overseeing—might just be her salvation.

Well, that and Macmillan's physical condition. He was a big man, but beefy; a bear, not a tiger. And she could outrun a bear. All day long, if she needed to. But she didn't have all day.

She stopped, caught her breath, listened. Yes, there was Macmillan, bashing his way through the brush, following the trail she was carefully leaving for him to follow. *Keep running, big guy; keep pushing and sweating and gasping.* She angled away from Eid's position: *can't get there too soon. Have to make sure Macmillan is exhausted first. So let's you and I take the scenic route, you traitorous asshole.*

Dora stretched her almost disproportionately long legs into an easy, deerlike stride. As she ran, she chose her path by the terrain: first a patch of rough ground, then a large clearing—*yeah, you'll see that and try to make up the distance between us by sprinting.* She stopped again, listened for Macmillan's approach, heard it faintly. *He's less tired than I thought; probably got a little stamina back when he was talking with Riordan. Well, you'll be running out of that second wind any time now. And you can't afford to let me go, can you? Not only would that displease your masters, but knowing your story, I might pop up on Earth someday, surrounded*

449

by Slaasriithi diplomats, and ruin you. Or your sacred memory, if the bastards who hired you clean up their loose ends.

Dora swung back toward the clearing where Nasr Eid was waiting. Or rather, where he was supposed to be waiting. *Either way, though, that little glade is the ace up my sleeve.* From the start, she had been worried that the unknown traitor might become active once the attackers arrived. So she had not gone immediately when Riordan had sent them to their first defensive positions, but had lagged behind, had heard Caine instruct Nasr "to watch a large clearing that is on our other flank—and you'll have some local help." Intrigued, she had stayed around long enough to learn about the nature of that local help. And now she was very glad that she had.

Macmillan's thumping progress was a bit louder. *Good; spend yourself.* She picked up the pace: she'd need a few extra minutes to locate Nasr and set her plan in motion.

She scanned for anything that would serve as a reasonable weapon as she ran, but was disappointed: no serviceable rocks amongst the few she passed, and the plants on this planet did not tend toward hardwoods with heavy branches or shoots. No crude clubs or spears lying ready to hand, therefore.

As she neared the clearing, she called out to Nasr, concerned that if she approached too quietly, he'd be startled, let out a shout, and ruin *everything.*

Eid responded, rising up from the blind that the convectorae has fashioned for him. "Ms. Veriden, what has happened? I have heard much shooting and then—"

"The battle is not over yet, but it will be soon. You only have to do one thing."

Eid visibly shivered. "And what is that?"

"Run through the bait zone."

Nasr turned, eyed the winding path she had indicated. "I am not sure if—"

"Nasr, have the Slaasriithi biomarkings ever failed to work? And you got a special dose from Unsymaajh, so you are perfectly safe. So what I want you to do is run down that path"—she took his arm, both leading him in that direction and blending the tracks she was leaving with his—"and keep running. As far and as fast as you can." *That's probably what you're best at, from what I've seen.*

"But what good does—?"

"Just do it." He looked uncertain. Time to change the incentive. "Nasr, if you do this, it's a near-certainty that you'll survive this battle."

Eid's eyes widened. He turned and raced down the path, flinching as he traversed the bait ground. Which of course, elicited no response, thanks to Unsymaajh's marking.

Dora retraced her progress, backed up by stepping into each of the tracks she had made just before. When she drew alongside a thick patch of foliage, she took a wide sideways step off the path, ensuring that the first footprint she made in leaving her prior tracks was obscured behind a sizable frond. She moved carefully into the taller growth, checking to make sure she left no obvious trace of her exit from the main trail. Paralleling it, she crept to a position seven meters back from the bait ground. Once there, she lowered herself into a sprinter's crouch, calmed her breathing, and listened.

She didn't have long to wait. Macmillan, thrashing his way through the closely spaced bushes and fronds, was audible fifty meters away. At thirty he slowed, then stopped. *Probably sees the clearing up ahead. Figuring out how he wants to approach it.* Which prompted Dora to review what she knew of her adversary: a career soldier, tough, smart, a little past his prime, probably chosen for the legation because despite a few extra pounds, he had absolute determination. And, they had probably thought, absolute integrity. But whatever his fitness or ethical flaws might be, he was a dangerous opponent: quick reflexes, even if he wasn't a particularly fast runner, and daunting upper body strength coupled with some kind of martial arts training. But, looking at his build, she eliminated a variety of styles of self-defense: anything that required extreme flexibility of the torso, or that relied heavily on kicking, was unlikely. He was too heavily built for the first, and didn't have the leg snap for the latter. Which, together with his exhaustion, determined her tactics.

Pandora Veriden was not accustomed to being surprised; indeed, she prided herself on not being subject to that reaction. Consequently, she was not only alarmed but annoyed when she heard a dried frond snap very nearby. Rather than turn her head, she moved her eyes in that direction.

Keith Macmillan had clearly seen her path, but had been cautious in following it; he was paralleling it four meters to the right.

Which would bring him within three meters of where she was crouching. *Damn it; can I take him here? In this thicket? Can't tell. Just gotta wait and see what he does.*

Macmillan, surprisingly stealthy, was unable to fully conceal his labored breathing as he approached and passed within two meters of where Dora was crouched behind a fan-shaped fern. He stopped a meter further on. Dora could see his feet under the lowest leaf covering her: he was still facing further along the trail she had made—well, the one Nasr Eid had made at her behest. Which meant he was looking at the tight foliage hemming in the bait ground.

She waited, ignored the sweat running down from her brow, her armpits. *Okay, Macmillan, so you're trying to calculate if that brush is so thick that it would obstruct a surprise attack, prevent an ambush. And you're balancing that against your tactical training and instincts: to never take an apparently unavoidable path. But the clock is ticking, you're exhausted, and if you don't have my head on a stake when you meet your masters—*

Macmillan slipped out of the undergrowth and back on to the trail, glancing at the scattered leaves and bent fronds that marked Nasr's passage. Decided, he hefted his combitool and moved forward quickly, entering the bait ground.

Macmillan got three meters farther along the path before a thin, shrill keening rose around him. Surprised, puzzled, he stopped, lifted the axe—

And was suddenly at the center of a cloud of what looked like flying, fanged salamanders with far too many eyes. Landing in his hair, on his florid face and arms, they began biting, darting off, flying back in for another mouthful. Macmillan swung the axe fruitlessly—

Despite the uneven ground and obtruding foliage, Dora sprinted the twelve yards separating them in just over four seconds. He clearly heard something behind him; he'd half turned when her flying kick hit him like a jackhammer, dropping him. She rolled up, backed away—and was surprised at how fast Macmillan recovered. But he was being swarmed by flying, biting salamanders, and Dora was not. A few ventured near her but, upon coming closer—particularly where she'd rubbed up against the water-strider—they shied away with an annoyed snap of their translucent wings. Macmillan feinted with the axe; she backed up a step, but did not watch his eyes, or even his elbows. Peripherally, her attention was riveted on his feet: where and when he committed to an attack with an axe would be decisively signaled by his stance.

Macmillan was sly; he shuffle-stepped. But Dora had been in far too many melees to be fooled; the arch of his first foot remained high when his toes hit the ground, a physical sign that this was not to be his last step.

He swung, missed, planted his feet as he pulled back the axe to swing again.

Gotcha.

With Macmillan's body twisted away, the axe still cocking back for a lethal blow, Dora jumped in with a side-kick that punched directly into her opponent's kneecap. He yowled, faltered; she let split-second instinct inform her that there was no ruse in either, and followed with the hardest spinning roundhouse she could deliver. *An idiot attack, really, unless you know—know—you have the time to deliver it.* At which point, it was like hitting your adversary with a sledgehammer.

Which was the result. With his knee already buckling at an unnatural angle, the kick caught Macmillan in the ribs. Two snaps—one small and reedy, the other heavier—accompanied the impact. Dora both grimaced and grinned: *lost my little toe; he lost his ribs. I'll take the trade.*

Macmillan had also lost the grip on his weapon; Veriden kicked it away. When he brought his head up—eyes desperate, pleading—she gauged his probable reach, danced to the outside of his left arm and front-kicked him square in the face. He went back with a grunt, his eyes unsteady. *Good*, she thought, pushing away some of her sweaty hair. *Now, to get permanent control of the situation—*

The howl of pain with which Macmillan came back to his senses was sure to call down his employers, so Dora made her speech quickly. "So how's it feel having a freshly broken leg, bitch?"

Macmillan's face was a rictus of pain; his left tibia was not merely broken, but splintered. A tooth of bone peeked through the savage wound.

"So here's what I want to know, loving father: when your leash-holders come and find their dog laid out, immovable, what do you think they're going to do? Take you back so you can lick your wounds in their kennel?"

"Don't care," Macmillan groaned. "Did this. For. Katie."

"Yeah, well, I hope it was worth it. You've killed a lot of good people. Well, I've got to get going; don't want to be here when your owners show up and find I've lamed their bitch." She turned and darted out the other side of the bait ground, his curses following her. She ran until he was completely out of sight, then doubled back and padded toward her first ambush point, but further into the woods, virtually invisible behind the canopy of a small cone-tree.

Dora only had to wait two minutes before she saw the first signs of the attackers: movement in the brush on the eastern side of the glade. Meaning they had probably not found Riordan; if they had stumbled across that first clearing, they would have seen and followed the trail that she and Macmillan had left. In which case they would have entered this glade from the north.

It was another minute before two clones emerged, sweeping the tree line with their weapons, then staring at the occasional winged newt-gators that landed on Macmillan, took a savage tear at his flesh, and flew off again. The Scotsman, between swatting them away and occasional groans, produced and choked down a mix of pills that looked like painkillers and the amphetamines that Riordan had been popping.

After walking the perimeter of the clearing and detecting where Dora's and Macmillan's tracks had entered it, the clones waved an all-clear. Four more figures entered the open space.

Dora did not even have to think about identifying their leader. His weapon, a liquimix Jufeng, marked his status as clearly as his height and distinctive facial features: angular, with prominent cheekbones and a high forehead. Not only taller than the clones, he had the tigerlike build of a decathlete on steroids. The clones hung at his heels, alert to his commands, like a pack of hounds following a hunter.

The leader approached Macmillan, gestured for him to be pulled beyond the ready reach of his winged tormentors, looked down at the broken man.

"You are Macmillan." It was a statement that bordered on a question as he assessed the man's shattered leg. "You have been bested in a fight. And you have failed in your mission."

Macmillan gasped out responses through his pain. "I carried out the instructions I decrypted from the file that your people added to my palmtop, the one that was in my coldcell. I got rid of the first saboteur after he crippled the Slaasriithi ship. I sabotaged the group as best I could down here, made their leader sick—"

"Not so sick that he couldn't mount a disappointingly effective defense. Well, let us call it a delaying action. The automated weapons platform we found. It was of Slaasriithi manufacture?"

"Yes. They brought it up about an hour before you arrived. There was no way for me to—"

"Failure is failure," the leader decreed. "I understand what you attempted to do: cripple them, yet keep them together so we could easily locate and exterminate them."

"Yes, after *you* failed to take care of them in orbit and the legation split up. After that, I had no way of getting the job done myself. There were too many survivors planetside, and Riordan and Veriden were both dangerous enough on their own. No opportunity arose where I could be sure of killing one without the other being aware that I had done it. And then I would have had to kill the second one and finish off all the other survivors. So I did the one thing that ensured they would all be destroyed: I remained with them. So I could be your beacon."

"You mean, so we could do your job. Typical low breed."

"No, damn it. Think it through: you had the necessary force to do the entire job with no chance of failure. I was one against many and not well-armed. Besides, the longer we were here, the more the wildlife seemed to—well, adopt Riordan. I think he may be—"

"Silence. I am even less interested in your hypotheses than I am in your excuses. I agree that your concept was reasonable, but it did not succeed. There is nothing more to be said. The agreement you made was a favor for a favor. You have failed to deliver your favor to us. We shall now fail to deliver ours to you."

Despite the pain, Macmillan heard the floating, generalized tone in the leader's voice. "You already *have* delivered my favor."

"Have we? Our factotum was overly generous, or careless, then. We shall correct this."

Macmillan stared at the tall man. "You have no idea what deal I made, do you?" When the man's decisiveness faltered for one crucial second, Macmillan jumped in. "You're not even connected to the people who hired me."

The leader shrugged. "You are relatively insightful, for an Aboriginal. No, I 'stole' you from the factors who originally suborned you. But I assure you that the favor was not complete. That is not how we operate."

"You're lying. I saw it myself. My daughter was cured of cancer." The certainty of Macmillan's words were undercut by the tense, desperate uncertainty in his voice.

"Oh, I'm sure she was cured—for a while. But upon returning to Earth, you would have discovered that without further service to us, she would have sickened again. And so we would own you permanently. This is our way. It has been so for many thous—for a very long time."

Macmillan tried to lunge at the leader from his hopeless position on the ground; he didn't even reach the toe of the other man's boot. "You bastards. You right fucking bastards."

The leader shouldered his weapon, waved a clone over to him. "For us family is strength. For you, it is a weakness. We recognize family—indeed, all affiliation—for what it is: an enabler of dominion, a path to power. But you confuse family bonds with love, sacrifice, and desperate tears of hope and joy." He held out his hand for the waiting clone's Pindad assault rifle, leveled it at Macmillan. "And so you are, inevitably, the architects of your own misguided miseries."

Macmillan could not physically reach the leader, but now, his spittle did. "I should have killed the sniveling bastard who offered me the deal a year ago."

The leader stared at the saliva on the leg of his duty suit. "Yes, I suppose you should have." With strange—inhuman—speed, he raised the Pindad and fired once. A small hole appeared in Macmillan's forehead; the big man slumped over.

Despite herself, despite the many horrors she had seen in many parts of the world, Dora sucked in her breath sharply at the calm barbarity of the scene just concluded.

The leader paused, chin raising—then turned in her general direction.

She was too well-trained to flinch back; if any part of her was exposed, he was more likely to detect movement than discriminate her shape from the surrounding foliage. She remained frozen, felt sweat run down her back.

The leader turned back to the clones, gave hasty orders: they arranged themselves into an open formation and headed toward the trail that would lead them back to the first clearing.

Back to Caine.

Chapter Fifty

SOUTHERN EXTENTS OF THE THIRD SILVER TOWER and FAR ORBIT
BD +02 4076 TWO ("DISPARITY")

Caine Riordan awakened with a gasp, struggling for air, couldn't get his lungs to expand enough. Frantic, he grasped about, hitting the two fallen logs on either side with his elbows. And then the sun went away. Alarmed, he looked up.

The water-strider that had entered the glade a minute—an hour?—ago was standing over him, crouching down. Having become accustomed to the creatures during the days of travel down the river, Riordan felt a strange sensation of relief, almost as if a friendly dog had trotted over to check on his well-being. *Strange, the bonds we forge—*

Then the sun was back; the water-strider had risen abruptly, rotated towards the west side of the clearing. Something was coming from that direction; Caine could hear it too, albeit faintly.

The water-strider spread its legs in a stance Riordan had observed during their occasional dominance tests; a kind of four-legged sumo come-and-get-me posture. *Oh Christ, no, you poor beast; you can't hope to—*

The water-strider turned slightly. The two full eyes on its right side, both the one above and below the jaw, gazed steadily at him. The creature emitted a low, mewling grunt—a sound of affection between water-striders—and backed up a step, its rear legs just clearing the far side of the two thick logs between which Riordan was coffined. Then it turned to face the west again.

A babble of voices speaking in a mishmash of English and Javanese-accented *behasa* grew, then quickly stilled as they

457

entered the clearing. Caine rose up high on one elbow, a broad leaf concealing everything but his eye.

Five clones and one other person had entered the treeless expanse—and the hair on the nape of Riordan's neck rose: that other person was not a human. Not a terrestrial human; that was a Ktor. The angular features, the build, the strange, almost archaic habits of speech, and above all, the aura of imperious disdain for his soldiers, made his identity as clear as if he had been wearing a sign on his back. *But what the hell are* you *doing out here, with Optigene clones—?*

The six spread out into a broad arc, the leader at the center, keeping slightly greater distance from the water-strider. Overhead, Caine could not only smell, but almost feel, a strong release of musk from the creature. Was it fear? Aggression? Dismay?

It peaked when the humans approached to twenty meters. The water-strider swiftly raised its long, graceful back-sails. Suddenly limned in orange bioluminescence, they shuddered as the creature released a long ululating hoot, both from its spine-paralleling respiratory ducts and its steam-shovel mouth. The humans stopped and raised their weapons.

God, no—

The water-strider stamped one wide foot, made to move forward—

The clones unleashed a stream of automatic fire into the body of the creature, which ducked, writhed, bucked—but neither charged nor fled. Nor did it fall; the Pindads, while effective weapons, were not elephant guns. The wounds they were inflicting would no doubt eventually prove mortal, but "eventually" might mean hours or even days.

The Ktor stepped forward, adjusted the Jufeng dustmix battle rifle, raised it, fired a single shot. Riordan knew from the sound what settings he'd chosen: semiautomatic fire, maximum propellant per shot, and expanding warheads.

The water-strider shuddered under the extraordinary impact of that round, which did approximate that of an elephant gun. As the stricken creature tried to right itself, the Ktor fired the Jufeng as steadily as the relentless pulse of a metronome.

After the fifth shot, the swaying water-strider exhaled heavily; its knees unlocked, bent, and the huge body started falling— directly toward Caine.

Who thought, *better this way than at the hands of that bastard Ktor.* The falling trunk of the water-strider rushed down, growing along with blackness of its widening shadow.

Which swallowed him.

Jesel checked his weapon after waving two of the clones over to inspect the body of the ungainly beast he had just slain. Perhaps a tooth would make a good trophy? No; there wasn't the time—

"Leader, the targets must have used this as a staging area. Note their packs."

"Yes," Jesel replied but wasn't really listening. This entire attack had gone miserably awry. There were still at least three or four Aboriginals unaccounted for. At the clearing there were signs that one had run further west. That could have been the one that had crippled Macmillan or a different one. Two of the humans that had skirmished with them during their approach and Pyrrhic assault had been silenced, but their bodies had not been located. There was no way of knowing if other humans had been on hand for what he had to assume was the complete annihilation of Pehthrum's riverside flanking attack. The only reasonable option was to return to the shuttle and risk nap-of-earth flight to scan for fleeing Aboriginal biosigns. Since they were no longer packed in among Slaasriithi signatures, they could now be hunted down one by one. It might be dangerous to stay that long, but if he returned with so profound a failure to report—

The first impact was so sharp and forceful that Jesel was on the ground even before he was aware he'd been hit. He rolled over, grasping for his weapon, saw a red crater of mashed gray snakes where the left side of his abdomen had been. He tried to control the blood flow, tried to make sense of what was happening.

He watched three of his clones go down: one round into each center of mass. So: a counterattack by professionals. Incapacitating each and then—

The last two clones, the ones that had been inspecting the dead water-strider, bounded deeper into the bush. *Cowards,* he wished he could shout after them, but he had to conserve his strength, focus his senses.

The fire was coming from the south edge of the clearing. He brought up his rifle, switched the propellant feed to fifty percent, the rate of fire to two hundred rounds per minute, swung it toward the bushes—

And fell back heavily, his neck and head riddled by eight-millimeter Colt Browning jacketed expanders.

Bannor Rulaine rose up, hand-motioned Peter Wu to circle around the clearing while staying within the tree line. Now to get the two clones who had—

A short stutter of gunfire from yet another eight-millimeter CoBro sent Bannor diving into the loam. It was usually a friendly sound, but today, that didn't prove anything.

However, the small, limping silhouette that emerged from the northwest edge of the glade near the survival kits confirmed everything that Bannor could have hoped for: Miles O'Garran.

"Are we clear?" Rulaine asked, keeping his prone position, but crabbing around until he was covering the southeast end of the glade. "Always watch your back" was an axiom by which he lived, and had survived.

"Far as I know," answered Dora Veriden, who emerged behind O'Garran.

Wu leaned out of the brush. "Bad landing?" he asked the pint-sized SEAL.

"I've had worse," O'Garran replied. "Can't remember when, though."

Bannor rose up on one knee. "We're going to have a hell of a time finding everyone."

"If anyone else is left," Wu amended faintly.

"Yeah, there's that."

"Look, guys, let's save our own lives first." Dora threw a hand up toward the sky. "This can't be all of them. I'm pretty sure some beat feet back toward their shuttle."

"They did." Bannor felt a smile bending his mouth, a smile that his first DI had told him would terrify any human under the age of fourteen. "They aren't going anywhere."

Dora's smile wasn't any more heart-warming. "Oh. Good. And by the way," she added, glancing at the dead Ktor, "lucky timing."

"Not luck," Wu corrected. "First we heard a shot, much farther inland." He pointed west. "We were heading there when this area started sounding like New Year's in Taipei. We just followed the sound of trouble."

But Veriden was no longer listening; she was pacing around the glade, searching, frowning. "Where's Riordan?"

Wu crossed the clearing to the northeast corner. "He was here?" He looked, saw the discarded filter mask.

Veriden looked up. "Yeah, I think—"

Wu saw a faint impression in the ground cover, a spatter of vomit, and, looking more closely, a faint trail of broken or bent ferns that led out of the clearing and straight toward—

Wu stood up sharply. "Everyone. We are going to need some help."

"Help doing what?" Rulaine asked.

"Lifting this dead water-strider."

Nezdeh Srina Perekmeres already knew what Zurur Deosketer would report: "Still no reply on the lascom from the strike team."

Nezdeh leaned back in her command chair, watched the two new cannonballs race to fill the orbital gap above the assault zone. Jesel's shuttle had signaled a safe landing three and a half hours ago. Fifteen minutes later, her sensors had picked out the thermal flare of the supposedly destroyed human corvette, performing what might well have been a suicidal maneuver that brought it briefly over the same zone. And then they had waited. And waited.

Nezdeh suppressed a sigh, turned toward Idrem, who was no longer at gunnery. He was here for counsel and, though she dared not even admit it to herself, for comfort. "Jesel has failed."

"It seems so."

"It was wise that we did not equip them with any of our technology. It would have fallen into the Aboriginals' hands."

Idrem nodded carefully. "The Terrans have been denied access to any conclusively incriminating evidence or advanced knowledge."

"You are guarded in your words, Idrem."

"I am hesitant to consider our exposure fully controlled. There are two corpses planetside whose genelines were on the threshold of Elevation. Their genetics will yield much to sustained examination."

Nezdeh frowned. "Agreed. But what options do we have? We could fire a missile spread in an attempt to obliterate that evidence, but that presumes that the Slaasriithi do not have unrevealed planetary defense batteries, in addition to their drone ships. We might achieve nothing other than blatantly bombarding their world."

"This is true." Idrem nodded. "And I concur that the Slaasriithi, while reluctant to deploy offensive systems, seem quite ready to commit their defensive technologies. I suspect we do not have enough missiles to saturate the assault zone and eliminate the spoor of Jesel's assault team."

"So you agree that we must live with the marginal exposure that has occurred?"

Tegrese Hreteyarkus interrupted from her station at gunnery. "We do have one nuclear weapon," she pointed out.

Nezdeh and Idrem exchanged surprised, then carefully neutral glances. Nezdeh turned toward Tegrese. "We are in a system adjacent to the Slaasriithi homeworld. We have trodden a terribly fine line between plausible deniability and overt responsibility for the attacks here. And you would have us 'correct' the faint evidence of our possible presence with a nuclear weapon?"

Tegrese looked away, her jaw bunching. "I merely mentioned the option."

Nezdeh turned away, did not want Tegrese to see what might be in her eyes at this moment: the ruthless calculation behind her unbidden thought, *She might have to be liquidated; she is worse than the males of this House. And she is only of a subsidiary gene line.* Nezdeh shifted her attention to the holosphere. "Ulpreln."

"Yes, Nezdeh."

"Plot a rendezvous with the *Arbitrage*. We are done here."

PART FIVE

October 2120–February 2121

Chapter Fifty-One

THE THIRD SILVER TOWER
BD +02 4076 TWO ("DISPARITY")

Ben Hwang leaned away from where Caine Riordan lay among, and in some cases fused with, a bewildering array of biots, all presided over by two small but efficient medical monitors. He stepped away from the living bed in which his friend was held, shook his head as the transparent osmotic membrane-dome lowered back down and sealed seamlessly into the rim of the cushion.

Etienne Gaspard hovered near the entry of the room. "Well, Dr. Hwang?"

Hwang shook his head. "I can't tell much. I'm not a medical doctor, and I've only had a day to absorb the details on half of what they're using to keep him alive. And they won't explain the other half. 'Culturally destabilizing technology,' they call it."

"Yes, yes, but will he recover?" Gaspard stepped closer, glancing up into the soaring, asymmetrical ceiling that was typical of the chambers within the Third Silver Tower. Seeing it the first time, Hwang had wondered if Gaudí had been coached by the Slaasriithi when he was building *La Sagrada Família*. At any rate, Hwang didn't want to answer Gaspard's question.

"Doctor, will Riordan recover; yes or no?"

Hwang turned to look the ambassador in the eyes. "Etienne, he's dying. There's too much compromised tissue, too little respiratory capacity. I wish I had the skill, the knowledge, to help him—but I don't."

Gaspard nodded curtly. "Then I shall talk to those who do. Forcibly." He turned on his heel, stalked toward the exit.

Hwang stared after him.

The Silver Towers, the cognitive hive of Slaasriithi life, were also renowned for their serenity, their simplicity. The Towers were objects, yes. They depended upon, and functioned as, machines, yes. But that was why such pains had been taken to create them as artifacts that invoked ancient feelings of safety and repose. They soared up beyond where predators might threaten, presenting adamantine walls to the world while, within, their chambers strove gracefully upward toward the sky.

But serenity was in short supply in the Third Silver Tower, Mriif'vaal reflected sadly as he entered the neoaerie. From the moment that Yiithrii'ah'aash's shift-carrier had been attacked in orbit, and the human survivors had landed in the reaches overseen by the Tower, its many halls and chambers had been in comparative turmoil. Calls for urgent decisions on urgent matters—a rarity in themselves—had flooded in at an increasing rate. And then in the last forty-eight hours—

Another orbital attack. An atmospheric intrusion. Requests for help and consequent protocol challenges. Consultations with the First Silver Tower. Responses and debates. Transfers of equipment and authority. Bloody battle. And now a collection of bedraggled and bruised humans, their eyes furtive and cautious, dwelling within the Third Silver Tower like so many truant predators, uncertain of what they should trust, if anything. It was most unsettling, Mriif'vaal admitted wearily.

But when the neoaerie's spore-transfer ducts wafted the approach of W'th'vaathi and Thnessfiirm, he signaled his receptivity. They, of all Slaasriithi, were the most knowledgeable about the humans and had the most right to make inquiries or reports, given the harrowing days they had just lived through.

To Mriif'vaal's right, Hsaefyrr gestured subtly with one tendril tip when the pair appeared in the entrance. "Note the cerdor, Thnessfiirm. She appears distressed."

Mriif'vaal allowed that "distressed" was a charitable description. Thnessfiirm evinced more than the typical quick motions and eager activity of her taxon; she seemed ready to tremble. Her sensor cluster did not merely move swiftly, but abruptly; gone was the smooth steadiness of a neurologically healthy cerdor. Her neck skin was haggard and her pelt beginning to tuft, in patches. Mriif'vaal grieved her obvious distress, greeted the two with a greater measure of affinity and empathy spores as they arrived at the Ratiocinator's Ring and sat.

"I am most gratified to see you, W'th'vaathi and Thnessfiirm. I trust you are recovering from your ordeal."

W'th'vaathi's sensor cluster angled briefly toward Thnessfiirm. "I do not believe I may call *my* experience of the last days an ordeal, Senior Ratiocinator. Not in comparison to my companion."

If Thnessfiirm had any reaction to, or had even registered, the conversation thus far, she gave no indication of it. She seemed intent on gazing up into the soaring heights of the neoaerie.

W'th'vaathi settled into the framed stool that Slaasriithi preferred as chairs. "Mriif'vaal, I have a—a difficulty to report."

Mriif'vaal's tendrils were a soothing current of invitation. "Please do so."

"I speak without preamble, though much might be wanted. In short, the human ambassador Gaspard has learned that we have a cure for Caine Riordan's condition."

Mriif'vaal peripherally noticed Hsaefyrr's sensor cluster rotate toward W'th'vaathi and remain focused there. "And how did the human ambassador learn of this?"

"I alluded to it in a conversation, Senior Ratiocinator. During the final leg of our journey here, he asked me to confirm my earlier assurance that we had cures for Caine Riordan's affliction. I answered that we did. He specifically followed by asking if we were certain that our cures would be sufficient to deal with a condition as severe and advanced as Captain Riordan's."

Mriif'vaal resisted the impulse to retract his sensor cluster sharply. "And you answered in the affirmative?"

"Not precisely, but I assured him that there were several different therapies we could apply, and that our records indicated that the strongest of them was efficacious against the spores which afflicted Riordan. Even unto the last hours of a human's life."

Mriif'vaal closed his many eyes. W'th'vaathi was skilled and a fast learner. However, the skill of dissembling—even in so small a degree as prudently keeping one's silence, or electing not to share crucial information—was always difficult for Slaasriithi to acquire, no matter their taxon, no matter their role. "This places us in a difficult position," he admitted to W'th'vaathi.

W'th'vaathi's voice was surprisingly firm in reply. "With all due regard, Senior Ratiocinator, we are complicit. The humans requested, on multiple occasions, stronger and faster intervention on our part. And we did nothing."

Mriif'vaal waved two tendrils in temporizing agreement. "There are always casualties, even amongst the most deserving, when contention erupts, W'th'vaathi. It is one of the great truths which has driven our evolution away from the conflicts you witnessed in these past days."

"Yes, but I wonder if Yiithrii'ah'aash will feel similarly. The humans were our guests here, invited explicitly to this planet. Although their misfortunes may illuminate and underscore the benefits of our evolutionary path, that does not absolve us from having failed to intervene in a timely fashion." She paused. "I presume you are also aware of how strongly, and uniquely, Caine Riordan is marked."

Mriif'vaal was quiet. "And the human ambassador is also aware of Riordan's atypical marking?"

"Yes, and it has emboldened him. He is adamant that we save the captain or, to quote Mr. Gaspard, 'the relations between our two species may be strained to such a point where they cannot be productively pursued at this time.' He also wondered how Yiithrii'ah'aash would react if he were to learn that we had not used every resource to save Riordan's life."

As well he might wonder. As must we all.

Mriif'vaal was startled out of his thoughts by Thnessfiirm's sudden interjection; there was no spore-warning that she had even intended to speak. "Caine Riordan is a brave being. His ways may not be ours, but he sought to minimize harm to all of us. He did not fight to kill, not as a predator; he fought to protect, to preserve. I—I wish I had his instincts for that."

And now the source of Thnessfiirm's misery and distress was clear. It was the age-old risk that accompanied all contact between Slaasriithi and other species. *Our natural empathy is perturbed when we Affine ourselves to creatures whose ways are praiseworthy, yet not our own. It can tear us in two, if we are not careful.* "Thnessfiirm, I assure you: the conduct of Caine

Riordan is known to us and shall weigh greatly upon our decision in this matter, as it would upon any boon these humans would ask of us."

Hsaefyrr's age-thready voice was aimed down at W'th'vaathi, but was canted for Mriif'vaal's benefit as well. "However, the request for this cure is not so simple as it sounds. It involves matters of ancient and grave consequence."

W'th'vaathi's neck oscillated once. "I do not understand."

"At this point, that is as it should be." Hsaefyrr settled back, buzzing faintly. Then, more quietly to Mriif'vaal. "We must, I think, compare our thoughts on this matter."

Mriif'vaal let his tendrils interlace slowly, carefully. "I think you are correct, old friend. For I fear we have a more difficult conversation before us."

Hsaefyrr's respiration slits widened in surprise for a moment. "I am ever your friend and mentor, Mriif'vaal, but if you refer to a conversation involving the First Silver Tower—"

"—I do—"

"Then that is one conversation I am not eager to undertake with you. Or in your stead."

"Of course not." Mriif'vaal sent a light dusting of affinity and amusement at his old friend. "You are too sane to wish such a thing upon yourself, Hsaefyrr."

Outside the room that seemed part ICU and part laboratory, Bannor Rulaine sat with folded hands, staring at the living membrane which covered Caine's body. With the setting of the sun, the membrane had phased from transparent to dimly translucent. He hadn't heard Pandora Veriden approach, started when she sat next to him.

After a full minute, she muttered. "You can't stay here forever, you know."

"Just watch me."

Her sigh was an audial monument to exasperation. "Jeez, what is it with you military guys? You don't have to stand watch over him, and being here isn't going to determine whether Riordan lives or— Look; you weren't even supposed to make it down to the planet. That was an insane stunt. Saved all our asses, yes, but insane nonetheless. You did everything you could. Now give it, and yourself, a rest."

Rulaine was not angry when he turned toward her, hoped that lack of animus was clear in his voice and his eyes, because he wasn't sure how she'd hear his words. "Ms. Veriden, you just don't get it. Despite all your training, you were never military—or raised around that ethos—so you'll allow my conjecture that you just don't understand what makes us tick."

"Sure I do; duty and honor. Responsibility. In another minute, you're going to be telling me that it doesn't matter that the corvette was stuck in orbit; that Riordan's safety was your assignment and that you failed. End of story."

"And it pretty much does come to that, Ms. Veriden. But it doesn't stop there. In fact, that doesn't even begin to touch the surface. That's the recruiting slogan, the ad jingle; that's not our life. And that's the part a civilian, even a civilian combat veteran, is not likely to understand because the only way you get to know it is to live it.

"Look: I like Caine. A lot. But that's not why I'm here. I'd be here even if I hated his guts. I've sat this kind of, well, vigil, I guess you'd call it, more than a few times before. There's always one of the team there. So your brother or sister doesn't wake up alone. Or face the dark alone. They might not know you're there, but *you* know. That's what matters. And when everyone in a unit is committed that way, then, when the shit starts hitting the fan and you look around the hole or the hooch or the bunker and you see the fear of death in everyone else's eyes, you can still hold on to something: each other. It's the knowledge that we will not break. That our bond is stronger than the death facing us. It has to be, otherwise all hope is lost."

Rulaine leaned back against the smooth, metallic wall of the Third Silver Tower. "You see, Ms. Veriden, it's not just about honor and fellowship and brotherhood. It's about survival, too. You tend the bonds that keep you strong, and not just for yourself or your fallen friend, but for the morale, the sense of unity, that binds the whole unit." He folded his hands, leaned forward, stared at the oval fusion of machine and plant that held Riordan. "And you tend them most, well, punctiliously, at times like this."

Veriden physically started when Rulaine used the word "punctiliously." "You're not just a grunt, are you, Major?"

Bannor shook his head. "Ms. Veriden, that question is wrong in so many ways, including the mere asking of it, that I don't know where to begin."

She frowned. "Yeah. I guess that was pretty shitty. Sorry. Didn't mean it that way."

Rulaine resisted the urge to ask, *"Then just how* did *you mean it?"* and instead speculated that Dora Veriden probably had a long history of putting her foot in her mouth. She did not have a winning way with people and seemed uninterested in improving the related skill sets. Of course, she was a solo operator, so maybe that lack of reliance upon, or even toleration of, other people was a professional advantage. She wouldn't have been the first field agent whose specialization had been driven by inborn predispositions and personality traits. He turned toward her. "So did you come to keep me company?" *As if.*

She actually seemed a bit abashed. "No. I've got some news."

"Oh?"

"Thanks to our forensics fan Peter Wu, Ben Hwang found some weird critter in a hermetic cell sealed inside Macmillan's right boot. Turned to goo the moment he breached the little chamber."

Bannor nodded. "Like the one you found on Danysh's body, after the shuttle crashed?"

"Just like that one. Hwang tried to get it into a sealed container, evacuate the air. Didn't do it in time; after an hour, it was paste. Just like the other one."

"What else?"

"We found one live clone. We're delaying the debrief until you give input."

"No more wounded? Just one alive and the rest dead? That's pretty peculiar."

Veriden shook her head. "Not so peculiar when they kill their own. Seven or eight were maimed or incapacitated by the rockets; a few by gunfire. All stabbed in the heart. Real professional, too."

Bannor nodded. *Professionals, indeed.* He would have liked to tell Veriden that the moment O'Garran saw the corpses of the two enemy leaders—one by the shuttle, the other in the clearing—he'd identified them as Ktor. But Veriden wasn't cleared to know that the Ktor were humans, yet. And might never have that clearance. But the charade of Ktor being subzero, ammonia-based worms was beginning to wear perilously thin. "Debriefing that clone should be very revealing," Bannor observed.

"Should be," Veriden observed with a nod, "as well as tracking down all the serial numbers on all the equipment. But we already know what ship he, and that armored shuttle, were from: the *Arbitrage*."

Rulaine frowned. "Isn't the *Arbitrage* a CoDevCo shift-carrier? Their newest?"

Veriden nodded. "It is. Which is going to make questioning the clone all that much more interesting."

A long silence passed. The distant hum of the medical monitors at Riordan's bedside—or would that be podside?—was the only sound.

Veriden sighed, leaned forward so her head was parallel with Rulaine's. "That's all the news I've got to report."

"Thanks."

More silence. Then: "Okay, aren't you going to ask me?"

Here it comes. "Ask you what?"

She sounded gratifyingly annoyed. "Ask me when I became a part of IRIS? Shit, when I dropped that little secret on you just before we left the clearing you barely blinked."

"Were you hoping I'd go slack-jawed or do something equally melodramatic?"

"Damn it, you're a hard case." She moved to leave.

"There *is* one thing I'd like to know."

She stayed put. "Yeah?"

"Why didn't you tell me at the start? Why didn't you tell any of us?"

Pandora sighed, leaned back. "Because I was only supposed to tell Riordan. Well, Downing, too—I was recruited after he'd left Earth—but who knew things would happen so quickly? Or that I'd wake up inside Slaasriithi space, instead of at Sigma Draconis?"

"Yeah, well, since the rules of the game had changed, and we traveled together for a few weeks, don't you think you might have been able to slip it in somewhere along the way?"

"No, because the whole damn mission was so irregular and last-second that there was no way to separate the crazy stuff going on from the hinky stuff."

"What 'hinky stuff'?"

"Hinky stuff like the way I woke up, checked the legation records, and discovered that the secure EU shuttle that was supposed to transfer all our cold cells to Yiithrii'ah'aash's ship had last second 'engine trouble.' Hinky like there was a TOCIO shuttle that just happened to have been cleared for operations and was on call, but without any particular flight order pending. Hinky that most of the personnel who staffed the legation were transferred as corpsicles, so there was no way for Downing to eyeball and debrief them, or to see if they acted in the flesh as they were written on paper. And then we lost Buckley, which might or might not have been a result of his being a saboteur, or running afoul of one."

"So, now I understand why you chased after the response team Caine led to rescue Buckley: to protect Riordan. But at least Buckley doesn't seem to be part of the conspiracy."

"Yeah, as it turns out. But that's hindsight. So, to answer your question about why I didn't announce my credentials: after all that, and not having a crystal ball, I figured I'd better play it cool."

"And not tell Caine. Or anyone else."

"Precisely. Look: Riordan's okay, I guess, but he's not a pro. If I had just sidled up to him and said, 'Hey, I'm on your side,' and showed him my credentials, he might not have even believed me. Actually, that would have been the most professional thing he could have done, because he's not experienced enough to pick out a genuine solo operator from a crowd. Don't give me that look, Rulaine. Yeah, I know Caine's got good instincts. But he's been pretty lucky, too. Given his lack of training, he could have been dead three or four times if he didn't think quickly on his feet."

"Thinking quickly is a skill in itself." Bannor offered the rebuttal more out of loyalty to Riordan than conviction in its accuracy.

"Well, yeah, sure, it is. But that skill wasn't the one Riordan had to have if I was going to tip my hand and tell him I was on his team. Because *if* he had believed me, then he would probably have given me away to the real traitors in the group."

"How so?"

"By changing the way he behaved toward me."

"In what way?"

"See? This is what I mean: you're a professional field operator, but you still don't get it because you're just a striker. My world is different. And here's how Riordan would have messed up my world: if I had revealed my identity, he'd probably become careless in ways he wouldn't realize. He'd start showing an unwonted trust in me, casual speech, relaxed body language, all that. If an enemy pro had infiltrated our team, he or she would spot those changes, and so, would have sniffed me out. Or Caine would have been too careful, would start distancing himself from me—and again, a rival pro would have sensed that overcompensatory reaction and I'd be fingered. So my motto in these cases—better safe than sorry—meant not revealing who I was."

Rulaine nodded slowly. "Okay, I get it. But I have to tell you: between that strategy and your, well, winning ways around people, I was half-convinced you were our traitor."

She nodded back. "Good."

"Good?"

"Sure. Figure it out, genius: I wanted to be the one that no one trusts. I *wanted* any spoken or unspoken suspicion centered on me. Because if it was, then everyone else isn't so worried about someone watching them—including the *real* traitor. Humans, even pros in my field, tend to have that blind spot; they presume that someone who is under scrutiny is too worried about proving their own innocence to be watching anyone else. Problem was, Macmillan didn't give me much to go on. Probably the only thing he ever did that would have incriminated him I wasn't on hand to see."

"Which was?"

"When he sabotaged Riordan's filter mask. I'm guessing he did that right after we crashed. During our salvage work, we had to take off our masks to keep them from getting soaked. I'll bet in all the activity, and then the confusion after Hirano was attacked by those pirhannows, he had plenty of opportunity to take care of Riordan's mask. It was a shrewd plan: let Caine sicken by degrees, weaken the group by taking out our leader—who we're not likely to leave behind—and freeze us in place. But the water-striders ruined it. Suddenly we had mobility independent of effort. But Macmillan never tipped his hand after that."

"Where'd you learn your fieldcraft?"

"Officially? I spent some weeks in training with the DGSE at Noisy-le-Sec, but mostly at the School of Hard Knocks."

"Starting in early childhood, if Mr. Gaspard is correct."

"He is, although the bastard has no right to talk about it."

"It doesn't sound as though you like your employer very much. Well, your ostensible employer."

"Oh, he's my real employer, all right. I took his coin *and* I took IRIS' and didn't much mind; I deserved them both, and more besides. But no, why should I like him? He's a prissy classist manbitch who thinks the world was better off when everyone who doesn't share his complexion was safely under the administration of colonial masters."

"Gaspard?"

"Sure. Part of the postwar wave of NeoImperialists."

Rulaine scratched his head. "I'm not even sure what that refers to."

"That's because you were on the counterinvasion fleet to Sigma Draconis. Those of us who lagged behind, even by a few weeks, got an earful of rhetoric about how humanity could no longer afford the inequities and inefficiencies which had plagued humankind for so long. So what's their answer? Any country that they felt couldn't pull its weight or hadn't been able to create an orderly government was essentially put on probation."

"Probation?"

"Yeah; as in, 'fix your shit or we're coming in and fixing it for you.' *Coño*, if that's how it was going to be, why the hell did the Western powers ever leave their colonies? They lost almost two centuries of fun oppressing, raping, and exploiting." Her terribly bright smile was as bitter and vitriolic as Bannor had ever seen on a human face.

He shrugged. "Then what's your answer? If we do get into another scrap with our new interstellar neighbors, and that seems likely, then how do we get everyone mobilized, working toward the common goal of speciate survival?"

"I don't know, but you sure as shit don't accomplish it by taking away some of your own peoples' national sovereignty!"

Rulaine sighed. "Gaspard is a pragmatist. And he probably has a better sense than we do about how much time we have to get our house in order before the wolf comes sniffing around the door again."

"Yeah, well, it took centuries to make this mess. Only seems fair that it would take centuries to unmake it."

Bannor nodded. "I get that. But what if we don't *have* centuries?"

"Look, I'm not saying I've got the answers. But the five blocs are going about this all wrong, and they're not losing a lot of sleep over it, either. The only thing they've all been able to agree on is that they should take the unproductive nations out behind the shed and whup them. Yeah, just like old times."

"So, you hate the nation-states. Surprised you're not working for the megacorporations."

"*Them?*" Bannor thought Dora might have expectorated along with her utterance of that word. "Look: nations screw up like people do; sometimes they mean well, sometimes they're selfish or delusional bitches on a spree, and sometimes they just plain make mistakes. But the megacorporations don't make mistakes; if they do damage, it's because they like the cost-to-benefit ratios, dead innocents notwithstanding. Nations are bulls in the global china shop; corporations are sharks."

"Yeah, but what about the—?"

Veriden rose. "Rulaine, I didn't come here to debate politics, the world, and everything. I came to make a report, explain why I didn't let anyone know I was IRIS, and try to get along. But as you've pointed out, I don't do that very well." She looked over her shoulder at Caine. "I hope he pulls through. But there doesn't seem much chance of it now." She turned and padded away, dwindling down the long hallway that was shaped by walls which swept up into high and impenetrable shadows.

Chapter Fifty-Two

Mriif'vaal approached the Rapport Sphere and thought: *Twice in the same week; this is unprecedented in the annals of Disparity. Woe that I should live in such times.*

He touched the outer layer of the sphere. The transparent membrane began allowing his tendrils to move through it. Moving very slowly, his whole body passed to the other side of the barrier much as oxygen passed through it by osmosis.

Between the osmotic Outer Sphere, and the hard, hermetic Inner Sphere, the air was thick: an overpressure environment that ensured that none of the spores and pheromones within the Inner Sphere would escape when the seam into it was opened. Mriif'vaal sighed, stared at the swirling vapors on the other side of the hard, clear surface. Those many airborne transmitters and receptors of meaning were not to be braved by the unprepared. The unrestricted sensory wave that perfused both the body and mind of any Slaasriithi that entered was powerful, paralyzing to the untrained.

Mriif'vaal did not welcome his imminent contact with the OverWatchling's mind. He did not know any ratiocinator that did. And none of the other taxae had contact with it at all. Indeed, it was probably wrong to even think of the OverWatchling as having a mind. It was more akin to a highly detailed awareness. It deduced, but hardly reasoned; it learned, but was rarely capable of generalizing lessons learned within one domain of knowledge to any other; and while it was capable of change, it was disposed to resist it, in the interest of maintaining the stability of the polytaxic order and the synergies of macroevolution.

But this was not what made the consciousness of the OverWatchling such a ubiquitous source of discomfort among ratiocinatorae; it was the unsettling impression that its awareness *could* have been a mind, but had not been allowed to become one. This invariably led any perspicacious ratiocinator to wonder what dark path of inducement had produced this biomechanical hybrid, this being that was not a being. It did not help matters that the source of the OverWatchlings was not shared with the whole of the Slaasriithi polytaxon, not even with all Senior Ratiocinatorae. It was only known to those Prime Ratiocinatorae whose domains of responsibility transcended the boundaries of an individual world and extended into the interconnections between planets, star systems, and species. It was they who delivered new OverWatchlings to planets that had been sufficiently bioformed to warrant one. They did not divulge where the OverWatchlings originated, or how their biological and mechanical parts were, ultimately, fused. None of which helped diminish the disquiet that other ratiocinatorae felt when in contact with the awareness of these pseudosophonts. Mriif'vaal splayed his tendrils wide across the Inner Sphere. A seam opened where none had been evident; he entered the pungent miasma.

Moments after he had seated himself, Mriif'vaal smelled a change in the pheromones; Disparity's newly reactivated satellite grid had linked this chamber of the Third Silver Tower to that one which housed the OverWatchling beneath the First Silver Tower. The room's audio converter and playback systems activated, but they were rarely significant in communicating with the OverWatchling. Having no mouth, no real body, it could communicate quantitatively through data streams or, when qualitative comparisons or discussions were required, through remote manipulation of the organic emissions within the Inner Chamber. Given the nature of this particular contact, the latter would predominate, or possibly be the sole vector of exchange.

"I am aware of your situation, Senior Ratiocinator Mriif'vaal," was the verbal equivalent of what the OverWatchling conveyed, albeit over the period of half a minute: it took considerable time for the Inner Sphere's changed spores to perfuse Mriif'vaal's receptors, then stimulate electrochemical changes the same way that sights and sounds produced meaning in one's brain. And in referring to "this situation," the OverWatchling transmitted meaning that went far beyond that simple word, but invoked a signification-matrix that encompassed all the relevant reports, data, lists, and analyses that were resident in its awareness. Resident, but mostly inert, since its prior experience had not prepared it for such a complicated and nuanced situation as the one it now faced.

"I requested this communing to alert you to the significance of the impending demise of the human named Caine Riordan."

"Your reason for contact is included in my awareness of the situation. But I do not perceive why a single being's impending demise warrants this concern."

"You are aware of the role of the human, of the tacit assurances we provided him and his group for their safety on Disparity, and of his possible further significance to Yiithrii'ah'aash's mission?"

"The ratiocinatorae have relayed these data points, but I do not understand the implicit connection between a single being and these greater significances."

Mriif'vaal breathed deeply: it had already been five minutes, and the OverWatchling's inability to perceive the social and cultural ramifications of the matter promised that it would take much, much longer. "I shall explain. Firstly, you may recall that we counseled you regarding the importance of individual human lives when they first crashed upon this world."

"I am aware of the content of our prior contact."

Aware of it in the sense of being an immense but uncomprehending recording device. "What we were not aware of at that time was that this particular being, Caine Riordan, was already Affined to us by an old mark—an unthinkably old mark. We are uncertain of the origin of this mark, but believe it may be connected to the profound sense of importance and urgency that Yiithrii'ah'aash imparted to us about this mission."

"I have much data that was initially relayed from Yiithrii'ah'aash's ship, the *Tidal-Drift-Instaurator-to-Shore-of-Stars.* There is no record of any human passenger bearing such a mark."

"I cannot account for that discrepancy," Mriif'vaal sent wearily. "It may be that Yiithrii'ah'aash did not wish to call attention to this factor in our communications. It may be that he was unaware of just how old, or just how powerful, this marking was upon Caine Riordan. Conceivably, it did not fully express itself until the human was fully in our environment. That would not be uncommon; many marks sleep until touched by microbiota they recognize and only demonstrate their full intensity when fully awakened thereby. It could have been so here on Disparity."

The OverWatchling did not respond for a long time; Mriif'vaal estimated it to be a delay of ten minutes. "What may be done? Given this new data, I would have agreed to many of your initial suggestions for action, or for release of assets, which I refused. But the past is past and may not be changed."

"True." Mriif'vaal took his time, allowed his body to replenish its pheromones and spore sacs to make his next message particularly clear and forceful. "But you may still change the future, may change the unfortunate course of events that has resulted from the recent past you now regret."

"I do not understand."

Mriif'vaal felt the OverWatchling's growing willingness to alter protocols and precedents, and so, proceeded carefully, like a tracker attempting not to startle skittish game. "There are other old marks, spores, and antidotes. They are resident in your awareness. You may summon the Emitters to produce them. And they are precisely what Caine Riordan needs to survive, for he is dying not from the wounds inflicted by his own kind, but from our own defensive spores. Which, as we communicated to you before, could have been suspended. But that was not done."

"To do so would have deviated from protocol." This time, the OverWatchling's reply was evasive, less resolute.

"Clearly," Mriif'vaal agreed. "But we must weigh that deviation against other concerns. I shall enumerate these concerns. If we allow this human to die when it is known that we may preserve his life, how will this particular group of humans Affine with us? Indeed, given their nonpolytaxic origins and perceptions of life and death, why should they? These beings fought to survive and indirectly defend the sovereignty of our planet. How will we explain to them and the rest of their species that Caine Riordan, an ancient-marked envoy, must be allowed to die—and not from wounds inflicted in the battle, but because of our unwillingness to correct an ailment caused by our own spores? If you would salvage this situation, if you would preserve the chance of an alliance between our races, then you must cure him." Mriif'vaal realized as he released the last fervent wash of pheromones that he might have pushed too hard.

The OverWatchling's reply was not brusque, but it was more firm than the prior ones. "What you ask is without precedent. The antidote to which you refer, the prime theriac, has not been used in millennia and there are many injunctions against doing so."

Carefully now. "Those injunctions arose from vastly different exigencies than the ones which face us now. They pertain to wars fought in the distant past, wars in which our antagonists were not true humans, but, rather, a malign subspecies derived from them. But *these* humans, the ones who were invited to Disparity, are the originals of their breed. Their genecode predates that of the self-warped subspecies that tormented us, and which recent intelligence suggests is one and the same as the exosapients who have masqueraded as the Ktor." Mriif'vaal paused, let the OverWatchling process these concepts. Then he circled back to the key assertion. "If the Slaasriithi polytaxon would be Affined to these natural humans of Earth, we must preserve the life of this being whom we ourselves have unwittingly brought to the edge of death. If we do not bear the responsibility of action to undo such a mistake, why would his kind believe or trust us in any other particular?"

The OverWatchling was slow in responding. Clearly, the arguments were wearing upon its inclination to remain in compliance with normative protocols. "I still do not perceive the urgency you presume to reside in the life of this single being. Is it not his fate, even desire, to devote his existence—including the surrender of it—to the welfare of his taxon?"

"No. That is not how humans have evolved, either biologically or socially. Because they are not polytaxic, their priorities are radically different. The importance we put upon the collective, they put upon the individual."

"And we wish to ally with such creatures?"

"Most urgently, I believe."

"I require confirmation of that assertion."

"If Yiithrii'ah'aash were here to provide it, I would never have contacted you myself. Consequently, your request for confirmation is, with apologies, illogical." *Not to say specious.*

The answer was very long in coming. "That is true." As Mriif'vaal waited, it felt as though the world breathed in and out deeply. Then: "Your counsel is prudent. I shall comply."

✧   ✧   ✧

Caine started awake, started again when he discovered Yiith-rii'ah'aash's sensor cluster focused on him, only a meter away. It drew back. "I did not mean to frighten you, Caine Riordan. My apologies."

"I wasn't frightened. Not exactly." Caine was suddenly and acutely conscious of still being in shorts and a tee shirt, the only recuperation clothing he had. Upon recovering consciousness two days ago, he had awakened to find himself lying stark naked in a strange amalgam of a bed, a couch, and an oversized sponge that smelled vaguely like citrus and bergamot. The Slaasriithi had been startled by his attempt to cover himself. His sudden, urgent motions without (for them) ready explanation led them to conclude he might be having a seizure of some sort. When Riordan groggily asked them for a hospital gown, much buzzing and sibilant speech ensued. After thirty minutes, they brought him an otherwise featureless black slate, which, when activated, displayed any number of gowns: wedding, formal, debutante ball. The attempt to find clothing had gone downhill from there, largely because the Slaasriithi, being unconcerned with personal coverings of any kind and quite unfamiliar with human sociology, presumed that all Earth garb was fundamentally a form of signification. To them, the concept of "modesty" was as foreign as the term "nudity" was redundant.

Yiithrii'ah'aash's sensor cluster regarded him steadily. "I am most gratified and glad that your health returns to you. And to those of your fellows who were wounded."

Caine nodded; Gaspard, the only human the Slaasriithi had permitted to see Riordan so far, had summarized the aftermath of the battle at the river. Eid had indeed fled to safety. Salunke had been knocked senseless when the explosion of a rifle grenade had blown down a rotting tree which fell upon her. Prior health concerns were also resolving: the wounds inflicted upon Hirano by the pirhannows were healing nicely, and it was speculated that she would not lose her eye. Hwang's internal injuries had not been so severe that they were beyond the ability of his own body to heal.

But Trent Howarth was dead. No one knew what had happened, but the speed of his exit from *Puller* was reasonably suspected of having compromised his HALO rig. Qwara and Xue had been buried and Riordan himself had been excavated from beneath the bulk of the slain water-strider that had, it seemed, sacrificed itself to conceal him from the Ktor and the clones. The loss of Macmillan was not mentioned. Caine suspected that many simply wrote him off as one of the enemy dead. Riordan was of the opinion that he, too, was a fallen fellow-traveler; the only difference was that he had been a casualty from the time he had left Earth, his soul torn asunder when forced to choose between his daughter's life and the fate of his planet. Caine wondered if he himself would have fared any better against that most terrible weapon of all: one's own greatest loves turned against each other.

Gaspard had made many vicariously proud noises about the extraordinary underdog outcome of the engagement beside the river, pointing to the scant losses among the humans and the Slaasriithi. But Caine's memories kept showing him very different pictures: Unsymaajh toppling from his downward swoop, Qwara pitching backward with only a fragment of her head remaining, Xue's limp collapse, or the imagined bird's-eye view of Trent falling, falling, falling. And unbidden, Keith Macmillan's tortured face rose up as well.

Gaspard eventually noticed that his references to the "wondrous deliverance" Riordan had effected for the legation did not seem to cheer the recipient of those panegyrics. But when the ambassador inquired if something was amiss, Caine deflected the inquiry, citing exhaustion. During his command of insurgents in Indonesia, Riordan had learned not to share regrets and remorse except with select persons, in private places, and after some time had passed. And Etienne Gaspard was never going to be such a person, despite how well he had ultimately risen to the challenges of their disastrous journey.

Riordan's reveries ended abruptly when Yiithrii'ah'aash shifted in his framed stool. "You are uncharacteristically silent, Caine Riordan. Do your require more rest? Should I return later?"

"No, no. I was just . . . thinking. I had not been informed that you were coming today, although Ambassador Gaspard informed me that you shifted in-system three days after our engagement with the—with our enemies."

"With the Ktor," Yiithrii'ah'aash corrected.

Caine was silent, considered: Yiithrii'ah'aash's identification of the Ktor as their attackers—and as humans—was not a probe, not a conjecture to elicit either confirmation or denial. It was uttered as a statement of fact. So it didn't seem as though that extremely classified piece of information was so classified anymore. Indeed, maybe it never had been for the Slaasriithi. "How long have you known? About the Ktor, I mean."

"'Know' is too strong a word. We suspected, some of us strongly. We Slaasriithi were not alone in this. We intuit that similar suspicions reside in the Dornaani Collective, particularly amongst the Custodians."

"Then why has the issue not been raised?"

"The Accord is an organization that rightly connects the assurance of privacy to the assurance of peace. Races that presume no rights to impede upon each other tend to be able to coexist."

"But if it turns out that one of them is a liar, that same coexistence can splinter in a second. With grave consequences."

Yiithrii'ah'aash's sensor cluster inclined slightly. "This is also true. As some of us have pointed out. However, over time, many Slaasriithi who suspected the true identity of the Ktor became hopeful that they had been mistaken, or that the Ktor had changed. It is difficult to imagine how so warlike and aggressive a subspecies could endure for so long without evolving into a less self-destructive social organism. But perhaps the more powerful inclination against seeking direct evidence of their biology arose from our own societies' desire for tranquility. The question of Ktoran identity was a very unnerving topic, and full of dire consequences if it was revealed that they had misrepresented their nature, as has now occurred, here on Disparity. However, we did not foresee that the confirmation would take such a brutal shape, or how quickly it would follow the conclusion of the recent war. Yet perhaps this has been, as your idiom has it, a blessing in disguise."

Riordan nodded. "But your suspicions of the true identity of the Ktor were hardly something you could ever fully forget."

"Why do you say so, Caine Riordan?"

"Because, during the journey with W'th'vaathi, we had a conversation which indicated that your defense spores were tailor-made to work upon human biochemistry. That, in turn, suggests that we were among your most dangerous enemies in the distant past.

"But Earth wasn't launching attacks against other species twenty millennia ago; it was still busy inventing fire. So the human threat which prompted you to devise these spores must have come from elsewhere. And then, when you joined the Dornaani in their Accord, there was already one other member race. A race that was both reclusive and secretive, but also aggressive, and for which no prior record existed: the Ktor. So you had to wonder: 'is the Ktor claim that they are ammonia-based worms inside big metal tanks just a masquerade?'"

Yiithrii'ah'aash's tone puzzled Riordan; the Slaasriithi inflections did not resemble those of humans, and this was one he had not heard before. "This is indeed what some of us wondered."

Riordan sighed. "And now two humans have continued that fine tradition of treachery and aggression. Danysh sabotaged your ship and almost killed you along with us. Macmillan enabled a raid against the surface of a world that is, in interstellar terms, right next door to your home system. I'm half expecting you to tell me that our visit to Beta Aquilae, and this whole diplomatic envoy, has been called off after what my species has done to yours. Again."

Yiithrii'ah'aash raised a tendril. "You misperceive. Our only concern is with your compromised subspecies, the Ktor."

Caine frowned. "Compromised?"

Yiithrii'ah'aash's tendrils waved, one following the other slowly. "The Ktor are not natural, not entirely."

"In what way? And how can you tell?"

"Many of our biota can 'taste' other genecodes, particularly the difference between those which arise from mechanistic genetic alteration, and those which arise from natural evolution or inducement. The latter leaves no genetic detritus, to put the matter crudely. However, the former process—mechanistic alteration— restructures genes through externally forced or crudely imposed addition, removal, or modification of target codes." Yiithrii'ah'aash may have read Riordan's frown as incomprehension. "Let us put it this way: natural processes change genetics the way a hand smooths a clay pot on a turning wheel. Mechanistic processes are the blows of hammers, the cuts of knives, the gnawings of nanites. Many of our biota can, for lack of a better description, smell or taste the ragged code left by these artificial processes."

Riordan suppressed a host of questions that this revelation stimulated about the Ktor, as well as about the genetic research opportunities that might arise through a partnership with the Slaasriithi. "I'm glad that you distinguish between us and the Ktor, Yiithrii'ah'aash, but the fact remains that two of *my* people brought war and death to Disparity. And the Ktor were using our clones and our equipment."

Yiithrii'ah'aash oscillated his neck lazily: the equivalent of a shrug. "These statements are true, but they are also unimportant." Perhaps perceiving the surprised expression on Riordan's face, Yiithrii'ah'aash held up several didactic tendrils. "If I were to take a dead branch from the forest, and slay my clutch-sibling with it, may I then blame the forest for committing the murder? The forest only provided the object I used. The hand and the will that wielded it show us the culprit. The same holds true of what transpired on Disparity: it was not your doing. The Ktor were the hand and the will behind the treachery and the murder. They simply found the weak and the vulnerable among you and corrupted them to use as their tools."

"Then isn't human corruptibility at least partly to blame?"

Yiithrii'ah'aash's neck wobbled diffidently once again. "Any social creature that is not part of a polytaxon is ultimately corruptible. The survival imperative of disparate individuals is particularly acute and so the values of self-preservation and self-hood may overpower any instinct toward communal preservation and group identity. Conversely, the inevitable outcome of our polytaxic evolution is that the group is more important than the individual; this makes the Slaasriithi unique among the races of the Accord. On the other hand, while human individualism is not unique, its extraordinary intensity also makes your species the most readily corruptible."

Riordan was tempted to shake his head in dismay. "Then why not presume that we will eventually become just like the Ktor?"

"Because although the countervailing communal impulses of altruism and empathy may not be as strong in your society as in ours, those impulses nonetheless remain intact and uncompromised. However, this balance between egoism and altruism was disrupted by whatever mechanistic modification was used to alter your genecode into that of the Ktor. Possibly this disruption was an unintended artifact of the modification. It is no less likely that it was one of the explicit objectives of the process. However, undamaged, that dynamic tension between love of self and love of others is the guarantor of your social equilibrium."

Caine leaned back. "I confess I never associated these issues with 'love.'"

"Indeed? No other word or concept in your species is so powerful, so universal, and yet so variform. Its ends and objects are neither simple nor consistent. Yet your dogged embrace of what you love is ultimately the source of the greatest power, the greatest virtue, of your species."

"And what is that virtue?"

"It is compounded of two traits. Because your evolution emphasized the importance and survival of the individual, you make new decisions and take new actions with extraordinary rapidity and autonomy. But because your reflex to love transcends self-interest, so do your survival instincts and imperatives. Were this not so, how could you have saved your legation? You and your group, far away from the counsel of the rest of your species, innately employed a mix of individual and collective actions to respond quickly and innovatively to great dangers and obstacles."

"The Ktor did the same."

"True. But if both history and current implications are reliable, their sole motivation was self-interest. They are like viruses; they are self-interested and self-perpetuating engines unencumbered by extraneous concerns, least of all love. You are perpetually active engines as well, but it is in your nature to turn that power to many purposes. And in the record we have of your recent centuries, of the wars you have fought and the social changes you have wrought, we see the unremitting influence of the dynamic equilibrium—and struggle—between self-interest and altruism." Yiithrii'ah'aash leaned forward. "You are not the Ktor. We know this. Possibly better than you do."

Riordan inclined his head. "You are very generous in your opinion of us."

"It is not generosity to understand the characteristics of a species. Perhaps, in the future, if you wish to alter your own innate proclivities to further distance yourself from the possibility of becoming similar to the Ktor, we may be able to help. We would certainly be able to reduce the possibility that you might inadvertently propagate the expression of negative traits within your genecode. Conversely, we could assist you in any attempts to amplify the positive traits."

Caine kept himself from shuddering. *Social conditioning on the genetic level, courtesy of the Slaasriithi? No thank you.*

Yiithrii'ah'aash had not noticed Riordan's reaction, but kept speaking. "And insofar as an apology is concerned, if either of us owes one to the other, it is we, the Slaasriithi, who must apologize to your legation."

Riordan waved away Yiithrii'ah'aash's concern. "We did not accept your invitation on the presumption that there would be no hazards on the journey. You protected us as well as you could—"

"That is not what prompts my apology, although our failure to ensure your safety also warrants one."

Caine's hand stopped in midwave. "Go on."

"We told you that the only way to know us was to visit our worlds, that in experiencing how we spread biota, and with what results, you would come to understand us."

Riordan frowned. "And you have done just that. What you have shown us has imparted far more insight than anything we could have gleaned from reading files and data packets."

"Yes. But there was another reason for our insistence upon that method of acculturation, one we could not initially reveal."

Caine felt a cool chill on his back, a sensation he'd come to associate with those moments in first contact when, invariably, a crucial and often dangerous new wrinkle insinuates itself into the budding relationship. "And what is this reason?"

"We wanted to watch you."

"Well, that only stands to reason. You wouldn't want to allow just any bunch of—"

"You misperceive, Caine Riordan. We wanted to watch *you*. I mean the singular pronoun."

Caine stopped. "Oh." Then: "Why?"

"Because our contact with your people is not just motivated by our desire to open normal diplomatic relations. We have another crucial objective, and we needed to be certain—beyond any doubt—that when the time came to reveal it, that we could do so to an individual who had demonstrated powerful affinity with our species, without the benefit of any of our pheromones or spores. When we learned of your travels on Delta Pavonis Three, it raised our interest and hopes. When I met you briefly at Sigma Draconis, it confirmed much, not only because of the easy amity of our discourse, but because of the mark you bear. It meant that you had been touched by, and Affined to, a lost branch of our family tree, a fallen branch. But now, also a cru-cial branch. This was the other reason we were eager to mount this mission so quickly; not only did we fear the machinations of the Ktor—"

Well, you certainly called that *correctly.*

"—we also realized that, with you, we had a fleeting opportunity to reveal our needs to the liaison we sought. And we were aware that it might be years, or longer, before so promising a candidate as yourself arose again." Yiithrii'ah'aash seemed to become distracted. "Besides, time is short. Which is quite ironic: our current urgency arises not from the events of this moment, but from those of past, and largely forgotten, epochs."

Riordan held up a pausing hand. "Forgotten by you, perhaps. But for us, that past is a blank. So if you want my help, you'll have to explain *how* events from those lost epochs are creating urgent problems now."

"I took the liberty of disturbing your rest, Caine Riordan, so that I might unfold that paradox," Yiithrii'ah'aash answered. "Because until you know its origins, you cannot fully comprehend why we wish you to be our liaison. Nor can you fully understand why we exhorted your legation to meet us." He paused. "Or rather, to save us."

Chapter Fifty-Three

Wait: to save *them? Damn, what's* that *about?* "You have my full attention, Yiithrii'ah'aash."

The Slaasriithi ambassador sat very straight. Riordan had the impression that he was preparing to strive for absolute precision and clarity in what he said, that he was possessed by a terrible need to impart this information *correctly.* "Long ago, my species lost something: the ability to defend itself against aggressors who were too large or fast or bold for us to ameliorate, and then constrain, with our various strategies of inducement.

"However, as your own people have begun to conjecture given the age of the ruins you found on Delta Pavonis Three, our people were in the stars before we lost that ability. Our races—yours and mine, certainly—were transplanted, much as we transplant biota to different worlds to achieve different ends. We have no concrete knowledge of that earlier epoch, or of what those ends were, but we conjecture that we were, in your vernacular, the preferred terraformers of that time."

Caine discovered he was squinting. "And what was humanity's function?"

"We can make even fewer conjectures about that, and those we have must wait for a later conversation. But be assured that it was not simply to be blood-drenched killers such as the Ktor. What evidence we do have suggests that the Ktor were a later aberration. You might call them the flawed result of a weapons development program."

490

Yiithrii'ah'aash's neck seemed to sag. "Sadly, what you uncovered on Delta Pavonis Three suggests that the Ktor were used to eliminate the enemies of one side in the great conflagration which ended that distant arc of history. Specifically, we believe that the human ruins you discovered belonged to the Ktor, who had been sent to exterminate us. And almost did so. Indeed, given the devolved subtaxon you encountered, the Ktor so damaged our population that it was unable to remain fully polytaxic; it regressed to a much earlier, simpler state. That is why you observed no discrete taxae there.

"I see you are eager to ask questions about this war, what caused it, what followed. It is in the nature of the way you narrativize the past to ask such questions. I must disappoint you. I have no such information. I doubt any of my species do. But this much is manifestly evident: the Ktor did not exterminate all Slaasriithi, everywhere." He gestured around him at the high ceilings of the Third Silver Tower. "I do not know when we devised the defense spores that almost killed you, Caine Riordan. It might have been during that war. It might have been later, as a means of making our remaining planets too difficult and costly to invade. But the spores do date from those days.

"Our historical record, such as it is, commences well after that war ended. We found ourselves alone in a silent universe. Never overly concerned with machinery, we did not find our loss of technological acumen terribly distressing. Rather, we pursued our efforts to build harmony between our polytaxon and the biota with which we shared the biosphere of what we call our homeworld. In time, of course, we reexpanded to other systems—by slower-than-light craft, at first—and often discovered worlds which still had vestiges of our earlier bioforming. There was much work, and much purpose, and we throve, although the pace of our 'thriving' is very different from humanity's.

"Well before the Dornaani recontacted us, we had progressed to the point where our synergistic balances had become so refined, so stable, that there were no longer any new regions to explore quickly, no crises that needed swift address, no species that required prompt suppression. In short, we had achieved the harmony we had sought. All the notes in the symphony of our many biospheres were in tune and consonant with the leitmotif we had heard and now, had created."

Riordan rested his chin in his hand. "Why do I suspect that there is a problem in this paradise?"

Yiithrii'ah'aash's voice was rueful but also gently agreeable. "Because you are the liaison, Caine Riordan; because you see the stories of other beings not from the outside, but from the inside. We have many words for this trait and its subtle shadings and variations. In your language, the closest term is 'empathy,' but that only touches the surface of a far more complicated matrix of phenomena. But to return to the problem in this paradise:

"Because conflicts, crises, and exploration had become uncommon, my species found itself confronted with a problem it had never faced: the existence of a taxon which had outlived its function. We called the members of this taxon the indagatorae, which comes closest to your term 'explorers.' That taxon had descended from our earliest days; they were our scouts, guards, trail-blazers. They were unique among us in that they sought challenge and uncertainty, conditions that the other taxae wished to avoid. They preferred rootless solitude or small groups over fixed communities. Furthermore, for the indagatorae to have optimal chances of survival and success, they required a trait that was also unique to their taxae: a pronounced self-preservation instinct that prompted them to be more innovative and more decisive than any other taxon when faced with a crisis."

Yiithrii'ah'aash's neck waggled slightly; his limbs drooped somewhat. Was it the onset of melancholy? "So here is the problem you foresaw in our paradise. In essence, the indagatorae had done their job too well. All Slaasriithi now dwelt in biospheres which held no threats, in which there were no undiscovered countries, and in which the only crises were natural disasters for which we had developed excellent contingency plans. The indagatorae's innovation and boldness was no longer needful or pertinent, except in rare rescue operations."

Riordan nodded. "But you still had a taxon with an acute self-preservation instinct and whose focus was as much, or more, upon the individual as upon the community."

"Perceiving this problem, and what it portends, is why we hope you shall consent to be our liaison. As you no doubt conjecture, we reduced the indagatorae over time. It was not difficult. The demographic balance of our breeding is driven by chemistries more than cognitive determination, and the almost vanished need for the abilities of this taxon had already made it the smallest of our taxae. And, having had no contact with any other intelligent races for many millennia, we believed that the past wars had very possibly wiped out all the others. Meanwhile, the indagatorae were constantly disrupting our polytaxic harmonies, always pushing for faster solutions, deviations from protocols and norms, seeking challenges where the community sought tranquility."

"And so they dwindled and were gone."

"Just so. But recent events have swelled the number of voices which, as a few always had, caution that no species should willingly divest itself of any skills, that no state of existence is so permanent that once-useful traits may be said to have outlived their usefulness."

"A point that no doubt became more pertinent at the last Convocation."

Yiithrii'ah'aash emitted a weary hum. "We had noted the increasing Ktor aggressiveness for some time, but the events of the past two years exceeded our worst projections. Now, the wisdom of the most senior ratiocinatorae is that although the indagator did become a disruptive element of our polytaxon, it still had a purpose. And this purpose did not reside solely, or even primarily, in the utilitarian skills it possessed. Rather, the nature of the indagator itself was a reminder of what we are in toto: a harmony among all things, because all things do have their place. In the case of the indagatorae, the variables they introduced into our existence were, ultimately, more beneficial to the long-term health of our polytaxon than they were disruptive to its smaller, short-lived particularities. The indagatorae may problematize the overarching strategies whereby we hope to achieve a universal synergy among all biota, but they are also a reminder that surprise, serendipity, and chance are powers that ineluctably shape us—and require special management—over time."

Riordan nodded. "So you are going to reintroduce the indagatorae."

"That is our intent. But we need you in order to do it."

Caine leaned back. "I don't understand."

"It has been at least ten millennia since the indagatorae walked amongst us. The genome for that taxae has been heavily compromised. It was repressed whenever it attempted to naturally reexpress in our communities. What is left of its coding is inconsistent, incomplete: insufficient."

"So you can't reintroduce the indagator?"

"Not by ourselves, no."

Caine shook his head. "I don't understand. How can I help? What do you need?"

Yiithrii'ah'aash spoke slowly, carefully. "We must have access to the original genome, to a genecode which was not altered by our repeated and forceful suppression of the indagator."

Caine frowned—and then understood. "The beings I met on Delta Pavonis Three, the devolved versions of your species: although they are regressed, they still carry that genome."

"Precisely. Indeed, I suspect that their population is heavily shaped by the genecodes particular to the indagator taxon. It is unlikely any other taxon could survive in isolation for so long."

Caine nodded. "And you need me to get permission to acquire a sample and—"

Yiithrii'ah'aash was buzzing softly but steadily. When Caine grew silent, Yiithrii'ah'aash said, "No. That would not be sufficient. We cannot know if every cell, or any cell, in one Pavonian's body or blood would carry the entirety of the code we require. It may only reside in what you would call stem cells, or in the nuclei of other specialized cell types. And only our experts will be able to make that determination."

Finally Caine understood what Yiithrii'ah'aash was asking of him. "You need me to take you to Delta Pavonis Three to meet, and abscond with, one or more Pavonians."

"Not abscond," Yiithrii'ah'aash insisted. "We would not compel compliance. But we will not need to. The mark they placed upon you tells me that. They will still recognize rapport spores; they will understand."

"Okay," Caine allowed, "but what if they *don't* understand? As you said, Ambassador, the Pavonians may be 'of' you, but they are not Slaasriithi anymore. So the way I look at it, that makes them free agents. Even if it's best that they cooperate with you, they're under no obligation to do so. And I won't support any attempts to coerce or compel their compliance."

"And I will never ask you to, Caine Riordan, because we are in absolute accord on this point: the Pavonians must be free to choose their own path. However, the mark on you tells me that they will hear our call and will come with us."

"All of them?"

"Only if they so wish. But eventually, I believe they all shall. However, I suspect that we will not be able to tarry to determine this during our first visit."

Caine mentally checked how this scenario would impact the clockwork gears of humanity's own political machinery. Yiithrii'ah'aash was right about not tarrying: Earth needed Slaasriithi technical assistance as quickly and as profoundly as the Slaasriithi needed the return of their indagatorae. But doing so promptly was going to involve a territorial violation, no way around it.

Trying to process a formal request for access was a nonstarter. It would take months, maybe years, to be cleared by the fledgling Terran Republic's inchoate and still-decentralized bureaucratic and diplomatic services. The upside of the violation was that, once the deed was done, the resulting agreement might provide an easy way to send most or all of the Pavonians to a good home, leaving DeePeeThree wide open for unrestricted human settlement. That would make everyone happy—eventually. But in the meantime...

"Yiithrii'ah'aash, you are aware that if we do this, it will be without any official permission or knowledge. In short, I will be violating the laws of my own government."

Yiithrii'ah'aash bobbed slowly. "I have examined the ramifications of what I ask. That is why I only ask it now, after you have seen us in our worlds: peaceful, productive, and woefully incapable of protecting ourselves. Or of being truly useful allies to you. To change that, we must reintroduce the indagator. And to accomplish that, we must act in stealth and in violation of your laws." He rose slowly, stiffly; was it a formal gesture of some sort, perhaps a supplication? "I would not ask this of you if there was any other way for our need to be met, or if the consequences were not so great. For both our peoples. And so I ask: would you do us the honor of consenting to be our Liaison with humanity?"

Caine stared at the tubes running into his arms, many without the benefit of needles or other mechanical interfaces. What had made this mission—a deep contact—different from a first contact was that the strangest and most unexpected challenges were those that percolated within oneself, not in exchanges with the exosapients. In this case, the questions and consequences spawned by Yiithrii'ah'aash's request were so immense, and so intertwined with humanity's uncertain and rapidly unfolding future, that it was impossible to separate and dissect them all discretely. At some point, the person on the spot just had to go with their gut feelings and choose a path.

"I will be your Liaison," Caine answered. He felt a little giddy, a little as if he were trying to walk a tightrope at a very high altitude. "Now what?"

"Now," Yiithrii'ah'aash answered slowly, "I believe we must converse with Ambassador Gaspard."

Not quite two hours later, Gaspard stared after Yiithrii'ah'aash's receding form, rubbing his chin meditatively.

"Well?" asked Riordan. "Will you support it?"

The ambassador quirked a smile. "Was my decision ever truly in doubt, Captain?"

"As far as I'm concerned, it still is. Nothing's settled until you agree to the mission explicitly. And on the record."

A single short laugh escaped from Gaspard's thin-lipped mouth. "You have become cautious of administrators and bureaucrats, *Monsieur* Riordan: good for you. So, yes: I explicitly and formally agree to the mission Yiithrii'ah'aash asks you to undertake to Delta Pavonis Three, and release the legation staff you require for that purpose. Of course, you understand that my approval is still but a legal fig leaf. I do not explicitly have the power to agree to a covert foreign entry into our space. Even permission to overtly receive their ship into one of our systems would require final confirmation and scheduling, although it is within my powers as a plenipotentiary ambassador to *agree* to it."

Riordan nodded carefully. "Yes, but you are still giving your consent. Which means you are instructing me to carry out this mission. If anyone is displeased, they will be coming after your hide, Etienne, no matter how much you protest, rightly, that it was my idea."

"I will claim derangement," Gaspard waved airily, "brought on by the stress of our ordeals upon Disparity and so forth." The ambassador smiled. Caine found that he was starting to like this man that he had originally dismissed as a nuisance and a popinjay. "Seriously, Captain, I have my reservations about what Yiithrii'ah'aash has requested. The same ones you have voiced, in fact. Since we were unable to detect the marking the Pavonians had impressed upon you, it only stands to reason that the Slaas-riithi could deposit more subtle markers, or perhaps biochemical agents, upon any of us or in any of the planetary environments with which they come into contact."

The ambassador sighed, leaned back in his chair. "But ironically, it is this very fact which decides me in favor of bypassing the appropriate quarantine and assessment protocols upon which our bureaucrats would insist. Not because they are unduly worried by such exposures: their concerns over surreptitious xenobiological intrusion could hardly be more justified than in this case. But by the time they arrive at an independent means of detecting the microorganisms or diffuse organic traces in question, this political moment will be long past."

"Which is why you showed only mild enthusiasm for Yiithrii'ah'aash's offer of providing the technology for detecting their markings."

"*Vraiment.* So the estimable Yiithrii'ah'aash provides us with the detection systems and biological guidelines he promised: what of it? How do we know that these are truly the only ones we require? Can we trust that he will not withhold those which are necessary to screen for agents and organics to which we have not yet been exposed, or have not yet detected? No, our quarantine administrators would rightly insist upon developing the machinery and protocols themselves. And that could require years, even decades." Gaspard cut the air with a decisive hand. "*Non*; we must cement this alliance now. And what the quarantine administrators do not know—and which has no traction upon their science, only upon this political moment—is that if the Slaasriithi had wished to make us plague carriers of one form or another, they have had months of opportunity to do so. Which we knew at the outset. And the only mitigating factor that would protect the entirety of the legation from an extended, or even lifelong, quarantine was the measure of genuine good will and mutual enlightened benefit that the Slaasriithi's own actions portended. This was the barometer we were forced to trust from the very beginning."

"In short, if the Slaasriithi really need us, then they aren't trying to poison us on the sly."

"Exactly so. And perhaps Yiithrii'ah'aash anticipated these very reservations. Perhaps that was why he insisted that we see their biospheres, their way of life, and their biological imperatives: so that we might understand the full significance of this mission he sends you upon now. For it is clear that without this indagator added back into their polytaxon, they lack not only the skills to protect themselves adequately, they lack the instincts."

Riordan nodded. "Those were my assessments, too." He sighed, leaned back into a posture not too different from Gaspard's own. "But even with your authority behind me, this mission is still going to be a tricky dance. I don't actually *possess* your authority personally, and I'm likely to be trying to bluff and bluster my way past colonial and military authorities. Particularly at Delta Pavonis."

Gaspard shook his head. "It may not be as difficult as you expect, Captain. I have official prerogatives of which you have not been made aware." Etienne obviously enjoyed the surprised look that Riordan was unable to suppress. "Oh, yes, not even *you* know all the provisions and entitlements of my appointment as the ambassador plenipotentiary to the Slaasriithi. For instance, I am able to confer upon you a limited measure of that pleni-potentiality: you have a measure of authority equal to my own if you are tasked to carry out initiatives that I authorize but for which I cannot be present. So, in instructing you to undertake this mission, you will enjoy my power and authority in matters directly pertaining to its execution."

"I could see no small amount of debate arising over the question of whether any given action 'directly pertains' to the execution of my mission."

"Naturally; that is the nature of diplomacy and diplomats. We dwell in a world where there is no black, no white; we navigate among shades of gray. However, I have been conferred broad powers—and the latitude to employ them—in order to secure an alliance with the Slaasriithi by the end of this journey. Fur-thermore, I am fully within my rights to transfer that aegis of authority to you for this special mission. So you may exercise the same broad latitude of action, and expect the same congenial interpretations of your prerogatives and authority."

Riordan smiled. "That's nice to know. It will be even nicer having a document that spells it all out for anyone who might be less than fully cooperative."

"With which I shall provide you, of course. I shall also pro-vide you with a means of being on more equal footing with most of the civilian and military authorities that you are likely to encounter. *Monsieurs* Sukhinin and Downing solicited and received a special writ from Admiral Lord Halifax on the day of our departure. It was to be employed in the event that I was killed, incapacitated, or that I was compelled to have you pursue legation business on what they term 'detached duty.'" Gaspard removed an envelope from the breast pocket within the liner of his duty suit, handed it to Riordan.

Who, frowning, opened it and discovered papers assigning him a brevet rank of commodore "for the duration of any detached duty to which he has been duly and officially assigned by Ambassador Plenipotentiary Etienne Gaspard, Consul of the Consolidated Terran Republic, in the furtherance of the objectives of the first legation to the Slaasriithi." Caine stared at the paper, the signatures and seals for a very long time. "This is wrong."

Gaspard glanced at him. "I beg your pardon? Everything is in order; I made certain of it."

Riordan shook his head. "No, I'm not referring to the legality of the document. I mean I've been boosted up the ranks far too quickly. Even if this is just a diplomatic convenience to give me necessary authority, I don't have the command experience or training to warrant this."

Gaspard frowned, folded his hands, thought for several very long seconds. "I am not eager to share this with you, *Monsieur* Riordan—it is not my way—but I must be frank: I consider your concerns largely unfounded. Firstly, I have worked with many flag rank officers who have never seen combat at all—or worse yet, with others who have commanded contingents with dire results. You, on the other hand, have distinguished yourself on this mission, and earlier, in the battles for both Barnard's Star and Earth itself. Have you commanded large warships? No, but neither have most of those so-called admirals."

Gaspard's frown deepened. "But that is merely the formal part of my argument. I must add my personal observation as well, and it is this: your innate abilities will more than compensate for the unevenness of your professional preparation. I do not pretend to be an expert on military matters, but as a diplomat, one of my most important skills is to be able to assess the character and capabilities of the individuals around me. Yours are beyond reproach; you are, as the American expression has it, the right person for this job, Captain—no: *Commodore*—Riordan."

"Well, I guess we'll find out if you're right." Riordan shook his head. "But I'll never be much of a diplomat."

Gaspard's smile widened. "So you keep claiming, in blatant disregard of all the evidence to the contrary. What you mean to say is that you do not wish to be a diplomat and that you have never claimed that as your career. But it has apparently chosen you. With enviable clarity, it would seem to me."

Riordan discovered that he was smiling slightly. "If I didn't know better," he commented, "I'd say that sounds like a compliment."

"I suppose it does." Gaspard almost smiled back. "Come; we must inform the others of what roles they will play when the legation is divided."

Chapter Fifty-Four

After Gaspard left the room with the members of the legation who were continuing on to Beta Aquilae, Riordan sat in silence, letting the others absorb all that they'd been told. The entirety of the surviving security contingent—Bannor, Tygg, Peter Wu, and Miles O'Garran—had received the news with the disinterested detachment of professional soldiers. So much of their life had been defined by getting unceremoniously shipped from one strange place to another that it hardly made any impression on them now.

Karam Tsaami didn't react much differently. He'd been piloting in different systems for almost ten years. Probably the only way in which this was a change from his accustomed routine was that he was going to keep seeing a lot of the same faces: in his line of work, that had been a rarity.

Tina Melah and Phil Friel sat close together and had actually smiled upon hearing the news; anything that kept them together was apparently fine by them. Melissa Sleeman's exchange of glances with Tygg strongly suggested that, although their mutual attraction might be at an earlier stage of development, it was every bit as strong.

The only person who looked at all ill-at-ease was also the only person whom Caine had been surprised to be named to his team, and apparently at her express request, Pandora Veriden. Her arms crossed, she furtively looked at the others, her frown contrasting oddly with the surprised expression on her face. Riordan had the distinct impression that the source of her surprise was herself, or more specifically, that she had asked for this posting. She certainly could have elected to continue her lucrative contract as Etienne's personal security expert, and Riordan suspected that if Downing were here, he would have been of the opinion that she should continue on in that role.

But she had chosen otherwise once Yiithrii'ah'aash had assured Gaspard and Caine, repeatedly and effusively, that the legation would not be exposed to further risk. A Slaasriithi shift-carrier designed for war—*Unassailable Aerie*—had arrived to carry them to Beta Aquilae. And several security ROVs that seemed to be almost as autonomous as robots now followed the remaining legation personnel everywhere, their sensors alert, the crowns of their small pop-turrets just barely visible.

Karam was the first to speak. "Morgan's not coming with us? He could be pretty handy if we run into any trouble—and if he can keep from shitting his shorts."

Despite her hard-assed self, Dora giggled. Positively giggled.

Riordan smiled. "No: he can't be spared. Part of the deal we worked out with Yiithrii'ah'aash is that Morgan gets to look at a variety of shipboard systems while traveling with them, and later on as well. Including their shift-drive."

"Which seems to have better than a one-light-year range advantage over the Arat Kur drive," Bannor murmured with a satisfied nod.

"Exactly. With all the technical intelligence we got from the Arat Kur, and now the Slaasriithi, we'll be a lot closer to achieving parity with the Ktor."

Dora folded her arms again. "Exactly what is *our* end of this deal you worked out with the Slaasriithi? And why do I think it has to do with our heading to Delta Pavonis Three?"

Riordan shook his head. "I'd like to be able to answer that, Dora, but I can't."

Neither Dora's face, nor her eyes, moved. "You can't answer, or you *won't* answer?"

Riordan just smiled.

Dora nodded. "Yeah. I thought so. Okay, no surprises. So how do we get there?"

"Yiithrii'ah'aash is taking us. We bring all our gear, the armored shuttle the Ktor left behind, all their gear, the clone for continued debriefing, and they repair *Puller* on the way. According to your specifications, Karam. Morgan's going over the finer points of our engineering and our weapon systems with them right now, but I don't expect any problems; our technology is embarrassingly basic compared to theirs."

Tina's face had contracted into a vinegary frown. "Why are we taking the clone equipment with us? Hardly seems to be worth the space."

"Well, firstly, it's all evidence. And we're taking everything of forensic value back with us, including the bodies." *And particularly the two mostly-intact Ktor. We didn't get a chance to harvest any usable DNA from Shethkador, but now we've got sources that can't invoke diplomatic privilege and immunity.* "But secondly, in a pinch, we might have want of their gear. Any gear, for that matter."

"What, us? Hell, you're a commodore now. Bannor's a major. We should be able to whistle up whatever we need, I figure!"

Phil smiled, slipped a hand in Tina's. "And how are we going to do that? Just dock *Puller* wherever we please and draw from any installation's stores? We won't have business being in any system we pass through. They won't have any record of *Puller* on any inbound carrier's manifest. And if they did have any record of us, they're not going to be rolling out the welcome mat; they're going to hit the alarm button, because we'll be about fifty light-years away from our last reported position. And if they were to ask us how we got there—"

Her eyes opened wide. "God, yes: we won't have arrived in a human shift carrier."

Karam leaned back, scowling. "Hell, considering just how far under the radar this mission will have to run, our side won't have any indication that any shift-carrier arrived in the system at all. Given what I've seen of Slaasriithi shift precision, they're going to be coming in behind gas giants, run slow and silent while they take on fuel, and then begin preacceleration for the next shift."

Riordan nodded. "That's the expectation. The Slaasriithi are also loaning us some of their technology and technical specialists to help make our job a little easier, but we won't get a chance to look *inside* their machinery. Their technical specialists are also duennas for their high-tech toys."

"What kind of toys?" Sleeman asked eagerly.

"We'll have a few of those high-speed drone-fighters we saw in orbit: 'cannonballs,' according to the apt Ktoran slang. And a few of the autonomous munitions platforms like the one we used at the river battle, but larger."

Dora leaned far back in her chair. "All weaponry. Why do I not like the sound of that and what it implies about our mission for Yiithrii'ah'aash?"

Riordan shrugged. "With any luck at all, we'll have no reason to use it as anything other than insurance or leverage. But if we do, then we let the Slaasriithi ROVs both dish out and take the heat instead of us."

O'Garran nodded. "I like the sound of *that*."

Karam scratched his left ear. "There's something I *don't* like the sound of: the length of the trip."

Caine nodded. "Yeah, it's long."

"How long?" Dora asked quickly.

"Six shifts to get back into human space at 70 Ophiuchi. Another three shifts to our, uh, final destination."

Veriden rolled her eyes. "Yeah, like I don't know it's Delta Pavonis."

Caine smiled but ignored her. "All told, we'll be lucky to get there by the second week of February."

"That's another four goddamned months!" Tina Melah cried.

"It is," Caine agreed. "And you'll be spending them in cold-sleep, just like you did on the way out here."

Melissa's eyes were wide with interest. "Can the Slaasriithi cold cells be adjusted to handle us?"

Caine shrugged. "They seem to think so, but we're not going to find out. Since our best medical tests and scanners haven't been able to detect their organics in our bloodstreams, we're not about to take the risk of giving them our whole body to infuse. So we'll rig the long-duration escape pods on *Puller* for the job."

Dora folded her arms again. "They're quad pods. That leaves two of us without a berth."

"There's a medical cold-cell in sick bay; that will provide for a ninth person."

"There are ten of us," Dora persisted.

Riordan smiled. "So we'll draw straws. In the meantime, I'll brief you on what I know of our mission during the preacceleration toward our first shift. That way, when everyone is awakened, we'll be ready for an update and can hit the ground running. And once we're done, we should be able to get back home to Earth a lot faster than before."

Tygg frowned. "How?"

"Just before we left Sigma Draconis, I heard talk about the Republic setting up an express service using one or two of the captured Arat Kur shift carriers. With their greater range and reduced turnaround time, travel back to Earth should be reduced from six shifts to four, and only twelve weeks, total."

"That's still a long time," Dora complained, "even from *Delta Pavonis*."

Riordan just nodded: every day was a long time when you hadn't seen your soulmate in nine months and hadn't seen your son in—well, forever. "It will be good to get home," he sighed. "We've been away too long." He hung his head and laughed. "As I count it, I now owe my son Connor fourteen birthday presents. And his mother a proper proposal."

Noticing the sudden silence, Caine looked up, discovered an oddly changed scene. Bannor, Tygg, Peter, Miles, and Karam were staring at the floor, faces wooden; the rest were staring at them, baffled.

"What is it with you guys?" Dora leaned forward. "Did someone die?"

Rulaine looked up, quick and hard. "Shut up."

Dora blinked, frowned, opened her mouth.

"Just shut up, Dora." He turned to Caine—who, seeing Bannor's eyes, had the sudden sense that he might vomit: he'd seen eyes like that before. At funeral homes and intensive care wards.

"What is it?" Riordan asked. "What haven't I been told?"

"Look," started Bannor, hands opening into an appeal. "I didn't know—none of us did—that you didn't know about it. Not at first, and then—"

"That I didn't know about *what*, goddamn it?" Riordan held his voice level, wasn't sure if he'd be able to manage that measure of self-control again.

"Caine, if you go back to Earth, you won't find her—Elena—there."

Riordan's thoughts spun off on their own, uncertain, inchoate. "Not on Earth? Why?"

Bannor opened his mouth, then looked away. Peter Wu took up the tale. "Commodore, back in Jakarta, after we took the Arat Kur headquarters, how much do you recall right after Shethkador shot you in the back with his environmental suit's manipulator arm?"

Riordan frowned. "I—I don't remember much. I remember falling. I remember most of you were there. I remember Elena screaming, her brother Trevor trying to call in a med-team. I remember feeling that arm sticking out of my back..."

The arm that was no longer attached to Shethkador's faux environmental suit when Caine had confronted him again at Sigma Draconis, where the Ktor was still masquerading as a cold-planet entity calling itself Apt-Counsel-of-Lenses, and where—

—Apt-Counsel rolled closer to the platform. Caine watched for the angle of the manipulator arm, saw that it had not been replaced. And saw that the other arm was missing as well: a prudent precaution...

But what if the other arm *hadn't* been removed as a prudent precaution? What if—?

"Shethkador shot Elena with the other arm a moment after you fell in Jakarta." It was Rulaine's voice again: bitter, tight, hating every word. "She was turning when he shot her. It hit her in the spleen, and a piece of the arm lodged in her spine. The two of you were assessed; our docs thought they might be able to save you, tried, had to ice you so that the Dornaani could work their medical magic later on.

"But they didn't spend one second wondering if they could save Elena; she would have been dead within the hour. The Dornaani offered to mend her if they could, and our docs turned her over to them. They put her in one of their own ICU cold cells and took her away. At first, we thought Downing must have told you when they woke you up. We never guessed—"

"No, the son of a bitch never told me. Of course, he never tells me anything, never commits to anything." Riordan didn't remember getting to his feet. "But that's going to change next time I meet him. Or he won't walk away from that meeting."

Riordan wasn't paying attention to his tone of voice, wasn't even bothering to choose his words. When he looked around the room again, he had paced halfway across the ring of chairs. The other nine were sitting up very straight; O'Garran had grown pale, Dora looked like she was ready to run, Tina's eyes were wide.

Tygg's voice rose behind him. "Caine, I was with Trevor when they took Elena away. Downing was right to do it. There wasn't any other choice."

"Maybe not. But he could have left me on Earth to be with her, to take care of Connor. And he sure as shit had the choice to tell me about it when they yanked me out of my cold cell."

Rulaine's voice dragged like a lame dog, moving in a direction it had to go, but wanted very badly not to. "I'm not sure Downing really had a choice then, either, Caine."

"Why? Was he under some kind of gag order?"

"He didn't have to be under any order, Caine. He simply had to read the strategic tea leaves."

Riordan turned. "What sort of bullshit are you talking, Bannor?"

"No bullshit; straight, hard facts, Caine. Come on, think it through. First of all, they needed you at Sigma Draconis. Downing knew that, and he was right. If it hadn't been for you, would we have found out that the Ktor were human? More to the point, would we have learned it in time to keep that bastard Shethkador from tricking us into bombing the Arat Kur out of existence? You were the linchpin that day, Caine; your presence was the indispensable variable."

"Bullshit."

"You can say 'bullshit' all you want, and wear that combination of real and false modesty all day long, but you know I'm telling the truth. You smelled the lie that Shethkador was peddling; you pieced it together. That was the moment we stepped back from xenocide, Caine—and not a moment before. And you're going to tell me Downing wasn't right to have you there? But he had to have you in that room undistracted by the knowledge that your lover was frozen on death's doorstep light-years away, and your son was a veritable orphan." Bannor, seeing Riordan paralyzed by the terrible truth of his words, stopped abruptly, hung his head to stare at his tightly clasped hands.

It was Phil Friel who broke the silence with a sigh. "And within twenty-four hours, you were meeting with Yiithrii'ah'aash. And within another four, we were being scraped together into this legation. So when was Downing supposed to tell you, Caine? Was there ever a reasonable moment, a moment when you didn't need all your attention and faculties, both for yourself and for the mission?" He paused. "I don't know Downing, but withholding this information doesn't sound like something he *chose* to do: it sounds like something he *had* to do. And then the rush of events did the rest."

Riordan did not remember returning to his seat, was not sure how long he'd been sitting there before he looked up and said, through a tight, parched throat, "I'd like to be alone." And then he was lost again: lost in one image after another of Elena, occasionally interspersed with the one photo he'd ever seen of his son Connor.

Out of the silence, as if happening at the other end of a long tunnel, he vaguely heard a chair leg scrape on the floor, then Dora's voice. "Hey, you."

It was Karam who answered. "Me?"

"You see anyone else sitting where I'm looking? Let's go get dinner. And don't get any ideas. I'm just hungry, is all."

Karam must have risen and left with her. At some point the others did as well.

Riordan didn't see or hear them leave; all he could see was Elena.

Mriif'vaal accompanied Yiithrii'ah'aash to the flight operations section of the Third Silver Tower. They approached the waiting shuttle in silence. Yiithrii'ah'aash sent forth a thin wave front of amity pheromones, and turned to board and begin his journey back to the *Tidal-Drift-Instaurator-to-Shore-of-Stars* and, ultimately, human space.

"Yiithrii'ah'aash, a question, if I may."

Yiithrii'ah'aash turned back toward Mriif'vaal. "Of course. You have been most silent today, and I have not wanted to distract you from your thoughts."

"They are not thoughts so much as they are concerns. Anxieties, even."

Yiithrii'ah'aash's interlaced his tendrils, made sure that his posture was relaxed. "Please share these with me; perhaps I may help."

"My gratitude, Yiithrii'ah'aash. The events surrounding the humans, and particularly Caine Riordan—I am not sure I understand all the consequences of the choice we made to preserve his life by applying the ancient theriac."

Ah: Mriif'vaal is both subtle and wise. He will be an excellent Prime Ratiocinator, when his day comes. "What consequences do you fear or foresee?"

"My reservations are not specific, but general."

"Please elucidate."

"Gladly, Yiithrii'ah'aash. I have never before encountered so many safeguards against the use of any resource that is at our disposal, and so many limiting protocols for its application. Even our employment of nuclear weapons has fewer, or at least less narrow, constraints. And yet, the danger one would presume to necessitate such extreme precautions is nowhere evident in the action of the theriac itself."

Clever. Excellent. But I may not fully satisfy your curiosity, and so apologize for the lie of omission that I must now employ. "The consequences of the theriac are difficult to foresee; they may take different forms, it is said. However, we created these potential problems by acting hastily in bringing the humans to us." *That we had no good alternative to that haste is a separate matter.* "What I commend to your further consideration is this: what problems we may have made for ourselves, and for Caine Riordan, by raising him from near-death with the theriac are in the future. Obversely, we had to act to solve urgent problems that beset us in the present. And Caine Riordan was, and remains, the key to their solution. In short, there was no choice. Besides, Mriif'vaal, beyond his utility to our purposes, Caine is also a great friend to our species and will prove even more so in the years to come, I foresee."

Mriif'vaal buzzed faintly. "And you are fond of him."

Yiithrii'ah'aash's neck wiggled. "And I am fond of him. But beyond any personal feeling in the matter, there is the need for our two species to be Affined. A powerful need." Yiithrii'ah'aash paused, let that pause alter the tenor of the conversation as he resumed with a casual, almost speculative tone. "I, and others, have been contemplating how the humans both problematize and adorn our macroscopic perspective of the universe, and how that points toward a long-term solution to our current problems. In contemplating the humans, I find myself unfurling tendrils of logic into the fibers of the cosmos as it is revealed to us through our challenges."

"And what does this reflection show you?"

Yiithrii'ah'aash was silent for a second, elected to answer Mriif'vaal's question with one of his own. "It is odd, is it not, how each of the sapient species in this region of space has a special talent?"

"I am not sure I perceive your meaning."

"It is as though the way our own species has distributed our need for different skills over our taxae and subtaxae recalls and resonates with the cosmos' own distribution of special talents and abilities among the other species we have encountered." He sent a final wave of affinity pheromones at Mriif'vaal. "You might contemplate this, in quiet moments."

Not daring to say more, Yiithrii'ah'aash dipped his neck in farewell, turned and boarded the waiting shuttle.

Chapter Fifty-Five

Brenlor glanced at Ayana Tagawa, the only Aboriginal who was still on the bridge of the *Arbitrage*. "Your shift-plot is sufficient. Leave us."

The small Asian female nodded her way into a reasonable bow that never did become fully submissive, Nezdeh noted. *She is the best of them and the most dangerous. And having lost one of our two Intendants and two near-Evolved, we need her even more than before. That does not bode well.*

Arbitrage's preacceleration burn caused them all to lean slightly toward the aft bulkhead; in eight hours they would terminate thrust and engage the shift drive to the system designated as G-22-26. But after that . . . Brenlor had not announced their subsequent course, which made Nezdeh nervous. His decisions had improved recently, but he had closeted himself over the matter of their further destinations and ultimate objective. Thus shielded from counsel, Brenlor would decide their fate. Possibly disastrously.

Brenlor Srin Perekmeres crossed his arms, leaned over the star-plot, shrank its scale to show more stars in the same volume. "Our mission to disrupt the establishment of an alliance between the Aboriginals and the Slaasriithi has failed. While our loss of Terran equipment and clones is negligible, we shall continue to feel the loss of our own team members. However, we still have a way to achieve our primary objective: to undermine any postwar stability between the various powers. We must ensure that the Aboriginals' recovery from the war is problematic and that they are unable to fully capitalize upon both the spoils of their victory over the Arat Kur and the benefits of any alliance with the Slaasriithi. And in so doing, we shall implicate House Shethkador as providing woefully insufficient leadership in this area of space."

So we will achieve the same ends with far fewer means—including the inestimable advantage of surprise? This, thought Nezdeh, *should prove most interesting.*

"Firstly, our defeat in this system provides our foes with no decisive forensic evidence, so it is unlikely to register with the Autarchs as more than a nuisance. Because Jesel and Suzruzh were not the product of optimized genelines, we left no definitive genetics. The Catalysites were expended and hence, deliquesced. We did not lose any of our own technology on their mission. In summary, any accusation against the Ktoran Sphere will be circumstantial and unsubstantiatable. The incident will become at most a cavil, not a decisive argument, against us, either within the Sphere or the Accord. Indeed, all the evidence we left behind is of Aboriginal origin."

Idrem nodded, folded his own arms. "Yes, but the Aboriginals still lack the shift range, to say nothing of the astrographic charts, to make their way to this system. So the question will be asked: how did they get there?"

"To which every responsible party must presently answer: 'Who knows?' Every power of the Accord will deny involvement, especially our own Sphere. And so, discord is sown. Let them concoct whatever hypothetical plots they wish. It shall not point back to the Ktoran Sphere or our patrons."

Sehtrek rubbed his chin. "And yet, Srin Shethkador, the Autarchs and the Hegemons will all know—*know*—who did this."

Brenlor smiled. "Yes, they will know. And part of what they will know is that Shethkador failed. We stole a ship of his in order to commandeer the *Arbitrage*, and although he was charged with calming the postwar waters, they instead roiled and frothed due to his inability to establish full dominion."

Idrem nodded. Nezdeh could tell that he was impressed with Brenlor's growth as a schemer. "That is so. But despite insufficient evidence, the other powers of the Accord will also know."

"Of course they will…and what could be better for generating the suspicions and tensions that are the precursors to the resumption of war? The humans will point incessantly to the impossibility of their involvement. The Slaasriithi must already conjecture it was us, the Arat Kur will be cast into greater turmoil, and the Hkh'Rkh will not care. But the greatest impact will be among the Aboriginals themselves, who will be torn between concealing or revealing the implicating clones and landers and guns we left behind."

"Yes, which could ultimately align the still disparate and factious nations of the Aboriginals strongly *against* us."

"Perhaps, but only if they have the luxury of time, of clarity, in which to consider the relevant facts. However, we shall ensure that the reports of what occurred here will be thoroughly mixed with new, more perplexing and distressing reports."

"And your plan can sow this profound confusion?"

Brenlor nodded, leaned away from the plot. For the first time his posture suggested hesitation. "I know of a project, a false flag operation left in sleeper mode, that was established by the next to last Hegemon of House Perekmeres. It was developed intermittently, opportunistically, starting approximately two centuries ago. It fell by the wayside a century later and was all but forgotten. Indeed, it was not referenced in any of the records that were arrogated during our Extirpation. When our House died, so did all the memories of this project. Except for mine."

"And you know of it how?" Tegrese asked.

Brenlor stared at her. "My father was one of those few who had overseen the project. And if all the pieces of this hidden ploy remain where they were deposited, it only requires my touch to set it in motion and thereby draw the Aboriginals into another disastrous war. In the bargain, we shall assure the Ktoran Sphere of the continued alliance of the Hkh'Rkh and gain access to badly needed resources. In the meantime, as we make our journey, we may reanimate the many UnDreamers of the *Arbitrage* and train them properly." He leaned back. "It will be risky, but it can be done. And it is so bold that none will look for it."

Sehtrek stared at the star plot. "So how do we get to the place where these assets were deposited?"

"With our tug, it is but four shifts before we stand on the threshold of our final destination. From G-22-26, we proceed to

HU Delphini, thence to AC+17 534-105, further to EQ Pegasi, and on to our penultimate destination G 130-4."

Nezdeh almost rolled her eyes. *Enough drama, or caution, Brenlor:* "And what is the *ultimate* destination?"

"BD +56 2966, to use the designation given on the Aboriginal charts."

Nezdeh started. "That is the location of the Hkh'Rhh colony world, Turkh'saar. It is also the system directly adjacent to their homeworld." She managed to suppress *"Are you mad?"*

Brenlor's leonine smile did not put her at ease. "I told you it would be too bold to be predicted."

"That is...one way of putting it."

He leaned across the table; there was both a threat and an appeal in his voice, his eyes. "Think of it this way, Nezdeh: where, in all of known space, may we go now? If we go to our patrons they will dispose of us themselves. We are too weak, we hold no leverage, and we are certain to become an embarrassment. We are otherwise friendless. But the Hkh'Rkh are the most rudimentary race technologically and eager for allies who prefer direct, vigorous action as they do. Allies like us. Specifically, like House Perekmeres.

"If we train our Aboriginals well enough to win one easy engagement on the behalf of the Hkh'Rkh, we shall see the seeds of war germinate in the fertile field my father prepared for us on Turkh'saar, seeds that will be brought by the Terrans themselves."

Nezdeh crossed her arms. "And how can we be sure that the Terrans will sow these seeds?"

"When I activate the sleeper cell on Turkh'saar, the Terrans will have to send an uninvited envoy to ensure that the diplomatic consequences do not spiral out of hand. And when they do, we shall be there to serendipitously catch them in the act: to repel invaders of Hkh'Rkh space." He leaned back. "We shall have defended the property and the honor of the Hkh'Rkh, and they, by their codes, shall owe us an honor-debt for doing so in their absence—or for succeeding where their outclassed forces could not. Suddenly we, not the failed Shethkador and his Autarchal lackeys, will have the greatest influence over the Hkh'Rkh's loyalty, and with that, we will become a force to be reckoned with, even if neither the Autarchs nor the Hegemons wish us to be so."

Idrem frowned. "The resulting war will be absolute, uncontainable."

"Of course it shall. And that war will ultimately return us to power. The Ktoran Sphere will be forced to exert its dominion aggressively in order to preserve its hold on its Hkh'Rkh allies. And the Hegemons will not be able to touch us without triggering an honor-war with those same indispensable allies." He turned to Nezdeh. "What is your opinion, Srina Perekmeres?"

"I think it just might succeed," she admitted. *I also think it might get us all killed, but I can't think of a better plan at the moment.* "Now, tell us more about this false-flag sleeper cell—"

Caine Riordan checked the medical cryocell's readings. After three days, Bannor's core temperature had been reduced to three-quarters of a degree centigrade, with blood substitute infusions at nominal levels. The glycol perfusion was deemed complete and internal sensors at full function. He nodded at his pale, unconscious friend and closed the long lid of the white oblong, adorned with blue and green status lights.

Behind Riordan, Yiithrii'ah'aash commented, "I hope it will not annoy you that I offer, one final time, the option of spending this journey in one of our cryogenic suspension units. It is fully adaptable to your species in every regard."

Caine smiled. *I'm sure it is, which is precisely what worries me. You know our biology too damned well and could manipulate it too damned easily.* "I appreciate the offer, Yiithrii'ah'aash, but a good commander always watches over his troops. Particularly when they are especially vulnerable." He smiled.

Yiithrii'ah'aash may have read Riordan's expression. "I perceive. We intended nothing by offering you the use of our modified cold cells, but at least this way, there can be no questions."

Riordan leaned back against Bannor's high-tech sarcophagus. "And you and I will have plenty of time to converse, maybe to forge the kind of bonds that should exist between allied species."

Yiithrii'ah'aash's tendrils were a wave falling in slow motion. "Would that I could participate as you intend, but I follow the instructions of others even as you do. It is incumbent upon me to sleep through these many weeks as well. But I shall be awakened periodically to assess our situation and review our navigational choices, and then again in the preacceleration phase before our last shift to Delta Pavonis itself. Perhaps on those occasions, we may begin the exchange you envision."

"I'd like that. So the Ktoran ship shifted out-system?"

"Over a day ago." Seeing the surprised look on Riordan's face, he explained. "I did not wish to bother you as you prepared your friends for their suspension. You were especially solicitous of them."

"Yeah, well, they're my responsibility."

"You also have a responsibility to yourself, Caine Riordan. I have consulted with those of my crew who are monitoring your caloric intake. It is insufficient."

Riordan grinned crookedly. "I mean no slight, Yiithrii'ah'aash, but your cuisine is not, er, the most appetizing."

"It is as I warned you. We simply do not have enough of your accustomed viands, and it was reported to me that your group did not find our genetically matched foodstuffs agreeable."

Riordan rubbed his stomach. "You heard right."

Yiithrii'ah'aash began walking toward the forward hatchway that would lead him back into his own ship. "What shall you do during this long journey, Caine Riordan?"

Caine glanced at *Puller*'s bridge stations as they passed that compartment. "I didn't start out as a military officer or a diplomat, Yiithrii'ah'aash. I fell into it, pretty much by accident. But now that I am a captain—hell, a bloody commodore—and a diplomat, there are some skills I should acquire and hone. It's only book and simulator knowledge, of course. But it's the best—and the least—I can do. A good combat commander tries to prepare as much as possible."

"You are a defense analyst. And you have fought. Do you not know enough already?"

Riordan smiled: it was a question that only a near-pacifist with no speciate concept of a military could ask. "Yiithrii'ah'aash, I know just enough about being a naval officer to be aware that I know almost nothing. I have reasonable familiarity with the various services, their various missions, but now I need depth, genuine expertise." Riordan sighed, thought of all the reading and sims ahead of him. "It's ridiculous that I'm going to try to teach myself. People with a lifetime of experience should be the ones imparting the knowledge. They're the ones who know where all the fine-sounding theory breaks down and the messy reality begins. But I can only work with what I've got. So I'll learn what

I can, keep my limitations in mind, and do my best when the time comes. Or die trying."

"One may only train so much, Caine Riordan. All creatures require rest or reflection."

"I'll have plenty of time to rest. And as concerns reflection"— passing his ready room, he saw the photo of Connor's young teenaged face, recognizably a fusion of his own and Elena's—"I have a lot of letters to write. A lifetime's worth, you might say." Three more steps brought them to the forward hatch. Riordan raised his hand in farewell. "I look forward to talking when you awaken, Yiithrii'ah'aash."

Yiithrii'ah'aash was evidently staring at Caine, then glanced back to the photo of Connor, flanked by one of Elena. "I look forward to our conversations as well, Caine Riordan. Until then, be well. And, if you can, be at peace."

The hatch closed automatically while Caine was still considering Yiithrii'ah'aash's parting words. Or would that be his parting benediction? He glanced back at the photos the Slaasriithi had noticed, wondered how often the exosapient had glimpsed him staring at them. Being at peace was a whole lot easier when your loved ones were close, safe, healthy, cared for. *A common trait among all species, I'll bet,* Caine reflected. *Maybe that will be our first topic of conversation.*

Or maybe it will be about the limits of responsibility for others and their *loved ones.* Riordan reached inside his duty-suit, slid a photograph out of an inner pocket: Keith Macmillan's little girl, Katie. Found on Macmillan's person, it was much-seamed and marked by the slowly erosive oils of fingertips. *And who shall save you now, little Katie, with a front tooth missing and a smile as wide as the Scottish highland skies?* Riordan started to replace the photograph but stopped: *no. You're going to put it next to Connor's. You're going to look at those laughing eyes of hers every day. And you're going to ask yourself: what must be done?*

Caine felt his stomach sink; he'd come close to putting the picture with the rest of the forensic materials, the evidence, several times, but had always held back. Held back from conveniently filing away that smile and those eyes and letting the cruel events set in motion by the Ktor run their tragic course. *No, he decided, no; you stay with me, Katie. And teach me about the limits of our responsibilities to others, to the innocent. If there are any limits.*

Caine dogged the hatch, leaned into his stateroom, and affixed Katie's photo between those of Elena and Connor. He touched their faces and then moved with a lengthening stride toward the bridge simulators. He had a lot of catching up to do.

And only four months in which to do it.

Tlerek Srin Shethkador wanted to ignore the privacy chimes but could not afford to do so. It was the unpleasant duty of a captain to respond to the summons of any who had sufficient rank to consult with him directly. He suppressed a sigh. "Enter."

Olsirkos entered in a rush, bowed his obeisance. "Word has arrived at the Convocation station located at EV Lacertae. The internecine friction among the Hkh'Rkh is reaching dangerous levels."

"Is a cause attributed?"

"Reportedly, there is an incursion of Aboriginal raiders in their codominium system with the Arat Kur at BD +56 2966."

Shethkador frowned. "That is absurd. The Aboriginals have no way to reach that system. And if they could, such an act would be folly. It is in the Aboriginals' interests to encourage calm relations and secure an extended peace for both reconstruction and technological upgrades. They are not behind this madness."

"Your wisdom guides my opinions, Potent Srin. But if it is not the Aboriginals, then who could it be?"

"That, Olsirkos, is a most interesting question. And one to which you shall find the answer."

"Me, Fearsome Srin?"

"Yes, you. The shift-destroyer *Will-Breaker* is due within the week. You shall take command of her and surreptitiously investigate what is transpiring in that system, especially its main world, Turkh'saar."

"Of course, Fearsome Srin. But what of maintaining a watch for the renegade Perekmeres who absconded with *Red Lurker* and the Aboriginal shift-carrier *Arbitrage*?"

"That is part of why I must remain here at Sigma Draconis. That, and to be on hand for the postsurrender talks that the Autarchs have instructed me to request. But I would not at all be surprised if, in the course of investigating the current insanity arising on Turkh'saar, you come across the spoor of these Perekmeres curs."

"You think that they may be behind this disturbance, Honored Srin?"

"Possibly. There is a smell of desperation about this 'raiding,' and the renegades of an Extirpated House would certainly bear that reek, themselves. Besides, they might correctly perceive that a precipitous plunge into another war with the Aboriginals and their allies could be parlayed into a rise in their fortunes."

"If I find evidence of the Perekmeres' involvement, shall I seek them out and destroy them, Srin Shethkador?"

"Your primary task is to observe and report, Olsirkos." *The Progenitors only know that the subtleties of statecraft are not within the compass of your abilities.* "Then I shall determine how we shall respond. But presently, I have a most unpleasant task to attend to."

"Further analysis of the peace treaty between the Aboriginals and the Arat Kur?"

"Worse. I must update the Autarchs on the situation here. Give word to ready the Sensorium. I will Contact the Autarchs by Reification within the hour. Now leave me. There is much work to be done if these Aboriginals are not to get out of hand."

Chapter Fifty-Six

Commodore Steven Cameron, skipper of the Commonwealth cruiser *Valiant*, acting C-in-C for the Delta Pavonis system—and therefore, its glorified traffic control supervisor—frowned when his comm officer, Lieutenant Stephanie Souders, turned to him with a deep frown. She handed him the transponder code, tail number, and supplementary Commonwealth identifiers relayed by the incoming Wolfe-class corvette. He stared at the unfamiliar data strings. "What the hell is this? Or more to the point, *who* the hell is this?"

"I wish I could tell you, Skipper," Souders replied with crossed arms. "Not on the list of craft that have entered Delta Pavonis. Ever."

"Bloody hell," Cameron muttered. And right at the end of his duty shift. Almost as if someone had planned it that way. Which gave him pause: was it possible that someone *had* planned it that way? *Bollocks, I'm starting at shadows now.* "Raise this, eh, UCS *Puller*, Lieutenant. Let's hear their story."

"Better be a good one," Souders grumbled. "Line is open, sir."

"UCS *Puller*, this is Commodore Steven Cameron, acting CINCPAV and captain of the UCS *Valiant*. Please confirm identity, and report mission and status."

The flat screen brightened and revealed a vaguely familiar face sitting at the center of a patched-up bridge; *Puller* had evidently seen some action in the late war. "This is Commodore Caine

Riordan, temporarily in command of UCS *Puller* on detached duty. Special operations. Relaying ops codes and authorizations now."

Souders turned towards Cameron, eyebrows raised, and tilted her head at the supplementary screen where the new data and codes were scrolling in. Cameron put on his best poker face. "Commodore Riordan—" and then he knew why he recognized the face. "Commodore, are you the same Caine Riordan who presented at the Parthenon Dialogs last year?"

Riordan's expression was a fusion of a smile and a grimace. "Guilty as charged."

"A pleasure to meet you, si—Commodore. But your OpOrds are, well, most irregular. And incomplete."

Riordan's smile was amiable. "They sure are, Commodore Cameron. Wish I could share it all with you, but I can't. Here's the classification level for the redacted components of the op, and my own, er, non-Naval clearance level." He nodded to someone off screen.

Souders' frown deepened. "Commodore," she muttered, "I don't even recognize his code."

"I do," Cameron replied.

"What is it?"

"I was told that if I ever see this code and this classification level, I have one relevant directive: not to ask a damn thing about it. Run it through the black box; if it checks out, he's got all the authority he needs to do whatever he wants."

Souders waited for the secure cypher check to finish. "Comes back green, sir."

Cameron nodded, glanced up at Riordan. "Sorry about the delay, Commodore. Protocols."

Riordan's smile was broad, easy. "I fully understand, Commodore. Do I have permission to initiate descent to the Shangri La subcontinent on DeePeeThree?"

"You do, but before you dip your nose into the cloud-tops, I wonder if you could give me a broad picture of what to expect?"

Riordan raised an eyebrow. "Pardon?"

Cameron leaned back. "Commodore, you're about to head dirtside to the same place where you made first contact. You might say, to the source of all the troubles we've had since then. And from what I understand of your last visit, the Colonial Development Combine was not particularly enamored of you when you left."

Riordan's smile became rueful. "You have a talent for understatement, Commodore Cameron."

"So I've been told. What I'm asking is: should I be prepared for a firestorm on Shangri La or elsewhere?"

Riordan steepled his fingers. "That is an excellent question. I wish I had an excellent answer. Part of why we're going in unannounced is because we don't really know what we're going to find. Sure, we get groundside reports, but those are from civilian observers who could be very, very bribable. That's why the cloak-and-dagger approach, Commodore."

"Which raises another question: just how did you get here at all? I've no record of *Puller,* or any Wolfe-class corvette, deploying here."

"That's because we were containerized for security purposes before shift, then were cut loose in our container shortly after we were carried in-system."

"Carried in-system by what carrier, Commodore?"

Riordan smiled. "Wish I could tell you."

"Does that mean you can't or you *won't* tell me?"

"Both, actually. As you can see, various elements of our full orders are classified, including our assignment to this detached duty. Fleet didn't want any CoDevCo stooges inside our ranks to be able to pass along a warning that we're about to show up to run a compliance check here. So everything pertaining to our reassignment and transport to this system was kept under wraps. But frankly, I couldn't tell you who gave us the ride even if I was allowed to. Naval ops boxed us up, let us sit, and then some shift-carrier came and picked us up. It never identified itself. We were handled by an intelligence cell, not the skipper of the ship, and those folks didn't share out any info. Once we got here, we were told to lay doggo until our secure mission clock ran down. That happened three days ago. And here we are."

Cameron frowned. "That's a lot of skullduggery for a visit to a corporate compound."

"Sure is. On the other hand, site intel suggests CoDevCo may have resumed hunting down the locals—who are soon to be recategorized, definitively, as exosapients. And you know what that means."

Cameron nodded. "Murder charges. Very well, Mr.—er, Commodore Riordan. Down you go, and we'll keep a channel open. I imagine they might not take very kindly to your visit, and we'd be all too happy to lend a hand if you need it."

"I just might, Commodore Cameron. Thanks, and we'll keep you posted."

The line closed. Souders frowned at the screen. "He'll 'keep us posted' in a pig's ass." She looked ready to spit. "I think I believe just slightly less than half of everything he said, sir. And I don't care *who* he is."

"That's as may be," Cameron temporized, "but his clearance code and authorization string checks out as legit. You think *those* are false?"

Souders' frown deepened. "No," she admitted finally. "I just don't like being lied to by people with big ranks and bigger clearance ratings."

Then you've chosen the wrong line of work, Steph. "Keep that channel open, Lieutenant. I don't think we've heard the last of Commodore Riordan on this matter."

"Hell," Souders sighed, "I suspect that was just the opening act."

"It must feel strange, being back here." Bannor Rulaine ran his targeting binoculars over the CoDevCo complex a kilometer away.

Riordan, waiting for word that *Puller* was in position, shrugged. "That's not what's on my mind right now."

"No? Seeing the locals again, maybe?"

Riordan shook his head. "No. Lying. I had to lie to Commodore Cameron to get us down here."

"Well, you knew that was coming."

Riordan shouldered his liquimix battle rifle, jacked it into the HUD on his helmet, watched it pick out targets based on thermal signatures and silhouette analysis. "Knowing you'll have to lie is different than doing it. I'm not saying there was any choice; not saying the stakes aren't high enough. Just saying it disgusts me, particularly when I have to do it to someone wearing the same uniform."

"Yes," Bannor agreed. "That's the worst." He raised his head slightly. "The stragglers are starting to run back into the compound, now."

Caine nodded, swept his scope over the familiar facility. Almost two and a half years ago, he had walked those dusty lanes, dined in that refectory, swum in that executive pool. It was all a bit shabby now. After the Parthenon Dialogues, the then-World Confederation had suspended all operations other than petrochemical prospecting with vertical drilling. The Hague had also tried to mount an investigation into the willful extermination of the local population of Pavonians, now known to be regressed Slaasriithi, but was stymied by procedural challenges. Then the Arat Kur and Hkh'Rkh had invaded and everything other than speciate autonomy, and possibly survival, was set aside. Now, as some semblance of calm was returning, there had been inquiries into whether CoDevCo's Site One facility had remained in compliance with the suspension order. No direct answer to the question was ever received. However, much verbiage about soliciting advice of counsel before vouchsafing a reply was sent in its place. Which, Riordan was sure, meant that the moment CoDevCo had no longer been under direct official oversight, they had returned to their rapacious ways.

Close passes by *Puller* confirmed it. Digging around the archaeological site reminiscent of a half-sized Acropolis had clearly resumed, and thermal sensors showed a number of small teams up near the hidden valley that was the preferred refuge of the Pavonians. Whether CoDevCo's henchmen had resumed hunting them to extinction or were simply containing them was unclear, but it was an absolute violation of the restrictions that had been placed upon their activities.

As *Puller* had swung around to make its initial approach, missiles had swarmed up out of the jungle at her. Melissa Sleeman had knocked them all down. She had become a pretty fair hand running the lasers in the point-defense fire mode.

Karam had lowered *Puller* on its vertifans, dropped off the Slaasriithi autonomous munitions platform, and fired a few beams into the bushes. That had sent the SAM teams scurrying back toward base, where they were finally arriving. And where CoDevCo was likely to either make a last stand or capitulate. But Riordan couldn't give them much time to make up their minds about which; they would have already earmarked any incriminating evidence for speedy elimination.

Bannor ran through a radio check. "Everyone's ready for the show to begin, Commodore," he reported. "Time to provide some pretext for pacification."

Riordan leaned towards his own collarcom. "Melissa, shift over to the ROV controls."

"Got it."

"Advance the Slaasriithi AMP to waypoint two and hold position."

"Acknowledged. And Commodore?"

"Yes, Melissa?"

"Is Tygg there with you?"

Riordan suppressed a smile while Bannor rolled his eyes. "No, he's about three hundred meters to our left, Melissa."

"Oh. Well, tell him to be careful. Please."

"Will do. Stand ready to activate the PA system we've rigged on the AMP." Riordan leaned down over his CoBro eight-millimeter's scope. Site One was relatively quiet; the fleeing SAM teams had repositioned themselves around the central marshalling area where a defunct fountain stood bleaching in the unrelenting yellow-amber sun. There were two prepared positions flanking the open ground, which had already been there when Riordan was an unwanted guest at the facility. Their relatively basic rocket launchers—tripod-mounted, with simple guidance packages—had been swiveled around to guard the main approach. Perfect. Just enough illegal ordnance to crucify CoDevCo in court, but not enough to really be a bother today.

Caine's collarcom crackled. "Commodore?"

"Yes, Melissa?"

"The AMP has now reached waypoint two."

"Good. Advance to waypoint three and hold."

"Do you want me to activate the PA system yet?"

"No, but I'll be calling for it soon. Riordan out."

"And there's our spider-monster, right on time," Bannor announced.

Sure enough, the much heavier, hexapedal Slaasriithi autonomous munitions platform emerged from the tree line and advanced toward the marshalling ground at a leisurely pace.

From the windows of the refectory, one of the more solidly built structures, small arms barked like a pack of warning dogs. The AMP showed no effect and did not stop. Riordan saw hints of what might have been loading and target tracking movements in the two defensive berms flanking the open ground, but none of the hurried motions consistent with an imminent attack.

The AMP came to a stop just the other side of the fountain.

Riordan leaned his mouth towards his collarcom. "PA, please, Melissa. And please activate the AMP's PDF system."

"You are live on the mic, Commodore. PDF coming up." The

back of the radially symmetric automated weapons platform segmented, extruded a pintle-mounted tube, resealed around it. "PDF coil gun is armed and ready. Go ahead, sir."

Bannor grinned at him. "Show time."

Riordan nodded, did not smile; he'd seen evidence of too many atrocities against the Pavonians to feel anything other than the heat of an anger he'd had to suppress but which had never guttered out. "This is Commodore Caine Riordan of the United Commonwealths and Allied States, acting on behalf of the Consolidated Terran Republic. You are hereby ordered to lay down your weapons, quit your positions, and present yourself for detention until such time as your individual culpability may be determined in the matter of any and all violations of Emergency Action Order 12509-C, issued by the World Confederation and transferred by political supersedence to the appropriate administrative agencies of the CTR."

A single shot rang out from the refectory, spanged harmlessly off one of the AMP's legs.

Riordan did not pause at all. "Failure to follow these instructions will be taken as an indication of continued hostile intent. You have thirty seconds to signal your intent to comply."

A rocket sped at the AMP from the left-hand berm; the PDF tube swung toward it with eye-defying speed, hissed briefly. The rocket detonated halfway between the berm and the Slaasriithi ROV, the explosion shattering half of the facing windows in the refectory.

"Seems like a pretty clear signal to me," Tygg drawled over the open channel.

"Hold your fire, everyone. We're going to give them the full thirty seconds."

"Why?" O'Garran sounded both eager and annoyed. He was well out on the right flank.

"Because we can afford to do so," Riordan answered, "and because we need to take the high road on this right up until we engage."

"Prudent," affirmed Wu, who was working through the jungle around to the rear of the compound, ready to laser-tag any runners with changed-phase pulses so that *Puller*'s sensors had immediate targeting discrimination between potential hostiles and noncombatants.

"Thirty seconds have elapsed...now," Bannor announced.

As if to confirm that timing, muzzle flashes from half a dozen small arms glittered along the shattered line of the refectory's windows. The rounds rang off the smooth legs of the AMP.

"PA off," Riordan ordered. "Melissa, is Phil on Puller's railgun?"

"Standing by," Phil answered.

"Okay. You keep standing by until I call for you. Peter, are you in position?"

"In position."

"I want you to paint the motor pool so we've got overlapping impact points. Melissa, you send each paint-point to the AMP's targeting computer."

Wu was silent for three seconds. "Done."

"I have the target-points," Melissa confirmed.

"Excellent. Slave and fire the AMP's full inventory of HE missiles to those target points."

"Commodore, please say again: *all* HE missiles?"

"Yes, Melissa: all HE missiles. Is our Slaasriithi technical advisor perturbed?"

"No, sir. The question was mine."

Of course it was yours. You're a human; you're used to fighting, to holding weapons in reserve, to keeping your options open. Our exosapient technical advisor is a wiz with machinery, but the pace and exigencies of combat overload and disorient him. Which is just what we need if we're going to make the AMP truly useful to us... "In the event of counterfire, miniature antipersonnel heatseekers are to be expended one per attacker. Engage."

For a moment, it looked as if the AMP had exploded: the plumes of a dozen tactical rockets hid it in a roiling cloud of smoke. But as the exhaust cleared and the rockets arced sharply over Site One's long, low administrative complex, the AMP stood revealed once again, half of its solid body—the part that had held the rockets—now an open framework.

Assault rifles stuttered at it from the refectory; the platform fired a MAPH at each flashing muzzle. Each fell silent.

The rockets hit the motor pool in a long, ragged roar followed immediately by an upward rush of smoke and debris. An instant later, the left berm launched a rocket, which the AMP's backmounted PDF knocked down easily. "Keep the PDF focused on that berm, Melissa," Riordan ordered.

Her voice was as alarmed as Bannor Rulaine's sudden sideways glance: "But, sir—"

"Just do it. I haven't forgotten about the rockets in the other berm."

The CoDevCo mercenaries indicated that their memory was similarly unimpeded: two rockets launched from the right-hand berm, hit the AMP, staggering it. One leg seemed to be unresponsive.

"Sir—?" began Melissa.

"Caine—?" began Bannor.

He ignored them. "Tygg, Miles; paint each berm. Phil, do you have target lock for the railgun?"

"I do."

"Good," replied Caine as another rocket rushed at the AMP. "Light 'em up."

As the last rocket blew two legs off the crippled ROV and sent it cartwheeling away, two flaming bolts shot over their heads, ripping through the sound barrier with an earsplitting crash. Both went into the left-hand berm, which literally flew apart. Another rush of thunder and flame; the right-hand berm vanished in a second cyclone of dirt, bodies, torn machinery.

"Karam, do you have an eye on your sensors?"

"Precisely one eye on them, Commodore."

"Tell me what you see."

"No combat effectives bearing upon the marshalling ground. Panicked civvies streaming out the back, dodging the inferno that used to be the motor pool, scattering into the jungle. Sure hope they don't meet any pavonosaurs out there."

"We'll make sure they don't."

"You're a killjoy. Sir."

"So true. Condition of the main complex?"

"Just some superficial blast damage, Commodore. All their records and dirty little local-killing secrets should still be in pristine condition when you get to them."

"No. Commodore Cameron is going to get first access and credit for the operation. If he wants it. We were just here to expedite, unless he's worried about taking heat for the op and wants to keep his hands clean." *For which I could not blame him one bit.* "Tygg, O'Garran, close on the compound; Major Rulaine and I will provide a base of fire to cover your advance if any hostiles show up again." *Although I'd say what little loyalty is bought with mercenary coin has long since been expended.* "Karam, when Tygg and Little Guy give you an all-clear, I want you on site in one minute to scoop up that disabled AMP."

"Aye, aye, Commodore. I've clued Tina in; she's ready in the bay with a robot stevedore."

"Excellent. I'll keep this channel open. Riordan out."

Bannor Rulaine, looking down the scope of his own liquimix battle rifle, alert for any thermal signatures or movement, did not look at Caine when he asked, "Why did you put that AMP out as a Judas Goat?"

"Well, the Slaasriithi Great Ring forbade Yiithrii'ah'aash from giving us any functional weapons to look at, remember? But when I pressed him, he admitted they hadn't said anything about us collecting any trash they left behind." Caine nodded at the stricken AMP. "So I figure we'll just do a good deed and clean up their trash."

Rulaine smiled. "Which our miltech brain trust will dissect and get messy drooling over. Commodore, I hope you never choose to become a statesman."

"Why's that?"

"Because you're just sneaky enough to be good at it."

"Maybe," answered Caine, "but today, I was only interested in one thing: getting us access to every weapon available, given the years to come."

Bannor heard the implication. "So despite the Arat Kur surrender, you don't think we're going to have 'peace in our time'?"

Riordan just watched *Puller* swing in on fans and open its bay, ready to scoop up the battered AMP like a mechanical bird retrieving an injured fledgling into its own body.

Sixty kilometers north of the mini-Acropolis that had been the first mute evidence of other intelligences in the universe, Riordan's team stood watch for the return of Yiithrii'ah'aash and his assistants. Despite repeated warnings about the dangers posed by pavonosaurs, the Slaasriithi had elected to search for the locals on their own. The presence of humans, Yiithrii'ah'aash explained, would only complicate what could yet prove to be a very simple matter.

Caine was part of the external anchor watch when Karam called him with news that Commodore Cameron was on the line. "Patch him through."

"Commodores, you are both on; the line is encrypted and private."

Encrypted and private? Hmmm—"Commodore Cameron, glad to hear from you."

"Just Steve, please, Commodore Riordan."

"Then it's Caine, Steve. What can I do for you?"

"Firstly, I wanted to update you on what we found at Site One."

"Incriminating evidence?"

"The mother lode. Apparently, the clever fellow they had running the show when you visited, Helger, was summoned home when it was anticipated that Shangri La was going into a deep freeze as far as profit-making was concerned. The drongo who took over was nowhere near so shrewd about what information he kept and what he didn't. We have full records of 'secure' communications and cypher keys from CoDevCo's top brass, instructing a resumption of Site One's campaign of 'indigenous wildlife elimination,' in which the locals are definitively listed. And this after they were designated a protected species by the Hague, pending a scientific measurement of their sapience. CoDevCo has screwed itself well and good, Caine."

"Couldn't happen to a more deserving pack of jackals," Caine observed. "But you wouldn't need a cypher on this line to tell me that. What's coming down the path towards me, Steve?"

There was a short silence. "You must have majored in reading between the lines, Riordan. But you're right. You've got a situation inbound."

"Big trouble or little trouble?"

"Might not be trouble at all. Or it might be worse trouble than I can imagine. Only you'd know."

"Me? Why me?"

"Because the trouble asked about you by name. Seemed to expect he'd find you here."

Ah. "So you got a call from Richard Downing."

"I did. Seems he came in-system two days ago, behind the further gas giant, had the codes to override our remote sensors out there. I didn't even know that was possible."

"Richard can do a lot of things that don't seem possible. What else?"

"Asked about you, what your mission was, showed me credentials even more extraordinary than yours. A *lot* more extraordinary. And he's on his way to see you."

"When?"

"About twenty minutes from now. He's putting down at Site One. Good luck, Caine."

The line went dead. *Twenty minutes before I have to deal with Richard Downing? Well, that just makes my day.*

Karam's voice was back. "Caine, group coming in from the west. Traveling tight, casual pace. Looks like Yiithrii'ah'aash, his party, maybe three others."

"Okay. Alert the rest of the watch; we don't want any friendly fire foul-ups. And spin up the fans; we've got a date back at Site One."

When Downing emerged from the dust kicked up by the vertifans of his shuttle, Caine and Yiithrii'ah'aash were waiting for him. Alone. Downing motioned for his security escort to stay back, resumed his approach.

"Richard," Caine called to him. "I'd like you to finally meet Prime Ratiocinator Yiithrii'ah'aash of the Slaasriithi Great Ring, with whom I believe you coordinated our legation's journey to Beta Aquilae."

Downing started to put out his hand, was about to pull it back, hesitated again when Yiithrii'ah'aash extended his tendrils. "I have become accustomed to your ways, Mr. Downing, and am pleased to make your personal acquaintance. You obviously received our message."

"In fact, Ambassador Yiithrii'ah'aash, I was already in transit when it arrived, but was able to divert here to Delta Pavonis." He glanced at the worn ramp leading up into *Puller*. "I take it you have found what you came for?"

"Indeed. It is gratifying to find such swift rapport with our distant kin despite the passage of so much time. We feared that the estrangement would be greater, that perhaps their pheromones had become hopelessly recidivistic. But the markings upon Caine Riordan gave us countervailing hope. After all, if the mark impressed upon him here was still recognizable—and powerfully so—to us, we had reason to conjecture that ours might still be recognizable to them."

He waved at *Puller*. "Three of the locals you call Pavonians have consented to come with us. It is a brave thing they do; their people have not ventured beyond this valley for many generations.

However, their myth tells them that we are all from the stars, and they wish to see the home of the biota that gave rise to them. They shall be honored among us and, if it is not objectionable to you, we shall return to repatriate any others that might wish it, once our respective governments have agreed to the conditions under which that might occur."

"I am sure that can be arranged swiftly, Ambassador," Downing affirmed with a nod. "We have no desire to keep you and your distant relatives apart any longer than absolutely necessary."

The Slaasriithi's neck dipped very low and remained so for several seconds before he raised it and spoke again. "Ultimately, we have humanity's curiosity to thank for our reunification. Naturally, all intelligence arises from curiosity, from exploring novel solutions to problems. But only humanity avidly, even restlessly, seeks out so many challenges and mysteries. For you, nothing calls more strongly than the unknown, or so it seems."

"Thank you," said Caine, unsure of what else to say. "But it's a shame that your reunion must take place under the likely shadow of war."

Yiithrii'ah'aash's neck wiggled slightly. "I suspect we would not have realized our need of the indagatorae until such a threat arose, so there may be an unavoidable connection between the approach of strife and our desire to reembrace our lost taxon. Which we shall now undertake to restore."

"But it will require some time to breed sufficient numbers of indagatorae, won't it?"

Yiithrii'ah'aash's sensor cluster focused on Caine. "'Sufficient numbers?' I am uncertain what you mean."

Downing stepped in. "Enough to field an army or expand your naval formations."

Yiithrii'ah'aash stared at them for a long time. "I am sorry; you misperceive. We do not need the indagatorae to breed an army. As you say, that would take too long and we lack the requisite skills to train such forces in time, or at all."

Riordan felt adrift. "Then why do you need the indagatorae?"

Yiithrii'ah'aash waved tendrils to take in everything around him. "To act as our liaisons to those members of the macrocommunity who are soldiers already. That is, the indagatorae will be our liaisons to humanity."

Caine had stepped backward before he realized he had done

so. "You mean, you consider us part of your community? And that our role is to be your soldiers?"

"All things are part of the community of life. And all have their roles."

And our role is to die for you? Wait just a goddamned minute— But Caine remembered that he was a diplomat, and that the Slaasriithi would be unlikely to see the situation in those terms. "Assuming we are even willing to take up that role, there is a further complication: you Slaasriithi shape your community without consulting all its members. Without anything like a referendum."

Yiithrii'ah'aash did not blink. "That is true," he said.

"And you presume we would be willing to be enter into that kind of relationship?"

"Caine Riordan, I have clearly alarmed you. Be calmed: we presume nothing. But we have observed, with great clarity, just how deficient we are in warfare. The speed with which your species is willing to destroy assets in order to achieve objectives—such as the way you prevailed upon me to destroy Disparity's antimatter depot to hamper the efforts of the Ktor—is utterly alien to us. We acknowledge our limitations. But we also see areas where we may make fair and balanced contributions in exchange. We may assist you in accelerating the speed with which your green and brown worlds become self-sufficient. We have technological capabilities which may be selectively shared. We may construct various defensive and sensor systems and ROVs that shall aid your forces, or allow you to secure vast areas without wasting precious personnel to do so. These contributions are merely the treetops of a deep forest of possibilities, and we shall explore all of them together."

"That sounds like a reasonable starting point," Downing answered, sending a warning glance at Caine.

Who could only think: *my God, with friends like these, who needs enemies? Unless we can trust them... but how would we ever know for sure? And no matter what Yiithrii'ah'aash says, we'd be doing all the fighting, even while wondering: who's really driving the bus? What if our "allies" are subtly changing our genome to make us more tractable, more willing to blend ourselves into a panspeciate polytaxic order?*

Of course, that was the human perspective. Caine could readily imagine an identical Slaasriithi perspective that was not intentionally malign or insidious, but was simply an outgrowth of their evolutionary successes. Just as humans evolved toward political unity to accrue collective power, the Slaasriithi were simply following the well-established groove of their own paradigm: that polytaxism is the natural means of expanding safety and stability for all species. For them, it deductively followed that all species should be linked in a figurative or even literal polytaxon.

But, as true as that might be for the Slaasriithi, Riordan doubted that it would ever be a good fit for humanity. And more so, he could not foresee any benefit so great that the mothers and fathers of Terra should be asked to accept that only *their* offspring would pay for the collective good in blood.

But these thoughts were not suitable for what was still a careful, diplomatic exchange, so Riordan replied with a harmlessly oblique truth: "I think the perspective you articulate will be the starting place for many enlightening discussions."

Yiithrii'ah'aash's sensor cluster remained fixed upon him. "I understand you are troubled, Caine Riordan. You have my assurance of this: we Slaasriithi understand the limits of cooperative relationships. Biota which are not both happy with a symbiosis are not symbiots for long. As we move forward together, we will always seek, and endeavor to productively address, the reservations of your species. Nothing else would be stable. Nothing else would be wise or prudent." He shifted his attention toward Downing. "It has been a pleasure making your acquaintance, Mr. Downing. I perceive you have separate matters to discuss with the commodore. I shall take my leave."

Chapter Fifty-Seven

Downing motioned toward a folding table that Commodore Cameron's teams had set up to process the CoDevCo employees into detention groups. "Mind if we sit?"

Caine shook his head, pulled out a chair, let Downing settle into his own before he declared, "Let's not play charades, Richard. Just tell me why you're out here. You told Yiithrii'ah'aash that you were already on the move, but were able to 'divert' to Delta Pavonis. But every time you're on the move, you seem to be coming to find me. So, let's get that out in the open and dealt with: what do you need from me, Richard?" *Because after we finish our business, we've got some personal matters to settle.*

Richard looked down at his folded hands. "Well, it just so happens we have a situation—"

Caine threw his head back and laughed. "Downing, you are too much. I haven't even finished this mission, and you've come out here to send me on another?"

"This isn't my doing, Caine. You were asked for by name."

"Oh? By whom?"

"By the New Families of the Hkh'Rkh. Specifically, by Yaargraukh."

Caine straightened. "Yaargraukh survived Jakarta?" The two-and-a-half meter Hkh'Rkh, a pipsqueak for his species, had been a confidante, a being of great honor, a friend.

Downing nodded. "He survived and was repatriated. His

534

circumstances are difficult, since the Hkh'Rkh leadership that brought him on the campaign was decimated. Their First Fist was killed in Indonesia and First Voice remains missing. With no one to vouch for Yaargraukh, or his version of the events in Jakarta, he was returned—ignominiously, I believe—to his home on a colony world in a system they share with the Arat Kur. Turkh'saar, they call it."

"I appreciate the news, but I don't see what—"

"Caine, the situation developing on Turkh'saar could have extremely serious repercussions for the Consolidated Terran Republic and possibly the peace. Yaargraukh has asked that we send you to help." Downing leaned forward. "You two always understood each other, had a bond from the first time you met. I don't think he fully trusts any other human to be impartial, given what's happening in his home system."

"And *what* is happening there?"

"According to him, offworld raiders have been striking at various targets on Turkh'saar, and they're leaving scorched earth behind."

Riordan frowned. "Well, that's definitely a bad situation, but why do they want to get humans involved in their own internal affairs?"

"Because," replied Richard, producing his palmtop, "the affair in question is not purely internal. This is part of what the Hkh'Rkh defenders recorded from the raiders' own tactical channels—just before they swooped in and destroyed another town." Downing activated the playback function, put the palmtop on the table between them. Sinuous music began rising, uncoiling from it: primitive drums savagely split apart a plaintive guitar solo, leaving a rift through which a seductively menacing voice flowed. Its words were dark, enigmatic.

Riordan started, stared at Downing. "That's—that's twentieth-century rock. Early in the movement. I think it's—uh, it's—"

"'Paint it Black' by a group called the Rolling Stones. Original recording, the archivists at Langley tell me."

Riordan shook his head. "Okay, but—but what do you want *me* to do about it?"

"I, and Yaargraukh, want you to go to Turkh'saar and find out why humans playing twentieth-century rock music over their tactical channels are attacking the Hkh'Rkh—and how that's even possible, since we can't reach that area of space yet. And it's got to be handled right away, because this has landed in the Hkh'Rkhs' political powderkeg like a lit firecracker. With First Voice still missing on Earth amid accusations that he is secretly being held by us, this incident has whipped up their hardliners into a xenophobic frenzy, convinced them that we have sent a raiding team into their space."

Caine stared at the palmtop. "But to achieve what?"

Downing shrugged. "They haven't offered any coherent hypotheses about that, but they also don't seem to care. Their internal debates—about just how duplicitous we really are, how to respond to this incursion, and who is to succeed First Voice—are primed to tear them apart. According to Yaargraukh, there is increasing talk of a multisided civil war."

Riordan nodded. "Which could propel them just that much deeper into the Ktoran camp."

"Exactly."

"And how do I get to Turkh'saar to investigate this?"

"I plan on asking Yiithrii'ah'aash. Since I will cut some official corners to retroactively 'allow' his trip here, he might return the favor by conveying you to the system in question: BD +56 2966. The Slaasriithi conducted a fair amount of commerce raiding against the Hkh'Rkh during the war. Consequently they have both the shift range and the local familiarity to deliver you where you need to go."

"Operational assets?"

"I've brought some personnel who can accompany you. Not a lot, I'm afraid. Clearance for this operation rather limited the selection pool."

Caine turned, stared back up at *Puller*, saw a few faces looking down at them from the bridge windows. "And what about the crew who came out here with me?"

"Them? Well, I should think they'll be happy to go home."

"Yeah? Will they?" Caine opened his collarcom, his eyes on Downing's. "Hey everyone, I need you to listen to a situation that's come up. Richard, tell them what you just told me."

"Caine, if I do that—"

"Richard, since they are already intelligence risks because of what we saw during our trip into Slaasriithi space, how much more hot water can they get into by hearing about current events on Turkh'saar?"

Downing returned Riordan's stare, then shrugged and told the whole tale again.

There was a long silence, broken by Miles O'Garran: "Man, that is some serious shit."

Caine couldn't help but grin. "Yes, it is. And here's why I had Mr. Downing share it with you: you've got a choice to make. Either you go straight back to Earth or you go straight back out into the field to investigate this very serious shit. I have no idea what we'll find there or if we'll make it back. Frankly, I'm not sure of anything about this mission; my ignorance is absolute. But you all know what going back to Earth could mean: extended debriefs, protective custody, God knows how many years living in secure facilities, safe houses, whatever. You've seen, and you know, too much to be allowed out in general circulation. Or am I exaggerating, Richard?"

"Caine, I would not impose that kind of cloistering on any of your—"

"I'm not talking about you, Richard. I'm talking about the people you answer to, who can trump any assurances you might give us. On a whim. Am I exaggerating what *they* are likely to do?"

Downing looked away. "No."

Caine turned and stared up at the nine faces now crowded against the bridge windows, spoke into his collarcom. "I can't guarantee you anything except that whatever we face, we face together. And maybe, when we come back, we can cut a deal to stay out of a facility for people who know too much. If, on the other hand, you want to go back to Earth, I can get Richard to promise you, with one hand on his heart and the other on the Bible, that you won't wind up in one of those ultra-secluded country clubs. But how much that promise is worth—well, you'll have to make that decision for yourself. I realize you might need some time to think about it, so there's no ru—"

"We're coming with you." It was Karam. "We're not stupid; we know how this would go down."

Bannor's voice went over the top of Tsaami's. "We all make a pretty good team. We think it best if we keep it that way, if that's all right with you. Commodore."

Caine felt a tightness behind his eyes, nodded at them, turned back to Downing. "They're coming along for the ride."

Downing was gazing steadily at Riordan. "So I hear. They seem a fine group, Caine."

"They are. Every damned one of them." He realized his collar-com was still on, slapped it off. "So are we done with business?"

"We are."

"Then I've got some personal questions to—"

Downing suddenly looked nervous. And tortured. "Caine, about Elena, about what happened—"

"Richard. This is not a prelude to recriminations." Riordan swallowed; it felt like there was a baseball in his throat. "I get it; I get what happened. I thought about it a lot on the way out here. You didn't really have any—"

"No, Caine. No. Enough is enough. My culpability goes deeper than you know and I'd rather have you angry—homicidally furious—at me, than live with this any longer." Downing's eyes were suddenly red-rimmed, almost rheumy. "Elena should never have been in Jakarta; she should never have been involved in any of this. For bloody Christ's sake, she's my godchild; I held her on my knee. She called me Uncle Richard as soon as she could talk."

"Richard, I know you must feel—"

"You know what I feel? Really?" Downing jabbed a finger at Caine. "You have every right to hate me, to despise what I've done and how I've failed her. But don't tell me you know what I feel, Riordan. Added all together, you've known Elena Corcoran a few weeks. I knew her for almost her entire life. If I had one meal with her, I have had, literally, a thousand. She babysat my daughter, took her around with Connor sometimes when they were both small—and when she was still devastated by losing you, though none of us knew anything about that at the time." His face contorted, grew red. "And this, *this,* is the life to which I led her? Boxed up somewhere in a Dornaani medical facility, hovering in a twilight between life and death?" He looked at Caine, furious and pleading. "Why was she ever inducted into IRIS? Why was she a member of the delegation to the Convocation? Why was she in Jakarta? Why was she part of the team who entered the Arat Kur headquarters with you? Why was she anywhere in range of that murdering bastard Shethkador? Because of me, goddamn it. Because of me." He averted his head, his teeth clenched, his whole body leaning sharply away as if he was trying to get out of it, somehow. "God, I could use a drink."

Caine nodded, then stopped. Come to think of it, Richard's desperation didn't look merely emotional, but tinged with need, dependence. And was he putting on weight, the kind of waste-flab that comes from drinking too much?

But there wasn't the time or the opportunity to surreptitiously look for other signs of a man who might be descending into a bottle. There was just enough time for Caine to say the words that had to be said, no matter how much he didn't want to utter them, but which Downing needed to hear: "Richard, you were just the accomplice. It was her own father who performed the deeds, who got her tangled up in IRIS, albeit indirectly. Who put her through all the misery. You weren't in a position to stop it. Ever."

Downing was only half listening. "This is a dirty game, a dirty life, Caine. I'm sorry I got you into it, into all the lies and manipulation and secrets. I'm sorry I ever—"

"Listen," Riordan said sharply, which got Downing's attention. Which had been Riordan's intent: he needed to steer Downing away from the edge of what might become a self-destructive precipice of grief. "Listen," Caine repeated, "long before any battles were joined, we were at war. But only you and Nolan Corcoran and a handful of others knew it. And you had to get us ready, had to prepare all of humanity. Without us knowing you were doing so. We had to be ready to fight species that were more advanced and expansive than we were. That didn't give you two any margin for error. And if you and Nolan made mistakes along the way—well, hindsight is twenty-twenty, but real-time is a bitch. The bottom line is, we're all still alive to complain about it. And maybe patch together a few pieces of our normal lives." He reached into the front pocket of his duty suit. "Here. I want you to take this back to Earth. It's for Connor."

Downing, his eyes still haunted but his face no longer contorted, took the data chip. "What is it?"

"A collection of letters. I wrote one every day of the journey from Disparity to here. Some recordings as well; anything to give him a sense of who I am."

Downing turned it around in his fingers. "Did you—did you know we were going to send you right out again?"

Riordan shrugged. "I didn't *know*. But like I told you, it always seems to happen that way. I just presumed that nothing would really be that different this time. And see? It wasn't." He exhaled. "So, Elena's in a Dornaani facility?"

Downing nodded. "On their homeworld, according to Alnduul."

"Her recuperation seems to be taking a long time."

Downing raised a hand, let it fall. "Too bloody long, if you ask me. But I haven't been in direct touch with Alnduul for six months now, and none of the Dornaani I come into contact with have any knowledge of Elena. I'm not even sure her transfer was approved by the Dornaani Collective. Or the Custodians. Alnduul may just have done it on his own authority. May have been skinned alive for it, too."

Riordan closed his eyes, asked the next awful question. "Who's taking care of Connor?"

"Trevor mostly, but Connor spends a lot of time with my family. We—we're doing the best we can by him. But it's hard. He's a tough lad, but with his mother dozens of light-years away in the care of exosapients—" He raised his hand in an appeal to the skies. Let it fall again.

And Caine thought: *I've got to get home. Now.* But Riordan pushed that gut-reflex down with a principled riposte: *No: you've got to take care of business, first. And while you do, you've got to get enough leverage to make sure that those nine human beings on board the corvette don't pay for their loyalty to you by spending half of their natural lives as gagged canaries in semi-gilded security cages.* Caine could not meet Downing's eyes. "Tell Connor I'm coming home as soon as I can. I promise."

"I will, Caine. You have my word on it."

"Good. I'd like to have your word on one more thing, Richard."

Downing immediately became wary. "And what is that?"

"Since you received Yiithrii'ah'aash's message about what happened on Disparity, you know about Keith Macmillan, right?"

Downing looked, and sounded, like he was swallowing glass. "I do."

"He has a daughter. Katie."

"I know. I pulled his dossier."

"So you know about the quid pro quo that the Ktor used to turn him: his cooperation in exchange for her life."

Richard's eyes were hard, unblinking. "They are right bastards."

Caine wasn't sure whether Downing was referring to the Ktor, their megacorporate lackeys, or both. And didn't care, at the moment. "If my guess is right, they didn't give Katie a full cure; Dora overheard one of the Ktor say as much. And frankly, that's exactly what I'd expect of them: to let the disease come back, clean up all their loose ends."

"I agree. And it's an awful situation. But what do you want me to do?"

Caine leaned forward. "I want you to use your authority, your power, to make it right."

Downing leaned away sharply. "Caine, assuming that I could get permission to—"

"Fuck permission. You've got the leads you need. Macmillan was approached in a hospital waiting room. That gives you a place and a face. And that face is sure to be all over the security cameras. I suspect that face didn't arrive at the hospital by public transport, so that face is also connected to a vehicle. You track down that vehicle, and that face. You grab that face from whatever well-appointed apartment or sybaritic retreat it happens to be occupying and you put a bag over it. And you take that bag off when you have that face in a cold, well-lit room and you squeeze that mother-fucker for everything he knows. Someplace, there is a connection between that face—that malicious bastard— and whatever cure he slipped into Katie. I'll even bet there are still some samples out there, just waiting to be used to turn some other desperate parent into a traitor. So you find that face, and that drug, and you save that poor girl's life."

"Caine, what you're asking—I can't just—"

"Richard, I will not listen to your bullshit. Not this time. This is a little girl who was a victim of our enemies. The timing makes it a near-certainty that they bred the cancer that was in her. And then they turned her father against everything else he loved to save her. You will do this, you will save that girl, or I will hold you—I will hold *our* side—responsible. Do you understand?" When Downing hesitated, Riordan lifted his hand to the table. He deposited its contents—a holstered CoBro liquimix sidearm—immediately to his right. "I asked: do you *understand*?"

Downing leaned even further away, eyes wide. "Bloody hell, Caine, what's come over—?"

"I am going to ask this. One. More. Time. Do you *understand*?"

"Yes, yes, of course. But I—"

"No buts, Richard. And no excuses or backsliding or consulting with your superiors. If you don't save her, then I will—and then I become your worst problem. Your *worst* problem. Do the right thing and—who knows?—we might actually become real friends. But I'm giving you a choice, right here, and right now: you can obey your precious rules and regulations and intelligence protocols and let Keith's little girl die, or you can stand up for basic human compassion and loyalty, and resolve not to allow these monsters to screw with our children." Caine felt his face grow suddenly hot. "With our *children*, for fuck's sake." Riordan rose so swiftly that his chair fell over. He spun and stalked away. If Downing called after him, he wasn't aware of it.

Because all he could hear, again and again, was what Dora had told him about Macmillan's death, about what the Ktor commander on Disparity had said: "Family is our strength, but it is your weakness." Riordan walked through the dust and postcombat debris littering the marshalling area of Site One, and thought: *and you Ktor actually believe that, too. Because part of the price you've paid for all your enhancements is love. But that love—and the loyalty it breeds—is not just our best virtue:*

It is the weapon I will use to destroy you.

Appendix A

Dramatis Personae

The Humans
(Traditional Chinese and Japanese names list family names first.)

Qwara Betul: Archivist/recorder; legation to Beta Aquilae

Piet Brackman: First Pilot, SS *Arbitrage*

Joe Buckley: Quartermaster/Purser; legation to Beta Aquilae

Oleg Danysh: Physicist; legation to Beta Aquilae

Richard Downing: Director, Institute of Reconnaissance, Intelligence Security; Riordan's handler:

Philip Friel: Engineer, legation to Beta Aquilae

Etienne Gaspard: Ambassador Plenitpotentiary, legation to Beta Aquilae; CTR Consul

Hirano Mizuki: Planetology/exobiome expert; legation to Beta Aquilae

Trent Howarth: Staff Sergeant, NZSAS; security staff for legation to Beta Aquilae

Ben Hwang: Biologist and senior scientist; legation to Beta Aquilae

Emil Kozakowski: Former master of the SS *Arbitrage*; (former) employee of CoDevCo

Morgan Lymbery: Aerospace and drive expert; legation to Beta Aquilae

Keith Macmillan: Warrant Officer Class 2, British Army/IRIS; legation to Beta Aquilae

Tina Melah: Engineer; legation to Beta Aquilae

Miles O'Garran: Master CPO, SEAL/IRIS; security staff for legation to Beta Aquilae

Caine Riordan: Commander, IRIS/USSF; security chief of legation to Beta Aquilae

Christopher "Tygg" Robin: Lieutenant, SAAS/IRIS; security staff of legation to Beta Aquilae

Bannor Rulaine: Major, US Special Forces/IRIS; security staff for legation to Beta Aquilae

Melissa Sleeman: Advanced science and technology expert; legation to Beta Aquilae

Vassily Sukhinin: Chief negotiator and Deputy Director of IRIS, Sigma Draconis; CTR Consul

Ayana Tagawa: Executive Officer of SS *Arbitrage*

Karam Tsaami: Pilot; legation to Beta Aquilae

Jorge Velho: Captain of SS *Arbitrage*

Dora Veriden: Personal security for Ambassador Gaspard; legation to Beta Aquilae

Peter Wu: Lieutenant, Taiwanese Army/IRIS; security staff for legation to Beta Aquilae

Xue Heng: EMT and assistant quartermaster; legation to Beta Aquilae

The Ktor

Ulpreln Balkether: Evolved; Crew of *Red Lurker*

Vranut Balkether: Evolved; Crew of *Red Lurker*

Zurur Deosketer: Evolved; Crew of *Red Lurker*

Tegrese Hreteyarkus: Evolved; Crew of *Red Lurker*

Pehthrum: Intendant; Crew of *Red Lurker*

Brenlor Perekmeres: Evolved and Srin; Captain of *Red Lurker*

Nezdeh Perekmeres: Evolved, Aware, and Srina; Executive officer of *Red Lurker*

Idrem Perekmeresuum: Evolved; Second Officer of *Red Lurker*

Jesel sul-Perekmeres: Aspirant; Crew of *Red Lurker*

Suzruzh sul-Perekmeres: Aspirant; Crew of *Red Lurker*

Sehtrek: Intendant, Crew of *Red Lurker*

Tlerek Shethkador: Evolved, Aware, Srin, and Ambassador to Earth/CTR; Captain of *Ferocious Monolith*

Olsirkos Shethkador-vah: Evolved; Acting Master of *Ferocious Monolith*

The Slaasriithi

Hsaefyrr: Third Ratiocinator of the Third Silver Tower

Mriif'vaal: Senior Ratiocinator; Overseer of the Third Silver Tower

Thnessfiirm: spokesperson for the cerdorae assisting the human survivors on Disparity

Unsymaajh: spokesperson for the convectorae assisting the human survivors on Disparity

W'th'vaathi: spokesperson for the ratiocinatorae assisting the human survivors on Disparity

Yiithrii'ah'aash: Prime Ratiocinator; Ambassador to Earth/CTR

Appendix B

Useful Acronyms and Slang

ACS: attitude control thruster

AMP: automated munitions platform

CIC: combat information center

CINC or C-in-C: Commander in Chief or Commander in Charge

CoDevCo: Colonial Development Combine

CTR: Consolidated Terran Republic

HALO: high altitude/low opening

MAP: magnetically (or magnetohydrodynamically) accelerated plasma

PDF: point defense fire

RFS: Russlavic Federation ship

ROV: remote operated vehicle

TOCIO: TransOceanic Commercial and Industrial Organization

UCS: United Commonwealth(s) ship

Appendix C

Ktoran Glossary

Aboriginal: a low breed of original Earth stock; unmodified *homo sapiens*

Agra: a junior officer who is neither Evolved nor an Intendant

Aspirant: the progeny of a particularly accomplished and genetically preferred huscarl; these children are being considered for Elevation to Intendant; rarely, directly to Aspirant. If they fail the first step of Elevation (to 'vah or Aspirant), they are typically demoted.

Aware: an Evolved that can exercise the power of Reification (self-reference; *homo transcendens*)

Berem(a): (m./f.) A generic term that indicates aristocratic birth or station, but which does not signify any particular rank (and usually implies an absence of special rank within that social class). Akin to "sir" or "madame."

Catalysite: a symbiot or "catalyst" that amplifies Reification control and power

Devolysite: a devolved version of the "catalyst" symbiot that is sensitive to various quantum entanglement alterations

Evolved: a member of the Ktor master geneline (*homo imperiens*)

Elevation: the process and rite by which low-breeds (usually Intendants) become Evolved

helot: a low-bred servitor, typically commanded by huscarls; many subclassifications exist

huscarl: direct, prized low-bred servitors; the class from which Intendants are usually drawn

jur: prefix; a particularly promising individual of one of the low-bred classes (a jur-huscarl, for instance, is likely to be the father of a sur-Intendant)

lictor: a junior officer rank, particular to the Aegis forces that answer solely to the Autarchs

Srin/Srina: an aristocrat of the Evolved, whose accomplishments, geneline, or both qualify them for elevation to Hegemon or Autarch. (pl.; Srinu)

sul: the prefix or short-form referent ('sul) signifying an Aspirant

Tval: one whose geneline has become corrupt, distant from the core line, or is otherwise not suitable to become the Hegemon of a House or Head of a Family, but who is otherwise unrestricted in their ambitions

-uum/'m: no longer of the core or progenitorial geneline of a House

vah: suffix added to a name that indicates the progeny of an Elevated Aspirant. Also shortened as 'vah, this status may be extended in the event of disappointing achievement, or other failures. Only in extreme cases, or several generations of a geneline remaining as 'vahs, is a 'vah demoted.

Wilding: a low breed that was not raised under Ktoran dominion